The city in these pages is imaginary.
The people, the places are all fictitious.
Only the police routine is based on established
investigatory technique.

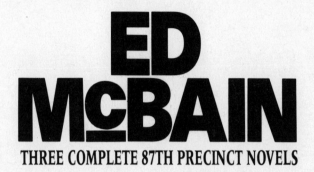

ED McBAIN

THREE COMPLETE 87TH PRECINCT NOVELS

ED McBAIN

THREE COMPLETE 87TH PRECINCT NOVELS

TRICKS

ICE

8 BLACK HORSES

WINGS BOOKS

New York • Avenel, New Jersey

This edition contains the complete and unabridged texts of the
original editions. They have been completely reset for this volume.

This omnibus was originally published in separate volumes
under the titles:
Tricks, copyright © 1987 by HUI Corporation
Ice, copyright © 1983 by HUI Corporation
8 Black Horses, copyright © 1985 by HUI Corporation.

This 1992 edition is published by Wings Books, distributed by
Outlet Book Company, Inc., a Random House Company,
40 Engelhard Avenue, Avenel, New Jersey 07001, by arrangement
with William Morrow & Company.

Printed and bound in the United States of America

Library of Congress Cataloging-in-Publication Data
McBain, Ed, 1926-
    Ed McBain—three complete novels / Ed McBain.
        p.   cm.
    Contents: Tricks—8 black horses—Ice.
    1. Detective and mystery stories, American. 2. Police—Fiction.
I. Title. II. Title: Three complete novels.
PS3515.U585A6   1992
813'.54—dc20   92-7598
                                          CIP

8 7 6 5 4 3 2 1

CONTENTS

This is for
RUSSELL WM. HULTGREN

__TRICKS__

1

The pair of them came down the street streaming blood.

No one paid any attention to them.

This was the city.

The taller of the two wore a blood-stained blue bathrobe. Blood appeared to be oozing from a half-dozen crosshatched wounds on his face. His hands were covered with blood. The striped pajama bottoms that showed beneath the hem of the robe were spattered with blood that seemed to have dripped from an open wound in his belly, where a dagger was plunged to the hilt.

The shorter person, a girl—although it was difficult to tell from the contorted mask of her face—wore only a paisely-patterned nightgown and high-heeled, pink pompommed bedroom slippers. Her garments screamed blood to the unusually mild October night. An ice pick was stuck into her chest, the handle smeared with blood. Blood was matted in her long stringy hair, bright red blood stained her naked legs, and her ankles, and the backs of her hands, and her narrow chest where it showed above the top of the yoke-necked nightgown.

She couldn't have been older than twelve.

The boy with her was perhaps the same age.

They were both carrying shopping bags that seemed stained with blood as fresh as that of their wounds. There could have been something recently severed from a human body inside each of those bags. A hand perhaps. Or a head. Or perhaps the bags had become blood-soaked only from proximity to their own bodies.

They came running up the street as though propelled by the urgency of their wounds.

"Let's try here," the boy said.

Several teeth appeared to be missing from his mouth. The black gaps were visible when he spoke. A thin line of red painted a trail from his lower lip to his chin. The flesh around his right eye was discolored red and black and blue and purple. He looked as if someone had beaten him severely before plunging the dagger into his belly.

"This one?" the girl asked.

They stopped before a street-level door.

They knocked frantically on the door.

It opened.

"Trick or treat!" they shouted in unison.

It was 4:10 P.M. on Halloween night.

The four-to-midnight shift at the 87th Precinct was only ten minutes old.

"Halloween ain't what it used to be," Andy Parker said.

He was sitting behind his desk in the squadroom, his feet up on the desk, his chair

3

tilted dangerously, as if burdened by the weight of the shoulder holster slung over its back. He was wearing rumpled trousers, an unpressed sports jacket, unshined black shoes, dingy white socks, and a wash-and-wear shirt with food stains on it. He had got his haircut at a barber's college on the Stem. There was a three-day-old beard stubble on his face. He was talking to Hawes and Brown, but they were not listening to him. That didn't stop Parker.

"What it is, Devil's Night steals from it," he said, and nodded in agreement with his observation.

At their own desks, the other detectives kept typing.

"Years ago," Park said, "*tonight* was when the kids raised hell. Nowadays, you got church dances, you got socials at the Y, you got all kinds of shit to keep the kids out of trouble. So the kids figure Okay, they want us to be good on Halloween, so we'll pick another night to behave like little bastards. So they invented Devil's Night, which was last night, when we got all the windows busted and the eggs thrown."

Across the room, the typewriters kept clacking.

"You guys writing books or what?" Parker asked.

No one answered him.

"I'm gonna write a book one of these days," Parker said. "Lots of cops write books, they make a fortune. I had plenty experience, I could prolly write a terrific book."

Hawes looked up for a moment, and then scratched at his back. He was sunburned and peeling. He had returned only Monday morning from a week's vacation in Bermuda, but his skin was still the color of his hair. Big red-headed man with a white streak in the hair over the left temple, where he'd once been slashed. He had not yet told Annie Rawles that he'd spent some very pleasant hours with a girl he'd met down there on the pink sands.

"This guy Wamburger in L.A., he used to be a cop," Parker said, "I think with Hollywood Division. He writes these big best-sellers, don't he? This other guy, Kornitch, he writes them, too, he used to be a cop in New York. Ain't nobody who didn't used to be a cop can write books sound real about cops. One of these days, I'm gonna write a big fuckin' best-seller, I'll go live on a yacht in the south of France. Get these naked broads diving off the boat while I sit there doing nothing."

"Like now," Brown said.

"Yeah, bullshit, I already finished my work," Parker said. "This shift's been too fuckin' quiet. Whose idea was it to put on extra men, anyway?"

"The lieutenant's."

"So what's the use of seven guys when nothin's happening? Who's on, anyway? And where the fuck are they?"

"Cruising," Hawes said. "Out there looking for trouble."

He was thinking he himself would be looking for trouble if he told Annie what had happened in Bermuda, even though his arrangement with her was a loose one. Separate apartments, occasional conjugal visits, like they gave prisoners down in Mexico. Anyway, he'd *asked* Annie to come with him to Bermuda, hadn't he? Annie said her vacation wasn't till February. He asked her to change her vacation. She said she had to be in court all that week. She also said she hated Bermuda. He went down alone. Met this girl who practiced law in Atlanta. She'd taught him some legal tricks.

"It's so quiet, you could hear a pin drop," Parker said. "I coulda been home sleeping."

"Instead of sleeping here," Brown said, and went to the water cooler. He was a hefty, muscular black man, standing some six-feet four-inches tall and weighing two hundred and twenty pounds. There was a glowering look on his face as he pulled a paper cup from the holder and then stabbed at the faucet button. He always looked glowering, even when he was smiling. Brown could get an armed robber to drop his piece just by glowering at him.

"Who's sleeping?" Parker said. "I'm resting, is all. I already finished my work."

"Then why don't you start writing your book?" Hawes said.

"You could write all about how Halloween ain't what it used to be," Brown said, crumpling the paper cup and going back to his desk.

"It ain't," Parker agreed.

"You could write about it's so quiet on Halloween, your hero has nothing to do," Hawes said.

"That's the truth," Parker said. "This phone ain't rung once since I come in."

He looked at the phone.

It did not ring.

"I'll bet that bothers you a lot," Brown said. "The phone not ringing."

"Nothing to do," Hawes said.

"No ax murders out there," Brown said.

"I had an ax murder once," Parker said, "I could maybe write about that."

"It's been done," Hawes said.

"Be a big fuckin' best-seller."

"I don't think it was."

" 'Cause maybe a cop didn't write it. You got to be a cop to write best-sellers about cops."

"You got to be an ax murderer to write best-sellers about ax murders," Brown said.

"Sure," Parker said, and looked at the phone again.

"You got nothing to do," Hawes said, "whyn't you go down the hall and shave?"

"I'm working on my Miami Vice look," Parker said.

"You look like a bum," Brown said.

"I *am* a bum," Parker said.

"You got to be a bum to write best-sellers about bums," Brown said.

"Tell that to Kennedy," Hawes said.

"Teddy? I didn't know he wrote books," Parker said. "What does he write about? Senators?"

"Go shave," Hawes said.

"Or go write a book about a barber," Brown suggested.

"I ain't a barber," Parker said.

He looked at the phone again.

"You ever see it this quiet?" he asked.

"I never even *heard* it this quiet," Brown said.

"Me, neither," Parker said. "It's like a paid vacation."

"Like always," Brown said.

"I once had a lady choked to death on a dildo," Parker said. "Maybe I could write about that. I had a lot of cases I could write about."

"Maybe you could write about the case you're working on now," Brown said.

"I ain't working nothing right now."

"No kidding?"

"I finished all my work. Everything wrapped up till the phone rings."

"Maybe the phone's out of order," Hawes said.

"You think so?" Parker said, but he made no move to lift the receiver and listen for a dial tone.

"Or maybe none of the bad guys are doing anything out there," Brown said.

"Maybe all the bad guys went south for the winter," Hawes said, and thought again about Bermuda, and wondered if he should come clean with Annie.

"Fat chance," Parker said. "This weather? I never seen an October like this in my entire life. I once had a case, this guy strangled his wife with the telephone cord. I'll bet I could write about that."

"I'll bet you could."

"Hit her with the phone first, knocked her cold. Then strangled her with the cord."

"You could call it *Long Distance,*" Brown said.

"No, he was standing close to her when he done it."

"Then how about *Local Call?*"

"What's wrong with *Sorry, Wrong Number?*" Parker asked.

"Nothing," Hawes said. "That's a terrific title."

"Or I could write about this guy got drowned in the bathtub. His wife drowned him in the bathtub. That was a good case."

"You could call it *Glub,*" Brown said.

"*Glub* ain't a best-selling title," Parker said. "Also, she cut off his cock. The water was all red with his blood."

"Why'd she do that?" Brown asked, truly interested now.

"He was fuckin' around with some other broad," Parker said. "You shoulda seen the guy, he was a tiny little runt. His wife came in while he was taking a bath, she shoved him under the water, good-bye, Charlie. Then she cuts off his cock with his own straight razor, throws it out the window."

"The razor?"

"No, the cock. Hit an old lady walking by in the street. Hit her right on top of the head, knocked this plastic flower off her hat. She bends down to pick up the flower, she sees the cock laying on the sidewalk. Right away she wonders who she can sue. She picks it up, runs to her lawyer with it. Goes running down the street with this cock in her fist, in this city nobody even blinked."

"Carella and I once worked a case," Hawes said, "where this guy cut off another guy's hands."

"Why'd he do that?"

"Same reason. Love."

"That's *love?*"

"Love or money," Hawes said, and shrugged. "The only two reasons there are."

"Plus your lunatics," Brown said.

"Well, that's a whole 'nother ball game," Parker said. "Your lunatics. I once had a lunatic, he killed four priests before we caught up with him. We ast him why he was killing priests. He told us his father was a priest. How could that be, his father a priest?"

"Maybe his mother was a nun," Brown said.

"No, his mother was a registered nurse. Fifty years old, but gorgeous. Peaches Muldoon, her name was. Her square handle, I mean it, she was from Tennessee. Told me her son was nuts for sure, and she was glad I nailed him. Peaches Muldoon. A red-head. A real racehorse."

"Who'd *she* say the father was?"

"Her brother," Parker said.

"Nice case," Hawes said.

"Yeah. Maybe I oughta write about that one."

"You're not a priest."

"Sometimes I *feel* like a priest," Parker said. "You know the last time I got laid? Don't ask."

"Maybe you oughta go look up Peaches," Brown suggested.

"She's prolly dead by now," Parker said, giving the idea serious consideration. "This was maybe ten years ago, this case."

"She'd be sixty by now," Hawes said.

"If she ain't dead, yeah. But sixty ain't old, you know. I laid a lot of sixty-year-old broads. They have lots of experience, they know what they're doing."

He looked at the phone again.

"Maybe I *will* go shave," he said.

The two women knew each other well.

Annie Rawles was a Detective/First working out of the Rape Squad.

Eileen Burke was a Detective/Second who worked out of Special Forces.

They were in Annie's office discussing murder.

The clock on the wall read 4:30 P.M.

"Why'd they drag *you* in?" Eileen asked.

"My experience with decoys," Annie said. "I guess Homicide's getting desperate."

"Who caught the squeals?"

"Guy named Alvarez at the Seven-Two."

"In Calm's Point?"

"Yes."

"All three?"

"All three."

"Same area of the precinct?"

"The Canal Zone, down by the docks. You'd think you were in Houston."

"I've never been to Houston."

"Don't go."

8   **Ed McBain**

Eileen smiled.

She was five-feet nine-inches tall, with long legs, good breasts, flaring hips, flaming red hair, and green eyes. There was no longer a scar on her left cheek. Plastic surgery had taken care of that. But Annie wondered if there were still internal scars.

"You don't have to take this one," she said. "I know it's short notice."

"Well, tell me some more," Eileen said.

"Or it can wait till *next* Friday. Shit, Homicide only called me an hour ago. Told me Alvarez wasn't making any headway, maybe the spic needed a helping hand. Homicide's words, not mine."

"Good old Homicide," Eileen said, and shook her head knowingly.

She wondered if Annie had doubts about her handling this one. She hadn't handled a really difficult one since the accident. Calling it an "accident" made it easier to think about. An accident was something that could happen to anyone. Something that needn't necessarily happen again. An accident wasn't a rapist slashing open your left cheek and then taking you by force.

Annie was watching her.

Eyes the color of loam behind glasses that gave her a scholarly look, black hair cut in a wedge, firm cupcake breasts on a slender body. About the same age as Eileen, a bit shorter. As hard and as brilliant as a diamond. Annie used to work out of Robbery, where she'd blown away two guys holding up a midtown bank. Blew them out of the air. If she hadn't been frightened by two seasoned hoods facing a max of twenty, would she have any sympathy for a decoy cop running scared?

Well, I've been on the job, Eileen thought, I'm *not* running scared.

But she was.

"When was the first one?" she asked.

"The tenth. A Friday night, full moon. Alvarez thought maybe a loonie. Then the second one turned up a week later, the seventeenth. And another one last Friday night."

"Always Friday night, huh?"

"So far."

"So tonight's Friday, so Homicide wants a decoy."

"So does Alvarez. I spoke to him right after I got the call. He sounds smart as hell, but so far he hasn't got a place to hang his hat."

"What's his thinking on it?"

"You don't know the Zone, huh?"

"No."

"Then you missed what I was saying about Houston."

"I guess so."

"There's an area bordering the Ship Canal down there, it's infested with hookers and dope. Sleaziest dives I've ever seen in my life. The docks on the Calm's Point Canal run a close second."

"Are they hookers then? The victims?"

"Yes. Hookers."

"All three?"

"One of them only sixteen years old."

Eileen nodded.

"What'd he use?" she asked.

Annie hesitated.

"A knife," she said.

And suddenly it all played back again in Eileen's head. . . .

Her hand going for the Browning .380 automatic tucked into her boot, Don't force me to cut you, *the pistol coming free of its holster, moving into firing position—and he slashed her face. Sudden fire blazed a trail across her cheek. She dropped the gun at once.* Good girl, *he said. And slashed her pantyhose and the panties underneath. . . .*

And . . .

And thrust the cold flat side of the knife against her . . . against her . . .

"Want me to cut you here, too?"

She shook her head.

No, please, *she thought.*

And mumbled the words incoherently, No, please, *and said them aloud at last,* "No, please. Please. Don't . . . cut me again. Please."

"Want me to fuck you instead?"

"Don't cut me again."

Annie was watching her intently.

"Slit their throats with a knife," she said.

Eileen was covered with cold sweat.

"So . . . I . . . I guess they want me to play hooker, is that it?" she said.

"That's it."

"New girl in town, huh?"

"You've got it."

"Cruising? Or have they set up . . . ?"

"They're planting you in a place called Larry's Bar. On Fairview and East Fourth."

Eileen nodded.

"Tonight, huh?"

"Starting around eight."

"That's early, isn't it?"

"They want to give him enough rope."

"Where do I check in?"

"The Seven-Two. You can change there."

"Into what? The hookers today look like college girls."

"Not the ones working the Canal Zone."

Eileen nodded again.

"Has Alvarez picked my backups?"

"One. A big beefy guy named . . ."

"I want at least two," Eileen said.

"I'm your other one," Annie said.

Eileen looked at her.

"If you want me."

Eileen said nothing.

"I'm not afraid of using the piece," Annie said.

"I know you're not."

"But if you'd feel better with another man . . ."

"Nothing's going to make me feel better," Eileen said. "I'm scared shitless. You could back me with the Russian army, and I'd still be scared."

"Then don't do it," Annie said.

"Then when do I stop being scared?" Eileen asked.

The room went silent.

"Homicide asked me to get the best decoy I knew," Annie said softly. "I picked you."

"Thanks a lot," Eileen said.

But she smiled.

"You *are,* you know."

"I *was.*"

"Are," Annie said.

"Sweet talker," Eileen said.

And smiled again.

"So . . . it's up to you," Annie said, and looked up at the clock. "But you've got to let me know right away. They want everything in place by eight tonight."

"Who's this big beefy guy?"

"His name's Shanahan. Irish as Paddy's underwear, six-feet tall, weighs at least two hundred pounds. I wouldn't want to meet him in a dark alley, believe me."

"I *would,*" Eileen said. "I'd like an hour with him before I hit the street. Can he be in the squadroom by seven?"

"You'll do it then?"

"Only 'cause you're the other backup," Eileen said, and smiled again.

But she was trembling inside.

"This guy who killed them," she said. "Do they have any idea what he looks like?"

"Alvarez says he's got some statements that seem to jibe. But who knows what he'll look like tonight? If he comes in at all."

"Terrific," Eileen said.

"One thing for sure, though."

"Yeah?"

"He's passing himself off as a trick."

The saw ripped through wood, ripped through flesh and bone along the middle of the wooden box and the middle of the woman. Blood gushed from the track the saw made, following the sharp teeth. The saw itself was bloody when at last he withdrew it from box and woman. He looked up at the wall clock. 5:05 P.M. He nodded in grim satisfaction.

And lifted the lids on both sides of the box.

And the woman stepped out in one piece, grinning, and held her arms over her head, and the audience began to applaud and cheer.

"Thank you, thank you very much," the man said, bowing.

The audience was composed mostly of boys and girls between the ages of thirteen and eighteen because the performance was being held at the high school on North Eleventh. The principal of the school, Mr. Ellington, beamed contentedly. Hiring the magician had been his idea. A way to keep these restless teenagers happy and occupied for an hour or so before they hit the streets. He would make a little speech after the performance was over, which should be any minute now. He would tell them all to go home and have a good dinner and then put on their costumes and go out for a safe and sane Halloween in the secure knowledge that among the rights granted in a democracy was freedom of assembly—like the assembly they'd had this evening—and also freedom of assembly in the streets, but *not* the freedom to perform malicious mischief, definitely not. That would be his pitch. The kids, grateful for an hour's entertainment, would—he hoped—follow his directives. No one from Herman Raucher High would become involved in vandalism tonight. Nossir.

He watched now as the magician's assistant rolled the wooden box off the stage. She was a good-looking blonde, in her late twenties Ellington guessed, wearing a sequined costume that exposed to good advantage her long, long legs and her exuberant breasts. Ellington noticed that most of the boys in the auditorium could not take their eyes off the assistant's long legs and the popping tops of her creamy white breasts. He himself was having a little difficulty doing that. She was back on stage now, wheeling a tall box. A vertical one this time. The magician—whose name was Sebastian the Great—was wearing tails and a top hat. Ellington looked up at the clock. This was probably the closing number of the act. He hoped so because he wanted to make his little speech and get the kids the hell out of here. He had promised Estelle he would stop by on the way home from school. Estelle was the lady he stopped by to see every Wednesday and Friday afternoon, when his wife thought he had meetings with the staff. Estelle's legs weren't as long, nor were her breasts as opulent as those on the magician's assistant, but then again Estelle was forty-seven years old.

"Thank you, kids," Sebastian the Great said, "thank you. Now I know you're all anxious to get out there in the streets for a safe and sane Halloween, and so I won't keep you much longer. Ah, thank you, Marie," he said to his assistant.

Her name's Marie, Ellington thought, and wondered what her last name was, and wondered if she was listed in the phone book.

"You see here a little box—well, not so little because I'm a pretty tall fellow—which I'm going to step into in just a moment . . . thank you, Marie, you can go now, you've been very helpful, let's have a nice round of applause for Marie, kids."

Marie held her hands up over her head, legs widespread, big smile on her mouth, and the kids applauded and yelled, especially the boys, and then she did a cute little sexy turn and went strutting off the stage in her high heels.

"That's the last you'll see of Marie tonight," Sebastian said.

Shit, Ellington thought.

"And in just a few minutes, you'll see the last of me, too. What I'm going to do, kids, I'm going to step inside this box . . . ."

He opened the door on the face of the box.

"And I'm going to ask you all to count to ten . . . out loud . . . one, two, three, four, and so on—you all know how to count to ten, don't you?"

Laughter from the kids.

"And I'm going to ask your principal, Mr. Ellington, to come up here—Mr. Ellington, would you come up here now, please?—and when you reach the number ten, he's going to open the door of this box, and Sebastian the Great will be gone, kids, I will have disappeared, vanished, poof! So . . . ah, good, Mr. Ellington, if you'll just stand here beside the box, thank you. That's very good." He took off his top hat. Stepping partially into the box, he said, "I'm going to say good-bye to you now . . ."

Applause and cheering from the kids.

"Thank you, thank you," he said, "and I want to remind you again to please have a safe and sane Halloween out there. Now the minute I close this door, I want you to start counting out loud. And when you reach ten, Mr. Ellington will open the door and I'll be gone but not forgotten. Mr. Ellington? Are you ready?"

"Ready," Ellington said, feeling like an asshole.

"Good-bye, kids," Sebastian said, and closed the door behind him.

"One!" the kids began chanting. "Two! Three! Four! Five! Six! Seven! Eight! Nine! Ten!"

Ellington opened the door on the box.

Sebastian the Great had indeed vanished.

The kids began applauding.

Ellington went to the front of the stage, and held up his hands for silence.

He would have to remind the kids not to try sawing anybody in half, because that had been only a trick.

The station wagon pulled up to the curb in front of the liquor store on Culver and Ninth. The big woman behind the wheel was a curly-haired blonde in her late forties, wearing a blue dress with a tiny white floral print, a cardigan sweater over it. A kid was sitting beside her on the front seat. Three more kids were in the back of the car. The kids looked perhaps eleven or twelve years old, no older than that.

They threw open the doors and got out of the car.

"Have fun, kids," the blonde behind the wheel said.

The kids were all dressed like robbers.

Little black leather jackets, and little blue jeans, and little white sneakers, and little billed caps on their little heads, and little black masks over their eyes. They were all carrying shopping bags decorated with little orange pumpkins. They were all holding little toy pistols in their little hands. They went across the sidewalk in a chattering little excited group, and one of them opened the door to the liquor store. The clock on the wall behind the counter read 5:15 P.M. The owner of the store looked up the moment the bell over the door sounded.

"Trick or treat!" the little kids squealed in unison.

"Come on, kids, get out of here," the owner said impatiently. "This is a place of business."

And one of the little kids shot him in the head.

Parker had shaved and was back in the squadroom, rummaging through the file cabinets containing folders for all the cases the detectives had successfully closed.

In police work, there was no such thing as a solution. You never *solved* a case, you closed it out. Or it remained *open,* which meant the perpetrator was already in Buenos Aires or Nome, Alaska, and you'd *never* catch him. The Open File was the graveyard of police detection.

"I feel like a new man," Parker said. In fact, he looked like the same old Parker, except that he had shaved. "Muldoon," he said, "Muldoon, where are you, Muldoon?"

"You really gonna call a sixty-year-old lady?" Brown asked.

"Peaches Muldoon, correct," Parker said. "If she was well-preserved at fifty, she's prolly still got it all in the right places. Where the fuck's the file?"

"Look under Aging Nurses," Hawes said.

"Look under Decrepit Broads," Brown said.

"Yeah, bullshit, wait'll you see her picture," Parker said.

The clock on the squadroom wall read 5:30 P.M.

"Muldoon, here we go," Parker said, and yanked a thick file from the drawer.

The telephone rang.

"Who's catching?" Parker asked.

"I thought you were," Brown said.

"Me? No, no. You're up, Artie."

Brown sighed and picked up the phone.

"Eighty-Seventh Squad," he said, "Brown."

"Artie, this is Dave downstairs."

Sergeant Murchison, at the muster desk.

"Yeah, Dave."

"Adam Four just responded to a 10-20 on Culver and Ninth. Liquor store called Adams Wine & Spirits."

"Yeah?"

"They got a homicide there."

"Okay," Brown said.

"You got some people out, don't you?"

"Yes."

"Who? Can you take a look for me?"

Brown reached across the desk for the duty chart.

"Kling and Carella are riding together," he said. "Meyer and Genero are out solo."

"Any idea which sectors?"

"No."

"Okay, I'll try to raise them."

"Keep in touch."

"Will do."

Brown hung up.

"What?" Hawes asked.

"Homicide on Culver. There goes the neighborhood."

The telephone rang again.

"Take a look at this picture," Parker said, coming over to Brown's desk. "You ever see a body like this one?"

"Eighty-Seventh Squad, Hawes,"

"Look at those tits," Parker said.

"Hello, who am I talking to, please?" a woman's voice asked.

"Detective Hawes."

"Legs that won't quit," Parker said.

"My husband's gone," the woman said.

"Yes, ma'am," Hawes said, "let me give you the number for ..."

"My name is ..."

"It'll be best if you call Missing Persons, ma'am," Hawes said. "They're specially equipped to deal with ..."

"He disappeared here in *this* precinct," the woman said.

"Still ..."

"Docs that look like a fifty-year-old broad?" Parker asked.

The telephone rang again. Brown picked up.

"Eighty-Seventh Squad, Brown," he said.

"Artie? This is Genero."

"Yeah?"

"Artie, you won't believe this."

"What won't I believe?" Brown asked. He looked up at Parker, covered the mouthpiece, and whispered, "Genero."

Parker rolled his eyes.

"It happened again," Genero said.

"My name is Marie Sebastiani," the woman on Hawes's phone said. "My husband is Sebastian the Great."

Hawes immediately thought he was talking to a bedbug.

"Ma'am," he said, "if your husband's really gone ..."

"I'm at this restaurant, you know?" Genero said. "On Culver and Sixth?"

"Yeah?" Brown said.

"Where they had the holdup last night? I stopped by to talk to the owners?"

"Yeah?"

"My husband is a magician," Marie said. "He calls himself Sebastian the Great. He's disappeared."

Good magician, Hawes thought.

"And I go out back to look in the garbage cans?" Genero said. "See maybe somebody dropped a gun in there or something?"

"Yeah?" Brown said.

"I mean he's *really* disappeared," Marie said. "Vanished. I went out back of the high school where he was loading the car, and the car was gone, and so was Frank. And all his tricks were dumped in the driveway like ..."

"Frank, ma'am?"

"My husband. Frank Sebastiani. Sebastian the Great."

"It happened again, Artie," Genero said. "I almost puked."

"What happened again?"

"Maybe he just went home, ma'am," Hawes said.

"No, we live in the next state, he wouldn't have left without me. And his stuff was all over the driveway. I mean, expensive *tricks.*"

"So what are you saying, ma'am?"

"I'm saying somebody must've stolen the car and God knows what he did to Frank."

"Artie?" Genero said. "Are you with me?"

"I'm with you," Brown said, and sighed.

"It was in one of the garbage cans, Artie."

"What was in one of the garbage cans?"

"Which high school is that ma'am?" Hawes asked.

"Herman Raucher High. On North Eleventh."

"Are you there now?"

"Yes. I'm calling from a pay phone."

"You stay right there," Hawes said, "I'll get somebody to you."

"I'll be waiting out back," Marie said, and hung up.

"Artie, you better come over here," Genero said. "The Burgundy on Culver and Sixth."

"What is it you find in . . . ?"

But Genero had already hung up.

Brown slipped into his shoulder holster.

Hawes clipped his holster to his belt.

Parker picked up the telephone receiver.

"Peaches Muldoon, here I come," he said.

5:40 P.M. on Halloween night, the streets dark for almost an hour now, the city off daylight savings time since the twenty-sixth of the month. All the little monsters and goblins and devils and bats out in force, carrying their shopping bags full of candy from door to door, yelling "Trick or Treat!" and praying no one would give them a treat with a double-edged razor blade in it.

Brown looked at his watch.

Along about now, his wife, Caroline, would be taking Connie around. His eight-year-old daughter had previewed her costume for him last night. She'd looked like the most angelic witch he'd ever seen in his life. All next week, there'd be sweets to eat. The only people who profited from Halloween were the candymakers and the dentists. Brown was in the wrong profession.

He had chosen to walk to the Burgundy Restaurant on Culver and Sixth. It wasn't too far from the station house, and a cop—if Genero could be considered one—was already on the scene.

The night was balmy.

God, what an October this had been.

Leaves still on the trees in the park, dazzling yellows and reds and oranges and browns, daytime skies a piercing blue, nighttime skies pitch-black and sprinkled with stars. In a city where itchy citizens took off their overcoats far too early each spring, it now seemed proper and fitting that there was no need to put them on again quite yet. He walked swiftly toward Culver, turning to glance at E.T. hurrying by with Frankenstein's monster on one side and Dracula on the other. Smiling, he turned the corner onto Culver and began walking toward Sixth.

Genero was waiting on the sidewalk outside the restaurant.

He looked pale.

"What is it?" Brown asked.

"Come on back," Genero said. "I didn't touch it."

"Touch what?" Brown asked. But Genero was already walking up the alleyway on the right-hand side of the restaurant.

Garbage cans flanked either side of the restaurant's back door, illuminated by an overhead flood light.

"That one," Genero said.

Brown lifted the lid on the can Genero was pointing to.

The bloody upper torso of a human body was stuffed into the can, on top of a green plastic garbage bag.

The torso had been severed at the waist from the rest of the body.

The torso had no arms.

And no head.

"Why does this always happen to me?" Genero asked God.

2

"**I** once found a hand in an airlines bag," Genero said.

"No shit?" Monoghan asked without interest.

Monoghan was a Homicide cop. He usually worked in tandem with his partner Monroe, but there had been two homicides in the Eight-Seven tonight, a few blocks apart from each other, and Monoghan was here behind the restaurant on Culver and Sixth, and Monroe was over at the liquor store on Culver and Ninth. It was a shame; Monoghan without Monroe was like a bagel without lox.

"Cut off at the wrist," Genero said. "I almost puked."

"Yeah, a person could puke, all right," Monoghan said.

He was looking down into the garbage can where the bloody torso still rested on the green plastic bag.

"Nothing but a piece of fresh meat here," he said to Brown. Brown had a pained look in his eyes. He merely nodded.

"M.E. on the way?" Monoghan asked.

"Called him ten minutes ago."

"You won't need an ambulance for this one," Monoghan said.

"All you'll need is a shopping bag."

He laughed at his own little witticism.

He sorely missed Monroe.

"Looks like a man, don't it?" he said. "I mean, no knockers, all that hair on the chest."

"This hand I found," Genero said, "it was a man's, too. A great big hand. I nearly puked."

There were several uniformed cops in the alley now, and a couple of technicians sniffing around the back door of the restaurant, and a plainclothes lady cop from Photo taking her Polaroids. Crime Scene signs already up, even though this *wasn't* a crime scene in the strictest sense of the word, in that the crime had almost certainly taken place elsewhere. All they had here was the detritus of a crime, a piece of fresh meat—as Monoghan had called it—lying in a garbage can, the partial remains of what had once been a human being. That and whatever clues may have been left by the person who'd transported the torso to this particular spot.

"It's amazing the number of dismembered stiffs you get in this city," Monoghan said.

"Oh, boy, you're telling *me?*" Genero said.

Monoghan was wearing a black homburg, a black suit, a white shirt, and a black tie. His hands were in his jacket pockets, only the thumbs showing. He looked like a sad, neat undertaker. Genero was trying to look like a hip big-city detective disguised as a college boy. He was wearing blue slacks and a reindeer-patterned sweater over a sports shirt open at the throat. Brown penny loafers. No hat. Curly black hair, brown eyes. He resembled a somewhat stupid poodle.

Monoghan looked at him.

"You the one found this thing here?" he asked.

"Well, yes," Genero said, wondering if he should have admitted this.

"Any other parts in these other garbage cans?"

"I didn't look," Genero said, thinking one part had been plenty.

"Want to look now?"

"Don't get prints on any of those garbage-can lids," one of the techs warned.

Genero tented a handkerchief over his hand and began lifting lids.

There were no other parts.

"So all we got here is this chest here," Monoghan said.

"Hello, boys," the M.E. said, coming up the alley. "What've we got here?"

"Just this chest here," Monoghan said, indicating the torso.

The M.E. pecked into the garbage can.

"Very nice," he said, and put down his satchel. "Did you want me to pronounce it dead, or what?"

"You could give us a postmortem interval, that'd be helpful," Monoghan said.

"Autopsy'll give you that," the M.E. said.

"Looks of this one," Monoghan said, "somebody already *done* the autopsy. What'd he use, can you tell?"

"Who?" the M.E. said.

"Whoever cut him up in pieces."

"He wasn't a brilliant brain surgeon, I can tell you that," the M.E. said, looking at the torn and jagged flesh where the head, arms, and lower torso had been.

"So what was it? A cleaver? A hacksaw?"

"I'm not a magician," the M.E. said.

"Any marks, scars, tattoos?" Brown asked quietly.

"None that I can see. Let me roll it over."

Genero noticed that the M.E. kept referring to it as "it."

The M.E. rolled it over.

"None here, either," he said.

"Nothing but a piece of fresh meat," Monoghan said.

Hawes was wearing only a lightweight sports jacket over a shirt open at the throat, no tie, no hat. A mild breeze riffled his red hair; October this year was like springtime in the Rockies. Marie Sebastiani seemed uncomfortable talking to a cop. Most honest citizens did; it was the thieves of the world who felt perfectly at home with law enforcement officers.

Fidgeting nervously, she told him how she'd changed out of her costume and into the clothes she was now wearing—a tweed jacket and skirt, a lavender blouse and high-heeled pumps—while her husband, Sebastian the Great, a.k.a. Frank Sebastiani, had gone out behind the high school to load the car with all the *little* tricks he used in the act. And then *she'd* gone out back to where she was supposed to meet him, and the car was gone, and he was gone, and his tricks were scattered all over the driveway.

"By *little* tricks ..." Hawes said.

"Oh, you know, the rings, and the scarves, and the balls, and the bird cage ... well, all this stuff all over the place here. Jimmy comes with the van to pick up the boxes and the bigger stuff."

"Jimmy?"

"Frank's apprentice. He's a jack of all trades, drives the van to wherever we're performing, helps us load and unload, paints the boxes when they need it, makes sure all the spring catches are working properly ... like that."

"He dropped you both off today, did he?"

"Oh, yes."

"And helped you unload and all?"

"Same as always."

"And stayed for the performance?"

"No, I don't know where he went during the performance. Probably out for a bite to eat. He knew we'd be done here around five, five-thirty."

"So where is he now? Jimmy?"

"Well, I don't know. What time do you have?"

Hawes looked at his watch.

"Five after six," he said.

"Gee, I don't know *where* he is," Marie said. "He's usually very punctual."

"What time *did* you get done here?" Hawes asked.

"Like I said, around five-fifteen or so."

"And you changed your clothes ..."

"Yes. Well, so did Frank."

"What does he wear on stage?"

"Black tie and tails. And a top hat."

"And he changed into?"

"Is this important?"

"Very," Hawes said.

"Then let me get it absolutely correct," Marie said. "He put on a pair of blue slacks, and a blue sports shirt, no pattern on it, just the solid blue, and blue socks, and black shoes, and a . . . what do you call it? Houndstooth, is that the weave? A sort of jagged little black and blue weave. A houndstooth sports jacket. No tie.''

Hawes was writing now.

"How old is your husband?" he asked.

"Thirty-four."

"How tall is he?"

"Five-eleven."

"Weight?"

"One-seventy."

"Color of his hair?"

"Black."

"Eyes?"

"Blue."

"Does he wear glasses?"

"No."

"Is he white?"

"Well, of *course,*" Marie said.

"Any identifying marks, scars or tattoos?"

"Yes, he has an appendectomy scar. And also a menisectomy scar."

"What's that?" Hawes asked.

"He had a skiing accident. Tore the cartilage in his left knee. They removed the cartilage—what they call the meniscus. There's a scar there. On his left knee."

"How do you spell that?" Hawes asked. "Menisectomy?"

"I don't know," Marie said.

"On the phone, you told me you live in the next state . . ."

"Yes, I do."

"Where?"

"Collinsworth."

"The address?"

"604 Eden Lane."

"Apartment number?"

"It's a private house."

"Telephone number, area code first?"

"Well, I'll give you Frank's card," she said, and dug into her shoulder bag and came up with a sheaf of cards. She took one from the stack and handed it to Hawes. He scanned it quickly, wrote both the home and office phone numbers onto his pad, and then tucked the card into the pad's flap.

"Did you try calling home?" he asked.

"No. Why would I do that?"

"Are you sure he didn't go home without you? Maybe he figured this Jimmy would pick you up."

"No, we were planning on eating dinner here in the city."

"So he wouldn't have gone home without you."

"He never has."

"This Jimmy . . . what's his last name?"

"Brayne."

"Brain? Like in somebody's head?"

"Yes, but with a Y."

"B-R-A-*Y*-N?"

"With an E on the end."

"B-R-A-Y-N-E?"

"Yes."

"James Brayne."

"Yes."

"And his address?"

"He lives with us."

"Same house?"

"A little apartment over the garage."

"And *his* phone number?"

"Oh, gee," she said. "I'm not sure I remember it."

"Well, try to remember," Hawes said, "because I think we ought to call back home, see if either of them maybe went back there."

"They wouldn't do that," Marie said.

"Maybe they got their signals crossed," Hawes said. "Maybe Jimmy thought your husband was going to take the stuff in the car . . ."

"No, the big stuff won't fit in the car. That's why we have the van."

"Or maybe your husband thought you were getting a ride back with Jimmy . . ."

"I'm sure he didn't."

"What kind of a car was your husband driving?"

"A 1984 Citation. A two-door coupe."

"Color?"

"Blue."

"License-plate number?"

"DL 74-3681."

"And the van?"

"A '79 Ford Econoline."

"Color?"

"Tan, sort of."

"Would you know the license-plate number on that one?"

"RL 68-7210."

"In whose name are the vehicles registered?"

"My husband's."

"Both registered across the river?"

"Yes."

"Let's find a phone okay?" Hawes said.

"There's one inside," she said, "but calling them won't do any good."

"How do you know?"

"Because Frank wouldn't have dumped his tricks all over the driveway this way. These tricks cost money."

"Let's try calling them, anyway."

"It won't do any good," Marie said. "I'm telling you."

He dialed Sebastiani's home and office numbers, and got no answer at either.

Marie at last remembered the number in the room over the garage, and he dialed that one, too. Nothing.

"Well," he said, "let me get to work on this. I'll call you as soon as . . ."

"How am I going to get home?" Marie asked.

They always asked how they were going to get home.

"There are trains running out to Collinsworth, aren't there?"

"Yes, but . . ."

"I'll drop you off at the station."

"What about all those tricks outside in the driveway?"

"Maybe we can get the school custodian to lock them up someplace. Till your husband shows up."

"What makes you think he'll show up?"

"Well, I'm sure he's okay. Just some crossed signals, that's all."

"I'm not sure I want to go home tonight," Marie said.

"Well, ma'am . . ."

"I think I may want to . . . could I come to the police station with you? Could I wait there till you hear anything about Frank?"

"That's entirely up to you, ma'am. But it may take a while before we . . ."

"And can you lend me some money?" she asked.

He looked at her.

"For dinner?"

He kept looking at her.

"I'll pay you back as soon as . . . as soon as we find Frank. I'm sorry, but I've only got a few dollars on me. Frank was the one they paid, he's the one who's got all the money."

"How *much* money, ma'am?"

"Well, just enough for a hamburger or something."

"I meant how much money does your husband have on him?"

"Oh. Well, we got a hundred for the job. And he probably had a little something in his wallet, I don't know how much."

Which lets out robbery, Hawes thought. Although in this city, there were people who'd slit your throat for a nickel. He suddenly wondered how much money he himself was carrying. This was the first time in his entire life that a victim had asked him for a loan.

"I'm sort of hungry myself," he said. "Let's find the custodian and then go get something to eat."

Monroe looked bereft without Monoghan.

The clock on the liquor-store wall read 6:10 P.M.

He was standing behind the cash register, where the owner of the store had been shot dead a bit more than an hour earlier. The body was already gone. There was only blood and a chalked outline on the floor behind the counter. The cash register was empty.

"There was four of them," the man talking to Meyer said.

Meyer had been cruising the area when Sergeant Murchison raised him on the radio. He had got here maybe ten minutes after it was all over, and had immediately radioed back with a confirmed D.O.A. Murchison had informed Homicide, so here was Monroe, all alone, and looking as if he'd lost his twin brother. He was wearing a black homburg, a black suit, a white shirt, and a black tie. His hands were in his jacket pockets, only the thumbs showing. He looked like a sad, neat undertaker. Meyer wondered where Monoghan was. Wherever he was, Meyer figured he'd be dressed exactly like Monroe. Even if he was home sick in bed, he'd be dressed like Monroe.

Meyer himself was wearing brown slacks, a brown cotton turtleneck, and a tan sports jacket. He thought he looked very dapper tonight. With his bald head and his burly build, he figured he looked like Kojak, except more handsome. He was sorry Kojak was off the air now. He'd always felt Kojak gave bald cops a good name.

"Little kids," the man said.

This was the third time he'd told Meyer that four little kids held up the liquor store and shot the owner.

"What do you mean, little kids?" Monroe asked from behind the cash register.

"Eleven, twelve years old," the man said.

His name was Henry Kirby, and he lived in a building up the street. He was perhaps sixty, sixty-five years old, a thin, graying man wearing a short-sleeved sports shirt and wrinkled polyester slacks. He'd told first Meyer and then Monroe that he was coming to the store to buy a bottle of wine when he saw these little kids running out with shopping bags and guns. Monroe still couldn't believe it.

"You mean *children?*" he said.

"Little kids, yeah," Kirby said.

"Grade-schoolers?"

"Yeah, little kids."

"Pre-pubescent twerps?" Monroe said.

He was doing okay without Monoghan. Without Monoghan, he was being Monoghan and Monroe all by himself.

"Yeah, little kids," Kirby said.

"What were they wearing?" Meyer said.

"Leather jackets, blue jeans, sneakers and masks."

"What kind of masks?" Monroe asked. "Like these monster masks? These rubber things you pull over your head?"

"No, just these little black masks over their eyes. Like robbers wear. They were robbers, these kids."

"And you say there were four of them?"

"Four, right."

"Ran out of the store with shopping bags and guns?"

"Shopping bags and guns, right."

"What kind of guns?" Monroe asked.

"Little guns."

"Like twenty-twos?"

"I'm not so good at guns. These were little guns."

"Like Berettas?"

"I'm not so good at guns."

"Like little Brownings?"

"I'm not so good at guns. They were little guns."

"Did you hear any shots as you approached the store?" Meyer asked.

"No, I didn't. I didn't know Ralph was dead till I walked inside."

"Ralph?" Monroe said.

"Ralph Adams. It's his store. Adams Wine & Spirits. He's been here in this same spot for twenty years."

"Not no more," Monroe said tactfully.

"So where'd these kids go when they came out of the store?" Meyer asked.

He was thinking this sounded like Fagin's little gang. The Artful Dodger, all that crowd. A cop he knew in England had written recently to say his kids would be celebrating—if that was the word for it—Halloween over there this year. Lots of American executives living in England, their kids had introduced the holiday to the British. Just what they need, Meyer thought. Maybe next year, twelve-year-old British kids'd start holding up liquor stores.

"They ran to this car parked at the curb," Kirby said.

"A vehicle?" Monroe said.

"Yeah, a car."

"An automobile?"

"A car, yeah."

"What kind of car?"

"I'm not so good at cars."

"Was it a big car or a little car?"

"A regular car."

"Like a Chevy or a Plymouth?"

"I'm not so good at cars."

"Like an Olds or a Buick?"

"A regular car, is all."

"They all got in this car?" Meyer asked.

"One in the front seat, three in the back."

"Who was driving?"

"A woman."

"How old a woman?"

"Hard to say."

"What'd she look like?"

"She was a blonde."

"What was she wearing?"

"I really couldn't see. It was dark in the car. I could see she was a blonde, but that's about all."

"How about when the kids opened the doors?" Monroe asked. "Didn't the lights go on?"

"Yeah, but I didn't notice what she was wearing. I figured this was maybe a car pool, you know?"

"What do you mean?"

"Well, the kids were all about the same age, so they couldn't all be *her* kids, you know what I mean? So I figured she was just driving maybe her own kid and some of his friends around. For Halloween, you know?"

"You mean the kid's mother was a wheelman, huh?"

"Well . . ."

"For a stickup, huh? A wheelman for four eleven-year-olds."

"Or twelve," Kirby said. "Eleven or twelve."

"These kids," Meyer said. "Were all of them boys?"

"They were *dressed* like boys, but I really couldn't say. They all went by so fast. Just came running out of the store and into the car."

"Then what?" Monroe asked.

"The car pulled away."

"Did you see the license plate?"

"I'm not so good at license plates," Kirby said.

"Was it you who called the police?" Meyer asked.

"Yes, sir. I called 911 the minute I saw Ralph lying dead there behind the counter."

"Did you use this phone here?" Monroe asked, indicating the phone alongside the register.

"No, sir. I went outside and used the pay phone on the corner."

"Okay, we've got your name and address," Monroe said, "we'll get in touch if we need you."

"Is there a reward?" Kirby asked.

"For what?"

"I thought there might be a reward."

"We're not so good at rewards," Monroe said. "Thanks a lot, we'll be in touch."

Kirby nodded glumly and walked out of the store.

"Halloween ain't what it used to be," Monroe said.

"You just got yourself another backup," Kling said.

"No," Eileen said.

"What do you mean no? You're going into one of the worst sections in the city . . ."

"Without you," she said.

". . . looking for a guy who's already killed . . ."

"Without *you*, Bert."

"Why?"

They were in an Italian restaurant near the Calm's Point Bridge. It was twenty minutes past six; Eileen had to be at the Seven-Two in forty minutes. She figured five minutes over the bridge, another five to the precinct, plenty of time to eat without hurrying. She probably shouldn't be eating, anyway. In the past, she'd found that going out hungry gave her a fighter's edge. Plenty of time to eat *after* you caught the guy. Have two martinis after you caught him, down a sirloin and a platter of fries. After you caught him. If you caught him. Sometimes you didn't catch him. Sometimes he caught you.

She was carrying her hooker threads and her hardware in a tote bag sitting on the floor to the left of her chair. Kling was sitting opposite her, hands clasped on the tabletop, leaning somewhat forward now, blond hair falling onto his forehead, intent look in his eyes, wanting to know why she didn't need a tagalong boyfriend tonight.

"Why do you think?" she asked.

The chef had overcooked the spaghetti. They'd specified *al dente* but this was the kind of dive where the help thought Al Dente was some guy with Mafia connections.

"I think you're crazy is what I think."

"Thanks."

"Damn it, if I can throw some extra weight your way . . ."

"I don't want you throwing anything my way. I've got a guy who's twice your size and a woman who can shoot her way out of a revolution. That's all I need. Plus myself."

"Eileen, I won't get in your way. I'll just . . ."

"No."

"I'll just be there if you need me."

"You really don't understand, do you?"

"No, I don't."

"You're not just another cop, Bert."

"I know that."

"You're my . . ."

She debated saying "boyfriend" but that sounded like a teenager's steady. She debated saying "lover" but that sounded like a dowager's kept stud. She debated saying "roommate" but that sounded like you lived with either another woman or a eunuch. Anyway, they weren't actually living together, not in the same apartment. She settled for what had once been a psychologist's term, but which had now entered the jargon as a euphemism for the guy or girl with whom you shared an unmarried state.

"You're my S.O." she said.

"Your what?"

"Significant Other."

"I should hope so," Kling said. "Which is why I want to . . ."

"Listen, are you dense?" she asked. "I'm a cop going out on a job. What the hell's the matter with you?"

"Eileen, I . . ."

"Yes, *what?* Don't you think I can cut it?"

She had chosen an unfortunate word.

Cut.

She saw the look on his face.

"That's just what I mean," she said.

"What are you talking about?"

"I'm going to get cut again," she said, "don't worry about it."

He looked at her.

"This time I shoot to kill," she said.

He took a deep breath.

"This spaghetti tastes like a sponge," she said.

"What time are you due there?"

"Seven."

He looked up at the clock.

"Where are they planting you?"

"A bar called Larry's. On Fairview and East Fourth."

"This guy Shanahan, is he any good?"

"I hope so," she said, and shoved her plate aside. "Could we get some coffee, do you think? And how come you're chalking off Annie?"

"I'm not . . ."

"I'd trade a hundred Shanahans for Annie."

"Calm down, Eileen."

"I'm calm," she said icily. "I just don't like your fucking attitude. You want to hand wrestle me? Prove you can go out there tonight and do the job better than I can?"

"Nobody said . . ."

"I can do the job," she said.

He looked into her eyes.

"I can do it," she said.

He didn't want to leave the parts where they'd be found too easily, and yet at the same time he didn't want to hide them so well that they wouldn't be discovered for weeks. This was tricky business here. Putting the pieces of the jigsaw in different places, making sure he wasn't spotted while he was distributing the evidence of bloody murder.

He'd dropped the first one behind a restaurant on Culver, near Sixth, figuring they'd be putting out more garbage when they closed tonight, hoping they'd discover the upper torso then and immediately call the police. He didn't want to scatter the various parts in locations too distant from each other because he wanted this to remain a strictly local matter, one neighborhood, one precinct, *this* precinct. At the same time, he couldn't risk someone finding any one of the parts so quickly that there'd be police crawling all over the neighborhood and making his job more difficult.

He wanted them to put it all together in the next little while.

Two, three days at the most, depending on how long it took them to find the parts and make identification.

By then, he'd be far, far away.

He cruised the streets now, driving slowly, looking for prospects.

The other parts of the body—the head, the hands, the arms, the lower torso—were lying on a tarpaulin in the trunk.

More damn kids in the streets tonight.

Right now, only the little ones were out. In an hour or so, you'd get your teenyboppers looking for trouble, and later tonight you'd get your older teenagers, the ones *really* hoping to do damage. Kick over a garbage can, find a guy's arm in it. How does that grab you, boys?

He smiled.

Police cars up ahead, outside a liquor store.

Bald guy coming out to the curb, studying the sidewalk and then the street.

Trouble.

But not *his* trouble.

He cruised on by.

Headed up to the Stem, made a right turn, scanning the storefronts. Kids swarming all over the avenue, trick or treat, trick or treat. Chinese restaurant there on the right. All-night supermarket on the corner. Perfect if there was a side alley. One-way side street, he'd have to drive past, make a right at the next corner, and then another right onto Culver, come at it from there. Stopped for the red light at the next corner, didn't want some eager patrolman pulling him over for a bullshit violation. Made the right turn. Another light on Culver. Waited for that one to change. Turned onto culver, drove up one block, made another right onto the one-way street. Drove up it slowly. Good! An alley between the corner super-market and the apartment house alongside it. He drove on by, went through the whole approach a second time. Guy in an apron standing at the mouth of the alley, lighting a cigarette. Drove by again. And again. And again and again until the alley and the sidewalk were clear. He made a left turn into the alley. Cut the ignition, yanked out the keys. Came around the car. Unlocked the truck. Yanked out one of the arms. Eased the trunk shut. Walked swiftly to the nearest garbage can. Lifted the lid. Dropped the arm in it. Left the lid slightly askew on top of the can. Got back in the car again, started it, and backed slowly out of the alley and into the street.

Two down, he thought.

3

The police stations in this city all looked alike. Even the newer ones began looking like the older ones after a while. A pair of green globes flanking the entrance steps, a patrolman standing on duty outside in case anybody decided to go in with a bomb. White numerals lettered onto each of the globes: 72. Only the numbers changed. Everything else was the same. Eileen could have been across the river and uptown in the Eight-Seven.

Scarred wooden entrance doors, glass-paneled in the upper halves. Just inside the doors was the muster room. High desk on the right, looked like a judge's bench, waist-high brass railing some two feet in front of it, running the length of it. Sergeant sitting behind it. On the wall behind him, photographs of the mayor and the police commissioner and a poster printed with the Miranda-Escobedo warnings in English and in Spanish. Big American flag on the wall opposite the desk. Wanted posters on the bulletin board under it. She flashed her shield at the sergeant, who merely nodded, and then she headed for the iron-runged steps at the far end of the room.

Rack with charging walkie-talkies on the wall there, each unit stenciled PROPERTY OF 72ND PRECINCT. Staircase leading down to the holding cells in the basement, and up to the Detective Division on the second floor, hand-lettered sign indicating the way. She climbed the steps, apple green walls on either side of her, paint flaking and hand-smudged. She was wearing sensible, low-heeled walking shoes, a cardigan sweater over a white cotton blouse and a brown woolen skirt. The hooker gear was still in the tote bag, together with her hardware.

Down the corridor past the Interrogation Room, and the Clerical Office, and the men's and women's toilets, and the locker rooms, through a wide doorway, and then to the slatted wooden rail divider with green metal filing cabinets backed up against it on the inside. Stopped at the gate in the railing. Flashed the potsy again at the guy sitting behind the closest desk.

"Eileen Burke," she said. "I'm looking for Shanahan."

"You found him," Shanahan said, and got to his feet and came around the desk, hand extended. He was not as big as Annie had described him, five-eleven or so, maybe a hundred and seventy pounds, a hundred and eighty. Eileen wished he were bigger. Black hair and blue eyes, toothy grin, what Eileen's father used to call a black Irishman. "Mike," he said, and took her hand in a firm grip. "Glad to have you with us. Come on in, you want some coffee?"

"Sounds good," she said, and followed him through the gate in the railing and over to his desk. "Light with one sugar."

"Coming right up," he said, and went to where a Silex pot of water was sitting on a hot plate. "We only got instant," he said, "and that powdered creamer stuff, but the sugar's real."

"Good enough," she said.

He spooned instant coffee and creamer into a cup, poured hot water over it, spooned sugar into it with the same white plastic spoon, stirred it, and then carried the cup back to his desk. She was still standing.

"Sit down, sit down," he said. "I'll buzz Lou, tell him you're here."

He looked up at the clock.

Ten minutes to seven.

"I thought you and Annie might be coming over together," he said, and picked up the phone receiver. "Good lady, Annie, I used to work with her in Robbery." He stabbed at a button on the base of the phone, waited, and then said, "Lou? Eileen Burke's here, you want to come on back?" He listened. "No, not yet." He looked at the clock again. "Uh-huh," he said. "Okay, fine." He put the receiver back on the cradle. "He'll be right here," he said to Eileen. "He's down the hall in Clerical, thought you might want to look over the reports on the case. We been working it together, Lou and me, not that we're getting such hot results. Which is why Homicide's on our backs, huh?"

She registered this last silently. She did not want a backup harboring a grudge over Homicide's interference. Some cops treated a tough case as if it were a sick child. Nurse it along, take its temperature every ten minutes, change the sheets, serve the hot chicken soup. Anybody else went near it, watch out. She hoped that wasn't the situation here. She wished the Seven-Two had *asked* for assistance, instead of having it dumped on them.

"How's the coffee?" Shanahan asked.

She hadn't touched it. She lifted the cup now. Squadroom coffee cups all looked alike. Dirty. In some squadrooms, the detectives had their initials painted on the cups, so they could tell one dirty cup from another. She sipped at the coffee. The imprint of her lipstick appeared on the cup's rim. It would probably still be there a month from now.

"Okay?" he said.

"Yes, fine," she said.

"Ah, here's Lou," he said, looking past her shoulder toward the railing. She turned in the chair just in time to see a slight, olive-complexioned man coming through the gate. Small mustache under his nose. Thick manila file folder in his right hand. Five-nine, she estimated. Moved like a bullfighter, narrow shoulders and waist, delicate hands. But you could never tell. Hal Willis at the Eight-Seven was only five-eight and he could throw any cheap thief on his ass in three seconds flat.

"Burke?" he said. "Nice to see you." No trace of an accent. Second- or third-generation American, she guessed. He extended his hand. Light, quick grip, almost instant release. No smile on his face. "Lou Alvarez," he said. "Glad to have you with us, we can use the help."

Party manners? Or a genuine welcome? She wished she knew. It would be her ass on the line out there tonight.

"I've got the file here," he said, "you might want to take a look at it while we're waiting for Rawles." He looked up at the clock. Still only five minutes to seven, but he nodded sourly. Was this an indication that he thought all women were habitually late? Eileen took the manila folder from him.

"You can skip over the pictures," he said.

"Why?"

Alvarez shrugged.

"Suit yourself," he said.

She was looking at the photographs when Annie walked in.

"Hi," Annie said, and glanced up at the clock.

Seven sharp.

"Hello, Mike," she said, "how's The Chameleon these days?"

"Comme-ci, comme-ça," Shanahan said, and shook her hand.

"We used to call him The Chameleon," she explained to Eileen, and then said, "Annie Rawles," and offered her hand to Alvarez.

"Lou Alvarez."

He took her hand. He seemed uncomfortable shaking hands with women. Eileen was suddenly glad it would be Shanahan out there with her tonight.

"Why The Chameleon?" she asked.

"Man of a thousand faces," Annie said, and looked at the photograph in Eileen's hand. "Nice," she said, and grimaced.

"Never mind the pictures," Alvarez said, "the pictures can't talk. We got statements in there from a couple of girls working the Zone, they give us a pretty good idea who we're looking for. Homicide's been pressuring us on this from minute one. That's 'cause the mayor made a big deal in the papers about cleaning up the Zone. So Homicide dumps it on us. You help us close this one out," he said to Eileen, "I'll personally give you a medal. Cast it in bronze all by myself."

"I was hoping for gold," Eileen said.

"You'd better take a look at those other pictures," Shanahan said.

"She don't have to look at them," Alvarez said.

"Which ones?" Eileen asked.

"You trying to spook her?"

"I'm trying to prepare her."

"She don't have to look at the pictures," Alvarez said.

But Eileen had already found them.

The earlier photographs had shown slashed faces, slit throats.

These showed rampant mutilation below.

"Used the knife top and bottom," Shanahan said.

"Uh-huh," Eileen said.

"Slashed the first girl in the doorway two blocks from the bar."

"Uh-huh."

"Second one in an alleyway on East Ninth. Last one on Canalside."

"Uh-huh."

"What I'm saying is watch your step," Shanahan warned. "This ain't your garden variety weirdo jumpin' old ladies in the park. This is a fuckin' animal, and he means business. You get in the slightest bit of trouble, you holler. I'll be there in zero flat."

"I'm not afraid to holler," Eileen said.

"Good. We ain't trying to prove nothing here, we only want to catch this guy."

"I'm the one who catches him," Alvarez said, "I'll cut off his balls."

Eileen looked at him.

"What'd these other girls tell you?" Annie asked.

She did not want Eileen to keep studying those pictures. Once around the park was once too often. She took them from her hand, glanced at them only cursorily, and put them back into the folder. Eileen looked up at her questioningly. But Alvarez was already talking.

"You familiar with the Canal Zone, you know most of the girls work on the street," he said. "A car pulls up, the girl leans in the window, they agree on a price, and she does the job while the trick drives them around the block. It's Have Mouth, Will Travel, is what is it. But there's a bar near the docks where you get a slightly better-class hooker. We're talking comparative here. None of these girls are racehorses."

"What about this bar?" Annie said.

"It's called Larry's, on Fairview and East Fourth. The girls working the cars go in there every now and then, shoot up in the toilet, fix their faces, whatever. But there's also some girls a little younger and a little prettier who hang out there looking for tricks. Again, we're talking comparative. The girls on the meat rack outside get only five bucks for a handjob and ten for a blowjob. The ones working the bar get double that."

"The point is," Shanahan said, "the three girls he ripped were working the bar."

"So that's where you're planting me," Eileen said.

"Be safer all around," Alvarez said.

"I'm not looking for safe," she said, bristling.

"No, and you're not a real hooker, either," Alvarez said, bristling himself. "You stand out there on the street, you keep turning down tricks, the other girls'll make you for fuzz in a minute. You'll be standing out there all alone before the night's ten minutes old."

"Okay," she said.

"I want this guy," he said.

"So do I."

"Not the way I want him. I got a daughter the age of that little girl in there," he said, wagging his finger at the folder.

"Okay," Eileen said again.

"You work the bar," Alvarez said, "you get a chance to call your own shots. You played hooker before?"

"Yes."

"Okay, so I don't have to tell you how to do your job."

"That's right, you don't."

"But there are some mean bastards down there in the Zone, and not all of them are looking to carve you up. You better step easy all around. This ain't Silk Stocking work."

"None of it is," Eileen said.

They both glared at each other.

"What'd they say about him?" Annie asked, jumping in.

"What?" Alvarez said.

Still angry. Figuring Homicide had sent him an amateur. Figuring she'd be spotted right off as a plant. Fuck you and your daughter both, Eileen thought. I know my job. And it's still *my* ass out there.

"These girls you talked to," Annie said. "What'd they say?"

"What?"

"About the guy, she means," Shanahan said. "This ain't gospel, Annie, this is maybe just hookers running scared, which they got every right to be. But on the nights of the murders, they remember a guy sitting at the bar. Drinking with the victims. The three he ripped. Same guy on three different Friday nights. Big blond guy, six-two, six-three, maybe two hundred pounds, dressed different each time, but blending in with everybody else in the joint."

"Meaning?"

"Meaning Friday-night sleaze. No uptown dude looking for kicks."

"Do you get any of those?" Eileen asked.

"Now and then," Shanahan said. "They don't last long in the Zone. Hookers ain't the only predators there. But this guy looked like one of the seamen off the ships. Which don't necessarily mean he *was,* of course."

"Anything else we should know about him?"

"Yeah, he had them in stitches."

"What do you mean?"

"Kept telling them jokes."

Eileen looked at him.

"Yeah, I know what you're thinking," Shanahan said. "A stand-up comic with a knife."

"Anything else?"

"He wears eyeglasses," Alvarez said.

"One of the girls thinks he has a tattoo on his right hand. Near the thumb. She's the only one who mentioned it."

"What kind of tattoo?"

"She couldn't remember."

"How many girls did you talk to?"

"Four *dozen* altogether," Alvarez said, "but only two of them gave us a handle."

"What time was this?" Annie asked. "When they saw him at the bar with the victims?"

"Varied. As early as nine, as late as two in the morning."

"Gonna be a long night," Annie said, and sighed.

Shanahan looked up at the clock.

"We better work out our strategy," he said. "So we can move when he docs. Once he gets Eileen outside . . ."

He let the sentence trail.

The clock ticked into the silence of the squadroom.

"Do they know you down there in the Zone?" Eileen asked.

Shanahan looked at her.

"Do they?"

"Yes, but . . ."

"Then what the hell . . . ?"

"I'll be . . ."

"What good's a backup who . . . ?"

"You won't recognize me, don't worry."

"No? What does the bartender say when you walk in? Hello, Detective Shanahan?"

"Six-to-five right this minute, you won't know me when I walk in," Shanahan said.

"Don't take the bet," Annie said.

"Will I know you if I have to holler?"

"You'll know me then. Because I'll be there."

"You're on," Eileen said. "But if I make you, I go straight home. I walk out of there and go straight home. Understood?"

"I'd do the same. But you won't know me."

"I hope not. I hope I lose the bet."

"You will," Annie promised.

"I didn't like your shooting him," the blonde at the wheel of the station wagon said. "That wasn't at all necessary, Alice."

Alice said nothing.

"You fire the guns in the air to scare them, to let them know you mean business, that's all. If that man you shot is dead, the rest of the night could be ruined for us."

Alice still said nothing.

"The beauty part of this," the blonde said, "is they never expect lightning to strike twice in the same night. Are you listening, kiddies?"

None of the kids said a word.

The digital dashboard clock read 7:04.

"They figure you do a stickup, you go home and lay low for a while. That's the beauty part. We play our cards right tonight, we got home with forty grand easy. I mean, a Friday night? Your liquor stores'll be open, some of them, till midnight, people stocking up for the weekend. Plenty of gold in the registers, kids, there for the taking. No more shooting people, have you got that?''

The kids said nothing.

The eyes behind the masks darted, covering both sides of the avenue. The slits in the masks made all the eyes look Oriental, even the blue ones.

''Especially you, Alice. Do you hear me?''

Alice nodded stiffly.

''There she is,'' the blonde said, ''number two,'' and began easing the station wagon in toward the curb.

The liquor store was brightly lighted.

The lettering on the plate-glass window read FAMOUS BRANDS WINE & WHISKEY.

''Have fun, kids,'' the blonde said.

The kids piled out of the car.

''Trick or treat, trick or treat!'' they squealed at an old woman coming out of the liquor store.

The old woman giggled.

''How *cute!*'' she said to no one.

Inside the store, the kids weren't so cute.

The owner had his back to them, reaching up for a half-gallon of Johnny Walker Red.

Alice shot him at once.

The thirty-year-old account executive standing in front of the counter screamed. She shot him, too.

The kids cleaned out the cash register in less than twelve seconds. One of them took a fifth of Canadian Club from the shelves. Then they ran out of the store again, giggling and yelling, ''Trick or treat, trick or treat!''

''Hello, Peaches?'' the man on the telephone said.

''Yes?''

''I've been trying to reach you all day. My secretary left your number, but she didn't say which agency you're with.''

''Agency?''

''Yes. This is Phil Hendricks at Camera Works. We're shooting some stuff next week, and my secretary thought you might be right for the job. How old are you, Peaches?''

''Forty-nine,'' she said without hesitation. Lying a little. Well, lying by eleven years, but who was counting?

''That's perfect,'' he said, ''this is stuff for the Sears catalogue, a half-dozen mature women modeling house-dresses. If you'll give me the name of your agency, I'll call them in the morning.''

''I don't have an agency,'' Peaches said.

''You don't? Well, that's strange. I mean ... well, how long have you been modeling?''

''I'm not a model,'' Peaches said.

"You're not? Then how'd my secretary . . . ?"

There was a long, puzzled silence on the line.

"This *is* Peaches Muldoon, isn't it?" he said.

"Yes," she said, "but I've never . . ."

"349-4040?"

"That's the number. But your secretary must've . . ."

"Well, here's your name and number right here in her handwriting," he said. "But you say you're not a model?"

"No, I'm an RN."

"A what?"

"A registered nurse."

"Then how'd she . . . ?"

Another puzzled silence.

"Have you ever *thought* of modeling?" he asked.

"Well . . . not seriously."

"Because maybe you mentioned to someone that you were looking for modeling work, and this got to my secretary somehow. That's the only thing I can figure."

"What's your secretary's name?"

"Linda. Linda Greeley."

"No, I don't know anyone by that name."

"*Did* you mention to someone that you might be interested in modeling?"

"Well . . . you know . . . people are always telling me I should try modeling, but you know how people talk. I never take them seriously. I mean, I'm not a kid anymore, you know."

"Well, forty-nine isn't exactly *ancient*," he said, and laughed.

"Well, I suppose not. But people try to flatter you, you know. I'm not really beautiful enough to do modeling. There's a certain type, you know. For modeling."

"What type *are* you, Peaches?" he asked.

"Well, I don't know how to answer that."

"Well, how tall are you, for example?"

"Five-nine," she said.

"How much do you weigh?"

"I could lose a little weight right now," she said, "believe me."

"Well, there isn't a woman on earth who doesn't think she could stand to lose a few pounds. How much *do* you weigh, Peaches?"

"A hundred and twenty," she said. Lying a little. Well, lying by ten pounds. Well, twenty pounds, actually.

"That's not what I'd call *obese*," he said. "Five-nine, a hundred-twenty."

"Well, let's say I'm . . . well . . . zoftig, I guess."

"Are you Jewish, Peaches?"

"What?"

"That's a Jewish expression, zoftig," he said. "But Muldoon isn't Jewish, is it?"

"No, no. I'm Irish."

"Red hair, I'll bet."

"How'd you guess?" she asked, and laughed.

"And isn't that a faint Southern accent I detect?"

"I'm from Tennessee originally. I didn't think it still showed."

"Oh, just a trace. Which is why zoftig sounded so strange on your lips," he said. "Well, I'm sorry you're not a model, Peaches, truly. We're paying a hundred and twenty-five a hour, and we're shooting something like two dozen pages, so this could've come to a bit of change. Do you work full time as a nurse?"

"No. I do mostly residential work."

"Then you might be free to . . ."

He hesitated.

"But if you're not experienced . . ."

He hesitated again.

"I just don't know," he said. "What we're looking for, you see, is a group of women who are mature and who could be accepted as everyday housewives. We're not shooting any glamor stuff here, no sexy lingerie, nothing like that. In fact . . . well, I don't really know. But your inexperience might be a plus. When you say you're a zoftig type, you don't mean . . . well, you don't look *too* glamorous, do you?"

"I wouldn't say I look glamorous no. I'm forty-nine, you know."

"Well, Sophia Loren's what? In her fifties, isn't she? And she certainly looks glamorous. What I'm saying is we're not looking for any Sophia Lorens here. Can you imagine Sophia Loren in a housedress?" he said, and laughed again. "Let me just write down your dimensions, okay? I'll discuss this with the ad agency in the morning, who knows? You said five-nine . . ."

"Yes."

"A hundred and twenty pounds."

"Yes."

"What are your other dimensions, Peaches? Bust size first."

"Thirty-six C."

"Good, we don't want anyone who looks *too*, well . . . you get some of these so-called *mature* models, they're big-busted, but very flabby. You're not flabby, are you?"

"Oh, no."

"And your waist size, Peaches?"

"Twenty-six."

"And your hips?"

"Thirty-six."

"That sounds very good," he said. "Are your breasts firm?" he asked.

"What?"

"Your breasts. Forgive me, but I know the ad agency'll want to know. They've had so many of these so-called mature models who come in with breasts hanging to their knees, they're getting a little gun-shy. Are your breasts good and firm?"

Peaches hesitated.

"What did you say your name was?" she asked.

"Phil Hendricks. At Camera Works. We're a professional photography firm, down here on Hall Avenue."

"Could I have your number there, please?"

"Sure. It's 847-3300."

"And this is for the Sears catalogue?"

"Yes, we begin shooting Monday morning. We've already signed two women, both of them in their late forties, good firm bodies, one of them used to model lingerie in fact. Do me a favor, will you, Peaches?"

"What's that?" she said.

"Is there a mirror in the room there?"

"Yes?"

"Does the phone reach over there? To where the mirror is?"

"Well, it's right there on the wall."

"Stand up, Peaches, and take a look at yourself in that mirror."

"Why should I do that?"

"Because I want an objective opinion. What are you wearing right now, Peaches?"

"A blouse and a skirt."

"Are you wearing shoes?"

"Yes?"

"High-heeled shoes?"

"Yes?"

"And a bra? Are you wearing a bra, Peaches?"

"Listen, this conversation is making me a little nervous," she said.

"I want your objective opinion, Peaches."

"About what?"

"About whether your breasts are good and firm. Can you see yourself in the mirror, Peaches?"

"Listen, this is really making me *very* nervous," she said.

"Take off your blouse, Peaches. Look at yourself in your bra, and tell me . . ."

She hung up.

Her heart was pounding.

A trick, she thought. He tricked me! How could I have been so dumb? Kept *talking* to him! Kept *believing* his pitch! Gave him all the answers he . . .

How'd he know my first name?

I'm listed as P. Muldoon, how'd he . . . ?

The answering machine. Hi, this is Peaches, I can't come to the phone just now. Of course. Said he'd been trying to reach me all day. Hi, this is Peaches, I can't come to the phone just now. Got the Muldoon and the number from the phone book, got my first name from the answering . . .

Oh, God, my *address* is in the book, too!

Suppose he *comes* here?

Oh dear God . . .

The telephone rang again.

Don't answer it, she thought.

It kept ringing.

Don't answer it.

Ringing, ringing.

But Sandra's supposed to call about the party.

Ringing, ringing, ringing.

If it's him again, I'll just hang up.

She reached out for the phone. Her hand was trembling. She lifted the receiver.

"Hello?" she said.

"Peaches?"

Was it him again? The voice didn't sound quite like his.

"Yes?" she said.

"Hi, this is Detective Andy Parker. I don't know if you remember me or not, I'm the one who locked up your crazy . . ."

"Boy, am I glad to hear from *you!*" she said.

"How about that?" Parker said, putting up the phone. "Remembered me right off the bat, told me to hurry on over!"

"You're unforgettable," Brown said. He was at his desk, typing a report on the torso they'd found behind the Burgundy Restaurant. Genero was looking over his shoulder, trying to learn how to spell dismembered.

The squadroom was alive with clattering typewriters.

Meyer sat in his dapper tan sports jacket typing a report on the kids who'd held up the liquor store and killed the owner.

Kling was at his own desk, typing a follow-up report on a burglary he'd caught three days ago. He was thinking about Eileen. He was thinking that right about now Eileen was in Calm's Point, getting ready to hit the Zone. He was thinking he might just wander over there later tonight. He looked up at the clock. Seven-fifteen. Maybe when he got off at midnight. See what was happening over there. She didn't have to know he was there looking around. A third backup never hurt anybody.

"So," Parker said, "if nobody needs me here, I think I'll mosey on over."

"Nobody needs you, right," Meyer said. "We got two homicides here, nobody needs you."

"Tell me the truth, Meyer," Parker said. "You think those two homicides are gonna be closed out tonight? In all your experience, have you ever closed out a homicide the same day you caught it? Have you?"

"I'm trying to think," Meyer said.

"In all my experience, that never happened," Parker said. "Unless you walk in and there's the perp with a smoking gun in his hand. Otherwise it takes weeks. Months sometimes. Sometimes *years.*"

"Sometimes *centuries,*" Brown said.

"So what's your point?" Meyer said.

"My point is . . . *here's* my point," he said, opening his arms wide to the railing as Carella came through the gate. "Steve," he said, "I'm very glad to see you."

"You are?" Carella said.

He was a tall slender man with the build and stance of an athlete, brown hair, brown eyes slanting slightly downward to give his face a somewhat Oriental look. Tonight he was wearing a plaid sports shirt under a blue windbreaker, light cotton corduroy trousers, brown loafers. He went directly to his desk and looked in the basket there for any telephone messages.

"How's it out there?" Brown asked.

"Quiet," Carella said. "You got back okay, huh?" he asked Kling.

"I caught a taxi."

Carella turned to Parker. "Why are you so happy to see me?" he asked.

" 'Cause my colleague, Detective Meyer Meyer there, sitting at his desk there in his new jacket and his bald head, is eager to crack a homicide he caught, and he needs a good partner."

"That lets me out," Carella said. "What kind of homicide, Meyer?"

"Some kids held up a liquor store and shot the owner."

"Teenagers?"

"Eleven-year-olds."

"No kidding?"

"You gotta get yourself some lollipops," Brown said, "bait a trap with them."

"So is everybody all paired up nice now?" Parker asked. "You got Genero . . ."

"Thanks very much," Brown said.

"Meyer's got Steve . . ."

"I only stopped by for some coffee," Carella said.

"And I got Peaches Muldoon."

"Who's that?"

"A gorgeous registered nurse who's dying to see me."

"Sixty years old," Brown said.

"That's an old *lady!*" Genero said, shocked.

"Tell him."

"You ever date a nurse?" Parker said.

"Me?" Genero said.

"You, you. You ever date a nurse?"

"No. And I never dated a sixty-year-old lady, either."

"Tell him," Brown said.

"There is nothing like a nurse," Parker said. "It's a fact that in the book business if you put the word nurse in a title, you sell a million more copies."

"Who told you that?"

"It's a fact. A publisher told me that. In this office where they stole all his typewriters, this was maybe a year ago. A nurse in the title sells a million more copies."

"I'm gonna write a book called *The Naked and the Nurse,*" Brown said.

"How about *Gone with the Nurse?*" Meyer said.

"Or *Nurse-22?*" Carella said.

"Kid around, go ahead," Parker said. "You see me tomorrow morning, I'll be a wreck."

"I think you'd better stick around," Brown said. "Cotton's all alone out there."

"Bert can go hold his hand, soon as he finishes writing his book there."

"What book?" Kling asked, looking up from his typewriter.

"Me," Parker said, "I'm gonna go do a follow-up on a homicide investigation."

"Ten years old," Brown said.

"I thought you said eleven," Carella said, puzzled.

"The homicide. Ten years ago. He arrested a nut was killing priests. The nurse is his mother."

"The *kids* are eleven years old," Meyer said. "The ones who did the liquor store guy. Or twelve."

"That's what I thought," Carella said. He still looked puzzled.

"Any further objections?" Parker asked.

They all looked at him sourly.

"In that case, gentlemen, I bid you a fond adoo."

"You gonna leave a number where we can reach you?" Brown asked.

"No," Parker said.

The phone rang as he went through the gate and out into the corridor.

Watching him go, Brown shook his head and then picked up the phone receiver.

"Eighty-Seventh Squad, Brown."

"Artie, this is Dave downstairs," Murchison said. "You're handling that body in the garbage can, ain't you?"

"*Piece* of a body," Brown said.

"Well, we just got another piece," Murchison said.

Hawes had to keep telling himself this was strictly business.

Bermuda had been one thing, Bermuda was a thousand miles away, and besides he'd asked Annie to go along with him. This was another thing. This was the big bad city, and Annie lived here and besides he had a date with her tomorrow night, and furthermore Marie Sebastiani was married.

As of the moment, anyway.

The possibility existed that her husband had run off on his own to get away from her, though why anyone would want to abandon a beautiful, leggy blonde was beyond Hawes. If that's what had happened, though—Sebastian the Great tossing his junk all over the driveway and then taking off in the Citation—then maybe he was gone forever, in which case Marie wasn't as married as she thought she was. Hawes had handled cases where a guy went out for a loaf of bread and never was heard from since. Probably living on some South Sea island painting naked natives. One case he had, the guy told his wife he was going down for a *TV Guide*. This was at eight o'clock. The wife sat through the eleven o'clock news, and then the Johnny Carson show, and then the late movie and still no hubby with the *TV Guide*. Guy turned up in California six years later, living with two girls in Santa Monica. So maybe Sebastian the Great had pulled the biggest trick of his career, disappearing on his wife. Who knew?

On the other hand, maybe the lady's concern was well-founded. Maybe somebody had come across Frank Sebastiani while he was loading his goodies in the car, and maybe he'd zonked the magician and thrown his stuff out of the car and took off with the car and the magician both. Dump the magician later on, dead or alive, and sell the car to a chop shop. Easy pickings on a relatively quiet Halloween night. It was possible.

Either way, this was strictly business.

Hawes wished, however, that Marie wouldn't keep touching him quite so often.

The lady was very definitely a toucher, and although Hawes didn't necessarily buy the psychological premise that insisted casual body contact was an absolute prerequisite to outright seduction, he had to admit that her frequent touching of his arm or his shoulder or his hand was a bit unsettling. True enough, the touching was only to emphasize a conversational point—as when she told him again how grateful she was that he was taking her to dinner—or to indicate this or that possible restaurant along the Stem. He had parked the car on North Fifth, and they were walking westward now, heading downtown, looking for a place to eat. At seven thirty-five on a Friday night there were still a lot of restaurants open, but Marie had told him she felt like pizza and so he chose a little place just south of the avenue, on Fourth. Red-checkered tablecloths, candles in Chianti bottles, people waiting in line for tables. Hawes rarely pulled rank, but now, he casually mentioned to the hostess that he was a detective working out of the Eight-Seven and he hadn't had anything to eat since he came on at four o'clock.

"This way, officer," the hostess said at once, and led them to a table near the window.

As soon as the hostess was gone, Marie said, "Does that happen all the time?"

"Does what happen?"

"The royal treatment."

"Sometimes," Hawes said. "You sure you only want pizza? There's plenty other stuff on the menu."

"No, that's what I really feel like. Cheese and anchovies."

"Would you like a drink?" he asked. "I'm on duty, but . . ."

"Do you really honor that?"

"Oh, sure."

"I'll just have beer with the pizza."

Hawes signaled to the waiter, and then ordered a large pizza with cheese and anchovies.

"Anything to drink?" the waiter asked.

"A draft for the lady, a Coke for me."

"Miller's or Michelob?"

"Miller's," Marie said.

The waiter went off again.

"This is really very nice of you," Marie said, and reached across the table to touch his hand briefly. A whisper touch. There, and then gone.

"As soon as we get back to the squadroom," Hawes said, "I'll call Auto again, see if they turned up anything on either of the vehicles."

He had made a call to Auto Theft from the custodian's office at the high school, reporting both the Citation and the Econoline, but he knew what the chances were of finding either vehicle tonight. He didn't want to tell her that.

"That would be a start," she said. "If they found the cars."

"Oh, sure."

A pained look crossed her face.

"I'm sure he's okay," Hawes said.

"I hope so."

"I'm sure."

He wasn't at all sure.

"I just keep thinking something terrible has happened to him. I keep thinking whoever stole the car . . ."

"Well, you don't know that for a fact," Hawes said.

"What do you mean?"

"Well, that the car was stolen."

"It's gone, isn't it?"

"Yes, but . . ."

He didn't want to tell her that maybe her husband had driven off on his own, heading for the wild blue yonder. Let the lady enjoy her pizza and her beer. If her husband had in fact abandoned her, she'd learn it soon enough. If he was lying dead in an alley someplace, she'd learn that even sooner.

He didn't bring up Jimmy Brayne again until after they'd been served.

She was digging into the pizza as if she hadn't eaten for a week. She ate the way that woman in the *Tom Jones* movie ate. Licked her lips, rolled her eyes, thrust pizza into her mouth as if she were making love to it. Come on, he thought. Strictly business here.

"He's normally reliable, is that right?" he said.

"Who?"

"Jimmy Brayne."

"Oh, yes. Completely."

"How long has he been working for you?"

"Three months."

"Started this July?"

"Yes. We did the act at a big Republican picnic on the Fourth. That was the first time Jimmy helped us."

"Carrying the stuff over in the van . . ."

"Yes."

"Picking it up later."

"Yes."

"Did he know where he was supposed to pick you up tonight?"

"Oh, sure. He dropped the stuff off at the school, of course he knew."

"Helped you unload it?"

"Yes."

"When was that? What time?"

"We got there about three-fifteen."

"Drove into the city together?"

"Frank and I were following the van."

"And Jimmy left the school at what time?"

"As soon as everything was on stage."

"Which was when?"

"Three-thirty, a quarter to four?"

"And he knew he was supposed to come back at five-thirty?"

"Yes."

"Is it possible he went someplace with your husband?"

"Like where?"

"For a drink or something? While you were changing?"

"Then why was all the stuff on the sidewalk?"

"It's just that ... well, *both* of them disappearing ..."

"Excuse me," the waiter said. "Officer?"

Hawes looked up.

"Officer, I hate to bother you," the waiter said.

"Yes?"

"Officer, there's somebody's arm in one of the garbage cans out back."

It was ten minutes to eight on the face of the clock on the locker-room wall.

They could have been teenagers swapping stories about their boyfriends.

Nothing in their conversation indicated they were going out hunting for a killer.

"Maybe I should've gone down later," Annie said. "The trial ended on Wednesday, I could've gone down then." She stepped into her short skirt, pulled it over her blouse and pantyhose, zipped up the side, fastened the button at the waist. "Trouble is, I wasn't sure I *wanted* to go."

"But he asked you, didn't he?" Eileen said.

"Sure, but ... I don't know. I got the feeling he was just going through the motions. I'll tell you the truth, I think he wanted to go down there alone."

"What makes you think so?" Eileen asked.

She was wearing a low-cut blouse, and a wraparound skirt as short as Annie's, fastened on the right-hand side with a three-inch-long ornamental safety pin. The pin would be a last-ditch weapon if she needed it. If she needed it, she would poke out his eyes with it.

She was sitting on the bench in front of the lockers, pulling on high-heeled boots with floppy tops. A holster was strapped to her ankle inside the right boot. The pistol in the holster was a .25-caliber Astra Firecat automatic, with a two-and-a-half-inch barrel. It weighed a bit less than twelve ounces. Six-shot magazine, plus one in the firing chamber. She would pump all seven slugs into his face if she had to. There was a six-shot, .44-caliber Smith & Wesson hammerless revolver in her handbag. Plus a switchblade knife. Rambo, she thought. But it won't happen to me again. She was wearing two pairs of panties under her pantyhose. Her psychological weapons.

"I just ... I don't know," Annie said. "I think Cotton's trying to end it, I just don't know."

She reached into the locker for her handbag, took out her cosmetics kit.

Eileen was standing now, looking down into the boots.

"Can you see this gun?" she asked.

Annie came over to her, lipstick in her hand. She looked down into the floppy top of the boot on Eileen's right foot.

"You might want to lower the holster," she said. "I'm getting a glimpse of metal."

Eileen sat again, rolled down the boot top, unstrapped the holster, lowered it, strapped it tight again.

"Maybe you should've gone down there, had it out with him," she said.

"Well, that would've ended it for sure. A man doesn't want a showdown on his vacation."

"But if he *wants* to end it . . ."

"I'm not sure of that."

"Well, what makes you think he *might* want to?"

"We haven't made love in the past two weeks."

"Bert and I haven't made love since the rape," Eileen said flatly, and stood up and looked down into the boots again.

"I'm . . . sorry," Annie said.

"Maybe that'll change tonight," Eileen said.

And Annie suddenly knew she was planning murder.

The old lady's name was Adelaide Davis, and she had seen the kids going into the liquor store on Culver and Twelfth. She was now standing outside on the sidewalk with Carella and Meyer. Inside the store, two ambulance attendants were hoisting the body of the owner onto a stretcher. Monroe was watching the operation, his hands in his jacket pockets. A tech from the Mobile Lab unit was dusting the register for fingerprints. The M.E. was kneeling over the second body. One of the attendants said, "Up," and they both lifted the stretcher and then stepped gingerly around the M.E. and the other body.

A crowd had gathered on the sidewalk. This was still only eight o'clock on a balmy Friday night, a lot of people were still in the streets. The ambulance attendants went past Mrs. Davis and the two detectives. Mrs. Davis watched them as they slid the stretcher into the ambulance. She watched them as they carried another stretcher back into the store. Patrolmen were shooing back the crowd now, making sure everyone stayed behind the barriers. Mrs. Davis felt privileged. Mrs. Davis felt like a star. She could see some of her neighbors in the crowd, and she knew they envied her.

"I can't believe this," she said. "They looked so cute."

"How many were there, ma'am?" Carella asked.

Mrs. Davis liked Carella. She thought he was very handsome. The other detective was bald, she had never favored bald men. Wait'll she told her daughter in Florida that she'd witnessed a murder—*two* murders—and had talked to detectives like on television.

"Oh, just a handful of them," she said.

"How many would you say?" Meyer asked.

"Well, they went by very fast," she said. "But I'd say there were only four or five of them. They all jumped out of the station wagon and ran into the store."

"It was a station wagon, huh? The vehicle?"

"Oh, yes. For certain."

"Would you know the year and make?"

"I'm sorry, no. A blue station wagon."

"And these kids ran out of it with guns in their hands, huh?"

"No, I didn't see any guns. Just the shopping bags."

"No guns," Carella said.

"Not until they got inside the store. The guns were in the shopping bags."

"So when they got inside the store, these little boys pulled the guns and . . ."

"No, they were little girls."

Meyer looked at Carella.

"Girls?" he said.

"Yessir. Four or five little girls. All of them wearing these long dresses down to their ankles and little blonde wigs. They looked like little princesses."

"Princesses," Carella said.

"Yes," Mrs. Davis said. "They had on these masks that covered their entire faces, with sort of Chinese eyes on them—slanted, you know—well, maybe Japanese, I guess. Well, like *your* eyes," she said to Carella. "Slanted, you know?"

"Yes, ma'am."

"And rosy cheeks painted on the masks, and bright red lips, and I think little beauty spots near the mouth. They were absolutely beautiful. Like little Chinese princesses. Or Japanese. Except that they were blonde."

"So they had on these Chinese-looking masks . . ."

"Or Japanese . . ."

"Right," Meyer said, "and they were wearing blonde wigs . . ."

"Yes, curly blonde wigs. Like Little Orphan Annie, except she's a redhead."

"Curly blonde wigs, and long dresses."

"Yes, like gowns. They looked like darling little princesses."

"What kind of shoes, ma'am?" Carella asked.

"Oh. I don't know. I didn't notice their shoes."

"They weren't wearing *sneakers,* were they?"

"Well, I really couldn't see. The gowns were very long."

The ambulance attendants were coming out with the second body now. The M.E. was still inside, talking to Monroe. Mrs. Davis looked down at the body as it went past. Before tonight, she had never seen a dead body except in a funeral home. Tonight, she'd just seen two of them close up.

"So they ran into the store," Carella said.

"Yes, yelling 'Trick or treat.' "

"Uh-huh," Carella said. "And pulled the guns . . ."

"Yes. And shot Mr. Agnello and the man who was in the store with him."

"Shot them right off?" Meyer said.

"Yes."

"Didn't say it was a stickup or anything, just started shooting."

"Yes. Mr. Agnello and the man with him."

"What happened next, ma'am? In the store. Did you keep watching?"

"Oh, yes. I was scared to death, but I kept watching."

"Did you see them clean out the cash register?"

"Yes. And one of them took a bottle of whiskey from the shelf."

"Then what?"

"They came running out. I was standing over there, to the left, over there, I'm not sure they saw me. I guess maybe they would've shot me, too, if they'd seen me."

"You were lucky," Carella said.

"Yes, I think I was."

"What'd they do then?" Meyer asked.

"They got back in the station wagon, and the woman drove them off."

"There was a woman driving the car?"

"Yes, a blonde woman."

"How old, would you know?"

"I really couldn't say. A sort of heavyset woman, she might've been in her forties."

"By heavyset . . ."

"Well, sort of stout."

"What was she wearing, would you remember?"

"I'm sorry."

Monroe was coming out of the liquor store.

"This the witness here?" he asked.

"A very good witness," Carella said.

"Well, thank you, young man," Mrs. Davis said, and smiled at him. She was suddenly glad she hadn't told him she'd wet her pants when she saw those little girls shooting Mr. Agnello.

"So what've we got here?" Monroe said. "An epidemic of kindergarten kids holding up liquor stores?"

"Looks that way," Carella said. "Where's your partner?"

"Who the hell knows where he is?" Monroe said. "Excuse me, lady."

"Oh, that's perfectly all right," she said. This was just like cable television, with the cursing and all. She couldn't wait to phone her daughter and tell her about it.

"Same kids, or what?" Monroe asked.

"What?" Mrs. Davis said.

"Excuse me, lady," Monroe said, "I was talking to this officer here."

"Little girls this time," Meyer said. "But it sounds like the same bunch. Same blonde driving the car."

"Nice lady, that blonde," Monroe said. "Driving kids to stickups. What kind of car, did you find out?" He turned to Carella. "What it is, the fart at the other store couldn't . . . excuse me, lady."

"Oh, that's perfectly all right," she said.

"A blue station wagon," Meyer said.

"You happen to know what year and make, lady?"

"I'm sorry, I don't."

"Yeah," Monroe said. "So all we got is the same big blonde driving four kids in a blue station wagon."

"That's about it," Meyer said.

"There wasn't homicides involved here, I'd turn this over to Robbery in a minute. You better give them a buzz, anyway."

"I already did," Meyer said. "After the first one."

One of the techs ambled out of the store.

"Got some bullets here," he said. "Who wants them?"

"What do they look like?" Monroe asked.

The technician showed him the palm of his hand. A white cloth was draped over it, and four spent bullets rested on it.

"Twenty-twos maybe," he said, and shrugged.

Mrs. Davis leaned over to look at the technician's palm.

"So, okay, lady," Monroe said, "you got any further business here?"

"Cool it," Carella said.

Monroe looked at him.

"I'll have one of our cars drop you home, Mrs. Davis," Carella said.

"A taxi service, they run up here," Monroe said to the air.

"Cool it," Carella said again, more softly this time, but somehow the words carried greater menace.

Monroe looked at him again and then turned to Meyer.

"Bag them bullets and get them over to Ballistics," he said. "Call Robbery and tell them we got another one."

"Sounds like good advice," Meyer said.

Monroe missed the sarcasm. He glared again at Carella, and then walked to where his car was parked at the curb.

Wait'll I tell my daughter! Mrs. Davis thought. A ride in a police car!

The patrolmen riding Charlie Four were approaching the corner of Rachel and Jakes, just cruising by, making another routine run of the section when the man riding shotgun spotted it.

"Slow down, Freddie," he said.

"What do you see, Joe?"

"The van there. Near the corner."

"What about it?"

Joe Guardi opened his notebook. "Didn't we get a BOLO on a Ford Econoline?" He snapped on the roof light, scanned the notebook. "Yeah, here it is," he said. In his own handwriting, he saw the words "BOLO tan '79 Ford Econoline, RL 68-7210. Blue '84 Citation, DL 74-3681." The word BOLO stood for Be On the Lookout.

"Yeah," he said again. "Let's check it out."

The two men got out of the car. They flashed their torches over the van. License plate from the next state, RL 68-7210.

They tried the door closest to the curb.

Unlocked.

Freddie slid it all the way open.

Joe came around to the passenger side of the van. He slid the door open there, leaned in, and thumbed open the glove compartment.

"Anything?" Freddie asked.

"Looks like a registration here."

He took the registration out of a clear-plastic packet containing an owner's manual and a duplicate insurance slip.

The van was registered to a Frank Sebastiani whose address was 604 Eden Lane in Collinsworth, over the river.

The movie had let out at seven o'clock, and they had stopped for a drink on the Stem later. They had begun arguing in the bar, in soft, strained voices, almost whispers, but everyone around them knew they were having a fight because of the way they leaned so tensely over the small table between them. At first, the fight was only about the movie they'd seen. She insisted it had been based on a novel called *Streets of Gold,* by somebody or other, and he insisted the movie'd had nothing whatever to do with that particular novel, the movie was an original. "Then how come they're allowed to use the same title?" she asked, and he said, "They can do that 'cause you can't copyright a title. They can make the shittiest movie in the world if they want to, and they can call it *From Here to Eternity* or *The Good Earth* or even *Streets of Gold,* like they did tonight, and nobody in the world can do a damn thing about it." She glared at him for a moment, and then said, "What the hell do you know about copyright?" and he said, "A hell of a lot more than you know about *anything,*" and by now they were really screaming at each other in whispers, and leaning tensely over the table, eyes blazing, mouths drawn.

They were still arguing on the way home.

But by now the argument had graduated to something more vital than an unimportant little novel called *Streets of Gold* or a shitty little movie that hadn't been based upon it.

They were arguing about sex, which is what they almost always argued about. In fact, maybe that's what they'd really been arguing about back there in the bar.

It was almost eight-thirty but the streets were already beginning to fill with teenagers on the prowl. Not all of them were looking for trouble. Many of them were merely seeking to let off adolescent energy. The ones out for fun and games were wearing costumes that weren't quite as elaborate as those the toddlers and later the teenyboppers had worn. Some of the teenage girls, using the excuse of Halloween to dress as daringly as they wished, walked the streets looking like hookers or Mata Haris or go-go dancers or sexy witches in black with slits up their skirts to their thighs. Some of the teenage boys were dressed like combat marines or space invaders or soldiers of fortune, most of them wearing bandoliers and carrying huge plastic machine guns or huge plastic death-ray guns. But these weren't the ones looking for trouble. The ones looking for trouble weren't dressed up for Halloween. They wore only their usual clothing, with perhaps a little blackening on their faces, the better to melt into the night. These were the ones looking to smash and to burn. These were the ones who had caused Lieutenant Byrnes to double-team his detectives tonight. Well, *almost* double-team them. Seven men on instead of the usual four.

The arguing couple came up the street toward the building where they lived, passing a group of teenage girls dressed like John Held flappers, sequined dresses with wide sashes, long cigarette holders, beaded bands around their foreheads, giggling and acting stoned, which perhaps they were. The couple paid no attention to them. They were too busy arguing.

"What it is," he said, "is there's never any spontaneity to it."

"Spontaneity, sure," she said. "What you mean by spontaneity is jumping on me when I come out of the shower ..."

"There's nothing wrong with ..."

"When I'm all clean."

"When do you *want* to make love?" he asked. "When you're all dirty?"

"I sure as hell don't want to get all *sweaty* again after I've just taken a shower."

"Then how about *before* you take your shower?"

"I don't like to make love when I feel all sweaty."

"So you don't like to do it when you're sweaty and you don't like to do it when you're *not* sweaty. When *do* you . . . ?"

"You're twisting what I'm saying."

"No, I'm not. The point I'm trying to make . . ."

"The point is you're a sex maniac. I'm trying to cook, you come up behind me and shove that humongous thing at me . . ."

"I don't see anything wrong with spontaneous . . ."

"Not while I'm cooking!"

"Then how about when you're *not* cooking? How about when I get home, and we're having a martini, how about . . . ?"

"You know I like to relax before dinner."

"Well, what the hell is making love? *I* find making love relaxing, I have to tell you. If *you* think making love is some kind of goddamn strenuous *obstacle* course . . ."

"I can't enjoy my cocktail if you're pawing me while I'm trying to re . . ."

"I don't consider *fondling* you *pawing* you."

"You don't know how to be gentle. All you want to do is jump on me like a goddamn *rapist!*"

"I do not consider passion *rape!*"

"That's because you don't know the difference between making love and . . ."

"Okay, what's this all about? Tell me what it's all about, okay? Do you want to quit making love *entirely*? You don't want to do it *before* your shower, you don't want to do it *after* your shower, you don't want to do it while we're *drinking* or while you're *cooking* or while we're watching television, or when we wake up in the morning, when the hell *do* you want to do it, Elise?"

"When I feel like doing it. And stop shouting!"

"I'm not *shouting,* Elise! When do you want to do it? Do you *ever* want to do it, Elise?"

"Yes!" she shouted.

"When?"

"Right now, Roger, okay? Right here, okay? Let's do it right here on the sidewalk, okay?"

"Fine by me!"

"You'd do it, too, wouldn't you?"

"Yes! Right here! *Anywhere!*"

"Well, I wouldn't! You'd have done it at the goddamn *movies* if I'd let you."

"I'd have done it in the bar, too, if you hadn't started *arguing* about that dumb movie!"

"You'd do it in church!" she said. "You're a maniac, is what you are."

"That's right, I'm a maniac! You're driving me crazy is why I'm a maniac!" They were entering their building now. He lowered his voice.

"Let's do it in the elevator, okay?" he said. "You want to do it in the elevator?"

"No, Roger, I don't want to do it in the goddamn elevator."

"Then let's take the elevator up to the roof, we'll do it on the roof."

"I don't want to do it on the goddamn roof, either."

He stabbed angrily at the elevator button.

"Where *do* you want to do it, Elise? *When* do you want to do it, Elise?"

"Later."

"When later?"

"When Johnny Carson goes off."

"If *we* were on television," he said, "and Johnny Carson was watching *us,*" he said, "and he had a big hard-on . . ."

"We happen to *live* here, Roger."

". . . do you think Johnny Carson would wait till *we* were off to do it? Or would Johnny Carson . . . ?"

"I don't care what Johnny Carson would do or wouldn't do. I don't even *like* Johnny Carson."

"Then why do you want to wait till he's off?"

The elevator doors opened.

At first they thought it was a stuffed dummy. The lower half of a scarecrow or something. Blue pants, blue socks, black shoes, black belt through the trouser loops. A Halloween prank. Some kids had tossed half a stuffed dummy into the elevator.

And then they realized that a jagged, bloody edge of torn flesh showed just above the dummy's waist, and they realized that they were looking at the lower torso of a human being and Elise screamed and they both ran out of the lobby and out of the building and up to the pay phone on the corner, where Roger breathlessly dialed 911.

The cruising cops in Boy Two responded within three minutes.

One of the cops got on the walkie-talkie to the Eight-Seven.

The other cop, although he should have known better, went through the stiff's trousers and found a wallet in the right hip pocket.

Inside the wallet, which he also shouldn't have touched, he found a driver's license with a name and an address on it.

"Well, here's who he is, anyway," he said to his partner.

5

"What this is," Parker said, "you had an obscene phone call, is what this is."

"That's what I figured it was," Peaches said.

She still looked pretty good. Maybe like a woman in her early fifties. Good legs—well, the legs never changed—breasts still firm, hair as red as he remembered it, maybe with a little help from Clairol. Wearing a simple skirt and blouse, high-heeled shoes. Legs tucked up under her on the couch. He was glad he'd shaved.

"They're not all of them what you think they're gonna be," Parker said. "I mean, they don't get on the phone and start talking dirty right away—well, some of them do—but a lot of them have a whole bagful of tricks, you don't realize what's happening till they already got you doing things."

"That's *just* what happened," Peaches said. "I didn't realize what was going on. I mean, he gave me his *name* and . . ."

"Phil Hendricks, right?" Parker said. "Camera Works."

"Right. And his address and his phone number . . ."

"Did you try calling that number he gave you?"

"Of *course* not!"

"Well, I'll give it a try if you like, but I'm sure all that was phony. I had a case once, this guy would call numbers at random, hoping to get a baby-sitter. He'd finally get a sitter on the phone, tell her he was doing research on child abuse, smooth-talked these fifteen-, sixteen-year-old girls into slapping around the babies they were sitting."

"What do you mean?"

"He'd tell them how important it was in their line of work to guard against their own tendencies, everybody has such tendencies—this is him talking—and child abuse is an insidious thing. And he'd have them interested and listening, and he'd say, 'I know you yourself must have been tempted on many an occasion to slap the little kid you're sitting, especially when he's acting up,' and the fifteen-year-old sitter goes, 'Oh, boy, you said it,' and he goes, 'For example, haven't you been tempted at least once tonight to smack him around?' and she goes, 'Well . . .' and he goes, 'Come on, tell me the truth, I'm a trained child psychologist,' and before you know it, he's got her convinced that the best way to *curb* these tendencies is to *release* them, you know, in a therapeutic manner, slap the kid gently, why don't you go get the kid now? And she runs to get the kid and he tells her to give the kid a gentle slap, and before you know it he's got her beating the daylights out of the kid while he's listening and getting his kicks. That was this one case I had, I may write a book about it one day."

"That's fascinating," Peaches said.

"Another case I had, this guy would look in the paper for ads where people were selling furniture. He was looking for somebody selling a kid's bedroom set, you know? Getting rid of the kiddy furniture, replacing it with more mature stuff. He knew he'd get either a youngish mother or a teenager girl on the phone—it's usually the girls who want their furniture changed when they get into their teens. And he'd start talking to them about the furniture, either the mother if she was home, or the teenage girl if the mother was out, and while he was talking to them, because it would be a long conversation, you know, what kind of bed is it, and how's the mattress, and how many drawers in the dresser, like that, while he was on the phone he'd be . . . well . . ."

"He'd be masturbating," Peaches said.

"Well, yes."

"Do you think the man who called me tonight was masturbating while he talked to me?"

"That's difficult to say. From what you told me, he either *was* already, or was leading up to it. He was trying to get you to talk about your body, you see. Which is still very nice, by the way."

"Well, thank you," Peaches said, and smiled.

"Sounds to me like that's what would've set him off. Getting you to strip in front of the mirror there. You'd be surprised how many women go along with something like that. He hooks them into thinking they've got a shot at modeling—there isn't a woman alive who wouldn't like to be a model—and then he gets them looking at themselves while he does his number.''

''That's when I began to realize,'' Peaches said.

''Sure.''

''When he told me to take off my blouse.''

''Sure. But lots of women don't realize even then. You'd be surprised. They just go along with it, thinking it's legit, never guessing what's happening on the other end.''

''I'm afraid he might come here,'' Peaches said.

''Well, these guys don't usually do that,'' Parker said. ''They're not your rapists or your stranglers, usually. Don't quote me on that, you got all *kinds* of nuts out there. But usually your telephone callers aren't your violent ones.''

''Usually,'' Peaches said.

''Yes,'' Parker said.

''Because he has my address, you see.''

''Um,'' Parker said.

''And my name is on the mailbox downstairs. With the apartment number.''

''I know. I saw it when I rang the bell. But that says P. Muldoon.''

''Sure, but that's what's in the phone book, too. P. Muldoon.''

''Well, I doubt he'll be coming around here. He may not even call again. What I'd do, though, if I was you, I'd change that message on your answering machine. Lots of single girls, they do these fancy messages, music going in the background, they try to sound sexy, it makes the caller think he's got some kind of swinger here. Better to just put a businesslike message on the machine. Something like, 'You've reached 123-4567,' and then, 'Please leave a message when you hear the beep.' Strictly business. You don't have to explain that you can't come to the phone because everybody *knows* they caught the machine. And of course you shouldn't say, 'I'm out just now,' or anything like that, because that's an invitation to burglars.''

''Yes, I know.''

''The point is most people today are familiar with answering machines, they *know* they're supposed to leave a message when they hear the beep, so you don't have to give them a whole list of instructions, and you don't have to sound cute, either. Your friends hear that cute little message a coupla hundred times, they want to shoot you. An obscene caller hears that cute little message, he figures he's got a live one, and he'll keep calling back till he can get you talking.''

''I see,'' Peaches said.

''Yeah,'' Parker said. ''Do you have any male friends who can record a message for you?''

''Well . . .''

''Because that's usually the best thing. That way any nut who's running his finger down the book for listings with only a first initial, he comes across P. Muldoon, he gets a man's voice on the answering machine, he figures he got a Peter Muldoon or a Paul Muldoon, but not a Peaches Muldoon. He won't call back. So that's a good way to go unless you're afraid it'll scare off any men who may be calling you legitimately. That's up to you.''

"I see," Peaches said.

"Yeah," Parker said. "Now with this guy who called you tonight, he already knows there's a Peaches Muldoon living here, and he already got you going pretty far with his little routine, so he may call you back. What we'll do if he keeps calling you, we'll put a trap on the line . . ."

"A trap?"

"Yeah, so we can trace the call even if he hangs up. You've got to let me know if he calls again."

"Oh, I *will*," Peaches said.

"So that's about it," Parker said. "Though maybe he won't call again."

"Or come here."

"Well, like I said, I don't think he'll do that. But you know how to reach me if he does."

"I really appreciate this," Peaches said.

"Well, come on, I'm just doing my job."

"Are you on duty right now?" she asked.

"Not exactly," he said.

"Wanna come to a party?" she said.

Marie Sebastiani was showing them another card trick.

"What we have is three cards here," she said. "The ace of spades, the ace of clubs, and the ace of diamonds." She fanned the cards out, the ace of diamonds under the ace of spades on the left and the ace of clubs on the right. "Now I'm going to put these three aces face down in different parts of the deck," she said, and started slipping them into the deck.

Five detectives were watching her.

Carella was on the phone to Ballistics, telling them he wanted a fast comeback on the bullets the techs had recovered at Famous Brands Wine & Liquors. The guy at Ballistics was giving him a hard time. He told Carella this was almost a quarter to nine already, and he went off at midnight. The lab would be closed till eight tomorrow morning. He was telling Carella the report could wait till then. Carella was telling him he wanted it right away. Meanwhile, he was watching Marie's card trick at the same time.

The other four detectives were either standing around Carella's desk, or else sitting on parts of it. His desk resembled a convention center. Brown was standing just to the left of Carella, his arms folded across his chest. He knew this was going to be another good trick. She had done four card tricks since Hawes came back to the squadroom with her. This was after Hawes had called Brown from a little pizza joint on North Fourth to say one of the people there had found an arm in a garbage can out back. Brown had rushed on over with Genero. Now they had three pieces. Or rather the Medical Examiner had them. The upper torso and a pair of arms. Brown was hoping the M.E. would be able to tell him whether or not the parts belonged to each other. If the parts didn't match, then they were dealing with maybe three separate corpses. Like the three cards Marie Sebastiani now slipped face down into various places in the deck.

"The ace of spades," she said. "The ace of diamonds." Sliding it into the deck. "And the ace of clubs."

Genero was watching the cards carefully. He felt certain he'd be able to catch the secret here, though he hadn't been able to on the last four tricks. He wondered if they were breaking some kind of regulation, having a deck of cards here in the squadroom. He was hoping the M.E. would call to say they were dealing with a single corpse here. Somehow, the idea of a single chopped-up corpse was more appealing than three separate chopped-up corpses.

Meyer was standing beside him, watching Marie's hands. She had long slender fingers. The fingers slipped the cards into the deck as smoothly as a drug dealer running a knife into a competitor. Meyer was wondering why those little kids had changed their clothes before pulling the second stickup. He was also wondering whether there'd be a third stickup. Were they finished for the night? Nitey-nite, kiddies, beddy-bye time. Or were they just starting?

Hawes was standing closest to Marie. He could smell her perfume. He was hoping her husband had abandoned her and run off to Hawaii. He was hoping her husband would call her from Honolulu to say he had left her. This would leave a cold, empty space in Marie's bed. Her proximity now was stupefyingly intoxicating. Hawes guessed it was her perfume. He had not yet told her that the blues had located the van. No word on the Citation yet. Maybe hubby and his apprentice had flown off to Hawaii together. Maybe hubby was gay. Hawes glanced at Marie's pert little behind as she leaned over the desk to pick up the deck of cards. He was sorely tempted to put his hand on her behind.

"Who'd like to shuffle?" she asked.

"Me," Genero said. He was sure the secret of all her tricks had something to do with shuffling.

Marie handed the deck to him.

Meyer watched her hands.

Genero shuffled the cards and then handed the deck back to her.

"Okay, Detective Brown," she said. "Pick one of those three cards. Either the ace of clubs, the ace of diamonds, or the ace of spades."

"Clubs," Brown said.

She riffled through the deck, the cards face up, searching for it. When she found the ace of clubs, she pulled it out, and tossed it onto the desk. "Detective Meyer?" she said. "How about you?"

"The ace of spades," he said.

"I don't get it," Genero said.

Marie was looking through the deck again.

"Where's the trick?" Genero said. "If you're looking at the cards, of *course* you're going to find them."

"Right you are," she said. "Here's the ace of spades."

She tossed it onto the deck.

"Which card do *you* want?" she asked Genero.

"There's only one card left."

"And which one is that?"

"The ace of diamonds."

"Okay," she said, and handed him the deck. "Find it for me."

Genero started looking through the deck.

"Have you found it yet?" she asked.

"Just hold on a minute, okay?" he said.

He went through the entire deck. No ace of diamonds. He went through it a second time. Still no ace of diamonds.

"Have you got it?" she asked.

"It isn't here," he said.

"Are you sure? Take another look."

He went through the deck a third time. Still no ace of diamonds.

"But I saw you put it back in the deck," he said, baffled.

"Yes, you did," she said. "So where is it?"

"I give up, where is it?"

"Right here," she said, grinning, and reached into her blouse, and pulled the ace of diamonds out of her bra.

"How'd you do that?" Hawes asked.

"Maybe I'll tell you sometime," Marie said, and winked at him.

The telephone rang. Carella was sitting closest to it. He picked up.

"Eighty-Seventh Squad, Carella," he said.

"Steve, this is Dave downstairs. Let me talk to either Brown or Genero, okay? Preferably Brown."

"Hold on a sec," Carella said, and extended the receiver to Brown. "Murchison," he said.

Brown took the receiver.

"Yeah, Dave?"

"I just got a call from Boy Two," Murchison said. "It looks like we maybe got an ID on that body been turning up in bits and pieces. A couple found the lower half in their building, in the elevator. *If* it's the same body. Wallet in the guy's hip pocket, driver's license in it. You better run on over there, I'll notify Homicide."

"What's the address?" Brown asked, and listened. "Got it," he said, writing. "And the couple's name?" He listened again. "Okay. And the name on the license? Okay," he said, "we're rolling." He put the receiver back on the cradle. "Let's go, Genero," he said, "the pieces are coming together. We just got ourselves the lower half. Name tag on it, this time."

"This trick is called The Mystic Prediction," Marie said, and began shuffling the cards.

"What do you mean, name tag?" Genero asked.

"The dead man's carrying a wallet," Brown said.

"How?"

"What do you mean *how?* In his *pocket* is how."

"I'm going to ask anyone of you to write down a three-figure number for me," Marie said.

"You mean he's wearing pants?" Genero said.

"Unless there's a pocket sewn on his ass," Brown said.

"You mean there's *pants* on the lower half of the body?"

"Whyn't we run on over and see for ourselves, okay?"

"Who wants to write down three numbers for me?" Marie asked. "Any three numbers?"

"And his name's in the wallet?" Genero said.

"On his driver's license," Brown said. "Let's go."

Both men started for the railing. Kling was coming back from the men's room down the hall. He opened the gate and made a low bow, sweeping his arm across his body, ushering them through.

"So what's his name?" Genero asked.

"Frank Sebastiani," Brown said.

And Marie fainted into Kling's arms.

Annie Rawles was already in place when Eileen pulled up outside Larry's. The clock behind the bar, a big ornate thing rimmed with orange neon, read five minutes to nine. Through the plateglass window, Annie could see the white Cadillac edging into the curb. The bartender could see it, too. They both watched with casual interest as the driver cut the engine, Annie nursing a beer, the bartender polishing glasses. The man behind the wheel of the car was big and black and wearing pimp threads.

They both watched as Eileen got out of the car on the curb side, long legs flashing and signaling, little hidden pistol tucked into one of those soft sexy boots, high-stepping her way toward the entrance door now.

Mr. Pimp leaned across the seat, rolled down the window on the curb side.

Yelled something to Eileen.

Eileen sashayed back, bent over to look in the window.

Short skirt tight across her ass, flashing, advertising.

Started shaking her head, waving her arms around.

"She's givin' him sass," the bartender said.

Southern accent you could cut with a butter knife. Maybe this wasn't so far from Houston after all.

"An' he don't like it none," the bartender said.

Mr. Pimp came storming out of the car on the driver's side, walked around the car, stood yelling at her on the sidewalk.

Eileen kept shaking her head, hands on her hips.

"Won't stop sassin' him, will she?" the bartender said. And suddenly Mr. Pimp slapped her.

"Whomp her good," the bartender said, nodding encouragement.

Eileen staggered back from the blow, her green eyes blazing. She bunched her fists and went at him as if she'd kill him, but he shoved her away, turned her toward the bar, shoved her again, toward the door of the bar this time, and then strutted back to the Caddy, lord of all he surveyed. Eileen was nursing her cheek. She glared at the Caddy as it pulled away from the curb.

Act One had begun.

Four pieces had become one piece.

Maybe.

They showed her the bundle of clothing first.

Black shoes, blue socks. Blue trousers. Black belt. White Jockey undershorts. Blood stains on the waistband of the trousers and the shorts.

"I . . . I think those are Frank's clothes," Marie said.

Some coins in one of the pants pockets. A quarter, two dimes, and a penny.

No keys. Neither house keys nor car keys.

A handkerchief in another pocket.

And a wallet.

Black leather.

"Is this your husband's wallet?" Brown asked.

"Yes."

Her voice very soft. As if what they were showing her demanded reverence.

In the wallet, a driver's license issued to Frank Sebastiani of 604 Eden Lane, Collinsworth. No credit cards. Voters Registration card, same name, same address. A hundred and twenty dollars in twenties, fives, and singles. Tucked into one of the little pockets was a green slip of paper with the words MARIE'S SIZES hand-lettered onto it, and beneath that:

Hat:	22
Dress:	8
Bra:	36B
Belt:	26
Panties:	5
Ring:	5
Gloves:	6½
Stockings:	9 ½ (Medium)
Shoes:	6½B

"Is this your husband's handwriting?" Brown asked.

"Yes," Marie said. Same soft reverential voice.

They led her inside.

The morgue stank.

She reeled back from the stench of human gasses and flesh.

They walked her past a stainless-steel table upon which the charred remains of a burn-victim's body lay trapped in a pugilistic pose, as though still trying to fight off the flames that had consumed it.

The four pieces of the dismembered corpse were on another stainless-steel table. They were casually assembled, not quite joining. Lying there on the table like an incomplete jigsaw puzzle.

She looked down at the pieces.

"There's no question they're the same body," Carl Blaney said.

Lavender-eyed, white-smocked. Standing under the fluorescent lights, seeming neither to notice nor to be bothered by the intolerable stink in the place.

"As for identification . . ."

He shrugged.

"As you see, we don't have the hands or the head yet."

He addressed this to the policemen in the room. Ignoring the woman for the time being. Afraid she might puke on his polished tile floor. Or in one of the stainless-steel basins containing internal organs. Three cops now. Hawes, Brown, and Genero. Two cases about to become one. Maybe.

The lower half of the torso was naked now.

She kept looking down at it.

"Would you know his blood type?" Blaney asked.

"Yes," Marie said. "B."

"Well, that's what we've got here."

Hawes knew about the appendectomy and meniscectomy scars because she'd mentioned them while describing her husband. He said nothing now. First rule of identification, you didn't prompt the witness. Let them come to it on their own. He waited.

"Recognize anything?" Brown asked.

She nodded.

"What do you recognize, ma'am?"

"The scars," she said.

"Would you know what kind of scars those are?" Blaney asked.

"The one on the belly is an appendectomy scar."

Blaney nodded.

"The one on the left knee is from when he had the cartilage removed."

"That's what those scars are," Blaney said to the detectives.

"Anything else, ma'am?" Brown asked.

"His penis," she said.

Neither Blaney nor any of the detectives blinked. This wasn't the Meese Commission standing around the pieces of a corpse, this was a group of professionals trying to make positive identification.

"What about it?" Blaney asked.

"There should be a small . . . well, a beauty spot, I guess you'd call it," Marie said. "On the underside. On the foreskin."

Blaney lifted the corpse's limp penis in one rubber-gloved hand. He turned it slightly.

"This?" he asked, and indicated a birthmark the size of a pinhead on the foreskin, an inch or so below the glans.

"Yes," Marie said softly.

Blaney let the penis drop.

The detectives were trying to figure out whether or not all of this added up to a positive ID. No face to look at. No hands to examine for fingerprints. Just the blood type, the scars on belly and leg, and the identifying birthmark—what Marie had called a beauty spot—on the penis.

"I'll work up a dental chart sometime tomorrow," Blaney said.

"Would you know who his dentist was?" Hawes asked Marie.

"Dentist?" she said.

"For comparison later," Hawes said. "When we get the chart."

She looked at him blankly.

"Comparison?" she said.

"Our chart against the dentist's. If it's your husband, the charts'll match."

"Oh," she said. "Oh. Well . . . the last time he went to a dentist was in Florida. Miami Beach. He had this terrible toothache. He hasn't been to a dentist since we moved north."

"When was that?" Brown asked.

"Five years ago."

"Then the most recent dental chart . . ."

"I don't even know if there *is* a chart," Marie said. "He just went to somebody the hotel recommended. We had a steady gig at the Regal Palms. I mean, we never had a *family* dentist, if that's what you mean."

"Yeah, well," Brown said.

He was thinking Dead End on the teeth.

He turned to Blaney.

"So what do you think?" he said.

"How tall was your husband?" Blaney asked Marie.

"I've got all that here," Hawes said, and took out his notebook. He opened it to the page he'd written on earlier, and began reading aloud. "Five-eleven, one-seventy, hair black, eyes blue, appendectomy scar, menisectomy scar."

"If we put a head in place there," Blaney said, "we'd have a body some hundred and eighty centimeters long. That's just about five-eleven. And I'd estimate the weight, given the separate sections here, at about what you've got there, a hundred-seventy, a hundred-seventy-five, in there. The hair on the arms, chest, legs, and pubic area is black—which doesn't necessarily mean the *head* hair would match it exactly, but at least it rules out a blonde or a redhead, or anyone in the brown groupings. This hair is very definitely *black.* The eyes—well, we haven't got a head, have we?"

"So have we got a positive ID or what?" Brown asked.

"I'd say we're looking at the remains of a healthy white male in his late twenties or early thirties," Blaney said. "How old was your husband, madam?"

"Thirty-four," she said.

"Yes," Blaney said, and nodded. "And, of course, identification of the birthmark on the penis would seem to me a conclusive factor."

"Is this your husband, ma'am?" Brown asked.

"That is my husband," Marie said, and turned her head into Hawes' shoulder and began weeping gently against his chest.

The hotel was far from the precinct, downtown on a side street off Detavoner Avenue. He'd deliberately chosen a fleabag distant from the scene of the crime. *Scenes* of the crime, to be more accurate. Five separate scenes if you counted the hand and the hands. Five scenes in a little playlet entitled "The Magical and Somewhat Sudden Disappearance of Sebastian the Great."

Good riddance, he thought.

"Yes, sir?" the desk clerk said. "May I help you?"

"I have a reservation," he said.

"The name, please?"

"Hardeen," he said. "Theo Hardeen."

Wonderful magician, long dead. Houdini's brother. Appropriate name to be using. Hardeen had been famous for his escape from a galvanized iron can filled with water and secured by massive locks. Failure Means a Drowning Death! his posters had proclaimed. The risks of failure here were even greater.

"How do you spell that, sir?" the clerk asked.

"H-A-R-D-E-E-N."

"Yes, sir, I have it right here," the clerk said, yanking a card. "Hardeen, Theo. That's just for the one night, is that correct, Mr. Hardeen?"

"Just the one night, yes."

"How will you be paying, Mr. Hardeen?"

"Cash," he said. "In advance."

The clerk figured this was a shack-up. One-night stand, guy checking in alone, his bimbo—or else a hooker from the Yellow Pages—would be along later. Never explain, never complain, he thought. Thank you, Henry Ford. But charge him for a double.

"That'll be eighty-five dollars, plus tax," he said, and watched as the wallet came out, and then a hundred-dollar bill, and the wallet disappeared again in a wink. Like he figured, a shack-up. Guy didn't want to show even a glimpse of his driver's license or credit cards, the Hardeen was undoubtedly a phony name. Theo Hardeen? The names some of them picked. Who cared? Take the money and run, he thought. Thank you, Woody Allen.

He calculated the tax, made change for the C-note, and slid the money across the desk top. Wallet out again in a flash, money disappearing, wallet disappearing, too.

"Did you have any luggage, sir?" he asked.

"Just the one valise."

"I'll have someone show you to your room, sir," he said, and banged a bell on the desk. "Front!" he shouted. "Checkout time is twelve noon, sir. Have a nice night."

"Thank you."

A bellhop in a faded red uniform showed him to the third-floor room. Flicked on the lights in the bathroom. Taught him how to operate the window air-conditioning unit. Turned on the television set for him. Waited for the tip. Got his fifty cents, looked at it on the palm of his hand, shrugged, and left the room. What the hell had he expected for carrying that one bag? Rundown joint like this—well, that's why he'd picked it. No questions asked. In, out, thank you very much.

He looked at the television screen, and then at his watch.

A quarter past nine.

Forty-five minutes before the ten o'clock news came on.

He wondered if they'd found the four pieces yet. Or either of the cars. He'd left the Citation in the parking lot of an A & P four blocks north of the river, shortly after he'd deep-sixed the head and the hands.

Something dumb was on television. Well, *everything* on television was dumb these days. He'd have to wait till ten o'clock to see what was happening, if anything.

He took off his shoes, lay full length on the bed, his eyes closed, and relaxed for the first time today.

By tomorrow night at this time, he'd be in San Francisco.

6

Eileen came out of the ladies' room and walked toward the farthest end of the bar, where a television set was mounted on the wall. Quick heel-clicking hooker glide, lots of ass and ankle in it. She didn't even glance at Annie, sitting with her legs crossed at the cash-register end of the bar. Two or three men sitting at tables around the place turned to look at her. She gave them a quick once-over, no smile, no come-on, and took a stool next to a guy watching the television screen. She was still fuming. In the mirror behind the bar, she could still see the flaming imprint of his hand on her left cheek. The bartender ambled over.

"Name it," he said.

"Rum-Coke," she said. "Easy on the rum."

"Comin'," he said, and reached for a bottle of cheap rum on the shelf behind him. He put ice in a glass, short-jiggered some rum over it, filled the glass with Coke from a hose. "Three bucks even," he said, "a bargain. You be runnin' a tab?"

"I'll pay as I go," she said, and reached into her shoulder bag. The .44 was sitting under a silk scarf, butt up. She took out her wallet, paid for the drink. The bartender lingered.

"I'm Larry," he said. "This's my place."

Eileen nodded, and then took a sip of the drink.

"You're new," Larry said.

"So?" she said.

"So I get a piece," he said.

"You get shit," Eileen said.

"I can't have hookers hangin' around in here 'cept I get a piece."

"Talk to Torpedo," she said.

"I don't know nobody named Torpedo."

"You don't, huh? Well, ask around. I got a feeling you won't like talking to him."

"Who's Torpedo? The black dude was slapping you around?"

"Torpedo Holmes. Ask around. Meanwhile, fuck off."

"You see the lady sittin' there at the end of the bar?" Larry said.

Eileen looked over at Annie.

"I see her."

"She's new, too. We had a nice little talk minute she come in. I'm gettin' twenty percent of her action, just for lettin' her plant her ass on that stool."

"She ain't got Torpedo," Eileen said. "You want to get off my fuckin' back, or you want me to make a phone call?"

"Go make your phone call," Larry said.

"Mister," Eileen said, "you're askin' for more shit than you're worth."

She swung off the stool, long legs reaching for the floor, picked up her bag, shouldered it, and swiveled toward the phone booth. Watching her, Annie thought God, she's good.

In the phone booth, Eileen dialed the hot-line number at the Seven-Two.

Alvarez picked up.

"Tell Robinson to get back here," she said. "The bartender's hassling me."

"You got him," Alvarez said, and hung up.

Detective/Second Grade Alvin Robinson worked out of the Seven-Three, near the park and the County Court House. The team at the Seven-Two was certain he wouldn't be made for a cop here in the Canal Zone, and were using him tonight only to establish Eileen's credentials as a bona fide hooker. He wouldn't be part of the backup team, though Eileen might have wished otherwise. She was still annoyed that he'd hit her that hard—even though she knew he'd been going for realism—but in the Caddy on the way over he'd sounded like a tough, dependable cop who knew his business.

He walked into the bar not ten minutes after she placed her call. Eyes challenging, sweeping the room under the wide brim of his hat, everyone in the joint looking away. He did a cool pimp shuffle over to where Eileen was sitting, and put his hand on her shoulder.

"That him?" he asked, and cocked his head to where Larry was filling a jar with tomato juice. Eileen merely nodded. "You," Robinson said, and pointed his finger. "Come here."

Larry took his time ambling over.

"You givin' my fox trouble?" Robinson said.

"You got a phone in that pussy wagon of yours?" Larry said, toughing it out though he'd never seen a meaner-looking black man in his life. Everybody in the bar was looking at them now. The guys at the tables, the one who'd been watching television a minute earlier.

"I ast you a question," Robinson said.

"I read her the rules, pal," Larry said. "The same rules . . ."

"Don't pal *me,* pal," Robinson said. "I ain't your fuckin' pal, and I don't live by no rules. If you never heard of Torpedo Holmes, then you got some quick learnin' to do. Nobody cuts my action, man. Nobody. Less he's lookin' for some *other* kinda cut I'd be mighty obliged to supply. You got that?"

"I'm tellin' you . . ."

"No, you ain't *tellin',* me nothin', mister. You *list'nin'* is what you doin'." He reached into his wallet, took a frayed piece of glossy paper from it, unfolded it, and smoothed it flat on the bar. "This's from *L.A. Magazine,*" he said. "You recognize that picture there?"

Larry looked down at a color photograph of a big black man wearing a red silk lounge robe and grinning cockily at the camera. The room in the background was opulent. The caption under the picture read: *Thomas "Torpedo" Holmes at Home.*

Robinson thought the resemblance was a good one. But even if it hadn't been, he firmly believed that most white men—especially a redneck like this one—thought all niggers looked alike. Thomas "Torpedo" Holmes was now doing ten years at Soledad. The article didn't mention the bust and conviction, because it had been written three years earlier, when Holmes was riding too high for his own good. You don't shit on cops in print, not even in L.A.

"I'm assumin' you don't know how to read," Robinson said, "so I'll fill you in fast." He snatched the article off the bartop before it got too much scrutiny, folded it, put it back into his wallet again. Eileen sat looking bored. "Now what that article says, man, is that not even L.A.'s finest could lay a finger on me, is what that article says. An' the same applies right here in *this* city, ain't no kinda law can touch me, ain't no kinda shitty bartender . . ."

"I *own* this place!" Larry said.

"You list'nin' to me, man, or you runnin' off at the mouth? I'm tellin' you I don't cut my action with nobody, not the law, not nobody else runnin' girls, and most of all not *you*."

"This ain't L.A." Larry said.

"Well, no shee-it?" Robinson said.

"I mean, I got rules here, man."

"You want me to shove your rules up your ass, man? Together with that jar of tomato juice? Man, don't tempt me. This little girl here, she's gonna sit here long as she likes, you dig, man? An' if I'm happy with the service she gets, then maybe I'll drop some other little girls off every now an' then, give this fuckin' dump some class." His wallet came out again. He threw a fifty-dollar bill on the counter. "This is for whatever she wants to drink. When that's used up, I'll be back with more. You better pray I don't come back with somethin' has a sharp end. You take my meanin', man?"

Larry picked up the bill and tucked it into his shirt pocket. He figured he'd won a moral victory. "What's all this strong-arm shit?" he asked, smiling, playing to the crowd now, showing them he hadn't backed down. "We're two gentlemen here, can't we talk without threatening each other?"

"Was you threatenin' me?" Robinson said. "I didn't hear nobody threatenin' me."

"What I meant . . ."

"We finished here, man? You gonna treat Linda nice from now on?"

"All I said to the lady . . ."

"What you said don't mean shit to me. I don't want no more phone calls from her."

"I don't mind a nice-looking girl in the place," Larry said.

"Good. An' I don't mind her bein' here," Robinson said, and grinned a big watermelon-eating grin. He put his hand on Eileen's shoulder again. "Now, honey," he said, "go easy on the sauce. 'Cause Daddy got some nice candy for you when the night's done."

"See you, Torp," she said, and offered her cheek for his kiss.

Robinson gave Larry a brief, meaningful nod, and then did his cool pimp shuffle over to the door and out to the white Cadillac at the curb.

From the other end of the bar, Annie said, "I wish *I* had a man like that."

The third liquor-store holdup took place while Alvin Robinson was doing his little dog-and-pony act for the owner of Larry's Bar, but the blues didn't respond till nine-thirty, and Carella and Meyer didn't arrive at the scene till nine thirty-five, by which time Robinson was already driving back toward the Seventy-Third Precinct.

This time, nobody had been killed—but not for lack of trying. Martha Frey, the forty-year-old woman who owned and operated the store on Culver and Twentieth, told them that four of them—wearing clown suits, and pointed pom-pommed clown hats, and white clown masks with bulbous red noses and wide grinning red mouths— had started shooting the minute they walked in. She'd grabbed for her heart and fallen down behind the counter in what she hoped was a very good imitation of someone who'd been mortally wounded. It had occurred to her, while they were cleaning out the cash register, that one of them might decide to put a "coop dee gracie," as she called it, in her head while she was lying there playing possum. None of them had. She considered it a miracle that she was still alive, four little guns opening up that way, all of them at the same time. She wondered if maybe they'd hit her after all. Was it possible she was now in shock and didn't know she'd been hit? Did the detectives see any blood on her?

Meyer assured her that she was still in one piece.

"I can't believe they missed me," she said, and made the sign of the cross. "God must have been watching over me."

Either that, or they were nervous this time around, Carella thought. Three times in the space of four hours, even your seasoned pro could spook. No less a handful of grade-schoolers.

"Did you see who was driving the car?" Carella asked.

"No," Martha said. "I was tallying the register for the night. I usually close at nine on Fridays, but this is Halloween, there's lots of parties going on, people run short of booze, they make a last-minute run to the store. This was maybe twenty after when they came in."

The Mobile Lab van was pulling up outside the store.

"Techs'll be here a while," Carella said. "They'll want to see if there's anything on that register."

"There ain't anything *in* it, that's for sure," Martha said mournfully.

"Did they say anything to you?" Meyer asked. "When they came in?"

"Just 'Trick or Treat!' Then they started shooting."

"Didn't say, 'This is a stickup,' anything like that?"

"Nothing."

"Hello, boys," one of the techs said. "Kiddy time again?"

"School let out again?" the other tech said.

"How about when they were cleaning out the register?" Meyer asked, ignoring them.

"One of them said, 'Hold it open, Alice.' I guess he meant the shopping bag."

"Alice?" Carella said. "A girl?"

"A woman, yes," Martha said.

Carella thought this was carrying feminism a bit too far.

"Well, this little girl . . ." he started to say, but Martha broke in at once.

"A *woman*," she said. "Not a little girl. These weren't *children*, Detective Carella, they were *midgets*."

He looked at her.

"I used to work the high-wire with Ringling," she said. "Broke my hip in a fall, quit for good. But I still know midgets when I see them. These were *midgets*."

"What'd I tell you, Baz?" one of the techs said. "I shoulda taken your bet."

"Midgets," the other tech said. "I'll be a son of a bitch."

Me, too, Carella thought.

But now they knew what they were looking for.

And now they had a pattern.

Peaches and Parker were the only ones not in costume.

"What are you supposed to be?" a man dressed like a cowboy asked.

"I'm a cop," Parker said.

"I'm a victim," Peaches said.

"I'll be damned," the cowboy said.

Parker showed his shield to everyone he met.

"Looks like the real McCoy," a pirate said.

Peaches lifted her skirt and showed a silent-movie director a black-and-blue mark on her thigh.

"I'm a victim," she said.

She had got the black-and-blue mark banging against a table on her way to the bathroom one night.

The silent-movie director, who was wearing jodhpurs and carrying a megaphone, said, "That's some leg, honey. You wanna be in pictures?"

The girl with him was dressed as Theda Bara. "That's an anagram for Arab Death," she said.

Parker looked into the front of her clinging satin, low-cut dress, and said, "You're under arrest," and showed her his shield.

In the kitchen, Dracula and Superman and Scarlett O'Hara and Cleopatra were snorting cocaine.

Parker didn't show them his shield. Instead, he snorted a few lines with them.

Peaches said, "You're kinda fun for a cop."

This was the first time in a good many years that anyone had told Parker he was kind of fun, for a cop or anything else. He hugged her close.

She went, "Oooooo."

A white man in blackface, dressed as Eddie Murphy dressed as the Detroit detective in *Beverly Hills Cop* said, "I'm a cop," and showed Parker a fake shield.

"I'll go along quietly," Parker said, and hugged Peaches again.

"Way I figure it," Kling said, "we go over there soon as we're relieved. Maybe get to the Zone around midnight, a little after."

"Uh-huh," Hawes said, and looked up at the wall clock.

Ten minutes to ten. Less than two hours before the relieving shift began filtering in.

"They don't even need to know we're there," Kling said. "We take one of the sedans, just cruise the streets."

They were sitting at his desk, talking in whispers. Across the room, Brown was getting a description of Jimmy Brayne. He was right now ready to bet the farm that

Sebastian the Great's apprentice was the one who'd done him in and chopped him up in pieces.

"This guy's extremely dangerous," Kling said. "Juked three people already."

"And you think they may need help, huh?" Hawes said. "Annie and Eileen?"

"More the merrier," Kling said.

"White or black?" Brown asked.

"White," Marie said.

"His age?"

"Thirty-two."

"Height?"

"About six feet."

"Annie never even mentioned she was going out on this," Hawes said. "I talked to her must've been . . ."

"She didn't get the call from Homicide till late this afternoon. That's the thing of it, Cotton. They pulled this whole damn thing out of a Cracker Jack box."

"Weight?" Brown said.

"About a hundred and eighty? Something like that."

"Color of hair?"

"Black."

"Eyes?"

"Brown."

"I mean would *you* go out there with only two back-ups?" Kling said. "Where the guy's armed with a knife, and already boxed three people?"

"Those don't sound like bad odds," Hawes said. "Three to one? All three of them loaded. Against only a knife."

"*Only,* huh? My point is, if Annie and this Shanahan guy stay too close to her," Kling said, "he won't make his move. So they have to keep their distance. But if he breaks out, who's covering the backfield?"

"Any identifying scars, marks, or tattoos?" Brown asked.

"Not that I know of."

"Any regional accent or dialect?"

"He's from Massachusetts. He sounds a little like the Kennedys."

"What was he wearing when you left the house today?"

"Let me think."

She was sitting on a bench under the squadroom bulletin board, her hands folded on her lap. Her face was still tear-stained. Brown had one foot up on the bench, a clipboard resting on his knee. He waited.

"Blue jeans," she said. "And a woolen sweater, no shirt. A V-necked sweater. Sort of rust-colored. And sneakers. And . . . white socks, I think. Oh, yes. He wears a sort of medallion around his neck. A silver medallion, I think he won it in a swim meet. A high school swim meet."

"Wears it all the time?"

"I've never seen him without it."

"Have you discussed this with Eileen?" Hawes asked.

"Yeah, I mentioned it at dinner," Kling said.

"Told her you want to go over there?"

"Yeah."

"To the Zone?"

"Yeah."

"What'd she say?"

"She told me she could handle it."

"But you don't think she can, huh?"

"I think she can handle it better with a few more people on the job. They shoulda known that themselves, Homicide. And also the Seven-Two. Putting two women on the street against . . ."

"Plus Shanahan."

"Well, I don't know this Shanahan, do you?"

"No, but . . ."

"For all I know . . ."

"But you can't automatically figure he's a hairbag."

"I don't know what he is. I *do* know he's not gonna care as much about Eileen as *I* care about her."

"Maybe that's the problem," Hawes said.

"Does he wear a wristwatch?" Brown asked.

"Yes," Marie said.

"Would you know what kind?"

"One of those digital things. Black with a black band. A Seiko, I think. I'm not sure."

"Any other jewelry?"

"A ring. He wears it on his right pinky. A little gold ring with a red stone. I don't think it's a ruby, but it looks like one."

"Is he right-handed or left-handed?"

"I don't know."

"What do you mean?" Kling said.

"I mean, why don't you leave it to them?" Hawes said.

Kling looked at him.

"They're experienced cops, all of them. If Homicide or the Seven-Two hasn't put an army out there, it's maybe 'cause they think they'll spook him."

"I don't see how two more guys is gonna make an *army,*" Kling said.

"Thee guys can smell traps," Hawes said, "they're like animals in the jungle. Anyway, they'll be carrying walkie-talkies, won't they? Annie, Shanahan? Maybe even Eileen. There'll be rmp's cruising the Zone, they're not gonna be alone out there. Any one of 'em calls in a 10–13 . . ."

"I don't want her getting cut again," Kling said.

"You think *she* wants to get cut again?" Hawes said.

"Tell me what happened before you left the house today," Brown said. "Was he behaving differently in any way?"

"Same as always," Marie said.

"Did he get along okay with your husband?"

"Yes. Well, he wants to be a magician, you see. He studies all the tricks the famous magicians did—Dai Vernon, Blackstone, Audley Walsh, Tommy Windsor,

Houdini, Ballantine—all of them. He keeps up with all the new people, too, tries to dope out their tricks. And my husband is . . .''

Her face almost broke.

''My husband . . . was . . . very patient with him. Always willing to explain a sleight, or a pocket trick, or a stage illusion . . . helping him with his patter . . . taking the time to . . . to . . . show him and . . . and guide him. I don't know how he could've done something like this. I'll tell you the truth, Detective Brown, I'm willing to give you anything you need to find Jimmy, but I can't believe he did this.''

''Well, *we* don't know that for sure, either,'' Brown said.

''That's just what I mean,'' Marie said. ''I just pray to God something hasn't happened to *him,* too. I just hope somebody hasn't . . . hasn't killed them *both.*''

''How do *you* get along with him?'' Brown asked.

''Jimmy? I think of him as a brother.''

''No friction, huh? I mean, the three of you living in the same house?''

''None whatever.''

''So what does that mean?'' Kling asked. ''You won't go with me?''

''I don't think *you* should go, either,'' Hawes said.

''Well, I'm going.''

''She knows her job,'' Hawes said flatly. ''And so does Annie.''

''She *didn't* know her job when that son of a bitch . . .''

Kling caught himself. He took a deep breath.

''Take it easy,'' Hawes said.

''I'm going out there tonight,'' Kling said. ''With you or without you.''

''Take it easy,'' Hawes said again.

Brown walked over.

''Here's the way I figure it,'' he said to Hawes. ''You caught the Missing P, I caught the pieces. Turns out it's the same case. I figure maybe Genero ought to go back to cruising, find all that trouble in the streets the loot's worried about. You and me can team up on this one, how does that sound to you?''

''Sounds good,'' Hawes said.

''I'll go tell Genero,'' Brown said, and walked off.

''You okay?'' Hawes asked Kling.

''I'm fine,'' Kling said.

But he walked off, too.

The precinct map was spread out on the long table in the Interrogation Room. Meyer and Carella were hunched over the map. They had already asked Sergeant Murchison to run a check on any circuses or carnivals that happened to be in town. They did not think there'd be any at this time of year. In the meantime, they were trying to figure out where the midgets would hit next.

''Midgets,'' Meyer said, shaking his head. ''You ever bust a midget?''

''Never,'' Carella said. ''I busted a dwarf once. He was a very good burglar. Used to crawl into vents.''

''What's the difference?'' Meyer asked.

''A midget is a person of unusually small size, but he's physically well-proportioned.''

"So? Dopey and Doc were well-proportioned, too."

"That's the movies," Carella said. "In real life, a dwarf has abnormal body proportions."

"Can you name all the Seven Dwarfs?" Meyer asked.

"I can't even name Snow White," Carella said.

"Go on, give it a try."

"Anyone can name the Seven Dwarfs," Carella said.

"Go ahead, name them."

"Dopey, Doc . . ."

"I gave you those two free."

"Grumpy, Sleepy, Sneezy . . . how many is that?"

"Five."

"Bashful."

"Yeah?"

"And . . ."

"Yeah?"

"Who's the seventh one?" Carella said.

"Nobody can name all seven of them," Meyer said.

"So tell me who he is."

"Think about it," Meyer said, smiling.

Carella hunched over the precinct map. Now the goddamn seventh dwarf would bother him all night long.

"First hit was here," he said, indicating the location on the map. "Culver and Ninth. Second one here. Still on Culver, three blocks east. Next one was Culver and Twentieth."

"They're working their way uptown on Culver."

"First one at . . . have you got that timetable?"

Meyer opened his notebook. "Five-fifteen," he said. "Second one at a little after seven. Third one about forty minutes ago."

"So what's the interval?"

"Five-fifteen, seven-oh-five, nine-twenty. Figure two hours, more or less."

"Time to change their costumes . . ."

"Or maybe we're dealing with *three* gangs here, did that occur to you?"

"There aren't that many midgets in the world," Carella said.

"You figured out the seventh dwarf yet?"

"No." He looked at the map again. "So the next one should be further uptown on Culver, and they should hit around eleven, eleven-thirty."

"*If* there's a next one."

"And unless they speed up the timetable."

"Yeah," Meyer said, and shook his head again. "Midgets. I always thought midgets were law-abiding citizens."

"Just be happy they aren't giants," Carella said.

"You got it," Meyer said.

"Huh?" Carella said.

"Happy. That's the seventh dwarf."

"Oh. Yeah."

"So what do you want to do?"

"First let's check Dave, see if he came up with any circuses or carnivals."

"That's a long shot," Meyer said.

"Then let's call Ballistics again, see if they got anything on the bullets."

"We'll maybe get a caliber and make," Meyer said, "but I don't see how that's gonna help us."

"And then I guess we better head uptown," Carella said, "case Culver, see which stores are possible for the next hit."

"You figuring on a plant?"

"Unless there's a dozen of them."

"Well, it's getting late, there won't be many open."

Carella folded the map.

"So," he said. "Murchison first."

She was still sitting on the bench, weeping softly, when Hawes approached her.

"Mrs. Sebastiani?" he said.

Marie looked up. Face tear-streaked, blue eyes rimmed with red now.

"I'm sorry to bother you," he said.

"No, that's all right," she said.

"I wanted to tell you . . . we found the van, but we still haven't located the Citation. You said Brayne drove the van into the city today . . ."

"Yes."

"So maybe the techs'll be able to lift his prints from the wheel. He hasn't got a criminal record, has he?"

"Not that I know of."

"Well, we'll run him through the computer, see what we come up with. Meanwhile, if the techs lift anything, and if we find the Citation, then maybe we'll know if he's the one who drove it away from the school. By comparing prints from the two wheels, do you see?"

"Yes. But . . . well, we *all* drove both cars a lot. I mean, you'll probably find my prints and Frank's together with Jimmy's. If you find any prints."

"Uh-huh, yes, that's a possibility. But we'll see, okay? Meanwhile, Detective Brown has already put out a bulletin on Brayne, and we'll be watching all railroad stations, bus terminals, airports, in case he . . ."

"*You'll* be watching?"

"Well, not Brown and me personally. I mean the police. The bulletin's gone out already, as I said, so maybe we'll get some results there. If he's trying to get out of the city."

"Yes," Marie said, and nodded.

"Brown and I are gonna run back to the high school, see if anybody there saw what happened in that driveway."

"Well . . . will anyone *be* there? I mean, won't the teachers . . . ?"

"And the kids, yes, they'll be gone, that'll have to wait till morning. But the custodian'll be there, and maybe *he* saw something."

"Will it be the same custodian who was there this afternoon?"

"I don't know, but we're going to check it out, anyway."

"Yes, I see."

"Meanwhile, I wanted to know what *you* plan to do. Do you have any relatives or friends here in the city?"

"No."

"Then will you be going back home? I know you're short of cash . . ."

"Yes, but there was money in Frank's wallet."

"Well, the lab'll be running tests on the wallet and everything in it, so I can't let you have that. But if you want me to lend you train fare, or bus fare . . . what I'm asking is whether or not you plan on going home, Mrs. Sebastiani. Because, honestly, there's nothing more you can do here."

"I . . . I don't know what I want to do," she said, and began crying again, burying her face in an already sodden handkerchief.

Hawes watched her, awkward in the presence of her tears.

"I'm not sure I want to go home," she said, her voice muffled by the handkerchief. "With Frank gone . . ."

The sentence trailed.

She kept sobbing into the handkerchief.

"You have to go home sometime," Hawes said gently.

"I know, I know," she said, and blew her nose, and sniffed, and wiped at her eyes with the back of her hand. "There are calls I'll have to make . . . Frank's mother in Atlanta, and his sister . . . and I guess . . . I supposed I'll have to make funeral arrangements . . . oh God, how are they going to . . . what will they . . . ?"

Hawes was thinking the same thing. The body was in four separate pieces. The body didn't have hands or a head.

"That'll have to wait till autopsy, anyway," he said. "I'll let you know when . . ."

"I thought they'd already done that."

"Well, that was a prelim. We asked for a preliminary report, you see. But the M.E.'ll want to do a more thorough examination."

"Why?" she asked. "I've already identified him."

"Yes, but we're dealing with a murder here, Mrs. Sebastiani, and we need to know . . . well, for example, your husband may have been *poisoned* before the body was . . . well . . ."

He cut himself short.

He was talking too much.

This was a goddamn grieving widow here.

"There are lots of things the M.E. can tell us," he concluded lamely.

Marie nodded.

"So . . . *will* you be going home?" he asked.

"I suppose."

Hawes opened his wallet, pulled out two twenties and a ten. "This should get you there," he said, handing the money to her.

"That's too much," she said.

"Well, tide you over. I'll give you a ring later tonight, make sure you got home okay. And I'll be in touch as we go along. Sometimes these things take a little while, but we'll be work . . ."

"Yes," she said. "Let me know."

"I'll have one of the cars drop you off," he said. "Will you be going home by train or . . . ?"

"Train, yes."

She seemed numb.

"So . . . uh . . . whenever you're ready, I'll buzz the sergeant and he'll pull one of the cars off the street. I'd drive you myself, but Brown and I want to get over to the school."

Marie nodded.

And then she looked up and said—perhaps only to herself—"How am I going to live without him?"

Genero was annoyed.

He was the one who'd found the first piece of the body, and now all *four* pieces were out of his hands. So to speak. He blamed it on seniority. Both Brown and Hawes had been detectives longer than he had, and so they'd immediately taken charge of a juicy homicide. So here he was, back on the street again, cruising like a goddamn patrolman. He was more than annoyed. He was enormously pissed.

The streets at a quarter past ten were still teeming with people . . . well, sure, who expected this kind of weather at the end of October? Guys in shirt sleeves, girls in summer dresses, everybody strolling up the avenue like it was summertime in Paris, not that he'd ever been there. Lady there on the corner with a French poodle, letting the dog poop right on the sidewalk, even though it was against the law. He wondered if he should arrest her. He considered it beneath his dignity, a Detective/Third having to arrest a lady whose dog was illegally pooping. He let the dog poop, drove on by.

Made a cursory tour of the sector.

Who else was out here?

Kling?

Came onto Culver, began heading east.

Past the first liquor store got robbed tonight, then the second one . . .

What had they been talking about back there in the squadroom? Meyer and Carella. Midgets? Was it possible? Midgets holding up liquor stores? Those little Munchkins from *The Wizard of Oz* holding up *liquor* stores, for Christ's sake? He didn't know what kind of a world this was getting to be. He thanked God every night before he went to sleep that he had been chosen to enforce law and order in the kind of world this was getting to be. Even if sometimes he had a good ripe murder yanked out of his hands. The only way to get ahead in the Department was to crack a good homicide every now and then. Not that it had done Carella much good, all the homicides he'd cracked. Been a detective for how many years now? Still only

Second Grade. Well, sometimes people got passed over. The meek shall inherit the earth, he thought. Still, he wished he'd had an honest crack at that homicide tonight. He was the one found the first piece, wasn't he?

Onto Mason Avenue, the hookers out in force, well, Halloween, lots of guys coming uptown to look for the Great Pumpkin. Went home with the Great Herpes and maybe the Great AIDS. He wouldn't screw a Mason Avenue hooker if you gave him a million dollars. Well, maybe he would. For a million, maybe. That one on the corner looked very clean, in fact. But you could never tell. Anyway, she was Puerto Rican, and his mother had warned him against fooling around with any girls who weren't Italian. He wondered if Italian girls ever got herpes. He was positive they never got AIDS.

Swinging north again, up one of the side streets, then onto the Stem, all gaudy and bright, he really loved this part of the . . .

"Boy One, Boy One . . ."

The walkie-talkie lying on the seat beside him. Dispatcher trying to raise . . .

"Boy One."

Answering.

"10–21 at one-one-four-one Oliver, near Sixth. Apartment four-two. 10–21 at one-one-four-one Oliver, near Sixth. See the lady."

"What was that apartment again?"

"Four-two."

"Rolling."

A burglary past, couple of blocks down and to the south. No need for a detective on the scene. If it had been a 10–30, an armed robbery in progress, or even a 10–34, an assault in progress, he'd have responded along with the blues. He guessed. Sometimes it was better not to stick your nose into too many things. A 10–13—an assist officer—sure. Man called in for help, you got to the scene fast, *wherever* you were.

Ran uptown on the Stem for a couple of blocks, made a right turn at random, heading south toward the park. He'd swing onto Grover there, parallel the park for a while, then run north to the river, come back down Silvermine, take a run around the Oval, then back south on . . .

Up ahead.

Four teenagers.

Running into the building on the corner.

Just a glimpse of them.

Blue jeans and denim jackets.

Something in their hands.

Trouble?

Shit, he thought.

He eased the car over. No parking spaces on the street, he double-parked in front of the building and picked up the walkie-talkie.

"Eight-Seven," he said, "D.D. Four."

Calling home, identifying himself. One of the six unmarked sedans used by the Detective Division.

"Go ahead, Four."

"Genero," he said. "10–51, four in number, at twelve-seventeen North Eleventh."

"Stay in touch, Genero."

He'd identified the four teenagers as a roving band, a noncrime incident, and he hoped that was what it turned out to be. Getting out of the car, he pulled back the flap of his jacket and was clipping the walkie-talkie to his belt when a loud whooshing sound erupted from inside the building. He almost dropped the walkie-talkie. He looked up sharply. Flames! In the lobby there! And running out of the building, the four teenagers, one of them still carrying in his right hand what looked like a Molotov cocktail. Instinctively, Genero yelled, "Stop! Police!" and yanked his service revolver from its holster.

The kids hesitated for only a moment.

"Police!" he shouted again.

The one with the firebomb held a Zippo lighter to the wick and hurled the bottle at Genero.

The bottle crashed at his feet. Flames sprang up from the sidewalk. He threw both hands up to protect his face, and then immediately stepped back and brought his right hand down again, pistol level, firing into the wall of fire, through the wall of fire, two quick shots in succession.

Somebody screamed.

And suddenly they were on him. They jumped through the flames like circus performers, three of them hitting him almost simultaneously, knocking him to the pavement. He rolled away from the fire, tried to roll away from their kicks. He brought the gun hand up again, fired again, three shots gone now, heard someone grunt. Don't waste any, he thought, and one of them kicked him in the head. He went blank for an instant. His finger tightened reflexively on the trigger. The gun exploded wild, close to his own ear. He blinked his eyes. He was going. He fought unconsciousness. Someone kicked him in the shoulder, and the sharp pain rocketed into his brain and brought him back. Four shots gone, he thought. Make the next ones count. He rolled away again. He blinked them into focus. Only two of them on their feet now. The third one flat on his back near the entrance to the building. Fourth one lying on the sidewalk dangerously close to the fire. He'd hammered two of them, but there were still two to go, and only two shots left in the gun.

His heart was pounding.

But he took his time.

Waited till the lead kicker was almost on him, and then shot for his chest.

Second one right behind him, almost knocked off his feet when his buddy blew back into him. Genero fired again. Took the second one in the left shoulder, sent him spinning around and staggering back toward the wall of the building.

Genero could hardly breathe.

He got to his feet, fanned the empty gun at them.

Nobody seemed to be going anywhere.

He backed off a pace, pulled cartridges from his belt, loaded them into the cylinder, counting . . . four, five, six and ready again.

"Move and you're dead," he whispered, and yanked the walkie-talkie from his belt.

Detective/Third Grade Richard Genero had come of age on the eve of All Hallows' Day.

The school custodian who answered the night bell was the same one who'd locked Sebastian the Great's tricks in a storeroom earlier this afternoon. Peering through the grilled upper glass panel of the door at the back of the building, he recognized Hawes at once, unlocked the door, and let him in.

" 'Evening, Mr. Buono," Hawes said.

"Hey, how you doing?" Buono said.

He was a man in his late sixties, thinning gray hair, thin gray mustache over his upper lip. Pale blue eyes, somewhat bulbous nose. He was wearing coveralls. A flashlight was in one of the pockets. He clipped his ring of keys to a loop on the pocket.

"This is my partner, Detective Brown," Hawes said.

"Nice to meetcha," Buono said. "You come back for the stuff?"

"Well, no," Hawes said. "Few questions we'd like to ask you."

Buono immediately figured they knew he was stealing supplies from the classroom closets.

"Hey, sure," he said, and tried to look innocent. He locked the door behind them, and said, "Come on over the office, we can talk there. My friend and me were playing checkers."

They walked down a yellow-tiled, locker-lined corridor. They passed a wall clock that read twenty minutes past ten. They made a left turn. More students' lockers on either wall. A bulletin board. A poster reading:

COME CHEER THE TIGERS!
Saturday, Nov. 1, 2:00 P.M.
RAUCHER FIELD

To the right of that, another poster announcing:

SEBASTIAN THE GREAT!
HALLOWEEN MAGIC!
Auditorium. 4:00 P.M.

Beneath the lettering was a black-and-white photograph of a good-looking young man wearing a top hat and bow tie, grinning into the camera.

"Okay to take that poster?" Brown asked.

"Which one?" Buono said.

"The magician."

"Sure," Buono said, and shrugged.

Brown began pulling out the tacks.

"Come in handy, we find the head," he said to Hawes, and then folded the poster and put it in his inside jacket pocket.

Buono led them further down the hall, opened a door at the end of it. A sparsely furnished room. An upright locker, green in contrast to the reds, yellows, and oranges of the lockers in the halls. Long oak table, probably requisitioned from one of the administration offices. Four straight-backed chairs around it, checkerboard on one end of it. Coffee pot on a hot plate on one wall of the room, clock over it. Framed picture of Ronald Reagan on the wall opposite.

"This here's my friend, Sal Pasquali," Buono said.

Pasquali was in his late sixties, early seventies, wearing brown trousers, brown shoes and socks, a pale yellow sports shirt, and a brown sweater buttoned up the front. He looked like a candy-store owner.

"These people here are detectives," Buono said, and looked at Pasquali, hoping he would understand what the look meant: Watch your onions about the chalk, and the paste, and the pencils, and the erasers, and the reams of paper.

Pasquali nodded sagely, like a Mafia don.

"Pleased to meetcha," he said.

"So," Buono said, "sit down. You want some coffee?"

"Thanks, no," Hawes said.

The detectives pulled out chairs and sat.

Buono could see Brown's gun in a shoulder holster under his jacket.

"We were just playing checkers here," Pasquali said.

"Who's winning?" Brown asked.

"Well, we don't play for money or nothing," Pasquali said.

Which meant that they did.

Brown suddenly wondered what these two old farts were hiding.

"I wanted to ask whether you saw anything that happened outside there this afternoon," Hawes said.

"Why?" Buono said at once. "Is something missing?"

"No, no. Missing? What do you mean?"

"Well, what do *you* mean?" Buono said, and glanced at Pasquali.

"I meant when the cars were being loaded."

"Oh."

"When Mr. Sebastiani was out there loading his tricks in the Citation."

"I didn't see him doing that," Buono said.

"You weren't out there after he finished the act, huh?"

"No. I didn't come on till four o'clock."

"Well, he'd have been out there around five-thirty."

"No, I didn't see him."

"Then you have no idea who might've dumped that stuff out of his car . . ."

"No idea at all."

"And driven off with it."

"No. Five-thirty, I was prolly down the north end of the building, starting with the classrooms there. I usually start cleaning the classrooms down the north end, it's like a routine, you know. Tradition."

"That's near the driveway, isn't it? The north end?"

"Yeah, the back of the building. But I didn't see anything out there. I mean, I *mighta* seen something if I was looking—there's windows in the classrooms, you know. But I wasn't looking for nothing. I was busy cleaning up the classrooms."

"You say you came on at four . . ."

"That's right. Four to midnight."

"Like us," Brown said, and smiled.

"Yeah?" Buono said. "Is that your shift? Whattya know? You hear this, Sal? They got shifts like us."

"What a coincidence," Pasquali said.

Brown still wondered what they were hiding.

"So you came on at four . . ." Hawes said.

"Yeah. Four to midnight. There's a man relieves me at midnight." He looked at the clock on the wall. "Be here in a few hours, well, less. But he's like just a watchman, you know."

"If you came on at four . . ."

"Yeah." A nod.

"Then you weren't here when the Sebastianis arrived, were you? They would've got here about a quarter after three. You weren't here then, is that right?"

"No. Sal was here."

Pasquali nodded.

"Sal works from eight to four," Buono said. "He's the *day* custodian."

"Shifts," Pasquali said. "Like you."

"He can't stay away from the place," Buono said. "Comes back to play checkers with me every night."

"I'm a widower," Pasquali explained, and shrugged.

"Did you see the cars when they arrived?" Brown asked him. "Tan Ford Econoline, blue Citation?"

"I seen one of them out there," Pasquali said. "But not when it came in."

"Which one did you see?"

"Light blue car."

"When was this? When you saw it?"

"Around . . . three-thirty, was it?"

"You asking me?" Buono said. "I wasn't here three-thirty."

"Three-thirty, it musta been," Pasquali said. "I remember I was heading out front, where the school buses come in. I usually go out there, talk to the drivers."

"They'd have been setting up the stage by then," Hawes said. Brown nodded.

"And the van was already gone."

Brown nodded again.

"Did you see any people out there?" Hawes asked Pasquali. "Carrying things in? Unloading the cars?"

"All I saw was the one car."

"Blonde woman in her late twenties? Two men in their early thirties?"

"No," Pasquali said, and shook his head.

"Were the doors open?"

"What doors?"

"On the car."

"They looked closed to me."

"Anything lying in the driveway there?"

"Nothing I could see. What do you mean? Like what?"

"Tricks," Hawes said.

"Tricks?" Pasquali said, and looked at Buono.

"They done a magic show this afternoon," Buono said. "For the kids."

"Oh. No, I didn't see no tricks out there."

"You didn't happen to wander by that driveway later on, did you? Around five-thirty? When they were loading the . . ."

"Five-thirty I was home eating my dinner. I made a nice TV dinner for myself."

Hawes looked at Brown.

"Anything?" he asked.

Brown shook his head.

"Well, thanks a lot," Hawes said, and shoved back his chair.

"I'll let you out the building," Buono said.

The detectives followed him out of the office.

As soon as they were gone, Pasquali took out his handkerchief and mopped his brow.

At twenty minutes past ten, Larry's Bar was buzzing with activity.

Not a table empty. Not a stool unoccupied at the bar.

Eileen was sitting at one of the tables now, talking to a blonde hooker named Sheryl who was wearing a red skirt slit up one side, and a white silk blouse unbuttoned three buttons down. There was nothing under the blouse. Sheryl sat with her legs spread, her high heels hooked on the chair's top rung. Eileen could see track marks on her naked white thighs. She was telling Eileen how she'd come to this city from Baltimore, Maryland. Eileen was scanning the room, trying to figure out which one of these guys in here was her backup. Two waitresses, who could have passed for hookers themselves—short black skirts, high heels, overflowing white peasant blouses—were busily scooting back and forth between the tables and the bar, avoiding grabs at their asses.

"Got off the bus," the girl said, "first thing happens to me is this kindly old man asks can he help me with my valise. Had to be forty years old, am I right, a nice old man being friendly. Asks me have I got a place to stay, offers to get me a taxi to the Y, says 'I'll bet you're starving,' which I was, takes me to a hamburger joint, stuffs me with burgers and fries, tells me a nice young girl like me—I was only seventeen—had to be careful in the big, bad city, lots of people out there waiting to victimize me."

"Same old bullshit," Eileen said.

She figured there were only two men who could be Shanahan. Guy sitting there at one of the tables, talking up a hooker with frizzied brown hair, he had a hook nose that could've been a phony, black hair and blues eyes like Shanahan's, about his height and weight, wearing horn-rimmed eyeglasses. He could've been Shanahan.

"Well, sure, you know the story already," the girl said. "Mr. Nice turns out to be Big Daddy, takes me to his apartment, introduces me to two other girls living there, nice girls like me, he says, has me smoking pot that same night and shooting horse before the week is out. Turned me out two days later with a businessman from Ohio. Guy ast me to blow him, I didn't know what the fuck he meant. Man, that seems like ages ago."

"How old are you now?" Eileen asked.

"Twenty-two," Sheryl said. "I'm not with Lou no more . . . that was his name, Lou . . . I got me a new man, takes good care of me. Who you with?"

"Torpedo Holmes," Eileen said.

"Is he black, or what?"

"Black."

"Yeah, mine, too. Lou was white. I think the white ones are meaner, I really do. Lou used to beat the shit out of me. That first time, after the guy from Ohio, you know, where I didn't know what to do, Lou beat me so I couldn't walk. Had a dozen of his buddies come up the next morning, one after the other, twelve of them, teach the little hayseed from Baltimore how to suck a cock. Broke in my ass, too. That was when I *really* got turned out, believe me. The guy from Ohio was child's play. In fact, everything after that night with Lou's buddies was child's play."

"Yeah, they can be rotten when they want to," Eileen said.

Guy sitting there talking to Annie was the other possibility, though she doubted Shanahan would've made such obvious contact. Brown eyes, but those could be contacts if he was playing this real fancy. Wearing a plaid jacket that made him look wider than Shanahan. Sitting on a stool, so Eileen couldn't tell how tall he was. But he was a possibility.

"This guy I got now . . . you know Ham Coleman?"

"I don't think so."

"Hamilton? Hamilton Coleman?"

"Yeah, maybe."

"Black as his name. Coal, you know. Coleman. Hung like a stallion, likes to parade around the pad with only a towel around him, dares the girls to snatch it off. Quick as a bullfighter. You snatch off the towel, he gives you a little treat. My poison is still hoss—well, you know, that's what Lou hooked me on. But some of the girls—there's six of us with him—they dig the nose candy, and he gets them whatever they need, good stuff too, I think he has Columbian connections. It's like a game he plays with the towel, snatch it off, suck his big dick, he lays the dope on you. I mean, it's just a game, 'cause he keeps us supplied very nice, anyway. It's kind of cute, though, the way he struts around in that towel. He's really okay. Ham Coleman. You ever think of moving, you might want to come over. We don't have any redheads. That your real hair?"

"Yeah," Eileen said.

" 'Cause mine is straight from a bottle," Sheryl said, and laughed.

She still had a little-girl's laugh. Twenty-two years old, hooked on heroin, in the life since she was seventeen. Thought Ham Coleman with his towel was "kind of cute."

"What I'm really hoping for . . . well, this is just a *dream,* I know," she said, and rolled her eyes, "but I keep asking Ham about it all the time, who knows, it might really come true one day. I keep asking him to set us up like real call girls, you know, hundred-buck tricks, maybe two hundred, never mind dropping us here in the Zone where we're like common *whores,* you know what I mean? I mean, you and me, we're just common whores, ain't we? When you get right down to it?"

"Uh-huh. And what does he say?"

"Oh, he says we ain't got the class yet to be racehorses. I tell him class, shit. A blowjob's a blowjob. He says we still got a lot to learn, all six of us. He says maybe in time he'll set up a class operation like what I got in mind. So I tell him *when?* When we're all scaley-legged hookers, thirty, forty years old? Excuse me, I guess maybe you're in your thirties, I didn't mean no offense, Linda."

"Don't worry about it," Eileen said.

"Well, we all have our dreams, don't we?" Sheryl said, and sighed. "My dream when I first came to this city was I'd become an actress, you know? I was in a lot of plays in high school, in Baltimore, I figured I could make it big as an actress here. Well, that was just a dream. Like being a hundred-dollar call girl is probably just a dream, too. Still, you got to have dreams, am I right? Otherwise . . ."

"You girls gonna sit here talking to each other all night?"

The man standing by the table had padded up so quietly that he startled both of them. Blond guy, Eileen figured him at five-eleven, around a hundred and seventy pounds, just like Shanahan. Wearing dark glasses, she couldn't see the color of his eyes. The blond hair could be a wig. Moved a bit like Shanahan, too, maybe he *was* Shanahan. If so, he'd just won the bet. One thing he wasn't was the killer. Not unless he'd lost three, four inches, thirty pounds, a pair of eyeglasses, and a tattoo near his right thumb.

He pulled out a chair.

"Martin Reilly," he said, and sat. "What's a nice Irish lad doing in a joint like this, right?"

Voice heavier than Shanahan's. Calm's Point accent. Turtle Bay section, most likely. Lots of Irish families still there.

"Hi, Morton," Sheryl said.

"Martin," he corrected at once.

"Ooops, sorry," Sheryl said. "I'm Sheryl, I know just how you feel. When people call me Shirley, it really burns my ass."

"You know what really burns my ass?" Reilly said.

"Sure. People calling you Morton."

"No," Reilly said. "A little fire about this high."

He held out his hand, palm down, to indicate a fire only high enough to burn a man's ass.

"That one has hair on it," Eileen said, looking bored.

"Like the palm of my hand," Reilly said, and grinned. "All those months at sea, ladies, a man marries his hand."

Still grinning. Rows of even white glistening teeth, the better to eat you with, my dear. If Shanahan had capped teeth like that, he'd be starring on *Hill Street Blues*.

"You just get in?" Sheryl asked.

"Docked tonight."

"From where?"

"Lebanon."

"Ain't there no girls there in Lebanon?" Sheryl said, and rolled her eyes.

"Not like you two," he said.

"Oooo, my," she said, and leaned over the table so he could look into the front of her blouse. "So what are you looking for?" she asked, getting straight to the point. "A handjob's fifteen," she said, quoting high, "a blowjob's twenty-five and Miss Puss is forty."

"How about your friend here? What's your name, honey?" he asked, and put his hand on Eileen's thigh.

"Linda," she said.

She let his hand stay on her thigh.

"That means beautiful in Spanish."

"So they tell me."

"How much for both of you? Do I get a better price for both of you?"

"You're getting a bargain as it is," Sheryl said.

"Tell you what," Reilly said, and slipped his hand up under Eileen's skirt. "I'll give you ..."

"Mister," Eileen said, and caught his hand at the wrist. "You ain't given us *nothing yet,* so don't grope the goods, okay?"

"I'm sampling it."

"You get what you see, you don't need samples. This ain't a grocery store honors coupons."

Reilly laughed. He folded his hands on the table top.

"Okay, let's talk numbers," he said.

"We're listening," Sheryl said, and glanced at Eileen.

"Fifty for the both of you," Reilly said. "Around the world."

"You talking fifty for *each* of us?" Sheryl said.

"I said *both* of you. Twenty-five each."

"No way," Sheryl said at once.

"Okay, make it *thirty* each. And you throw in a little entertainment."

"What kinda entertainment?" Sheryl asked.

"I wanna see you go down on the redhead here."

Sheryl looked at Eileen appraisingly.

"I hardly know her," she said.

"So? You'll get to know her."

Sheryl thought it over.

"Make it fifty apiece, we'll give you a good show," she said.

"That's too much," he said.

"Then fuck off," Sheryl said. "You're wasting our time here."

"I'll tell you what," Reilly said. "I'll make it forty apiece, how's that?"

"What are you?" Sheryl said. "A Lebanese rug merchant?"

Reilly laughed again.

"Forty-five," he said. "For each of you. And a ten-dollar bonus for whoever brings me off first."

"Count me out," Eileen said.

"What's the matter?" Reilly asked, looking offended. "That's a fair and honest deal."

"It really is, you know," Sheryl said.

"Sheryl can show you a good time all by herself," Eileen said, doing a fast tap dance. "I don't work doubles."

"Then what the fuck were we talking about here?" Reilly asked.

"You were doing all the talking," Eileen said. "I was only listening."

Reilly dismissed her at once.

"You got any other girlfriends in here?" he asked Sheryl.

"How about the frizzied brunette over there?" she said.

Reilly looked over to where the brunette was still in conversation with one of the other Shanahan possibilities.

"That's Gloria," Sheryl said. "I worked with her before."

"Is she a muff-diver?" Reilly said. "Or is she like your friend here?"

"She *loves* pussy," Sheryl said, lying. "You want me to talk to her?"

"Yeah, go talk to her."

"That's forty-five apiece," Sheryl said, cementing the deal, "and a ten-buck bonus." She was figuring they'd do a little show, then take turns blowing him, and share the extra ten for fifty each. Which wouldn't be bad for an hour's work. Maybe less than an hour if he'd been at sea as long as he'd said. "A hundred in all, right?"

"A hundred is what I said, ain't it?"

"It's just I have to tell Gloria," Sheryl said, and got up, long leg and thigh flashing in the slit skirt. "Don't go away, honey," she said, and walked over to the other table.

"You're in the wrong business," Reilly said to Eileen.

Maybe I am, Eileen thought.

There were four liquor stores on Culver Avenue between the last one hit on Twentieth, and the eastern edge of the precinct territory on Thirty-Fifth. After that, it was the neighboring precinct's problem, and welcome to it. They drove up Culver to the last store, and then doubled back to the one on Twenty-Third. The digital dashboard clock read 10:32 P.M.

The store was empty except for a man behind the counter who was slitting open a carton of Jack Daniels sour mash. He looked up when the bell over the door sounded, saw a burly bald-headed guy and another big guy with him, and immediately placed his hand on the stock of the shotgun under the counter.

"What'll it be, gents?" he asked.

Hand still on the shotgun stock, finger inside the trigger guard now.

Meyer flashed the potsy.

"Police," he said.

The hand under the counter relaxed.

"Detective Meyer," he said. "Detective Carella. Eighty-Seventh Squad."

"What's the problem?" the man said.

He was in his early fifties, not quite as bald as Meyer, but getting there. Brown eyes, slight build, wearing a gray cotton work jacket with the words ALAN'S WHISKIES stitched in red on the breast pocket.

"Who are we talking to, sir?" Meyer asked.

"I'm Alan Zuckerman."

"Is this your store, sir?"

"It is."

"Mr. Zuckerman," Carella said, "there've been three liquor-store holdups on

Culver Avenue tonight. Starting on Ninth and working uptown. If there's a pattern—and there may not be—your store's next in line.''

"I'm closing in half an hour," Zuckerman said, and turned to look at the clock on the wall behind the counter.

"They may come in before then," Meyer said.

"You don't know me, huh?" Zuckerman said.

"Should I know you?" Meyer said.

"Alan Zuckerman. I was in all the papers last year this time." He looked at Carella. "*You* don't know me, either, do you?"

"I'm sorry, sir, I don't."

"Some cops," Zuckerman said.

Meyer glanced at Carella.

"This very precinct, they don't know me."

"Why should we know you, sir?" Carella asked.

"Because last October I shot two people came in the store to rob me," Zuckerman said.

"Oh," Carella said.

"With *this!*" Zuckerman said, and yanked the shotgun from under the counter.

Both detectives backed away.

"*Bang!*" Zuckerman said, and Meyer flinched. "One of them falls on the floor screaming! *Bang,* the other barrel! And the second one goes down!"

"I seem to recall that now," Meyer said. "Mr. Zuckerman, you can put up the shotgun now, okay?"

"Made all the papers," Zuckerman said, the gun still in his hands, his finger inside the trigger guard. "Shotgun Zuckerman, they called me, the papers. They had the story on television, too. Nobody tried no tricks here since, I can tell you that. It's been a year already, a little more than a year."

"Well, these people tonight," Meyer said, "Mr. Zuckerman, could you please put up the gun?"

Zuckerman slid the gun under the counter again.

"Thank you," Meyer said. "These people tonight, there are four of them. All of them armed. So your shotgun there, if all four of them start shooting . . .''

"Shotgun Zuckerman can take care of them, don't worry."

"What we were thinking," Carella said, "is maybe we could lend you a hand."

"Sort of ride shotgun to your shotgun," Meyer said, nodding.

"Backups, sort of," Carella said.

"Only in case you need us."

"Otherwise we'll butt out."

Zuckerman looked at them.

"Listen," he said at last, "you want to waste your time, that's fine by me."

He yanked the phone from the receiver the moment it rang.

"Hello?" he said.

"Hi," Marie said.

"Where are you?"

"Metro West. I'm catching the ten forty-five home."

"How'd it go?"

"Tough night," she said. "Any trouble on your end?"

"Nope. They made identification, huh? I saw it on television."

"I was the one who made it. Where'd you leave the Citation?"

"Behind an A & P near the river."

" 'Cause I don't think they found it yet."

"Who's on the case?"

"A salt-and-pepper team. Brown and Hawes. Big redhead, big black guy. In case they come snooping."

"Why would they?"

"I'm saying in case. They're both dummies, but you oughta be warned. They got a bulletin out . . . they asked me for descriptions. They're gonna be watching all the airports. What flight are you on?"

"TWA's one twenty-nine. Leaves at twelve-oh-five tomorrow afternoon."

"What time do you get to Frisco?"

"Four forty-seven."

"I'll try you at the hotel around six-thirty. You'll be registered as Jack Gwynne, am I right?"

"All the dead ones," he said, and laughed. "Like Sebastian the Great."

"Give me the number of the Hong Kong flight again?"

"United eight-oh-five. Leaves Frisco at one-fifteen Sunday, gets there around eight the next morning."

"When will you call me?"

"Soon as I'm settled."

"You think that passport'll work?"

"It cost us four hundred bucks, it *better* work. Why? You running scared?"

"Nerves of steel," she said. "You shoulda seen me with the cops."

"No problem with the ID, was there?"

"None."

"You did mention the cock?"

"Oh, sure."

"Little birthmark and all?"

"Come on, we went over this a hundred times."

"*You* went over it a hundred times."

"And hated every minute of it."

"Sure."

"You *know* that, damn it."

"Sure."

"You going to start on me again?"

"I'm sorry."

"You oughta be. All we've been through."

"I said I was sorry."

"Okay."

There was a long silence on the line.

"So whattya gonna do till noon tomorrow?"

"Thought I'd go down for a drink, then come back and get some sleep."

"Be careful."

"Oh, yeah."

"They know what you look like."

"Don't worry."

Another silence.

"Maybe you oughta call me later tonight, okay?"

"Sure."

"Be careful," she said again, and hung up.

8

"Torpedoman ain't gonna like this," Larry said.

"Who asked you?" Eileen said.

"For a working girl, all you done so far is sit and drink."

"Guess it just ain't my lucky night," Eileen said.

"Whattya talkin' about? I already seen you turn down a dozen guys."

"I'm particular."

"Then you shouldn't be in this dump," Larry said. "Particular ain't for the Canal Zone."

Eileen knew he was only pointing out the obvious: the name of the game was money, and a hooker working a bar wasn't a girl at the Spring Cotillion. You didn't tell a prospective John your card was filled, even if he looked like Godzilla. Larry was already suspicious, and that was dangerous. Get a few more guys giving her the fish eye, and she could easily blow the *real* reason she was here.

Sheryl and the frizzied brunette were still out with the blond sailor, but Eileen was ready to bet her shield they'd be back in business the moment they returned. There was no way any enterprising girl could avoid making a buck in here. The bar was in incessant motion, a whorehouse with a liquor license and a transient crowd. Any man who came in alone walked out not five minutes later with a girl on his arm. According to Shanahan, the girls—even some of them on the Canalside meat rack— used either a hotbed hotel up the street or any one of fifty, sixty rooms for rent in the Zone. They usually paid five bucks for the room, got a kickback from the owner and also a share of the three bucks the John paid for soap and towels. That way, a twenty-dollar trick could net a girl the same twenty when all was said and done. Plus whatever tip a generous John might decide to lay on her for superior performance.

She glanced down the length of the bar to where Annie was sitting in earnest conversation with a little Hispanic guy wearing jeans, boots, and a black leather jacket studded with chrome. Looked like Annie was having the same problem. The only difference was that she could step outside every now and then, make it look like she was drumming up trade on the street. Eileen was glued to the bar. The bar was where the killer had picked up his three previous victims. She tried to catch Annie's eye. They had figured out beforehand that if they wanted to talk they'd do it in the ladies' room, not here in public. Eileen wanted to dope out a scam that would cool Larry's heat.

"Torpedoman's gonna whip your ass," he said.

"You wanna make a little side bet?" Eileen said. "You wanna bet I go home with six bills before the night's over?"

Annie finally looked over at her.

Eye contact.

Brief nod of her head.

Eileen got off the stool and started for the ladies' room. The Hispanic guy sitting next to Annie got off his stool at the same time. Good, Eileen thought, she's ditching him. But the Hispanic guy walked straight toward her, meeting her halfway down the bar.

"Hey, where you goin', Mama?" he said. Loud voice for a little twerp, Spanish accent you could cut with a machete. Little brown eyes, mustache under his nose, looked like an undernourished biker in his leather jacket.

"Got to visit my grandma," Eileen said.

"You gran'ma can wait," he said.

Behind him, down the bar, Annie was watching them.

Another brief nod.

All right already, Eileen thought. As soon as I *shake* this guy.

The guy wasn't about to be shaken. He gripped Eileen's elbow in his right hand, began steering her toward the stool she'd abandoned—"Come on, Mama, we ha' biss'niss to talk abou' "—same loud voice, you could hear him clear across the river, fingers tight on her elbow, plunked her down on the stool—"My name iss Arturo, I been watchin' you, Mama"—and signaled to Larry.

"You want me to wet my pants?" Eileen asked.

"No, no, I sornly don' wann you to do that," he said.

Larry ambled over.

"See wha' my frien' here iss drinkin'," Arturo said.

She couldn't make a fuss about the ladies' room now, not with Larry standing right here and already believing she was turning down tricks left and right. Spot Annie trailing her in there, they'd *both* be out of business.

"Larry knows what I'm drinking," she said.

"Rum-Coke for the lady," Larry said, "it's still prom night. How about you, amigo?"

"Scotch on dee rahss," Arturo said. "Twiss."

Larry started pouring.

"So how much you get, Mama?" Arturo asked.

"What are you looking for?"

"This swee' lil' ting here," he said, and put his forefinger on her lips.

"That'll cost you twenty," she said.

Going price, in case Larry was listening. Which of course he was.

"You got someplace we can go, Mama?"

"Plenty of rooms for rent around here."

Everything kosher so far. But Larry was still here.

"How much do I pay for dee room?" Arturo asked.

"Five."

Larry raised his eyebrows. He knew the girls usually paid for the room themselves but he figured Linda here was hustling the little spic. Maybe she *would* go home with six bills tonight, who the hell knew?

"Muy bien, muchacha," Arturo said.

"Rum-Coke, scotch-rocks with a twist," Larry said, sliding the drinks closer to them. "Six bucks, a bargain."

Arturo put a ten-dollar bill on the counter. Larry started for the cash register at the far end. As soon as he was out of earshot, Arturo whispered, in perfect English, "I'm on the job, play along."

Eileen eyes opened wide.

At the far end of the bar, Annie gave another brief nod. Larry rang open the register, put the ten in the drawer, took four bills out of it, slammed the drawer shut again, and then started back toward where they were sitting, sipping at their drinks now. Arturo had his hand on Eileen's knee, and he was peering down the front of her blouse. She was saying, " 'Cause like, you know, I'm a working girl, Artie, so I'd like to get started, if that's okay with you."

"Hey, no sweat, Mama," he said. "We can tay dee booze wid us."

"Not in *my* good glasses," Larry said, and immediately began transferring the drinks to plastic cups.

Eileen was already off the stool. She turned to Larry and said, "Glad you didn't take that bet?"

Larry shrugged.

He watched them as they picked up the cups and walked away from the bar. He was thinking he wouldn't mind a piece of that himself. As they started out the door, they almost collided with a man coming in at the same time.

"Oh, I beg your pardon," he said, and stepped aside to let them through.

Larry was sure he'd seen the guy before. He was at least six-feet two-inches tall, with wide shoulders and a broad chest, thick wrists, big hands. He was wearing jeans, sneakers, a little tan cap, and a yellow turtleneck sweater that matched the color of his hair. He looked like a heavyweight fighter in training.

"You're not *leaving,* are you?" he asked Eileen.

She breezed right past him, ignoring him.

But her heart was suddenly pounding.

Annie sat at the bar wearing a short tight black skirt, purple tube top cradling her cupcake breasts, high-heeled black patent leather shoes, face heavily pancaked, blood-red lipstick on her mouth, eyes lined in black, lids tinted to match the blouse, looking more like a hooker than any of the real ones in the place.

She thought Terrific. Here he is.

All we need is this little trick of fate.

Eileen walking out while he walks in.

Eileen loaded to the gunnels, me wearing only a .38 in my handbag, terrific.

Eileen the decoy, me the backup, and in he walks.

Terrific.

If it's him.

He sure as hell looked like the blond guy Alvarez and Shanahan had described. No eyeglasses, but the same height and weight, the same bulk.

Standing just inside the doorway now, looking over the place, cool, confident in his size, ready to take on any guy in the place, mop up the floor with him, this cat had nothing to worry about, oh no, handsome as the devil, oh so cool, scanning the room, checking out the girls, then walking up toward the bar, passing the cash register where she sat . . .

"Hi," she said. "Wanna join me?"

"Danny Ortiz," Arturo said on the street outside.

"Detective/Second, Undercover Narcotics. I got a call from Lou . . ."

Lou, Eileen thought. Not Lou the friendly white man who'd turned out Sheryl, if that was her real name. In novels, everybody had different names so you could tell them apart. In real life, Lou could be a pimp and a detective at the same time. Lou Alvarez of the Seven-Two.

". . . said I ought to check out Larry's Bar, see his decoy needed some help. Described you and Rawles, sat with her, talked her up, she told me the Johns were hitting on you like locusts. Am I screwing anything up?"

Lou Alvarez, calling his buddy Danny Ortiz in Narcotics, asking him to run on over here, hit on the decoy, take her out of the joint to preserve her credibility.

"You saved my life," Eileen said.

Bit of an exaggeration, but at least he'd saved her cover.

"So you wanna neck or anything?" Ortiz said. "Pass the time?"

"That's the best offer I've had all night," she said. "But I gotta get back in there."

Ortiz looked at her.

"Our man just walked in," she said.

His size was intimidating. He filled the stool, filled the bar, seemed to fill the entire room. Sitting next to him, Annie was scared. If this was the guy . . .

"So what's your name?" she asked.

"What's yours?"

"Jenny," she said.

"I'll bet."

Deep voice rumbling up out of his barrel chest.

"Well," she said, "my straight handle is Antoinette Le Fevrier, but who'll believe that on a hooker?"

"Oh, is that what you are?" he asked.

Voice almost toneless. Bored attitude. Looking in the mirror, checking out the other girls in the place even as he talked to her.

"No, I'm a famous brain surgeon," Annie said, and smiled.

He did not smile back. Turned to look at her. Eyes the color of steel. A chill ran up her spine. Where the hell was Shanahan?

"You still didn't tell me your name," she said.

"Howie," he said.

Sounded square enough to be true.

"Howie what?"

"Howie's enough," he said, and folded his hands on the tabletop. No tattoo on either one of them. Was he, or wasn't he? "So what you do is make love to strangers, huh?" he said. "For money."

She didn't want this guy to ask her outside. Not with only the .38 in her bag and Shanahan nowhere in sight.

"That's my job. You interested?"

"You're not my type," he said.

"Oh? And what's your type?" she asked. Keep him talking. Keep him interested till Eileen walked back in. And if Eileen *didn't* walk in soon, then talk him into taking *her* outside to make his move. If Shanahan was anywhere around, he'd be tracking both of them.

"I like them younger," he said. "And fresher."

"Well, what you see is what you get," she said.

"You seem too far gone."

"Uh-huh," she said, "practically ancient." One of the dead girls had been sixteen. The others were in their twenties. Keep him here, she thought. Don't let him wander off to any of the younger girls in here, or they'll drift away together and he'll score another one tonight.

"I mean, what can I tell you?" she said. "I'm not a teenager, but I'm pretty good for an old lady."

He turned to look at her again.

No smile.

Christ, he was chilling.

"Really?" he said.

"Really."

Come-on look in her eyes. She licked her lips. But she had only the .38 in her bag. No backup artillery. And Shanahan God knew where. Ortiz heading back home soon as he cleared Eileen, wham, bam, thank you, ma'am, or so it would appear to Larry.

"Ten for a handjob," she said, "how about it? Twenty for a blowjob, thirty if you want the pearly gates."

"My, my," he said. "You really are a seasoned pro, aren't you?"

"Exactly what I am," she said. "How about it?"

"No, you're too far gone," he said.

Eyes on the mirror again. The blonde who'd been talking with Eileen earlier was back now, together with her frizzied brunette friend. Both of them young and looking for more action. His eyes checked them out. Stick with me, pal, she thought. Here's where the action is.

"Are you a cop?" he asked without even looking at her.

Mind-reader, she thought.

"Sure," she said. "Are you a cop, too?"

"I used to be," he said.

Oh, shit, she thought. A renegade. Or a malcontent.

"I can always tell a cop," he said.

"You wanna see my badge?" she said.

Deliberately using the word badge. A cop called it a shield.

"Are you with Vice?" he asked.

"Oh, man, *am* I," she said. "Clear down to my tonsils."

"I used to be with Vice," he said.

"So *I'm* the one who caught myself a cop, huh?" she said, and smiled. "Well, Howie, that makes no difference to me at all, the past is the past, all water under the bridge. What do you say we take a little stroll up the street, I'll show you a real good . . ."

"Get lost," he said.

"Let's get lost together, Howie," she said, and put her hand on his thigh.

"You understand English?" he said.

"French, too," she said. "Come on, Howie, give a working girl a . . ."

"Get *lost!*" he said.

A command this time.

Eyes blazing, big hands clenched on the bartop.

"Sure," she said. "Relax."

She got off the stool.

"Relax, okay?" she said, and walked down to the other end of the bar.

Inexplicably, her palms were wet.

Guy sitting next to him at the bar was running a tab, twenty-dollar bill tucked under the little bowl of salted peanuts. Big flashy Texan sporting a diamond pinky ring, a shirt as loud as he himself was, and a black string tie held with one of those turquoise-and-silver Indian clasps. He was drinking martinis, and talking about soybeans. Said soybeans were the nation's future. No cholesterol in soybeans.

"So what do *you* do?" he asked.

"I'm in insurance."

Which wasn't too far from the truth. Soon as Marie made the insurance claim . . .

"Lots of money in insurance," the Texan said.

"For sure."

At double indemnity, the policy came to two hundred grand. More money than he could make in eight years' time.

"By the way, my name's Abner Phipps," the Texan said, and extended a meaty hand.

He took the hand. "Theo Hardeen," he said.

"Nice to meet you, Theo. You gonna be in town long?"

"Leaving tomorrow."

"I'm stuck here all through next week," Phipps said. "I hate this city, I truly do. There're people who say it's a nice place to visit, but I can't even see it for that. Worth your life just walkin' the streets here. You see that thing on television tonight?"

"What thing is that?"

The black bartender was listening silently, standing some six feet away from them, polishing glasses. The clock on the wall read ten to eleven. Shows'd be breaking soon, he wanted to be ready for the crowd.

"Somebody chopping up a body, leaving pieces of it all over town," Phipps said, and shook his head. "Bad enough you *kill* somebody, you got to chop him up in pieces afterward? Why you suppose he did that, Theo?"

"Well, I'll tell you, Abner, there're all kinds of nuts in this world."

"I mean, there're two rivers in this city, Theo. Why didn't he just throw the whole damn *body* in one of them?"

That's where the head is, he thought. And the hands.

"Still," Phipps said, "if you got a body to get rid of, I guess it's easier to dump in sections. I mean, somebody sees you hauling a corpse around, that might raise suspicion, even in *this* city. An arm, a head, whatever, you can just drop in a garbage can or down the sewer, nobody'll pay any attention to you, am I right, Theo?"

"I guess maybe that's why he did it."

"Well, who can figure the criminal mind?" Phipps said.

"Not me, that's for sure. I have a hard enough time selling insurance."

"Oh, I'll bet," Phipps said. "You know why? Nobody likes to think he's gonna kick off one day. You sit there tellin' him how his wife's gonna be sittin' pretty once he's dead, he don't want to hear that. He wants to think he's gonna live forever. I don't care *how* responsible a man he is, it makes him uncomfortable talkin' about death benefits."

"You hit it right on the head, Abner. I talk myself blue in the face, and half the time they're not even listening. Explain, explain, explain, they don't know what the hell I'm talking about."

"People just don't listen anymore," Phipps said.

"Or they don't listen carefully enough. They hear only what they want to hear."

"That's for sure, Theo."

"I'll give you an example," he said, and then immediately thought Come on, he's too easy. On the other hand, it might teach him a valuable lesson. Chatting up a stranger in a bar, no real sense of how many con artists were loose and on the prowl in this city. Teach him something he could take back home to Horse's Neck, Texas.

He reached into his pocket, took out a dime and a nickel.

"What have I got here?" he asked.

"Fifteen cents," Phipps said.

"Okay, open your hand."

Phipps opened his hand.

"Now I'm putting this dime and this nickel on the palm of your hand."

"Yep, I see that, Theo."

"And I'm not touching them anymore, they're in your hand now, am I right?"

"Right there on the palm of my hand, Theo."

"Now close your hand on them."

Phipps closed his hand. The bartender was watching now.

"You've got that fifteen cents in your fist now, am I right?"

"Still there," Phipps said.

"A dime and a nickel."

"A dime and a nickel, right."

"And I haven't touched them since you closed your hand on them, right?"

"You haven't touched them, right."

"Okay I'll bet you when you open your hand, one of them won't be a dime."

"Come on, Theo, you're lookin' to lose money."

"Man's lookin' to lose money for sure," the bartender said.

"I'll bet you the twenty dollars under the peanut bowl, okay?"

"You got a bet," Phipps said.

"Okay, open your hand."

Phipps opened his hand. Fifteen cents still on his palm. Same dime, same nickel. The bartender shook his head.

"You lose," Phipps said.

"No, I win. What I said . . ."

"The bet was that one of these coins wouldn't be a dime no more."

"No, you weren't listening. The bet was that one of them wouldn't be a dime."

"That's just what . . ."

"And one of them isn't. One of them's a nickel."

He slid the twenty-dollar bill from under the peanut bowl, and tucked it into his jacket pocket. "You can keep the fifteen cents," he said, and smiled and walked out of the bar.

The bartender said, "That's a good trick to know, man."

Phipps was still looking at the fifteen cents on the palm of his hand.

Genero was a celebrity.

And he was learning that a celebrity is expected to answer a lot of questions. Especially if he shot four teenagers. There were two people waiting to ask questions now. One was a roving investigative reporter from Channel 6. The other was a Duty Captain named Vince Annunziato, who was filling in for the Eight-Seven's Captain Frick. The reporter was interested only in a sensational news story. Annunziato was interested only in protecting the Department. He stood by silently and gravely while the reporter set up the interview; one sure way to get the media dumping on cops was to act like you had something to hide.

"This is Mick Stapleton," the reporter said, "at the scene of a shooting on North Eleventh Street, here in Isola. I'm talking to Detective/Third Grade Richard Genero, who not forty-five minutes ago shot four teenagers who allegedly started a fire in the apartment building behind me."

Annunziato caught the "allegedly." Protecting his ass in case this thing blew up to something like the Goetz shootings in New York. Guy with a hand-held camera aimed at Stapleton, another guy working some kind of sound equipment, third guy handling lights, you'd think they were shooting a Spielberg movie instead of a two-minute television spot. Crowds behind the police barriers. Ambulances already here and gone, carting away the four teenagers. Annunziato was happy they weren't black.

"Detective Genero, can you tell us what happened here?" Stapleton asked.

Genero blinked into the lights, looked at the red light on the front of the camera.

"I was making a routine tour of the sector," he said. "This is Halloween night and the lieutenant put on extra men to handle any problems that might arise in the precinct."

So far, so good, Annunziato thought. Care and caution on the part of the commanding officer, concern for the citizenry.

"So you were driving past the building here . . ."

"Yes, and I saw the perpetrators running into the premises with objects in their hands."

"What kind of objects?" Stapleton asked.

Careful, Annunziato thought.

"What turned out to be firebombs," Genero said.

"But you didn't know that at the time, did you?"

"All I knew was a roving band running into a building."

"And this seemed suspicious to you?"

"Yes, sir."

"Suspicious enough for you to draw your gun and . . . ?"

"I did not unholster my revolver until fire broke out in the premises."

Good, Annunziato thought. Felony in progress, reason to yank the piece.

"But when you first saw these youngsters, you didn't know they were carrying firebombs, did you?"

"I found out when the fires went off inside there, and they came running out."

"What did you do then?"

"I drew my service revolver, announced that I was a policeman and warned them to stop."

"And did they stop?"

"No, sir, they threw one of the firebombs at me."

"Is that when you shot at them?"

"Yes, sir. When they ignored my warnings and came at me." Good, Annunziato thought. Proper procedure all the way down the line. Firearm used as a defensive weapon, not a tool of apprehension.

"When you say they came at you . . ."

"They attacked me. Knocked me over and kicked me."

"Were they armed?"

Careful, Annunziato thought.

"I did not see any weapons except the firebombs. But they had just committed a felony, and they were attacking me."

"So you shot them."

"As a last resort."

Perfect, Annunziato thought.

"Thank you, Detective Genero. For Channel Six News, this is Mick Stapleton on Eleventh Street."

With the edge of his hand, Stapleton made a throat-slitting gesture to his cameraman, and a brief "Thanks, that was swell" to Genero, and then walked quickly to where the mobile van was waiting at the curb.

Annunziato came over to where Genero was standing, looking surprised that it was over so fast.

"Captain Annunziato," he said. "I've got the duty."

"Yes, sir," Genero said.

"You handled that okay," Annunziato said.

"Thank you, sir."

"Handled *yourself* okay with them four punks, too."

"Thank you, sir."

"But you better call home now, tell 'em we're taking you off the street."

"Sir?"

"Few questions we'll have to ask you downtown. Make sure we get all the facts before the bleeding hearts come out of the woodwork."

"Yes, sir," Genero said.

He was thinking the goddamn shift would be relieved at a quarter to twelve, but he'd be downtown answering questions all night.

Train speeding through the night now, leaving behind the mills and factories just over the river, coming into rolling green land where you could see the lights of houses twinkling like it was Christmas instead of Halloween.

By Christmas they'd be sitting fat and pretty in India someplace.

Person could live on ten cents a day in India—well, that was an exaggeration. But you could rent yourself a luxurious villa, staff it with all the servants you needed, live like royalty on just the interest the two hundred thousand would bring. New names, new lives for both of them. Never mind trying to live on the peanuts Frank had earned each year.

She sighed heavily.

She'd have to call his mother as soon as she got home, and then his sister, and then she guessed some of his friends in the business. Had to get in touch with that detective again, find out when she could claim the body, arrange for some kind of funeral, have to keep the casket closed, of course, she wondered how soon that would be. Today was Friday, she didn't know whether they did autopsies on the weekend, probably wouldn't get around to it till Monday morning. Maybe she could have the body by Tuesday, but she'd better call an undertaker first thing in the morning, make sure they could handle it. Figure a day in the funeral home—well, two days, she guessed—bury him on Thursday morning. She'd have to find a cemetery that had available plots, whatever you called them, maybe the undertaker would know about that. Had to have a stone cut, too, HERE LIES FRANK SEBASTIANI, REST IN PEACE—but that could wait, there was no hurry about a stone.

She'd call the insurance company on Friday morning.

Tell them her husband had been murdered.

Make her claim.

She didn't expect any problems. Sensational case like this one? Already on television and in one of the early morning papers she'd bought at the terminal. MAGICIAN MURDERED, the headline read. Bigger headline than he'd ever had in his life. Had to get himself killed to get it.

Two hundred thousand dollars, she thought.

Invest it at ten percent, that'd bring them twenty thousand a year, more than enough to live on like a king and queen. A maharajah and maharanee was more like it. Go to the beach every day, have someone doing the cleaning and the cooking, have a man polishing the car and doing the marketing, buy herself a dozen saris, learn how to wrap them, maybe get herself a little diamond for her nose. Even at eight percent, the money would bring in sixteen thousand a year. More than enough.

And all they'd had to do for it was kill him.

The train rumbled through the night, lulling her to sleep.

He approached Eileen almost the moment she sat down at one of the tables.

"Hi," he said. "Remember me?"

No eyeglasses, no tattoo, but otherwise their man down to his socks. The eyeglasses he'd worn on his earlier outtings could have been windowpane. The tattoo could have been a decal. Her heart was beating wildly. She didn't realize until this moment just how frightened she really was. You're a *cop,* she told herself. *Am* I? she wondered.

"I'm sorry," she said, "have we met?"

"Mind if I sit down?"

"Please do."

The prim and proper hooker.

But crossed her legs anyway, to show him thigh clear to Cincinnati.

"I'm Linda," she said. "Are you looking for a good time?"

"That depends," he said.

"On what?"

"On what you consider a good time."

"That's entirely up to you."

"I noticed you when I was coming in," he said. "You were leaving with a little Puerto Rican."

"You're very observant," she said.

"You're a beautiful woman, how could I miss you?"

"What's your name?" she asked.

"Howie."

"Howie what?"

"Howie gonna keep 'em down on the farm."

He had them in stitches. Shanahan's words. Kept telling them jokes. A stand-up comic with a knife.

"So what're you interested in, Howie?"

"Let's talk," he said.

"Candy store's open," she said. "You want to know how much the goodies cost?"

"Not right now."

"Just say when, Howie."

He folded his hands on the tabletop. Looked into her eyes.

"How long have you been hooking, Linda?"

"First time tonight," she said. "In fact, I'm a virgin."

Not a smile. Not even the *hint* of a smile. Some stand-up comic. Just sat there looking into her eyes, big hands folded on the table.

"How old are you?"

"You should never ask a woman her age, Howie."

"Early thirties, in there?"

"Who knows?" she said, and rolled her eyes.

"What's your real name?"

"What's yours?"

"I told you. Howie."

"But you didn't tell me Howie what."

"Howie Cantrell," he said.

"Eileen Burke," she said.

The name would mean nothing to him. If he was their man, he'd learn soon enough who Eileen Burke was. If he was looking for action, her name wouldn't mean beans to him.

"Why are you using Linda?" he asked.

"I hate the name Eileen," she said. Which wasn't true. She'd always thought the name Eileen was perfect for the person she was. "Linda sounds more glamorous."

"You're glamorous enough," he said, "you don't need a phony name. May I call you Eileen?"

"You can call me Lassie if you like."

Still no smile. Totally devoid of a sense of humor. So where was the comedian? Flat, steel-gray eyes reflecting nothing. But were they the eyes of a triple murderer?

"So where're you from, Howie?"

"I'll ask the questions," he said.

"Now you sound like a cop."

"I used to be one."

Bullshit, she thought.

"Oh?" she said. "Where?"

"Philadelphia," he said. "Do you see that girl sitting at the bar?"

"Which one?" Eileen asked.

"In the black skirt. With the short dark hair."

He was indicating Annie.

"What about her?"

"I think she's a cop," he said.

Eileen burst out laughing.

"Jenny?" she said. "You've got to be kidding."

"You know her?"

"She's been hooking since she was thirteen. Jenny a cop? Wait'll I tell her!"

"I already told her."

"Mister, let me tell *you* something about hookers and cops, okay?"

"I know all about hookers and cops."

"Right, you're a cop yourself."

"*Used* to be one," he said. "I can always tell a cop."

"Have it your way," she said. "Jenny's a cop, you're a cop, I'm a cop, when you're in love the whole world's a cop."

"You don't believe I used to be a cop, do you?"

"Howie, I'll believe anything you tell me. You tell me you used to be a Presbyterian minister, I'll believe you. An astronaut, a spy, a . . ."

"I was with the Vice Squad in Philly."

"So what happened? Didn't you like the work?"

"It was good work."

"So how come you ain't doing it no more?"

"They fired me."

"Why?"

"Who knows?" he said, and shrugged.

"Can't stay away from the job, though, huh?"

"What does that mean?"

"Well, here you are, Howie."

"Just thought I'd drop by."

"You been here before?"

First leading question she'd asked him.

"Couple of times."

"Guess you like it, huh?"

"It's okay."

"Come on, Howie, tell me the truth." Teasing him now. "You really dig the girls here, don't you?"

"They're okay. Some of them."

"Which ones?"

"Some of them. Lots of these girls, you know, they're in this against their will, you know."

"Oh, sure."

"I mean, they were forced into it, you know."

"You sure you were a Vice cop, Howie?"

"Yes."

"I mean, you sound almost *human*."

"Well, it's true, you know. A lot of these girls would get out of it if they knew how."

"Tell me the secret. How do I get out of it, Howie?"

"There are ways."

A big, wiry, gray-haired guy walked over from the bar. Had to be in his mid-fifties, grizzled look, sailor's swagger. Wearing jeans and white sneakers, blue T-shirt, gold crucifix hanging on a chain outside the shirt, metal-buttoned denim jacket open over it. Right arm in a plaster cast and a sling. Shaggy gray eyebrows, knife scar angling downward through the right brow, and partially closing the right eye. Brown eyes. Thick nose broken more than once. Blue watch cap tilted onto the back of his head. Shock of gray hair hanging on his forehead. He pulled out a chair, sat, and said, "Buzz off, Preacher."

Howie looked at him.

"Buzz off, I wanna talk to the lady."

"Hey mister," Eileen said, "we're . . ."

"You hear me, Preacher? Move!"

Howie shoved back his chair. He glared angrily at the guy with the broken arm, and then walked across the bar and out into the street. Annie was already up and after him.

"Thanks a lot," Eileen said. "You just cost me . . ."

"Shanahan," he said.

She looked at him.

"Put your hand on my knee, talk nice."

*   *   *

The midgets came in a minute before eleven.

Shotgun Zuckerman was ready to close the store.

They came in yelling "Trick or treat!"

Alice opened fire at once.

("It was us taking all the risk," she said at the Q & A later. "Never mind what Quentin told us. If anybody pegged us for little people, we were finished. It was better to kill them. Easier, too.")

Zuckerman didn't even have a chance to reach for the shotgun. He went down dead in the first volley.

Meyer and Carella broke out of the stockroom the moment they heard the bell over the door sound. By the time they came through the curtain shielding the front of the store from the back, Zuckerman was already dead.

In the station wagon outside, the blonde began honking the horn.

"Police!" Meyer shouted, and Alice opened up with a second volley.

This wasn't a cops-and-robbers movie, this was real life.

Neither of the detectives got off a shot.

Meyer went down with a bullet through his arm and another through his shoulder.

Carella went down with a bullet in his chest.

No tricks. Real blood. Real pain.

Three of the midgets ran out of the store without even glancing at the cash register. The only reason Alice ran out after them, without first killing the two cops on the floor, was that she thought there might be more cops in the place.

This came out during the Q & A at ten minutes past two on the morning of All Hallows' Day.

9

The more Parker presented himself as a *fake* cop, the more he began feeling like a *real* cop. Everybody at the party kept telling him he could pass for a detective anywhere in the city. Everybody told him his shield and his gun, a .38 Smith & Wesson Detective Special, looked very authentic. One of the women—a sassy brunette dressed as a Las Vegas cigarette girl, in a flared black skirt and a flimsy top, high-heeled black shoes, and seamed silk stockings—wanted to hold the gun but he told her cops didn't allow straights to handle dangerous weapons. He had deliberately used police jargon for "honest citizens." In this city, a straight was anyone victimized by a thief. In some cities, victims were called "civilians." In any city, a thief was anyone who wasn't a cop, a straight, or a civilian. To the cops in this city, most thieves were "cheap" thieves.

A homosexual wearing a blonde wig, a long purple gown, and amethyst earrings to match, objected to the use of the word "straight" to describe an honest citizen.

The homosexual, who said he was dressed as Marilyn Monroe, told Parker that all the *gays* he knew were also honest citizens. Parker apologized for his use of police terminology. "But, you see," he said, "I ain't a *real* cop." And yet he felt like one. For the first time in as long as he could remember, he felt like a bona fide detective on the world's finest police force.

It was peculiar.

Even more peculiar was the fact that he was having such a good time.

Peaches Muldoon had a lot to do with that.

She was the life of the party, and some of her exuberance and vitality rubbed off on Parker. She told everyone stories about what it was like growing up as a victim on a sharecropper's farm in Tennessee. She told them incest was a way of life on the farm. Told them her first sexual experience was with her father. Told them her *brother's* first sexual experience—other than with the sheep who was his steady girlfriend—had been with his sister Peaches Muldoon one rainy afternoon when they were alone together in the house. She told everyone that she'd enjoyed her brother more than she had her father. Everyone laughed. They all thought she was making up victim stories. Only Parker knew that the stories were true; she'd told him ten years earlier that her priest-killing son was the bastard child of her relationship with her brother.

The stories Peaches told encouraged Parker to tell stories of his own. Everyone thought he was making them up, the way Peaches had made up her stories about the *Tobacco Road* dirt farm. He told them the story about the woman who'd cut off her husband's penis with a straight razor. He said, "I substituted the word penis for cock, because I didn't want to offend anybody here who might be a vigilante for the Meese Commission." Everyone laughed at the story and also at his comment about the Meese Commission. Somebody wondered out loud if the Attorney General considered it pornographic that the unauthorized sale of arms to Iran had provided unauthorized funds for Nicaraguan rebels.

This was straying into intellectual territory beyond Parker's scope.

He laughed, anyway.

Pornography was something he dealt with on a daily basis, and he believed straights ought to keep their noses out of it, period. Complicated and illegal arms deals were something else, and he never wondered about them except as they might affect his line of work. When you dealt with cheap thieves day and night, you already knew that they weren't only in the streets but also in the highest reaches of government. He didn't say this to anyone here at the party because he was having too good a time, and he didn't want to get too serious about cause and effect. He didn't even think of it consciously as cause and effect. But he knew, for example, that when a star athlete was exposed as a coke addict, the kids playing pickup ball in the school yard thought, "Hey, I gotta try me some of that shit." He also knew that when somebody high up in government broke the law, then your punk dealing grams of crack in the street could justify his actions by saying, "See? *Everybody* breaks the law." Cause and effect. It only made Parker's job harder. Which was maybe why he didn't work too hard at the job anymore. Although tonight, *playing* at the job, he felt as if he was working harder at it than he had in years.

It was really very peculiar.

He told everybody that one day he was going to write a book about his experiences.

"Ah-ha!" somebody said, "you're a *writer!*"

"No, no, I'm a cop," he protested.

"So how come you want to be a writer?" someone else said.

" 'Cause I ain't got the guts to be a burglar," Parker said, and everyone laughed again.

He'd never realized he was so witty.

At a little after eleven, Peaches suggested that they move on to another party.

Which is how Parker got to meet the wheelman and one of the midgets on the liquor-store holdups.

There were a lot of things bothering Brown about the Sebastiani case.

The three most important things were the head and the hands. He kept wondering why they hadn't turned up yet. He kept wondering where Jimmy Brayne had dropped them.

He also wondered where Brayne was right now.

The blues from the Two-Three, armed with the BOLO that had gone out all over the city, had located the blue Citation in the parking lot of an A & P not far from the River Dix. The techs had crawled over the car like ants, lifting latent prints, collecting stain samples, vacuuming for hairs and fibers. Anything they'd got had already been bagged and sent to the lab for comparison with whatever had been recovered from the Econoline van. Brown had no illusions about the lab getting back to them before sometime Monday. Meanwhile, both cars had been dumped—which left Brayne without wheels. His last location had been in the Twenty-Third, where he'd dropped the Citation, way over on the south side of the city. Was he now holed up somewhere in that precinct? Had he cabbed east, west, or north to a hotel someplace else? Or was he already on an airplane, bus, or train heading for parts unknown?

All of this bothered Brown.

He also wondered why Brayne had killed his mentor and employer.

"You think they're making it?" he asked Hawes.

"Who?"

"Brayne and the woman."

"Marie?"

The possibility had never occurred to Hawes. She had seemed so honestly grieved by her husband's disappearance and death. But now that Brown had mentioned it—

"I mean, what I'm looking for is some motive here," Brown said.

"The guy could've just gone beserk, you know. Threw those tricks all over the driveway, ran off in the Citation . . ."

"Yeah, I'm curious about that, too," Brown said. "Let's try to dope out a timetable, okay? They come into the city together, Brayne in the van, Marie and her husband in the Citation . . ."

"Got to the school around a quarter past three."

"Unloaded the car and the van . . ."

"Right."

"And then Brayne went off God knows where, said he'd be back at five, five-thirty to pick up the big stuff.''

"Uh-huh."

"Okay, they finish the act around five-fifteen. Sebastiani changes into his street clothes, goes out back to load the car while Marie's getting out of her costume. She comes out later, finds the stuff all over the driveway and the Citation gone.''

"Right.''

"So we got to figure Brayne dumped the van on Rachel Street sometime between three-thirty and five-fifteen, grabbed a taxi back to the school, and cold-cocked Sebastiani while he was loading the car.''

"That's what it looks like,'' Hawes said.

"Then he chops up the body—where'd he do that, Cotton? Blood stains in the Citation's trunk, you know, but nowhere else in the car.''

"Coulda done it anywhere in the city. Found himself a deserted street, an abandoned building . . .''

"Yeah, you could do that in this city. So he chops up the corpse, loads the pieces in the trunk, and starts dropping them all around town. When he gets rid of the last one, he leaves the car behind the A & P and takes off.''

"Yeah.''

"So where's the motive?''

"I don't know.''

"She's an attractive woman,'' Brown said.

Hawes had noticed that.

"If she was playing house with Brayne in that apartment over the garage . . .''

"Well, you've got no reason to believe that, Artie.''

"I'm snowballing it, Cotton. Let's say they had a thing going. Brayne and the woman.''

"Okay.''

"And let's say hubby tipped to it.''

"You're thinking movies or television.''

"I'm thinking real-life, too. Hubby tells Brayne to lay off, Brayne's still hungry for her. He chops up hubby, and him and the woman ride off into the sunset.''

"Except Brayne's the only one who rode off,'' Hawes said. "The woman's . . .''

"You think she's home yet?'' Brown asked, and looked up at the clock.

Ten minutes past eleven.

"Half hour or so to Collinsworth,'' Hawes said. "She was catching the ten forty-five.''

"Whyn't we take a ride out there?'' Brown said.

"What for?''

"Toss that apartment over the garage, see we can't find something.''

"Like what?''

"Like maybe where Brayne's heading. Or better yet, something that links him to the woman.''

"We'll need a warrant to toss that garage.''

"We haven't even got jurisdiction across the river,'' Brown said. "Let's play it by ear, okay? If the lady's clean, she won't ask for a warrant.''

"You want to call her first?"

"What for?" Brown said. "I love surprises."

Kling waved so long to them as they headed out of the squadroom. He looked up at the clock. The graveyard shift should be here in half an hour or so—O'Brien, Delgado, Fujiwara and Willis. Fill them in on what had gone down on the four-to-midnight, grab one of the sedans, and head for Calm's Point. Make himself invisible in the Zone, just another John looking for a little Friday-night sport. But keep an eye out for Eileen.

He thought she was dead wrong about this one.

His being there in the Zone could only help an undercover situation that had been hastily planned and recklessly undermanned.

This time, *he* was the one who was dead wrong.

They sat at the table talking in whispers, just another hooker and a potential trick. Negotiating the deal, Larry figured. Never seen the guy with the broken arm in here before, wondered who'd be on top in the sack, might get a little clumsy with that arm in a sling. Wondered about that and nothing else. The place was still busy, there was booze to be poured.

"Howie Cantrell is his real name," Shanahan whispered. "Used to be with Vice in Philly, that's all straight goods. Went off his rocker six years ago, first started beating up hookers in the street, then began preaching salvation to them. The Philly P.D. didn't so much mind the beatings. Worse things than beatings go down in Vice. But they didn't like the idea of a plainclothes minister on the force. They sent him up for psychiatric, and the shrinks decided he was under considerable stress as a result of his proximity to the ladies of the night. Retired him with full pension, he drifted first to Boston, then here, started his missionary work all over again in the Zone. Everybody calls him the Preacher. He looks for the young ones, spouts Jesus to them, tries to talk them out of the life. Takes one of them to bed every now and then, for old times' sake. But he's harmless. Hasn't raised a hand to anybody since Philly let him go."

"I thought he was our man," Eileen said.

"We did, too, at first. Dragged him in right after the first murder, questioned him up and down, but he was clean as a whistle. Talked to him again after the second one, and again after the third. Alibis a mile long. We shoulda warned you about him. Be easy to make the mistake you made. How's it going otherwise?"

"I almost lost my virginity, but Alvarez bailed me out."

"Who'd he send?"

"Guy named Ortiz. Narcotics."

"Good man. Looks eighteen, don't he? He's almost thirty."

"You coulda told me I'd have help."

"We're just full of tricks," Shanahan said, and smiled.

"You gonna plant yourself in here?" Eileen asked.

"Nope. I'll be outside. Watching, waiting."

"Who grizzled up your hair?" she asked.

"The Chameleon," he said, and grinned.

"I hope you can *see* through that eye."

"I can see just fine."

"And I hope our man doesn't want to arm wrestle," she said, glancing at the cast.

Across the room, Annie was coming back into the bar. She walked to where Larry was standing, put four dollars on the bartop and said, "Your end, pal."

"Why, thank you, honey," he said, "much obliged," and tucked the bills into his shirt pocket, figuring the four represented twenty percent of whatever she'd got for her last trick. I *do* love an honest hooker, he thought, and immediately wondered if she'd short-changed him.

Annie wandered over to where Eileen and Shanahan were sitting.

"Your blond friend went home," she said. "Caught a bus on the corner."

"That's okay," Eileen said, "I'm still waiting for Mr. Right."

Annie nodded, and then walked over to a table on the other side of the room. She wasn't alone for more than a minute when a big black guy sat down next to her.

"She needs help," Eileen whispered.

"Bring her outside," Shanahan said, and then rose immediately and said in a voice loud enough for everyone in the bar to hear, "I'll see you around the corner, honey."

Eileen went over to Annie and the black man.

"I got a one-armed bandit waiting in a car around the corner," she said. "He's looking for a hands-on trio, me driving, him in the middle, both of us dancing his meat around the block. You interested in a dime for ten minutes' work?"

"Dimes add up," Annie said, and immediately got to her feet.

"Hurry on back, hear?" the black man said.

"I did not appreciate all the shooting," Quentin Forbes said, looking petulant. He was still wearing the dress, pantyhose, and low-heeled walking shoes he'd worn while driving the station wagon, but the long blonde wig was hooked over the arm of a ladder-backed wooden chair. "There was no need for such violence, Alice. I warned you repeatedly . . ."

"It was only insurance," she said, and shrugged.

"The costumes were all the insurance we . . ."

"The costumes were bullshit," Alice said.

She was a beautiful little blonde woman in her late thirties, blue eyes and a Cupid's-bow mouth, perfect legs and breasts, four-feet two-inches tall and weighing a curvaceous seventy-one pounds. In the circus, she was billed as Tiny Alice. This went over big with homosexual men. She had changed out of the clown costume they'd worn on the last two holdups, and was now wearing a dark green dress and high-heeled pumps. To Forbes, she looked wildly sexual.

"Did you want the cops to think three *separate* gangs of kids were holding up those stores?" she asked.

"I wanted to confuse the cops, was all," Forbes said. "If you want to know what *I* think, Alice, I think your shooting spree was what brought them down on us, is what I think."

"We should have finished them off," she said. "If you hadn't started honking the horn . . ."

"I honked the horn twice to warn you. The moment I saw them coming from the back room . . ."

"We should have finished them off," she said again, and took a tube of lipstick from her handbag and went to the mirror on the wall.

"The point of the costumes," Forbes insisted, "was to . . ."

"The point was you wanted to put on a dress," Alice said. "I think you enjoy being in drag."

"I do indeed," Forbes said. "First time I've been in a woman's pants in more than a month."

"Braggart," Corky said.

She was slightly taller than Alice, a bad failing for a midget, but she was prettier in a delicate, small-boned, almost Oriental way. She, too, had changed into street clothes, a black skirt and a white silk blouse, a pink cardigan sweater, high-heeled patent leather pumps. She looked like a tiny, young Debbie Reynolds.

The two men who'd been in on the holdups were sitting at the table, still wearing their clown suits, counting the money.

"That's five thousand here," one of them said.

High Munchkin voice, wearing glasses, brown eyes intent behind them. His name was Willie. In the circus, he was billed as Wee Willie Winkie. Next month, he'd be down in Venice, Florida, rehearsing for the season. Tonight he was helping to stack and count the money from four stickups—well, *three* actually, since they hadn't got anything but cops on the last one. The stickups had been Forbes' idea, but Corky was the one who talked Willie into going along, said it'd be a good way to pick up some quick off-season change. Corky was his wife, and Alice was her best friend. This made Willie nervous. Alice was the only one who'd shot anyone tonight. The others had all fired their pistols well over the heads of the store owners, the way Forbes had told them to.

"What we should do," Willie said to the other man at the table, "we should both of us count each stack."

His hands were sweating. He was still very nervous about this whole thing. He was sure the police would come breaking in here any minute. All because of Alice. He had never heard of a midget doing time in prison. Or getting the electric chair. He did not want to be the first one in history.

"Can I trust you little crooks to give me a true count?" Forbes asked.

"You can help count it, you want to," the other man at the table said.

He was older than the other midgets, shorter and more delicate than even the women. His name was Oliver. In the circus, he was billed as Oliver Twist. He never understood why. He had red hair and blue eyes, and he was single, which was just the way he wanted it. Oliver was a great ladies' man. Full-sized women loved to pick him up and carry him to bed. Full-sized women considered him too darling for words, and they were never threatened by his tiny erect pecker. Full-sized women were always amazed that they could swallow him to the hilt without gagging. In some ways, being a midget had its benefits.

"Here's another five," Willie said, and slid the stack to Oliver, who began riffling the bills like a casino dealer.

"My rough estimate," Forbes said, "is we took in something like forty thousand."

"I think that's high," Alice said.

Standing at the mirror, putting on her lipstick. Lips puckered to accept the bright red paint, pretty as a little doll. Forbes had tried making her last year when they were playing the Garden in New York. She'd turned him down cold, said he would break her in half, although he knew she was sleeping with half the Flying Dutchmen. Corky watched her intently, as if hoping to pick up some makeup tricks.

"Twelve, thirteen thousand each store," Forbes said, "that's what I figure. Thirty-five, forty thousand dollars."

"There wasn't any thirteen in that store with the lady owner," Oliver said.

He was the one who'd cleaned out the register after Alice shot that lady in the third store. They weren't supposed to talk in the stores, but he'd yelled, "Hold it *open,* Alice!" because Alice's hands were trembling, and the bag was shaking as if there was a snake in it trying to get out.

"Mark my words, forty," Forbes said.

"Here's another five," Willie said.

"Fifteen already," Forbes said. "Mark my words."

Turned out, when all was said and done, that there was only thirty-two thousand.

"What'd I tell you?" Alice said.

"Somebody must be skimming," Forbes said, and winked at her.

"What does that come to?" Corky asked. "Five into thirty-two?"

"Something like sixty grand apiece," Oliver said.

"You *wish,*" Alice said.

"Six, I mean."

Willie was already doing the long division on a scrap of paper.

"Six-four," he said.

"Which ain't bad for a night's work," Forbes said.

"We should've finished those cops," Alice said idly, blotting her lipstick with a piece of Kleenex. Willie shivered. He looked at his wife. Corky was staring at Alice's mouth, a look of idolatrous adoration on her face. Willie shivered again.

"What I'm gonna do right now," Forbes said, "is get out of this dress, and put on my own clothes, and then I'm gonna go partying. Alice? You wanna come along?"

She looked him up and down as if seeing him for the first time.

Then she shrugged and said, "Sure. Why not?"

She called her mother-in-law the moment she was in the house.

The place felt empty without him.

"Mom," she said. "This is Marie."

Crackling on the line to Atlanta.

"Honey," her mother-in-law said, "this is a *terrible* connection, can you get the operator to ring it again?"

Terrific, she thought. I'm calling to tell her Frank is dead, and she can't hear me.

"I'll try again," she said, and hung up, and then dialed the operator and asked her to place the call. Her mother-in-law picked up on the second ring.

"How's that?" Marie asked her.

"Oh, much better. I was just about to call *you,* this must be psychic." Susan Sebastiani believed in psychic phenomena. Whenever she held a seance in her house, she claimed to converse with Frank's father, who'd been dead and gone for twenty years. Frank's father had been a magician, like his son. "What it is," she said, "I had this terrible premonition that something was wrong. I said to myself, 'Susan, you'd better call the kids.' Are you okay? Is everything all right?"

"Well . . . no," Marie said.

"What's the matter?" Susan said.

"Mom . . ."

How to tell her?

"Mom . . . this is very bad news."

"What is it?"

"Mom . . . Frank . . ."

"Oh, my God, something's happened to him," Susan said at once. "I knew it." Silence on the line.

"Marie?"

"Yes, Mom."

"What happened? Tell me."

"Mom . . . he's . . . Mom, he's dead."

"What? Oh, my God, my God, oh, dear God," she said, and began weeping. Marie waited.

"Mom?"

"Yes, I'm here."

"I'm sorry, Mom. I wish I wasn't the one who had to tell you."

"Where are you?"

"Home."

"I'll come up as soon as I can. I'll call the airlines, find out when there's . . . what happened? Was it an automobile accident?"

"No, Mom. He was murdered."

"What?"

"Someone . . ."

"What? *Who?* What are you talking about? Murdered?"

"We don't know yet, Mom. Someone . . ."

She couldn't bring herself to tell his mother that someone had chopped up his body. That could wait.

"Someone killed him," she said. "After a show we did this afternoon. At a high school up here."

"Who?"

"We don't know yet. The police think it might have been Jimmy."

"Jimmy? Jimmy Brayne? Who Frank was teaching?"

"Yes, Mom."

"I can't believe it. Jimmy?"

"That's what they think."

"Well, where is he? Have they questioned him?"

"They're still looking for him, Mom."

"Oh, God, this is terrible," Susan said, and began weeping again. "Why would he do such a thing? Frank treated him like a brother."

"We both did," Marie said.

"Have you called Dolores yet?"

"No, you're the first one I . . ."

"She'll have a heart attack," Susan said. "You'd better let me tell her."

"I can't ask you to do that, Mom."

"She's my daughter, I'll do it," Susan said.

Still weeping.

"I'll tell her to come there right away, you'll need help."

"Thank you, Mom."

"What is it from her house? An hour?"

"Tops."

"I'll tell her to get right there. Are you okay?"

"No, Mom," she said, and her voice broke. "I feel terrible."

"I know, I know, sweetie, but be brave. I'll come up as soon as I can. Meanwhile, Dolores will be there. Oh, my God, so many people I'll have to call, relatives, friends . . . when is the funeral going to be? They'll want to know."

"Well . . . they'll be doing an autopsy first."

"What do you mean? Chopping him up?"

Silence on the phone.

"You didn't give them permission to do that, did you?"

Opportunity right there to tell her he was *already* chopped up. She let the opportunity pass.

"They have to do an autopsy in a murder case," she said.

"Why?"

"I don't know why, it's the law."

"Some law," Susan said.

Both women fell silent.

Susan sighed heavily.

"All right," she said, "let me call Dolores, let me get to work. She'll be there in a little while, will you be okay till then?"

"I'll be fine."

Another silence.

"I know how much you loved him," Susan said.

"I did, Mom."

"I know, I know."

Another sigh.

"All right, honey, I'll talk to you later. I'll try to get a plane tonight if I can. You're not alone, Marie. Dolores will be right there, and I'll be up as soon as I can."

"Thank you, Mom."

"All right now," Susan said, "I have to go now. Call me if you need me."

"Yes, Mom."

"Good night now, honey."

"Good night, Mom."

There was a small click on the line. Marie put the receiver back on the cradle. She looked up at the clock on the kitchen wall. Only forty minutes left to what had been the longest day of her life.

The clock ticked noisily into the stillness of the empty house.

The clock on the hospital wall read twenty-five minutes past eleven.

Lieutenant Peter Byrnes had not yet called the wives. He would have to call the wives. Speak to Teddy and Sarah, tell them what had happened. He was standing in the corridor with Deputy Police Commissioner Howard Brill, who'd come uptown when he'd heard that two detectives had been shot in a liquor-store stakeout. Brill was a black man in his early fifties; Byrnes had known him when they were both walking beats in Riverhead. About the same size as Byrnes, same compact head and intelligent eyes; the men could have been cast from the identical bullet mold, except that one was black and the other was white. Brill was upset; Byrnes could understand why.

"The media's gonna have a ball," Brill said. "Did you see this?"

He showed Byrnes the front page of one of the morning tabloids. The headline looked as if it had been written for a sensational rag that sold at the local supermarket. But instead of MARTIAN IMPREGNATES CAMEL or HITLER REINCARNATED AS IOWA HOUSEWIFE, this one read:

MIDGETS 2—COPS 0
POLICE CAUGHT SHORT

"Very funny," Byrnes said. "I got one cop in intensive care, and another one in surgery, and they're making jokes."

"How are they?" Brill asked.

"Meyer's okay. Carella . . ." He shook his head. "The bullet's still inside him. They're digging for it now."

"What caliber?"

"Twenty-two. That's according to the slugs we recovered in the store. Meyer took two hits, but the bullets passed through."

"He was lucky," Brill said. "They're worse than a goddamn forty-five, those low-caliber guns. Hit a man where there's real meat, the bullet hasn't got the force to exit. Ricochets around inside there like it's bouncing off furniture."

"Yeah," Byrnes said, and nodded bleakly.

"Lot of shooting tonight," Brill said. "You'd think it was the Fourth of July, 'stead of Halloween. Your man clean on that other one?"

"I hope so," Byrnes said.

"Four teenagers, Peter, the media *loves* kids getting shot. What's the report on their condition?"

"I haven't checked it. I ran over here the minute . . ."

"Sure, I understand."

Byrnes guessed he should have checked on those kids before he'd come over here—not that he really cared *how* they were, except as their condition reflected on his squad. On his block, if you were looking for trouble with a cop, you should be happy you found it. But if Genero had pulled his gun without prudent care and reasonable cause, and if one of those punks died, or worse yet ended up a vegetable . . .

"How smart is he?" Brill asked.

"Not very."

" 'Cause they'll be coming at him, you know."

"I realize that."

"Where is he now?"

"Still downtown. I think. I really don't know, Howie. I'm sorry, but when I heard about Meyer and Carella . . ."

"Sure, I understand," Brill said again.

He was wondering which of the incidents would cause the Department the biggest headache. A dumb cop shooting four kids, or two dumb cops getting shot by midgets.

"Midgets," he said aloud.

"Yeah," Byrnes said.

Tricky, he thought.

I know that.

Coming back to the same bar a fourth time.

But that's part of the fun.

Look the same, act the same, makes it more exciting that way. Big blond guy is who they're looking for, so Heeeeeere's *Johnny* folks! No description in the newspapers yet, but that's the cops playing it tricky, too.

Tricks all around, he thought.

Suits me fine.

By now they're thinking psycho.

Some guy who once had a traumatic experience with a hooker. Hates all hookers, is systematically eliminating them. They ought to boot up their computer, check with Kansas City. In Kansas City, it was only two of them. Well, when you're just starting, you start small, right? In Chicago, it was three. Good night, folks! Do my little song and dance in each city, listen to the newspaper and television applause, take my bow, and shuffle off to Buffalo. Slit their throats, carve up their pussies, the cops *have* to be thinking psycho. I'll do four of them here, he thought, and then move on. Two, three, four, a nice gradual escalation.

Let the cops think psycho.

A psycho acts compulsively, hears voices inside his head, thinks someone's commanding him to do what he's doing. Me, I never hear voices except when I'm listening to my Sony Walkman. Comedians. Walk along with the earphones on, listen to their jokes. Woody Allen, Bob Newhart, Bill Cosby, Henny Youngman . . .

Take my wife. Please.

For our anniversary, my wife said she wanted to go someplace she'd never been. I said, How about the kitchen?

My wife wanted a mink coat, and I wanted a new car. We compromised. I bought her a mink coat and we keep it in the garage.

Walk along, listen to the comics, laugh out loud, people probably think I'm nuts. Who cares? There isn't anyone *commanding* me to kill these girls—

Ooops, excuse me, I beg your parmigiana. Mustn't get the feminists on my back, they'd be worse to deal with than cops. Next city, maybe I'll do five. Get five of them and then move on. Two, three, four, five, nice arithmetical progression. Keep moving, keep having fun, just the way Mother wanted it. What's the sense of life if you can't enjoy it? Live a little, laugh a little, that's the thing. These women—got it right that time, Ms. Steinem—are *fun* to do.

Try to dope *that* one out, officers.

Keep on looking for a psycho, go ahead.

When all you're dealing with is somebody as sane as Sunday.

Larry's Bar.

Welcome home, he thought, and opened the door.

"What'll it be?" Larry asked him.

"This guy comes into a bar, has a little monkey on his shoulder."

"Huh?" Larry asked him.

"This is a joke," he said. "The bartender asks him 'What'll it be?' The guy says, 'Scotch on the rocks,' and the monkey says, 'Same for me.' The bartender looks at both of them and says, 'What are you a ventriloquist?' The monkey says, 'Were my lips moving?' "

"That's a joke, huh?" Larry said.

"Gin and tonic," he said, and shrugged.

"How about your monkey?"

"The monkey's driving," he said.

Larry blinked.

"That's another joke."

"Oh," Larry said, and looked at him. "You been in here before?"

"Nope. First time."

" 'Cause you look familiar."

"People tell me I look like Robert Redford."

"Now *that's* a joke," Larry said, and put the drink in front of him. "Gin and tonic, three bucks, a bargain."

He paid for the drink, sat sipping it, eyes on the mirror.

"Nice crop tonight, huh?" Larry said.

"Maybe."

"What are you looking for? We had a Chinese girl in here ten minutes ago. You dig Orientals?"

"This samurai comes home from the wars," he said.

"Is this another joke?"

"His servant meets him at the gate, tells him his wife's been making it with a black man. The samurai runs upstairs, breaks down the bedroom door, yanks out his sword, yells, 'Whassa this I hear, you make it with a brack man?' His wife says, 'Where you hear such honkie jive?' "

"I don't get it," Larry said.

"I guess you had to be there."

"Where?"

"Forget it."

"We got some nice black girls in here tonight, if that's what you're lookin' for."

Larry was thinking about his twenty-percent commission. Drum up a little trade here.

"This old man goes into a whorehouse . . ."

"This ain't a whorehouse," Larry said defensively.

"This is another joke. Old guy, ninety-five years old. He tells the madam he's looking for a blowjob. The guy's so frail he can hardly stand up. The madam says, 'Come on, mister, you've had it.' He says, 'I have? How much do I owe you?' "

"Now, *that's* funny," Larry said.

"I know a hundred jokes about old people."

"*That* funny, it wasn't."

"This old guy is sitting on a park bench, crying his heart out. Another guy sits next to him, says . . ."

"Hi."

He turned.

A good-looking blonde girl was sitting on the stool next to his.

"My name's Sheryl," she said. "Wanna party?"

10

The minute he saw her, he knew she was going to be more fun than any of the others. Something in her eyes. Something in her smile. Something in the way she plumped her cute little bottom down on the bar stool, and crossed her legs, and propped one elbow on the bar, and her chin on her hand, and looked him mischievously in the eye—a fun girl, he could tell that at once.

"Well, well, well, hello, Sheryl," he said.

"Well, well, well, hello to you," she said.

"Barkeep," he said, "see what the lady'll have."

"Barkeep, I love that," Sheryl said.

A fun girl. He knew it.

"So what'll it be?" he asked.

"What are *you* drinking?"

"Gin and tonic."

"I'll have the same," she said.

"A gin and tonic for the lady," he said to Larry, and then immediately, "This guy walks into a bar . . ."

"You already told this one," Larry said.

"This is another one. Guy walks into a bar, says, 'See that cat over there?' Everybody looks at the cat. Big tomcat with an enormous tail. The guy says, 'I'll bet any man in the house my penis is longer than that cat's tail.' Everybody wants to bet him. Hundred-dollar bills come out all over the place. The guy says to the bartender . . ."

"Gin and tonic," Larry said, "three bucks, a bargain."

"You should learn not to interrupt a story," he said.

"Tell 'im," Sheryl said.

"The guy says to the bartender, 'Okay, measure us.' So the bartender takes out a tape measure, goes over to the cat, measures the cat's tail, and says, 'Fourteen inches.' The guy nods and says, 'Okay, now measure my penis.' The bartender measures the penis. 'Eight inches,' he says. 'You lose.' The guy looks at him. 'Excuse me,' he says, 'but exactly *how* did you measure that cat's tail?' The bartender says, 'I put one end of the tape against his asshole and the other end . . .' and the guy says, 'Would you mind showing me the same consideration?' "

Sheryl burst out laughing.

Larry said, "I don't get it. You owe me three bucks."

He paid for the drink. Sheryl was still laughing.

A fun girl.

"What's your name?" she asked.

"Robert Redford," he said, which wasn't too far from the truth in that his first name really was Robert.

"I believe you," she said, and winked at Larry. "What do people call you? Rob? Bob? Bobby?"

"Bobby," he said, which was absolutely the truth.

"And how does *your* tail measure up against that cat's, Bobby?"

"Want to find out?" he said.

"Oooo, yes," Sheryl said, and rolled her eyes.

"Think that might be fun, huh?" he said.

"I think it'd be *loads* of fun," she said. "I'll tell you what I get, Bobby. A handjob's . . ."

"Not yet," he said.

"Well, you see, Bobby, I'm a working girl. So whereas there's nothing I'd enjoy more than sitting here all night with you . . ."

He put a twenty-dollar bill on the bartop.

"Let's say we're running a tab," he said.

"You mean you and me? Or you and Larry?"

"You and me. The twenty's yours. It buys twenty minutes, a dollar a minute. We'll talk about renewing the option when the meter runs out. How's that sound, Sheryl?"

"No problem," she said, and scooped up the bill.

"Four bucks of that is mine," Larry said, and held out his hand. Sheryl made a face, but she gave him the twenty, and watched him as he walked down to the cash register to make change.

"So where you from, Bobby?" she asked.

"Most recently? Chicago. Before that, Kansas City."

Playing it recklessly. Those were the two cities exactly. But that's what made this so exciting. Playing the game for the ultimate risk.

Larry was back with her change. "Here's your sixteen," he said, handing her three fives and a single.

"You take out a fourteen-inch whanger in here," she said, "Larry'll want twenty percent of it."

"I never yet seen nobody with a fourteen-incher," Larry said.

"You been looking?" she asked, and winked at Bobby and put the bills into her handbag. "What Larry does, he checks out the men's room for fourteen-inchers."

"This soldier is in the men's room taking a shower," Bobby said. "All the other guys in his company . . ."

"Is this another one?" Larry said.

"I thought I told you not to interrupt my stories," Bobby said.

"Stories like yours . . ."

"Be quiet," he said.

He spoke the words very softly.

Larry looked at him.

"Do you understand?" he said. "When I'm telling a story, be quiet."

Larry looked into his eyes.

Then he shrugged and walked to the other end of the bar.

"Serves him right," Sheryl said. "Let me hear the story, Bobby."

"This soldier is taking a shower. All the other guys in his company are crowded around the stall, looking in at him, craning for a look at him. That's because the guy has a penis that's only an inch long. Finally, the guy can't take it anymore. He turns to them and yells, 'What's the matter? You never seen anybody with a hard-on before?' "

Sheryl burst out laughing again.

From the other end of the bar, Larry grimaced sourly, and said, "Very funny."

"So which one are you, Bobby?" Sheryl asked. "The fourteen-incher or the inch-long wonder?"

"I thought we weren't going to hurry," he said.

"Listen, it's your money," Sheryl said. "Take all the time you need."

"I mean, I thought we were having fun here," he said.

"We are," she said.

"I mean, isn't this fun?"

"I love your stories, Bobby," she said.

"You're a fun girl," he said. "I can tell that."

"That's what I've been told, Bobby."

"I mean, I'll bet you like to do new and exciting things, don't you?"

"Oh, sure," she said. "I even did it with a police dog once."

"That's not what I meant. I meant *new* things. Exciting things."

"Well, to me that was new. Six guys watching while I did it with a police dog? That was new."

"It may have been new, but I'll bet it wasn't exciting," Bobby said.

"Well, I have to admit, when the dog went down on me that was sort of exciting. He had like this very raspy tongue, you know? Like sandpaper. I guess you could say that was sort of exciting. I mean, once you got past the idea of him being a *dog,* which was disgusting, of course."

"Sheryl," he said, "I think you're terrific, I really do. We're going to have a lot of fun together, you'll see."

"Oh, I'm sure."

"We're going to do some new and very exciting things."

"I can hardly wait," she said.

"Lots of laughs," he said.

"I already find you very funny," she said.

"This midget goes into a men's room," he said. "And there's a guy standing there at one of the . . ."

This second party was even better than the first one had been.

Parker was having the time of his life.

At the first party, he'd got drunk enough to believe he was really a writer passing himself off as a cop who only wanted to be a writer. At this party, he didn't tell anyone he was a cop because no one was in costume here, it wasn't that kind of a party. But even without the masquerade, he was having a marvelous time. Maybe because there were all sorts of interesting people here, most of them women. Or maybe because these interesting women all found *him* interesting.

This was very amazing to him.

He thought he was just being his usual shitty self.

It turned out that the woman whose apartment they were in was celebrating her sixty-third birthday tonight, which was why there was a party in the first place, never mind Halloween. Her name was Sandra, and she was the one Peaches had been expecting a call from earlier tonight, which was the only reason she'd answered the phone after that heavy-breathing creep got off the line. Sandra was her next-to-best friend; her best friend was the woman who'd thrown the costume party. Still, Peaches liked Sandra a lot, especially because she never expected a present on her birthday. She was a bit surprised, therefore, and somewhat annoyed, when Parker flatly and rudely expressed the opinion that no one over the age of sixty should be asked to blow out all the candles on a birthday cake in a single breath. And she was even more surprised when Sandra burst out laughing and said, "Oh, baby, how true! Who the hell needs such a humiliating stress test?"

Everyone laughed. Even Peaches.

Sandra then blew out all the candles in a single breath, and pinched Parker on the behind and asked him if he'd like the candles on *his* cake blown. "Out," she added.

Everyone laughed. Except Peaches.

A little later on, encouraged by the attention a lot of these very interesting women were paying to ideas he'd never even known he'd had, Parker ventured a bit closer to home and suggested to a lady trial lawyer that *anyone* committing a murder was at least a little bit crazy and that therefore the "legal insanity" defense was meaningless. The lady lawyer said, "That's very interesting, Andy. I had a case last week where . . ."

It was astonishing.

Parker said to a woman wearing horn-rimmed eyeglasses and no bra that he found pornographic movies more honest than any of the nighttime soaps on television, and the woman turned out to be a film critic who encouraged him to expand upon the idea.

Parker told a woman writer—a *real* writer—that he never spent more than five pages with any book if he wasn't hooked by then, and the woman expounded upon the importance of a book's opening, and closing paragraphs, to which Parker said,

"Sure, it's like foreplay and afterplay," and the woman writer put her hand on his arm and laughed robustly, which Peaches did not find at all amusing.

Peaches, in fact, was becoming more and more irritated by the fact that Sandra had invited her to a party where the women outnumbered the men by an approximate two-to-one and where Parker was suddenly the center of all this female attention. She had liked it better when they were a couple pretending to be a cop and a victim. They were *sharing* something then. Now Parker seemed to be stepping out on his own, the small-time flamenco dancer who'd been offered a movie contract provided he ditched his fat lady partner. This miffed Peaches because for Christ's sake she was the one who'd introduced him to show biz in the first place!

When the female midget walked in at twenty-five minutes to twelve, Peaches immediately checked out the man with her. Burly guy going a bit bald, but with a pleasant craggy face, and a seemingly gentle manner. Five-ten or -eleven, she guessed, merry blue eyes, nice speaking voice now that she heard him wishing Sandra a happy birthday. Sandra took their coats and wandered off, muttering something about mingling. Peaches moved in fast before the other sharks smelled blood on the water. She introduced herself to the man and the midget—

"Hi, I'm Peaches Muldoon."

"Quentin Forbes. Alice . . ."

—then took the man's arm before he could finish the midget's name, and said, "Come on, I'll get you a drink," and sailed off with him, leaving the midget standing there by the door looking forlornly and shyly into the room.

Parker had never seen a more beautiful woman in his life.

He went over to her at once.

"Small world," he said.

And to his enormous surprise—the night was full of surprises—she burst out laughing, and said, "I feel like a fire hydrant waiting for an engine company. Where's the bar?"

Hal Willis came into the squadroom at twenty minutes to midnight. The teams usually relieved at a quarter to the hour, and so he was early—which was a surprise. Nowadays, ever since he'd taken up with Marilyn Hollis, he was invariably late. And rumpled-looking. He was rumpled-looking tonight, too, giving the impression of a man who'd leaped out of bed and into his trousers not five minutes earlier.

"Getting a bit brisk out there," he said.

He was wearing a short car coat over slacks and a sports jacket, no tie, the top button of his shirt unbuttoned. At five-feet eight-inches tall, he was the shortest man on the squad—even shorter than Fjuiwara, who was of Japanese descent—but Willis knew judo and karate, and he'd fooled many a cheap thief who'd figured him for a pushover. He took off the coat and hung it on the coatrack, glanced idly at the bulletin board, and then looked at the duty chart to see who'd be sharing the shift with him. He moved like a man underwater nowadays. Kling attributed his eternal weariness to Marilyn Hollis. Eileen said Marilyn Hollis was poison. Maybe she was right. Kling looked up at the clock.

"Let me fill you in," he said.

He told Willis about the four teenagers Genero had shot.

"Genero?" Willis said, amazed.

He told Willis about the four midgets who'd held up a series of liquor stores.

"Midgets?" Willis said, amazed.

He told Willis that Carella and Meyer had taken three bullets between them and were both at Buenavista Hospital.

"You going over there?" Willis asked.

"Maybe later. I have to run out to Calm's Point."

He looked up at the clock again.

"Brown and Hawes caught a homicide," he said, "all the paperwork is on Brown's desk. There's a picture of the victim, too, a magician. They found him in four separate pieces."

"Four pieces?" Willis said, amazed.

"There's a number you can reach them at in Collinsworth, case anything breaks. They got an all-points out on a guy named Jimmy Brayne."

"Good evening, gentlemen," O'Brien said from the slatted rail divider, and then pushed his way through the gate into the squadroom. "Winter's on the way." He was indeed dressed for winter, wearing a heavy overcoat and a muffler, which he took off now and carried to the coatrack. Willis wasn't happy to be partnered with O'Brien. O'Brien was a hard-luck cop. You went on a call with O'Brien, somebody was bound to get shot. This wasn't O'Brien's fault. Some cops simply attracted the lunatics with guns. On Christmas Day, not too long ago—well, not too long ago by *precinct* time, where sometimes an hour seemed an eternity—O'Brien and Meyer had stopped to check out a man changing a flat tire on a moving van. A moving van? Working on Christmas Day? The man turned out to be a burglar named Michael Addison, who'd just cleaned out half a dozen houses in Smoke Rise. Addison shot Meyer twice in the leg. Brown later dubbed the burglar Addison and Steal. This was pretty funny, but the bullets in Meyer's leg weren't. Willis—and everyone else on the squad—was convinced Meyer had got himself shot only because he'd been partnered with O'Brien. Still, he'd been shot again tonight, hadn't he? And he'd been working with Carella. Maybe in this line of work, there were bullets waiting out there with your name on them. In any event, Willis wished O'Brien was home in bed, instead of here in the squadroom with him.

"Steve and Meyer took a couple, did you hear?" he said.

"What are you talking about?"

"Some midgets shot them," Kling said.

"Come on, midgets," O'Brien said.

Kling looked up at the clock again.

"I'll be checking out a car," he said to no one.

"You want a cup of coffee?" O'Brien asked Willis.

It was only fifteen minutes before the beginning of All Hallows' Day.

In the Roman Catholic and Anglican churches, the first day of November is a feast day upon which the church glorifies God for all his saints, known or unknown. The word "hallow" derives from the Middle English *halowen,* further derived from the Old English *hālgian,* and it means "to make or set apart as holy; to sanctify; to consecrate." All Hallows' Day and Hallowmass are now archaic names for this feast; today—except in novels—it is called All Saints' Day. But it has always been celebrated on the first day of November, which in Celtic times was coincidentally the first day of winter, a time of pagan witches and ghosts, mummery and masquerade. Wholly Christian in origin, however, are the vigil and fasting that occur on the day before.

On the eve of All Hallows' Day, a Christian and a Jew kept vigil in a corridor of the Ernest Atlas Pavilion on the fourth floor of Buenavista Hospital.

The Christian was Teddy Carella.

The Jew was Sarah Meyer.

The clock on the corridor wall read 11:47 P.M.

Sarah Meyer had brown hair and blue eyes and lips her husband had always considered sensual.

Teddy Carella had black hair and brown eyes, and lips that could not speak, for she had been born deaf and mute.

Sarah had not seen the inside of a synagogue for more years than she cared to count.

Teddy scarcely knew the whereabouts of her neighborhood church.

But both women were silently praying, and they were both praying for the same man.

Sarah knew that her husband was out of danger.

It was Steven Carella who was still in surgery.

On impulse, she took Teddy's hand and squeezed it.

Neither of the women said a word to the other.

Neither of the women said a word to the other.

They spotted him the moment they came back into the bar. Annie knew he was their man. So did Eileen. They headed immediately for the ladies' room.

A black hooker wearing a blonde wig was standing at the sink, looking into the mirror over it, touching up her lipstick. She was a woman in her early forties, Eileen guessed, wearing a black dress and a short, fake fur jacket, going a bit thick in the middle and around the ankles. Eileen was certain she had just come in off the meat rack on the street outside.

"Getting chilly out there, ain't it?" the woman said.

"Yeah," Annie said.

"I'd park in here a while, but Larry gets twenty percent."

"I know."

"My man take a fit I give away twenty percent of the store."

There was a knife scar across the bridge of her nose.

She must have been pretty once, Eileen thought.

"One last pee," she said, and went into one of the stalls.

Annie lighted a cigarette. They chatted idly about how cold it was. The black hooker chimed in from behind the closed door of the stall, reporting on the really cold weather in Buffalo, New York, where she used to work years ago. They waited for her to flush the toilet. They waited while she washed her hands at the sink.

"Have a nice night," she said, and was gone.

"He's our man, isn't he?" Eileen said at once.

"Looks like him."

"Hitting on the wrong hooker."

"You'd better move in," Annie said.

"Sheryl won't like it."

"She'll like a slab even less."

"Will Shanahan know he's here?" Eileen asked.

"He'll know, don't worry."

Eileen nodded.

"You ready for this?" Annie asked.

"I'm ready."

"You sure?"

"I'm sure."

Annie searched her face.

"Because if you . . ."

"I'm ready," Eileen said.

Annie kept searching her face. Then she said, "Let's go then," and tossed her cigarette into one of the toilet bowls.

The cigarette expired with a short tired hiss.

He was telling another joke when Eileen took the stool on his right.

Blond. Six-two, six-three. Two hundred and ten easy. Eyeglasses. A tattoo near his right thumb, a blue heart lined in red, nothing in it.

". . . so he says to the old man. 'What's the matter? Why are you crying?' The old man just keeps sitting there on the park bench, crying his eyes out. Finally he says, 'A year ago, I married this beautiful twenty-six-year-old girl. I've never been happier in my life. Before breakfast each morning, she wakes me up and blows me, and then she serves me bacon and eggs and toasted English muffins and piping hot coffee, and I go back to bed and rest till lunchtime. Then she blows me again before lunch, and she serves me a hot, delicious lunch, and I go back to bed again and rest till dinnertime. And she blows me again before dinner and serves me another terrific meal, and I fall asleep until morning when she wakes me up again with another blowjob. She's the most wonderful woman I've ever met in my life.' The guy looks at him. 'Then why are you crying?' he asks. And the old man says, 'I forgot where I *live!*' "

Sheryl burst out laughing.

Eileen was thinking about the dead hookers he'd had in stitches.

"This guy's marvelous," Sheryl said, still laughing, leaning over to talk across him. "Linda, say hello to Bobby, he's marvelous."

"Hello, Bobby," Eileen said.

Terrific name for a slasher, she thought.

"Well, well, well, hello, Linda," he said, turning to her.

"Me and Bobby's running a tab," Sheryl said. "Which by the way, time's almost up."

"That right?" Eileen said.

"Just having a little fun here," Bobby said.

"The real fun comes later, honey," Sheryl said. "This is just the warm-up."

"I hear redheads are a lot of fun," Bobby said. "Is that true?"

"I haven't had any complaints," Eileen said.

She was wondering how she could get rid of Sheryl. If they were running a bar tab . . .

"But they burn in the sun," Bobby said.

"Yeah, I have to watch that."

"Just don't go out except at night, that's all," Sheryl said. "Listen, Bobby, I hate to be pushy, but your time's running out. You said twenty bucks for twenty minutes, remember?"

"Uh-huh."

"So take a look at the clock. You got about a minute left."

"I see that."

"So what do you say? We're having fun here, am I right?"

"Lots of fun."

"So how about another twenty, take us into Saturday?"

"Sounds like a good idea," he said, but he made no move for his wallet. Sheryl figured she was losing him.

"Matter of fact," she said, "whyn't you put Linda on the tab, too?"

"Thanks, no, I've been drinking too much tonight," Eileen said.

"This ain't a booze tab," Sheryl said. "This is accounts receivable. What do you say, Bobby? Lay a couple of twenties on the bar there, you buy both of us till a quarter past. Double your pleasure, double your fun. And later on, you still interested, we do a triad."

"What's a triad?" he asked.

"I read it in a book. It's like a two-on-one. A triad."

"I'm not sure I could handle two of you," he said.

But Eileen could see the sudden spark of ambition in his eyes. Blue to match the blue in the tattooed heart near his thumb. Seriously considering the possibility now. Take them *both* outside, slash them both, maybe go for a third one later on, do the hat trick tonight.

She didn't want a civilian getting in the way.

She had to get rid of Sheryl.

"I don't work doubles," she said.

A risk.

"How come?" Bobby asked.

"Why should I share this?" she said, and put her left hand on his thigh. He thought she was going for the meat. She was frisking him for the knife. Found it, too. Outlined in his right-hand pants pocket, felt like a six-incher at least. Maybe eight.

A shiver ran up her spine.

Sheryl was getting nervous. Her eyes flicked up to the clock again. The twenty minutes were gone, and she didn't see another twenty bucks coming out of his wallet. She was afraid she'd already lost him. So she tried again, appealing not to *him* now, but to the redhead hooker sitting on his right, a sorority sister, so to speak, someone who knew how tough it was to earn a buck in a dog-eat-dog world.

"Change your mind, Linda," she said.

There was something almost plaintive in her voice.

"Come on, okay? It'll be fun."

"I think Linda might be more fun alone," Bobby said.

Eileen's hand was still on his thigh. Off the knife now, like finding the knife was an accident. Fingers spread toward his crotch.

Sheryl looked up at the clock again.

"Tell you what," she said. "I'll make it only ten bucks for the next twenty minutes, how's that? We'll sit here, I'll let you tell me some more of your jokes, be a lot of fun, what do you say?"

A last desperate try.

"I say it's up to Linda here. What do you say, Linda?"

"I told you. I don't do doubles."

Flat out. Get rid of her.

"You heard her," he said.

"Hey come on, what kinda . . . ?"

"So long, Sheryl," he said.

She got off the stool at once.

"You're some cunt, you know that?" she said to Eileen, and turned away angrily and walked toward a table where three men were sitting drinking beer. "Who wants me?" she said angrily, and pulled out a chair and sat.

"I hate it when the fun goes out of it," Bobby said.

"We'll have lots of fun, don't worry," Eileen whispered, and tightened her hand on his thigh. "You want to get out of here this minute? I get ten bucks for a handjob . . ."

"No, no, let's talk a while, okay?" He reached into his right hip pocket, pulled out his wallet. Big killer, she thought, keeps his wallet in the sucker pocket. "Same deal as with Sheryl, okay? A buck a minute, here's a twenty"—reaching into the wallet, pulling out a bill, looking up at the clock—"we'll see how it goes, okay?"

"What is this?" Eileen asked. "An audition?"

"Well, I'd like to get to know you a little before I . . ."

He cut himself short.

"Before you what?" she said.

"You know," he said, and smiled, and lowered his voice. "Do it to you."

"What would you like to do to me, Bobby?"

"New and exciting things," he said.

She looked into his eyes.

Another shiver ran up her back.

"You cold?" he asked.

"A little. The weather's changing all of a sudden."

"Here," he said. "Take my jacket."

He shrugged out of the jacket. Tweed. He was wearing a blue flannel shirt under it, open at the throat. Blue to match his eyes and the tattooed heart near his thumb. He draped the jacket over her shoulders. There was the smell of death on the jacket, as palpable as the odor of smoke hanging on the air. She shivered again.

"So what do you say?" he asked her. "A buck a minute, does that sound all right?"

"Sure," she said.

"Well, good," he said, and handed her the twenty-dollar bill.

"Thanks," she said, and looked up at the clock. "This buys you till twenty past," she said, and tucked the bill into her bra. She didn't want to open her bag. She didn't want to risk him spotting the .44 in her bag, under the silk scarf. She was going to blow his brains out with that gun.

"Nothing for our friendly barkeep?" he asked.

"Huh?"

"I thought he got twenty percent."

"Oh. No, we have an arrangement."

"Well, good. I'd hate to think you were cheating him. You don't cheat people, do you, Linda?"

"I try to give good value," she said.

"Good. 'Cause you promised me a lot of fun, didn't you?"

"Show you a real good time," she said, and nodded.

Across the room, Annie was in conversation with the frizzied brunette who'd earlier partnered with Sheryl. The place was beginning to thin out a bit. There'd be a new shift coming in, Eileen guessed, the morning people, the denizens of the empty hours. He'd paid for twenty minutes of her time, but he'd dumped Sheryl without a backward glance, and she couldn't risk losing him to any of the other girls here. Twenty minutes unless he laid another bill on the bar. Twenty minutes to get him outside on the street, where he'd moved on the other three women. Show him a real good time, all right. Punish him for what he'd done. Make him pay for the three women he'd killed. Make him pay, too, for what a man named Arthur Haines had done to her face . . . and her body . . . and her spirit.

"So where are all the jokes?" she asked.

"Jokes?"

"Sheryl said you're full of jokes."

"No, Sheryl didn't say that."

"I thought she said . . ."

"I'm sure she didn't."

A mistake? No. Back off a bit, anyway.

"She said she'd settle for ten bucks, sit here with you, let you tell her some more jokes . . ."

"Oh. Yeah."

"So let me hear one."

"I'd rather talk about you right now."

"Sure," Eileen said.

" 'Cause I find that fun, you know. Learning about other people, finding out what makes them tick."

"You sound like a shrink," she said.

"Well, my father's a shrink."

"Really?"

"Yeah. Practices in L.A. Lots of customers out there. You know what L.A. stands for?"

"What?"

"Lunatic Asylum."

"I've never been there, so I wouldn't . . ."

"Take my word for it. Every variety of nut in the—do you know the one about the guy who goes into a nut shop?"

"No."

"He stutters badly, he says to the clerk, 'I'd l-l-like to b-b-buy a p-p-pound of n-n-nuts.' The clerk says, 'Yes, sir, we have some very nice Brazil nuts at three dollars a pound.' The guy says, 'N-n-no, that's t-t-too high.' So the clerk says, 'I've also got some nice almonds at two dollars a pound.' The guy says, 'N-n-no, that's t-t-too high, t-t-too.' So the clerk says, 'I've got some peanuts at a dollar a pound,' and the guy says, 'F-f-fine.' The clerk weighs out the peanuts, puts them in a bag, and the guy pays for them. The guy says, 'Th-thank you, and I also w-w-want to th-thank you for n-n-not m-m-mentioning m-m-my im-p-p-pediment.' The clerk says, 'That's quite all right, sir, and I want to thank you for not mentioning my deformity.' The guy says, 'Wh-what d-d-deformity?' The clerk says, 'Well, I have a very large nose.' The guy says, 'Oh, is that your n-n-nose? Your n-n-nuts are so high, I th-thought it was your p-p-pecker.' "

Eileen burst out laughing.

The laughter was genuine.

For the briefest tick of time she forgot that she was sitting here at the bar with a man she felt reasonably certain had killed three women and would do his best to kill her as well if she gave him the slightest opportunity.

The laughter surprised her.

She had not laughed this heartily in a long time. She had not laughed since the night Arthur Haines slashed her cheek and forced himself upon her.

She could not stop laughing.

She wondered all at once if the laughter was merely a release of nervous tension.

But she kept laughing.

Tears were rolling down her cheeks.

She reached into her bag for a tissue, felt under the silk scarf, touched the butt of the .44, and suddenly the laughter stopped.

Dabbing at her eyes, she said, "That was very funny."

"I'm going to enjoy you," he said, smiling, looking into her eyes. "You're going to be a good one."

11

Alice was telling him that a lot of men got turned on by midgets, did he realize that?

Parker realized it. She was a perfect little doll, blonde hair and blue eyes, beautifully formed breasts and well-shaped legs. She was wearing a green dress that hugged the womanly curves of her body, legs crossed, one foot jiggling in a high-heeled green slipper.

He said, "I read a lot of these men's magazines, you know . . ."

"Uh-huh," she said, nodding encouragement. Drink in her right hand, cigarette in her left.

"And there's all sorts of letters from men who get turned on by all sorts of women."

"Uh-huh."

"Like, for example, there are many men who are sexually attracted to women with back problems."

"Back problems?" Alice said.

"Yes. Women who wear braces."

"I see," she said.

"And there are men who enjoy one-armed women."

"Uh-huh."

"Or even double amputees."

"Uh-huh."

"Or women who are color blind."

"Color blind, right."

"But I've never seen any letters from men who find *midgets* sexually attractive. I wonder why. I mean, I find *you* very attractive, Alice."

"Well, thank you," she said. "But that's what I was saying. A *lot* of men get turned on by midgets."

"I can understand that."

"It's what's called the Snow White Syndrome."

"Is that what it's called?"

"Yes, because she was living with those seven dwarfs, you know."

"That's right, I never thought of that. I mean, if you look at it that way, it could be a dirty story, couldn't it?"

"Well, sure. Not that dwarfs are midgets."

"No, no. They *aren't?*"

"No. Midgets are perfectly proportioned little people."

"You certainly are perfectly proportioned, Alice."

"Well, thank you. But my point is, with so many men being attracted to female midgets . . ."

"Uh-huh."

"You think you'd see midgets in ads and all."

"I never thought of it that way."

"I mean, wouldn't you like to see me modeling lingerie, for example?"

"Oh, I would."

"But instead, if you're a midget, you have to join a circus."

"I never thought of it that way," he said again.

"Have you ever seen a midget working as a clerk in a department store?"

"Never," he said.

"Do you know why?"

"Because you can't see over the counter?"

"Well, that's one reason, of course. But the main reason is there's a lingering prejudice against little people."

"I'll bet there is."

"Short has become a dirty word," Alice said. "Have you ever seen a short movie star?"

"Well, Al Pacino is short."

"On my block, Al Pacino is a *giant,*" she said, and giggled.

Parker loved the way she giggled.

"Have you ever seen a movie where there are midgets making *love?*" she asked.

"Never."

"We *do* make love, you know."

"Oh, I'll bet."

"Have you ever seen a midget fireman? Or a midget cop?"

He had not yet told her he was a cop. He wondered if he should tell her he was a cop.

"Well, they changed the requirements, you know," he said.

"What requirements?"

"The height requirements. It used to be five-eight."

"So what is it now?"

"You can be any height. I know cops you can fit them in your vest pocket."

"You mean a midget can become a cop?"

"Well, I don't know about *midgets.* But I guess . . ."

"Because I can shoot a gun as good as anybody else, you know. I used to do an Annie Oakley act in the circus. Little Annie Oakley, they called me. That was before I got to be Tiny Alice."

"You *are* tiny," he said. "That's one of the things I find very sexually attractive about you."

"Well, thank you. But what I'm asking, if I applied to the police department . . . to become a woman cop, you know . . . would they accept me? Or would they think *short?* Do you see what I mean?"

"I don't think of you as short," Parker said.

"Oh, I'm short, all right."

"I think of you as delicate."

"Well, thank you. There's this man Hans, he's one of the Flying Dutchmen, an aerial act, you know?"

"Uh-huh."

"He wrote me this very hot love letter, I memorized it. What made me think of it was your use of the word delicate."

"Well, you are delicate."

"Thank you. Would you like to hear the letter?"

"Well . . . sure," Parker said, and glanced over his shoulder to see where Peaches was. She was nowhere in sight. "Go ahead," he said.

"He said he wanted to disrobe me."

"Take off your clothes, you mean."

"Yes. He said he wanted to discard my dainty delicate under things . . . that's what made me think of it, delicate."

"Yes, I see."

"And pat my pubescent peaks . . . this is him talking now, in the letter."

"Yes."

"And probe my pithy pussy, and manipulate my miniature mons veneris and Lilliputian labiae . . ."

"Uh-huh."

"And caress my compact clitoris and crisp pauciloquent public patch. That was the letter."

"From one of the Flying Dutchmen, huh?"

"Yes."

"He speaks good English."

"Oh, yes."

"That isn't the guy you're with tonight, is it? The guy you came in with?"

"No, no. That's Quentin."

"He's not one of the Flying Dutchmen, huh?"

"No, he's a clown."

"Oh."

"A very good one, too."

"So how long have you been in town? I didn't even know the circus was here, I'll tell you the truth."

"Well, we're not here. We won't be here till the spring sometime. We go down to Florida next month to start rehearsing the new season."

"Oh, so you're just visiting then, is that it?"

"Yeah, sort of."

"You're not married or anything, are you?"

"No, no. No, no, no, no, no."

Shaking her head like a little doll.

"How long will you be in town?"

"Oh, I don't know. Why?"

"I thought we might get together," Parker said, and shrugged.

"How about the big redhead you're with?"

"Peaches? She's just a friend."

"Uh-huh."

"Really. I hardly know her. Alice, I've got to tell you, I've never met a woman as delicate and as attractive as you are, I mean it. I'd really like to get together with you."

"Well, why don't you give me a call?"

"I'd like that," he said, and took his pad from his pocket.

"That's *some* notebook," she said. "It's bigger than I am."

"Well, you know," he said, and wondered again if he should tell her he was a cop. Lots of women, you told them you were a cop, it turned them off. They figured all cops were on the take, all cops were crooks. Just because every now and then you accepted a little gift from somebody. "So where can I reach you?" he said.

"We're staying at Quentin's apartment. The four of us."

"Who's the four of us? Not the Flying Dutchmen, I hope."

"No, no, they went back to Germany, they'll be joining us in Florida."

"So who's the four of you?"

"Willie and Corky . . . they're married . . . and Oliver and me. And of course Quentin, whose apartment it is. Quentin Forbes."

"What's the address?" Parker asked.

"Four-oh-three Thompson Street."

"Downtown in the Quarter," he said, nodding. "The Twelfth."

"Huh?"

He wondered if he should explain to her that in this city you didn't call the Twelfth the "One-Two." Any precinct from the First to the Twentieth was called by its full and proper designation. After that, it became the Two-One, the Three-Four, the Eight-Seven, and so on. But that would have meant telling her he was a cop, and he didn't want to chance losing her.

"What's the phone number there?" he asked.

"Three-four-eight . . ."

"Ex*cuse* me."

Voice as cold as the second day of February, hands on her hips, green eyes blazing.

"I'd like to go home now," Peaches said. "Did you plan on accompanying me? Or are you going to play house all night?"

"Uh . . . sure," Parker said, and got to his feet. "Nice meeting you," he said to Alice.

"It's in the book," Alice said, and smiled up sweetly at Peaches.

Peaches tried to think of a scathing midget remark, but nothing came to mind. She turned and started for the door.

"I'll call you," Parker whispered, and ran out after her.

The house was a white clapboard building with a white picket fence around it. A matching white clapboard garage stood some twenty feet from the main structure. Both buildings were on a street with only three other houses on it, not too far from the turnpike. It was two minutes past midnight when they reached the house. The first day of November. The beginning of the Celtic winter. As if in accordance, the weather had turned very cold. As they pulled into the driveway, Brown remarked that all they needed was snow, the turnpike would be backed up all the way to Siberia.

There were no lights burning on the ground floor of the house. Two lighted windows showed on the second story. The men were inappropriately dressed for the sudden cold. Their breaths plumed from their mouths as they walked to the front door. Hawes rang the doorbell.

"Probably getting ready for bed," he said.

"You wish," Brown said.

They waited.

"Give it another shot," Brown said.

Hawes hit the bell button again.

Lights snapped on downstairs.

"Who is it?"

Marie's voice, just inside the door. A trifle alarmed. Well, sure, midnight already.

"It's Detective Hawes," he said.

"Oh."

"Sorry to bother you so late."

"No, that's all . . . just a minute, please."

She fumbled with the lock, and then opened the door. She *had* been getting ready for bed. She was wearing a long blue robe. Laced ruff of a nightgown showing in the V-necked opening. No slippers.

"Have you found him?" she asked at once.

Referring to Jimmy Brayne, of course.

"No, ma'am, not yet," Brown said. "Okay for us to come in?"

"Yes, please," she said, "excuse me," and stepped back to let them in.

Small entryway, a sense of near-shabbiness. Worn carpeting, scarred and rickety piece of furniture under a flaking mirror.

"I thought . . . when you told me who you were . . . I thought you'd found Jimmy," she said.

"Not yet, Mrs. Sebastiani," Hawes said. "In fact, the reason we came out here . . ."

"Come in," she said, "we don't have to stand here in the hall."

She backed off several paces, reached beyond the door jamb for a light switch. A floor lamp came on in the living room. Musty drapes, a faded rug, a thrift-shop sofa and two upholstered armchairs, an old upright piano on the far wall. Same sense of down-at-the-heels existence.

"Would you like some coffee or anything?" she asked.

"I could use a cup," Brown said.

"I'll put some up," she said, and walked back through the hall and through a doorway into the kitchen.

The detectives looked around the living room.

Framed photographs on the piano, Sebastian the Great doing his act hither and yon. Soiled antimacassars on the upholstered pieces. Brown ran his finger over the surface of an end table. Dust. Hawes poked his forefinger into the soil of a potted plant. Dry. The continuing sense of a house too run down to care about—or a house in neglect because it would soon be abandoned.

She was back.

"Take a few minutes to boil," she said.

"Who plays piano?" Hawes asked.

"Frank did. A little."

She'd grown used to the past tense.

"Mrs. Sebastiani," Brown said, "we were wondering if we could take a look at Brayne's room."

"Jimmy's room?" she said. She seemed a bit flustered by their presence, but that could have been normal, two cops showing up on her doorstep at midnight.

"See if there's anything up there might give us a lead," Brown said, watching her.

"I'll have to find a spare key someplace," she said. "Jimmy had his own key, he came and went as he pleased."

She stood stock still in the entrance door to the living room, a thoughtful look on her face. Hawes wondered what she was thinking, face all screwed up like that. Was she wondering whether it was safe to show them that room? Or was she merely trying to remember where the spare key was?

"I'm trying to think where Frank might have put it," she said. A grandfather clock on the far side of the room began tolling the hour, eight minutes late.

One . . . two . . .

They listened to the heavy bonging.

Nine . . . ten . . . eleven . . . twelve.

"Midnight already," she said, and sighed.

"Your clock's slow," Brown said.

"Let me check the drawer in the kitchen," she said. "Frank used to put a lot of junk in that drawer."

Past tense again.

They followed her into the kitchen. Dirty dishes, pots, and pans stacked in the sink. The door of the refrigerator smudged with handprints. Telephone on the wall near it. Small enamel-topped table, two chairs. Worn linoleum. Only a shade on the single window, over the sink. On the stove, the kettle began whistling.

"Help yourselves," she said. "There's cups there, and a jar of instant."

She went to a drawer in the counter, opened it. Hawes spooned instant coffee into each of the cups, poured hot water into them. She was busy at the drawer now, searching for the spare key. "There should be some milk in the fridge," she said. "And there's sugar on the counter there." Hawes opened the refrigerator. Not much in it. Carton of low-fat milk, slab of margarine or butter, several containers of yogurt. He closed the door.

"You want some of this?" he asked Brown, extending the carton to him.

Brown shook his head. He was watching Marie going through the drawer full of junk.

"Sugar?" Hawes asked, pouring milk into his own cup.

Brown shook his head again.

"This may be it, I really don't know," Marie said.

She turned from the drawer, handed Brown a brass key that looked like a house key.

The telephone rang.

She was visibly startled by its sound.

Brown picked up his coffee cup, began sipping at it.

The telephone kept ringing.

She went to the wall near the refrigerator, lifted the receiver from its hook.

"Hello?" she said.

The two detectives watched her.

"Oh, hello, Dolores," she said at once. "No, not yet, I'm down in the kitchen," she said, and listened. "There are two detectives with me," she said. "No, that's all right, Dolores." She listened again. "They want to look at the garage room." Listening again. "I don't know yet," she said. "Well, they . . . they have to do an autopsy first." More listening. "Yes, I'll let you know. Thanks for calling, Dolores."

She put the receiver back on its hook.

"My sister-in-law," she said.

"Taking it hard, I'll bet," Hawes said.

"They were very close."

"Let's check out that room," Brown said to Hawes.

"I'll come over with you," Marie said.

"No need," Brown said, "it's getting cold outside."

She looked at him. She seemed about to say something more. Then she merely nodded.

"Better get a light from the car," Hawes said.

Marie watched them as they went out the door and made their way in the dark to where they'd parked their car. Car door opening, interior light snapping on. Door closing again. A moment later, a flashlight came on. She watched them as they walked up the driveway to the garage, pool of light ahead of them. They began climbing the steps at the side of the building. Flashlight beam on the door now. Unlocking the door. Should she have given them the key? Opening the door. The black cop reached into the room. A moment of fumbling for the wall switch, and then the light snapped on, and they both went inside and closed the door behind them.

The bullet had entered Carella's chest on the right side of the body, piercing the pectoralis major muscle, deflecting off the rib cage and missing the lung, passing through the soft tissue at the back of the chest, and then twisting again to lodge in one of the articulated bones in the spinal column.

The X rays showed the bullet dangerously close to the spinal cord itself.

In fact, if it had come to rest a micrometer further to the left, it would have traumatized the cord and caused paralysis.

The surgical procedure was a tricky one in that the danger of necrosis of the cord was still present, either through mechanical trauma or a compromise of the arterial supply of blood to the cord. Carella had bled a lot, and there was the further attendant danger of his going into heart failure or shock.

The team of surgeons—a thoracic surgeon, a neurosurgeon, his assistant, and two residents—had decided on a posterolateral approach, going in through the back rather than entering the chest cavity, where there might be a greater chance of infection and the possibility of injury to one of the lungs. The neurosurgeon was the man who made the incisions. The thoracic surgeon was standing by in the event they had to open the chest after all. There were also two scrub nurses, a circulating nurse, and an anesthesiologist in the room. With the exception of the circulating nurse and the anesthesiologist, everyone was fully gowned and gloved. Alongside the operating table, machines monitored Carella's pulse and blood pressure. A Swan-Ganz catheter was in place, monitoring the pressure in the pulmonary artery. Oscilloscopes flashed green. Beeps punctuated the sterile silence of the room.

The bullet was firmly seated in the spinal column.

Very close to the spinal cord and the radicular arteries.

It was like operating inside a matchbox.

The River Dix had begun silting over during the heavy September rains, and the city had awarded the dredging contract to a private company that started work on the fifteenth of October. Because there was heavy traffic on the river during the daylight hours, the men working the barges started as soon as it was dark and continued on through until just before dawn. Generator-powered lights set up on the barges illuminated the bucketsful of river slime scooped up from the bottom. Before tonight, the men doing the dredging had been grateful for the unusually mild weather. Tonight, it was no fun standing out here in the cold, watching the bucket drop into the black water and come up again dripping all kinds of shit.

People threw everything in this river.

Good thing Billy Joe McAllister didn't live in this city; he'd have maybe thrown a dead baby in the river.

The bucket came up again.

Barney Hanks watched it swinging in wide over the water, and signaled with his hand, directing it in over the center of the disposal barge. Pete Masters, sitting in the cab of the diesel-powered dredge on the other barge, worked his clutches and levers, tilting the bucket to drop another yard and a half, two yards of silt and shit. Hanks jerked his thumb up, signaling to Masters that the bucket was empty and it was okay to cast the dragline out over the river again. In the cab, Masters yanked some more levers and the bucket swung out over the side of the barge.

Something metallic was glistening on the surface of the muck in the disposal barge.

Hanks signaled to Masters to cut the engine.

"What is it?" Masters shouted.

"We got ourselves a treasure chest," Hanks yelled.

Masters cut his engine, climbed down from the cab, and walked across the deck toward the other barge.

"Time for a coffee break, anyway," he said. "What do you mean a treasure chest?"

"Throw me that grappling hook," Hanks said.

Masters threw the hook and line to him.

Hanks tossed the hook at what appeared to be one of those aluminum cases you carried roller skates in, except that it was bigger all around. The case was half-submerged in slime, it took Hanks five tosses to snag the handle. He pulled in the line, freed the hook, and put the case down on the deck.

Masters watched him from the other barge.

Hanks tried the catches on the case.

"No lock on it," he said, and opened the lid.

He was looking at a head and a pair of hands.

Kling arrived in the Canal Zone at thirteen minutes past midnight.

He parked the car on Canalside and Solomon, locked it, and began walking up toward Fairview. Eileen had told him they'd be planting her in a joint called Larry's Bar, on Fairview and East Fourth. This side of the river, the city got all turned around. What could have been North Fourth in home territory was East Fourth here, go figure it. Like two different countries, the opposite sides of the river. They even spoke English funny over here.

Larry's Bar.

Where the killer had picked up his three previous victims.

Kling planned on casing it from the outside, just to make sure she was still in there. Then he'd fade out, cover the place from a safe vantage point on the street. Didn't want Eileen to know he was on the scene. First off, she'd throw a fit, and next she might spook, blow her own cover. All he wanted was to be around in case she needed him.

He had put on an old pea jacket he kept in his locker for unexpected changes of weather like the one tonight. He was hatless and he wasn't wearing gloves. If he needed to pull the piece, he didn't want gloves getting in the way. Navy-blue pea jacket, blue jeans—too lightweight, really, for the sudden chill—blue socks and black loafers. And a .38 Detective Special in a holster at his waist. Left hand side. Two middle buttons of the jacket unbuttoned for an easy reach-in and cross-body draw.

He came up Canalside.

The Beef Trust was out in force, despite the cold.

Girls huddled under the lamp posts as though the overhead lights afforded some warmth, most of them wearing only short skirts and sweaters or blouses, scant protection against the cold. A lucky few were wearing coats provided by mobile pimps with an eye on the weather.

"Hey, sailor, lookin' for a party?"

Black girl breaking away from the knot under the corner lamp post, swiveling over to him. Couldn't be older than eighteen, nineteen, hands in the pockets of a short jacket, high-heeled ankle-strapped shoes, short skirt blowing in the fresh wind that came off the canal.

"Almos' do it for free, you so good-lookin'," she said, grinning widely. "Thass a joke, honey, but the price is right, trust me."

"Not right now," Kling said.

"Well, *when* baby? I stann out here much longer, my pussy turn to ice. Be no good to neither one of us."

"Maybe later," Kling said.

"You promise? Slide your hand up under here, take a feel of heaven."

"I'm busy right now," Kling said.

"Too busy for *this?*" she said, and took his hand and guided it onto her thigh. "Mmmmm-*mmmmm,*" she said, "sweet chocolate pussy, yours for the takin'."

"Later," he said, and freed his hand and began walking off.

"You come on back later, man, hear?" she shouted after him. "Ask for Crystal."

He walked into the darkness. On the dock, he could hear rats rustling along the pilings. Another lamp post, another huddle of hookers.

"Hey, Blondie, lookin' for some fun?"

White girl in her twenties. Wearing a long khaki coat and high heels. Opened the coat to him as he went past.

"Interested?" she said.

Nothing under the coat but garter belt and long black stockings. Quick glimpse of rounded belly and pink-tipped breasts.

"Faggot!" she yelled after him, and twirled the coat closed as gracefully as a dancer. The girls with her laughed. Fun on the docks.

Made a right turn onto Fairview, began walking up toward Fourth. Pools of light on the sidewalk ahead. Larry's Bar. Two plate-glass windows, beer displays in them, entrance door set between them. He went to the closest window, cupped his hands on either side of his face, peered through the glass. Not too crowded just now. Annie. Sitting at a table with a black man and a frizzied brunette. Good, at least one backup was close by. There at the bar. Eileen. With a big blond guy wearing glasses.

Okay, Kling thought.

I'm here.

Don't worry.

From where Shanahan sat slumped behind the wheel of the two-door Chevy across the street, he saw only a big blond guy looking through the plate-glass window of the bar. Six feet tall, he guessed, give or take an inch, broad shoulders and narrow waist, wearing a seaman's pea jacket and blue jeans.

Shanahan was suddenly alert.

Guy was still looking through the window, hands cupped to his face, motionless except for the dancing of his blond hair on the wind.

Shanahan kept watching.

The guy turned from the window.

No eyeglasses.

Might not be him.

On the other hand . . .

Shanahan got out of the car. It was clumsy moving with the right arm in a cast, but he'd rather be made for a cripple than a cop. Guy walking up the street now. How come he wasn't going in the bar? Change of M.O.? Shanahan fussed with the lock of the car door, watching him sidelong.

Minute the guy was four cars lengths away, Shanahan took off after him.

The bar was baited with Eileen, but there were plenty of other girls out here on the street. And if this guy was suddenly changing his pattern, Shanahan didn't want *any* of them dying.

Eileen didn't like the tricks her mind was beginning to play.

She was beginning to like him.

She was beginning to think he couldn't possibly be a murderer.

Like the stories you read in the newspapers after the kid next door shot and killed his mother, his father, and his two sisters. Nice kid like that? all the neighbors said. Can't believe it. Always had a kind word for everyone. Saw him mowing the lawn and helping old ladies across the street. This kid a killer? Impossible.

Or maybe she didn't *want* him to be a murderer because that would mean eventual confrontation. She knew that if this was the guy, she'd have to end up face to face with him on the street outside. And the knife would come out of his pocket. And . . .

It was easier to believe he couldn't possibly be the killer.

You're tricking yourself, she thought.

And yet. . .

There really were a lot of likable things about him.

Not just his sense of humor. Some of his jokes were terrible, in fact. He told them almost compulsively, whenever anything in the conversation triggered what appeared to be a vast computer-bank memory of stories. You mentioned the tattoo near his thumb, for example—the killer had a tattoo near this thumb, she reminded herself—and he immediately told the one about the two girls discussing the guy with the tattooed penis, and one of them insisted only the word Swan was tattooed on it, whereas the other girl insisted the word was Saskatchewan, and it turned out they were both right, which took Eileen a moment to get. Or you mentioned the sudden change in weather, and he immediately reeled off Henry Morgan's famous weather forecast, "Muggy today, Toogy tomorrow," and then segued neatly into the joke about the panhandler shivering outside in the cold and another panhandler comes over to him and says, "Can you lend me a dime for a cup of coffee?" and the first guy says, "Are you kidding? I'm standing here bare-assed, I'm shivering and starving to death, how come you're asking *me* for a dime?" and the second guy says, "Okay, make it a nickel," which wasn't very funny, but which he told with such dramatic flair that Eileen could actually visualize the two panhandlers standing on a windy corner of the city.

Outside, the city beckoned.

The night beckoned.

The knife beckoned.

But inside, sitting here at the bar with the television set going, and the sound of voices everywhere around them, the world seemed safe and cozy and warm, and she found herself listening intently to everything he said. Not only the jokes. The jokes were a given. If you wanted to learn about him, you had to listen to his jokes. The jokes were some sort of defense system, she realized, his way of keeping himself at arm's distance from anyone. But scattered in among the incessant jokes, there were glimpses of a shy and somewhat vulnerable person longing to make contact—until another joke was triggered.

He had used up his first twenty dollars five minutes ago, and was now working on the second twenty, which he said should take them through to twelve-forty.

"After that, we'll see," he said. "Maybe we'll talk some more, or maybe we'll go outside, depends how we feel, right? We'll play this by ear, Linda, I'm really enjoying this, aren't you?"

"Yes," she said, and guessed she meant it.

But he's the killer, she reminded herself.

Or maybe not.

She hoped he wasn't.

"If you add up these twenties," he said, "a dollar a minute, you'll be getting a third of what my dad gets in L.A., he gets a hundred and fifty bucks for a fifty-minute hour, which ain't bad, huh? For listening to people tell you they have bedbugs crawling all over them? Don't brush them on me, right? Well, I guess you know that one, I guess I've already told that one."

He hadn't told that one. But suddenly, as he apologized for what he'd mistakenly thought was repetition, she felt oddly close to him. Like a married woman listening to the same jokes her husband had told time and again, and yet enjoying them each time as if he were telling them for the first time. She knew the "Don't-brush-them-on-me" joke. Yet she wished he would tell it, anyway.

And wondered if she was stalling for time.

Wondered if she was putting off that eventual moment when the knife came out of the pocket.

"My father was very strict," he said. "If you have any choice, don't get raised by a psychiatrist. How's your father? Is he tough on you?"

"I never really knew him," she said.

Her father. A cop. On the beat, they used to call him Pops Burke. Shot to death when she was still a little girl.

In the next instant, she almost told him that her *uncle* and not her father was the one who'd had the most telling influence on her life. Uncle Matt. Also a cop. Whose favorite toast was, "Here's to golden days and purple nights." An expression he'd heard repeated again and again on a radio show. Recently, Eileen had heard Hal Willis's new girlfriend using the same expression. Small world. Even smaller world when your favorite uncle is sitting off-duty in his favorite bar making his favorite toast and a guy walks in with a sawed-off shotgun. Uncle Matt drew his service revolver and the guy shot him dead. She almost told Bobby she'd become a cop because of her Uncle Matt. She almost forgot in that instant that she herself was a cop working undercover to trap a killer. The word "entrapment" flashed into her mind. Suppose he isn't the killer? she wondered. Suppose I blow him away and it turns out—

And realized again that her mind was playing tricks.

"I grew up in a world of don't do this, don't do that," Bobby said. "You'd think a shrink would've known better, well, I guess it was a case of the shoemaker's children. Talk about repression. It was my mother who finally helped me to break out. I make it sound like a prison, don't I? Well, it was. Do you know the one about the lady walking along the beach in Miami?"

She shook her head.

She realized she was already smiling.

"Well, she sees this guy lying on the sand, and she goes up to him and she says, 'Excuse me, I don't mean to intrude, but you're very white.' The guy looks up at her and says, 'So?' The lady says, 'I mean, most people they come down to Miami, they lie in the sun, they get a nice tan. But you're very white.' The guy says, 'So?' The lady says, 'So how come you're so white?' The guy says, 'This is prison pallor, I just got out of prison yesterday.' The lady shakes her head and says, 'How long were you in prison?' The guys says, 'Thirty years.' The lady says, 'My, my, what did you do, they put you in prison for thirty years?' The guy says, 'I killed my wife with a hatchet and chopped her up in little pieces.' The woman looks at him and says, 'Mmmm, so you're single?' "

Eileen burst out laughing.

And then realized that the joke was about murder.

And then wondered if a murderer would tell a joke about murder.

"Anyway, it was my mother who broke me out of prison," Bobby said, "and she had to die to do it."

"What do you mean?"

"Left me a lot of money. Do you know what she said in her will? She said, 'This is for Robert's freedom to risk enjoying life.' Her exact words. She always called me Robert. 'Robert's freedom to risk enjoying life.' Which is just what I've been doing for the past year. Pissed my father off, told him to shove it, told him I'd be happy if I never saw him again, and then left L.A. forever.''

She wondered if there were any warrants out on him in L.A.

But why would there be any warrants?

"Went to Kansas City, had a good time there . . . got the tattoo there, in fact, what the hell, I'd always wanted a tattoo. Then on to Chicago, lived it up there, too, plenty of money to take risks, Linda. I owe that to my mother." He nodded thoughtfully, and then said, "He's the one who killed her, you know."

She looked at him.

"Oh, not literally. I mean he didn't stick a knife in her or anything. But he was having an affair with our housekeeper, and she found out about it, and it broke her heart, she was never the same again. They said it was cancer, but stress can induce serious illness, you know, and I'm sure that's what caused it, his fooling around with Elga. The money my mother eventually left me was the money she'd got in the divorce settlement, which I think was poetic justice, don't you? I mean, him raising me so strictly—while he's fooling around with that Nazi hooker, mind you—and my mother giving me *his* money so I could lead a richer life, so I could risk enjoying life. I think that was the key word, don't you? In the will? Risk. I think she wanted me to take risks with the money, which is what I've been doing."

"How?" Eileen asked.

"Oh, not by investing in hog bellies or anything," he said, and smiled. "By living well. Living well is the best revenge, isn't it? Who said that? I know *some-body* said that."

"Not *me!*" Eileen said, and backed away in mock denial.

"Don't brush them on me, right?" he said, and they both laughed.

He looked at the clock.

"Five minutes left," he said. "Maybe we'll go outside then. Would you like to go outside then? When the five minutes are up?"

"Whatever you want," she said.

"Maybe that's what we'll do," he said. "Have a little fun. Do something new and exciting, huh? Risks," he said, and smiled again.

He had a very pleasant smile.

Transformed his entire face. Made him look like a shy little boy. Blue eyes soft, almost misty, behind the eyeglasses. Shy little kid sitting in the back row, afraid to raise his hand and ask questions.

"In a way, you know," he said, "it *has* been a sort of revenge. What I've been doing with the money. Traveling, having a good time, taking my risks. And getting even with him, in a way, for Elga. Our housekeeper, you know? The woman he tricked my mother with. Deceiving her all those years. A shrink, can you imagine? Holier than thou, and he's laying the goddamn housekeeper. I mean, my mother was the one who put him through medical school. She was a schoolteacher, you know, worked all those years to put him through school, do you know how long a psychiatrist has to go to school? It's very difficult to believe that women can be so callous toward other women. I find that very difficult to believe, Linda. I mean, Elga behaving like a common hooker . . . excuse me, I don't mean any offense. Excuse me, really," he said, and patted her hand. "But, you know, you hear all this talk about sisterhood, you'd think she might have had some sense of concern for my mother, I mean the woman was married to him for forty *years!*" He grinned suddenly. "Do you know the one about this man who comes to his wife, they've been married forty years, he says to her, 'Ida, I want to do it like dogs.' She says, 'That's disgusting, Sam, doing it like dogs.' He says, 'Ida, if you won't do it like dogs, I want a divorce.' She says, 'Okay, Sam, we'll do it like dogs. But not on our block.' "

Eileen nodded.

"Didn't like that one, huh?"

"Mezza' a mezza," she said, and see-sawed her hand on the air.

"I promise we won't do it like dogs, okay?" he said, smiling. "How would you like to do it, Linda?"

"You're the boss," she said.

"Have you ever seen a snuff movie?" he asked.

"Never," she said.

Here it comes, she thought.

"Does that scare you?" he said. "My asking about a snuff movie?"

"Yes," she said.

"Me, too," he said, and smiled. "I've never seen one, either."

Explore it, she thought.

But she was afraid to.

"Think you might like that?" she said.

Her heart was suddenly pounding again.

"Killing someone while you were laying her?"

He looked deep into her eyes as though searching for something there.

"Not if she knew it was going to happen," he said.

And suddenly she knew, for certain that he was their man, and there was no postponing what would happen tonight.

He looked up at the clock.

"Time's up," he said. "Let's go outside."

12

The call to the squadroom came at twenty minutes to one. The call came from Monoghan, who was in a phone booth on the edge of the River Dix. He asked to talk to either Brown or Genero. Willis told him Brown and Genero were both out.

"So who's this?" Monoghan asked.

"Willis."

"What I got here," Monoghan said, "is a head and a pair of hands. These guys dragging the river turned up this aluminum case, like it's big enough to hold a man's head. And his hands. So that's what I got here. A head cut off at the neck, and a pair of hands cut off at the wrists."

"Uh-huh," Willis said.

"So earlier tonight I was with Brown and Genero back out behind this restaurant the Burgundy, and what we had there was the upper part of a torso in a garbage can, is what we had. And now I got a head and a pair of hands, and it occurred to me this might be the same body here, this head and hands."

"Uh-huh," Willis said.

"So what I want to know, does Brown or Genero have a positive make on the stiff? 'Cause otherwise we now got a head to look at, and also some hands to print."

"Let me take a look at Brown's desk," Willis said. "I think he left some stuff here."

"Yeah, go take a look," Monoghan said.

"Hold on," Willis said.

"Yeah."

"Hold on, I'm putting you on hold."

"Yeah, fine," Monoghan said.

Willis pressed the hold button, and then went over to Brown's desk. He riffled through the papers there, and then stabbed at the light extension button, and picked up the receiver.

"Monoghan?"

"Yeah."

"From what I can gather, the body was identified as someone named Frank Sebastiani, male, white, thirty-four years old."

"That's what I got here, a white male around that age."

"I've got a picture here, too," Willis said.

"Whyn't you run on over with it?" Monoghan said. "We see we got the same stiff or not."

"Where are you?"

"Freezing my ass off on the drive here. Near the river."

"Which river?"

"The Dix."

"And where?"

"Hampton."

"Give me ten minutes," Willis said.

"Don't forget the picture," Monoghan said.

The apartment over the garage was perhaps twelve-feet wide by twenty-feet long. There was a neatly made double bed in the room, and a dresser with a mirror over it, and an upholstered chair with a lamp behind it. The wall surrounding the mirror was covered with pictures of naked women snipped from men's magazines banned in 7-Eleven stores. All of the women were blondes. Like Marie Sebastiani. In the bottom drawer of the dresser, under a stack of Brayne's shirts, the detectives found a pair of crotchless black panties. The panties were a size five.

"Think they're Brayne's?" Hawes asked drily.

"What size you think the lady wears?" Brown asked.

"Could be a five," Hawes said, and shrugged.

"I thought you were an expert."

"On *bras* I'm an expert."

Men's socks, undershorts, sweaters, handkerchiefs in the other dresser drawers. Two sports jackets, several pairs of slacks, a suit, an overcoat, and three pairs of shoes in the single small closet. There was also a suitcase in the closet. Nothing in it. No indication anywhere in the apartment that Brayne had packed and taken off in a hurry. Even his razor and shaving cream were still on the sink in the tiny bathroom.

A tube of lipstick was in the cabinet over the sink.

Brown took off the top.

"Look like the lady's shade?" he asked Hawes. "Pretty careless if it's her, leavin' her o.c.p.'s in the dresser and her . . ."

"Her *what?*"

"Her open-crotch panties."

"Oh."

"You think she was dumb enough to be makin' it with him right here in this room?"

"Let's see what else we find," Hawes said.

What else they found was a sheaf of letters rubberbanded together. They found the letters in a cardboard shoe box on the top shelf of the closet. The letters were inside lavender-colored envelopes, but none of the envelopes had been stamped or mailed. The name "Jimmy" was scrawled on the front of each envelope.

"Hand-delivered," Hawes said.

"Mmm," Brown said, and they began reading the letters.

The letters were written in purple ink.

The first letter read:

> Jimmy,
> Just say when.
> *Marie*

It was dated July 18.

"When did he start working for them?" Brown asked.

"Fourth of July."

"Fast worker, this lady," Brown said.

The second letter was dated July 21. It described in excruciatingly passionate detail all the things Marie and Jimmy had done together the day before.

"This is dirty," Brown said, looking up.

"Yes," Hawes said. He was reading over Brown's shoulder.

There were twenty-seven letters in all. The letters chronicled a rather active sex life between the lady and the sorcerer's apprentice, Marie apparently having been compulsive about jotting down everything she had done to Jimmy in the recent past, and then outlining everything she hadn't yet done to him but which she planned to do to him in the foreseeable future, which—if the chronology was faithful—she did indeed get around to doing to him.

She did a lot of things to him.

The last letter was dated October 27, four days before the murder and dismemberment of the lady's husband. She suggested in this last letter that one of the things she wanted to do to Jimmy on Halloween night was tie him to the bed in his black silk undershorts and spread herself open over him in her black crotchless panties and then—

"You see any black silk undershorts in the dresser there?" Brown asked.

"No," Hawes said. "I'm reading."

"A celebration, do you think?" Brown asked. "All this stuff she planned to do to him on Halloween?"

"Maybe."

"Do hubby in, chop him up in little pieces, then come back here and have a witch's sabbath."

"Where does she call it that?"

"Call it what?"

"Witch's sabbath."

"*I'm* calling it that," Brown said. "Black silk undershorts, black o.c.p's . . ."

"So where's Brayne?" Hawes asked. "If they were planning a celebration . . ."

"Did you look under the bed?" Brown asked, and then turned suddenly toward the window.

Hawes turned at exactly the same moment.

An automobile had just pulled into the driveway.

At ten minutes to one—ten minutes after Bobby had suggested that they go out-side—Eileen excused herself and went to the ladies room. Annie, sitting at a table with an Italian sailor who was having difficulty making his needs understood, watched her as she crossed the room and made a left turn at the phone booths.

"Excuse me," Annie said.

By the time she got to the ladies room, Eileen was already in one of the stalls. Annie did a quick check for feet. The other stalls were empty.

"Yes or no?" she asked.

"Yes," Eileen said.

Her voice from behind the closed door sounded odd.

"Are you sure?"

"I think so."

"You okay?"

"Fine. Checking out the hardware."

The door opened. Eileen looked pale. She went to the sink, touched up her lipstick, blotted it.

"You going out now?" Annie asked.

"Yes."

The same odd voice.

"Give me three minutes to get on the street," Annie said.

"Okay."

Annie went to the door.

"I'll be there," she said simply.

"Good," Eileen said.

Annie took one last look at her, and then went out.

*   *   *

"What I'm talking about is decency and honor," Peaches said.

It was very cold and they were walking along the street rapidly.

"I'm talking about a person's responsibility to another person," Peaches said, clinging to Parker's arm for warmth and nothing else.

Parker was beginning to feel married.

"You went to that party with *me,*" Peaches said, "and not with Little Miss Muffet."

"If a person can't have a simple conversation with another person . . ."

"That wasn't a conversation," Peaches said. "That was a person-and-a-half exchanging deep sighs and meaningful glances."

"I don't think it's nice of you to make midget jokes," Parker said.

"Oh, was she a midget?" Peaches said. "I thought maybe she'd shrunk in the wash."

"That's just what I mean," Parker said.

"I thought maybe she was E.T. in drag."

"I'm sorry if you're upset," he said.

"I am upset."

"And I'm sorry."

He *was* sorry. He was thinking it was getting to be a very cold night after a lovely day in the tropics, and he would much prefer spending the winter in Peaches' probably warm and generous bed here in town instead of in his own narrow, mean bed in his grubby little apartment away the hell out in Majesta. He was also thinking tomorrow was time enough to give Alice a call.

"What bothers me is I thought we were having such a good time together," Peaches said.

"We were. We still are. The night is young," he said.

"I thought you sort of liked me."

"I do like you. I like you a lot."

"I like you, too," Peaches said.

"So where's the problem? There's no problem. I don't see any problem. What we'll do," Parker said, "is we'll go back to your place, and we'll have a drink, and maybe watch some television . . ."

"That sounds nice," she said, and hugged his arm.

"It does, doesn't it?" he said. "It does sound nice."

"And we'll forget all about Eeansie-Beansie Spider."

"Who?" Parker said.

"Your little friend," Peaches said.

"I already forgot about her," Parker said.

They were just passing one of those subway-kiosk newsstands on the corner. The blind owner was kneeling over a stack of newspapers on the pavement, cutting the cord around them. Parker came up beside him. The blind man knew he was there, but he took his good sweet time cutting the cord. Parker waited; he prided himself on never having hassled a blind man in his life. The blind man finally hefted the papers up onto the newsstand and then walked around to the little door on the side of the stand and went in behind the counter.

"So?" he said.

Parker was looking down at the headline.

"You want a paper?" the blind man said.

The headline read:

2 COPS SHOT
4 MIDGETS SOUGHT

The car in the driveway of the Sebastiani house was a 1979 Cadillac Seville, silver-sided with a black hardtop, still in seemingly excellent condition. The woman who got out of the Caddy was in excellent condition herself, tall and leggy and wearing a black cloth coat the color of her hair. Hawes and brown watched her from the upstairs window of the garage as she went directly to the front door of the house and rang the bell.

Hawes looked at his watch.

A few minutes before one in the morning.

"Who the hell is that?" he said.

They came out of Larry's Bar at exactly 1:00 A.M., twenty minutes after Bobby had first suggested they leave. A strong wind was blowing off the canal. He had insisted that she continue wearing his jacket, and she still had it draped over her shoulders. She hoped it wouldn't get in the way when she yanked the gun. Her hand hovered over the open top of her bag, seemingly resting there close to the shoulder strap. But close to the butt of the gun, too.

Bobby had his right hand in his pants pocket.

On the knife, she thought.

He had slashed his first victim in a doorway two blocks from the bar.

The second one in an alleyway on East Ninth.

The third on Canalside itself, heavily trafficked with hookers.

"Pretty cold out here," he said. "Not exactly what I had in mind."

Annie was the first of the three detectives to spot them coming out of the bar.

She had hit the street the moment she'd left Eileen in the ladies' room, and had taken up position in the darkened doorway of a closed Chinese noodle factory. It was very cold out here on the street, and she wasn't dressed for it. Skirt too damn short, blouse too flimsy. Eileen came out of the bar like a flare, red hair blowing on the wind, the guy's jacket draped over her shoulders, made an immediate left turn, walking on the guy's right, her own right hand on the curb side and resting on her bag. The guy's right hand was in his pants pocket.

Two of the lamp posts on Fairview had been vandalized, and there were wide stretches of darkness between the light on the corner and the third one up. On the distant corner, a traffic light turned to red as flaming as Eileen's hair. The red hair was a plus. Easy to keep her in view. Annie gave them a twenty-yard lead, and then fell into step behind them, keeping close to the buildings on her left, the guy's blind side because he was turned to the right as he walked and talked. She cursed the hooker heels she was wearing because they made such a clatter on the sidewalk, but the guy seemed unaware of her presence behind them, just kept chatting up Eileen as they dissolved into the darkness between the lighted lamp posts.

Eileen's red hair was the beacon.

Kling, scanning the street from a vantage point diagonally across from the bar, was the second detective to spot them.

The street was dark where he waited in the shadow of an abandoned tool works, the lamp post globe shattered, but the woman was unmistakably Eileen. Never mind the red hair, he'd have known her if she was wearing a blonde wig. Knew every nuance of her walk, the long stride, the swing of her shoulders, the rhythmic jiggle of her buttocks. He was about to move out, cross the street and fall in behind them, when he saw Annie.

Good, he thought, she's in place.

He stayed on the opposite side of the street, ten feet behind Annie who was working hard to keep up without showing herself. Eileen and the guy were walking very fast, up toward the traffic light on the corner, which changed now, throwing a green wash onto the roadway. The formation could have been a classic tailing triangle—one cop behind the quarry, another cop ahead of them on the same side of the street, a third cop on the opposite side of the street—except that it was lacking the third cop.

Or so Kling thought.

Shanahan was the third cop.

He had been tailing Kling from the moment he'd spotted him peering through the plate-glass window of the bar. Pacing the street impatiently, always circling back to the bar, checking out the front door from across the street, then drifting off again, and back again, behaving very much like a person waiting for somebody to come out of there. When Eileen finally came out of the bar with a *second* blond guy, Shanahan's blond took off after them. Annie was up ahead, she had Eileen and her blond covered and in sight. But this other blond guy was still showing too much interest. Shanahan gave him a lead, and then fell in behind him again.

Up ahead, Eileen and her blond turned left at the traffic light, and disappeared around the corner.

Shanahan's blond hesitated only a moment.

Seemed undecided whether to make his move or not.

Then he pulled a gun and started across the street.

Annie recognized Kling at once.

He had a gun in his hand.

She didn't know whether she was more surprised by his presence here or by the gun in his hand. Too many thoughts clicked through her mind in the next three seconds. She thought He's going to blow it, the guy hasn't made his move yet. She thought Does Eileen know he's here? She thought—

But Eileen and her man were already around the corner and out of sight.

"Bert!" she shouted.

And in that instant Shanahan came thundering up yelling, "Stop! Police!"

                    *   *   *

Kling turned to see a man pointing an arm in a plaster cast at him.

He turned the other way and saw Annie running across the street.

"Mike!" Annie shouted.

Shanahan stopped dead in his tracks. Annie was waving her arms at him like a traffic cop.

"He's on the job!" she shouted.

Shanahan had earlier told Eileen that he and Lou Alvarez were just full of tricks. He hadn't realized, however, that Alvarez had sent another man to the Zone without telling him about it. That tricky, he didn't think Alvarez was. Shanahan's own little trick was a .32 revolver in his right hand, his finger inside the trigger guard, the gun and the hand encased in the plaster cast. He felt like an asshole now, the plaster cast still pointed at a guy Annie had just identified as a cop.

The realization came to all three of them in the same instant. The traffic light on the corner turned red again as though signaling the coming of their mutual dawn.

Without a word, they looked up the street.

It was empty.

Eileen and her man were gone.

A minute ago, she'd had three backups.

Now she didn't have any.

Dolores Eisenberg was Frank Sebastiani's older sister.

Five-feet ten-inches tall, black hair and blue eyes, thirty-eight, thirty-nine years old. Hugging Marie to her when Brown and Hawes came over from the garage. Tears in the eyes of both women.

Marie introduced her to the cops.

Dolores seemed surprised to see them there.

"How do you do?" she said, and glanced at Marie.

"We're sorry for your trouble," Brown said.

An old Irish expression. Hawes wondered where he'd picked it up.

Dolores said, "Thank you," and then turned to Marie again. "I'm sorry it took me so long to get here," she said. "Max is in Cincinnati, and I had to find a sitter. God, wait'll he hears this. He's crazy about Frank."

"I know," Marie said.

"I'll have to call him again," Dolores said. "When Mom told me what happened, I tried to reach him at the hotel, but he was out. What time was that, when you called Mom?"

"It must've been around eleven-thirty," Marie said.

"Yeah, she called me right afterward. I felt like I'd been hit by a locomotive. I tried to get Max, I left a message for him to call me, but then I left the house around midnight, as soon as the sitter got there. I'll have to call him again."

She was still wearing her overcoat. She took it off now, revealing a trim black skirt and a crisp white blouse, and carried it familiarly to the coatrack. They were still standing in the entrance hall. The house seemed exceptionally still at this hour of the morning. The heater came on with a sudden whooosh.

"Would anyone like some coffee?" Dolores asked.

A take-charge lady, Hawes thought. Tragedy in the family, here she is at one in the morning, ready to make coffee.

"There's some on the stove," Marie said.

"Officers?" Dolores said.

"Thank you, no," Brown said.

"No, thanks," Hawes said.

"Marie? Honey, can I get a cup for you?"

"I'm all right, Dolores, thank you."

"Poor baby," Dolores said, and hugged her sister-in-law close again. Her arm still around her, she looked at Brown and said, "My mother told me you think Jimmy did it, is that right?"

"That's a strong possibility," Brown said, and looked at Marie.

"You haven't found him, though?"

"No, not yet."

"It's hard to believe," Dolores said, and shook her head. "My mother said you have to do an autopsy. I wish you wouldn't, really. That's really upsetting to her."

It occurred to Brown that she did not yet know her brother's body had been dismembered. Hadn't Marie told the family? He debated breaking the news, opted against it.

"Well, ma'am," he said, "an autopsy's mandatory in any trauma death."

"Still," Dolores said.

Brown was still looking at Marie. It had further occurred to him that on the phone with Dolores not an hour ago, she herself advised her sister-in-law about the autopsy. Yet now Dolores sounded as if the information had come from her mother. He tried to remember the exact content of the phone conversation. Marie's end of it, anyway.

Hello Dolores, no, not yet, I'm down in the kitchen.

Which meant her sister-in-law had asked her if she was in bed, or getting ready for bed, or whatever, and she'd told her No, I'm down here with two detectives. Which meant that Dolores *knew* there were two detectives here, so why had she looked so surprised to *find* them here?

They want to look at the garage room.

So you had to figure Dolores had asked her what two detectives were doing there. And she'd told her. And then the business about the autopsy. Which Dolores had just now talked about as if it had come from her mother. But if Dolores had called her just before leaving the house . . . well, wait a minute.

On the phone, Marie hadn't said anything about expecting her, nothing like "See you soon then," or "Hurry on over," or "Drive safely," just "I'll let you know," meaning about the autopsy, "Thanks for calling."

Brown decided to play it flat out.

He looked Dolores dead in the eye and said, "Did you call here about an hour ago?"

And the telephone rang.

Brown figured there had to be a god.

Because if the earlier ringing of the phone had visibly startled Marie, this time the ringing caused an immediate look of panic to flash in her eyes. She turned toward the kitchen as if it had suddenly burst into flames, made an abortive start out of the entrance hall, stopped, said, "I wonder . . ." and then looked blankly at the detectives.

"Can't be Dolores again, can it?" Brown said.

"What?" Dolores said, puzzled.

"Better go answer it," Brown said.

"Yes," Marie said.

"I'll go with you," he said.

In the kitchen, the phone kept ringing.

Marie hesitated.

"Want me to get it?" Brown asked.

"No, I'll . . . it may be my mother-in-law," she said, and headed immediately for the kitchen, Brown right behind her.

The phone kept ringing.

She was thinking You goddamn fool, I *told* you the cops were here!

She reached out for the receiver, her mind racing.

Brown was standing in the doorway to the kitchen now, his arms folded across his chest.

Marie lifted the receiver from the hook.

"Hello?" she said.

And listened.

Brown kept watching her.

"It's for you," she said, sounding relieved, and handed the receiver to him.

13

Parker felt like a real cop again.

A working detective.

The feeling was somewhat exhilarating.

The newspaper story accompanying the headline told him everything he needed to know about the liquor-store holdups tonight. The story extensively quoted Detective Meyer Meyer who had been interviewed in his room at Buenavista Hospital. Meyer had told the reporter that the heists and subsequent felony murders had been executed by four midgets being driven by a big blonde woman in a blue station wagon. One of the holdup victims had described the thieves as midgets. She had further told the police that one of the midgets was named Alice.

Parker did not have to be a detective to know that there couldn't be too many midgets named Alice in this city. But making the connection so quickly made him feel like a real cop again. He put Peaches in a taxi—even though they were only four blocks from her apartment—told her he'd try to call her later, and then hailed a cruising patrol car. The two uniformed cops in the car advised Parker they were from the Three-One—which Parker knew anyway since the number of the precinct was on the side of the car—and they didn't know if they had authority to provide transportation for a detective from the Eight-Seven.

Parker said, "This is a homicide here, open the fucking door!"

The two uniformed cops looked at each other by way of consultation, and then the cop riding shotgun unlocked the back door for him. Parker sat in the back of the car like a common criminal, a metal grille separating him from the two cops up front.

"Four-oh-three Thompson Street," he told the driver.

"That's all the way down the Quarter," the driver complained.

"That's right, it should take you fifteen, twenty minutes."

"Half hour's more like it," the shotgun cop said, and then got on the walkie-talkie to tell his sergeant they were driving a bull from the Eight-Seven downtown.

The sergeant said, "Let me talk to him."

"He's in back," the shotgun cop said.

"Stop the car and let me talk to him," the sergeant said. He sounded very no-nonsense. Parker had met sergeants like him before. He loved trampling on sergeants like him.

They stopped the car and opened the back door. The shotgun cop handed the walkie-talkie in to Parker.

"What's the problem?" Parker said into it.

"Who's this?" the sergeant said.

"Detective Andrew Lloyd Parker," he said, "Eighty-Seventh Squad. Who's this?"

"Never mind who this is, what's the idea commandeering one of my cars?"

"The idea is homicide," Parker said. "The idea is two cops in the hospital. The idea is I gotta get downtown in a hurry, and I'd hate like hell for the media to find out a sergeant from the Three-One maybe stood in the way of a timely arrest. That's the idea. You think you got it?"

There was a long silence.

"Who's your commanding officer?" the sergeant asked, trying to save face.

"Lieutenant Peter Byrnes," Parker said. "We finished here?"

"You can take the car downtown, but I'll be talking to your lieutenant," the sergeant said.

"Good, you talk to him," Parker said, and handed the walkie-talkie to the shotgun cop. "Let's get rolling," he said.

They closed the back door again. The driver set the car in motion.

"Hit the hammer," Parker said.

The blues looked sidelong at each other. This kind of thing didn't seem to warrant use of the siren.

"Hit the fucking hammer," Parker said.

The driver hit the siren-switch.

They were sitting in the living room when Brown got off the phone. Marie and her sister-in-law side by side on the sofa, Hawes in an easy chair opposite them.

Brown walked in looking very solemn.

"Hal Willis," he said to Hawes.

"What's up?" Hawes said.

Brown tugged casually at his earlobe before he started talking again. Hawes picked up the signal at once. Little dog-and-pony act on the way.

"They found the rest of the body," Brown said.

Marie looked at him.

"Head and the hands," Brown said. "In the river. I'm sorry, ma'am," he said to Dolores, "but your brother's body was dismembered. I hate to break it to you this way."

"Oh my *God!*" Dolores said.

Marie was still looking at Brown.

"Guys dredging the river pulled up this aluminum case, head and the hands in it," he said.

Hawes was trying to catch the drift. He kept listening intently. "Did you know this?" Dolores asked Marie.

Marie nodded.

"You knew he'd been . . . ?"

"Yes," she said. "I didn't tell Mom because I knew what it would do to her."

"Monoghan responded," Brown said to Hawes, "phoned the squad. Willis went on over with the stuff on my desk."

The stuff on his desk, Hawes thought. The reports, the positive ID, the poster he'd taken from the high school bulletin board.

"I hate to have to go over this another time, Mrs. Sebastiani," Brown said, "but I wonder if you can give me a description of your husband again. So we can close this out."

"I have it right here," Hawes said. He was beginning to catch on. Nobody closed out a case while the murderer was still running around loose. He took his notebook from the inside pocket of his jacket, flipped through the pages. "Male, white, thirty-four years old . . ." he said.

"That right?" Brown asked Marie.

"Yes," she said.

"Five-eleven," Hawes said, "one-seventy . . ."

"Mrs. Sebastiani?"

"Yes."

Eyes flashing with intelligence now. Hawes figured she was beginning to catch on, too. Didn't know exactly what was coming, but was bracing herself for it. Hawes didn't know exactly what was coming, either. But he had a hunch.

"Hair black," he said, "Eyes . . ."

"Why do we have to go over this again?" she said. "I identified the body, you have everything you . . ."

"My brother's hair was black, yes," Dolores said softly, and patted Marie's hand.

"Eyes blue," Hawes said.

"Blue eyes, yes," Dolores said. "Like mine."

"Will I have to come into the city again?" Marie asked. "To look at . . . at what they . . . they found in the . . . ?"

"Mrs. Sebastiani," Brown said, "the head we found in the river doesn't match your husband's photograph."

Marie blinked at him.

Silence.

Then:

"Well . . . does . . . does that mean . . . what does that mean?"

"It means the dead man isn't your husband," Brown said.

"Has someone made a mistaken then?" Dolores asked at once. "Are you saying my brother isn't dead?"

"Mrs. Sebastiani," Brown said, "would you mind very much if I read you this description you gave me of Jimmy Brayne?"

"I really don't see why we have to go over this a hundred times," she said. "If you were doing your job right, you'd have *found* Jimmy by now."

Brown had already taken out his notebook.

"White male," he read, "thirty-two years old. Height, six feet. Weight, a hundred and eighty . . ."

"Yes," she said impatiently.

Eyes alert now. Hawes had seen those eyes before. Desperate eyes, trapped eyes. Brown was closing in, and she knew it.

"Hair black, eyes brown."

"Yes," she said again.

"Mrs. Sebastiani, the eyes were brown."

"Yes, I just told you . . ."

"On the head in the river. The eyes were brown." He turned to Dolores. "Does your brother have an appendectomy scar?" he asked.

"A what?"

"Did he ever have his appendix removed?"

"No. I don't understand what you . . ."

"Was he ever in a skiing accident? Did he ever tear the cartilage on his . . ."

"He never skied in his life," Dolores said.

She looked extremely puzzled now. She glanced at Marie.

"The techs printed the fingers and thumbs on both hands," Brown said. "We're running a comparison check right this minute. Was your brother ever in the service?"

"Yes. The Army."

"Would you know if Jimmy Brayne was ever in the service?"

"I don't know."

"Or in any security-sensitive job? How about you, Mrs. Sebastiani? You seem to know a lot about Jimmy Brayne, maybe you know whether he's ever been finger-printed."

"All I know about him . . ."

"Right down to his beauty spot," Brown said, and snapped the notebook shut.

"Marie, what is he talking about?" Dolores asked.

"I think she knows what I'm talking about," Brown said.

Marie said nothing.

"If the prints come up blank," Brown said, "we've still got the head. Someone'll identify him. Sooner or later, we'll get a positive ID."

She still said nothing.

"He's Jimmy Brayne, isn't he?" Brown asked.

Silence.

"You and your husband killed Jimmy Brayne, didn't you?" he said.

She sat quite still, her hands folded on the lap of her robe.

"Mrs. Sebastiani," Brown said, "would you like to tell us where your husband is?"

Parker opened the door with a skeleton key.

On the sofa bed in the living room, a male midget and a female midget were asleep. They jumped up the minute the door opened.

"Hello," Parker said softly, and showed them the gun.

Wee Willie Winkie was one of the midgets. He was wearing striped pajamas. He looked cute as a button, but his face went pale the moment he saw the gun. His wife, Corky, was wearing panties and a baby-doll nightgown. Pink. She grabbed a pillow and hugged it to her breasts as Parker approached the bed. Light from the hallway spilled illumination into the room. It glinted on the gun in Parker's hand. Corky's brown eyes were opened wide. She kept holding the pillow to her breasts. Parker thought she looked a little bit like Debbie Reynolds.

"Are the others asleep?" he whispered.

Willie nodded.

"Where?"

Willie pointed to a pair of closed doors.

"Up," Parker whispered.

They got out of bed. Corky looked embarrassed in only her nightgown and panties. She kept holding the pillow to her in front, but her back was exposed. Parker gestured with the gun.

"We're going to wake them up," he whispered. "Don't yell or I'll shoot you both."

In one of the bedrooms, Oliver Twist was asleep with a full-sized woman. The woman was very fat and very blonde. Parker remembered the old joke about the midget marrying the circus fat lady and running around the bed all night yelling, "Mine, all mine!"

He nudged the midget.

The midget popped up in bed.

Red hair all mussed, blue eyes wide.

"Shhhh," Parker said. "It's the police."

Oliver blinked. So did Willie. This was the first he was hearing of this. Up to now, he'd thought they were dealing with a burglar, which was bad enough. Now he knew it was a cop in here, his worst nightmare realized. He glanced at Corky, his eyes blaming his wife for her goddamn friendship with Little Annie Oakley and her trigger-happy finger.

"Wake up your lady," Parker said to Oliver.

Oliver nudged the fat blonde.

She rolled over.

He nudged her again.

"Go away," she said.

Parker pulled the blanket off her. She was wearing a long granny nightgown. She tried to pull the blanket back over her again, grasped futilely at only thin air, and then sat up, annoyed and still half-asleep.

"Police," Parker said, smiling.

"What?" she said, blinking.

"You the one did the driving?" he said.

"What driving?" she said.

"She don't know what driving," Parker said to Oliver, still smiling.

"Quentin did the driving," Oliver said. "This lady had nothing to do with any of it."

"Any of what?" the blonde said.

Quentin, Parker thought. The guy at the party.

"Where is he?" he asked.

"In the other room," Oliver said.

"Let's go tell him the party's over," Parker said. "Get out of bed. Both of you." They got out of bed.

"Is this a joke?" the blonde whispered to Oliver.

"I don't think it's a joke," Oliver whispered back.

Parker herded the four of them into the other bedroom. The radiator was hissing, and the room was suffocatingly hot. Parker snapped on the lights. Quentin Forbes was in bed with Alice. Neither of them stirred. They had thrown back the covers in their sleep, and they were both naked. Alice looked as pretty as a little doll, her blonde hair fanned out over the pillow.

"Police!" Parker shouted, and they both jumped up at the same time. "Hello, Alice," he said, and smiled.

"Hello, Andy," she said, and smiled back.

"We have to get dressed now," he said, as if to a child.

"Okay," she said, and reached under the pillow.

Parker said it even before he saw the gun in her hand.

"Don't."

She hesitated.

"Please, Alice," he said. "Don't."

She must have discerned something in his eyes. She must have known she was looking into the eyes of a cop who had seen it all and heard it all.

"Okay," she said, and put down the gun.

Forbes said, "This is an outrage."

"It is, I know," Parker said.

"Let me see your badge," the blonde said.

Parker showed her his shield.

"What is this?" she asked.

"Let's get dressed now," he said, and went to the window and yelled down for the two uniformed cops from the Three-One.

There were only three pairs of handcuffs among them, and six people to cuff. This was a problem in the law of supply and demand. One of the blues went downstairs again and radioed for assistance, making it clear this wasn't a 10-13, they just needed some more handcuffs. The sergeant at the Twelfth wanted to know what two blues from the Three-One and a detective from the Eight-Seven were doing on his turf, but he sent a car around with the extra cuffs. By the time the cuffs arrived, Parker had personally searched the apartment. He'd found a valise full of money. He'd found a trunk with costumes and masks and wigs in it. He'd found four .22-caliber Zephyr revolvers and a Colt .45-caliber automatic.

He figured he had a case.

When they put the cuffs on her, Alice was wearing a pair of tailored gray slacks, a long-sleeved pink blouse, a double breasted navy-blue jacket with brass buttons, blue patent leather shoes with French heels, and a little navy-blue overcoat. She looked adorable.

As they went out of the apartment together, she said, "It didn't have to happen this way, you know."

"I know," Parker said.

Willis hoped there wasn't a gun in the room here. He hoped there wouldn't be shooting. With O'Brien along . . .

"Police," O'Brien said, and knocked on the door again.

Silence inside the room there.

Then the sound of a window scraping open.

"He's moving!" Willis said.

He was already backing away from the door and raising his right leg for a piston-kick. Arms wide for leverage, he looked like a football player going for the extra point. His leg lashed out, the sole and heel of his shoe hitting the door flat, just above the knob. The latch sprang, the door swung inward, O'Brien following it into the room, gun extended. Don't let there be another gun in here, Willis thought.

A man in his undershorts was halfway out the window.

"That's a long drop, mister," O'Brien said.

The man hesitated.

"Mr. Sebastiani?" Willis said.

The man still had one leg over the windowsill. There was no fire escape out there. Willis wondered where the hell he thought he was going.

"My name is Theo Hardeen," he said.

"So your wife mentioned," Willis said.

"My wife? I don't know what you're talking about."

They never knew what anyone was talking about.

"Mr. Sebastiani," Willis said, "at this very moment, your wife is driving in from Collinsworth with two detectives from the Eighty-Seventh Squad, upon whose instructions and advice we're . . ."

"I don't have any wife in . . ."

"They also have a chain saw in the car," O'Brien said.

"They found a chain saw, in your garage," Willis said.

"There's a lot of blood on the saw," O'Brien said.

"Sir, we're arresting you for the crime of murder," Willis said, and then began reeling off Miranda-Escobedo by rote. Sebastiani listened to the recitation as though he were being lectured. He still had one leg over the windowsill.

"Mr. Sebastiani?" Willis said. "You want to come in off that window now?"

Sebastiani came in off the window.

"She blew it, huh?" he said.

"You both did," Willis said.

This time is for real, Carella thought.

No tricks this time.

This time I go west.

Swirling darkness, blinking lights, aurora borealis, murmuring voices, beeping sounds, everything so fake and far away, but everything so real and immediate, it was funny. Floating somewhere above himself, hovering above himself like the angel of death, "Wear this garlic around your neck," Grandma used to say, "it'll keep away the angel of death," but where's the garlic now, Grandma? Crisp white sheets and soft feather pillows, tomato sauce cooking on the old wood stove in the kitchen, your eyeglasses steaming up, the time Uncle Jerry ate the rat shit, thinking it was olives, everyone gone now, is Meyer dead, too?

Jesus, Meyer, don't be dead.

Please don't be dead.

Floating on the air above himself, looking down at himself, the big hero, some hero, open to the world, open to the hands and eyes of strangers, an open book, don't let Meyer be dead, let me hold you, Meyer, let me hold you, friend. Let's go in now, did someone say that years and years ago? Open him up now, open up the hero, big editorial conference out there, but no last minute editorial decisions this time, no one here to say you can't kill the hero, big hero, some hero, cold-cocked by midgets, bang-bang, gotcha, close the book.

Exit.

But . . .

Please save that for later, okay? Save the final curtain for somewhere down the line, I'm a married man, give me a break. He almost laughed though nothing was funny, tried to laugh, wondered if he was smiling instead, heard someone say something through the fog rolling in off the water, heavy storm brewing out there, I never even learned to sail, he thought, I never had a yacht.

All the things I never did.

All the things I never had.

Well, listen, who's . . . ?

All the treasures.

Thirty-seven five a year doesn't buy treasures.

Ah, Jesus, Teddy, I never bought you treasures.

All the things I wanted to buy you.

Forgive me for the treasures, bless me father for I have sinned, A is for amethyst and B is for beryl, C is for coral and D is for diamonds, F is for furs and G is for gold and H is for heaven and I is for . . .

E is missing.

E is for exit.

But . . .

Please don't get ahead of me, please don't rush me, just give me a little time to finish the rest of the alphabet, I beg of you, please.

I is for me.

"Careful," someone said.

There's one hot-bed hotel the girls use, plus fifty of sixty rented rooms all over the zone.

Shanahan talking.

Too many hours ago.

She had lost her backups, she knew that.

She didn't know what had happened on the street outside, but they were gone, that was for sure.

So here we are, she thought.

Alone at last.

You and me.

Face to face.

Not in that single hot-bed hotel, where there was a chance they might find her before the crack of dawn, but in one of those fifty or sixty rented rooms. Lady downstairs taking the money from him, looking at it on the palm of her hand as if she expected a tip besides, up the stairs to the third floor, the smells of cooking permeating the hallways, terrific spot for a honeymoon, key in the door, the door opening on a room with a bed and a dresser and a wooden chair and a lamp and a tattered window shade, and a small door at the far end leading into a bathroom with only a toilet bowl and a soiled sink.

"It's small, but it's cheerful," he'd said, grinning, and then he'd locked the door behind them and put the key into the same pocket with the knife.

That was almost an hour ago.

He'd been talking ever since.

She kept reminding him that time was money, wanting him to make his move, get it over with, but he kept laying twenty-dollar bills on her, "A dollar a minute, right?" he said, and the empty minutes of the night kept ticking away, and he made no move to approach her.

She wondered if she should bust him, anyway. Here we go, mister, it's the Law, run a lineup for the pair of hookers who'd described him, run the risk of them either chickening out or not remembering, run the further risk—even *with* a positive ID—that he'd talk his way out of it, walk away from it. Two hookers claiming they saw him chatting up the victims didn't add up to a conviction. No. If he was their man, he had to move on her before she could bust him. Come at her with the knife. No easy way out of this one, she thought. It's still him and me, alone together in this room. And all I can do is wait. And listen.

She was learning a lot about him.

He was lying on the bed with his hands behind his head, looking up at the ceiling, and she was sitting in the wooden chair across the room near the dresser, her bag on the floor near her dangling hand, and she felt like a psychiatrist listening to a patient. The room was warm enough, she had to say that for it. Sizzling hot radiator throwing heat, she was almost getting drowsy, that's all she needed. His jacket draped over the back of the wooden chair now, his voice droning into the room. She saw with both feet planted firmly on the floor, legs slightly apart, gun strapped to her ankle inside the right boot. She was ready for anything. But nothing came. Except talk.

". . . that maybe *she* was partly to blame for what happened, you know?" he said. "My mother. Listen, I love her to death, don't get me wrong, she's the one who made my freedom possible, may she rest in peace. But when you think of it another way, was it all my *father's* fault? Can I just hold him responsible? For laying Elga? I mean, isn't my *mother* partly to blame for what happened?"

Elga again.

Hardly a sentence out of his mouth without some mention of the housekeeper.

"She was a schoolteacher, you know, my mother, did I tell you that?"

Only a hundred times, Eileen thought.

"Put him through medical school, left me with Elga all the while I was growing up, well, listen, I don't blame her for that. She was teaching to support the family, you know, that was a lot of responsibility. Do you know the one about the kindergarten teacher who gets the obscene phone call? She picks up the phone, she says, 'Hello?' and the voice on the other end says, 'Doo-doo, pee-pee, ca-ca,' well, that's an old one, you probably heard it. My mother didn't teach kindergarten, she was a high school teacher, worked in a tough school, long, hard hours, sometimes didn't get home till six or seven, had to correct papers all night long. I *hated* Elga. But what I'm saying, responsibility is a two-way street. If my father was laying Elga, maybe part of the fault was my mother's, do you see what I mean? She always said she hated teaching, but then why did she take it so seriously? Her sense of responsibility, sure. But shouldn't she have been responsible to her husband, too? To her son? Shouldn't she have taken care of *our* needs, too? I mean, shit, teaching didn't have to become an *obsession* with her, did it?"

I don't want to be your shrink, Eileen thought. I don't want to hear anything else about you, make your goddamn move!

But he wouldn't stop talking.

"Children sense things, don't you think?" he said. "I must have *known* something was wrong in that house. My father yelling at me all the time, my mother never there, there was tension in that house, you could cut it with a knife."

Silence.

She watched him on the bed.

Hands behind his head, staring up at the ceiling.

"I'll tell you the truth, I sometimes felt like killing her."

More silence.

Here it comes, Eileen thought.

"When I was a kid," he said.

And the silence lengthened.

"Fucking dedicated schoolteacher," he said.

She watched him.

"Ignoring the people who loved her."

Kept watching him. Ready. Waiting.

"I tried to make sense of it later, after she died. Let me all that money. This is for Robert's freedom to risk enjoying life. That was guilt talking, wasn't it? That was her guilt for having ignored us both."

Silence again.

"Do you know what she did once? Elga?"

"What did she do?"

"I was eight years old."

"What did she do?"

"She took off her bloomers."

Bloomers. A child's expression.

"Showed herself to me."

Silence.

"I ran away from her and locked myself in the bathroom."

Silence.

"My mother found me in there when she got home from school. Elga said I'd been a bad boy. Told my mother I'd locked myself in the bathroom and wouldn't come out. My mother asked me why I'd done that. Elga was standing right there. I said I was afraid of the lightning. It was raining that day. Elga smiled. The next time we were alone together, she . . . she . . . forced me to . . ."

He sat up suddenly.

"Do you know the one about the guy who goes into a sex shop to buy a merkin? The clerk says, 'Did you want this sent, sir, or will you take it with you?' The guy says, 'No, I'll just eat it here.' " He laughed harshly and abruptly and then said, "How would you like me to eat *your* pussy?"

"Sure," she said.

"Then take off your bloomers."

He swung his legs over the side of the bed.

"Come over here and take off your bloomers."

"You come here," Eileen said.

He stood up.

He put his right hand in his pocket.

She thought Yes, take out the knife, you son of a bitch.

And then she thought No, don't, Bobby.

And was suddenly confused again.

"Bobby," she said wearily, "I'm a cop."

"Sure," he said, "a cop."

"I don't want to hurt you," she said.

"Then don't bullshit me!" he said angrily. "I've had enough bullshit in my life!"

"I'm a cop," she said, and took the gun out of her bag, and leveled it at him. "Let's go find some help for you, okay?"

He looked at her. A smile cracked over his face.

"Is this a trick?" he said.

"No trick. I'm a cop. Let's go, okay?"

"Go where? Where do you want to go, baby?" He was still smiling.

But his hand was still in his pocket.

"Find some people you can talk to," she said.

"About what? There's nothing I have to say to . . ."

"Put the knife on the floor, Bobby."

She was standing now, almost in a policeman's crouch, the gun still leveled at him.

"What knife?" he said.

"The knife in your pocket, Bobby. Put it on the floor."

"I don't have a knife," he said.

"You have a knife, Bobby. Put it on the floor."

He took the knife out of his pocket.

"Good, now put it on the floor," she said.

"Suppose I don't?" he said.

"I know you will, Bobby."

"Suppose I lock myself in the bathroom instead?"

"No, you won't do that, Bobby. You're going to put the knife on the floor . . ."

"Like a good little boy, huh?"

"Bobby . . . I'm not your mother. I'm not Elga. I'm not going to hurt you. Just drop the knife on the floor . . ."

"Listen to the shrink," he said. "You're a fucking *hooker* is what you are, who the fuck do you think you're kidding?"

"Bobby, please drop the knife."

"Say pretty please," he said, and the blade snicked open.

The gun was in her hand, she had him cold.

"Don't move," she said.

The policeman's crouch more defined now, more deliberate. He took a step toward her.

"I'm warning you, don't move!"

"Do you know the one about the guy who goes into a bank to hold it up? He sticks the gun in the teller's face and says, 'Don't muss a moovle, this is a fuck-up!' "

Another step toward her.

"This isn't fun anymore," he said, and sliced the knife across the air between them.

"Whoosh," he said.

And came at her.

Her first bullet took him in the chest, knocking him backward toward the bed. She fired again almost at once, hitting him in the shoulder this time, spinning him around, and then she fired a third time, shooting him in the back, knocking him over onto the bed, and then—she would never understand why—she kept shooting into his lifeless body, watching the eruptions of blood along his spine, saying over and over again, "I gave you a chance, I gave you a chance," until the gun was empty.

Then she threw the gun across the room and began screaming.

Some people never change.

Genero didn't even seem to know she couldn't hear him.

He was there at the hospital to tell Carella what a hero he'd been, shooting four teenagers who'd firebombed a building.

He sat in the hallway talking to Teddy, who was praying her husband wouldn't die, praying her husband wasn't already dead.

". . . and all at once they came running out," he said. "Steve would've been proud of me. They threw the firebomb at me, but that didn't scare me, I . . ."

A doctor in a green surgical gown was coming down the hallway.

There was blood on the gown.

She caught her breath.

"Mrs. Carella?" he said.

She read his lips.

At first she thought he said, "We shot him."

A puzzled look crossed her face.

He repeated it.

"We got it," he said.

She let out her breath.

"He'll be okay," the doctor said.

"He'll be okay," Genero repeated.

She nodded.

And then she cupped her hands to her face and began weeping.

Genero just sat there.

Annie talked to him in the hallway of the Seven-Two.

"The landlady called 911 because somebody was screaming upstairs," she said. "She caters to hookers, she wouldn't have called unless she thought it was very serious."

Kling nodded.

"She quieted down just a little while ago. She's down the hall in Interrogation. I'm not sure you ought to talk to her."

"Why not?" Kling said.

"I'm just not sure," Annie said.

He went down the hall.

He opened the door.

She was sitting at the long table in the Interrogation Room, the two-way mirror behind her. Just sitting there. Looking at her hands.

"I'm sorry if I screwed up," he said.

"You didn't."

He sat opposite her.

"Are you okay?" he asked.

"No," she said.

He looked at her.

"I'm quitting," she said.

"What do you mean?"

"The force."

"No, you're not."

"I'm quitting Bert. I don't like what it did to me, what it keeps doing to me."

"Eileen, you ..."

"I'm quitting this city, too."

"Eileen ..."

"This fucking city," she said, and shook her head.

He reached for her hand. She pulled it away.

"No," she said.

"What about me?" he said.
"What about me?" she said.

The phone rang at a little past two in the morning.

She picked up the receiver.

"Peaches?" the voice said. "This is Phil Hendricks at Camera Works, we talked earlier tonight."

Him again!

"What I want you to do," he said, "I want you to take off your blouse and go look at yourself in the mirror. Then I want you to . . ."

"Listen, you creep," she said, "if you call me one more time . . ."

"This is Andy Parker," he said. "I'm in a phone booth on the corner. Is it too late to come up?"

"You dope," she said.

It was the last trick of the night.

ICE

1

It was still snowing hard when she came out of the theater.

The snow, wind driven, struck her face sharply as she stepped into the alley and closed the stage door behind her. She glanced upward, shaking her head as though reprimanding God, and grimaced at the myriad tiny darts of white swirling in the reflected glow of the hooded light hanging over the door. Reflexively, she lifted the collar of her coat, and then yanked the muffler from around her throat and draped it over her head like a scarf. Holding the ends together just under her chin, she began walking toward the street at the end of the alley.

In this city, there were only two good seasons, and even they were sometimes lousy. Winter and summer, you could forget entirely; they were either too hot or too cold. Like *this* winter, which had started in November instead of when it was supposed to. London was worse, she supposed. No, London was better. Well, at last London was dependable; London was *always* lousy. Well, that wasn't quite true, either. She could remember days, when she was living there—ah, those lovely balmy summer days, strolling up Piccadilly, blond pony tail swishing behind her, nineteen years old then and worlds ahead to conquer. Summertime in London.

The snow underfoot was at least a foot deep.

Luckily, she had decided to put on boots before leaving her apartment for the performance tonight, not because she was expecting snow—the snow hadn't begun until sometime after the curtain went up—but only because it was so damn *cold.* The boots afforded at least some protection. They were shin-high, her blue jeans and leg warmers tucked into them, her long gray cavalry officer's coat coming almost to their leather tops. There wasn't a taxicab in sight. Naturally. This city. She had lingered too long in the dressing room, leisurely cold-creaming off her makeup, getting out of the silver-spangled costume all the dancers wore for the finale, and then into her sweater, jeans, socks, leg warmers, and boots. She'd made her big mistake in listening so long to Molly. Molly was having trouble with her husband again. Molly's husband was an unemployed actor who seemed to hold her responsible for having landed a part in a hit musical while *he* was still running around town auditioning. Never mind that Molly's weekly salary paid the rent and put food on the table. Never mind that Molly, like *all* the gypsies in the show, busted her ass doing complicated routines six nights a week, not to mention Wednesday and Saturday matinees. Molly's husband kept railing at her, and in the dressing room Molly kept repeating his angry tirades, and it was all you could do to get out of there by eleven if you weren't careful. It was twenty past eleven now; Molly had gone on *forever.*

All the cabs had been snatched up by audiences pouring out into the night when the shows broke all up and down the street. She could either walk north to Lassiter and hope to catch an uptown bus on the corner there, or she could walk south to the Stem, and then four blocks east to the subway station, where she could catch an uptown train. The avenue bordering the theater on the north was perhaps the roughest in the entire city, thronged with hookers and pimps at all hours of the day, but especially after dark. Besides, with this snow, would the buses be running on schedule? No, the subway would be best.

When she reached the brightly lighted Stem, however, she was surprised to find that it was still crowded with people, despite the rotten weather. She stood on the street corner for a moment, debating whether it wouldn't be simpler just to *walk* home. She lived only ten blocks from the theater. If she took the subway, it meant walking the four blocks to the station, and then another block to her apartment building when she got off the train. Besides, would the subway be safer than the Stem at this hour of the night?

She decided to walk.

She walked with a dancer's peculiarly duckfooted waddle. She had been a dancer ever since she was nine—sixteen years now—including four years of study at the Sadler's Wells in London. She had been living then with an oboe player, a young man who could never understand why dancers looked so graceful onstage and so oddly awkward off. Walking duck-footedly, but briskly, she smiled at the memory, and thought again of London, and longed idiotically for the wet and gloomy winters there—winters *without* the stubborn cold that held this city in its icy grip for months on end. This was February. Spring was only a bit more than a month away. But where was it? She paced herself as if she were doing a routine, head ducked against the wind and the snow, so many strides to the corner, so many strides to the corner after that, pause there for the traffic light—*five* six seven eight—striding out again, the tails of her gray coat flapping in the wind, the snow swirling around her, the blinking lights on the rooftop billboards flashing palely through the fierce sharp flakes.

It was ten minutes to midnight when she reached her own corner.

She turned left at the familiar phone booth, banked with snow now, and began walking toward her building in the middle of the block.

In this city, the neighborhoods changed rapidly. Ten blocks farther downtown, it would have been extremely dangerous to stand on a street corner waiting for a bus at this time of night. But here, only half a mile uptown from the theater, the block between the Stem and Lassiter was a safe, secluded enclave of juxtaposed brownstones, high rises, and small shops. Her own building was midway between the two avenues. The shops, at this hour, were shuttered and dark. She passed the streetlamp two buildings down from her own and was approaching her own building when the man stepped out of the shadowed doorway to the service entrance.

Her head was still ducked against the blinding snow; at first, she only *sensed* his presence. She stopped. He was holding a gun in his hand. She knew only sudden lurching terror. She opened her mouth to scream, or to plead, or to shout for help, but the gun exploded and she felt a searing sensation below her left breast, and then she fell over backward onto the sidewalk, into the snow, blood bubbling from the wound and soaking the gray cavalry officer's coat.

He stood over her.

He glanced briefly over his shoulder.

He leveled the pistol at her head then and fired two shots directly into her face.

The girl lay wet and gray and red against the white snow.

The snow was still falling. A patrol car was angled in against the curb, its blinking red dome lights flashing red onto the red-stained snow around the girl. Two detectives from Midtown East stood looking down at the dead girl. Behind them, the two patrolmen who'd first responded to the call were putting up wooden police barricades and cardboard "Crime Scene" placards. One of the detectives was named Henry Levine, and he had been working for the police department since he was twenty-one. He was now forty-six. He looked down at the dead girl's shattered face without blinking. His partner was twenty-eight years old. He had been a cop for six years, and had only recently been promoted to Detective/Third Grade. The plastic-encased card clipped to the lapel of his overcoat identified him as Ralph Coombes. In the color photograph behind the plastic, he looked like a teenager.

"I never saw anything like this in my life," he said.

"Yeah," Levine said.

"Did you?"

"Yeah," Levine said. He looked over his shoulder to where the two patrolmen were working on the barricades. One of the wooden crossplanks refused to seat itself properly on the sawhorses. The patrolmen were swearing.

"You gonna be all night here?" Levine asked.

"This thing don't fit right," one of the patrolmen said.

"Her face all blown away," Coombes said, shaking his head.

"Leave it alone," Levine said to the patrolmen. "Come here a minute, willya?"

The heavier of the two patrolmen left the stubborn plank to his partner. He walked over through the snow, and put his hands on his hips.

"Who reported it?" Levine asked.

"Guy coming home from work. Lives there in the same building."

"What's his name?"

"I didn't get his name. Frank!" he called to his partner. "You get that guy's name?"

"What guy?" his partner yelled back. He had finally managed to get the crossplank seated on the sawhorses. Dusting off his gloves, he walked to where the other patrolman, his hands still on his hips, was standing with Levine. "What guy you talking about?" he asked.

"The guy who called it in," Levine said.

"Yeah, I got it here in my pad, just a second." He took off one glove, and began leafing through his pad. "I can't find it," he said. "What the hell did I do with it?"

"But he lives in the girl's building, huh?" Levine said, sighing.

"Yeah."

"And he's the one who called nine-one-one?"

"Yeah. Whyn't you go ask him yourself? He's inside there with the Homicide dicks."

Levine looked surprised. "Homicide's here already?"

"Got here before you did."

"How come?"

"They were cruising, picked up the ten-twenty-nine on the squawk box."

"Come on," Levine said to his partner.

The two Homicide detectives were standing in the lobby of the building with a man wearing a plaid mackinaw and a blue watch cap. The man was tall and thin and he looked frightened. The two Homicide detectives were burly and broad and they looked self-assured. They framed the thin frightened man like belligerent bookends.

"What time was this?" one of the Homicide detectives asked. His name was Monoghan.

"About twelve-thirty," the man said.

"Half-past midnight?" the other Homicide detective asked. His name was Monroe."

"Yes, sir."

"How'd you happen to find her?" Monoghan asked.

"I was coming home from work. From the subway."

"You live in this building?" Monroe asked.

"Yes, sir."

"And you were walking home?" Monoghan asked.

"From the subway?" Monroe asked.

"Yes, sir."

"What kind of work do you do, you're getting home so late?"

"I'm a bank guard," the man said.

"You get home this time every night?" Monoghan asked.

"Half-past midnight?" Monroe asked.

"Yes, sir. I'm relieved at twelve, it takes me a half hour to get home by subway. The subway station's a block away. I always walk home from the subway."

"And that's when you found the girl?" Monoghan asked.

"Walking home from the subway?" Monroe asked.

"Yes, sir."

"Look who's here," Monoghan said, spotting Levine as he came toward them. Monroe looked at his watch. "What took you so long, Henry?"

"We were on a coffee break," Levine said, deadpan. "Didn't want to rush it."

"Who's this?" Monoghan said.

"My partner. Ralph Coombes."

"You look a little green around the gills, Coombes," Monroe said.

"A little Irish around the gills," Monoghan said.

"You sure you two guys'll be able to handle this without your mamas here to wipe your asses?" Monroe said.

"At least the cops in Midtown East *have* mamas," Levine said.

"Oh, hilarious," Monoghan said.

"Sidesplitting," Monroe said.

"This here's Dominick Bonaccio," Monoghan said. "Man who found the body. He was coming home from work."

"From the subway station," Monroe said.

"Right, Bonaccio?" Monoghan said.

"Yes, sir," Bonaccio said. He looked even more frightened now that two other detectives had joined them.

"You think you can take over now?" Monoghan asked Levine. "The squeal's officially yours, am I right?"

"That's right," Levine said.

"Better call your mamas first," Monroe said.

"Tell 'em you're gonna be freezin' your asses off tonight," Monoghan said, and laughed.

"You feel like pizza?" Monroe asked him.

"I thought Chink's," Monoghan said. "Okay, you guys, it's yours. Keep us informed. In triplicate, if you don't mind."

"We'll keep you informed," Levine said.

The Homicide detectives nodded. First Monoghan nodded and then Monroe nodded. They looked at each other, looked at the two detectives from Midtown East, looked at Bonaccio, and then looked at each other again.

"Okay, pizza," Monoghan said, and both cops walked out of the building.

"Choke on it," Levine said, under his breath.

Coombes already had his notebook in his hand.

"Do you know who the girl is?" Levine asked Bonaccio.

"Yes, sir."

"How come? Her face is gone."

"I recognize the coat, sir."

"Uh-huh," Levine said.

"It's a new coat. I met her in the elevator on the day she bought it. She told me she got it in a thrift shop."

"Uh-huh," Levine said.

Coombes was writing.

"What's her name?" Levine said.

"Sally. I don't know her last name."

"Lives here in the building, huh?"

"Yes, sir. Third floor. She always gets on and off the elevator on the third floor."

"Would you know what apartment?"

"No, sir, I'm sorry."

Levine sighed. "What apartment do *you* live in, sir?"

"Six-B."

"Okay, go to sleep, we'll get in touch with you if we need you. Would you know where the super's apartment is?"

"On the ground floor, sir. Near the elevator."

"Okay, thanks a lot. Come on," he said to Coombes.

The rest was routine.

They awakened the superintendent of the building and elicited from him the information that the dead girl's name was Sally Anderson. They waited for the assistant M.E. to pronounce the girl officially dead, and then they waited while the Crime Unit boys took their pictures and their prints. They went through the dead girl's shoulder bag after everyone else was through with her. They found an address book, a tube of lipstick, a small packet of Kleenex tissues, an eyebrow pencil, two sticks of gum, and a wallet containing several photographs, twenty-three dollars in fives and singles, and a card identifying her as a member of Actors Equity. The ambulance carted her off to the morgue while they were making their drawings of the crime scene.

It was not until later that morning that Detective Steve Carella and the 87th Precinct were drawn into the case.

2

Well, there it is, Carella thought. Same old precinct. Hasn't changed a bit since I first started working here, probably won't change even after I'm dead and gone. Same rotten precinct.

He was walking uptown from the subway kiosk on Grover Avenue, approaching the station house from the west. He normally drove to work, but the streets in Riverhead hadn't yet been plowed when he'd awakened this morning, and he figured the subway would be faster. As it was, a switch had frozen shut somewhere on the track just before the train plunged underground at Lindblad Avenue, and he'd had to wait with another hundred shivering passengers until the trouble on the line was cleared. It was now almost 9:00 A.M. Carella was an hour and fifteen minutes late.

It was bitterly cold. He could understand how a switch could freeze in this weather; his *own* switch felt shrunken and limp in his trousers, even though he was wearing long woolen underwear. Just before Christmas, his wife had suggested that what he needed was a willy-warmer. He had never heard it called a willy before. He asked her where she'd picked up the expression. She said her uncle had always called her cousin's wee apparatus a willy. That figured. She had been Theodora Franklin before he'd married her, four-fifths Irish with (as she was fond of saying) a fifth of Scotch thrown in. So naturally her cousin owned a "wee apparatus" and naturally her uncle called it a "willy" and naturally she'd suggested just before Christmas that what a nice Italian boy like Carella could use in his stocking on Christmas morning was a nice mink willy-warmer. Carella told her he already *had* a willy-warmer, and it was better than mink. Teddy blushed.

He climbed the steps leading to the front door of the station house. A pair of green globes flanked the wooden entrance doors, the numerals 87 painted on each in white. The doorknob on the one operable door was the original brass one that had been installed when the building was new, sometime shortly after the turn of the century. It was polished bright by constant hand-rubbings, like the toes of a bronze saint in St. Peter's Cathedral. Carella grasped the knob, and twisted it, and opened the door, and stepped into the huge ground-floor muster room that was always colder than anyplace else in the building. This morning, compared with the glacier outside, it felt almost cozy.

The high muster desk was on the right side of the cavernous room, looking almost like a judge's altar of justice except for the waist-high brass railing before it and Sergeant Dave Murchison behind it, framed on one side by a sign that requested all visitors to stop and state their business, and on the other by an open ledger that held the records—in the process known as "booking"—of the various and sundry criminals who passed this way, day and night. Murchison wasn't booking anyone at the moment. Murchison was drinking a cup of coffee. He held the mug in thick fingers, the steam rising in a cloud around his jowly face. Murchison was a man in his fifties, somewhat stout, bundled now in a worn blue cardigan sweater that made him look chubbier than he actually was and that, besides, was nonregulation. He looked up as Carella passed the desk.

"Half a day today?" he asked.

"Morning, Dave," Carella said. "How's it going?"

"Quiet down *here,*" Murchison said, "but wait till you get upstairs."

"So what else is new?" Carella said, and sighed heavily, and walked for perhaps the ten-thousandth time past the inconspicuous and dirty white sign nailed to the wall, its black lettering announcing DETECTIVE DIVISION, its pointing, crudely drawn hand signaling any visitors to take the steps up to the second floor. The stairs leading up were metal, and narrow, and scrupulously clean. They went up for a total of sixteen risers, then turned back on themselves and continued on up for another sixteen risers, and there he was, automatically turning to the right in the dimly lighted corridor. He opened the first of the doors labeled with a LOCKERS sign, went directly to his own locker in the row second closest to the door, twisted the dial on the combination lock, opened the locker door, and hung up his coat and muffler. He debated taking off the long johns. No, on a day like today, the squadroom would be cold.

He went out of the locker room and started down the corridor, passing a wooden bench on his left and wondering for the thousandth time who had carved the initials C.J. in a heart on one arm of the bench, passing a backless bench on the right and set into a narrow alcove before the sealed doors of what had once been an elevator shaft, passing a door also on the right and marked MEN'S LAVATORY, and a door on his left over which a small sign read CLERICAL. The detective squadroom was at the end of the corridor.

He saw first the familiar slatted wooden rail divider. Beyond that, he saw desks and telephones, and a bulletin board with various photographs and notices on it, and a hanging light glove, and beyond that more desks and the grilled windows that opened on the front of the building. He couldn't see very much that went on beyond the railing on his right because two huge metal filing cabinets blocked the desks on that side of the room. But the sounds coming from beyond the cabinets told him the place was a zoo this morning.

Detective Richard Genero's portable radio, sitting on the corner of his desk in miniaturized Japanese splendor, blasted a rock tune into the already dissonant din. Genero's little symphony meant that the lieutenant wasn't in yet. Without a by-your-leave, Carella went directly to Genero's desk, and turned off the radio. It helped, but not much. The sounds in this squadroom were as much a part of his working day as were the look and the feel of it. He sometimes felt he was more at home in this scarred and flaking, resonating apple green room than he was in his own living room.

Everyone on the squad thought Carella looked short when he wore a turtleneck. He was not short. He was close to six feet tall, with the wide shoulders, narrow hips, and sinewy movements of a natural athlete—which he was not. His eyes, brown and slanted slightly downward, gave his face a somewhat Oriental look that prompted the squadroom wags to claim he was distantly related to Takashi Fujiwara, the only Japanese-American detective on the squad. Tack told them it was true; he and Carella *were,* in fact, cousins—a blatant lie. But Tack was very young, and he admired Carella a great deal, and was really fonder of him than he was of his no-good *real* cousins. Carella knew how to say "Good morning" in Japanese. Whenever Tack came into the squadroom—morning, noon, or night—Carella said, "Oh-hi-oh." Tack answered, "Hello, cousin."

Carella was wearing a turtleneck shirt under his sports jacket that Saturday morning. The first thing Meyer Meyer said to him was, "Those things make you look short."

"They keep me warm," Carella said.

"Is it better to be warm or tall?" Meyer asked philosophically, and went back to his typing.

He did not, even under normal circumstances, enjoy typing. Today, because of the very pregnant lady across the room who was shouting Spanish obscenities at the world in general and at Detective Cotton Hawes and an appreciative chorus of early-morning drunks in particular, Meyer found it even more difficult to concentrate on the keyboard in front of him. Patiently, doggedly, he kept typing, while across the room the pregnant lady was loudly questioning Cotton Hawes's legitimacy.

Meyer's patience was an acquired skill, nurtured over the years until it had reached a finely honed edge of perfection. He had certainly not been born patient. He had, however, been born with all the attributes that would later make a life of patience an absolute necessity if he were to survive. Meyer's father had been a very comical man. At the *briss,* the classic circumcision ceremony, Meyer's father made his announcement. The announcement concerned the name of his new off-spring. The boy was to be called Meyer Meyer. The old man thought this was exceedingly humorous. The *moile* didn't think it was so humorous. When he heard the announcement, his hand almost slipped. In that moment, he almost deprived Meyer of something more than a normal name. Fortunately, Meyer Meyer emerged unscathed.

But being an Orthodox Jew in a predominantly gentile neighborhood can be trying even if your name isn't Meyer Meyer. As with all things, something had to give. Meyer Meyer had begun losing his hair when he was still rather young. He was now completely bald, a burly man with china blue eyes, slightly taller than Carella—even when Carella *wasn't* wearing a turtleneck. He was smoking a cigar as he typed, and wishing he could have a cigarette. He had begun smoking cigars on Father's Day last year when his daughter presented him with an expensive box in an attempt to break his cigarette habit. He still sneaked a cigarette every now and then, but he was determined to quit entirely and irrevocably. On a day like today, with the squadroom erupting so early in the morning, he found his patience a bit strained, his determination somewhat undermined.

Across the room, the pregnant lady—in a mixture of streetwise English and hooker's Spanish—yelled, "So how comes, *pendego,* you kippin me here when I couldn't make even a *blind* man happy in my condition?"

Her condition was imminent. Perhaps that was why the four drunks in the detention cage in the corner of the room found her so comical. Or perhaps it was because she was wearing nothing but a half-slip under her black cloth coat. The coat was unbuttoned, and the pregnant lady's belly ballooned over the elastic waistband of the peach-colored slip. Above that, her naked breasts, swollen with the threat of parturition, bobbed indignantly and rather perkily in time to her words, which the drunks found hilarious.

"Tell me, *hijo de la gran puta,*" she said grandly to Hawes, grinning at the detention cage, pleased with her receptive audience and playing to the house, "would *you* pay for somebody looks like me?" and here she grabbed both frisky breasts and squeezed them in her hands, the nipples popping between her index and middle fingers. "Would you? Hah?"

"Yes!" one of the drunks in the cage shouted.

"The arresting officer says you propositioned him," Hawes said wearily.

"So where *is* this arresting officer, hah?" the woman asked.

"Yeah, where *is* he?" one of the drunks in the cage shouted.

"Down the hall," Hawes said.

The arresting officer was Genero. Genero was a horse's ass. Nobody in his right mind would have arrested a pregnant hooker. Nobody in his right mind would have filled the detention cage with drunks at nine o'clock on a Saturday morning. There would be stale vomit in the cage tonight, when the citizenry began howling and the cage was *really* needed. Genero had first brought in the drunks, one at a time, and then he had brought in the pregnant hooker. Genero was on a crusade. Genero was a one-man Moral Majority. Which, perhaps, the *real* Moral Majority was as well.

"Sit down and shut up," Hawes said to the hooker.

"No, keep *standin',*" one of the drunks in the cage yelled.

"Turn this way, honey!" another one yelled. "Let's see 'em one more time!"

"Muy linda, verdad?" the hooker said, and showed her breasts to the drunks again.

Hawes shook his head. In a squadroom where fairness was an unspoken credo, it rankled that Genero had dragged in a pregnant hooker. He could be forgiven the cageful of drunks—*maybe*—but a pregnant hooker? Even Hawes's father would have looked the other way, and Jeremiah Hawes had been an extremely religious person, a man who'd felt that Cotton Mather was the greatest of the Puritan priests, a man who'd named his own son in honor of the colonial God-seeker who'd hunted witches with the worst of them. Hawes's father had chalked off the Salem witch trials as the personal petty revenges of a town feeding on its own ingrown fears, thereby exonerating Cotton Mather and the role the priest had played in bringing the delusion to its fever pitch. Would his father, if he were still alive, have similarly excused Genero for his zeal? Hawes doubted it.

The woman came back to his desk.

"So what you say?" she said.

"About what?"

"You let me walk, okay?"

"I can't," Hawes said.

"I got somethin' in the oven juss now," the woman said, and spread her hands wide on her belly. "But I pay you back later, okay? When this is all finish, okay?" She winked at him. "Come on, let me walk," she said. "You very cute, you know? We have a nice time together later, okay?"

"Cute?" one of the drunks in the cage yelled, insulted. *"Jesus,* lady!"

"He's *very* cute, this little *muchacho,"* the woman said, and chucked Hawes under the chin as though he were a cuddly little ten-year-old dumpling. He was, in fact, six feet two inches tall, and he weighed an even two hundred pounds now that he wasn't watching his diet too closely, and he had somewhat unnervingly clear blue eyes and flaming red hair with a white streak over the left temple—the result of a peculiar accident while he was still working as a Detective/Third out of the 30th Precinct downtown. He had responded to a 1021, a Burglary Past, and the victim had been a hysterical woman who came screaming out of her apartment to greet him, and the super of the building had come running up with a knife when he spotted Hawes, mistaking Hawes for the burglar, who was already eighteen blocks away, and lunging at him with the knife and putting a big gash on his head. The doctors shaved the hair to get at the cut, and when it grew back, it grew in white—which had been the exact color of Hawes's terror.

The streak in his hair had accounted for a great many different reactions from a great many different women—but none of them had ever thought he was "cute." Looking at the pregnant hooker's naked breasts and appraising eyes, he began to think that maybe he *was* cute, after all. He also began to think that it wouldn't be such a bad idea to let her walk and to take her up later on her fine proposition. She was a good-looking woman in her mid-thirties, he guessed, who carried her coming infant like a barrage balloon, but who had a good slender body otherwise, with long strong legs and very nice breasts indeed, swollen to bursting now and being flaunted with deliberate coercive intent as she sashayed past Hawes's desk, back and forth, back and forth, black coat open, belly and breasts billowing like the mainsail and jibsail of an oceangoing schooner. The drunks began to applaud.

If he *did* let her walk, of course, Genero would bring departmental charges or do something else stupid. Hawes was pondering the inequity of having to work with someone like Genero when Hal Willis pushed through the slatted rail divider, dragging behind him two people handcuffed to each other. Hawes couldn't tell whether the people were boys or girls because they were both wearing designer jeans and woolen ski masks. The drunks in the cage cheered again, this time in greeting to the masked couple. Willis took a bow, spotted the pregnant hooker with the open coat, said, "Close your coat, lady, you'll freeze those sweet little darlings to death," and then said, "Come in, gentlemen," to the two people in the designer jeans and the ski masks. "Hello, Steve," he said to Carella, "it's starting early today, isn't it? Who's that in the cage? The Mormon Tabernacle Choir?''

The drunks found this almost as amusing as they found the pregnant hooker. The drunks were having the time of their lives. First a topless floor show, and now a stand-up comic with two guys in funny costumes. The drunks *never* wanted to leave this place.

''What've you got?'' Carella asked.

''Two masked bandits,'' Willis said, and turned to them. ''Sit down, boys,'' he said. ''You won't believe this,'' he said to Carella, and then he turned to where Meyer was typing, and said, ''You won't believe this, Meyer.''

''*What* won't I believe?'' Meyer asked, and his words seemed to command the immediate respect of everyone in the squadroom, as though—like a superb ring-master—he had cracked a whip to call attention to the morning's star performers, diminutive Hal Willis and the two masked men. The pregnant hooker turned to look at them, and even closed her coat so that her *own* star performers would not detract from the action in the main ring. The drunks put their faces close to the meshed steel of the detention cage as if they were Death Row inmates in a B-movie, watching a fellow prisoner walk that Long Last Mile. Hawes looked, Carella looked, Meyer looked, everybody looked.

Willis, never one to shun the limelight, upstaged the two masked and manacled bandits, and said, ''I was heading in to work, you know? Snow tires in the trunk 'cause I planned to have them put on at the garage on Ainsley and Third, okay? So I stop there, and I tell the mechanic to put on the tires for me—don't ask why I waited till February, okay? The *Farmer's Almanac said* it was gonna be a harsh winter. So he starts jackin' up the car, and I take the key to the men's room, and I go out to take a leak—excuse me, lady.''

''*De nada,*'' the pregnant hooker said.

''And when I come back, these two guys are standin' there with cannons in their hands and yelling at the mechanic, who already crapped his pants, to open the safe. The mechanic is babbling he hasn't got the combination, and *these* two heroes here are yelling that he'd better *find* the combination fast or they'll blow his goddamn brains out, excuse me, lady. That's when I come out of the can zipping up my fly.''

''What happened?'' one of the drunks asked breathlessly and with sincere interest. This was really turning into a *marvelous* morning! First the topless dancer, then the stand-up comic, who was now becoming a very fine dramatic actor with a good sense of timing and a wonderful supporting cast of actors in masks as in the Japanese traditional No theater.

''Do I need an attempted armed robbery at nine in the morning?'' Willis asked the cageful of drunks. ''Do I need an armed robbery at *any* time of day?'' he asked the pregnant hooker. ''I stop in a garage to get my tires changed and to take a leak, and I run into *these* two punks.''

''So what'd you *do?*'' the drunk insisted. The suspense was unbearable, and all this talk about taking a leak was making *him* want to pee, too.

''I almost ran out of there,'' Willis said. ''What would you have done?'' he asked Hawes. ''You're zipping up your fly and suddenly there are two punks with forty-fives in their hands?''

"I'd have run," Hawes said, and nodded solemnly.

"Of *course,*" Willis said. "Any cop in his right *mind* would've run."

"I'd have run, too," Carella said, nodding.

"Me, too," Meyer said.

"No question," Willis said.

He was beginning to enjoy this. He was hoping the drunk would ask him again about what had happened back there at the garage. Like any good actor, he was beginning to thrive on audience feedback. At five feet eight inches tall, Willis had minimally cleared the height requirement for policemen in this city—at least when *he* had joined the force. Things had changed since; there were now uniformed cops, and even detectives, who resembled fire hydrants more than they did law enforcers. But until recently, Willis had most certainly been the smallest detective anyone in this city had ever seen, with narrow bones and an alert cocker-spaniel look on his thin face, a sort of younger Fred Astaire look-alike carrying a .38 Detective's Special instead of a cane, and kicking down doors instead of dancing up staircases. Willis knew judo the way he knew the Penal Code, and he could lay a thief on his back faster than any six men using fists. He wondered now if he should toss one of the masked men over his shoulder, just to liven up the action a bit. He decided instead to tell what had happened back there at the garage.

"I pulled my gun," he said, and to demonstrate, pulled the .38 from its shoulder holster and fanned the air with it. "These two heroes here immediately yell, 'Don't shoot!' You want to know why? Because their *own* guns aren't loaded! Can you imagine that? They go in for a stickup, and they're carrying empty guns!"

"That ain't such a good story," the previously interested drunk said.

"So go ask for your money back," Willis said. "Sit down, punks," he said to the masked men.

"We're handcuffed together. How can we sit?" one of them said.

"On two chairs," Willis said, "like Siamese twins. And take off those stupid masks."

"Don't," one of them said to the other.

"Why not?" the other one said.

"We don't have to," the first one said. "We know our constitutional rights," he said to Willis.

"I'll give you *rights,*" Willis said. "I could've got *shot,* you realize that?"

"How?" Meyer said. "You just told us the guns—"

"I mean *if* they'd been loaded," he said, and just then Genero came up the hall from the men's room. He said, "Who turned off my radio?" looked around for the pregnant hooker, the only one of his prisoners who wasn't in the detention cage, spotted her sitting on the edge of Hawes's desk, walked swiftly toward her, and was saying, "Okay, sister, let's . . ." when suddenly she began screaming at him. The scream scared Genero half out of his wits. He ducked and covered his head as if he'd suddenly been caught in a mortar attack. The scream scared all the drunks in the cage, too. In defense, *they* all began screaming as well, as if they'd just seen mice coming out of the walls and bats flying across the room to eat them.

The woman's strenuous effort, her penetrating, persistent, high-pitched angry scream—aside from probably breaking every window within an eight-mile radius—also broke something else. As the detectives and the drunks and the two masked men watched in male astonishment, they saw a huge splash of water cascade from between the pregnant hooker's legs. The drunks thought she had wet her pants. Willis and Hawes, both bachelors, thought so, too. Carella and Meyer, who were experienced married men, knew that the woman had broken water, and that she might go into labor at any moment. Genero, his hands over his head, thought he had done something to provoke the lady to pee on the floor, and he was sure he would get sent to his room without dinner.

"*Madre de Dios!*" the woman said, shocked, and clutched her belly.

"Get an ambulance!" Meyer yelled to Hawes.

Hawes picked up the phone receiver and jiggled the hook.

"My baby's comin'," the woman said, very softly, almost reverently, and then very quietly lay down on the floor near Meyer's desk.

"Dave," Hawes said into the phone, "we need a meat wagon, *fast!* We got a pregnant lady up here about to give birth!"

"You know how to do this?" Meyer asked Carella.

"No. Do you?"

"Help me," the woman said with quiet dignity.

"For Christ's sake, *help* her!" Hawes said, hanging on the phone.

"*Me?*" Willis said.

"Somebody!" Hawes said.

The woman moaned. Pain shot from her contracting belly into her face.

"Get some hot water or something," Carella said.

"Where?" Willis said.

"The Clerical Office," Carella said. "Steal some of Miscolo's hot water."

"Help me," the woman said again, and Meyer knelt beside her just as the phone on Carella's desk rang. He picked up the receiver.

"Eighty-Seventh Squad, Carella," he said.

"Just a second," the voice on the other end said. "Ralph, will you please pick up that other *phone,* please!"

In the detention cage, the drunks were suddenly very still. They pressed against the mesh. They watched as Meyer leaned over the pregnant woman. They tried to hear his whispered words. The woman screamed again, but this time they did not echo her scream with their own screams. This was not a scream of anger. This was something quite different. They listened to the scream in awe, and were hushed by it.

"Sorry," the voice on the phone said, "they're ringing it off the hook today. This is Levine, Midtown East. We had a shooting around midnight, D.O.A., girl named—"

"Listen," Carella said, "can you call back a little later? We've got a sort of emergency up here."

"This is a *homicide,*" Levine said, as if that single word would clear all the decks for action, cause whoever heard it to drop whatever else he was doing and heed the call to arms. Levine was right.

"Shoot," Carella said.

"Girl's name was Sally Anderson," Levine said. "That mean anything to you?"

"Nothing," Carella said, and looked across the room. Willis had come back from the Clerical Office not only with Miscolo's boiling water, but with Miscolo himself. Miscolo was now kneeling on the other side of the woman on the floor. Carella realized all at once that Miscolo and Meyer were going to try delivering the baby.

"Reason I'm calling," Levine said, "it looks like this may be related to something you're working."

Carella moved his desk pad into place and picked up a pencil. He could not take his eyes off what was happening across the room.

"I got a call from Ballistics ten minutes ago," Levine said. "Guy named Dorfsman, smart guy, very alert. On the slugs they dug out of the girl's chest and head. You working a case involving a thirty-eight-caliber Smith and Wesson?"

"Yes?" Carella said.

"A homicide this would be. The case you're working. You sent some slugs to Dorfsman, right?"

"Yes?" Carella said. He was still writing. He was still looking across the room.

"They match the ones that iced the girl."

"You're sure about that?"

"Right down the line. Dorfsman doesn't make mistakes. The same gun was used in both killings."

"Uh-huh," Carella said.

Across the room, Miscolo said, "Bear down now."

"Hard," Meyer said.

"However you want to," Miscolo said.

"So what I want to know is who takes this one?" Levine asked.

"You're sure it's the same gun?"

"Positive. Dorfsman put the bullets under the microscope a dozen times. No mistake. The same thirty-eight-caliber Smith and Wesson."

"Midtown East is a long way from home," Carella said.

"I know it is. And I'm not trying to dump anything on you, believe me. I just don't know what the regs say in a case like this."

"If they're related, I would guess—"

"Oh, they're related, all right. But is it yours or mine, that's the question. I mean, you caught the original squeal."

"I'll have to check with the lieutenant," Carella said. "When he comes in."

"I already checked with mine. He thinks I ought to turn it over to you. This has nothing to do with how busy we are down here, Carella. One more stiff ain't gonna kill us. It's that you probably already done a lot of legwork . . ."

"I have," Carella said.

"And I don't know what you come up with so far, if anything . . ."

"Not much," Carella said. "The victim here was a small-time gram dealer."

"Well, this girl's a dancer, the victim here."

"Was she doing drugs?"

"I don't have anything yet, Carella. That's why I'm calling you. If I'm gonna start, I'll start. If it's your case, I'll back off."

"That's the way," Meyer said. "Very good."

"We can see the head," Miscolo said. "Now you can push a little harder."

"That's the way," Meyer said again.

"I'll check with the lieutenant and get back to you," Carella said. "Meanwhile, can you send me the paper on this?"

"Will do. I don't have to tell you—"

"The first twenty-four hours are the most important," Carella said by rote.

"So if I'm gonna move, it's got to be today."

"I've got it," Carella said. "I'll call you back."

"Push!" Miscolo said.

"Push!" Meyer said.

"Oh, my God!" the woman said.

"Here it comes, here it *comes!*" Meyer said.

"Oh, my God, my God, my *God!*" the woman said exultantly.

"That's *some* little buster!" Miscolo said.

Meyer lifted the blood-smeared infant and slapped its buttocks. A triumphant cry pierced the stillness of the squadroom.

"Is it a boy or a girl?" one of the drunks whispered.

3

Carella did not call Levine back until ten minutes past eleven, because that was how long it took to straighten out the protocol regarding the two corpses. By that time, the squadroom had quieted down considerably. The no-longer-pregnant hooker and her operatic new daughter had been taken by ambulance to the hospital, and the four drunks had been booked for Public Intoxication and led out of the station house to the waiting van by a triumphant Detective Genero, who perhaps did not realize that Public Intoxication was a mere violation as opposed to a misdemeanor or a felony, and was punishable only by a sentence not to exceed fifteen days. There was not a man or woman in that squadroom on that bright February morning who did not realize that Genero was wasting the city's time and therefore money by dragging those drunks downtown, where they would undoubtedly be turned loose at once by a judge who knew that every available inch of cell space was needed for more serious offenders than a quartet of happy inbibers. Blithely, Genero went his way. The man—and the one woman who arrived at the squadroom at 11:00 A.M. that Saturday, just as Genero was leading his procession of prisoners out—shook their heads in unison and moved on to the more serious matters at hand.

The woman was a Detective/Second on loan from Headquarters Division's Special Forces Unit. Her name was Eileen Burke, and she worked out of the Eight-Seven only occasionally, usually on cases requiring a female decoy. Which meant that whenever Eileen worked up here, she walked the streets alone as bait for a mad rapist, or any other kind of degenerate person out there. Eileen had red hair and green eyes; Eileen had long legs, sleek and clean, full-calved and tapering to slender ankles; Eileen had very good breasts and flaring hips and Eileen was five feet nine inches tall, all of which added up to someone who could not be missed on a city street if someone else had rape on his mind. But Eileen had once worked a *mugging* case up here, too, with Hal Willis as her backup, and she'd coincidentally worked another case with Willis as her partner in a sleeping bag in the park, both of them pretending to be passionate lovers in a complicated stakeout that included Detectives Meyer and Kling dressed as nuns and sitting on a nearby bench.

Eileen could not later remember the *purpose* of the elaborate stakeout. She remembered only that Willis kept putting his hand on her behind while she tried to watch a third bench on which there was a lunch pail that was supposed to contain fifty thousand dollars but instead contained fifty thousand scraps of newspaper. Willis—in his role as ardent lover—kissed her a lot while they huddled together in the sleeping bag on that bitterly cold day. The necking came to an abrupt halt when a young man picked up the lunch-pail bait and began walking away toward the bench upon which the fake blind man Genero was sitting, whereupon Genero leaped to his feet, ripped off his dark glasses, unbuttoned the third button of his coat the way he had seen detectives do on television, reached in for his revolver, and shot himself in the leg. In the sleeping bag, Willis managed to slide the walkie-talkie up between Eileen's breasts and began yelling to Hawes, who was parked in an unmarked car on Grover Avenue, that their man was heading his way—it was always fun working out of the Eight-Seven, Eileen thought now. She also thought it was a shame she only got to see Willis every once in a while. Idly, she wondered if Willis was married. Idly, she wondered why she had begun thinking of marriage so *often* these past few days. Was it because no one had sent her a valentine this year?

The squadroom was relatively quiet with Genero and all of his prisoners (the delivered hooker had escaped his grasp—for the time being, anyway) gone their separate ways. Cotton Hawes, at his desk, was taking a complaint from a fat black man who insisted that his wife threw hot grits all over him every time he got home late because she thought he was larking around with another woman. Those were his words: larking around. Hawes found them somewhat poetic. Hal Willis had already gone down to book the two juves and was leading them into the alley running through the station house and adjacent to the detention cells on the street level, where Genero's drunks were already in the van that would take them downtown. The juves still refused to take off the ski masks. One of the drunks in the van asked them if they were going to a party. As Willis delivered them to the uniformed cop, who slammed the locked door of the van behind them, Eileen Burke perched herself on the edge of Willis's desk upstairs, and crossed her splendid legs, and then looked at her watch, and then lit a cigarette.

"Hello, Eileen," Hawes said to her as he led the fat black grits-victim past her and out of the squadroom, presumably to confront the grits-tossing wife in to sanctity of their own peaceful home. Eileen watched Hawes as he disappeared down the corridor. He had red hair, much like her own. She wondered idly if the progeny of two redheaded people would *also* be redheads. She wondered idly if Hawes was married. She began jiggling one foot.

Some three feet away from where she smoked her cigarette and impatiently jiggled her foot, Meyer was on the telephone with his wife, telling her he'd delivered a baby right here in the squadroom with a little—but *only* a little—help from Alf Miscolo, who was at the moment down the hall in the Clerical Office, brewing another pot of coffee now that his hot water was no longer urgently needed in maternity cases. On another telephone, at his own desk, Carella finally made contact with Levine at Midtown East, and began apologizing to him for having taken so long to get back.

It had taken him all this while to get back because a police department is like a small army, and a homicide is like a big battle in a continuing war. In big armies, even small battles get serious consideration. In a small army like a police department, a big battle like homicide commands a great deal of attention and participation from a great many people all up and down the line. In the city for which these men worked, the precinct detective assigned to any homicide was the one who'd caught the original squeal, generally assisted by any member of the detective team who'd been catching with him at the time. The moment a squadroom detective said, "I've got it," or, "I'm rolling," or some such other colorful jargon to that effect, the case was officially his, and he was expected to stick with it until he solved it, or cleared it (which was not the same thing as solving it) or simply threw up his hands in despair on it. But since homicide was such a big deal—a major offensive, so to speak—there were *other* people in the department who were terribly interested in the activity down there at the squadroom level. In this city, once a squadroom detective caught a bona fide or "good" homicide, he had to inform:

1. The Police Commissioner
2. The Chief of Detectives
3. The District Commander of the Detective Division
4. Homicide East or Homicide West, depending upon where the body was found
5. The Squad and Precinct Commanding Officers of the precinct in which the body was found
6. The Medical Examiner
7. The District Attorney
8. The Telegraph, Telephone and Teletype Bureau at Headquarters
9. The Police Laboratory
10. The Police Photo Unit

Not all of these people had to be consulted on protocol that Saturday morning. But the situation was knotty enough to cause Lieutenant Byrnes, in command of the 87th Squad, to wrinkle his brow and phone Captain Frick, in command of the entire 87th Precinct, who in turn hemmed and hawed a bit and then cleverly said, "Well, Pete, this would seem to be a matter of 'member of the force,' wouldn't it?" which Byrnes took to mean "member of the force handling the case," which is exactly what he'd called Frick about in the *first* place. Frick advised Byrnes to go to superior rank within the division on this, which necessitated a call to the Chief of Detectives, something Byrnes would have preferred avoiding lest his superior officer think he was not up on current regs. The Chief of Detectives did a little telephonic head scratching and told Byrnes he had not had one like this in a great many years and since the police department changed its rules and regulations as often as it changed its metaphoric underwear, he would have to check on what *current* procedure might be, after which he would get back to Byrnes. Byrnes, eager to remind his superior officer that the men of the Eight-Seven were conscientious law enforcers, casually mentioned that there were *two* homicides involved here, and *two* detectives in separate parts of the city waiting to get moving on the second and freshest of the killings (which wasn't quite true; neither Levine *nor* Carella were particularly hot to trot) so he would appreciate it if the Chief could get back to him as soon as possible on this. The Chief did not get back until close to 11:00 A.M., after he'd had a conversation with the Chief of Operations, whose office was two stories above the Chief's own in the Headquarters Building. The Chief told Byrnes that in the opinion of the Chief of Operations, the *former* homicide took priority over the *latter;* the member of the force handling the case should be the squadroom detective who'd caught the *initial* squeal, whenever that had been. Byrnes didn't know when it had been, either; he simply said, "Yes, whenever. Thank you, Chief," and hung up, and summoned Carella to his office and said, "It's ours," meaning not that it was actually *theirs* (although in a greater sense it was) but that it was *his*—Carella's. When Carella reported all this to Levine, Levine said, "Good luck," managing to convey an enormous sense of relief in those two simple words.

Hal Willis came back into the squadroom some five minutes later, just as a windblown and frostbitten patrolman from Midtown East was delivering the packet promised by Levine when he'd first spoken to Carella earlier this morning. Willis spotted Eileen sitting on the edge of his desk, smiled, and virtually tap-danced over to her. Grinning, he said, "Hey, they sent *you,* huh?"

"Here's that stuff from Levine," Carella said to Meyer.

"You were hoping for Raquel Welch maybe?" Eileen said.

"Who's complaining?" Willis said.

"Who raped who *this* time?" Eileen asked.

"Don't talk dirty in my squadroom," Meyer said, and winked at Carella.

"Looks very thin," Carella said, hefting the yellow manila envelope he had just signed for.

"That it?" the patrolman asked, rubbing his hands together.

"That's it," Carella said.

"Anyplace I can get a cup of coffee here?" the patrolman asked.

"There's a machine downstairs in the swing room," Carella said.

"I got no change," the patrolman said.

"Oh, the old Got-No-Change Ploy," Meyer said.

"Huh?" the patrolman said.

"Try the Clerical Office down the hall," Carella said.

"Is your insurance paid up?" Meyer said.

"Huh?" the patrolman said, and shrugged, and went down the hall.

"Oh, the old Your-Place-Or-Mine Ploy," Meyer said. He was feeling terrific! He had just delivered a baby! There was nothing like collaborating in an act of creation to make a man feel marvelous! "Is this the laundromat case?" he asked Willis.

"It's the laundromat case," Willis said.

"A rapist in a *laundromat?*" Eileen asked, and stubbed out her cigarette.

"No, a guy who's been holding up laundromats late at night. We figured we'd plant you in the one he's gonna hit next—"

"How do you know which one he'll hit next?" Eileen asked.

"Well, we're guessing," Willis said. "But there's sort of a pattern."

"Oh, the old Modus-Operandi Ploy," Meyer said, and actually burst out laughing. Carella looked at him. Meyer shrugged and stopped laughing.

"Dress you up like a lady with dirty laundry," Willis said.

"Sounds good to me," Eileen said. "You're the backup, huh?"

"I'm the backup."

"Where will *you* be?"

"In a sleeping bag outside," Willis said, and grinned.

"Sure," she said, and grinned back.

"Remember?" he said.

"Memory like a judge," she said.

"We'll leave you two to work out your strategy," Meyer said. "Come on, Steve, let's use the interrogation room."

"When do we start?" Eileen asked, and lit another cigarette.

"Tonight?" Willis said.

In the interrogation room down the hall, Meyer and Carella studied the single sheet of paper that had been in the envelope Levine sent them:

(DO NOT FOLD OR ROLL THIS REPORT)

CRIME CLASSIFICATION	**POLICE DEPARTMENT**	DETECTIVE SQUAD
Homicide	**SUPPLEMENTARY**	PRECINCT
HERETOFORE THIS CASE WAS CLASSIFIED AS FOLLOWS:	**COMPLAINT REPORT**	

CRIME CLASSIFICATION	**POLICE DEPARTMENT**	DETECTIVE SQUAD Midtown East
Homicide	**SUPPLEMENTARY COMPLAINT REPORT**	PRECINCT Midtown East
HERETOFORE THIS CASE WAS CLASSIFIED AS FOLLOWS: Homicide	(See Activity Report #379-61-0230)	COMPLAINT NUMBER 375-61-0241 DATE OF THIS REPORT Feb. 13
NAME OF COMPLAINANT Dominick Bonaccio re victim SALLY ANDERSON	ADDRESS OF COMPLAINANT 637 North Campbell	same DATE OF FIRST REPORT

Complainant Dominick Bonaccio discovered victim lying on her back in the snow at 12:30 AM on his way home from work. Recognized her from the coat she was wearing. Went up to his apartment, called 911, went down stairs again to wait for responding police officers. (P. O. Frank O'Neal, P.O. Peter Nelson, Midtown East, Charlie Car.) Victim D.O.A. on arrival. Officer O'Neal radioed dispatcher, requesting detectives on scene. (See Activity report #375-61-0230) Homicide detectives (Monoghan and Monroe) cruising area, responded to call, arrived at scene before M.E. Detectives Henry Levine and Ralph Coombes.

Victim identified as SALLY ANDERSON, white female, age 25. Hair blonde. Eyes blue. Pending exact autopsy measurements, height appears five-feet eight-inches, weight approximately one twenty-five. Assistant

M.E. David Lowenby pronounced victim dead at scene, apparent cause of
death gunshot wounds. Pending autopsy report, wounds appear to be
three: one in leftside of chest, two in face. No spent shell casings
recovered at scene. Contents girl's handbag: lipstick, eyebrow pencil, two sticks chewing gum, address book. Kleenex tissues, wallet with
three photographs, twenty-three dollars U.S. currency, Actors Equity I.D.
card. Canvas of tenants 637 North Campbell no eye witnesses, but
statements victim was a dancer employed in a musical called "Fatback,"
Wales Theater, 1134 North Adderley.

   Body sent to Haley Hospital Morgue. Personal effects in possession
Midtown East for transfer to Laboratory. Ballistics section informed
BOLO for any bullets recovered from body during autopsy, early report
requested.

Henry Levine

Detective (1st/Gr) Henry Levine
Shield #27842 (Midtown East)

"He types neat," Meyer said.

"Not much here though," Carella said.

"This must've been before he got that call from Dorfsman, huh?"

"Got fast action with his BOLO," Carella said.

"Let's see what we've got on the *other* one," Meyer said.

In the Clerical Office, Alf Miscolo was brewing the city's worst coffee. Its strong aroma assailed their nostrils the moment they stepped into the room.

"Halloween has come and gone," Meyer said.

"What's that supposed to mean?" Miscolo said.

"You can stop throwing newts and frogs in your coffeepot."

"Ha-ha," Miscolo said. "You don't like it, don't drink it." He sniffed the air. "This is a new Colombian blend," he said, and rolled his eyes appreciatively.

"Your coffee smells just like Meyer's cigars," Carella said.

"I give him all my old butts," Meyer said, and then realized his *cigars* were being attacked. "What do you mean?" he said. "What's the matter with my ci-gars?"

"Did you come in here to waste my time, or what?" Miscolo said.

"We need the file on Paco Lopez," Carella said.

"That was only a few days ago, wasn't it?"

"The homicide on Culver," Carella said, nodding. "Tuesday night."

"It ain't filed yet," Miscolo said.

"So where is it?"

"Here on my desk someplace," Miscolo said, and gestured toward the wilderness of unfiled reports covering its top.

"Can you dig it out?" Carella said.

Miscolo did not answer. He sat in the swivel chair behind the desk and began sorting out the reports. "My wife gave me that coffee for Valentine's Day," he said, sulking.

"She must love you a lot," Meyer said.

"What'd *your* wife give *you?*"

"Valentine's Day isn't until tomorrow."

"Maybe she'll give you some terrific cigars," Carella said. "Like the ones you're already smoking."

"Here's a *Gofredo* Lopez, is that who you're looking for?"

"Paco," Carella said.

"There's nothing wrong with my cigars," Meyer said.

"You know how many Lopezes we got up here in the Eight-Seven?" Miscolo said. "Lopez up here is just like Smith or Jones in the *real* world."

"Only one Lopez got shot last Tuesday," Carella said.

"I sometimes wish *all* of them would," Miscolo said.

"Give them a sip of your coffee instead," Meyer said. "Do 'em in as sure as a sawed-off shotgun."

"Ha-ha," Miscolo said. "Paco, where the hell's Paco?"

"When are you going to get around to filing all this stuff?" Meyer said.

"When I get around to it," Miscolo said. "If all our upstanding citizens out there would stop shooting each other, and robbing each other, and stabbing each other—"

"You'd be out of a job," Carella said.

"Shove the job," Miscolo said. "I've had the job up to here. Three more years, I'll be out of it. Three more years, I'll be living in Miami."

"No crime at all down there in Miami," Meyer said.

"Nothing that'll bother *me,*" Miscolo said. "I'll be out on my boat fishing."

"Don't forget to take your coffeepot with you," Meyer said.

"Here it is," Miscolo said. "Paco Lopez. Bring it back when you're finished with it."

"So you can file it next Friday," Meyer said.

"Ha-ha," Miscolo said.

In the late-morning stillness of the squadroom, they looked over the sheaf of papers on Paco Lopez. The shooting had taken place last Tuesday night, a bit more than seventy-three hours before Sally Anderson was killed with the same gun half a city away. The girl's body had been found at 12:30 A.M. on the morning of the thirteenth; Paco Lopez had been killed at 11:00 P.M. on the night of the ninth. The dead girl had been twenty-five years old, a white female, gainfully employed. Lopez had been nineteen, a Hispanic male, with one previous arrest for possession of narcotics with intent to sell; he had gotten off with a suspended sentence because he'd been only fifteen at the time. When they'd gone through his pockets on Tuesday night, they'd found six grams of cocaine and a rubber-banded roll of hundred-dollar bills totaling eleven hundred dollars. Sally Anderson's wallet had contained twenty-three dollars. There seemed very little connection between the two victims. But the same gun had been used in both slayings.

The supplementary reports on Lopez confirmed that he'd continued dealing drugs after his initial bust; his street name was El Snorto. No such word existed in the Spanish language, but the Hispanic residents in the 87th Precinct were not without their own wry sense of humor. The people Carella and Meyer had interrogated and interviewed all seemed to agree that Paco Lopez was a mean son of a bitch who'd deserved killing. Many of them suggested alternate means of death slower and more painful than the two .38 caliber bullets that had been fired into his chest at close range. One of his previous girlfriends unbuttoned her blouse for the detectives and showed them the cigarette burns Lopez had left as souvenirs on both her breasts. Even Lopez's mother seemed to agree (although she'd crossed herself when she admitted this) that the world would be much better off without the likes of her son around.

A round-up of known gram dealers had brought up the information that Lopez was truly a small-time operator, something slightly higher than a mule in the hierarchy of cocaine "redistribution"—as one of the dealers euphemistically called it. Lopez had enjoyed a small following of users whom he'd supplied on a modest basis, but if he pulled down ten, twelve bills a week, that was a lot. Listening to this, Meyer and Carella, who each and separately pulled down only twenty bills a *month,* wondered if perhaps they were not in the wrong profession. All of these more successful dealers agreed that Lopez hadn't even been *worth* killing. He was a threat to nobody, operating as he was on the fringes of gram-dealer society. They all figured some angry cokie had iced him. Maybe Lopez got fancy, started cutting his stuff too fine in an attempt to get more mileage out of the dust, and maybe an irate user had put the blocks to him. As simple as that. But how did a cocaine murder tie in with Sally Anderson?

"You know what I wish?" Carella said.

"What?"

"I wish we hadn't inherited this one."

But they had.

The superintendent of Sally Anderson's building on North Campbell Street was not happy to see them. He had been awakened at close to one in the morning and interrogated by two other detectives, and he had not been able to fall asleep again till almost two-thirty, and then he'd had to get up at six to put out the garbage cans before the Sanitation Department trucks arrived, and then he'd had to shovel the sidewalk in front of the building clear of snow, and now it was ten minutes to twelve, and he was hungry, and he wanted his lunch, and he didn't want to be talking to two *more* detectives when he hadn't even seen what happened and hardly knew the girl from a hole in the wall.

"All I know is she lives in the building," he said. "Her name's Sally Anderson, she lives in apartment three-A." He kept using the present tense when referring to her, as though her death had never happened, and even if it had was of small consequence to him—which was the truth.

"Did she live alone?" Carella asked.

"Far as I know."

"What does that mean?"

"These girls today, who knows *who* they live with? A guy, *two* guys, another girl, a cat, a dog, a goldfish—who knows, and who cares?"

"But as far as you know," Meyer said patiently, "she was living alone."

"As far as I know," the super said. He was a gaunt and graying man who had lived in this city all his life. There were burglaries day and night in this building and in all the other buildings he'd ever worked in over the years. He was no stranger to violence, and had little patience with the minor details of it.

"Mind if we take a look at the apartment?" Carella asked.

"Makes no matter to me," the super said, and led them upstairs, and unlocked the door for them.

The apartment was small and furnished eclectically, modern pieces and antiques rubbing elbows side by side, throw pillows on the black leather sofa and the carpeted floor surrounding it, framed three-sheets from various shows, including the current hit *Fatback,* hanging on all the walls. There were several framed professional photographs of the girl in ballet tights, in various ballet positions, hanging on the wall outside the bathroom. There was a poster for the Sadler's Wells Ballet. There was a bottle of white wine on the kitchen counter. They found her appointment calendar near the telephone in her bedroom, on a night table alongside a king-sized bed covered with a patchwork quilt.

"Did you call the lab?" Meyer asked.

"They're through here," Carella said, nodding, and picked up the appointment calendar. It was one of those large, spiral-bound books that, when opened, showed each separate day at a glance. A large, orange-colored, plastic paper clip allowed the calendar to fall open easily to the twelfth of February. Meyer took out his notebook and began listing her daily appointments since the beginning of the month. He had come through Thursday, February 4, when the doorbell rang. Both detectives looked at each other. Carella went to the door, half expecting the super would be standing out there in the hall, asking for a search warrant or something.

The girl outside the door looked at Carella and said, "Oh."

She looked at the numeral on the door as if somehow she'd made a mistake, and then she frowned. She was a tall, lissome Oriental girl, perhaps five nine or five ten, with midnight black hair and slanted eyes the color of loam. She was wearing a black ski parka over blue jeans tucked into knee-high black boots. A yellow watch cap was tilted saucily over one brow. A long yellow-and-black muffler hung loosely over the front of the parka.

"Do I know you?" she asked.

"I don't think so," Carella said.

"Where's Sally?" she asked, and peered past him into the apartment. Meyer had come out of the bedroom and stood in the living room now, within her frame of vision. Both men were still wearing overcoats. She glanced briefly at Meyer, and then looked back at Carella again.

"What *is* this?" she said. "What's going on here?"

She backed away a pace, and then quickly glanced over her shoulder toward the elevator. Carella knew just what she was thinking. Two strangers in overcoats, no sign of her girlfriend Sally—she was interrupting a burglary in progress. Before she could panic, he said, "We're policemen."

"Oh, *yeah?*" she said skeptically, and glanced again toward the elevator.

A native, Carella thought, and almost smiled.

He took a small leather case from his pocket, and opened it to show his shield and his I.D. card. "Detective Carella," he said, "Eighty-Seventh Squad. This is my partner, Detective Meyer."

The girl bent to look at the shield. She bent from the waist, her legs and her back stiff. A dancer, he thought. She straightened up again and looked him dead in the eye.

"What's the matter?" she said. "Where's Sally?"

"Can you tell us who *you* are, please?" Carella said.

"Tina Wong. Where's Sally?"

Carella hesitated.

"What are you doing here, Miss Wong?" he said.

"Where's Sally?" she said again, and moved past him into the apartment. She was obviously familiar with the place; she went first into the kitchen and then the bedroom and then came back into the living room, where the two detectives were waiting. "Where is she?" she said.

"Was she expecting you, Miss Wong?" Carella asked.

The girl did not answer him. Her eyes were beginning to reflect the knowledge that something was wrong. They darted nervously in her narrow face, moving from one detective to the other. Carella did not want to tell her, not yet, that Sally Anderson was dead. The story had not made the morning's papers, but it was certain to be in the afternoon editions, on the newsstands by now. If she already *knew* Sally was dead, Carella wanted the information to come from her.

"Was she expecting you?" he said again.

The girl looked at her watch. "I'm five minutes early," she said. "Would you mind telling me what's going on here? Was she robbed or something?"

A native for sure, he thought. In this city, burglary was always confused with robbery—except by the police. The police only had trouble distinguishing one *degree* of burglary from another.

"What were your plans?" Carella asked.

"Plans?"

"With Miss Anderson."

"Lunch and then the theater," Tina said. "It's a matinee day, half-hour is one-thirty." She planted her feet firmly, put her hands on her hips, and said again, "Where is she?"

"Dead," Carella said, and watched her eyes.

Only suspicion showed there. Not shock, not sudden grief, only suspicion. She hesitated a moment, and then said, "You're putting me on."

"I wish I were."

"What do you mean, *dead?*" Tina said. "I saw her only last night. *Dead?*"

"Her body was found at twelve-thirty A.M.," Carella said.

Something came into the eyes now. Belief. And then belated shock. And then something like fear.

"Who did it?" she asked.

"We don't know yet."

"How? Where?"

"Outside the building here," Carella said. "She was shot."

"Shot?"

And suddenly she burst into tears. The detectives watched her. She fumbled in her shoulder bag for a tissue, wiped her eyes, began crying again, blew her nose, and continued crying. They watched her silently. They both felt huge and awkward in the presence of her tears.

"I'm sorry," she said, and blew her nose again, and looked for an ashtray into which she could drop the crumpled tissue. She took another tissue from her bag, and dabbed at her eyes again. "I'm sorry," she mumbled.

"How well did you know her?" Meyer asked gently.

"We're very good . . ." She stopped, correcting herself, realizing she was talking about Sally Anderson as though she were still alive. "We were very good friends," she said softly.

"How long had you known her?"

"Since *Fatback.*"

"Are you a dancer, too, Miss Wong?"

She nodded again.

"And you'd known her since the show opened?"

"Since we went into rehearsal. Even longer ago than that, in fact. From when we were auditioning. We met at the first audition."

"When was that, Miss Wong?" Meyer asked.

"Last June."

"And you've been good friends since."

"She was my *best* friend." She shook her head. "I can't *believe* this."

"You say you saw her only last night . . ."

"Yes."

"Was there a performance last night?"

"Yes."

"What time did the curtain come down?"

"About a quarter to eleven. We ran a little long last night. Joey—he's our comic, I don't know if you're familiar with the show . . ."

"No," Carella said.

"No," Meyer said.

The girl looked surprised. She shrugged, dismissing their ignorance, and then said, "Joey Hart. He was bringing down the house in the second act, so he milked it for all it was worth. We ran fifteen minutes over."

"The curtain usually comes down at ten-thirty, is that it?" Meyer asked.

"Give or take, either way. It varies. It depends on the house."

"And is that the last time you saw Sally Anderson alive?"

"In the dressing room later," Tina said.

"Who else was in the dressing room?"

"All the gypsies. The girls, anyway."

"Gypsies?"

"The dancers in the chorus."

"How many of them?"

"There are sixteen of us altogether. Boys and girls. Eight of us were in the girls' dressing room. Five blonds, two blacks, and a token Chink—*me.*" She paused. "Jamie digs blonds."

"Jamie?"

"Our choreographer. Jamie Atkins."

"So you were in the dressing room . . ."

"All eight of us. Taking off our makeup, getting out of our costumes . . . like that."

"What time did you leave the dressing room, Miss Wong?"

"I got out as fast as I could." She paused. "I had a date."

"Who was in the dressing room when you left?" Meyer asked.

"Just Sally and Molly."

"Molly?"

"Maguire." She paused. "She changed her name. It used to be Molly Materasso, which isn't too terrific for the stage, am I right?" Carella guessed it was not too terrific for the stage. "In fact, that was her *maiden* name. She's married now, and her *real* name is Molly Boyd, but she still uses Molly Maguire on the stage. It's a good name. Because of the Molly Maguires, you know." Carella looked at her blankly. "It was a secret society in Ireland. In the 1840s," she said. Carella was still looking at her blankly. "And later in Pennsylvania," she said. "Anyway, you hear the name, you think you know her from someplace. The name gets her lots of jobs because directors and producers think, 'Hey, Molly *Maguire,* sure, *I* know *her.'* Actually, she's a pretty lousy dancer."

"But she was there alone in the dressing room with Sally when you left," Meyer said.

"Yes."

"What time was that?"

"About five after eleven."

"What were they talking about, do you know?"

"It was *Molly* who was doing all the talking."

"About what?"

"Geoffrey. Her husband. That's why I got out of there as fast as I could. Actually, I wasn't supposed to meet my date till midnight."

"I don't understand," Meyer said.

"Well, Molly keeps bitching about her husband, and it gets to be a drag. I wish she'd either shut up, or else divorce him."

"Uh-huh," Meyer said.

"And that's the last time you saw her, right?" Carella said.

"Yeah, right. I *still* can't believe this. I mean . . . *God!* We had a cup of *coffee* together just before half-hour last night."

"What'd you talk about then, Miss Wong?"

"Girl talk," Tina said, and shrugged.

"Men?" Carella said.

"Of course men," Tina said, and shrugged again.

"Was she living with anybody?" Meyer asked.

"Not in that sense."

"What sense is that?"

"Most of *her* clothes were here, most of *his* were there."

"Whose clothes?" Carella asked.

"Timmy's."

"Is he a boyfriend or something?" Meyer asked.

"Or something," Tina said.

"Timmy what?" Carella asked.

"Moore."

"Is the Timmy for Timothy?"

"I think so."

"Timothy Moore," Meyer said, writing the name into his notebook. "Do you know where he lives?"

"Downtown, just outside the Quarter. He's a med student at Ramsey U. His apartment is near the school someplace."

"You wouldn't know the address, would you?"

"I'm sorry," Tina said.

"When you say 'or something' . . ." Carella said.

"Well, they were sort of on-again off-again."

"But they *were* romantically involved?"

"Do you mean were they sleeping together?"

"Yes, that's what I mean."

"Yes, they were sleeping together," Tina said. "Isn't everybody?"

"I suppose," Carella said. "Did she ever mention a man named Paco Lopez?"

"No. Who's Paco Lopez? Is he in show business?"

Carella hesitated a moment, and then said, "Was Sally doing drugs?"

"I don't think so."

"Never mentioned drugs to you?"

"Are you talking about a little pot every now and then, or what?"

"I'm talking about the hard stuff. Heroin," he said, and paused. "Cocaine," he said, and watched her closely.

"Sally smoked pot," Tina said. "Who doesn't? But as for anything else, I don't think so."

"You're sure of that?"

"I couldn't swear to it in a court of law, if that's what you mean. But usually, you can get a pretty good idea of who's doing what when you're working in a show, and I don't think Sally was doing any kind of hard drugs."

"Are you suggesting that *some* members of the cast . . . ?"

"Oh, sure."

"Uh-huh," Carella said.

"Not heroin," Tina said, "nobody's *that* stupid anymore. But some coke here and there, now and then, sure."

"But not Sally."

"Not to my knowledge," Tina paused. "Not *me,* either, if that's your next question."

"That wasn't my next question," Carella said, and smiled. "Did Sally ever mention any threatening letters or telephone calls?"

"Never."

"Did she owe anybody money? To your knowledge?"

"Not that I know of."

"Anything seem to be troubling her?"

"No. Well, yes."

"What?"

"Nothing serious."

"Well, what?"

"She wanted to take singing lessons again, but she didn't know how she could find the time. She had dance every day, you know, and she was seeing a shrink three times a week."

"And that's it? That's all that was troubling her?"

"That's all she ever mentioned to me."

"Would you know her shrink's name?"

"I'm sorry, no."

"How'd she get along with the rest of the cast?"

"Fine."

"How about management?"

"Who do you mean? Allan?"

"Who's Allan?"

"Our producer, Allan Carter. I mean, who do you mean by management? The company manager? The general manager?"

"Any or all of them. How'd she get along with the people who were *running* the show?"

"Fine, I guess," Tina said, and shrugged. "Once a show opens, you rarely *see* any of those people anymore. Well, in our case, because we're such a big hit, Freddie comes around to check it out once or twice a week, make sure we aren't coasting. But for the most part—"

"Freddie?"

"Our director. Freddie Carlisle."

"How do you spell that?" Meyer asked, beginning to write again.

"With an *i* and an *s,*" Tina said. "C-a-r-l-i-s-l-e."

"And you said your producer's—"

"Allan Carter. Two *l*'s and an *a.*"

"Who's your company manager?"

"Danny Epstein."

"And your general manager?"

"Lew Eberhart."

"Anybody else we should know about?" Carella asked.

Tina shrugged. "The stage managers? We've got three of them." She shrugged again. "I mean, there are thirty-eight people in the cast alone, and God knows how many musicians and electricians and carpenters and property men and—"

"Any of them Hispanic?"

"In the crew, do you mean? I guess so. I don't know too many of them. Except to pass them in my underwear."

She smiled suddenly and radiantly, and then seemed to remember what they were talking about here. The smile dropped from her face.

"How about the cast? Any Hispanics in the cast?" Carella asked.

"Two of the gypsies," Tina said.

"Could we have their names, please?" Meyer said.

"Tony Asensio and Mike Roldan. Roldan doesn't *sound* like a Spanish name, but it is. Actually, it's *Miguel* Roldan."

"Was Sally particularly friendly with either of them?"

"The gypsies in a show get to know each other pretty well," Tina said.

"How well did she know these two men?" Carella asked.

"Same as the rest of us," Tina said, and shrugged.

"Did she ever date either of them?"

"They're both faggots," Tina said. "In fact, they're living together." As though talk of the show had suddenly reminded her of the afternoon performance, she looked swiftly at her watch. "Oh, my God," she said. "I've got to get out of here. I'll be late!" And suddenly a look of self-chastisement crossed her face, and it appeared as if she would burst into tears again. "The show must go on, huh?" she said bitterly, shaking her head. *"I'm* worrying about the goddamn *show,* and Sally's *dead."*

4

From where the two patrolmen sat in the patrol car parked at the curb, it seemed evident that the priest was winning the fight. They had no desire to get out of the car and break up the fight, not with it being so cold out there, and especially since the priest seemed to be winning. Besides, they were sort of enjoying the way the priest was mopping up the street with his little spic opponent.

Up here in the Eight-Seven, you sometimes couldn't tell the spics (*Hispanics,* you were supposed to say in your reports) from the whites because some of them had high Spanish blood in them and looked the same as your ordinary citizen. For all the patrolmen knew, the *priest* was a spic, too, but he had a very white complexion, and he was bigger than most of the cockroach-kickers up here. The two patrolmen sat in the heated comfort of the car and guessed aloud that he was maybe six three, six four, something like that, maybe weighing in at two hundred and forty pounds or thereabouts. They couldn't figure which church he belonged to. None of the neighborhood churches had priests who dressed the way this one was dressed, but maybe he was visiting from someplace in California—they dressed that way in California, didn't they, at those missions they had out there in the Napa Valley? The priest was wearing a brown woolen robe, and his head was shaved like a monk's head, its bald crown glistening above the tonsure that encircled it like a wreath. One of the patrolmen in the car asked the other one what you called that brown thing the priest was wearing, that thing like a dress, you know? The other patrolman told him it was called a *hassock,* stupid, and the first patrolman said, "Oh yeah, right." They were both rookies who had been working out of the Eight-Seven for only the past two weeks, otherwise they'd have known that the priest wasn't a priest at all, even though he was known in the precinct as Brother Anthony.

Clearly, Brother Anthony was in fact beating the man to a pulp. The man was a little Puerto Rican pool shark who'd made the enormous mistake of trying to hustle him. Brother Anthony had dragged the little punk out of the pool hall and first had picked him up and hurled him against the brick wall of the tenement next door, just to stun him, you know, and then had swung a pool cue at his kneecaps, hoping to break them but breaking only the pool cue instead, and was now battering him senseless with his hamlike fists as the two patrolmen watched from the snug comfort of the patrol car. Brother Anthony weighed a lot, but he had lifted weights in prison, and there wasn't an ounce of fat on his body. He sometimes asked people to hit him as hard as they could in the belly, and laughed with pleasure whenever anyone told him how hard and strong he was. All year round, even in the hot summer months, he wore the brown woolen cassock. During the summer months, he wore nothing at all underneath it. He would lift the hem of the cassock and show his sandals to the neighborhood hookers. "See?" he would say. "That's all I got on under this thing." The hookers would oooh and ahhh and try to lift the cassock higher, making believe they didn't think he was really naked under it. Brother Anthony was very graceful for such a big man; he would laugh and dance away from them, dance away.

In the winter, he wore army combat boots instead of the sandals. He was using those boots now to stomp the little Puerto Rican pool hustler into the icy sidewalk. In the patrol car, the two cops debated whether they should get out and break this thing up before the little spic got his brains squashed all over the sidewalk. They were spared having to make any decision because their radio erupted with a 1010, and they radioed back that they were rolling on it. They pulled away from the curb just as Brother Anthony leaned over the prostrate and unconscious hustler to take his wallet from his pocket. Only ten dollars of the money in that wallet had been hustled from Brother Anthony, but he figured he might as well take *all* of it because of the trouble the little punk had put him to. He was cleaning out the wallet when Emma came around the corner.

Emma was known in the neighborhood as the Fat Lady, and most of the people in the precinct tried to steer very clear of her because she was known to possess a short temper and a straightedge razor. She carried the razor in her shoulder bag, hanging from the left shoulder, so that she could reach in there with her right hand, and whip open the razor in a flash, and lop off any dude's ear, or lash his face or his hands, or sometimes go for the money, open the man's windpipe and his jugular with one and the same stroke. Nobody liked to mess with the Fat Lady, which was perhaps why the crowd began to disperse the moment she came around the corner. On the other hand, the crowd might have dispersed anyway, now that the action had ended; nobody liked to stand around doing nothing on a cold day, especially in *this* neighborhood, where somehow it always seemed colder than anyplace else in the city. This neighborhood could have been Moscow. The park bordering this neighborhood could have been Gorky Park. Maybe it was. Or vice versa.

"Hello, bro," the Fat Lady said.

"Hello, Emma," he said, looking up from where he was crouched over the unconscious hustler. He had stomped the man real good. A thin trickle of blood was beginning to congeal on the ice beneath the stupid punk's head. His face looked very blue. Brother Anthony tossed the empty wallet over his shoulder, stood up to his full height, and tucked the five hundred-odd dollars into the pouchlike pocket at the front of the cassock. He began walking, and Emma fell into step beside him.

Emma was perhaps thirty-two or thirty-three years old, in any event a good six or seven years older than Brother Anthony. Her full name was Emma Forbes, which had been her name when she was still married to a black man named Jimmy Forbes, since deceased, the unfortunate victim of a shoot-out in a bank he'd been trying to hold up. The man who'd shot and killed Emma's husband was a bank guard who'd been sixty-three years old at the time, a retired patrolman out of the 28th Precinct downtown. He'd never lived to be sixty-*four* because Emma sought him out a month after her husband's funeral, and slit his throat from ear to ear one fine April night when the forsythias were just starting to bud. Emma did not like people who deprived her or her loved ones of anything they wanted or needed. Emma was fond of saying, "The opera ain't over till the fat lady sings," an expression she used to justify her frequent vengeful attacks. It was uncertain whether the expression had preceded the nickname, or vice versa. When someone was five feet six inches tall and weighed a hundred and seventy pounds, it was reasonable to expect—especially in *this* neighborhood, where street names were as common as legal names—that sooner or later someone would begin calling her the Fat Lady, even without having heard her operatic reference.

Brother Anthony was one of the very few people who knew that the name on her mailbox was Emma Forbes, and that she had been born Emma Goldberg, not to be confused with the anarchist Emma Goldman, who'd been around long before Emma Goldberg was even born. Brother Anthony was also one of the very few people who called her Emma, the rest preferring to call her either Lady (not daring to use the adjective in her presence) or nothing at all, lest she suddenly take offense at an inflection and whip out that razor of hers. Brother Anthony was the only person in the precinct, and perhaps the entire world, who thought Emma Goldberg Forbes a.k.a. the Fat Lady was exceptionally beautiful and extraordinarily sexy besides.

"Listen, there's no accounting for taste," a former acquaintance once said to Brother Anthony immediately after he'd mentioned how beautiful and sexy he thought Emma was. The man's thoughtless comment was uttered a moment before Brother Anthony plucked him off his stool and hurled him through the plate glass mirror behind the bar at which they'd been sitting. Brother Anthony did not like people who belittled the way he felt about Emma. Brother Anthony saw her quite differently than most people saw her. Most people saw a dumpy little bleached blond in a black cloth coat and black cotton stockings and blue track shoes and a black shoulder bag in which there was a straightedge razor with a bone handle. Brother Anthony—despite empirical knowledge to the contrary—saw a natural blond with curly ringlets that framed a Madonna-like face and beautiful blue eyes; Brother Anthony saw breasts like watermelons and a behind like a brewer's horse; Brother Anthony saw thick white thighs and acres and acres of billowy flesh;

Brother Anthony saw a shy, retiring, timid, vulnerable darling dumpling caught in the whirlwind of a hostile society, someone to cuddle and cherish and console.

Just walking beside her, Brother Anthony had an erection, but perhaps that was due to the supreme satisfaction of having beaten that pool hustler to within an inch of his life; it was sometimes difficult to separate and categorize emotions, especially when it was so cold outside. He took Emma's elbow and led her onto Mason Avenue toward a bar in the middle of a particularly sordid stretch of real estate that ran north and south for a total of three blocks. There was a time when the Street (as the three-block stretch was familiarly defined) was called the Hussy Hole by the Irish immigrants and later Foxy Way by the blacks. With the Puerto Rican influx, the street had changed its language—but not its major source of income. The Puerto Ricans referred to it as La Vía de Putas. The cops used to call it Whore Street before the word *hooker* became fashionable. They now referred to it as Hooker Heaven. In any language, you paid your money, and you took your choice.

Not too long a time ago, the madams who ran the sex emporiums called themselves Mama-this or Mama-that. In those days, Mama Teresa's was the best-known joint on the street. Mama Carmen's was the filthiest. Mama Luz's had been raided most often by the cops because of the somewhat exotic things that went on behind its crumbling brick facade. Those days were gone forever. The brothel, as such, was a thing of the past, a quaint memory. Nowadays, the hookers operated out of the massage parlors and bars that lined the street, and turned their tricks in the hot-bed hotels that blinked their eyeless neon to the night. The bar Brother Anthony chose was a hooker hangout named Sandy's, but at two in the afternoon most of the neighborhood working girls were still sleeping off Friday night's meaningless exercise. Only a black girl wearing a blond wig was sitting at the bar.

"Hello, Brother Anthony," she said. "Hello, Lady."

"Dominus vobiscum," Brother Anthony said, cleaving the air with the edge of his right hand in a downward stroke, and then passing the hand horizontally across the first invisible stroke to form the sign of the cross. He had no idea what the Latin words meant. He knew only that they added to the image he had consciously created for himself. "All is image," he liked to tell Emma, the words rolling mellifluously off his tongue, his voice deep and resonant, "all is illusion."

"What'll it be?" the bartender asked.

"A little red wine, please," Brother Anthony said. "Emma?"

"Gin on the rocks, a twist," Emma said.

"See what the other lady will have," Brother Anthony said, indicating the black-and-blond hooker. He was feeling flush. His encounter with the ambitious pool hustler had netted him a five-hundred-dollar profit. He asked the bartender for some change, went to the juke box, and selected an assortment of rock-and-roll tunes. He loved rock-and-roll. He especially loved rock-and-roll groups that dressed up on stage so you couldn't recognize them later on the street. The black-and-blond hooker was telling the bartender she wanted another scotch and soda. As Brother Anthony went back to his stool at the other end of the bar, she said, "Thanks, Brother Anthony."

The bartender, who was also the Sandy who owned the place, wasn't too happy to see Brother Anthony in here. He did not like having to replace plate glass mirrors every time Brother Anthony took it in his head to get insulted by something somebody said. Luckily, the only other person in here today, besides Brother Anthony and his fat broad, was the peroxided nigger at the end of the bar, and Brother Anthony had just bought *her* a drink, so maybe there'd be no trouble this afternoon. Sandy hoped so. This was Saturday. There'd be plenty of trouble here tonight, whether Sandy wanted it or not.

In this neighborhood, and especially on this street, Saturday night was never the loneliest night of the week, no matter *what* the song said. In this neighborhood, and especially on this street, nobody had to go lonely on Saturday night, not if he had yesterday's paycheck in his pocket. Along about ten tonight, there'd be more hookers cruising this bar than there'd be rats rummaging in the empty lot next door, black hookers and white ones, blonds and brunettes and redheads, even some with pink hair or lavender hair, males and females and some who were AC/DC. Two by two they came, it took all kinds to make a world, into the ark they came, your garden variety scaly-legged twenty-dollar-a-blowjob beasts or your slinky racehorses who thought they were working downtown at a C-note an hour, it took all kinds to make a pleasant family neighborhood bar. Two by two they came and were welcomed by Sandy, who recognized that all those men drinking at the bar were here to sample the flesh and not the spirits, and who was anyway getting a piece of the action from each of the nocturnal ladies who were allowed to cruise here, his recompense (or so he told them) for having to pay off the cops on the beat and also their sergeant who dropped in every now and again. Actually, Sandy was ahead of the game, except when the weekend trouble assumed larger proportions than it normally did. He dreaded weekends, even though it was the weekends that made it possible for the bar to remain open on weekdays.

"This is on the house," he said to Brother Anthony, hoping the bribe would keep him away from here tonight, and then suddenly panicking when he realized Brother Anthony might *like* the hospitality and might decide to return for more of it later.

"I pay for my own drinks," Brother Anthony said, and fetched the roll of bills from the pouchlike pocket running across the front of his cassock, and peeled off one of the pool hustler's tens, and put it on the bar.

"Even so . . ." Sandy started, but Brother Anthony silently made the sign of the cross on the air, and Sandy figured who was he to argue with a messenger of God? He picked up the ten-spot, rang up the sale, and then put Brother Anthony's change on the bar in front of him. At the end of the bar, the black hooker in the frizzy blond wig lifted her glass and said, "Cheers, Brother Anthony."

"Dominus vobiscum," Brother Anthony said, lifting his own glass.

Emma put her fleshy hand on his knee.

"Did you hear anything else?" she whispered.

"No," he said, shaking his head. "Did you?"

"Only that he had eleven bills in his wallet when he caught it."

"Eleven bills," Brother Anthony whispered.

"And also, it was a thirty-eight. The gun."

"Who told you that?"

"I heard two cops talking in the diner."

"A thirty-eight," Brother Anthony said. "Eleven bills."

"That's the kind of bread I'm talking about," Emma said. "That's *cocaine* bread, my dear."

Brother Anthony let his eyes slide sidelong down the bar, just to make sure neither the bartender nor the black hooker were tuning in. The bartender was leaning over the bar, in deep and whispered conversation with the hooker. His fingertips roamed the yoke front of her dress, brushing the cleft her cushiony breasts formed. Brother Anthony smiled.

"The death of that little *schwanz* has left a gap," Emma said.

"Indeed," Brother Anthony said.

"There are customers adrift in the night," Emma said.

"Indeed," Brother Anthony said again.

"It would be nice if we could *fill* that gap," Emma said. "Inherit the trade, so to speak. Find out who the man was servicing, become their *new* candyman and candylady."

"There's people who might not like that," Brother Anthony said.

"I don't agree with you. I don't think the little pisher was killed for his trade. No, my dear, I definitely disagree with you."

"Then why?"

"Was he killed? My educated guess?"

"Please," Brother Anthony said.

"Because he was a stupid little man who probably got stingy with one of his customers. That's my guess, bro. But, ah, my dear, when *we* begin selling the nose dust it'll be a different story. We will be sugar-sweet to everybody; we will be Mr. and Mrs. Nice."

"How do we get the stuff to sell?" Brother Anthony asked.

"First things first," Emma said. *"First* we get the customers, *then* we get the candy."

"How many customers do you think he had?" Brother Anthony asked.

"Hundreds," Emma said. "Maybe thousands. We are going to get rich, my dear. We are going to thank God every day of the week that somebody killed Paco Lopez."

"Dominus vobiscum," Brother Anthony said, and made the sign of the cross.

Timothy Moore came into the squadroom not ten minutes after a package of Sally Anderson's effects was delivered by a patrolman from Midtown East. The accompanying note from Detective Levine mentioned that he had talked with the dead girl's boyfriend and they ought to expect a visit from him. So here he was *now,* standing just outside the slatted rail divider and introducing himself to Genero, who immediately said, "That ain't my case."

"In here, sir," Meyer said, signaling to Moore, who looked up, nodded, found the release catch on the inside of the gate, and let himself into the squadroom. He was a tall, angular young man with wheat-colored hair and dark brown eyes. The trench coat he was wearing seemed too lightweight for this kind of weather, but perhaps the long striped muffler around his neck and the rubber boots on his feet were some sort of compensation. His eyes were quite solemn behind the aviator eyeglasses he wore. He took Meyer's offered hand and said, "Detective Carella?"

"I'm Detective Meyer. *This* is Detective Carella."

"How do you do?" Carella said, rising from behind his desk and extending his hand. Moore was just a trifle taller than he was; their eyes met at almost the same level.

"Detective Levine at Midtown East . . ."

"Yes, sir."

"Told me the case had been turned over to you."

"That's right," Carella said.

"I went up there the minute I learned about Sally."

"When was that, sir?"

"This morning. I heard about it this morning."

"Sit down, won't you? Would you like some coffee?"

"No, thank you. I went up there at about ten o'clock, it must've been, right after I heard the news on the radio."

"Where was this, Mr. Moore?"

"In my apartment."

"And where's that?"

"On Chelsea Place. Downtown, near the university. Ramsey."

"We understand you're a medical student there," Carella said.

"Yes." He seemed puzzled as to how they already knew this, but he let it pass, shrugging it aside. "I went back up there a little while ago—"

"Up there?"

"Midtown East. And Mr. Levine told me the case had been turned over to you. So I thought I'd check with you, just to see if there was anything I could do to help."

"We appreciate that," Carella said.

"How long had you known Miss Anderson?" Meyer asked.

"Since last July. I met her shortly after my father died."

"How'd you happen to meet her?"

"At a party I crashed. She . . . the minute I saw her . . ." He looked down at his hands. The fingers were long and slender, the nails as clean as a surgeon's. "She was . . . very beautiful. I . . . was attracted to her from the first minute I saw her."

"So you began seeing her . . ."

"Yes . . ."

"Last July."

"Yes. She'd just gotten the part in *Fatback.*"

"But you weren't living together or anything," Meyer said. "Or *were* you?"

"Not officially. That is, we didn't share the same apartment," Moore said. "But we saw each other virtually every night. I keep thinking . . ." He shook his head. The detectives waited. "I keep thinking if only I'd been with her *last* night . . ." He shook his head again. "I usually picked her up after the show. Last night . . ." Again he shook his head. The detectives waited. He said nothing further.

"Last night . . ." Carella prompted.

"It's stupid the way things work sometimes, isn't it?" Moore said. "My grades were slipping. Too much partying. Okay. I made a New Year's resolution to spend at least *one* weekend night studying. Either Friday, Saturday, or Sunday. This week it was Friday.''

"You're saying—''

"I'm saying . . . look, I don't know *who* did this to her, but chances are it was just some lunatic who ran across her on the street, am I right? Saw her on the street and killed her, am I right? A chance victim.''

"Maybe," Carella said.

"So what I'm saying is if this had been *last* week, I'd have been there to pick her *up* on Friday night. Because last week I stayed home on *Sunday* to study. I remember there was a party she wanted me to go to on Sunday, and I told her no, I had to study. Or the week *before* that, it would've been a Saturday. What I'm saying is why did it have to be a *Friday* this week, why couldn't I have been *waiting* for her last night when she came out of that theater?''

"Mr. Moore," Meyer said, "in the event this *wasn't* a crazy—''

"It had to be," Moore said.

"Yes, well," Meyer said, and glanced at Carella, looking for some sort of expression on his face that would indicate whether or not it would be wise to mention Paco Lopez. Carella's face said nothing, which was as good as telling Meyer to cool it. "But we have to explore every possibility," Meyer said, "which is why the questions we're about to ask may sound irrelevant, but we have to ask them anyway.''

"I understand," Moore said.

"As the person closest to Miss Anderson—''

"Well, her mother is alive, you know," Moore said.

"Does she live in the city?''

"No, she lives in San Francisco.''

"Did Miss Anderson have any brothers or sisters?''

"No.''

"Then essentially—''

"Yes, I suppose you could say I was closest . . . to her.''

"I'm assuming you confided things to each other.''

"Yes.''

"Did she ever mention any threatening letters or telephone calls?''

"No.''

"Anyone following her?''

"No.''

"Or lurking about the building?''

"No.''

"Did she owe money to anyone?''

"No.''

"Did anyone owe *her* money?''

"I don't know.''

"Was she involved with drugs?''

"No.''

"Or any other illegal activity?''

"No.''

"Had she recently received any gifts from strangers?'' Carella asked.

"I don't know what you mean."

"At the theater," Carella said. "Flowers . . . or candy? From unknown admirers?"

"She never mentioned anything like that."

"Did she ever have any trouble at the stage door?"

"What kind of trouble?"

"Someone waiting for her, trying to talk to her, or touch her . . ."

"You don't mean autograph hounds?"

"Well, anyone who might have got overly aggressive."

"No."

"Or who was rejected by her . . ."

"No."

"Nothing you saw or that she later mentioned to you."

"Nothing."

"Mr. Moore," Carella said, "we've gone through Miss Anderson's appointment calendar and had a schedule typed up for every day this month. We've just now received her address book from Midtown East, and we'll be cross-checking that against the names on the calendar. But you might save us some time if you could identify—"

"I'll be happy to," Moore said.

Carella opened the top drawer of his desk and took out several photocopies of the sheet Miscolo had typed from their handwritten notes. He handed one of the copies to Moore and another to Meyer.

MONDAY, FEBRUARY 1

10:00 AM	Dance
12:00 Noon	Lunch, Herbie.
	Genelli's.
4:00 PM	Kaplan
6:00 PM	Groceries
7:30 PM	Theater

"Kaplan's her shrink," Moore said. "She saw him at four o'clock every Monday, Thursday, and Friday."

"Would you know his first name?"

"Maurice, I think."

"Know where his office is?"

"Yes, on Jefferson. I picked her up there once."

"Who's this Herbie she had lunch with?"

"Herb Gotlieb, her agent."

"Know where *his* office is?"

"Midtown someplace. Near the theater."

TUESDAY, FEBRUARY 2

10:00 AM	Dance
2:00 PM	Audition
	Théâtre des Étoiles
4:30 PM	Call Mother M.
7:30 PM	Theater

"That's when she was *due* at the theater," Moore said. "The curtain goes up at eight each night, two o'clock for the matinees. Half hour is one-thirty for the matinees, seven-thirty for the evening performances. That means the company gets to the theater a half hour before curtain."

"What's this audition at two o'clock?" Carella asked. "Do they audition for other parts when they're already working in a hit?"

"Oh, yes, all the time," Moore said.

"We've got her clocked for two calls a week to 'Mother M,' " Meyer said. "Would that be her mother in San Francisco?"

"No," Moore said. "That's *my* mother. In Miami."

"She called *your* mother twice a week?"

"Every week. Sally didn't get along too well with her own mother. She left home at an early age, went to London to study ballet. Things were never the same afterward."

"So your mother was . . . sort of a substitute, huh?"

"A surrogate, if you will."

"Mother M. Does that stand for? . . ."

"Mother Moore, yes."

"That's what she called her, huh?"

"Yes. We used to joke about it. Made my mother sound like a nun or something." He paused. "Has anyone contacted *Mrs.* Anderson? I'm sure she'd want to know. I guess."

"Would you know her first name?" Carella asked.

"Yes, it's Phyllis. Her number's probably in Sally's book. You *did* say Mr. Levine had sent you—"

"Yes, we have it here with some of her other stuff. The stuff the lab's finished with."

"What's the lab looking for?" Moore asked.

"Who knows *what* they look for?" Carella said, and smiled. He knew damn well what they looked for. They looked for anything that might shed a little light on either the killer or the victim. The killer because he was still loose out there and the longer he stayed loose the harder it would be to get him. And the victim because very often the more you knew about what a person had *been,* the easier it became to learn why anyone would want that person to *cease* being.

"But surely," Moore said, "nothing in Sally's personal effects could possibly tell you anything about the lunatic who attacked her."

Again, neither of the detectives mentioned that the same "lunatic" had attacked and killed a young cocaine dealer named Paco Lopez three nights before he'd killed Sally. Instead, both of them looked at the schedules in their hands. Taking his cue, Moore also looked at his schedule.

WEDNESDAY, FEBRUARY 3

10:00 AM	Dance
12:00 Noon	Antoine's
1:30 AM	Theater
5:00 PM	Herbie, Sands Bar
7:30 PM	Theater

"Two performances every Wednesday and Saturday," Moore said.

"Who's Antoine?" Carella asked.

"Her hairdresser," Moore said. "He's on South Arundel, six blocks from her apartment."

"There's Herbie again," Meyer said.

"Yes, she saw him often," Moore said. "Well, an agent is very important to an actress's career, you know."

The listings for the remaining nine days between Wednesday, February 3 and Friday, February 12—the last full day before she was murdered—followed much the same pattern. Dance class on Monday through Friday at ten in the morning. Kaplan at 4:00 P.M. three times a week. Calls to Moore's mother in Miami twice a week. Meetings with her agent Herbie at *least* twice a week, and sometimes more often. The page for Sunday, February 7, listed only the word "Del" without a time before it, and then the words "8:00 P.M. Party. Lonnie's."

"She's one of the black dancers in the show," Moore said. "Lonnie Cooper. That's the party Sally wanted me to go to last week."

"And who's Del?" Carella asked.

"Del?"

"Right there on the sheet," Carella said. "Del. No time, no place. Just Del."

"Del? Oh," Moore said. "Of course."

"Who is he? Or she?"

"Neither," Moore said, and smiled. "That stands for delicatessen."

"Delicatessen?" Meyer said.

"Cohen's Deli," Moore said. "On the Stem and North Rogers. Sally went up there every Sunday. To pick up bagels and lox, cream cheese, the works."

"And she put that on her calendar, huh?"

"Well, yes, she put *everything* on her calendar."

"Went up there every Sunday."

"Yes."

"What time?"

"It varied."

"Uh-huh," Carella said, and looked at the sheet again.

On Thursday, February 11, Sally had gone to her hairdresser again, and then later in the day to a meeting with a man named Samuel Lang at Twentieth Century-Fox. On the day before she was killed, she had taken her cat to the vet's at one in the afternoon. The listed calendar appointments naturally spilled over into the weeks beyond her death; even in this city, no one ever expected a gun exploding out of the night. She had, for example, meticulously noted "Dance" for every February weekday at 10:00 A.M. and had similarly noted her appointments with Kaplan, her twice-weekly calls to Moore's mother, and the times she was due at the theater. For Monday, February 15, she had noted that the cat had to be picked up at 3:00 P.M.

"Mr. Moore," Carella said, "I hope you won't mind if we ask some questions—"

"Anything," Moore said.

"Of a more personal nature," Carella said.

"Go ahead."

"Well . . . would you know whether or not there was any other man in her life?

Besides you. Someone who might have been jealous of the relationship she shared with you? Someone she might have known *before* she met you?''

"Not that I know of.''

"Or another woman?''

"No, of course not.''

"No one who might have resented—''

"No one.''

"How about her agent, Herb Gotlieb? How old a man is he?''

"Why?''

"I was just wondering,'' Carella said.

"Wondering what?''

"Well, she *did* see him a lot—''

"He was her agent; of *course* she saw him a lot.''

"I'm not suggesting—''

"Yes, you *are,* as a matter of fact,'' Moore said. "First you ask me whether there was another man—or even another *woman,* for God's sake—in Sally's life, and then you zero in on Herb Gotlieb, who has to be at *least* fifty-five years old! How can you *possibly* believe someone like Herb could have—''

"I don't believe anything yet,'' Carella said. "I'm simply exploring the possibilities.''

And one of the possibilities, it belatedly occurred to him, was that Mr. Timothy Moore himself was a possible suspect in at least the murder of Sally Anderson. Carella had learned a long time ago that some 30 percent of all reported homicides were generated by family situations, and 20 percent were eventually identified as stemming from lovers' quarrels. By his own admission, Timothy Moore had been Sally Anderson's lover, and never mind that he had voluntarily walked into the squadroom—*two* squadrooms, in fact, by the most recent count.

"As a matter of fact,'' Moore said, "the only thing that interests Herb is money. Sally could have danced for him naked and he wouldn't have noticed unless she was *also* tossing gold doubloons in the air.''

Carella decided to run with it.

"But she wouldn't have done that, right?'' he said.

"Done *what?*''

"Danced naked for Herb Gotlieb. Or for anyone else.''

"Is that a question?''

"It's a question.''

"The answer is no.''

"You're sure of that?''

"I'm absolutely positive.''

"No other men or women in her life?''

"None.''

"She told you that?''

"She didn't *have* to tell me. I *knew.*''

"How about you?''

"What about me?''

"Any other women in your life?"

"No."

"Or men?"

"No."

"Then this was pretty serious between you, is that right?"

"It was serious enough."

"How serious is serious enough?"

"I don't get this," Moore said.

"What don't you get?"

"I came up here to offer—"

"Yes, and we're grateful for that."

"You don't *seem* too grateful," Moore said. "What are you going to ask *next?* Where I was last night when Sally was getting killed?"

"I wasn't going to ask that, Mr. Moore," Carella said. "You already told us you were home studying."

"*Were* you home?" Meyer asked.

"You weren't going to ask, huh? I was home."

"All night long?"

"Here we go," Moore said, rolled his eyes.

"You were her boyfriend," Meyer said flatly.

"Which means I killed her, right?" Moore said.

"You seem to be asking the questions and giving the answers both," Meyer said. "*Were* you home all night?"

"All night."

"Anyone with you?"

"Not exactly."

"What does that mean, not exactly? Either someone is with you or you're alone. Were you alone?"

"I was alone. But I called a friend of mine at least a half a dozen times."

"What about?"

"The study material. Questions back and forth."

"Is he a med student, too? This friend you called?"

"Yes."

"What's his name?"

"Karl Loeb."

"Where does he live?"

"In the Quarter."

"Do you know his address?"

"No. But I'm sure he's in the phone book."

"What time did you call him?"

"Off and on, all night long."

"Did you call him at midnight?"

"I don't remember."

"Did he call *you* at any time last night?"

"Several times."

"When's the last time you spoke to him?"

"Just before I went to sleep. I called Sally first, I tried her number—"

"Had you called *her* before that?"

"On and off, yes."

"Last night, we're talking about."

"Yes, last night. I called her on and off."

"Were you worried when you didn't get her?"

"No."

"How come? When's the last time you tried her?"

"About three in the morning. Just before I called Karl for the last time."

"And you got no answer?"

"No answer."

"And you weren't worried? Three in the morning, and she doesn't answer the phone—"

"You're talking about theater people," Moore said. "Night people. Three o'clock is still early for them. Anyway, she knew I was studying. I figured she must've made other plans."

"Did she tell you *what* plans?"

"No, she didn't."

"When did you call her again?"

"I didn't. I heard about . . . when I woke up, I turned on the radio and I . . . I . . . heard . . . I heard . . ."

He suddenly buried his face in his hands and began weeping. The detectives watched him. Carella was thinking they'd been too harsh with him. Meyer was thinking the same thing. But why'd he come up here? Carella wondered. Meyer wondered the same thing. And why had a medical student expressed ignorance of what sort of evidence might be turned up by an examination of Sally's personal effects? Weren't medical schools teaching prospective doctors about bloodstains anymore? Or traces of semen? Or fingernail scrapings? Or human hair? Or any of the other little physical leftovers that could later lead to positive identification? Moore kept weeping into his hands.

"Are you all right?" Carella asked.

Moore nodded. He fumbled in his back pocket for a handkerchief, tossing the tails of his trench coat aside. There was a stethoscope in the right-hand pocket of his jacket. He found the handkerchief, blew his nose, dried his eyes.

"I loved her," he said.

The detectives said nothing.

"And she loved me," he said.

Still they said nothing.

"I know what you're trained to look for, I know all about it. But I had nothing to do with her murder. I came up here because I wanted to *help,* period. You might do better to go looking for the son of a bitch who *did* it, instead of—"

"I'm sorry, Mr. Moore," Carella said.

"I'll bet you are," Moore said. He put the handkerchief back in his pocket. He looked up at the wall clock. He stood up and began buttoning the trench coat. "I've got to to," he said. "You'll find my number in Sally's book, you can reach me at night there. During the day, I'm at Ramsey."

"We appreciate your help," Meyer said.

"Sure," Moore said, and turned and walked out of the squadroom.

Both men looked at each other.

"What do you think?" Carella said.

"The idea or the execution?"

"Well, I know I blew it, but the idea."

"Good one."

"I really *was* looking for a third party at first—"

"I know that. But the other way around, right?"

"Right. Some guy—"

"Or some lady—"

"Right, who was annoyed because Sally Anderson was seeing Moore—"

"Right."

"And who decided to put the blocks to her."

"A possibility," Meyer said.

"But then Moore blew sky-high—"

"Right, I could see the wheels clicking inside your head, Steve."

"Right, when I reversed field, right?"

"Right. You were thinking, 'Hey, maybe *Moore* is the jealous party, maybe *he's* the one who killed her.' "

"Well, yeah. But I blew it."

"Maybe not, maybe now he'll run a bit scared. Two things we've got to find out, Steve—"

"Right. The exact time he was on the phone talking to this guy Loeb—"

"Right, the other med student."

"Right. And where he was on Tuesday night, when Lopez was getting his."

"You decided not to go with Lopez, huh?"

"I wanted to see if Moore would *volunteer* an alibi for Tuesday."

"Listen, you know something?" Meyer said. "Who *says* the same gun means the same killer?"

"Huh?" Carella said.

"*I* use a gun to kill somebody on Tuesday night. I throw the gun away. Somebody picks it up, and it finds its way onto the street. *You* come along and buy the gun to use on Friday night. No connection at all between the two murders, do you get it?"

"I get it," Carella said, "and you're making life difficult."

"Only because I can't see any connection at all between Paco Lopez and Sally Anderson."

"Monday's a holiday, isn't it?" Carella asked abruptly.

"Huh?"

"Monday."

"What about it?"

"It's Washington's Birthday, isn't it?"

"No, that's the twenty-second."

"But we're celebrating it on the fifteenth. We're calling it 'Presidents' Day.'"

"What's that got to do with Moore?"

"Nothing. I'm thinking about the cat."

"What cat?"

"Sally's cat. She was supposed to pick it up on Monday. Will the vet be open on Monday?"

"I guess if she put it in her book—"

"She listed a pickup for three o'clock."

"Then I guess he'll be open."

"So who'll pick up the cat?" Carella asked.

"Not me," Meyer said at once.

"Maybe Sarah would like a cat," Carella said.

"Sarah doesn't like cats," Meyer said. His wife did not like *any* animals. His wife thought animals were *animals*.

"Maybe the girl's mother will take the cat," Carella said, very seriously.

"The girl's mother is in San Francisco," Meyer said, and looked at him.

"So who'll take the goddamn cat?" Carella said. He had once taken home a seeing eye dog he'd inherited on the job. Fanny, the Carella housekeeper, had not liked the dog. At *all*. The dog no longer resided at the big old house in Riverhead. Meyer was still looking at him.

"I just hate to think of that cat sitting there *waiting*," Carella said, and the telephone rang. He snatched the receiver from the cradle.

"Eighty-Seventh Squad, Carella," he said.

"This is Allan Carter," the voice on the other end said.

"Ah, Mr. Carter, good," Carella said. "I've been trying to reach you. Thanks for returning my call."

"Is this about Sally Anderson?" Carter asked.

"Yes, sir."

"I know nothing whatever about her death."

"We'd like to talk to you anyway, sir," Carella said. "As her employer—"

"I've never heard it described *that* way before," Carter said.

"Sir?"

"I've never heard a *producer* described as an *employer*," Carter said, raising his voice as though Carella hadn't quite heard him the first time around. "In any event, I was in Philadelphia last night. Her death came as a total surprise to me."

"Yes, sir, I'm sure it did," Carella said. He paused. "We'd *still* like to talk to you, Mr. Carter."

"We're talking now," Carter said.

"In *person*, Mr. Carter."

There was a silence on the line. Carella leaped into it.

"Can you see us at three?" he asked. "We won't take up much of your time."

"I have an appointment at three," Carter said.

"When *will* you be free, sir?"

"This is Saturday," Carter said. "I just got back from Philly, I'm calling you from home. Tomorrow's Sunday, and Monday's a holiday. Can we meet sometime Tuesday? Or Wednesday? I won't be going back to Philly till late Wednesday.''

"No, sir," Carella said, "I'm afraid we can't."

"Why not?" Carter said.

"Because a twenty-five-year-old girl's been murdered," Carella said, "and we'd like to talk to you *today,* sir—if that's all right with you."

Carter said nothing for several seconds.

Then he said, "Four o'clock," and gave Carella the address, and hung up abruptly.

5

Allan Carter lived in a high-rise apartment building snugly nestled into a row of luxury hotels overlooking Grover Park West. Because the streets had not yet been plowed entirely clear of snow, it took the detectives almost a half-hour to drive the fifty-odd blocks from the station house to Carter's building. Actually, if the forecast for more snow tomorrow was accurate, the sanitmen were laboring somewhat like Hercules in the Augean stables. The day was gloomy and bitterly cold. The snow had hardened and was difficult to move. As the detectives approached Carter's building, a uniformed doorman was trying to break away the ice that had formed in front of the doorway after the sidewalk had been shoveled. He worked with a long-handled ice-chipper that would have made a good weapon, Carella thought. Meyer was thinking the same thing.

Another uniformed man was sitting behind a desk in the lobby. Carella and Meyer identified themselves, and the man picked up a phone, said, "Mr. Carella and Mr. Meyer to see you, sir," and then cradled the receiver and said, "You can go right up, it's apartment thirty-seven."

The uniformed elevator man said, "They say it's gonna snow again tomorrow." Meyer looked at Carella.

They got off on the third floor, walked a long carpeted hallway to Carter's apartment, pressed the bell button set in the doorjamb, heard chimes sounding inside, and then a voice calling, "Come in, it's open!"

Carella opened the door, and almost tripped over a piece of brown leather luggage in the entrance hall. He stepped around the bag, motioned for Meyer to be careful, and then moved from the foyer into a vast living room with wall-to-wall windows overlooking the park. The naked branches of the trees beyond were laden with snow. The sky behind them was gray and roiling. Allan Carter was sitting on a long sofa upholstered in a pale green springtime fabric. He had a telephone to his ear. He was wearing a dark brown business suit over a lemon-colored shirt. Gold cufflinks showed at his sleeves. A chocolate brown tie hung loose over his massive chest. The top button of his shirt was unfastened. Listening to whoever was on the other end of the phone connection, he gestured for the detectives to come in.

"Yes, I understand that," he said into the phone. "But, Dave ... uh-huh, uh-huh." He listened impatiently, sighing, pulling a face, tugging simultaneously at a lock of thick white hair that crowned his head. The white hair was premature, Carella guessed; Carter seemed to be a man in his early forties. His eyes were a piercing blue, reflecting wan, fading winter light from the window wall. He looked suntanned. Carella wondered if the weather was better in Philadelphia than it was here. He suddenly thought of all the Philadelphia jokes he knew. He had never been to Philadelphia.

"Well, what did *Annie* get?" Carter said into the phone. He listened and then said, "That's exactly my point, Dave. This is a bigger hit than *Annie* ever was. Well, that's just too damn bad, things are tough all over. You tell Orion the price is firm, and if they can't meet it, tell them to pass, they're just wasting our time here. I recognize I'm talking deal-breaker, Dave, I'm not a babe in the woods. Tell them."

He hung up abruptly.

"Forgive me," he said, rising and coming to where the detectives were standing, his hand extended. "I'm Allan Carter, can I get either of you a drink?"

"No, thanks," Carella said.

"Thanks," Meyer said, shaking his head.

"So," Carter said. "Hell of a thing, huh?"

"Yes, sir," Carella said.

"Any idea yet who did it?"

"No, sir."

"Some lunatic," Carter said, shaking his head and walking toward the bar. He lifted a decanter. "Sure?" he said. "No?" He shrugged, poured two fingers of whiskey into a low glass, added a single ice cube to it, said, "Cheers," drank the entire contents of the glass in a single swallow, and poured more whiskey into it. "Philadelphia," he said, shaking his head as if simple *mention* of that city explained his need for alcoholic reinforcement.

"When did you learn about her death, Mr. Carter?" Carella asked.

"When I got off the train. I picked up a paper at the station."

"What were you doing in Philadelphia?"

"Trying out a new play there."

"Another musical?" Meyer asked.

"No, a straight play. Big headache," Carter said. "It's a thriller ... have you seen *Deathtrap?*"

"No," Meyer said.

"No," Carella said.

"It's sort of like *Deathtrap*. Except it's lousy. I don't know how I ever got talked into doing it. First time I've ever done a straight play." He shrugged. "Probably go right down the drain when it gets here. *If* it ever gets here."

"So you read about Miss Anderson in the papers," Carella prompted.

"Yes," Carter said.

"What'd you think?"

"What *could* I think? This city," he said, and shook his head.

"How well did you know her?" Carella asked.

"Hardly at all. Just another one of the dancers, you know? We've got sixteen of them in the show. Have you seen the show?"

"No," Meyer said.

"No," Carella said.

"I'll get you some house seats," Carter said. "It's a good show. Biggest hit this town has seen in a long time."

"Who hired her, Mr. Carter?"

"What? Oh, the girl. It was a joint decision."

"Whose?"

"Mine and Jamie's and—"

"Jamie?"

"Our choreographer, Jamie Atkins. But . . . are you asking who was actually *there* when the dancers were cast?"

"Yes."

"Well, as I said—this would be the final selection, you understand—*I* was there, and Freddie Carlisle, our director, and Jamie, and his assistant, and our musical director, and an Equity rep, I guess, and . . . let me see . . . two of the stage managers were there, and our press agent, I think, and, of course, a piano player. And . . . well, sure, the composer and the lyricist and the book writer."

"The book writer?"

"The librettist. I think that was about it. This was a long time ago. We went into rehearsal last August, you know. We must've been doing our final casting in July sometime."

"Quite a few people," Carella said.

"Oh, yes, decision by committee," Carter said, and smiled. "But when you figure a musical can cost anywhere between two and three million bucks—well, you've got to be cautious."

"So all these people got together and . . . well, what *did* they do?" Carella asked. "Vote?"

"Not really. It's more a sort of general agreement on a finalist, with the choreographer having the last word, of course. He's the one who's going to have to work with any given dancer, you know."

"How many dancers *didn't* get a part?"

"Thousands. Counting the cattle calls, and the Equity calls . . . sure. We must've seen every unemployed dancer in the city."

"Miss Anderson must've been a good dancer," Meyer said.

"I'm sure she was. She was, after all, hired for the part."

"How'd she get along with the rest of the cast?"

"You'd have to ask either Freddie or Jamie about that."

"Your director and choreographer."

"Yes. But I'm sure there was no friction . . . aside from the usual tension generated by a show in rehearsal. What I'm saying . . . let me try to explain this."

"Please," Carella said.

'''The company of any show, particularly a musical, has to perform as a tightly knit unit. I'm sure if there was any friction between Miss Anderson and anyone else in the cast, Jamie would've had a good long talk with her. When two million five is at stake, there's no room for fooling around with artistic temperament.''

"Is that how much *Fatback* cost?"

"Give or take."

"How long was the show in rehearsal, Mr. Carter?"

"Six weeks. Not counting previews. We did two weeks of previews before we felt we were ready for the critics."

"Were you present at all those rehearsals?"

"Not all of them. After Freddie had mounted a good part of the show, yes. Usually, you try to give your creative people a free hand in the beginning. Once the run-throughs start, a producer—well, *this* producer, anyway—tries to be present at all the rehearsals."

"Then you would have noticed if there was any friction between Miss Anderson and any other member of the cast."

"I detected no such friction. Gentlemen, I wish I could help you, believe me. But I hardly knew the girl. I'll confess something to you. When I read about her in the paper, I had difficulty recalling just which one of the dancers she was."

"I see," Carella said.

"Little redheaded thing, wasn't she?" Carter said.

"We didn't see the body, sir," Carella said.

"What?" Carter said.

"We weren't there at the scene, sir," Carella said.

"The body was found in another precinct," Meyer said at once.

"Sir," Carella said, "it would help us if we could get a list of names, addresses, and telephone numbers for everyone in the cast and crew, anyone who might have had even the slightest contact with Miss Anderson."

"You don't plan to visit them *all,* do you?" Carter said.

"Well . . . yes," Carella said.

Carter smiled. "Maybe I ought to give you some idea of what that would involve," he said. *"Fatback* is a very large show. We've got six principals, four featured players, sixteen dancers plus twelve *other* people in the chorus, eighteen stagehands, twenty-six musicians, three stage managers, three property men, fourteen wardrobe people, including the dressers, three electricians, two carpenters, one sound man, three lighting-board-and-follow-spot men, one makeup woman, and two standby dancers—what we call 'swing' dancers."

Carella looked at Meyer.

"That comes to a hundred and fourteen people," Carter said.

"I see," Carella said. He paused. Then he said, "But *does* such a list exist? Of all these people?"

"Well, yes, *several* lists, in fact. Our general manager has one, and our company manager, and the production secretary . . . in fact, I'm sure there's a list at the theater, too. Near the stage door phone. That might be your best bet. If you could stop by the theater . . ."

"Yes, sir, we'll do that."

"As a matter of fact, why don't you kill two birds with one stone?" Carter said.

"Sir?" Carella said.

"I mean, as long as you'll be at the theater."

The detectives looked at him, puzzled.

"I've guaranteed a pair for a friend of mine, but there was a message on my machine that he won't be coming into the city tonight because of the weather." Carter looked at their blank faces. "I'm talking about the show," he said. "Do you think you might like to see it? There's a pair of house seats guaranteed at the box office."

"Oh," Carella said.

"Oh," Meyer said.

"What do you think?" Carter said.

"Well, thank you," Meyer said, "but my wife and I are meeting some friends for dinner tonight."

"How about you?"

"Well . . ." Carella said.

"You'll enjoy it, believe me."

"Well . . ."

He was hesitating because he didn't know what "house seats" were and he didn't know what "guaranteed" meant, but it sounded to him as if these might be free tickets, and he sure as hell wasn't about to accept a gift from a man who claimed to believe a five-foot-eight blond murder victim was a "little redheaded thing." Carella had learned early on in the game that if you wanted to survive as a cop, you either took nothing at all or you took everything that wasn't nailed down. Accept a cup of coffee on the arm from the guy who ran the local diner? Fine. Then also take a bribe from the friendly neighborhood fence who was running a tag sale on stolen goods every Sunday morning. A slightly dishonest cop was the same thing as a slightly pregnant woman.

"How much do these tickets cost?" he asked.

"Forget it," Carter said, and waved the question aside, and Carella knew the man had figured he was seeking the grease; he was, after all, a *cop* in this fair city, wasn't he? And cops *copped;* anytime and anyplace they could."

"Are house seats free tickets?" Carella asked.

"No, no, we *do* have investors, you know, we can't go giving away seats to a hit," Carter said. "But these are taken care of, don't worry about them."

"Who's taking care of them?" Carella asked.

"I personally guaranteed them," Carter said.

"I don't know what that means," Carella said. "Guaranteed."

"I personally agreed to pay for them. Even if they weren't claimed."

"Claimed?"

"By law, house seats have to be claimed forty-eight hours before any performance. By guaranteeing them, I was—in effect—claiming them."

"But they haven't been paid for yet."

"No, they haven't."

"Then I'll pay for them myself, sir," Carella said.

"Well, really—"

"I'd like to see the show, sir, but I'd like to pay for the tickets myself."

"Fine, whatever you say. They're being held at the box office in my friend's name. Robert Harrington. You can claim them anytime before the curtain goes up."

"Thank you," Carella said.

"I'll call the stage door, meanwhile, tell them you'll be stopping by for that list."

"Thank you."

"I *still* don't understand what house seats are," Meyer said.

"Choice seats set aside for each performance," Carter said. "For the producer, director, choreographer, stars—"

"Set aside?"

"Reserved," Carter said, nodding. "By contract. So many seats for each performance. The higher you are in the pecking order, the more seats you're entitled to buy. If you don't claim them, of course, they go right back on sale in the box office, on a first-come, first-served basis."

"Live and learn," Meyer said, and smiled.

"Yes," Carter said, and glanced at his watch.

"Anything else?" Carella asked Meyer.

"Nothing I can think of," Meyer said.

"Then thank you, sir," Carella said. "And thanks for making those seats available to me."

"My pleasure," Carter said.

The detectives were silent in the elevator down to the street. The elevator operator, who had already informed them earlier that it was going to snow tomorrow, seemed to have nothing more to say. The sky was even more threatening when they stepped outside again. Darkness was coming on. It would be a moonless night.

"I just want to make sure I heard her right," Meyer said.

"Tina Wong, do you mean?"

"Yeah. She *did* say 'Five blonds, two blacks, and a token Chink,' didn't she?"

"That's what she said."

"So how could Carter think Sally Anderson was a *redhead?*"

"Maybe one of the understudies is a redhead."

"Maybe *I'm* a redhead, too," Meyer said. "Didn't Carter say that once they started run-throughs he was at every rehearsal?"

"That's what he said."

"So he *knows* that damn show. How could he *possibly* think there was a redhead up there?"

"Maybe he's color-blind."

"You *did* catch it, didn't you?"

"Oh, I caught it, all right."

"I was wondering why you didn't jump on it."

"I wanted to see how far he'd go with it."

"He didn't go *anywhere* with it. He let it lay there like a lox."

"Maybe he was just trying it for size."

"Backing up what he said about not knowing her from a hole in the wall. Just another one of the girls, another face in the crowd."

"Which may be true, Meyer. There are thirty-eight people in the cast. You can't expect a man to remember—"

"What's thirty-eight people, a *nation?*" Meyer said. "We've got close to two *hundred* cops in the precinct, and I know each and every one of them. By sight, at least."

"You're a trained observer," Carella said, smiling.

"How long does it take to get from Philadelphia by train?" Meyer asked.

"About an hour and a half."

"Easy to get here and back again," Meyer said. "Time enough to do anything that had to be done here. If a person had anything to do here."

"Yes," Carella said.

"Jamie digs blonds, remember?" Meyer said. "Isn't that what she told us? The choreographer digs blonds. So how come everybody in the world knows this but Carter? He was there when the whole *mishpocheh* was picking the dancers. Decision by committee, remember? So how come, all of a sudden, he has trouble remembering what color her *hair* is? A little redheaded thing, he calls her. All of a sudden, his choreographer—who likes them blond—ends up with a *redhead* in his chorus line. Steve, that stinks. I'm telling you it stinks. Do *you* buy it?"

"No," Carella said.

Buying the tickets came as something of a shock.

Carella had not seen a hit show in a long time, and he did not know what current prices were. When the woman in the box office shoved the little white envelope across the counter to him, he glanced at the yellow tickets peeking out, *thought* he saw the price on one of them, figured he must be wrong, and then had verbal confirmation when the woman said, "That'll be eighty dollars, please." Carella blinked. Eighty divided by two came to forty dollars a seat! "Will that be charge or cash?" the woman asked.

Carella did not carry a credit card; he did not know any cops who carried credit cards. He panicked for a moment. Did he *have* eighty dollars in cash in his wallet. As it turned out, he was carrying ninety-two dollars, which meant he would have to call home and ask Teddy to bring some cash with her tonight. He parted with the money reluctantly. This had better be *some* show, he thought, and walked to the pay phone in the lobby. Fanny, the Carella housekeeper, answered on the fourth ring.

"Carella residence," she said.

"Fanny, hi, it's me," he said. "Can you give Teddy a message? First tell her I've got tickets to a show called *Fatback,* and I thought we'd have dinner down here tonight before the show. Ask her to meet me at six-thirty, at a place called O'Malley's, she knows it, we've been there before. Next, tell her to bring a lot of cash; I'm running low."

"That's *three* messages," Fanny said. "How *much* cash?"

"Enough to cover dinner."

"I planned to make pork chops," Fanny said.

"I'm sorry," he said. "This came up all of a sudden."

"Mm," Fanny said.

He visualized her standing by the phone in the living room. Fanny Knowles was "fiftyish," as she put it in her faint Irish brogue, and she had blue hair, and she wore a pince-nez, and she weighed about 150 pounds, and she'd ruled the Carella household with an iron fist from the day she'd arrived there as a temporary gift from Teddy's father—ten years ago. Fanny was a registered nurse, and she'd originally been hired to stay with the Carellas for only a month, just long enough to give Teddy a hand till she was able to cope alone with the infant twins. It was Fanny who suggested that she ought to stay on a while longer, at a salary they could afford, telling them she never again wanted to stick another thermometer into a dying old man. She was still there. Her silence on the phone was ominous.

"Fanny, I'm really sorry," he said. "This is *sort* of business."

"What do I do with a dozen pork chops?" she said.

"Make a cassoulet," he said.

"What in hell is a cassoulet?" she asked.

"Look it up," he said. "Will you give her my message?"

"When she gets home," Fanny said, "which should be any minute now. She'll have to run a foot race to meet you downtown at six-thirty."

"Well, tell her, okay?"

"I'll tell her," Fanny said, and hung up.

He put the receiver back on the hook, went out of the theater, found the alley leading to the stage door, went to the door, and knocked on it.

An old man opened the door and peered out at him.

"Box office is up front," he said.

Carella showed him his shield and I.D. card. "I'm supposed to pick up a list," he said.

"What list?"

"Of everyone in the company."

"Oh, yeah, Mr. Carter phoned me about it. Come on in. I got one on the clipboard here, but I can't let you have it, it's the only one I got." The old man paused. "You can copy it down, if you like."

Carella went to the list hanging on the wall near the telephone, and looked at it. Four typewritten pages. He glanced at his watch.

"Okay if I take it out and have it Xeroxed?" he asked.

"No way," the old man said. "Only one I got."

"I was hoping—"

"How're we supposed to get in touch with anybody, case he don't show up for half hour? How we supposed to know to put in a swing dancer case somebody's sick or something? That list has to stay right *there,* right where it is." The old man paused. "You want my advice?"

Carella sighed, sat on the high stool near the wall telephone, and began copying the list into his notebook.

The laundromat was on the corner of Culver and Tenth, a neighborhood enclave that for many years had been exclusively Irish but that nowadays was a rich melting-pot mixture of Irish, black, and Puerto Rican. The melting pot here, as elsewhere in this city, never seemed to come to a precise boil, but that didn't bother any of the residents; they all knew it was nonsense, anyway. Even though they all shopped the same supermarkets and clothing stores; even though they all bought gasoline at the same gas stations and rode the same subways; even though they washed their clothes at the same laundromats and ate hamburgers side by side in the same greasy spoons, they all knew that when it came to socializing it was the Irish with the Irish and the blacks with the blacks and the Puerto Ricans with the Puerto Ricans and never mind that brotherhood-of-man stuff.

Eileen Burke, what with her peaches-and-cream complexion and her red hair and green eyes, could have passed for any daughter of Hibernian descent in the neighborhood—which, of course, was exactly what they were hoping for. It would not do to have the Dirty Panties Bandit, as the boys of the Eight-Seven had wittily taken to calling him, pop into the laundromat with his .357 Magnum in his fist, spot Eileen for a policewoman, and put a hole the size of a bowling ball in her ample chest. No, no. Eileen Burke did not want to become a dead heroine. Eileen Burke wanted to become the first lady Chief of Detectives in this city, but not over her own dead body. For the job tonight, she was dressed rather more sedately than she would have been if she'd been on the street trying to flush a rapist. Her red hair was pulled to the back of her head, held there with a rubber band, and covered with a dun-colored scarf knotted under her chin and hiding the pair of gold hoop earrings she considered her good-luck charms. She was wearing a cloth coat that matched the scarf, and knee-length brown socks and brown rubber boots and she was sitting on a yellow plastic chair in a very cold laundromat, watching her dirty laundry (or rather the dirty laundry supplied by the Eight-Seven) turn over and over in one of the washing machines while the neon sign in the window of the place flashed LAUNDROMAT first in orange, and then LAVANDERÍA in green. In the open handbag on her lap, the butt of a .38 Detective's Special beckoned from behind a wad of Kleenex tissues.

The manager of the place did not know Eileen was a cop. The manager of the place was the night man, who came on at four and worked through till midnight, at which time he locked up the place and went home. Every morning, the owner of the laundromat would come around to unlock the machines, pour all the coins into a big gray sack, and take them to the bank. That was the owner's job: emptying the machines of coins. The owner had thirty-seven laundromats all over the city, and he lived in a very good section of Majesta. He did not empty the machines at closing time because he thought that might be dangerous, which in fact it would have been. He preferred that his thirty-seven night men all over the city simply lock the doors, turn on the burglar alarms, and go home. That was part of their job, the night men. The rest of their job was to make change for the ladies who brought in their dirty clothes, and to call for service if any of the machines broke down, and also to make sure nobody stole any of the cheap plastic furniture in the various laundromats, although the owner didn't care much about that since he'd got a break on the stuff from his brother-in-law. Every now and then it occurred to the owner that his thirty-seven night men each had keys to the thirty-seven separate burglar alarms in the thirty-seven different locations and if they decided to go into cahoots with one of the crazies in this city, they could open the stores and break open the machines— but so what? Easy come, easy go. Besides, he liked to think all of his night men were pure and innocent.

Detective Hal Willis knew for damn sure that the night man at the laundromat on

Tenth and Culver was as pure and as innocent as the driven snow so far as the true identity of Eileen Burke was concerned. The night man did not know she was a cop, nor did he know that Willis himself, angle-parked in an unmarked green Toronado in front of the bar next door to the laundromat, was *also* a cop. In fact, the night man did not have the faintest inkling that the Eight-Seven had chosen his nice little establishment for a stakeout on the assumption that the Dirty Panties Bandit would hit it next. The assumption seemed a good educated guess. The man had been working his way straight down Culver Avenue for the past three weeks, hitting laundromats on alternate sides of the avenue, inexorably moving farther and farther downtown. The place he'd hit three nights ago had been on the south side of the avenue. The laundromat they were staking out tonight was eight blocks farther downtown, on the north side of the avenue.

The Dirty Panties Bandit was no small-time thief, oh no. In the two months during which he'd operated unchecked along Culver Avenue, first in the bordering precinct farther uptown, and then moving lower into Eight-Seven's territory, he had netted—or so the police had estimated from what the victimized women had told them—six hundred dollars in cash, twelve gold wedding bands, four gold lockets, a gold engagement ring with a one-carat diamond, and a total of twenty-two pairs of panties. These panties had not been lifted from the victim's laundry baskets. Instead, the Dirty Panties Bandit—and hence his name—had asked all those hapless laundromat ladies to please remove their panties for him, which they had all readily agreed to do since they were looking into the rather large barrel of a .357 Magnum. No one had been raped—yet. No one had been harmed—yet. And whereas there was something darkly humorous, after all, about an armed robber taking home his victims' panties, there was nothing at all humorous about the potential of a .357 Magnum. Sitting in the parked car outside the bar, Willis was very much aware of the caliber of the gun the laundromat robber carried. Sitting inside the laundromat, flanked by a Puerto Rican woman on her left and a black woman on her right, Eileen Burke was even more aware of the devastating power of that gun.

She looked up at the wall clock.

It was only ten-fifteen, and the place wouldn't be closing till midnight.

A little slip of paper in the program informed the audience that someone named Allison Greer would be replacing Sally Anderson that night, but none of the dancers in the show had character names, and they all looked very much alike with the exception of the two black girls (who in fact looked very much like each other) and Tina Wong, who looked like no one in the cast but herself. The blonds were indistinguishable one from the other. They were tall and leggy and, Carella thought, somewhat busty for dancers. They all had radiant smiles. They were all dressed in costumes that made them look even more alike, cut high on their thighs and hanging in tatters on their flashing legs, the sort of little nothing any young and ignorant southern girl might wear in the middle of a swamp, which was where *Fatback* was supposed to be taking place, and which was what the dancers in the cast were supposed to be. Given such a premise, given a curtain rising on what looked like a primeval bog, with mist floating in over it, and giant trees dripping moss onto slime-covered rocks, Carella had expected the worst. He turned to his right to look at Teddy. She was looking back at him. This was going to be yet another example of this city's critics praising yet another lousy show to the skies, and thereby turning straw into gold—for the *investors,* at any rate.

Teddy Carella was a deaf mute.

She often had difficulty at the theater. She could not hear what any of the performers were saying, of course, and usually she and Carella would be sitting too far back to read lips. Over the years, they had worked out a system whereby his hands—held chest high so as not to disturb anyone sitting behind them—flashed dialogue to her while she shifted her eyes back and forth from the stage to his rapidly moving fingers. Musicals, as a general rule, were somewhat easier for her. A singer usually faced the audience squarely when belting out a song, and his lip movements were more exaggerated than when he was simply speaking. Ballet was her favorite form of entertainment, and tonight she was delighted when—not ten seconds after the curtain had risen on that ominous bog—the entire stage seemed to fill with leaping, prancing, gyrating, twirling, frantically energetic dancers who virtually swung from the treetops and turned that steamy swamp into the sassiest, sexiest, most dazzling opening number Teddy had ever seen in her life. Spellbound, she sat beside Carella for what must have been ten full minutes of exposition through dance, squeezing his hand, her dark eyes flashing as she watched the story silently unfold. Carella sat there grinning. When the opening number ended, the house burst into tumultuous applause. He readied his hands for the translation he felt would be necessary as the act progressed, but he found that Teddy was impatiently nodding his moving fingers aside, understanding most of what was happening, able to read directly from the performers' lips because the seats were sixth row center.

She asked him some questions during intermission. She was wearing a black, wool-knit dress with a simple cameo just above her breasts, black leather boots, a gold bracelet on her wrist. She had pulled her long black hair to the back of her head and fastened it there with a gold barrette. Except for eye liner, shadow and lipstick, there was no makeup on her face. She needed none; she was the most beautiful woman he'd ever known in his life. He watched her hands, watched the accompanying expressions that crossed her face. She wanted to know if she'd been right in assuming that the trapper and the girl moonshiner had had an affair years ago, and that this was the first time they'd seen each other since? No? Then what was all that hugging and kissing about? Carella explained, responding with his voice so that she could read his lips, accompanying his voice with hand signals (and always there were the fascinated observers in the crowd, nudging each other—Hey, take a look, Charlie, see the grown man talking to the dummy?) and she watched his lips and watched his hands and then signed *Well, they seem awfully lovey-dovey for cousins,* and he explained that they were only *second* cousins, and she signed *Does that make incest legal?*

Now, forty-five minutes into the second act, Carella looked at his watch because he sensed the evening was coming to an end and he simply did not want it to. He was having too good a time.

Eileen Burke was having a splendid time watching her laundry go round and round. The night man thought she was a little crazy, but then again everybody in this town was a little crazy. She had put the same batch of laundry through the machine five times already. Each time, she sat watching the laundry spinning in the machine. The night man didn't notice that she alternately watched the front door of the place or looked through the plate glass window each time a car pulled in. The neon fixture splashed orange and green on the floor of the laundromat: LAVANDERÍA ... LAUNDROMAT ... LAVANDERÍA ... LAUNDROMAT. The laundry in the machines went round and round.

A woman with a baby strapped to her back was at one of the machines, putting in another load. Eileen guessed she was no older than nineteen or twenty, a slender attractive blue-eyed blond who directed a nonstop flow of soft chatter over her shoulder to her near-dozing infant. Another woman was sitting on the yellow plastic chair next to Eileen's, reading a magazine. She was a stout black woman, in her late thirties or early forties, Eileen guessed, wearing a bulky knit sweater over blue jeans and galoshes. Every now and then, she flipped a page of the magazine, looked up at the washing machines, and then flipped another page. A third woman came into the store, looked around frantically for a moment, seemed relieved to discover there were plenty of free machines, dashed out of the store, and returned a moment later with what appeared to be the week's laundry for an entire Russian regiment. She asked the manager to change a five-dollar bill for her. He changed it from a coin dispenser attached to his belt, thumbing and clicking out the coins like a streetcar conductor. Eileen watched as he walked to a safe bolted to the floor and dropped the bill into a slot on its top, just as though he were making a night deposit at a bank. A sign on the wall advised any prospective holdup man: MANAGER DOES NOT HAVE COMBINATION TO SAFE. MANAGER CANNOT CHANGE BILLS LARGER THAN FIVE DOLLARS. Idly, Eileen wondered what the manager did when he ran out of coins. Did he run into the bar next door to ask the bartender for change? Did the bartender next door have a little coin dispenser attached to *his* belt? Idly, Eileen wondered why she wondered such things. And then she wondered if she'd ever meet a man who wondered the same things she wondered. That was when the Dirty Panties Bandit came into the store.

Eileen recognized him at once from the police-artist composites Willis had shown her back at the squadroom. He was a short slender white man wearing a navy pea coat and watch cap over dark brown, wide-wale corduroy trousers and tan suede desert boots. He had darting brown eyes and a very thin nose with a narrow mustache under it. There was a scar in his right eyebrow. The bell over the door tinkled as he came into the store. As he reached behind him with his left hand to close the door, Eileen's hand went into the bag on her lap. She was closing her fingers around the butt of the .38 when the man's right hand came out of his coat pocket. The Magnum would have looked enormous in any event. But because the man was so small and thin, it looked like an artillery piece. The man's hand was shaking. The gun in it flailed the room.

Eileen looked at the Magnum, looked at the man's eyes, and felt the butt of her own pistol under her closing fingers. If she pulled the gun now, she had maybe a thirty/seventy chance of bringing him down before he sprayed the room with bullets that could tear a man's head off his body. In addition to herself and the robber, there were five other people in the store, three of them women, one of them an infant. Her hand froze motionless around the butt of the gun.

"All right, all right," the man said in a thin, almost girlish voice, "nobody moves, nobody gets hurt." His eyes darted. His hand was still shaking. Suddenly, he giggled. The giggle scared Eileen more than the gun in his hand did. The giggle was high and nervous and just enough off center to send a shiver racing up her spine. Her hand on the butt of the .38 suddenly began sweating.

"All I want is your money, all your money," the man said. "And your—"

"I don't have the combination to the safe," the manager said.

"Who asked *you* for anything?" the man said, turning to him. "You just shut up, you hear me?"

"Yes, sir," the manager said.

"You hear me?"

"Yes, sir."

"I'm talking to the ladies here, not you, you hear me?"

"Yes, sir."

"So shut up."

"Yes, sir."

"You!" the man said, and turned to the woman with the baby strapped to her back, jerking the gun at her, moving erratically, almost dancing across the floor of the laundromat, turning this way and that as though playing to an audience from a stage. Each time he turned, the woman with the baby on her back turned with him, so that she was always facing him, her body forming a barricade between him and the baby. She doesn't know, Eileen thought, that a slug from that gun can go clear through her *and* the baby *and* the wall behind them, too.

"Your money!" the man said. "Hurry up! Your rings, too, give me your rings!"

"Just don't shoot," the woman said.

"Shut up! Give me your panties!"

"What?"

"Your panties, take off your panties, give them to me!"

The woman stared at him.

"Are you deaf?" he said, and danced toward her,and jabbed the gun at her. The woman already had a wad of dollar bills clutched in one fist and her wedding ring and engagement ring in the other, and she stood there uncertainly, knowing she had heard him say he wanted her panties, but not knowing whether he wanted her to give him the money and the jewelry *first* or—

"Hurry up!" he said. "Take them off! Hurry up!"

The woman quickly handed him the bills and the rings and then reached up under her skirt and lowered her panties over her thighs and down to her ankles. She stepped out of them, picked them up, handed them to him, and quickly backed away from him as he stuffed them into his pocket.

"All of you!" he said, his voice higher now. "I want all of you to take off your panties! Give me your money! Give me all your money! And your rings! And your panties, take them off, hurry up!"

The black woman sitting on the chair alongside Eileen kept staring at the man as though he had popped out of a bottle, following his every move around the room, her eyes wide, disbelieving his demands, disbelieving the gun in his hand, disbelieving his very existence. She just kept staring at him and shaking her head in disbelief.

"You!" he said, dancing over to her. "Give me that necklace! Hurry up!"

"Ain't but costume jewelry," the woman said calmly.

"Give me your money!"

"Ain't got but a dollar an' a quarter in change," the woman said.

"Give it to me!" he said, and held out his left hand.

The woman rummaged in her handbag. She took out a change purse. Ignoring the man, ignoring the gun not a foot from her nose, she unsnapped the purse, and reached into it, and took out coin after coin, transferring the coins from her right hand to the palm of her left hand, three quarters and five dimes, and then closing her fist on the coins, and bringing her fist to his open palm, and opening the fist and letting the coins fall (disdainfully, it seemed to Eileen) onto his palm.

"Now your panties," he said.

"Nossir."

"Take off your panties," he said.

"Won't do no such thing," the woman said.

"What?"

"Won't do no such thing. Ain't just a matter of reachin' up under m'skirt way that lady with the baby did, nossir. I'd have to take off fust m'galoshes and then m'jeans, an' there ain't no way I plan to stan' here naked in front of two men I never seen in my life, nossir."

The man waved the gun.

"Do what I tell you," he said.

"Nossir," the woman said.

Eileen tensed.

She wondered if she should make her move now, a bad situation could only get worse, she'd been taught that at the academy and it was a rule she'd lived by and survived by all the years she'd been on the force, but a rule she'd somehow neglected tonight when this silly little son of a bitch walked through the door and pulled the cannon from his pocket, a bad situation can only get worse, make your move now, do it now, go for the money, go for broke, but now, *now!* And she wondered, too, if he would bother turning to fire at *her* once she pulled the gun from her handbag or would he instead fire at the black woman who was willing to risk getting shot and maybe killed rather than take off her jeans and then her panties in a room containing a trembling night man and an armed robber who maybe was or maybe wasn't bonkers, make your move, stop thinking, stop wondering—but what if the baby gets shot?

It occurred to her that maybe the black woman would actually succeed in staring down the little man with the penchant for panties, get him to turn away in defeat, run for the door, out into the cold and into the waiting arms of Detective Hal Willis— which reminds me, where the hell *are* you, Willis? It would not hurt to have my backup come in *behind* this guy right now, it would not hurt to have his attention diverted from me to you, two guns against one, the good guys against the bad guys, where the hell *are* you? The little man was trembling violently now, the struggle inside him so intense that it seemed he would rattle himself to pieces, crumble into a pile of broken pink chalk around a huge weapon—he's a closet rapist, she thought suddenly, the man's a closet rapist!

The thought was blinding in its clarity. She knew now, or felt she knew, why he was running around town holding up laundromats. He was holding up laundromats because there were *women* in laundromats and he wanted to see those women taking off their panties. The holdups had nothing at all to do with money or jewelry, the man was after *panties!* The rings and the bracelets and the cash were all his cover, his beard, his smoke screen, the man wanted ladies' panties, the man wanted the aroma of women on his loot, the man probably had a garageful of panties wherever he lived, the man was a closet rapist and she knew how to deal with rapists, she had certainly dealt with enough rapists in her lifetime, but that was her alone in a park, that was when the only life at stake had been her own, make your move, she thought, make it *now!*

"You!" she said sharply.

The man turned toward her. The gun turned at the same time.

"Take mine," she said.

"What?" he said.

"Leave her alone. Take *my* panties.

"What?"

"Reach under my skirt," she whispered. "Rip off my panties."

She thought for a terrifying moment that she'd made a costly mistake. His face contorted in what appeared to be rage, and the gun began shaking more violently in his fist. Oh, God, she thought, I've forced him out of the closet, I've forced him to see himself for what he is, that gun is his cock as sure as I'm sitting here, and he's going to jerk it off in my face in the next ten seconds! And then a strange thing happened to his face, a strange smile replaced the anger, a strange secret smile touched the corners of his mouth, a secret communication flashed in his eyes, his eyes to her eyes, *their* secret, a secret to share, he lowered the gun, he moved toward her.

"Police!" she shouted, and the .38 came up out of the bag in the same instant that she came up off the plastic chair, and she rammed the muzzle of the gun into the hollow of his throat and said so quietly that only he could hear it, "Don't even *think* it or I'll shoot you dead!" And she would remember later and remember always the way she shouted the word "Police!" had shattered the secret in his eyes, their shared secret, and she would always wonder if the way she'd disarmed him hadn't been particularly cruel and unjust.

She clamped the handcuffs onto his wrists and then stooped to pick up the Magnum from where he'd dropped it on the laundromat floor.

6

Carella could not fall asleep.

He kept thinking that too many people were involved. He kept thinking that even if the lieutenant was willing to put another man on the case, even *then* it would take them at least a week to question all those people in the show, that was if the lieutenant agreed to give him another man, *fat* chance he'd agree to that. Well, maybe he would. The death of Paco Lopez had gone by without a ripple, there weren't many people who cared about a two-bit dealer biting the dust—"Good riddance to bad rubbish," as Carella's mother used to say when he was but a mere lad coming along in this city he loved. He often wondered where his mother had picked up the expressions that had been her favorites. "Ike and Mike, they look alike," she would often say of him and his father. Or, whenever Carella managed to knock over a glass of milk at the dinner table, "Very good, Eddie." Or, regarding his Aunt Clara, whom Carella had positively adored, "She dresses like Astor's pet horse." Or (speaking of horses), whenever anyone became insulted about something, Carella's mother would describe it with the words, "He got on his high horse." Were Ike and Mike comic strip characters? Who in the world was Eddie? Good riddance to bad rubbish—was there such a thing as *good* rubbish?

Paco Lopez had been bad rubbish for sure, and no one had mourned his passing. But the Anderson girl's death had made headlines in the city's afternoon newspaper, and the muckracking journalists on that yellow sheet were beginning to clamor for a speedy arrest of the "maniac responsible." So maybe the lieutenant *would* give Carella the additional man he planned to request, maybe Pete himself was getting some pressure from upstairs.

The newspapers did not yet know, nor did Carella plan to tell them, that a man named Paco Lopez, whose death had gone unnoticed, had been killed with the same gun. There was nothing the journalists would have liked better than a possible romantic link (a possibility that had crossed Carella's mind) between a young blond dancer and a Puerto Rican dope dealer. A story like that would make even the *television* newscasters jump for joy. There were, after all, two Puerto Rican dancers in the show—well, not necessarily Puerto Rican, Carella had asked only if there were any *Hispanics* in the show, and Tina Wong had told him there were two, so they could be anything, Puerto Rican, Cuban, Dominican, Colombian, you name it, this city had it. Both of them faggots. Carella wondered if either of them was doing nose candy. Carella wondered if either of them had known Paco Lopez. That was the damn trouble. A hundred and fourteen people involved with that show, one or more of whom may have been the connection between Sally Anderson and Paco Lopez, if there *was* any connection at all besides the .38 caliber gun that had killed them both.

Please don't let it be a crazy, he thought.

Please let it be a nice sensible murderer who killed both those people for a very good reason.

He kept staring up at the ceiling.

There were just too many people involved, he thought.

Willis was trying to explain why he hadn't happened to notice the Dirty Panties Bandit when he entered the laundromat. They had sent down for pizza, and now they sat in the relative 1:00 A.M. silence of the squadroom, eating Papa Joe's really pretty good combination of anchovies and pepperoni and drinking Miscolo's really pretty lousy Colombian coffee; Detective Bert Kling was sitting with them, but he wasn't eating or saying very much.

Eileen remembered him as a man with a huge appetite, and she wondered now if he was on a diet. He looked thinner than she recalled—well, that had been several years back—and he also looked somewhat drawn and pale and, well, unkempt. His straight blond hair was growing raggedly over his shirt collar and his ears, and the collar itself looked a bit frayed, and his suit looked unpressed, and there were stains on the tie he was wearing. Eileen figured he was maybe coming in off a stakeout someplace. Maybe he was *supposed* to look like somebody who was going to seed. And maybe those dark shadows under his eyes were all part of the role he was playing out there on the street, in which case he should get not only a commendation but an Academy Award besides.

Willis was very apologetic.

"I'll tell you the truth," he said, "I figured we didn't have a chance of our man showing. Because on the other jobs, he usually hit between ten and ten-thirty, and it was almost eleven when this guy came running out of the bar—"

"Wait a minute," Eileen said. "*What* guy?"

"Came running out of the bar next door," Willis said. "Bert, don't you want some of this?"

"Thanks," Kling said, and shook his head.

"Yelling, 'Police, police,' " Willis said.

"When was this?" Eileen asked.

"I told you, a little before eleven," Willis said. "Even so, if I thought we had a chance of our man showing I'd have said screw it, let some other cop handle whatever it is in the bar there. But I mean it, Eileen, I figured we'd had it for tonight."

"So you went in the bar?"

"No. Well, yes. But not right away, no. I got out of the car, and I asked the guy what the trouble was, and he asked me did I see a cop anywhere because there was somebody with a knife in the bar and I told him I was a cop and he said I ought to go in there and take the knife away before somebody got cut."

"So naturally you went right in," Eileen said, and winked at Kling. Kling did not wink back. Kling lifted his coffee cup and sipped at it. He seemed not to be listening to what Willis was saying. He seemed almost comatose. Eileen wondered what was wrong with him.

"No, I still gave it a bit of thought," Willis said. "I would have rushed in *immediately,* of course—"

"Of course," Eileen said.

"To disarm that guy . . . who by the way turned out to be a girl . . . but I was worried about you being all alone there in the laudromat in case Mr. Bloomers *did* decide to show up."

"Mr. Bloomers!" Eileen said, and burst out laughing. She was still feeling very high after the bust, and she wished that Kling wouldn't sit there like a zombie but would instead join in the general post mortem celebration.

"So I looked through the window," Willis said.

"Of the bar?"

"No, the laundromat. And saw that everything was still cool, you were sitting there next to a lady reading a magazine and this other lady was carrying about seven tons of laundry into the store, so I figured you'd be safe for another minute or two while I went in there and settled the thing with the knife, *especially* since I didn't think our man was going to show anyway. So I went in the bar, and there's this very nicely dressed middle-class-looking lady wearing eyeglasses and her hair swept up on her head and a dispatch case sitting on the bar as if she's a lawyer or an accountant who stopped in for a pink lady on the way home and she's got an eight-foot-long switchblade in her right hand and she's swinging it in front of her like this, back and forth, slicing the air with it, you know, and I'm surprised first of all that it's a lady and next that it's a switchblade she's holding, which is not exactly a lady's weapon. Also, I do not wish to get cut," Willis said.

"Naturally," Eileen said.

"Naturally," Willis said. "In fact, I'm beginning to think I'd better go check on you again, make sure the panties nut hasn't shown up after all. But just then the guy who came out in the street yelling, 'Police, police,' now says to the crazy lady with the stiletto, 'I warned you, Grace, this man is a policeman.' Which means I now have to uphold law and order, which is the last thing on earth I wish to do."

"What'd you do?" Eileen asked.

She was really interested now. She had never come up against a woman wielding a dangerous weapon, her line of specialty being men, of sorts. Usually she leveled her gun at a would-be rapist's privates, figuring she'd threaten him where he lived. Tonight, she had rammed the gun into the hollow of the man's throat. The barrel of the gun had left a bruise there, she had seen the bruise when she was putting the cuffs on him. But how do you begin taking a knife away from an angry *woman?* You couldn't threaten to shoot her in the balls, could you?

"I walked over to her and I said, 'Grace, that's a mighty fine knife you've got there, I wonder if you'd mind giving it to me.' "

"That was a mistake," Eileen said. "She might've given it to you, all right, she might've *really* given it to you."

"But she didn't," Willis said. "Instead, she turned to the guy who'd run out of the bar—"

"The 'Police, police' guy?"

"Yeah, and she said, 'Harry,' or whatever the hell his name was, 'Harry, how can you keep cheating on me this way?' and then she burst into tears and handed the knife to the *bartender* instead of to *me,* and Harry took her in his arms—"

"Excuse me, huh?" Kling said, and got up from behind the desk, and walked out of the squadroom.

"Oh, God," Willis said.

"Huh?" Eileen said.

"I forgot," Willis said. "He probably thinks I told that story on purpose. I'd better go talk to him. Excuse me, okay? I'm sorry, Eileen, excuse me."

"Sure," she said, puzzled, and watched while Willis went through the gate in the slatted rail divider and down the corridor after Kling. There were some things she would never in a million years understand about the guys who worked up here. Never. She picked up another slice of pizza. It was cold. And she hadn't even got a chance to tell anyone about how absolutely brilliant and courageous and deadly forceful she'd been in that laundromat.

And whenever he couldn't sleep, Carella found himself thinking about Kling. Found himself wondering what Kling was doing at that moment. And to keep his mind off Kling, he started thinking about the case again, whichever case it happened to be, there was always some case or other he was working, some case or other that was driving him slowly crazy. And when he couldn't find an opening in the case, when he'd poked and pried and shaken the damn thing trying to find that one seam in the fabric that he could tear open with his hands—let some light in, climb in there inside the case, find out what the hell was making the case tick—when the case refused to yield he began thinking about Kling again, wondering about Kling, hoping that Kling would not decide to eat his own gun one night.

It was a possibility.

It was more than a remote possibility.

Carella had been a Detective/Second for several years already before he'd met Kling—well, *really* met him; before that, he'd known him as a patrolman, but only to say hello to. When Kling got promoted into the squadroom (youngest man on the team back then) Carella took an immediate liking to him, and recognized at once that his boyish good looks and quiet manner could be a tremendous asset to anyone partnered with him. Nor was he thinking only of your garden-variety Mutt-and-Jeff situations, where any cop in the world would be happy to play the heavy to Kling's apple-cheeked softie. It went beyond that. It involved something like basic decency that civilians could sense, a decency that encouraged them to open up in his presence where they might not have to another cop.

It was easy to allow this precinct to burn you out. When you dealt with it day and night, it could get to you. All the ideals you'd come in with, the lofty notions about maintaining law and order, preserving society, all of it seemed to fade deeper and deeper into an innocent past as you came to grips with what it was *really* all about, when you realized it was a *war* you were fighting out there, the good guys versus the bad guys, and in a war you got tired, man, in a war you burned out.

So, yes, the police work had left its mark on Kling, too; only a man like Andy Parker could remain unfazed by police work, and the way *he* remained unfazed was by abdicating it. Parker was the worst cop in the precinct, perhaps the worst one in the entire city. Parker's credo was a simple one: you can't drown if you don't go in the water. Maybe Parker had once been young and idealistic. If so, Carella hadn't known him then. All he saw now was a man who never went in the water. The police work had touched Kling the way it had touched them all, but it wasn't the police work that made Carella worry he would eat his gun one night, it was the women, the way Kling kept having such bad luck with women.

Carella had been with him that first time, in the bookshop on Culver Avenue, when Kling had knelt beside a dead girl wearing what appeared to be a red blouse, and had winced when he'd seen the two enormous bullet holes in the girl's side, the blood pouring steadily from those wounds, staining her white blouse a bright red. Kling had reached down to lift from the dead girl's face a book that had fallen from one of the shelves and lay tented over it, her broken string of pearls scattered on the floor like tiny luminescent islands in the sticky coagulation of her blood, his hand reaching out to lift the book, to reveal the girl's face, and then he'd whispered, "Oh, my Jesus Christ!" and something in his voice caused Carella to run toward the back of the shop at once. And then he heard Kling's cry, a single sharp anguished cry that pierced the dust-filled, cordite-stinking air of the shop.

"Claire!"

He was holding the dead girl in his arms when Carella reached him. His hands and his face were covered with Claire Townsend's blood, his fiancées blood, and he kissed her lifeless eyes and her nose and her throat, and he kept murmuring over and over again, "Claire, Claire," and Carella would remember that name and the sound of Kling's voice as long as he lived.

And he would remember, too, the kind of cop Kling became—or almost became—after her murder. He thought they'd lose him then. He thought Kling would go the way of the Andy Parkers of the world, if indeed he remained a cop at all. Lieutenant Byrnes had wanted to transfer him out of the Eight-Seven. Byrnes was normally a patient and understanding man, who could appreciate the reasons for Kling's behavior, but this in no way made Kling any nicer to have around the office. The way Byrnes figured it, psychology was certainly an important factor in police work because it helped you to recognize there were no longer any villains in the world, there were only disturbed people. It was a very nice tool to possess, psychology was, until a cheap thief kicked you in the groin one night. It then became somewhat difficult to imagine the thief as a put-upon soul who'd had a shabby childhood. In much the same way, though Byrnes completely understood the trauma that had been responsible for Kling's behavior (God, how many *years* ago was this? Carella wondered) he nonetheless was finding it more and more difficult to accept Kling as anything but a cop who was going to hell with himself.

He had not gone to hell with himself.

Not that time nor the time afterward, either, when the girl he'd begun dating and eventually living with decided to dump him once and for all on a Christmas Eve, which was not a particularly good time to finally and irrevocably end a relationship, especially if later that night you were forced to shoot somebody dead, which was just what happened with Kling on that Christmas Eve, the man lunging across the room toward him, Kling squeezing the trigger once, and then again, aiming for the man's trunk, both slugs catching him in the chest, one of them going directly through his heart and the other piercing his left lung. Kling had lowered his gun. He remained sitting on the floor in the corner of the room, and watched the man's blood oozing into the sawdust, and wiped the sweat from his lip, and blinked and then began crying.

Long ago, Carella thought. All of it long ago.

Meeting Augusta Blair—or so all the guys in the squadroom had thought at the time—was perhaps the best thing that ever could have happened to Kling. He'd been investigating a burglary—victim came home from a ski trip to find the apartment a shambles—and there she was, auburn-haired and green-eyed, the most beautiful woman he'd ever seen in his life. Augusta Blair. Whose face and figure only adorned every fashion magazine in America. How could a Detective/Second earning only $24,600 a year even *hope* to ask a famous fashion model for a date? Nine months later, he told Carella he was thinking of marrying her.

"Yeah?" Carella said, surprised.

"Yeah," Kling said, and nodded.

They were in an unmarked police car, heading for the next state. It was bitterly cold outside. The windows, except for the windshield, were entirely covered with rime. Carella busied himself with the heater.

"What do you think?" Kling asked.

"Well, I don't know. Do you think she'll say yes?"

"Oh, yeah, I think she'll say yes."

"Well then, ask her."

"Well," Kling said, and fell silent.

They had come through the tollbooth. Behind them, Isola thrust its jagged peaks and minarets into a leaden sky. Ahead, the terrain consisted of rolling, smoke-colored hills through which the road snaked its lazy way. As it turned out, Kling's doubts had largely to do with whether or not the relationship he then enjoyed with Augusta would somehow *change* once they were married. He finally got around to asking Carella why he himself had got married. Carella thought it over for a long while. Then he said, "Because I couldn't bear the thought of any other man ever touching Teddy."

And in the long run, that was what had ended the marriage between Kling and Augusta, wasn't it? Another man touching her? Not so long ago, that. No. Only last August. This was now February, and Kling had found his wife in bed with another man only last August, and had almost killed the man, but had hurled his gun away before he'd fired it. The divorce had been simple and clean. Augusta needed no alimony and wanted none from him; she had always earned more than three times what he did, anyway. They had split their possessions equally down the middle. It was Kling who'd moved out of the apartment they'd once shared. It was Kling who'd found a new apartment downtown, almost at the opposite end of the city, almost as though he wanted to put as much geographical distance between them as was humanly possible. It was Kling who'd carted all his possessions downtown with him, his clothes, his share of the records and books—and his guns. He owned two guns. They were both .38 caliber Police Specials. He preferred carrying the one with the burn mark on the walnut stock, and kept the other one only as a spare. It was the guns that bothered Carella.

He had never seen Kling this despondent, not even after the senseless murder of Claire Townsend in that bookshop. He had talked Byrnes into offering Kling two weeks' vacation immediately after the divorce was final, even though Kling wasn't up for another vacation till the summertime. Kling had refused the offer. He had invited Kling to several dinner parties at the Riverhead house. Kling had turned down the invitations. He had tried to work out his schedule so that he and Kling were partnered more often than any other two men on the squad, so that he could talk to Kling, help him through *this* bad time the way he had helped him through all the *other* bad times. But Kling had learned of the maneuver and had asked that he be put on "floater" status, filling in for whoever was off sick or in court or on vacation or whatever. Carella now believed that Kling was deliberately trying to avoid him, and only because he was a painful reminder of what had happened; he had, after all, been the first person to whom Kling had confided his suspicions.

Tomorrow was Valentine's Day—well, *today,* actually; the bedside clock read one-thirty in the morning. Holidays, even minor-league ones, were a bad time for anyone who'd lost a partner through death or divorce. Carella felt there was a fifty-fifty chance the lieutenant would give him the extra man he and Meyer desperately needed. So, all right, if the lieutenant *did* say okay, then why not zero in on Kling, tell the lieutenant Kling was the only man who could properly help them track down all those hundred and fourteen names on the company list, and then question a third of those people, and eliminate the ones who couldn't possibly have killed either Sally Anderson *or* Paco Lopez—damn it, where was the connection?

He fell asleep thinking that even if the lieutenant *did* assign Kling as a triple, the job would take them forever. He did not know that at that very moment the case was about to take a turn that would bring Kling into it, anyway, and would furthermore obviate the urgent need for questioning all those hundred and fourteen people.

The man was wearing under his overcoat a plaid jacket, gray flannel slacks, and a vest. He was also wearing a .32 caliber pistol in a holster on the left-hand side of his body. The overcoat button closest to his waist was unbuttoned so that he could reach in for a clean, right-handed draw if ever the need arose. He had never had to use the pistol since he'd got the carry permit for it, six years ago.

He should not have worked so late tonight.

When he'd closed his shop downtown, and then rolled down the metal grille and fastened the padlock in place, bolting the protective grille to the sidewalk, there had not been another soul anywhere on the street. He had walked quickly and nervously to the all-night garage where he normally parked his car, grateful for the gun at his waist. In the empty hours of the morning, the midtown area of this city turned into something resembling a moonscape. He had driven steadily uptown, stopping at each red light, nervously anticipating a sudden attack from any of the denizens who were abroad. When finally he entered the Grover Park transverse road, he felt a bit more secure; he would only have to stop at two traffic lights inside the park itself (if, in fact, they were red when he approached them) and a possible third one when he came out of the park farther uptown on Grover Avenue. He caught the first of the lights and waited impatiently for it to change. The next one was green. The one at the end of the exit ramp was also green; he made his right turn onto Grover Avenue, drove uptown several blocks, past the police station with its green globes flanking the front doorstep, the numerals 87 on each globe, and continued driving for another three blocks uptown before he made a left turn and headed north for Silvermine Road. He parked the car in the garage under his building, the way he always did, locking it and then heading for the elevator at the far end of the garage. It occurred to him, each and every time he parked the car under the building, that the security guard at the front door upstairs wasn't of very much use down here. But the distance from his assigned parking space to the red door of the elevator was perhaps fifty feet, if that, and rarely did he get home later than 7:00 P.M., when there were a great many other tenants coming and going.

There was no one else in the garage at a quarter to two in the morning.

The pillars supporting the roof stood like bulky sentinals spaced some ten feet apart from each other, four of them marking off the distance between him and the elevator. The garage was brightly lighted. His heels clicked on the cement floor as he moved toward the elevator. His footfalls echoed. He was passing the third pillar when a man with a gun in his hand stepped out from behind it, directly into his path.

He reached immediately into his coat for his own gun.

His hand closed on the stock.

He was starting to pull the gun free of its holster when the man standing in his path fired. The man fired directly into his face. He felt only the the fierce sharp pain of the first bullet. His body was already jerking backward with the force of the impact when the second bullet entered his head. He did not feel this bullet. He did not feel anything anymore. His hand was still inside his coat, the fingers wrapped around the butt of the pistol, when he collapsed to the cold cement floor of the garage.

It was beginning to snow again. Lightly. Fat fluffy flakes drifting down lazily from the sky. Arthur Brown was driving. Bert Kling sat beside him on the front seat of the five-year-old unmarked sedan. Eileen Burke was sitting in the back. She had still been in the squadroom when the homicide squeal came in, and she'd asked Kling if he'd mind dropping her off at the subway on his way to the scene. Kling had merely grunted. Kling was a charmer, Eileen thought.

Brown was a huge man who looked even more enormous in his bulky overcoat. The coat was gray and it had a fake black fur collar. He was wearing black leather gloves that matched the black collar. Brown was supposed to be what people nowadays called a "black" man, but Brown knew that his complexion did not match the color of either the black collar or the black gloves. Whenever he looked at himself in the mirror, he saw someone with chocolate-colored skin looking back at him, but he did not think of himself as a "chocolate" man. Neither did he think of himself as a Negro anymore; somehow, if a black man thought of himself as a Negro, he was thinking obsequiously. *Negro* had become a derogatory term, God alone knew when or how. Brown's father used to call himself "a person of color" which Brown thought was a very hoity-toity expression even when it was still okay for black men to call themselves Negroes. (Brown noticed that *Ebony* magazine capitalized the word *Black,* and he often wondered why.) He guessed he still thought of himself as colored, and he sincerely hoped there was nothing wrong with that. Nowadays, a nigger didn't know *what* he was supposed to think.

Brown was the kind of black man white men crossed the street to avoid. If you were white, and you saw Brown approaching on the same side of the street, you automatically assumed he was going to mug you, or cut you with a razor, or do something else terrible to you. That was partially due to the fact that Brown was six feet four inches tall and weighed two hundred and twenty pounds. It was also partially (*mostly*) due to the fact that Brown was black, or colored, or whatever you chose to call him, but he certainly was not white. A white man approaching Brown might not have crossed the street if Brown had also been a white man; unfortunately, Brown never had the opportunity to conduct such an experiment. The fact remained that when Brown was casually walking down the street minding his own business, white people crossed over to the other side. Sometimes even white *cops* crossed over to the other side. Nobody wanted trouble with someone who looked the way Brown looked. Even *black* people sometimes crossed the street when Brown approached, but only because he looked so bad-ass.

Brown knew he was, in fact, very handsome.

Whenever Brown looked in the mirror, he saw a very handsome chocolate-colored man looking back at him out of soulful brown eyes. Brown liked himself a lot. Brown was very comfortable with himself. Brown was glad he was a cop because he knew that the *real* reason white people crossed the street when they saw him was because they thought all black people were thieves or murderers. He frequently regretted the day he was promoted into the Detective Division because then he could no longer wear his identifying blue uniform, the contradiction to his identifying brown skin. Brown especially liked to bust people of his own race. He especially liked it when some black dude said, "Come on, brother, give me a break." That man was no more Brown's brother than Brown was brother to a hippopotamus. In Brown's world, there were the good guys and the bad guys, white or black, it made no difference. Brown was one of the good guys. All those guys breaking the law out there were the bad guys. Tonight, one of the bad guys had left somebody dead and bleeding on the floor of a garage under a building on fancy Silvermine Road, and Kling had caught the squeal, and Brown was his partner, and they were two good guys riding out into the gently falling snow, with another good guy (who happened to be a girl) sitting on the back seat—which reminded him; he had to drop her off at the subway station.

"The one on Culver and Fourth okay?" he asked her.

"That'll be fine, Artie," Eileen said.

Kling was hunkered down inside his coat, looking out at the falling snow. The car heater rattled and clunked, something wrong with the fan. The car was the worst one the squad owned. Brown wondered how come whenever it was his turn to check out a car, he got *this* one. Worst car in the entire *city,* maybe. Ripe tomato accelerator, rattled like a two-dollar whore, something wrong with the exhaust, the damn car always smelled of carbon monoxide, they were probably *poisoning* themselves on the way to the homicide.

"Willis says you nabbed the guy who was running around pulling down bloomers, huh?" Brown said.

"Yeah," Eileen said, grinning.

"Good thing, too," Brown said. "This kind of weather, lady *needs* her underdrawers." He began laughing. Eileen laughed, too. Kling sat staring through the windshield.

"Will you be all right on the subway, this hour of the night?" Brown asked.

"Yeah, I'll be fine," Eileen said.

He pulled the car into the curb.

"You sure now?"

"Positive. G'night, Artie," she said, and opened the door. "G'night, Bert."

"Good night," Brown said. "Take care."

Kling said nothing. Eileen shrugged and closed the door behind her. Brown watched as she went down the steps into the subway. He pulled the car away from the curb the moment her head disappeared from sight.

"What was that address again?" he asked Kling.

"One-one-one-four Silvermine," Kling said.

"That near the Oval?"

"Few blocks west."

There were two patrol cars parked at the curb when Brown pulled in. Their dome lights were flashing blue and red into the falling snow. Kling and Brown got out of the car, had a brief conversation with the patrolman who'd been left at the sidewalk to keep an eye on both cars (the theft of police cars not being unheard of in this city), and then walked down the ramp into the underground garage. The place was lighted with sodium lamps. The three patrolmen from the cars upstairs were standing around a man lying on the cement floor some eight feet from the elevator. The elevator door was red. The man's blood flowed from his open skull toward the matching red elevator door.

"Detective Brown," Brown said. "My partner, Detective Kling."

"Right," one of the patrolmen said, and nodded.

"Who was the first car on the scene?"

"We were," another patrolman said. "Boy Car."

"Anybody down here when you arrived?"

"Nobody."

"Nobody?" Kling said. "Who called it in? Who found the body?"

"Don't know, sir," the patrolman said. "Dispatcher radioed us a Ten-Ten— investigate shots fired. We didn't even know where we were supposed to look, they just gave us the address. So we asked the guy in the lobby, the security guard there, did he call nine-one-one to report a man with a gun, and he said no, he didn't. So we looked around the building and also the backyard, and we were about to call it back as a Ten-Ninety, when Benny here, he says, 'Let's check out the garage under the building.' By that time, Charlie Car was here—"

"We'd been checking out an alarm on Ainsley," one of the other patrolmen said.

"So the three of us come down here together," the first patrolman said.

"And there he is," the third patrolman said, nodding toward the body on the floor.

"Has Homicide been informed?" Kling asked.

"I guess so," the first patrolman said.

"What do you mean, you *guess* so?"

"I gave it to the desk sergeant as a D.O.A. It ain't my responsibility to inform Homicide."

"Who's talkin' about Homicide behind our backs?" a voice from the top of the ramp said.

"Speak of the devil," Brown said.

It was rare that Homicide detectives—or any detectives, for that matter—worked as triples, but the three men who came down the ramp now, advancing as steadily as Sherman tanks, were known throughout the city as the Holy Trinity, and it was rumored that they never did *anything* except as a trio. Their names were Hardigan, Hanrahan and Mandelbaum. It occurred to Brown that he had never learned their first names. It further occurred to him that he had never learned the first name of *any* Homicide detective. Did Homicide detectives *have* first names? The three detectives were all wearing black. Homicide detectives in this city favored black. There was a rumor afoot that the stylistic trend had been started years back by a very famous Homicide dick. Brown's surmise was a much simpler one: Homicide cops dealt exclusively with corpses; they were only wearing the colors of mourning. It occurred to him that Genero had begun wearing a lot of black lately; was Genero hoping for a transfer to Homicide? It further occurred to him that nobody in the squadroom ever called Genero by his first name, which was Richard. It was always, "Come here, Genero" or—more likely—"Go away, Genero." Occasionally, he was called Genero the Asshole, the way an ancient king might have been dubbed affectionately Amos the Simple or Herman the Rat. If Homicide cops had no first names, and if Genero had a first name no one ever used, then perhaps Genero might one day enjoy a successful career with the Homicide Division. Brown devoutly hoped so.

"This here the victim here?" Hardigan asked.

"No, this here is a paper doily here," Brown said.

"I forgot I was dealing with the Eight-Seven," Hardigan said.

"Comedians," Hanrahan said.

"*Morons,*" Mandelbaum said. "Two o'clock in the *morning.*"

"We get you out of your little beddie?" Brown asked.

"Shove it up your ass," Mandelbaum said pleasantly.

"In spades," Hardigan said, and Brown wondered if he was making a racist remark.

"Who *is* he?" Hanrahan asked.

"We haven't tossed him yet," Kling said.

"So do it," Hanrahan said.

"Not until the M.E.'s finished with him."

"Who says?"

"New regs—only a year old already."

"Hell with the regs, we'll freeze out here waiting for the M.E. here. This is Saturday night, you know how many people are getting themselves killed out there tonight?"

"How many?" Kling said.

"Toss him. Do what I tell you. This is Homicide here," Hanrahan said.

"Put it in writing," Kling said. "That I should toss him before the M.E. pronounces him dead."

"You can *see* he's dead, can't you? What do you need? The man's got no face left, why do you need an M.E. to tell you he's *dead?*" Hardigan said, backing his partner.

"Then *you* toss him," Brown said, backing *his* partner.

"Okay, we'll wait for the M.E., okay?" Hanrahan said.

"We'll freeze down here waiting for the M.E., okay?" Mandelbaum said.

"Will that make you guys happy?" Hardigan said.

Neither Brown nor Kling answered.

The M.E. did not arrive until almost 3:00 A.M. By that time the Mobile Crime Unit was on the scene doing everything they *could* do without touching the body itself. The boys from the Photo Unit were taking their pictures, and the Crime Scene signs were up, and Brown and Kling were making their drawings, and everybody was freezing to death but nobody had yet come to pronounce the stiff (very *literally* stiff) dead. The M.E. made a grand entrance, striding down the ramp like a stand-up burlesque comic ready to pitch popcorn and prizes.

"Sorry to be late, gentlemen," he said, and Hardigan farted.

The M.E. bent over the corpse. He unbuttoned the corpse's overcoat. The first thing all of them saw was the corpse's hand clutched around the butt of a pistol in a holster.

"Well, well," Hanrahan said.

With some difficulty, the M.E. unbuttoned the man's plaid jacket. He was about to slide his stethoscope under the man's vest and then under his shirt and onto his chest, the better to determine that the bullets pumped into his face had caused his heart to cease functioning, when he noticed—as did the five detectives and the three patrolmen and the photographer and the two lab technicians—that the man's vest had perhaps a dozen pockets sewn into it.

"Last time I saw that was on a pickpocket," Mandlebaum said. "Had all these pockets on his vest, used to drop stolen goods in them."

The man was not a pickpocket.

Not unless he'd been very fortunate that day.

As soon as the M.E. was finished with him (and he *was* indeed dead), they went through all those little pockets sewn into his vest. And in each one of those little pockets, they found little plastic packets. And in each one of those little plastic packets, they found diamonds of various sizes and shapes.

"The guy's a walking jewelry store," Hardigan said.

"Only he ain't walking no more," Hanrahan said.

"*Look* at all that ice, willya?" Mandelbaum said.

7

They had promised only snow, but by morning the snow had changed to sleet and then to freezing rain, and the streets were dangerously slick. Carella almost slipped on his way to the subway, catching his balance a moment before he flew into the air. His mother had told him two atrocity stories when he was a child, and both of them had remained with him into his adult years. The first had to do with his Uncle Charlie, whom he'd never met, who had accidentally blinded himself in one eye with the point of a scissors while trying to trim his eyebrows. Carella occasionally had his eyebrows trimmed in a barber shop, but never did he attempt that dangerous task himself. His mother had also told him how his Uncle Salvatore had slipped on the ice outside his haberdashery in Calm's Point, and landed on his back, which was why he was confined to a wheelchair. Whenever Carella spotted a patch of ice on a sidewalk or a road, he walked or drove over it very, very carefully.

Carella *had* known (and incidentally had loved) his Uncle Salvatore, and whenever his uncle asked him why he didn't wear a hat, Carella felt a bit guilty. "You should wear a hat," his uncle said. "If you don't wear a hat, forty percent of your body heat escapes from your head, and you feel cold all over." Carella did not like hats. He told his uncle he did not like hats. His uncle tapped his temple with his forefinger. "*Pazzo,*" he said, which meant "crazy" in Italian. It was Carella's uncle who'd told him the only haberdashery joke he'd ever heard in his life. "A man walks into a haberdashery," his uncle said. "The haberdasherer comes over to him and says, 'Yes, sir, do you have anything in mind?' The man says, 'I have *pussy* in mind, but let me see a hat.' " Carella was sixteen years old when his uncle told him that story. They were in his uncle's haberdashery, which he was still running from a wheelchair. He died three years later.

It took Carella two hours to get to work that morning. He spent the time on the subway trying to figure out what he would buy Teddy for Valentine's Day—which was today, a Sunday, when most of the city's shops would be closed. He had expected to pick up something yesterday, but that was before he'd inherited the Sally Anderson homicide. Teddy had told him at breakfast this morning, a secretive smile on her mouth, her hands flashing, that she would be getting him *his* gift sometime this afternoon, and would present it to him tonight when he got home from work. He told her there was no rush; despite the makeshift Presidents' Day holiday tomorrow, many of the stores would be open, and besides, the roads would be cleared and sanded by then. Teddy told him she'd already made the appointment. An appointment for *what?* he wondered.

Meyer Meyer was wearing his Valentine's Day present.

His Valentine's Day present was a woolen watch cap that would have caused Carella's Uncle Salvatore to beam with pride. Meyer's wife Sarah had knitted the watch cap herself. It was a white cap with a border of linked red hearts. Meyer was marching around the squadroom with the hat pulled down over his ears, showing it off.

"You can hardly tell you're bald with that hat," Tack Fujiwara said, and noticed Carella coming through the gate in the railing. "Hello, cousin," he said.

"Oh-hi-oh," Carella said.

"What do you mean *'hardly'?*" Meyer said. "Do I look bald?" he asked Carella.

"You look hairy," Carella said. "Where'd you get that hat?"

"Sarah made it. For Valentine's Day."

"Very nice," Carella said. "Is the Loot in?"

"Ten minutes ago," Fujiwara said. "What'd *you* get for Valentine's Day?"

"A murder," Carella said.

"Shake hands with Kling," Fujiwara said, but Carella was already knocking on the lieutenant's door, and he didn't catch the words.

"Come!" Byrnes shouted.

Carella opened the door. The lieutenant was sitting behind his desk studying the open lid of a box of candy. "Hello, Steve," he said. "This chart tells you what each piece of candy in the box is. Would you like a piece of candy?"

"Thanks, Pete, no," Carella said.

Byrnes kept studying the chart, running his finger over it. He was a compact man with a head of thinning iron gray hair, flinty blue eyes, and a craggy nose that had been broken with a lead pipe when he was still a patrolman in Majesta, but that had miraculously knitted itself together without any trace of the injury save a faintly visible scar across the bridge. No one ever noticed the scar except when Byrnes touched it, as he sometimes did during a particularly knotty skull session in his office. He was touching it now as he studied the varied selection promised by the chart on the inside lid of the candy box.

"My Valentine's present," he said, fingering the scar on his nose, studying the list of goodies to be sampled.

"I'll be getting mine tonight," Carella said, feeling somehow defensive.

"So have some candy now," Byrnes said, and plucked a square-shaped piece of chocolate from the box. "The square ones are always caramels," he said. "I don't need a chart to tell me this is a caramel." He bit into it. "See?" he said, smiling and chewing. "Good, too. Have one," he said, and shoved the box across his desk.

"Pete, we've got a hundred and fourteen people to track down," Carella said. "That's how many people are in the *Fatback* company, and that's how many people Meyer and I have got to question if we're going to get any kind of a lead on this dead dancer."

"What's her connection with this Lopez character?" Byrnes asked, chewing.

"We don't know yet."

"Dope?" Byrnes asked.

"Not that we know. The lab's checking."

"Was he her boyfriend or something?"

"No, her boyfriend is a med student at Ramsey."

"Where was *he* when the girl was cashing it in?"

"Home studying."

"Who says?"

"He says."

"Check it."

"We will. Meanwhile, Pete—"

"Let me guess," Byrnes said. "You sure you don't want one of these?" he said, and took another chocolate from the box.

"Thanks," Carella said, and shook his head.

"Meanwhile," Byrnes said, "I'm trying to guess what you want from me."

"Triple us," Carella said.

"Who'd you have in mind?"

"Bert Kling."

"Bert's got headaches of his own just now."

"What do you mean?"

"He caught a homicide last night."

"Well, that takes care of that," Carella said. "Who *can* you spare?"

"Who said I can spare anybody?"

"Pete, this girl is all over the newspapers."

"So what?"

"She'll be making news as long as that show runs . . . and that'll be forever."

"So what?"

"So how long do you think it'll be before the Chief of Detectives picks up the telephone and gives you a little jingle? 'Hello, Pete, about this dancer? In that big hit musical? Any leads yet, Pete? Lots of reporters calling here, Pete. What are your boys doing up there, Pete, besides sitting on their duffs while people go around shooting other people?"

Byrnes looked at him.

"Never mind the Chief of Detectives," he said. "The Chief of Detectives doesn't have to come to work up *here* every day, the Chief of Detectives has a nice big corner office in the *Headquarters* Building downtown. And if the Chief of Detectives thinks we're moving too slowly on this one, then maybe we ought to remind him it wasn't even *ours* to begin with, the girl was shot and killed in Midtown *East,* if the Chief of Detectives would like to know, and not up here in the Eight-Seven. What we have as our very own up *here* is the murder of a crumby little gram dealer, if that would interest the Chief of Detectives, though I doubt he could care less. Now if you want to make your request to me on the basis of something *sensible,* Steve, like how talking to a hundred and fourteen people—are there *really* that many people attached to that show?"

"A hundred and fourteen, yes."

"If you want to come to me and tell me it'll take you and Meyer a week, ten days, two weeks, *however* long to question all hundred and fourteen of those people while a murderer is running around out there with a gun in his hand, if you want to present your case sensibly and logically and not threaten me with what the Chief of *Detectives* is going to think . . ."

"Okay, Pete, how's this?" Carella said, smiling. "It's going to take Meyer and me at least ten days to question all those people while a murderer is running around out there with a gun in his hand. We can cut the working time to maybe five days, unless we hit pay dirt before then, so all I'm asking for is *one* other man on the case, triple us up, Pete, and turn us loose out there. Okay? Who can you spare?''

"Nobody," Byrnes said.

She tried to remember how long ago it had been. Years and years, that was certain. And would he think her frivolous now? Would he accept what she had done (what she was *about* to do, actually, since she hadn't yet done it, and could still change her mind about it) as the gift she intended it to be, or would he consider it the self-indulgent whim of a woman who was no longer the young girl he'd married years and years ago? Well, who *is?* Teddy thought. Even Jane Fonda is no longer the young girl she was years and years ago. But does Jane Fonda worry about such things? Probably, Teddy thought.

The section of the city through which she walked was thronged with people, but Teddy could not hear the drifting snatches of their conversations as they moved past her and around her. Their exhaled breaths pluming on the brittle air were, to her, only empty cartoon balloons floating past in a silent rush. She walked in an oddly hushed world, dangerous to her in that her ears could provide no timely warnings, curiously exquisite in that whatever she saw was unaccompanied by any sound that might have marred its beauty. The sight (and aroma) of a bluish-gray cloud of carbon monoxide, billowing onto the silvery air from an automobile exhaust pipe, assumed dreamlike proportions when it was not coupled with the harsh mechanical sound of an automobile engine. The uniformed cop on the corner, waving his arms this way and that, artfully dodging as he directed the cross-purposed stream of lumbering traffic, became an acrobat, a ballet dancer, a skilled mime the moment one did not have to hear his bellowed, *"Move* it, let's keep it *moving!"* And yet—

She had never heard her husband's voice.

She had never heard her children's laughter.

She had never heard the pleasant wintry jingle of automobile skid chains on an icy street, the big-city cacophony of jackhammers and automobile horns, street vendors and hawkers, babies crying. As she passed a souvenir shop whose window brimmed with inexpensive jade, ivory (illegal to import), fans, dolls with Oriental eyes (like her husband's), she did not hear drifting from a small window on the side wall of the shop the sound of a stringed instrument plucking a sad and delicate Chinese melody, the notes hovering on the air like ice crystals—she simply did not hear.

The tattoo parlor was vaguely anonymous, hidden as it was on a narrow China-town side street. The last time she'd been here, the place had been flanked by a bar and a laundromat. Today, the bar was an offtrack betting parlor and the laundromat was a fortune-telling shop run by someone named Sister Lucy. Progress. As she passed Sister Lucy's emporium, Teddy looked over the curtain in the front window and saw a Gypsy woman sitting before a large phrenology poster hanging on the wall. Except for the poster and the woman, the shop was empty. The woman looked very lonely and a trifle cold, huddled in her shawl, looking straight ahead of her at the entrance door. For a moment, Teddy was tempted to walk into the empty store and have her fortune told. What was the joke? Her husband was very good at remembering jokes. What was it? Why couldn't women remember jokes? Was that a sexist attitude? What the hell was the *joke?* Something about a Gypsy band buying a chain of empty stores?

The name on the plate glass window of the tattoo parlor was Charlie Chen. Beneath the name were the words Exotic Oriental Tattoo. She hesitated a moment, and then opened the door. There must have been a bell over the door, and it probably tinkled, signaling Mr. Chen from the back of his shop. She had not heard the bell, and at first she did not recognize the old Chinese man who came toward her. The last time she'd seen him, he had been a round fat man with a small mustache on his upper lip. He had laughed a lot, and each time he laughed, his fat little body quivered. He had thick fingers, she remembered, and there had been an oval jade ring on the forefinger of his left hand.

"Yes, lady?" he said.

It was Chen, of course. The mustache was gone, and so was the jade ring, and so were the acres of flesh, but it was surely Chen, wizened and wrinkled and shrunken, looking at her now out of puzzled brown eyes, trying to place her. She thought *I've* changed, too, he doesn't recognize me, and suddenly felt foolish about what she was here to do. Maybe it was too late for things like garter belts and panties, ribbed stockings and high-heeled, patent leather pumps, merry widows and lacy teddies, too late for Teddy, too late for silly, sexy playfulness. Was it? Oh my God, *was* it?

She had asked Fanny to call yesterday, first to find out if the shop would be open today, and next to make an appointment for her. Fanny had left the name Teddy Carella. Had Chen forgotten her name as well? He was still staring at her.

"You Missa Carella?" he said.

She nodded.

"I know you?" he said, his head cocked, studying her.

She nodded again.

"You know me?"

She nodded.

"Charlie Chen," he said, and laughed, but nothing about him shook, his laughter was an empty wind blowing through a frail old body. "Everybody call me Charlie *Chan,"* he explained. "Big detective Charlie Chan. But me Chen, *Chen.* You know Charlie Chan, detective?"

The same words he had spoken all those years ago.

Oddly, she felt like weeping.

"Big detective," Chen said. "Got stupid sons." He laughed again. "Me got stupid sons, too, but me no detec—" And suddenly he stopped, and his eyes opened wide, and he said, "Detective wife, you detective *wife!* I make butterfly for you! Black lacy butterfly!"

She nodded again, grinning now.

"You no can talk, right. You read my lips, right?"

She nodded.

"Good, everything hunky-dory. How you been, lady? You still so pretty, most beautiful lady ever come my shop. You still got butterfly on shoulder?"

She nodded.

"Best butterfly I ever make. Nice small butterfly. I want do *big* one, remember?

You say no, small one. I make tiny delicate black butterfly, very good for lady. Very sexy in strapless gown. You husband think was sexy?''

Teddy nodded. She started to say something with her hands, caught herself—as she so often had to—and then pointed to a pencil and a sheet of paper on Chen's counter.

"You wanna talk, right?'' Chen said, smiling, and handed her the pencil and paper.

She took both, and wrote: *How have you been, Mr. Chen?*

"Ah, well, not so good,'' Chen said.

She looked at him expectantly, quizzically.

"Old Charlie Chen gotta Big C, huh?'' he said.

She did not understand for a moment.

"Cancer,'' he said, and saw the immediate shocked look on her face and said, "No, no, lady, don't worry, old Charlie be hunky-dory, yessir.'' He kept watching her face. She did not want to cry. She owed the old man the dignity of not having to watch her cry for him. She opened her hands. She tilted her head. She raised her eyebrows ever so slightly. She saw on his face and in his eyes that he knew she was telling him how sorry she was. "Thank you, lady,'' he said, and impulsively took both her hands between his own, and, smiling, said, "So, why you come here see Charlie Chen? You write down what you like, yes?''

She picked up the pencil and began writing again.

"Ah,'' he said, watching. "Ah. Very smart idea. Very smart. Okay, fine.''

He watched the moving pencil.

"Very good,'' he said, "come, we go in back. Charlie Chen so happy you come see him. My sons all married now, I tell you? My oldest son a doctor in Los Angeles. A *head* doctor!'' he said, and burst out laughing. "A shrink! You believe it? My oldest *son!* My other two sons . . . come in back, lady . . . my other two sons . . .''

From where Captain Sam Grossman stood at the windows looking down at High Street, he could see out over almost all of the downtown section of the city. The new Headquarters Building was a structure made almost entirely of glass (or so it appeared from the outside) and Grossman sometimes wondered if anyone down there in the street was watching him as he went about his daily commonplace chores—like trying to get through to the Eight-Seven on the telephone, which was both commonplace *and* irritating. Actually, Grossman rarely thought of his work in the lab as being anything but important and exciting and very far from commonplace, but he would not have admitted that to anyone in the world, with the possible exception of his wife. The number was still busy. He momentarily pressed one of the receiver rest buttons, got a fresh dial tone, and dialed the number again. He got another busy signal. Sighing, Grossman cradled the receiver and looked at his watch. I shouldn't even *be* here today, he thought. This is Sunday.

He was here today because someone thought it might be amusing to restage the Valentine's Day Massacre right here in *this* city instead of in Chicago, where it had originally taken place in 1929. What had happened back then, if Grossman's memory of history served, was that some nice fellows from Al Capone's gang forced seven unarmed but equally nice fellows from the Bugs Moran gang to line up against a garage wall and then shot them down with machine guns. Oh boy, that was some massacre. It was also a pretty good joke since the guys from the Capone gang were all dressed as policemen. There were some wags in Chicago at the time who maintained that the hoods were only *behaving* like policemen, too, but that was mere conjecture. Nonetheless, at nine o'clock this morning—which by Grossman's watch was almost three hours ago—several uniformed "policemen" had broken into a garage housing not bootleggers but instead narcotics traffickers, and had asked them to line up against the wall, and had shot them down in cold blood. One of the surprise-shooters had spray-painted the outline of a big heart on the wall. The killers hadn't even bothered to take with them the estimated four kilos of heroin the traffickers had been processing when they'd broken in; perhaps they felt the red heart on the wall, and the red blood all over the floor, complimented the pristine white of the uncut heroin on the table. Either way, there were seven dead men on the Lower Platform, as the area closest to the city's Old Quarter was called, and those men had bullets in them, and those bullets had been recovered from their respective cadavers and sent to the laboratory together with the empty spray can and a slew of fingerprints lifted from hither and yon, not to mention some paint scrapings taken from the lamppost opposite the garage, presumably left there when the get-away car backed into it, leaving as well a deposit of tail light glass splinters on the pavement, all in all a nice batch of material for the lab to ponder on a nice Sunday morning.

Grossman dialed the number again.

Would miracles never? It was actually ringing!

"Eighty-Seventh Squad, Genero," a harried-sounding voice said.

"Detective Carella, please," Grossman said.

"Can he call you back?" Genero said. "We're very busy up here just now."

"I've been trying to get through for the past ten minutes," Grossman said.

"Yeah, that's 'cause the lines've been busy," Genero said. "All hell is busting loose up here. Give me your name and I'll ask him to call back."

"No, give him my name and tell him I'll on the line *waiting*," Grossman said, annoyed.

"Well, what *is* your name, mister?" Genero said, somewhat snottily.

"Captain Grossman," Grossman said. "What's *your* name?"

"He'll be right with you, sir," Genero said, forgetting to tell Grossman his name. Grossman heard the receiver clattering onto a hard surface. There was a great deal of yelling and hollering in the background, but that was usual for the Eight-Seven, even on a Sunday.

"Detective Carella," Carella said. "Can I help you, sir?"

"Steve, this is Sam Grossman."

"*Sam?* He told me it was Captain *Holtzer.*"

"No, it's Captain Grossman. What's going on up there? It sounds like World War Three."

"We have a delegation of angry citizens," Carella said.

"Angry about what?"

"A person shitting in the hallways."

"Don't send me samples," Grossman said at once.

"*You* may think it's comical," Carella said, lowering his voice, "and frankly, so do I. But the tenants of 5411 Ainsley do not find it amusing at all. They are here en masse, demanding police action."

"What do they want you to *do*, Steve?"

"Apprehend the Mad Shitter," Carella said, and Grossman burst out laughing. Carella started laughing, too. In the background, over Carella's laughter, Grossman could hear someone yelling in Spanish. He thought he detected the word *mierda*.

"Steve," he said, "I hate to take you away from matters of great moment—"

"Matters of great *movement*, you mean," Carella said, and both men burst out laughing again; there was nothing a grown cop liked better than a scatalogical joke unless it was a joke about a cop on the take. Both cops laughed for what must have been a full two minutes while behind them everyone was shouting like the Bay of Pigs. At last, the laughter subsided. So did all the Spanish voices in the background.

"Where'd they all *go*, all of a sudden?" Grossman asked.

"*Home!*" Carella said, and burst out laughing again. "Genero told them he'd arrange a *lineup* for them! Can you picture eight cops and a possible perp throwing moons at twenty-six concerned Hispanic tenants?"

Grossman began laughing so hard he thought he would wet his pants. Another two minutes went by before either of the men could speak. It was not always like this when Carella and Grossman got on the phone together, but both men were grateful for those times when it was. Usually, Grossman presented a much soberer demeanor to the detectives with whom he worked. Tall and blue eyed, rather somber looking in his unrimmed spectacles, he resembled a New England farmer more than he did a scientist, and his clipped manner of speaking did little to belie the notion. Standing face to face with Sam Grossman in the sterile orderliness of his laboratory, you had the feeling that if you asked him directions to the next town, he'd say you couldn't get there from here. But every so often, perhaps because he liked Carella so much, Grossman seemed to forget momentarily that his job was often inextricably linked with violent death.

"About this girl's handbag," he said, and Carella knew he was getting down to business.

"The Anderson girl?" he said.

"Sally Anderson, right," Grossman said. "I'll send you the full report later, right down to what brand of cigarettes she smoked. But for now . . . this was flagged for possible cocaine, wasn't it?"

"Because the other victim was a—"

"That's what the card says, anyway."

"Did you find anything that *might* be cocaine?"

"A residue on the bottom of the bag. Not enough to run as many tests as I'd have liked."

"How many *did* you run?"

"Four. Which in the process of elimination—you should pardon the expression—isn't a hell of a lot. But I knew what you were looking for, so I deliberately chose my color tests for the most dramatic reactions. For example, cocaine shows colorless on both the Mercke and the Marquis, so I avoided those. Instead, I went with nitrosylsulfuric acid for my first color test. I got a pale yellow reaction, with no change when ammonia was added, and with a change to colorless when water was added. That's a cocaine reaction. For the second color test—am I boring you?''

"No, no, go on,'' Carella said. He considered himself a scientific nitwit and was in fact fascinated whenever Grossman began spewing formulas and such.

"For the second color test, I used tetrabitromathane, which again—if we're looking for cocaine—would give us a more dramatic reaction than some of the other tests. Sure enough, we initially got yellow with an orange cast to it, turning eventually to full yellow. Cocaine,'' Grossman said.

"Cocaine,'' Carella repeated.

"And when I ran my tests for precipitation and crystallization, I got virtually the same results. With platinum chloride as my reagent and normal acetic acid as my solvent, I got an immediate cocaine reaction—thousands of aggregate crystalline blade forms, arranged in bizarre fashion, moderate birefringence, predominantly—''

"You're losing me, Sam,'' Carella said.

"No matter. It was typically cocaine. When I used gold chloride with the acid, I got ruler-edged crystals forming from amorphous . . . again, no matter. It, too, was typically cocaine.

"So . . . are you saying the substance you found at the bottom of her bag *is* cocaine?''

"I'm saying there's a very strong *likelihood* it's cocaine. I can't say positively, Steve, without having run a great many more tests, but I simply ran out of available substance before I could. If it makes you any happier . . . you *are* looking for a drug connection here, I assume.''

"I am.''

"Well, we found shreds of marijuana, as well as marijuana seeds at the bottom of the bag. Ladies' handbags are wonderful receptacles for all *kinds* of crap.''

"Okay, thanks, Sam.''

"Would it help further to know that the girl chewed sugarless gum?''

"Not in the slightest.''

"In that case, I won't mention that she chewed sugarless gum. Good luck, Steve, I have bullets here from seven people who were shot by cops today.''

"What?'' Carella said, but Grossman had hung up.

Smiling, Grossman stood with his hand on the cradled receiver for a moment, and then looked up when he heard the door opening. He was surprised to see Bert Kling coming into the room, not because Kling never visited the lab, but only because Grossman had not ten seconds earlier been talking to *another* cop from the Eight-Seven. Considering the laws of probability, Grossman would have guessed . . . well, no matter.

"Come in, Bert,'' he said. "How's it going?''

He knew how it was going. Everyone in the department knew how it was going. Bert Kling had found his wife in bed with another man last August, *that's* how it was going. He knew that Kling and his wife were now divorced. He knew that Carella was concerned about him because Carella had expressed concern to Grossman, who had suggested that he talk to one of the department psychologists, who in turn had advised Carella to try to get Kling to come in personally, which Carella had not been able to convince Kling to do. Grossman liked Kling. There were not many cops in the Eight-Seven he disliked, as a matter of fact—well, yes, Parker, he guessed. Parker very definitely. Parker was meanspirited and lazy and altogether a person to dislike passionately. Grossman liked Kling and he hated seeing him *looking* this way, like a man who'd just been released from the state penitentiary at Castleview and was still wearing the ill-fitting civilian threads the state gave him gratis with his parole papers and his minimum-wage check. Like a man who needed a shave, even though the blond stubble on Kling's cheeks and jaws was less noticeable than it might have been on a man with a heavier beard. Like a man carrying an enormous weight on his shoulders. Like a man whose eyes appeared a trifle too moist, a bit too precariously poised on the edge of tears. Grossman looked into those eyes as the men shook hands. Was Carella's concern a legitimate one? *Did* Kling look like a man who might one day decide to chew on the barrel of his gun?

"So," Grossman said, smiling, "what brings you down here?"

"Some bullets," Kling said.

"More bullets? We had the Valentine's Day Massacre all over again this morning," Grossman said. "Seven guys killed in a garage down on the Lower Platform. Guys who did it were dressed like cops. I have to admit it took style, but I don't like the extra work it's given us on a weekend. What bullets?"

"We caught a homicide last night on Silvermine Road," Kling said. "Man named Marvin Edelman, gunshot victim. I asked the morgue to send whatever they recover over to you. I thought I might mention it."

"You came all the way down here to tell me some *bullets* are on the way?" Grossman said.

"No, no, I was in the area, anyway."

Grossman knew that the Criminal Court Building was right next door, and at first he figured Kling might be down here on court business. There was only one court open on Sunday, though, and that strictly for the arraignment of anyone arrested the day before. And then Grossman remembered that the Psychological Counseling Unit had recently moved into new quarters on the third floor of the building. Had Carella finally convinced Kling to see someone about his obvious depression?

"So what *did* bring you down here on a Sunday?" Grossman asked in what he hoped was a casual way.

"I had a lady in yesterday, her husband . . . well, it's a long story," Kling said.

"Let me hear it," Grossman said.

"No, you've got bullets to worry about," Kling said. "Anyway, keep an eye out for whatever comes from the morgue, will you? The guy's name is Edelman."

"A *landsman,*" Grossman said, smiling, but Kling did not return the smile.

"See you," Kling said, and walked out of the lab and into the marble corridor outside. The story he'd been about to tell was about this woman who'd come to see him yesterday because her husband's former girlfriend had accosted him on the street and slashed his arm from the shoulder to the wrist with a bread knife she'd pulled from her handbag. In describing the former girlfriend, the woman used the words "black as that telephone there" and then went on to describe her further as an extremely thin woman whose name was Annie—she didn't know Annie *what,* and neither did her husband. Her husband, according to the woman's story, was a

Dutch seaman who came into this city's port every other month or so and who, until they'd met and married, used to spend his wages on various prostitutes either uptown on La Vía de Putas or else downtown on a stretch of hooker-paced turf known as Slit City. The wife had been witness to the knifing, and had heard the girl Annie say, "I'm goan juke you good," and it was perhaps the use of the word *juke* that rang a bell for Kling.

A working cop doesn't always know *how* he remembers the myriad little details of the numberless criminal transgressions that cross his desk and his path every day of the week. To remember them is enough. The fact that the knife wielder had been black had not been enough to trigger recall. Neither had the name Annie, or the knowledge that the girl was extremely thin and a working prostitute. But the first time Kling had ever heard the word *juke* in his life was on Mason Avenue, when an anorectic black whore who'd slashed a customer's face later claimed, "I di'n juke that dumb trick." Cotton Hawes, who had answered the squeal with him, informed Kling that he himself had first heard the expression in New Orleans, and that it meant, of course, "to stab." The hooker's name had been Annie Holmes. The moment the victim's wife repeated what Annie had said as she carved up her former playmate's arm, Kling snapped his fingers.

He was down here today—even though it was his day off—because: (a) he lived only six blocks away, in a small apartment in the shadow of the Calm's Point Bridge, and (b) he could not question Marvin Edelman's widow until tomorrow because she was on her way home from the Caribbean after receiving a call from her daughter informing her that Edelman had been shot and killed last night, and (c) there was not much more he could do on the homicide until Grossman's people came up with some information on the gun used in the slaying, and (d) he knew the Identification Section was open seven days a week (although the Mayor had been threatening cutbacks) and he hoped he might be able to pick up a picture of Annie Holmes, which he could then show to the man she'd stabbed and his wife, who'd witnessed the stabbing, hoping for a positive I.D. that would be good enough for an arrest.

That was why he was here.

He had not told Grossman why he was here, even though he'd started to, because somehow the triangle of Dutch Seaman—Present Wife—Former Bedmate recalled vividly and blindingly the scene in the bedroom of the apartment Kling had shared with Augusta as man and wife, the triangular scene in that room, Augusta naked in their bed, absurdly clutching the sheet to her breasts, hiding her shame, protecting her nakedness from the prying eyes of her own husband, her green eyes wide, her hair tousled, a fine sheen of perspiration on the marvelous cheekbones that were her fortune, her lip trembling the way the gun in Kling's hand was trembling. And the man with Augusta, the *third* side of the triangle, was in his undershorts and reaching for his trousers folded over a bedside chair, the man was short and wiry, he looked like *Genero,* for Christ's sake, with curly black hair and brown eyes wide in terror, but he was not Genero, he was Augusta's lover, and as he turned from the chair where his trousers were draped, he said only, "Don't shoot," and Kling leveled the gun at him.

I *should* have shot him, he thought now. If I'd shot him, I wouldn't still be living with the shame. I wouldn't have to stop telling a story about a Dutch seaman and his hooker girlfriend for fear that even a decent man like Sam Grossman will remember, will think, Ah yes, Kling and his cheating wife, Ah yes, Kling did *nothing*, Ah yes, Kling did not *kill* the man who was—

"Hey, hi!" the voice said.

He was approaching the elevators, his head bent, his eyes on the marble floor. He did not recognize the voice, nor did he even realize at first that it was he who was being addressed. But he looked up because someone had stepped into his path. The someone was Eileen Burke.

She was wearing a simple brown suit with a green blouse that was sort of ruffly at the throat, the green the color of her eyes, her long red hair swept efficiently back from her face, standing tall in high-heeled brown pumps a shade darker than the suit. She was carrying a shoulder bag, and he could see into the bag to where the barrel of a revolver seemed planted in a bed of crumpled Kleenexes. The picture of her plastic I.D. card, clipped to the lapel of her suit, showed a younger Eileen Burke, her red hair done in the frizzies. She was smiling—in the picture, and in person.

"What are you doing down *here?*" she asked. "Nobody comes here on a Sunday."

"I need a picture from the I.S.," he said. She seemed waiting for him to say more. "How about you?" he added.

"I work here. Special Forces is here. Right on this floor, in fact. Come on in for a cup of coffee," she said, and her smile widened.

"No, thanks, I'm sort of in a hurry," Kling said, even though he was in no hurry at all.

"Okay," Eileen said, and shrugged. "Actually, I'm glad I ran into you. I was going to call later in the day, anyway."

"Oh?" Kling said.

"I think I lost an earring up there. Either there or in the laundromat with the panty perpetrator. If it *was* the laundromat, good-bye, Charlie. But if it was the squadroom, or maybe the car—when you were dropping me off last night, you know . . ."

"Yeah," Kling said.

"It was just a simple gold hoop earring, about the size of a quarter. Nothing ostentatious when you're doing dirty laundry, right?"

"Which ear was it?" he asked.

"The right," she said. "Huh? What difference does it make? I mean, it *was* the right ear, but earrings are interchangeable, so—"

"Yeah, that's right," Kling said. He was looking at her right ear, or at the space beyond her right ear, or wherever. He was certainly not looking at her face, certainly not allowing his eyes to meet her eyes. What the hell is *wrong* with him? she wondered.

"Well, take a look up there, okay?" she said. "If you find it, give me a call. I'm with Special Forces—well, you know that—but I'm in and out all the time, so just leave a message. That is, if you happen to find the earring." She hesitated, and then said, ''The *right* one, that is. If you find the *left* one, it's the *wrong* one.'' She smiled. He did not return the smile. ''Well, see you around the pool hall,'' she said, and spread her hand in a farewell fan, and turned on her heel, and walked away from him.

Kling pressed the button for the elevator.

Tina Wong had been jogging in the snow, and she was surprised to find the detectives waiting in the lobby of her building when she came out of the park. She was wearing a gray sweat suit and a woolen hat that was less colorful than the one Meyer had received as a present. Her track shoes were wet, as were the legs of the sweat suit pants. She said, ''Oh,'' and then inexplicably looked over her shoulder, as though her car were illegally parked at the curb or something.

''Sorry to bother you, Miss Wong,'' Meyer said. He was not wearing his Valentine's Day gift. Instead, he had on a blue snap-brim fedora that he felt made him look more stylish if a trifle more bald than the watch cap did.

''Just a few questions we'd like to ask,'' Carella said. They had been standing in the lobby for close to forty minutes, after having been advised by Tina's doorman that Miss Wong was ''out for her run.''

''Sure,'' Tina said, and gestured toward an array of furniture clustered around an imitation fireplace. The lobby was very hot. Tina's face was flushed red from the cold outside and the energetic jogging she had done. She yanked off the woolen hat and shook out her hair. All three sat in chairs around the fake fireplace. At the switchboard across the room, the doorman looked bored as he read the headline on the morning paper. There was a mechanical hum in the room; the detectives could not locate its source. The lobby had the feel and smell of slightly damp clothes in a cloistered alcove. Outside the glass entrance doors, the wind blew fiercely, its rising and falling keen counterpointing the steady hum.

''Miss Wong,'' Carella said, ''when we spoke to you yesterday, do you remember our asking whether or not Sally was doing anything like cocaine?''

''Uh-huh,'' Tina said.

''And you remember you told us—''

''I said that to my knowledge she wasn't.''

''Does that mean you never *saw* her using cocaine?''

''Never.''

''Does that also mean she never mentioned it to you?''

''Never.''

''*Would* she have mentioned something like that?''

''We were close friends. There's nothing so terrible about snorting a few lines every now and then. I suppose if she'd been using it, she might have mentioned it.''

''But she didn't.''

''No, she didn't.''

''Miss Wong, according to Timothy Moore, there was a party Sally Anderson went to last Sunday night. Someone named Lonnie. One of the black dancers in the show.''

''Yes?'' Tina said.

"Were you at that party?"

"Yes, I was."

"But Mr. Moore wasn't."

"No, he wasn't. He had to study. He made this New Year's Eve resolution—"

"Yes, he told us. At any time that night, did you notice Miss Anderson sniffing coke?"

"No, I didn't."

"How about anyone else?"

"I don't know what you mean."

"Were there any other cast members there?"

"Oh, sure."

"Do you remember when we talked yesterday, you mentioned that some people in the cast *were* doing coke."

"Yes, I may have said that."

"Well, you said that some of them were doing a little coke, here and there, now and then."

"I suppose that's what I said."

"Were any of them doing coke last Sunday night? That you may have noticed?"

"I'm not sure I ought to answer that," Tina said.

"Why not?" Meyer said.

"Anyway, why do you think *Sally* was into cocaine?"

"*Was* she?" Carella asked at once.

"I told you, not to my knowledge. But all these questions you're asking . . . what *difference* does it make if she was or she wasn't? She's dead, she was shot to death. What does *cocaine* have to do with anything?"

"Miss Wong, we have good reason to believe she was a user."

"How? What reason?"

"We tested a residue of powder from her handbag."

"And it was cocaine?"

"We're reasonably certain it was."

"What does that mean? Was it or wasn't it?"

"The tests weren't exhaustive, but from what—"

"Then it could have been *anything,* right? Face powder or—"

"No, it wasn't face powder, Miss Wong."

"Why are you so anxious to prove she was doing coke?"

"We're not. We simply want to know who *else* was."

"How am *I* supposed to know who else was?"

"When we talked to you yesterday—"

"Yesterday, I didn't know this would turn into a third degree."

"This isn't a third degree, Miss Wong. When we talked to you yesterday, you said—and I think I'm quoting you exactly—'Usually, you can get a pretty good idea of who's doing what when you're working in a show.' Isn't that what you said?"

"I don't remember my exact words."

"But that's what you meant, isn't it?"

"I suppose so."

"Okay. If you have a pretty good idea of who's doing what, we'd like you to share it with us."

"What for? So I can get decent people in trouble for no reason at all?"

"*Which* decent people?" Carella asked.

"I don't know anybody who was involved with drugs, okay?"

"That's not what you said yesterday."

"It's what I'm saying today." She looked at them steadily, and then added, "I think I'd better call my lawyer."

"We're not looking for a drug bust here," Meyer said.

"I don't know what you're looking for, but you're not going to get it from me."

"Your best friend was murdered," Carella said softly.

She looked at him.

"We're trying to find the person who did it," Carella said.

"Nobody in the show did it."

"How do you know that?"

"I *don't* know it. I just know . . ." She fell silent. She folded her arms across her chest. She lifted her chin stubbornly. Carella looked at Meyer. Meyer nodded almost imperceptibly.

"Miss Wong," Carella said, "on the basis of what you told us yesterday, we have good cause to believe you know who, if anyone, in the cast was using cocaine. This is a murder we're investigating. We can subpoena you before a grand jury, who'll ask you the same questions we've been asking you—"

"No, you can't," she said.

"Yes, we can," Carella said, "and we *will* if you continue refusing to—"

"What is this, Russia?" Tina asked.

"This is the United States," Carella said. "You've got *your* rights, but we've also got *ours*. If you refuse to answer a grand jury, you'll be held in contempt of court. Take your choice."

"I can't believe this," she said.

"Believe it. If you know who's doing coke—"

"I hate strong-arm macho shit," Tina said.

Neither of the detectives said anything.

"*Mafia* tactics," Tina said.

Still, they said nothing.

"As if it has anything at *all* to do with who killed her," Tina said.

"Let's go, Meyer," Carella said, and stood up.

"Just a minute," Tina said.

He did not sit down again.

"There were maybe half a dozen people snorting at that party."

"Anyone in the cast?"

"Yes."

"Who?"

"Sally, of course."

"Who else?"

"Mike."

"Mike who?"

"Roldan. Miguel Roldan."

"Thank you," Carella said.

"If you cause him any trouble—"

"We're not looking to cause him trouble," Meyer said. "How well did Sally Anderson know your producer?"

The question took her totally by surprise. Her eyes opened wide. She hesitated a moment before answering. "Allan?" she said.

"Allan Carter," Carella said, nodding.

"Why?"

"Did Sally ever mention him in anything but a professional way?"

"I don't know what that means."

"I think you know what it means, Miss Wong."

"Are you asking if she was *involved* in some way with him? Don't be ridiculous."

"Why do you think that's ridiculous, Miss Wong?"

"Because . . . well, she had a boyfriend. You *know* that, I told you that yesterday."

"Why would that exclude an involvement with Mr. Carter?"

"I just know there was nothing going on between them."

"How do you know that?"

"There are some things you just *know.*"

"Did you ever see them together?"

"Of course."

"Outside of the theater, I mean."

"Occasionally."

"When's the *last* time you saw them together?"

"Last Sunday night."

"Under what circumstances?"

"He was at Lonnie's party."

"Is that usual? For the producer of a show to attend a party given by one of the dancers?"

"You're not going to stop till you get *everybody* in trouble, are you?"

"Who are we getting in trouble now?" Meyer asked.

"Allan was with *me,*" Tina said, "okay? *I* asked him to the party."

The detectives looked at each other, puzzled.

"He's *married,* okay?" Tina said.

At this point, they only wanted to talk to two people connected with the show.

The first was Miguel Roldan, who, coincidentally, was both Hispanic and a cocaine user. Sally Anderson had been a cocaine user, and Paco Lopez had been Hispanic. They wanted to ask Roldan where he got his stuff and whether Sally got it from the same place and whether that place happened to be Paco Lopez's little candy stand. The second was Allan Carter, married producer of *Fatback,* who— according to Tina Wong—had been enjoying a little backstage romance with the Chinese dancer ever since September, when they'd discovered each other at the show's opening-night party. They wanted to ask Carter why he had thought Sally Anderson was "a little redheaded thing." Had Carter been involved in an *extra* extramarital fling with the blond dancer as well? If not, why had he gone to such lengths to indicate he'd scarcely known her? They had not asked Tina anything at all about Carter's seeming confusion. If there *had* existed any sort of relationship between him and the dead girl, it was entirely possible that Tina knew nothing about it, in which case they did not want her to alert him. They knew intuitively that he'd been lying when he denied remembering Sally Anderson. Now they wanted to find out *why* he'd been lying.

They did not find out that late Sunday afternoon.

The doorman at Carter's building on Grover Park West told the detectives that both he and Mrs. Carter had left at close to 4:00 P.M. He did not know where they'd gone or when they'd be back. He suggested that perhaps Mr. Carter had gone down to Philadelphia again, but that didn't seem to tie in with the fact that a chauffeured limousine had picked up the couple; Mr. Carter usually took the train to Philadelphia, and besides, he always went down alone. The Philadelphia possibility seemed unlikely to Carella as well. Carter had mentioned on the phone yesterday that he would not be going back to Philadelphia until late Wednesday. The detectives drove uptown and crosstown to the brownstone Miguel Roldan shared with Tony Asensio, the other Hispanic dancer in the show. No one was home there, either, and there was no doorman to offer suggestions or possibilities.

Carella said good night to Meyer at ten minutes past six, and only then remembered he had not yet bought Teddy a present. He shopped the Stem until he found an open lingerie shop, only to discover that it featured panties of the open-crotch variety and some that could be eaten like candy, decided this was not quite what he had in mind, thank you, and then shopped fruitlessly for another hour before settling on a heart-shaped box of chocolates in an open drugstore. He felt he was letting Teddy down.

Her eyes and her face showed no disappointment when he presented the gift to her. He explained that it was only a temporary solution, and that he'd shop for her *real* present once the pressure of the case let up a little. He had no idea when that might be, but he promised himself that he would buy her something absolutely mind-boggling tomorrow, come hell or high water. He did not yet know that the case had already taken a peculiar turn or that he would learn about it tomorrow, when once again it would postpone his grandiose plans.

At the dinner table, ten-year-old April complained that she had received only one Valentine's card, and that one from a doofus. She pronounced the word with a grimace her mother might have used more suitably, managing to look very much like Teddy in that moment—the dark eyes and darker hair, the beautiful mouth twisted in an expression of total distaste. Her ten-year-old brother Mark, who resembled Carella more than he did either his mother or his twin sister, offered the opinion that anyone who would send a card to April *had* to be a doofus, at which point April seized her half-finished pork chop by its rib, and threatened to use it on him like a hatchet. Carella calmed them down. Fanny came in from the kitchen and casually mentioned that these were the same pork chops she'd taken out of the freezer the night before and she hoped they tasted okay and wouldn't give the whole family trichinosis. Mark wanted to know what trichinosis was. Fanny told him it was related to a cassoulet and winked at Carella.

They put the children to bed at nine.

They watched television for a while, and then they went into the bedroom. Teddy was in the bathroom for what seemed an inordinately long time. Carella guessed she was angry. When she came into the bedroom again, she was wearing a robe over her nightgown. Normally, she wasn't quite so modest in their own bedroom. He began to think more and more that his gift of chocolates without even a selection chart under the lid had truly irritated her. So deep was his own guilt (''Italians and Jews,'' Meyer was fond of saying, ''are the guiltiest people on the face of the earth'') that he did not remember until she pulled back the covers in the dark and got into bed beside him that *she* hadn't given *him* anything at *all*.

He snapped on the bedside lamp.

''Honey,'' he said, ''I'm really sorry. I know I should have done it earlier, it was stupid of me to leave it for the last minute. I promise you tomorrow I'll . . .''

She put her fingers to his lips, silencing him.

She sat up.

She lowered the strap of her nightgown.

In the glow of the lamplight, he saw her shoulder. Where previously there had been only a single black butterfly tattoo, put there so long ago he could hardly remember when, he now saw *two* butterflies, the new one slightly larger than the other, its wings a bright yellow laced with black. The new butterfly seemed to hover over the original, as though kissing it with its outstretched wings.

His eyes suddenly flooded with tears.

He pulled her to him and kissed her fiercely and felt his tears mingling with hers as surely as did the butterflies on her shoulder.

For some people, it was still St. Valentine's Day.

Many people do not believe a day ends at midnight. It is still the same day until they go to sleep. When they wake up in the morning, it is the next day. Two people who thought it was still St. Valentine's Day were Brother Anthony and the Fat Lady. Even though it was 1:00 A.M. on the morning of February 15, they thought of it as still being a day for lovers, especially since they had learned the name of Paco Lopez's girlfriend. Actually, they had learned her name when it *was* still St. Valentine's Day, which they considered a good omen. But it was not until 1:00 A.M. that Brother Anthony knocked on the door of Judite Quadrado's apartment.

In this neighborhood, a knock on the door at 1:00 A.M. meant only trouble. It meant either the police coming around to ask about a crime that had been committed in the building, or it meant a friend or neighbor coming to tell you that a loved one had either hurt someone or *been* hurt by someone. Either way, it meant bad news. The people in this neighborhood knew that a knock on the door at 1:00 A.M. did not mean a burglar or an armed robber. Thieves did not knock on doors unless it was going to be a shove-in and in this neighborhood most thieves knew that doors were double-locked and often reinforced as well with a Fox lock, the steel bar hooked into the door and wedged into a floor plate. Brother Anthony knew that someone awakened at one in the morning would be frightened; that was why he and Emma had waited until that time, even though they'd had their information at 10:00 P.M.

From behind the door, Judite said, "Who is it?"

"Friends," Brother Anthony said.

"Friends? Who? What friends?"

"Please open the door," he said.

"Go away," Judite said.

"It's important that we speak to you," Emma said.

"Who are you?"

"Open the door just a little," Emma said, "and you'll see for yourself."

They heard lock tumblers falling. One lock, then another. The door opened just a crack, held by a night chain. In the wedge of the open door, they saw a woman's pale face. A kitchen light burned behind her.

"Dominus vobiscum," Brother Anthony said.

"We have money for you," Emma said.

"Money?"

"From Paco."

"Paco?"

"He said to make sure we gave it to you if anything happened to him."

"Paco?" Judite said again. She had not seen Paco for at least two months before he was killed. It was Paco who had scarred her breasts, the rotten bastard. Who was this priest in the hallway? Who was this fat woman claiming they had money for her? Money from Paco? Impossible.

"Go away," she said again.

Emma took a sheaf of bills from her pocketbook, the money remaining from what Brother Anthony had taken from the pool hustler. In the dim hallway light, she saw Judite's eyes widen.

"For you," Emma said. "Open the door."

"If it's for me, hand it to me," Judite said. "I don't need to open the door."

"Never mind," Brother Anthony said, and put his hand on Emma's arm. "She doesn't want the money."

"How much money is it?" Judite asked.

"Four hundred dollars," Emma said.

"And Paco said he wanted *me* to have it?"

"For what he did to you," Emma said, lowering her voice and her eyes.

"Just a minute," Judite said.

The door closed. They heard nothing. Brother Anthony shrugged. Emma returned the shrug. Had their information been wrong? The man who'd told them about Judite was her cousin. He said she'd been living with Paco Lopez before he was killed. He said Paco had burned her breasts with cigarettes. Which was one of the reasons Brother Anthony had suggested they call on her at one in the morning. It was Brother Anthony's opinion that no woman allowed herself to be treated brutally unless she was a very frightened woman. One o'clock in the morning should make her even more frightened. But where was she? Where had she gone? They waited. They heard the night chain being removed. The door opened wide. Judite Quadrado stood in the open doorway with a pistol in her fist.

"Come in," she said, and gestured with the pistol.

Brother Anthony had not expected the pistol. He looked at Emma. Emma said, *"No hay necesidad de la pistola,"* which Brother Anthony did not understand. Until that moment, in fact, he hadn't known Emma could speak Spanish.

"Hasta que yo sepa quien es usted," Judite said, and again gestured with the gun.

"All right," Emma answered in English. "But *only* until you know who we are. I don't like doing favors for a woman with a gun in her hand."

They went into the apartment. Judite closed and locked the door behind them. They were in a small kitchen. A refrigerator, sink, and stove were on one wall, below a small window that opened onto an areaway. The window was closed and rimed with ice. A table covered with white oilcloth was against the right-angled wall. Two wooden chairs were at the table.

Brother Anthony did not like the look on Judite's face. She did not look like a frightened woman. She looked like a woman very much in command of the situation. He was thinking they'd made a mistake coming up here. He was thinking they'd lose what was left of the money he'd taken from the pool hustler. He was thinking maybe the ideas he and Emma hatched weren't always so hot. Judite was perhaps five feet six inches tall, a slender, dark-haired, brown-eyed girl with a nose just a trifle too large for her narrow face. She was wearing a dark blue robe; Brother Anthony figured that was why she'd left them waiting in the hall so long. So she could go put on the robe. And get the gun from wherever she kept it. He did not like the look of the gun. It was steady in her hand. She had used a gun before; he sensed that intuitively. She would not hesitate to use it now. The situation looked extremely bad.

"So," she said. "Who are you?"

"I'm Brother Anthony," he said.

"Emma Forbes," Emma said.

"How did you know Paco?"

"A shame what happened to him," Emma said.

"How did you know him?" Judite said again.

"We were friends for a long time," Brother Anthony said. It kept bothering him that she held the gun so steady in her hand. The gun didn't look like any of the Saturday-night specials he had seen in the neighborhood. This one was at *least* a .38. This one could put a very nice hole in his cassock.

"If you're his friends, how come *I* don't know you?" Judite said.

"We've been away," Emma said.

"Then how did you get the money, if you've been away?"

"Paco left it for us. At the apartment."

"What apartment?"

"Where we live."

"He left it for *me?*"

"He left it for you," Emma said. "With a note."

"Where's the note?"

"Where's the note, Bro?" Emma said.

"At the apartment," Brother Anthony said, assuming an attitude of annoyance. "I didn't know we'd need a *note*. I didn't know you need a *note* when you came to deliver four hundred dollars to—"

"Give it to me then," Judite said, and extended her left hand.

"Put away the gun," Emma said.

"No. First give me the money."

"Give her the money," Brother Anthony said. "It's hers. Paco wanted her to have it."

Their eyes met. Judite did not notice the glance that passed between them. Emma went to the table and spread the bills in a fan on the oilcloth. Judite turned to pick up the bills and Brother Anthony stepped into her at the same moment, smashing his bunched fist into her nose. Her nose had not looked particularly lovely beforehand, but now it began spouting blood. Brother Anthony had read somewhere that hitting a person in the nose was very painful and also highly effective. The nose bled easily, and blood frightened people. The blood pouring from Judite's nose caused her to forget all about the pistol in her hand. Brother Anthony seized her wrist, twisted her arm behind her back, and yanked the pistol away from her.

"Okay," he said.

Judite was holding her hand to her nose. Blood poured from her nose into her fingers. Emma took a dish towel from where it was lying on the counter and tossed it to her.

"Wipe yourself," she said.

Judite was whimpering.

"And stop crying. Nobody's going to hurt you."

Judite didn't exactly believe this. She had *already* been hurt. She had made a mistake, opening the door at one in the morning, even *with* the gun. Now the gun was in the priest's hand, and the fat woman was picking up the money on the table and stuffing it back into her shoulder bag.

"Wh . . . what do you want?" Judite said. She was holding the towel to her nose now. The towel was turning red. Her nose hurt; she suspected the priest had broken it.

"Sit down," Brother Anthony said. He was smiling now that the situation was in his own capable hands.

"Sit down," Emma repeated.

Judite sat on the table.

"Get me some ice," she said. "You broke my nose."

"Get her some ice," Brother Anthony said.

Emma went to the refrigerator. She took out an ice tray and cracked it open into the sink. Judite handed her the bloodstained towel, and Emma wrapped it around a handful of cubes.

"You broke my nose," Judite said again, and accepted the towel and pressed the ice pack to her nose. On the street outside, she could hear the rise and fall of an ambulance siren. She wondered if she would need an ambulance.

"Who were his customers?" Brother Anthony asked.

"What?" She didn't know who he meant at first. And then it occurred to her that he was talking about Paco.

"His *customers*," Emma said. "Who was he *selling* to?"

"Paco, do you mean?"

"You know who we mean," Brother Anthony said. He tucked the gun into the pouchlike pocket at the front of his robe, and gestured to the fat woman. The fat woman reached into her bag again. For a dizzying moment, Judite thought they were going to let her go. The priest had put the gun away, and now the fat woman was reaching into her bag again. They were going to give her the money, after all. They were going to let her go. But when the fat woman's hand came out of the bag, there was something long and narrow in it. The fat woman's thumb moved, and a straight razor snapped open out of its case, catching tiny dancing pinpricks of light. Judite was more afraid of the razor than she had been of the gun. She had never in her life been shot, but she'd been cut many, many times, once even by Paco. She bore the scar on her shoulder. It was a less hideous scar than the ones he had burned onto her breasts.

"Who were his customers?" Brother Anthony asked again.

"I hardly even knew him," Judite said.

"You were living with him," Emma said.

"That doesn't mean I knew him," Judite said, which, in a way, was an awesome truth.

She did not want to tell them who Paco's customers had been because *his* customers were now *her* customers, or at least *would* be as soon as she got her act together. She had reconstructed from memory a list of an even dozen users, enough to keep her living in a style she thought would be luxurious. Enough to have caused her to buy a gun before she embarked on her enterprise; there were too many bastards like Paco in the world. But the gun was now in the priest's pocket, and the fat woman was turning the razor slowly in her hand, so that its edge caught glints of light. Judite thought, and this in itself was an awesome truth, that life had a peculiar way of repeating itself. Remembering what Paco had done to her breasts, she pulled the robe instinctively closed over her nightgown, using her free left hand. Brother Anthony caught the motion.

"Who were his customers?" Emma said.

"I don't know. *What* customers?"

"For the nose candy," Emma said, and moved closer to her with the razor.

"I don't know what that means, nose candy," Judite said.

"What you *sniff,* my dear," Emma said, and brought the razor close to her face. "Through your *nose,* my dear. Through the nose you won't *have* in a minute if you don't tell us who they were."

"No, not her face," Brother Anthony said, almost in a whisper. "Not her face."

He smiled at Judite. For another dizzying moment, Judite thought he was the one who would let her go. The woman seemed menacing, but surely the priest—

"Take off the robe," he said.

"What for?" she asked, and clutched the robe closed tighter across her chest.

"Take it off," Brother Anthony said.

She hesitated. She pulled the towel away from her nose. The flow of blood seemed to be tapering. She put the towel back again. Even the pain seemed to be ebbing now. Perhaps this would not be so bad, after all. Perhaps, if she just went along with them, played along with them—surely the fat woman wasn't *serious* about cutting off her nose? Were the names of Paco's customers really that important to them? Would they risk so much for so little? Anyway, they were *her* customers now, damn it! She would give them whatever else they wanted, but not the names that were her ticket to what she imagined as freedom. She did not know what kind of freedom. Just freedom. She would never give them the names.

"Why do you want me to take off the robe?" she asked. "What is it you want from me?"

"The customers," Emma said.

"Do you want to see my body?" she asked. "Is that it?"

"The customers," Emma said.

"You want me to blow you?" she asked Brother Anthony.

"Take off the robe," Brother Anthony said.

"Because if you want me to—"

"The robe," he said.

She looked at him. She tried to read his eyes. Paco had told her she gave better head than most of the hookers he knew. If she could reach the priest—

"Can I stand up?" she asked.

"Stand up," Emma said, and retreated several steps. The open razor was still in her hand.

Judite put down the towel. Her nose had stopped bleeding entirely. She took off the robe and draped it over the back of the chair. She was wearing only a pale blue baby-doll nightgown. The nightgown ended just an inch below her crotch. She was not wearing the panties that had come with the nightgown when she'd bought it. The nightgown and panties had cost her twenty-six dollars. Money she could easily get back from her new cocaine trade. She saw where the priest's eyes went.

"So what do you say?" she asked, arching one eyebrow and trying a smile.

"I say take off the nightgown," Brother Anthony said.

"It's cold in here," Judite said, hugging herself. "The heat goes off at ten." She was being seductive and bantering, she thought. She had captured the priest's eye—they were all supposed to be celibate, some joke—and now she thought she'd make it a bit more interesting and spicy, tease him along a little, make a big production out of taking off the nightgown. The fat woman would go along with whatever the priest decided; Judite knew women, and that's the way it was.

"Just take it off," Brother Anthony said.

"What for?" Judite said, the same light tone in her voice. "You can *see* what you're getting, can't you? I'm practically naked here, you can practically see right through this thing, so why do I have to take if off?"

"Take off the fucking nightgown!" Emma said, and all at once Judite thought she'd made a big error in judgment. The fat woman was moving closer to her again, the razor flashing.

"All right, don't . . . just don't get . . . I'll take it off, okay? Just . . . take it easy, okay? But, really, I don't know what you're talking about, Paco's customers, I swear to God I don't know what you mean by—"

"You know what we're talking about," Brother Anthony said.

She pulled the gown up over her waist, lifted it over her breasts and shoulders, and without turning placed it on the seat of the wooden chair. Gooseflesh erupted immediately on her arms and across her chest and shoulders. She stood naked and trembling in the center of the kitchen, her bare feet on the cold linoleum, the ice-rimed window behind her. She was quite well formed, Brother Anthony thought. Her shoulders were narrow and delicately turned, and there was a gently rounded swell to her belly, and a ripe flare to her hips. Her breasts, too, were large and firm, quite beautiful except for the angry brown burn scars on their sloping tops. Very well formed, he thought. Not as opulent a woman as Emma, but very well formed indeed. He noticed that there was a small knife scar on her left shoulder. She was a woman who'd been abused before, perhaps regularly, a very frightened woman.

"Cut her," he said.

The thrust of the razor came so swiftly that for a moment Judite didn't even realize she'd been cut. The slash drew a thin line of blood across her belly, not as frightening as the blood pouring from her nose had been, really just a narrow line of blood oozing from the flesh, nothing so terribly scary. Even the searing aftermath of the razor slash was less painful than the blow to her nose had been. She looked down at her belly in amazement. But somehow, she was less frightened now than she'd been a moment earlier. If this was what it would be like, if this was the *worst* they would do to her—

"We don't want to hurt you," the priest said, and she knew this meant they *did* want to hurt her, would in *fact* hurt her more than they already had if she did not give them the names they wanted. Her mind worked quickly, frantically searching for a way to protect her own interests, give them the names of the customers, why not, but withhold the name of the ounce dealer—you could always find new customers if you knew where to get the stuff. Hiding her secret, hiding her fear as well, she calmly gave them all the names they wanted, all of the twelve she had memorized, writing them down at their request, scribbling the names and addresses on a sheet of paper, trying to conceal the shaking of her fist as she wrote. And then, after she had given them all the names, and had even clarified the spelling of some of them, after she thought it was all over, thought they had what they wanted from her now, and would leave her alone with her broken nose and the bleeding slash across her belly, she was surprised to hear the priest ask, "Where did he get the stuff?" and she hesitated before answering, and realized all at once that her hesitation had been another mistake, her hesitation had informed them that she knew the source of Paco's supply, knew the name of his ounce dealer and wanted it from her now.

"I don't know where," she said.

Her teeth were beginning to chatter. She kept looking at the razor in the fat woman's hand.

"Cut off her nipple," the priest said, and her hands went instinctively to her scarred breasts as the fat woman approached with the razor again, and suddenly she was more frightened than she'd ever been in her life, and she heard herself telling them the name, heard herself giving away her secret and her freedom, saying the name over and over again, babbling the name, and thought that would truly be the end of it, and was astonished to see the razor flashing out again, shocked beyond belief when she saw blood spurting from the tip of her right breast and knew, *Oh dear Jesus,* that they were going to hurt her anyway, *Oh sweet Mary,* maybe kill her, *Oh sweet mother of God,* the razor glinting and slashing again and again and again until at last she fainted.

In the station house, the squadroom looked exactly the same every day of the week, weekends and holidays included. But on Monday mornings, everyone *knew* it was Monday, the feel was just different. Like it or not, it was the start of another week. Sameness or not, it was somehow different.

Carella was at his desk at 7:30 A.M., fifteen minutes before he was scheduled to relieve the graveyard shift. The men on the night watch were wrapping it up, winding down over coffee and crullers from an all-night greasy spoon on Crichton, talking softly about the events that had transpired in the empty hours of the night. The shift had been a relatively quiet one. They kidded Carella about coming in fifteen minutes early; was he bucking for Detective/First? Carella was bucking for a conversation with Karl Loeb, the med-student friend Timothy Moore claimed to have telephoned several times on the night Sally Anderson was shot to death.

There were three columns of Loebs in the Isola telephone directory, but only two of the listings were for men named *Karl* Loeb, and only one of those listed an address on Perry Street, three blocks from Ramsey University. Moore had told Carella that he could be reached at the school during the daytime. Carella didn't know whether or not Ramsey would be observing a cockamamie holiday like President's Day, but he didn't want to take any chances. Besides, if the school *was* closed today, Loeb might decide to go out for a picnic or something. He wanted to catch him at home, before he left one way or the other. He dialed the number.

"Hello?" a woman said.

"Hello, may I speak to Karl Loeb, please?" Carella said.

"Who's this, please?" the woman asked.

"Detective Carella of the Eighty-Seventh Squad."

"What do you mean?" the woman said.

"Police department," Carella said.

"Is this a joke?" she said.

"No joke."

"Well . . . just a sec, okay?"

She put down the phone. He heard her calling to someone, presumably Loeb. When Loeb came onto the line, he sounded puzzled.

"Hello?" he said.

"Mr. Loeb?"

"Yes?"

"This is Detective Carella, Eighty-Seventh Squad."

"Yes?"

"If you have a few minutes, I'd like to ask you some questions."

"What about?" Loeb said.

"Do you know a man named Timothy Moore?"

"Yes?"

"Were you at home Friday night, Mr. Loeb?"

"Yes?"

"Did Mr. Moore call you at any time on Friday night? I'm talking now about Friday, February twelfth, this past Friday."

"Well . . . can you tell me what this is about, please?"

"Is this an inconvenient time for you, Mr. Loeb?"

"Well, I was shaving," Loeb said.

"Shall I call you back?"

"No, but . . . I *would* like to know what this is about."

"Did you speak to Mr. Moore at any time this past Friday night?"

"Yes, I did."

"Do you remember what you discussed?"

"The exam. We have a big exam coming up. In Pathology. Excuse me, Mr. Coppola, but—"

"Carella," Carella said.

"Carella, excuse me. Can you tell me what this is about, please? I'm not really in the habit of getting mysterious phone calls from the police. In fact, how do I even *know* you're a policeman?"

"Would you like to call me back here at the precinct?" Carella said. "The number here—"

"Well, no, I don't think that's necessary. But, really—"

"I'm sorry, Mr. Loeb, but I'd rather *not* tell you what it's about just yet."

"Is Timmy in some kind of trouble?"

"No, sir."

"Then what . . . I just don't understand."

"Mr. Loeb, I'd appreciate your help. Do you remember *when* Mr. Moore called you?"

"He called me several times."

"How *many* times, would you estimate?"

"Five or six? I really couldn't say. We were swapping information back and forth."

"Did you call *him* at any time?"

"Yes, two or three times."

"So between the two of you—"

"Maybe four times," Loeb said. "I really couldn't say. We were sort of studying together on the phone."

"So you exchanged calls nine or ten times, is that right?"

"Roughly. Maybe a dozen times. I don't remember."

"Throughout the night?"

"Well, not *all* night."

"When was the first call?"

"Around ten o'clock, I guess."

"Did you call Mr. Moore, or did—"

"He called me."

"At ten o'clock."

"Around ten. I'm not sure of the exact time."

"And the next call?"

"I called him back about a half hour later."

"To swap information."

"To ask him a question, actually."

"And the next one?"

"I really couldn't say with any accuracy. We were on the phone together constantly that night."

"When you made *your* three or four calls . . . was Mr. Moore at home?"

"Yes, of course."

"You called him at his home number?"

"Yes."

"When was the *last* time you spoke to him?"

"It must've been about two in the morning, I guess."

"Did you call him? Or did he—"

"I called him."

"And you got him at home?"

"Yes, Mr. Carella, I *would* like to—"

"Mr. Loeb, did you exchange any phone calls between eleven o'clock and midnight this past Friday night?"

"With Timmy, do you mean?"

"Yes, with Mr. Moore."

"Between eleven and midnight?"

"Yes, sir."

"I believe so, yes."

"Did he call you, or did you call him?"

"He called me."

"Can you remember the exact times?"

"Well, no, not the *exact* times."

"But you're certain those calls came between eleven and midnight."

"Yes, I am."

"How *many* calls during that hour?"

"Two, I believe."

"And Mr. Moore made both those calls?"

"Yes."

"Can you try to remember the precise times of—"

"I really couldn't say with any accuracy."

"Approximately then."

"I guess he called at . . . it must've been a little past eleven, the first call. The news was just going off. It must've been about five past eleven, I guess."

"The news?"

"On the radio. I was studying with the radio on. So was Timmy. I like to study with background music, do you know? I find it soothing. But the news was on when he called."

"And you say *he* was listening to the radio, too?"

"Yes, sir."

"How do know that?"

"I could hear it. In fact, he said something about turning it down."

"I'm sorry, turning it—"

"His radio. He said something like . . . I really don't remember exactly . . . 'Let me turn this down a minute, Karl,' something like that."

"And then he turned down the radio?"

"Yes, sir."

"The volume on the radio?"

"Yes, sir."

"And you had your conversation."

"Yes, sir."

"How long did you talk to him during that call? This was at five after eleven, you say?"

"Yes, sir, approximately. We talked for five or ten minutes, I guess. In fact, when he called *back,* there were still some things he didn't understand about—"

"When was that, Mr. Loeb? The next call, I mean."

"A half hour later? I can't say exactly."

"Sometime around eleven thirty-five?"

"Approximately."

"Was his radio still on?"

"What?"

"His radio. Could you still hear it in the background?"

"Yes, sir, I could."

"What did you talk about *that* time?"

"The same thing we'd talked about at eleven. Well, five *after* eleven, actually. The test is on diseases of the bone marrow. We went over the material on luekemia. How specific do you want me to get?"

"Went over the same material again, is that it?"

"Well, leukemia isn't quite as simple as it may sound, Mr. Carella."

"I'm sure it isn't," Carella said, feeling reprimanded. "And you say the last time you spoke to him was at two in the morning or thereabouts?"

"Yes, sir."

"Did you speak to him at any time between eleven thirty-five and two A.M.?"

"I believe so, yes."

"Who called who?"

"We called each other."

"At what time?"

"I don't remember exactly. I know the phone was busy at one point, but—"

"When you called him?"

"Yes, sir."

"What time would that have been?"

"I really couldn't say with any accuracy."

"Before midnight? After midnight?"

"I'm not sure."

"But you *did* speak again after that eleven-thirty-five call?"

"Yes, sir. Several times."

"Calling back and forth."

"Yes, sir."

"To discuss the exam again."

"Yes, the material that would be on the exam."

"Was his radio still on?"

"I think so."

"You could hear the radio?"

"Yes, sir. I could hear music."

"The same sort of music you'd heard earlier?"

"Yes, sir. He was listening to classical music. I heard it in the background each time he called."

"And the last time you spoke was at two in the morning."

"Yes, sir."

"When *you* called him."

"Yes, sir."

"At home."

"Yes, sir."

"Thank you very much, Mr. Loeb, I really appreciate—"

"Well, what *is* this all about, Mr. Carella? I really—"

"Routine," Carella said, and hung up.

Blue Monday.

The threatening blue glare of ice. The brilliant robin's-egg blue of a sky that stretched from horizon to horizon over the city's towers and peaks, the kind of sky that always came as a surprise in January and February even though—like the snow and wind and the freezing rain—it was not an unusual occurrence in this city. The darker blue of smoking pouring from the tall stacks of the factories across the river Dix in Calm's Point. The almost-black blue of the uniforms on the cops who stood outside the tenement on Ainsley Avenue and looked down at the mutilated woman on the icebound sidewalk.

The woman was naked.

A trail of blood led from where she lay on the sidewalk to the front door of the tenement behind her, and into the tenement hallway, bloody palm prints on the inner vestibule door, blood on the stairs and banisters leading to the upper stories.

The woman was still bleeding profusely.

The woman's breasts had been brutally slashed.

There was a giant bleeding across on the woman's belly.

The woman had no nose.

"Jesus!" one of the patrolmen said.

"Help me," the woman moaned, and blood bubbled from her mouth.

The woman who answered the door to Allan Carter's apartment was perhaps thirty-five years old, Carella guessed, wearing a brocaded housecoat at ten in the morning, her long black hair sleekly combed and hanging straight on either side of a delicate oval face, her brown eyes slanted enough to give her the same faintly Oriental appearance that caused the cops of the Eight-Seven to kid Carella about being Fujiwara's cousin. She could have been an older Tina Wong; it always amazed Carella that when a man began cheating on his wife, he often chose a woman who looked somewhat *like* her.

"Mr. Carella?" she said.

"Yes, ma'am."

"Come in, please, my husband's expecting you." She extended her hand. "I'm Melanie Carter."

"How do you do?" Carella said, and took her hand. It felt extremely warm to the touch, perhaps because his own hand was so icy cold after walking gloveless (*and hatless, yes, I know,* Uncle Sal) from where he'd parked the police sedan.

Carter came out of what Carella assumed to be a bedroom. He was wearing a Japanese-style kimono over dark blue pajamas. Carella idly wondered if the kimono had been a gift from Tina Wong. He let the thought pass.

"Sorry to bother you so early in the morning," he said.

"No, no, not at all," Carter said, and took his hand. "Some coffee? Melanie?" he said. "Could we get some coffee?"

"Yes, certainly," Melanie said, and went out into the kitchen.

"No partner today?" Carter asked.

"There are only two of us," Carella said, "and we have a lot of people to see."

"I'll bet," Carter said. "So. What can I do for you?"

"I was hoping we could talk privately," Carella said.

"Privately?"

"Yes, sir. Just the two of us," he said, and nodded toward the kitchen.

"My wife can hear anything we have to say," Carter said.

"I'm not sure of that, sir," Carella said, and their eyes met and held. Carter said nothing. Melanie came out of the kitchen carrying a silver tray on which there was a silver coffeepot, a silver sugar bowl and creamer, and two cups and saucers. She set the tray down on the coffee table before them, said, "I forgot spoons," and went out into the kitchen again. Neither of the men said a word. When she came back, she said, "There we are," and put two spoons onto the tray. "Would you like anything else, Mr. Carella? Some toast?"

"No, thank you, ma'am," Carella said.

"Melanie," Carter said, and hesitated. "I'm sure this will bore you to tears. If you have anything you need to do . . ."

"Of course, dear," Melanie said. "If you'll forgive me, Mr. Carella." She nodded briefly, smiled, and went out into the bedroom, closing the door behind her. Carter rose suddenly and went to the bank of stereo equipment set into a bookcase on the far wall. He knows what we're going to talk about, Carella thought. He wants a sound cover. The door between the rooms isn't enough for him. Carter turned on the radio. Music flooded the room. Something classical. Carella could not place it.

"That's a little loud, isn't it?" he said.

"You said you wanted to talk privately."

"Yes, but I don't want to *shout* privately."

"I'll lower it," Carter said.

He went to the radio again. Carella remembered that there had been classical music in the background when Loeb had spoken to Moore on the telephone Friday night. There was only one classical music station in this entire cultured city. Apparently it had more listeners than it realized.

Carter came back to where Carella was sitting on the sofa upholstered in the pale green springtime fabric, and took the chair opposite him. The chair was upholstered in a lemon-colored fabric. Outside the windows at the far end of the room, the sky was intensely blue, but the wind howled fiercely.

"This is about Tina, huh?" Carter said at once.

Carella admired him for getting directly to what he surmised was the point, but actually he wasn't here to talk about Tina Wong. Tina Wong was only his form of official blackmail. Coercion, it might have been called in the Penal Code. Carella was not above a little coercion every now and again.

"Sort of," he answered.

"So you know," Carter said. "So what? Actually, my wife *could* have heard this."

"Oh?" Carella said.

"She isn't exactly a nun," Carter said.

"Oh?" Carella said again.

"She finds ways to busy herself while I'm occupied elsewhere, believe me. Anyway, what does Tina have to do with Sally Anderson?"

"Well, gee," Carella said, "that's just what *I'd* like to know."

"That was very nicely delivered," Carter said, unsmiling. "The next time I have a part for a shit-kicking bumpkin, I'll call you. What are you after, Mr. Carella?"

"I want to know why you thought Sally Anderson was a redhead."

"Isn't she?" Carter said.

"Very nicely delivered," Carella said. "The next time *I* have a role for a smart-ass liar, I'll call *you.*"

"Touché," Carter said.

"I didn't come here to fence," Carella said.

"Why *did* you come here? So far, I've been very patient with you. I'm not without legal resources, you know. I have a lawyer on retainer, and I'm sure he'd like nothing better than to—"

"Go ahead, call him," Carella said.

Carter sighed. "Let's cut the crap, okay?" he said.

"Fine," Carella said.

"Why did I think Sally was a redhead. That was your question, wasn't it?"

"That was my question."

"Is it a crime to believe a redhead was a redhead?"

"It's not even a crime to think a *blond* was one."

"Then what's the problem?"

"Mr. Carter, you *know* she was a blond."

"What makes you think so?"

"Well, for one thing, your choreographer favors blonds, and every white girl in the show *is* a blond. It was a nice show, by the way. Thanks for making those tickets available to me."

"You're welcome," Carter said and nodded sourly.

"For another thing, you were present at the final selection of all the dancers . . ."

"Who told you that?"

"You did. And you *had* to know there were no redheads in the show, especially since you attended all the run-throughs after the show was put together . . . which you *also* told me."

"So?"

"So I think you were lying when you told me you thought she was a redhead. And when someone is lying, I begin wondering why."

"I *still* think she was a redhead."

"No, you don't. Her picture's been in the papers for the past three days. She's clearly shown as a blond, and she's described as such. Even if you thought she was a redhead on the day after she was murdered, you certainly don't think so now."

"I haven't seen the papers," Carter said.

"How about television? They showed her picture on television, too. In full color. Come on, Mr. Carter. I told you I wasn't here to fence."

"Let me hear what *you* think, Mr. Carella."

"I think you knew her better than you're willing to admit. For all I know, you were playing around with *her* as *well* as Tina Wong."

"I wasn't."

"Then why'd you lie to me?"

"I didn't. I thought she was a redhead."

Carella sighed.

"I did," Carter said.

"I'll tell you something, Mr. Carter. Shit-kicking bumpkin that I am, I nonetheless believe that if a man *continues* lying even after he's been *caught* in a lie, then he's *really* got something to hide. I don't know what that something might be. I know that a girl was shot to death last Friday night, and you're lying about having known her better than you *did* know her. Now what would *you* think, Mr. Carter, big-shot producer that you are?"

"I would think you're way off base."

"Were you at a party on the Sunday before the murder? A party given by a dancer named Lonnie Cooper? One of the black girls in the cast?"

"I was."

"Was Sally Anderson there?"

"I don't remember."

"She was there, Mr. Carter. Are you telling me you didn't recognize her *then*, either? There are only *eight* female dancers in your show, how could you *not* know Sally Anderson if you ran into her?''

''*If* she was there—''

''*If* she was there—and she *was*—she sure as hell wasn't wearing a red wig!'' Carella said, and stood up abruptly. ''Mr. Carter, I hate to sound like a clichéd detective in a B-movie, but I wouldn't advise you to go to Philadelphia this Wednesday. I'd suggest, instead, that you stay right here in this city, where we can reach you if we want to ask you any other questions. Thanks for your time, Mr. Carter.''

He was starting for the door when Carter said, ''Sit down.''

He turned to look at him.

''Please,'' Carter said.

Carella sat.

''Okay, I knew she was a blond,'' Carter said.

''Okay,'' Carella said.

''I was simply afraid to say I'd known her, that's all.''

''Why?''

''Because she was murdered. I didn't want to get involved, not in any way possible.''

''In what way *could* you have got involved? You didn't kill her, did you?''

''Of course not!''

''Were you having an affair with her?''

''No.''

''Then what were you afraid of?''

''I didn't want people poking around. I didn't want anyone to find out about Tina and me.''

''But we *have* found out, haven't we? And besides, Mr. Carter, your wife isn't exactly a nun, remember? So what difference would it have made?''

''People behave strangely when murder is involved,'' Carter said, and shrugged.

''Is that a line from the play you're rehearsing in Philadelphia?''

''It's a lame excuse, I know—''

''No, it happens to be true,'' Carella said. ''But usually, the only people who behave strangely are the ones with something to hide. I *still* think you have something to hide.''

''Nothing, believe me,'' Carter said.

''*Did* you, in fact, see Sally at that party last Sunday night?''

''I did.''

''Did you talk to her?''

''I did.''

''What about?''

''I don't remember. The show, I suppose. When people are involved in a show—''

''Anything besides the show?''

''No.''

''Were you present when Sally and some other people began snorting cocaine?''

''I was not.''

''Then how do you know they were doing it?''

"What I'm saying is I didn't *see* anyone doing anything of the sort. Not while I was there."

"What time did you leave the party, Mr. Carter?"

"At about midnight."

"With Tina Wong?"

"Yes, with Tina."

"Where'd you go from there?"

"To Tina's place."

"How long did you stay there?"

"All night long."

"Tina saw Sally Anderson snorting. Together with a group of other people including Mike Roldan, who's *also* in your show. If *Tina* saw them, how come *you* didn't see them?"

"Tina and I are *not* Siamese twins. We are *not* joined at the hip."

"Meaning what?"

"Lonnie has one of these big old rent-controlled apartments on the park. There were sixty or seventy people there that night. It's entirely possible that Tina was in one part of the apartment while I was in another."

"Yes, that's entirely possible," Carella said. "And I guess Tina would be willing to swear you weren't with her when she witnessed Sally Anderson using cocaine."

"I don't know *what* Tina would be willing to swear."

"Do *you* use cocaine, Mr. Carter?"

"I certainly do not!"

"Do you know who was supplying Sally?"

"I do not."

"Do you know a man named Paco Lopez?"

"No."

"Where were you last Friday night between eleven and twelve midnight?"

"I told you. In Philadelphia."

"Where were you on Tuesday night at about the same time?"

"Philadelphia."

"I suppose there are any number of people—"

"Any number."

"What are you trying to hide, Mr. Carter?"

"Nothing," Carter said.

At St. Jude's Hospital—familiarly called St. Juke's by the cops, because of the many knifing victims carted there day and night—Judite Quadrado kept calling for a priest. At least that's what they thought she wanted. They thought she knew she was dying and wanted a priest to administer the rites of extreme unction. Actually, she was trying to tell them that a priest had come into her apartment together with a fat woman and that the two of them had done this terrible thing to her.

Judite was in the Intensive Care Unit, with tubes coming out of her nose and her mouth, and tubes running from her arms to a galaxy of machines that beeped and glowed with electronic oranges and blues all around her bed. It was difficult to talk around the tube in her mouth. When she tired to say, "Brother Anthony," which was the name the priest had given her, it came out as a scrambled "Branny," and when she tired to say "Emma Forbes," which had been the fat woman's name, it came out only as what sounded like a cross between a mumble and a hum. She went back to saying "priest," which came out as "preese," but which at least they seemed to understand.

The priest came into the unit at seven minutes past eleven that Monday morning. He was a little too late.

Judite Quadrado had died six minutes earlier.

If there is one thing criminals and cops alike share—aside from the symbiotic relationship that makes each of their jobs possible—it is the sense of smell that tells them when someone is frightened. The moment they catch that whiff, cops and criminals alike turn into savage beasts of prey, ready to tear out the throat and devour the entrails. Miguel Roldan and Antonio Asensio were scared witless, and Meyer smelled their fear the instant Roldan, unsolicited, told him that he and Asensio had been living together as man and wife for the past three years. Meyer didn't care *what* their persuasion was. The offered information told him only that the two men were frightened. He knew they weren't afraid they'd be busted as homosexuals; not in *this* city. So what *were* they afraid of? Until that moment, he had been calling them, respectively and respectfully, Mr. Roldan and Mr. Asensio. He now switched to "Mike" and "Tony," an old cop trick designed to place any suspect to a disadvantage, a ploy somewhat similar to the one nurses used in hospitals. "Hello, Jimmy, how are we feeling this morning?" they would say to the chairman of the board of a vast conglomerate, immediately letting him know who was boss around here, and who was privileged to take your rectal temperature. It worked even better with policemen and anyone who came into their purlieu. Calling a man Johnny instead of Mr. Fuller was the same thing as calling him Boy. It put him in his place at once, and instantly made him feel (a) inferior, (b) defensive, and (c) oddly dependent.

"Mike," Meyer said, "why do you think I'm here?"

They were sitting in the living room of the brownstone Roldan and Asensio shared. The room was pleasantly furnished with antiques Meyer wished he could have afforded. A fire was going on the hearth. The fire crackled and spit into the room.

"You're here about Sally, of course," Roldan said.

"Is that what *you* think, Tony?"

"Yes, of course," Asensio said.

Meyer wasted no time.

"You know she was using cocaine, don't you?" he said.

"Well . . . no," Roldan said. "How would we know that?"

"Well, come on, Mike," Meyer said, and smiled knowingly. "You were at a party with her a week ago Sunday, and she was doing cocaine, so you *must* know she was a user, right?"

Roldan looked at Asensio.

"You were using it that night, too, weren't you, Mike?"

"Well . . ."

"I know you were," Meyer said.

"Well . . ."

"How about you, Tony? You snort a few lines last Sunday night?"

Asensio looked at Roldan.

"Who were you and Sally getting your stuff from?" Meyer asked.

"Listen," Roldan said.

"I'm listening."

"We had nothing to do with her murder."

"Didn't you?" Meyer said.

"We didn't," Asensio said, shaking his head, and then looking at Roldan. Meyer wondered which of them was the wife and which was the husband. They both seemed very demure. He tried to reconcile this with the fact that the homosexual murders in the precinct were among the most vicious and brutal the cops investigated.

"Do you know who *might* have killed her?" he asked.

"No, we don't," Roldan said.

"We don't," Asensio agreed.

"So who do you get your stuff from?" Meyer asked again.

"Why is that important?" Roldan asked.

"That's assuming we're users," Asensio said quickly.

"Yes," Roldan said, *"If* we're users . . ."

"You are," Meyer said, and again smiled knowingly.

"Well, *if* we are, what does it matter *who* we were getting it from?"

"Were?" Meyer asked at once.

"Are," Roldan said, correcting himself.

"Assuming we're users, that is," Asensio said.

"Did something happen to your dealer?" Meyer asked.

"No, no," Roldan said.

"That's assuming we even *needed* a dealer," Asensio said.

"Needed?" Meyer said.

"Need, I mean," Asensio said, and looked at Roldan.

"Well, Tony," Meyer said, "Mike . . . assuming you *are* users, and assuming you *do* have a dealer, or *did* have a dealer, who *is* the dealer? Or *was* the dealer, as the case may be."

"Cocaine isn't habit-forming," Roldan said.

"A sniff every now and then never hurt anybody," Asensio said.

"Ah, I know," Meyer said. "It's a shame it's against the law, but what can you do? Who are you getting it from?"

The two men looked at each other.

"Something *did* happen to your dealer, huh?" Meyer said.

Neither of them answered.

"Were you getting it from Sally Anderson?" Meyer asked, taking a wild stab in the dark, and surprised when both men nodded simultaneously. "From *Sally?"* he said. The men nodded again. *"Sally* was dealing cocaine?"

"Well, not what you'd call *dealing*," Roldan said. "Would you call it *dealing*, Tony?"

"No, I wouldn't call it *dealing*," Asensio said. "Besides, the coke had nothing to do with her murder."

"How do you know?" Meyer said.

"Well, it wasn't that big a deal."

"How big a deal was it?"

"I mean, she wasn't making any *money* from it, if that's what you think," Roldan said.

"What *was* she doing?" Meyer asked.

"Just bringing a few grams a week, that's all."

"How many grams?"

"Oh, I don't know. How many grams, Tony?"

"Oh, I don't know," Asensio said.

"By bringing it in—"

"To the theater. For whichever of the kids needed it."

"Well, I wouldn't say *needed* it," Roldan said. "Cocaine isn't habit-forming, you know."

"Whoever *wanted* it, I should have said," Asensio agreed, nodding.

"How many people *wanted* it?" Meyer asked.

"Well . . . Tony and I," Roldan said. "And some of the other kids."

"How many other kids?"

"Not many," Asensio said. "Six or seven? Would you say six or seven, Mike?"

"I'd say six or seven," Roldan said. "Not including Sally herself."

"So what are we talking about here?" Meyer said. "A dozen grams a week, something like that?"

"Something like that. Maybe two dozen."

"Two dozen grams," Meyer said, nodding. "What was she charging?"

"The going street price. I mean, Sally wasn't *making* anything on the deal, believe me. She just picked up *our* stuff when she was getting her *own*. She may have even got a discount for a bulk purchase, who knows?"

"I think, in fact," Roldan said to Asensio, "that we were getting it cheaper than the going street price."

"Maybe so," Asensio said.

"How much were you paying?" Meyer said.

"Eighty-five dollars a gram."

Meyer nodded. A gram of cocaine was the approximate equivalent of one twenty-eighth of an ounce. The going street price ranged from a hundred to a hundred and a quarter a gram, depending on the purity of the cocaine.

"Who was *she* getting it from?" he asked.

"I don't know," Roldan said.

"I don't know," Asensio said.

"Who's Paco Lopez?" Meyer asked.

"Who is he?" Roldan said.

Asensio shrugged.

"Are we supposed to know him?" Roldan said.

"You don't know him, huh?"

"Never heard of him."

"How about you, Tony?"

"Never heard of him," Asensio said.

"Is he a dancer?" Roldan asked.

"Is he gay?" Asensio asked.

"He's dead," Meyer said.

Rebecca Edelman was a woman in her late forties, splendidly tanned and monumentally grief stricken. The detectives had called her early this morning, eager to talk to her after her flight back from Antigua the night before, but they had been advised by a daughter-in-law that Marvin Edelman's funeral would be taking place at eleven that morning, in keeping with the Jewish tradition of burying a person within twenty-four hours after his death. As it was, the funeral and burial had been delayed, anyway, by the mandatory autopsy required in any cases of traumatic death.

Neither Kling nor Brown had ever witnessed a family sitting shiva before. The windows in the Edelman living room faced the river Harb. The sky beyond was still intensely blue, the light less golden than it might have been in that it was partially reflected from the icebound water below. There was a knife-edged clarity to the atmosphere that afternoon; Brown could make out in the sharpest detail the high rises that perched atop the cliffs on the shore opposite, in the next state. Farther uptown, he could see the graceful curves of the Hamilton Bridge, its lacy outlines etched against the brilliant blue of the sky. In the living room, the family and friends of Marvin Edelman sat on wooden boxes and talked to each other in hushed voices.

She led them into a small room she obviously used a sewing room, a machine in one corner, a basket of brightly colored fabrics sitting left of the treadle. She sat in the chair before the machine. They sat on a small sofa facing her. Her brown eyes were moist in her tanned face. She kept wringing her hands as she spoke. The sun had not been kind to her. Her face was wrinkled, her hands were wrinkled, her lips looked parched without lipstick. She directed her entire conversation to Kling, even though Brown asked most of the questions. Brown was used to this; sometimes even the *blacks* turned to the white cop, as though he himself were invisible.

"I told him he should come with me," Mrs. Edelman said. "I told him he could use the vacation, he should be good to himself, am I right? But no, he said he had too much work to do just now, planning for his trip to Europe next month. He told me he'd take a vacation when he got back, in April sometime. Who needs a vacation in April? In April, we have flowers, even here in the city. So he wouldn't come. Now he'll *never* have another vacation, never," she said, and turned her head away because tears were beginning to form in her eyes again.

"What sort of work did he do, ma'am?" Brown asked. "Was he in the jewelry business?"

"Not what you would call a regular jeweler," Mrs. Edelman said, and took a paper tissue from her bag and dabbed at her eyes with it.

"Because he was wearing this vest—" Brown started.

"Yes," Mrs. Edelman said. "He bought and sold gems. That's what he did for a living."

"Diamonds?"

"Not only diamonds. He dealt in all kinds of precious gems. Emeralds, rubies, sapphires—diamonds, of course. Precious gems. But he neglected the most precious thing of all. His life. If he'd come with me . . ." She shook her head. "A stubborn man," she said. "God forgive me, but he was a stubborn man."

"Was there any *special* reason he wanted to stay here in the city?" Brown asked. "Instead of going with you to Antigua." He pronounced the word "An-tee-gwa."

"It's a hard g," Mrs. Edelman said.

"What?"

"It's the British pronunciation they use. An-*tee*-ga."

"Oh," Brown said. He looked at Kling. Kling said nothing. "But in any event," Brown said, "*was* there?"

"Only the usual. Nothing he couldn't have left for a week. So look what happens," she said, and again dabbed at her eyes.

"By the usual—" Brown said.

"His usual business. Buying and selling, selling and buying." She was still directing all of her conversation to Kling. Brown cleared his throat, to remind her *he* was here, too. It had no effect.

Perhaps prompted by her steady gaze, Kling said, "Did he go very often to Europe?"

"Well, when he had to. That's the diamond center of the world, you know. Amsterdam. For emeralds, he went to South America. He could run all over the world for his business, am I right?" she said. "But when it comes to flying only four, five hours away, for a week in the sun, this he can't do. He has to stay here instead. So someone can shoot him."

"Do you have any idea who might have—"

"No," Mrs. Edelman said.

"No enemies you can think of?" Brown said.

"None."

"Any employees he might have—"

"He worked alone, my husband. That's why he could never take any time off. All he wanted to do was make money. He told me he wouldn't be happy till he was a multimillionaire."

"Did the possibility exist in his business?" Brown said. "Making millions of dollars, I mean?"

"Who knows? I suppose. We lived comfortably. He was always a good earner, my husband."

"But when you're talking about millions of dollars—"

"Yes, it was possible to make such money," Mrs. Edelman said. "He had a very sharp eye for quality gems. He turned a very good profit on almost anything he bought. He knew what he was buying, and he drove very hard bargains. Such a dope," she said. "If only he'd come with me, like I wanted him to."

Her eyes were misting with tears again. She dabbed at them with her crumpled tissue, and then reached into her bag for a fresh one.

"Mrs. Edelman," Kling said, "where was your husband's place of business, can you tell us?"

"Downtown. On North Greenfield, just off Hall Avenue. What they call the Diamond Mart, the street there."

"And he worked alone there, you said?"

"All alone."

"In a street-level shop?"

"No, on the second floor."

"Was he ever held up, Mrs. Edelman?"

She looked at him in surprise.

"Yes," she said. "How did you know that?"

"Well, being a diamond merchant . . ."

"Yes, last year," she said.

"When last year?" Brown asked.

"August, I think it was. The end of July, the beginning of August, sometime in there."

"Was the perpetrator apprehended?" Brown asked.

"What?" Mrs. Edelman said.

"Did they catch the man who did it?"

"Yes."

"They *did?*"

"Yes, two days later. He tried to pawn the gems in a shop three doors down from my husband's, can you believe it?"

"Would you remember the man's name?"

"No, I wouldn't. He was a black man," she said, and—for the first time during their visit—turned to look at Brown, but only fleetingly. Immediately, she turned her attention back to Kling again.

"Can you be more exact about the date?" Kling asked. He had taken out his pad and was beginning to write.

"Why? Do you think it was the same person? They told me nothing was stolen. He had diamonds in his vest, nobody touched them. So how could it be anybody who wanted to rob him?"

"Well, we don't know, really," Kling said, "but we'd like to follow up on that robbery if you can give us a few more details."

"All I know is he was working late one night, and this black man came in with a gun and took everything from the work table. He didn't bother with the safe, he just told my husband to dump everything from the work table into this little sack he had. The *good* stuff was in the safe, my husband was tickled to dea—"

She cut herself short before she could finish the word. The tears began again. She busied herself with searching for another tissue in her bag. The detectives waited.

"You say it was sometime toward the end of July, the beginning of August," Kling said at last.

"Yes."

"The last week in July, would that have been? The first week in August?"

"I can't say for sure. I think so."

"We can track it from the address," Brown said to Kling. "It'll be on the computer."

"*Could* we have the address, please?" Kling said.

"Six-twenty-one North Greenfield," Mrs. Edelman said. "Room two-oh-seven."

"Was the man convicted, would you know?" Brown asked.

"I think so, I don't remember. My husband had to go to court to identify him, but I don't know whether he was sent to jail or not."

"We can check with Corrections," Brown said to Kling. "Mrs. Edelman, had you spoken to your husband at any time since you left for Antigua?" This time, he pronounced it correctly.

"No. Do you mean, did we *call* each other? No. Antigua's not around the corner, you know."

"*Before* you left, did he mention anything that might have been disturbing him? Threatening telephone calls or letters, quarrels with customers, anything like that? Was anything at *all* troubling him, that you know of?"

"Yes," Mrs. Edelman said.

"What?" Brown asked.

"How he could make his millions of dollars," Mrs. Edelman said to Kling.

This time, the call came from Dorfsman himself.

It came at twenty minutes past four that Monday, the day after Valentine's Day, but Dorfsman apparently was still enjoying the influence of the brief lovers' holiday. The first thing he said to Carella was, "Roses are red, violets are blue, wait'll you hear what *I've* got for *you!*"

Carella thought Dorfsman had lost his marbles; it happened often enough in the police department, but he had never heard of it happening to anyone in Ballistics.

"What *have* you got for me?" he asked warily.

"Another one," Dorfsman said.

"Another what?"

"Another corpse."

Carella waited. Dorfsman sounded as if he was enjoying himself immensely. Carella did not want to spoil his fun. A corpse on the day of the observance of Washington's Birthday, even if it was a week *before* Washington's Birthday, was certainly amusing.

"I haven't even called Kling yet," Dorfsman said. "You're the first one I'm calling."

"Kling?" Carella said.

"Kling," Dorfsman said. "Don't you guys ever *talk* to each other up there? Kling caught the squeal Saturday night. Sunday morning, actually. Two o'clock Sunday morning."

"What are you talking about?" Carella asked.

"A homicide on Silvermine Oval. Guy named Marvin Edelman, two slugs pumped into his head." Dorfsman still sounded as if he was smiling. "I'm calling you first, Steve," he said.

"So I gather. How come?"

"Same gun as the other two," Dorfsman said cheerfully.

It was beginning to look like they had a crazy on their hands.

Crazies make police work difficult.

When you've got a crazy on your hands, you might just as well throw away the manual and work the case by the seat of your pants, because that's the way the crazy is working *his* case. There were a lot of crazies in this city, but thankfully most of them were content to walk up and down Hall Avenue carrying signs about doomsday or else muttering to themselves about the Mayor and the weather. The crazies in this city seemed to think the Mayor was responsible for the weather. Maybe he was.

Detective Lieutenant Peter Byrnes seemed to think his squad was responsible for the lack of communication on what now appeared to be *three* linked murders. Byrnes, when apprised of what Dorfsman had said on the telephone, agreed emphatically with him: Didn't the guys up here ever *talk* to each other?

"Yet get a murder last Tuesday night and another one on Saturday night, Sunday morning, when*ever* it was," Byrnes said. "The first one is on Culver Avenue, and the next one is on Silvermine Road, just a few blocks *away!* Both of them are *gunshot* murders, but does it ever occur to you masterminds to do an in-house *cross*-check? I'm not even *mentioning* the little girl who got killed downtown on *Friday* night, I wouldn't *dream* of mentioning a *third* gunshot murder to sleuths of such remarkable perception," Byrnes said, gathering steam, "but does anyone up here even *glance* at the activity reports, which is why we *keep* activity reports in the *first* place, so that every cop in this precinct, uniformed *or* plainclothes, will know what the hell is going *on* up here!"

In the squadroom outside, Miscolo and a handful of uniformed patrolmen were milling about apprehensively, listening to Byrnes's angry voice from behind the frosted glass door to his office, and knowing that someone in there was getting chewed out mightily. Actually, there were *four* someones in there, but none of the squadroom eavesdroppers knew that because the detectives had been called at home early that Tuesday morning and asked to report at the crack of dawn (well, 7:30 A.M.) and the uniformed force hadn't begun trickling in until 7:45 A.M., when roll call took place every morning in the muster room downstairs. The four plainclothes someones were, in alphabetical order, Detectives Brown, Carella, Kling, and Meyer. They were all looking at their shoes.

Byrnes's rage was comprised of one part pressure from "rank" downtown and one part sheer indignation over the stupidity of men he had hoped, after all these years, could to their jobs with at least a modicum of routine efficiency. Secretly, he suspected Kling was more at fault than any of the others because of the clamlike posture he had developed after his divorce. But he did not want to single out Kling as the sole perpetrator here because that would only serve to embarrass him and perhaps cause disharmony among four detectives who now seemed fated to work together on solving three separate murders. So Byrnes ranted and raved about simple procedures, which—if only followed to the letter—would dispel confusion, elimi-nate duplication, and ("A consummation devoutly to be wished," he actually said) maybe solve a *case* every now and then around here.

"All right," he said at last, "that's that."

"Pete—" Carella started.

"I said all right, that's the end of it," Byrnes said. "Have a piece of candy," he said, shoving the half-depleted box across the desk toward his surprised detectives. "Tell me what you've got."

"Not much," Carella said.

"Is this a crazy we're dealing with here?"

"Maybe," Brown said.

"Have you got a line on that thirty-eight yet?"

"No, Pete, we've been—"

"Round up your street gun dealers, find out who was shopping for a gun that fits the description."

"Yes, Pete," Carella said.

"How does Lopez tie in with these other two?"

"We don't know yet."

"Were either of them doing drugs?"

"The girl was. We don't know about Edelman yet."

"Was Lopez supplying her?"

"We don't know yet. We *do* know she was bringing coke in for some of the other people in the show."

"This last one was a diamond merchant, huh?"

"Precious gems," Kling said.

"Did he know either Lopez or the girl?"

"We don't know yet," Kling said. "But he was held up sometime last summer, and that may be something to go on. We'll be running it through the computer this morning."

"Don't go squeezing them," Byrnes said to Meyer, who was reaching for a chocolate in the box. "Take all you want, but *eat* the ones you touch, and don't go squishing up the whole box."

Meyer, who had in fact been about to squeeze one of the chocolates, gave Byrnes an offended look.

"What's with her boyfriend?" Byrnes said. "The girl's boyfriend."

"He was on the phone most of last Friday night," Carella said. "The night the girl was killed."

"On the phone? Who with?"

"Another student. The boyfriend's a med student at Ramsey."

"What's his name again?"

"Timothy Moore."

"And his friend's name?"

"Karl Loeb."

"You checked with him?"

"Loeb? Yes. They were gabbing till almost two in the morning."

"Who called who?" Byrnes asked.

"Back and forth."

"What else?"

"The producer of the show, man named Allan Carter, is playing house with one of the dancers."

"So what?" Byrnes asked.

"He's married," Meyer said.

"So what?" Byrnes asked again.

"We think he's lying to us," Meyer said.

"About his little tootsie?" Byrnes said, using one of the quaint, archaic terms that sometimes crept into his vocabulary, for which the younger men on the squad almost always forgave him.

"No, he was straight on about that," Carella said. "But he claims to have known the dead girl only casually, and it doesn't smell right."

"Why would he lie about that?" Byrnes asked.

"We don't know yet," Carella said.

"You think they were doing a two-on-one?" Byrnes asked, using one of the more voguish terms that sometimes crept into his vocabulary.

"We don't know yet," Meyer said.

"What the hell *do* you know?" Byrnes asked heatedly, and then gained control of himself once again. "Have some candy, for Christ's sake!" he said. "I'll get fat as a horse here."

"Pete," Carella said, "this is a complicated one."

"Don't tell *me* it's a complicated one. Don't I know a complicated one when I see a complicated one?"

"Maybe it *is* a crazy," Brown suggested.

"That's the easy way out," Byrnes said, "blaming it on a crazy. You want to know something? In *my* book, *anybody* who kills anybody is a crazy."

The detectives had no quarrel with him there.

"Okay," Byrnes said, "start vacuuming the street. Or, better yet, call some of our snitches, see if they can come up with a line on that goddamn gun. Bert, Artie, run your computer check on that holdup . . . have you been to that guy's shop yet? Edelman's?"

"Not yet," Brown said.

"Go there, go through everything in the place. You come across even a *speck* of white dust, shoot it over to the lab for a cocaine test."

"We're not sure cocaine is the connection," Meyer said.

"No? Then what *is?* The girl was doing coke and supplying half the cast with it . . ."

"Not that many, Pete."

"How*ever* goddamn many! I don't care if she was the *star* of that show, which I gather she wasn't. On my block, she was delivering dope, and that made her a *mule*. We *know* Lopez was in the business of selling cocaine, he had six grams and eleven hundred bucks in his pocket when he was killed. So find out some more about little Miss Goody Two Shoes. Where'd she get the stuff she was spreading around the cast? Was she turning a profit or just doing a favor? And put the blocks to this producer, whatever the hell his name is, Carter. If he was sleeping with both that other dancer *and* the dead girl, I want to know about it. That's it. Call Danny Gimp, call Fats Donner, call any snitch who's in town instead of in Florida, where *I* should be. I want this case moved off the *dime,* have you got that? The next time the Chief calls me, I want to tell him something *positive.*"

"Yes, Pete," Carella said.

"Don't 'Yes, Pete' me. Just *do* it."

"Yes, Pete."

"And another thing. I'm not buying this as a crazy until you guys can convince me there was absolutely *no* connection between the three victims."

Byrnes paused.

"Find that connection," he said.

They arranged to meet on a bench in Grover Park, not too far from the skating rink and the statue of General Ronald King, who had once stormed a precious hill during the Spanish-American War, thereby shortening the tenure of the foreign tyrants who (according to William Randolph Hearst and Joseph Pulitzer) were oppressing the honest Cuban cane cutters and fishermen. A bygone Mayor had commissioned the statue of the general, not because of his indisputable gallantry, but only because King (like the Mayor himself) was reputed to have been a card *mayvin* whose specialty had been poker and whose favorite game within the genre had been something called "Shove," which was also the Mayor's favorite. For his patience in standing out there in bronze in all sorts of weather, the general had been further honored by the city's Hispanic (though not Cuban) population, who scrawled their names in spray paint across his bold chest and who occasionally pissed on his horse's legs.

School had been canceled today because of hazardous road conditions. As Carella waited for Danny Gimp on the bench near the statue of the general, he could hear the voices of young boys playing ice hockey on the outdoor rink. He was frozen to the marrow. He was not normally a philosophical man, but as he sat huddled inside his heaviest coat—*and* his jacket beneath that, *and* a sweater beneath that, *and* his jacket beneath that, *and* a sweater beneath that, *and* a flannel shirt beneath that, *and* woolen underwear beneath that—he thought that winter was a lot like police work. Winter wore you down. The snow, and the sleet, and the freezing rain, and the ice just kept coming at you till you were ready to throw up your hands in surrender. But you hung in there somehow until the spring thaw came and everything seemed all right again—till *next* winter.

Where the hell was Danny?

He saw him limping slowly up the path, turning his head this way and that to check the snow-covered terrain, just like an undercover agent out in the cold, which—to tell the truth—Danny sometimes fancied himself to be. He was wearing a red-and-blue plaid mackinaw and a red watch cap pulled down around his ears, and blue woolen gloves and green corduroy trousers tucked into the tops of black galoshes, a somewhat garish costume for someone trying to appear inconspicuous. He walked directly past the bench on which Carella sat freezing (there were times when he carried this spy stuff a *bit* too far), walked almost to the statue of the general, peered around cautiously, and then came back to the bench, sat beside Carella, took a newspaper from the side pocket of his mackinaw, opened it to hide his face, and said, "Hello, Steve. Cold, huh?"

Carella took off his glove and offered his hand to Danny. Danny lowered the newspaper, took off his glove, and reached out for Carella's hand. They shook hands briefly and put on their gloves again. There were not too many detectives who shook hands with informers. Most cops and their informers were business associates of a sort, but they did not shake hands. Not many cops held snitches in a very high regard. A snitch was usually someone who "owed" something to the cops. The cops were willing to look the other way in return for information. Some of the snitches who provided information were among the city's worst citizens. But if politics made strange bedfellows, criminal investigation made even stranger ones. Hal Willis's favorite snitch was a man named Fats Donner, whose penchant for twelve-year-old girls made him universally despised. But he was a good and valuable informer. Of all the snitches Carella worked with, he liked Danny Gimp best. And he would never forget that once upon a time, more years ago than he cared to remember, Danny had come to see him in the hospital when he was recovering from a bullet wound. That was why he always shook hands with Danny Gimp. He would shake hands with Danny Gimp even if the Commissioner were watching.

"How's the leg?" he asked.

"It hurts when it's cold," Danny said.

"Just once," Carella said, "I would like to meet someplace that isn't Siberia."

"I have to be careful," Danny said.

"You can be careful *inside.*"

"Inside there are ears," Danny said.

"Well, let's make this fast, okay?"

"It's your nickel," Danny said, inappropriately in that they were not on the telephone, and anyway a nickel telephone call had gone the way of the buggy whip.

"I'm looking for a thirty-eight Smith and Wesson that was used in three murders," Carella said.

"When was this?" Danny asked.

"The first one was a week ago today, the ninth. The second one was last Friday night, the twelfth. The last one was on Saturday night, the thirteenth."

"All of them up here?"

"Two of them."

"Which two?"

"A coke dealer named Paco Lopez—ever hear of him?"

"I think so."

"And a diamond merchant named Marvin Edelman."

"Doing business up here?"

"No, downtown. He lived on Silvermine Road."

"Fancy," Danny said.

"Who's the *third* party?"

"A girl named Sally Anderson. Dancer in a musical downtown."

"So where's the connection?" Danny asked.

"That's what we're trying to find out."

"Mmm," Danny said. "Lopez, huh?"

"Paco," Carella said.

"Paco Lopez," Danny said.

"Ring a bell?"

"Did he burn some chick's tits a while back?"

"That's the guy."

"Yeah," Danny said.

"Do you know him?"

"I seen him around. This was months ago. He must've been living with the chick, they were together all the time. So he bought it, huh? That's no great loss, Steve. He was bad news all around."

"How so?"

"Mean," Danny said, "I don't like people who are mean, do you? Did you talk to the chick yet?"

"The day after Lopez got killed."

"And?"

"Nothing. She told us what he'd done to her . . ."

"Something, huh?" Danny said, and shook his head.

"But they'd stopped living together two months ago. She didn't know anything."

"Nobody *ever* knows anything when it comes to cops in this neighborhood. Maybe *she's* the one who done it. For marking her that way."

"I doubt it, Danny, but be my guest. Frankly, I'm more interested in knowing whether a thirty-eight changed hands sometime during this past week."

"Lots of thirty-eights in this city, Steve."

"I know that."

"Changing hands all the time." He was silent for a moment. "The first one was last Tuesday, huh? What time?"

"Eleven o'clock."

"P.M.?"

"P.M."

"Where?"

"On Culver Avenue."

"Inside or out?"

"On the street."

"Not too many people out doing mischief in this weather," Danny said. "The cold keeps them home. Murderers and thieves like their comfort," he said philosophically. "Nobody seen the killer, huh?"

"Would I be here freezing my ass off if we had a witness?" Carella said.

"*I'm* freezing, too, don't forget," Danny said, somewhat offended. "Well, let me see what I hear. How urgent is this?"

"Urgent," Carella said.

" 'Cause there's a bet I want to place before I get to work."

"Anything good?" Carella asked.

"Only if he wins," Danny said, and shrugged.

Brother Anthony and Emma were smoking dope and drinking wine and going over the list of names and addresses Judite Quadrado had given them two days ago. A kerosene heater was going in one corner of the room, but the radiators were only lukewarm, and the windows were nonetheless rimed with ice. Brother Anthony and Emma were sitting very close to the kerosene heater, even though both of them insisted that cold weather never bothered them. They were both in their underwear.

They had smoked a little pot an hour ago, before making love in the king-sized bed in Brother Anthony's bedroom. Afterward, they had each and separately pulled on their underwear and walked out into the living room to open the bottle of wine and to light two more joints before sitting down again with the list of potential customers. Brother Anthony was wearing striped boxer shorts. Emma was wearing black bikini panties. Brother Anthony thought she looked radiantly lovely after sex.

"So what it looks like to me," Emma said, "is that he had a dozen people he was servicing."

"That's not so many," Brother Anthony said. "I was hoping for something bigger, Em, I'll tell you the truth. Twelve rotten names sounds like very small potatoes for all the trouble we went to." He looked at the list again. "Especially in such small quantities. Look at the quantities, Em."

"Do you know the joke?" she asked him, grinning.

"No. What joke?" He loved it when she told jokes. He also loved it when she went down on him. Looking at her huge breasts, he was beginning to feel the faintest stirrings of renewed desire, and he began thinking that maybe he would let her tell her joke and then they would forget all about Lopez's small-time list and go make love again. That sounded like a very good thing to do on a cold day like today.

"This lady is staying at a Miami Beach hotel, you know?" Emma said, still grinning.

"I wish *I* was staying at a Miami Beach hotel," Brother Anthony said.

"You want to hear this joke or not?"

"Tell it," he said.

"So she eats a couple of meals in the dining room, and then she goes to the front desk and starts complaining to the manager."

"What about?" Brother Anthony said.

"Will you let me tell it, please?"

"Tell it, tell it."

"She tells the manager the food in the dining room is absolute poison. The *eggs* are poison, the *beef* is poison, the *potatoes* are poison, the *salads* are poison, the *coffee* is poison, everything is poison, poison, poison, she says. And you know what *else?*"

"What else?" Brother Anthony asked.

"The *portions* are so small!" Emma said, and burst out laughing.

"I don't get it," Brother Anthony said.

"The lady is complaining the food is *poison* . . ."

"Yeah?"

"But she's *also* complaining the portions are too small."

"So what?"

"If it's *poison,* why does she want bigger portions?"

"Maybe she's crazy," Brother Anthony said.

"No, she's not crazy," Emma said. "She's complaining about the food, but she's *also* telling the manager the portions—"

"I understand," Brother Anthony said, "but I still don't get it. Why don't we go in the other room again?"

"You're not ready yet," Emma said, glancing at his lap.

"You can make me ready."

"I know I can. But I like it better when you're ready *before* I make you ready."

"Sweet mouth," Brother Anthony said, lowering his voice.

"Mmm," Emma said.

"So what do you say?"

"I say business before pleasure," Emma said.

"Anyway, what made you ever *think* of that joke?" he asked.

"You said something about the small quantities."

"They *are* small," Brother Anthony said. "Look at them," he said, and handed the list to her. "Two or three grams a week, most of them. We ain't gonna get rich on two, three grams a week."

"We don't have to get rich all at once, Bro," Emma said. "We'll take things slow and easy at first, start with these people who used to be Lopez's customers, build from there."

"How?"

"Maybe the lady can put us onto some other customers."

"What lady? The one eating poison?"

"The one who was supplying Lopez. His ounce dealer."

"Why would she want to help us that way?"

"Why not? There has to be a chain of supply, Bro. An ounce dealer needs gram dealers, a gram dealer needs users. The lady puts us onto some users, we buy our goods from her, and everybody's happy."

"I think you're dreaming," Brother Anthony said.

"Would it hurt to ask?" Emma said.

"She'll tell us to get lost."

"Who knows? Anyway, first things first. First we have to let her know we've taken over from Lopez and would like to continue doing business with her. That's the first thing."

"That's the first thing, for sure."

"So what I think you should do," Emma said, "is get dressed and go pay this Sally Anderson a little visit."

"Later," Brother Anthony said, and took her in his arms.

"Mmm," Emma said, and cuddled closer to him, and licked her lips.

Eileen Burke called the squadroom while Kling was still on the phone with Communications Division. Brown asked her to wait, and then put a note on Kling's desk, advising him that Detective Burke was on six. Kling nodded. For a moment, he didn't know who Detective Burke *was*.

"I've got the printout right here in my hand," the supervisor in the Dispatcher's Office said. "That was last July twenty-eighth, eight-oh-two P.M., six-twenty-one North Greenfield, room two-oh-seven. Adam Car responded at eight-twelve."

"What'd they find?"

"Radioed back with a Ten-Twenty. That's a Robbery Past."

Kling knew what a 10-20 was.

"Which precinct was that?"

"Midtown East," the supervisor said.

"Would you know who handled the case there?"

"That's not on the printout."

"Okay, thanks," Kling said, and pressed the lighted 6 button in the base of his phone. "Kling," he said.

"Bert, it's Eileen."

"I didn't get a chance to look for that earring," he said.

"Didn't turn up in the squadroom, huh?"

"Well, we've got a lost-and-found box, but there's nothing in it."

"How about the car?"

"I haven't checked the car yet," he said. "I haven't used that particular car since Saturday night."

"Well, if you *do* get a chance . . ."

"Sure," he said.

"It's just that . . . they're sort of my good-luck earrings."

Kling said nothing.

"I feel naked without them," she said.

He still said nothing.

"Can't go around wearing just *one* good-luck earring, can I?" she said.

"I guess not," he said.

"Cut my luck in half," she said.

"Yeah," he said.

"How's the weather up there?" she asked.

"Cold."

"Here, too," she said. "Well, let me know if you find it, okay?"

"I will."

"Thanks," she said, and hung up.

On the same slip of paper Brown had placed on his desk, Kling scrawled "E's earring," and then put the slip of paper in his jacket pocket. He flipped his precinct directory till he found the number for Midtown East, dialed it, told the desk sergeant there what he was looking for, and was put through to a detective named Garrido,

who spoke with a Spanish accent and who remembered the case at once because he
himself had been staked out in the back of the Greenfield Street pawnshop when the
armed robber walked in trying to hock all the stuff he'd stolen from Edelman two
days earlier and three doors south.

"The whole list," Garrido said, "ever'ting on it from soup to nuts. We had him
cold."

"So what happened?" Kling asked.

"Guess who we got for the jutch?" Garrido asked.

"Who?" Kling asked.

"Harris."

Kling knew the Honorable Wilbur Harris. The Honorable Wilbur Harris was
known in the trade as Walking Wilbur. His specialty was allowing criminals to
march out of his courtroom.

"What happened?" Kling asked.

"The kid was a junkie, first time he did anything like this. He wass almos' cryin'
in the cour'room. So Harris less him off with a suspended sentence."

"Even thought you caught him with the goods, huh?"

"*All* of it!" Garrido said. "Ever'ting on the list! Ah, what's the sense?"

"What was the kid's name?"

"Andrew someting. You wann me to pull the file?"

"If it's not any trouble."

"Sure," Garrido said, "Juss a secon', okay?"

He was back five minutes later with a name and a last known address for the
seventeen-year-old boy who had held up Marvin Edelman the summer before.

The apartment Allan Carter had described as "one of those big old rent-controlled
apartments on the park" was in fact on the park, and most certainly old, and
possibly rent-controlled, but only a dwarf would have considered it "big." Lonnie
Cooper, one of the two back dancers in *Fatback,* was almost as tall as the two
detectives she admitted into her home that late Tuesday morning; together, the three
of them caused the tiny place to assume the dimensions of a clothes closet. Com-
pounding the felony, Miss Cooper had jammed the place chock-full of furniture,
knickknacks, paintings, and pieces of sculpture so that there was hardly an uncovered patch of wall or floor surface; both Meyer and Carella felt they had wandered
into the business office of a fence selling stolen goods.

"I like clutter," the dancer explained. "Most dancers don't, but I do. On stage,
I can fly. When I'm home, I like to fold my wings."

She was even more beautiful than Carella remembered her on stage, a lissome
woman with skin the color of cork, high cheekbones, a nose like Nefertiti's, a
generous mouth, and a dazzling smile. She was wearing a man's red woolen shawl-
collared sweater over a black leotard top and black tights. She was barefooted, but
she was wearing striped leg warmers over the tights. She asked the detectives if they
would like some coffee or anything, and when they declined, she asked them to
make themselves comfortable. Carella and Meyer took seats beside each other on a
sofa cluttered with throw pillows. Lonnie Cooper sat opposite them in an easy chair
with antimacassars pinned to the back and the arms. A coffee table between them

was covered with glass paperweights, miniature dolls, letter openers, campaign buttons, and a trylon-and-perisphere souvenir ashtray from New York City's 1939 World's Fair. Catching Carella's glance, she explained, "I collect things."

"Miss Cooper," he said, "I wonder if—"

"Lonnie," she said.

"Fine," he said. "Lonnie, I—"

"What's *your* first name?" she asked.

"Steve," he said.

"And yours?" she asked Meyer.

"Meyer," he said.

"I thought that was your last name."

"It is. It's also my first name."

"How terrific!" she said.

Meyer shrugged. He had never thought of his name as being particularly terrific, except once when a lady fiction writer used it as the title of a novel about a college professor. He had called Rollie Chabrier in the D.A.'s office, wanting to know if he could sue. Chabrier told him he should feel honored. Meyer guessed he'd felt a *little* bit honored. But it continued to bother him that somebody out there had used the name of a *real* person for a mere character in a work of fiction. A college professor, no less.

"Are you sure you don't want any coffee?" Lonnie asked.

"Positive, thanks," Carella said.

"We're about coffeed out," Meyer said. "This weather."

"Yeah, do you find yourself drinking a lot of coffee, too?" Lonnie said.

"Yes," Meyer said.

"Me, too," she said. "Gee."

There was something very girlish about her, Carella decided. She looked to be about twenty-six or twenty-seven, but her movements and her facial expressions and even her somewhat high-pitched voice were more like those of a seventeen-year-old. She curled up in the easy chair now, and folded her legs under her, the way his daughter April might have.

"I guess you realize we're here about Sally Anderson," Carella said.

"Yes, of course," she said, and her face took on the studied, sober look of a child trying to cope with grown-up problems.

"Miss Cooper—"

"Lonnie," she said.

"Lonnie—"

"Yes, Steve?"

Carella cleared his throat. "Lonnie, we understand there was a party here a week ago last Sunday, that would've been the seventh of February. Do you recall such a party?"

"Yeah, wow," she said, "it was a *great* party!"

"Was Sally Anderson here?"

"Yeah, sure."

"And Tina Wong?"

"Yep."

"And Allan Carter?"

"Sure, lots of people," Lonnie said.

"How about Mike Roldan and Tony Asensio?" Meyer asked.

"You guys really do your homework, don't you?" Lonnie said.

Meyer had never thought of it as homework; he smiled weakly.

"They were here, too, Meyer," Lonnie said, and smiled back—dazzlingly.

"From what we've been able to determine," Carella said, "there was some cocaine floating around that night."

"Oh?" she said, and the smile dropped from her face.

"Was there?"

"Who told you that?"

"Several people."

"Who?"

"That's not important, Miss Cooper."

"It's important to *me,* Steve. And please call me Lonnie."

"We've had it from three different sources," Meyer said.

"Who?"

He looked at Carella. Carella nodded.

"Tina Wong, Mike Roldan, and Tony Asensio," Meyer said.

"Boy," Lonnie said, and shook her head.

"Is it true?" Carella said.

"Listen, who am I to contradict them?" Lonnie said, and shrugged and grimaced, and then shifted her position in the chair. "But I thought this was about Sally."

"It is."

"I mean, is this going to turn into a *cocaine* thing?"

"It's *already* a cocaine thing," Meyer said. "We know Sally was doing coke that night, and we also know—"

"You're talking about last Sunday?"

"A week ago last Sunday, yes. You *do* remember that Sally was doing coke, don't you?"

"Well . . . yes. Now that you mention it."

"Plus some other people as well."

"Well, a few others."

"Okay. Where'd the stuff come from?"

"How would I know?"

"Miss Cooper—"

"Lonnie."

"Lonnie, we're not looking for a drug collar here. Sally Anderson was *murdered,* and we're trying to find out *why.* If cocaine had anything to do with her death—"

"I don't see how it could have."

"How do you know that?"

"Because she's the one who *brought* the coke."

"We know that. But where'd *she* get it, would you know?"

"Uptown someplace."

"Where uptown?"

"I have no idea."

"How far uptown? Are we talking about below the park or—"

"I really don't know."

"How often did she bring the stuff in?"

"Usually once a week. On Monday nights, before the show. We're dark on Sunday—"

"Dark?"

"No performances. So she usually got the stuff on Sundays, I guess, went uptown for it on Sundays, or else had it delivered, I really don't know. Anyway, she brought it to the theater on Monday nights."

"And distributed it among the cast."

"Those who wanted it, yes."

"How many of those were there?"

"Half a dozen? Seven? Something like that."

"How much money was involved here, would you say?"

"You don't think she was in this for the *money,* do you?"

"Why *was* she in it?"

"She was doing us a favor, that's all. I mean, why duplicate the effort? If you've got a good contact and he delivers good dust,why not make one *big* buy every week instead of six or seven *small* buys from dealers you maybe can't trust? It only makes sense."

"Uh-huh," Carella said.

"Well, doesn't it?"

"So what are we talking about here?" Meyer said. "For the six or seven grams, what'd she—"

"Well, sometimes more than that. But she only charged what she herself was paying for it, believe me. I know street prices, and that's all she was getting."

"Nothing for all the trouble of having to go uptown?"

"What trouble? She had to go anyway, didn't she? And besides, maybe the man was delivering it, who knows? You're really barking up the wrong tree if you think *that's* how Sally—"

She stopped suddenly.

"How Sally what?" Carella asked at once.

"How she . . . uh—"

Lonnie grimaced and shrugged as though utterly baffled as to how she might finish the sentence she had started.

"Yes?" Carella said. "How she *what?*"

"Earned her living," Lonnie said, and smiled.

"Well, we *know* how she earned her living, don't we?" Meyer said. "She was a dancer."

"Well, yes."

"Then why would we think she earned her living some *other* way?"

"Well, you've been talking about coke here, and asking how much money was involved—"

"Yes, but you told us she wasn't making any profit on the coke."

"That's right."

"Was she earning extra cash someplace *else?*" Carella asked.

"I don't know anything about any extra cash."

"But there *was* extra cash someplace, wasn't there?"

"Gee, did *I* say that?" Lonnie said, and rolled her eyes.

"You seemed to indicate—"

"No, you misunderstood me, Steve."

"Where'd she get this extra cash?" Carella asked.

"What extra cash?" Lonnie said.

"Let's start all over again," Carella said. "What did you mean when you used the words 'how she earned her living'?"

"As a dancer," Lonnie said.

"That's not what I'm asking you."

"I don't know what you're asking me."

"I'm asking you where she earned additional income."

"Who said she did?"

"I thought that's what you implied."

"Anyway," Lonnie said, "sometimes a performer will do a nightclub gig or something. While she's still in a show that's running."

"Uh-huh," Carella said. "*Was* Sally doing nightclub gigs?"

"Well . . . no. Not that I know of."

"Then what *was* she doing?"

"I only said . . ."

Lonnie shook her head.

"You said he was doing something that earned her a living. What was it?"

"It goes on all over town," Lonnie said.

"What does?"

"If Sally was lucky enough to get cut in on it, more power to her."

"Cut in on *what?*"

"It isn't even against the law, that I know of," Lonnie said. "Nobody gets hurt by it."

"What are talking about?" Meyer asked. It sounded as if she'd been describing prostitution, but surely she knew *that* was against the law. And besides, who *said* nobody got hurt by it?

"Tell us what you mean," Carella said.

"I don't have anything else to tell you," she said, and folded her arms across her chest like a pouting six-year-old.

"We can subpoena you before a grand jury," Carella said, figuring if the ploy had worked at least a thousand times before, it might work yet another time.

"So subpoena me," Lonnie said.

When Brown went out back to where the precinct's vehicles were parked, he was surprised first to see that it was the same rotten decrepit automobile they'd pulled last Saturday night, and next to see Kling on his hand and knees in the back seat.

"I told them I didn't want this car again," he said to Kling's back. "What are you doing?"

"Here it is," Kling said.

"Here's what?"

"Eileen's earring," he said, and held up a small gold circle.

Brown nodded. "You want to drive?" he asked. "I *hate* this car."

"Sure," Kling said.

He put the earring in his coat pocket, dusted off the knees of his trousers, and then climbed in behind the wheel. Brown got in beside him on the passenger side. "This door doesn't close right," he said, slamming and reslamming the door until it seemed at last to fit properly into the frame. He turned on the heater at once. The heater began rattling and clanging. "Terrific," he said. "Where we headed?"

"Diamondback," Kling said, and started the car.

"Terrific," Brown said.

A police department adage maintained that the best time and place to get killed in this city was at twelve midnight on a Saturday in the middle of August on the corner of Landis Avenue and Porter Street. Brown and Kling were happy that they reached that particular corner at twelve noon on a freezing day in February, but they weren't particularly delighted to be in Diamondback at all. Brown appreciated their destination even less than did Kling. Diamondback, in the 83rd Precinct, was almost exclusively black, and many of the residents here felt that a black cop was the worst kind of cop in the world. Even the honest citizens up here—and they far outnumbered the pimps, pushers, junkies, armed robbers, burglars, hookers, and assorted petty thieves—felt that if you had any kind of law trouble it was better to go to Whitey than to one of your own brothers. A black cop was like a reformer hooker who'd gone tight and dry.

"What's this kid's name?" Brown asked.

"Andrew Fleet," Kling said.

"White or black?"

"Black," Kling said.

"Terrific," Brown said.

The last known address for Fleet was in a row of grimy tenements on St. Sebastian Avenue, which started at the eastern end of Grover Park, and then ran diagonally northward and eastward for a total of thirteen blocks between Landis and Isola avenues, to become—inexplicably—*another* thoroughfare named Adams Street, presumably after the second president of the United States, or perhaps even the sixth. St. Sab's, as it was familiarly called by everyone in the neighborhood, looked particularly dismal that Tuesday afternoon. You could always tell a neighborhood of poor people in this city because the streets were always the last to be plowed and sanded, and the garbage, especially in bad weather, was allowed to pile up indefinitely, presumably as an inducement to free enterprise among the rat population. It was not unusual in Diamondback to see rats the size of alley cats striding boldly across an avenue at high noon. It was ten minutes past twelve when Kling pulled up alongside a snowbank outside Fleet's building. There was not a rat in sight, but all the garbage cans along the street were overflowing, and the sidewalks were cluttered with the loose debris of urban waste, much of it frozen into the icy pavement. Up here, people didn't use plastic garbage bags. Plastic garbage bags cost money.

Two old black men were standing around a fire in a sawed-off gasoline drum, warming their hands as Brown and Kling approached the front stoop of the building. The men knew immediately that Brown and Kling were detectives. There's a smell. Brown and Kling knew immediately that the men around the gasoline drum knew immediately they were detectives. There's a symbiosis. The two men didn't even look up at Brown and Kling as they climbed the front steps. Brown and Kling didn't look at the two men. The unspoken rule was that if you hadn't done anything wrong, you had no bona fide business with each other.

In the small vestibule, they checked the mailboxes. Only two of them had name-plates.

"Have we got an apartment for him?" Brown asked.

"Three-B," Kling said.

The lock on the inner vestibule door was broken. Naturally. The socket hanging from the ceiling just inside the door had no light bulb in it. Naturally. The hallway was dark and the steps leading upstairs were darker, and there was the aggressive aroma of tight cramped living, a presence as tangible as the brick walls of the building.

"Shoulda taken a flash from the car," Brown said.

"Yeah," Kling said.

They climbed the steps to the third floor.

They listened outside the door to Fleet's apartment.

Nothing.

They listened some more.

Still nothing.

"Johnny?" a voice said.

"Police," Brown said.

"Oh."

"Open it up," Brown said.

"Sure, just a second."

Brown looked at Kling. Both men shrugged. They heard footsteps inside, approaching the door. They heard someone fumbling with a night chain. They heard the tumblers of a lock falling. The door opened. A thin young black man wearing blue jeans and a tan V-necked sweater over a white undershirt stood in the door-frame, peering out into the hallway.

"Yeah?" he said.

"Andrew Fleet?" Brown said, and showed him his shield and I.D. card.

"Yeah?"

"*Are* you Andrew Fleet?"

"Yeah?"

"Few questions we'd like to ask you. Okay to come in?"

"Well, uh, sure," Fleet said, and glanced past them toward the stairwell.

"Or were you expecting somebody?" Kling asked at once.

"No, no, come on in."

He stepped aside to allow them entrance. They were standing in a small kitchen. A single ice-rimed window opened onto the brick wall of the tenement opposite. There were dirty dishes stacked in the sink. An empty wine bottle was on the small table. A clothesline was stretched across the room from one wall to the wall opposite. A single pair of Jockey shorts was draped over the line.

"It's a little chilly in here," Fleet said. "The heat's slow coming up today. We already called the Ombudsman's Office."

"Who's *we?*" Brown asked.

"A guy on the tenant's committee."

Through an open door off the kitchen, they could see an unmade bed. The floor around the bed was heaped with dirty clothes. On the wall over the bed, there was a framed picture of Jesus Christ with his hand hovering in blessing over his exposed and bleeding heart.

"You live here alone?" Brown asked.

"Yes, sir," Fleet said.

"Just these two rooms?"

"Yes, sir."

He was suddenly all "sirs"; the formality was not lost on the two detectives. A glance passed between them. They were both wondering what he was afraid of.

"Okay to ask you a few questions?" Brown said.

"Sure. But ... uh ... you know, like you said, I *was* kind of expecting someone."

"Who?" Kling said. "Johnny?"

"Well, yeah, actually."

"Who's Johnny?"

"A friend."

"You still doing heroin?" Brown asked.

"No, no. Who told you that?"

"Your record, for one thing," Kling said.

"I ain't *got* a record. I never done time in my life."

"Nobody said you did time."

"You were arrested last July," Brown said. "Charged with Rob One."

"Yeah, but—"

"You walked, we know."

"Well, it was a suspended sentence."

"Because you were a poor, put-upon junkie, right?" Brown said.

"Well, I was hooked pretty bad back then, that's true."

"But no more, huh?"

"No. Hey, no. You gotta be crazy to fool around with that shit."

"Uh-huh," Brown said. "So who's this friend Johnny?"

"Just a friend."

"Not a dealer by any chance?"

"No, no. Hey, come on, man."

"Where were you last Saturday night, Andrew?" Kling asked.

"Last Saturday night?"

"Actually Sunday morning. Two o'clock on the morning of the fourteenth."

"Yeah," Fleet said.

"Yeah what?"

"I'm trying to remember. Why? What happened last Saturday night?"

"You tell us," Brown said.

"Saturday night," Fleet said.

"Or Sunday morning, take your choice."

"Two o'clock in the morning," Fleet said.

"You've got it," Kling said.

"I was here, I think."

"Anybody with you?"

"Is this an Article Two-Twenty?" Fleet asked, using the penal law number for the section defining drug abuses.

"Anybody with you?" Kling repeated.

"Who remembers? That was . . . what was it? Three days ago? Four days ago?"

"Try to remember, Andrew," Brown said.

"I'm trying."

"Do you remember the name of the man you held up?"

"Yeah."

"What was his name?"

"Edelbaum."

"Try again."

"That was his name."

"Ever see him since the holdup?"

"Yeah, at the trial."

"And you think the name is Edelbaum, huh?"

"That *is* his name."

"Do you know where he lives?"

"No. Where does he live?"

"No idea where he lives, huh?"

"How would I know where he lives?"

"Do you remember where his shop is?"

"Sure. On North Greenfield."

"But you don't remember where he lives, huh?"

"I *never* knew where, so how can I *remember* where?"

"But if you wanted to find *out* where, you'd look it up in the phone book, right?" Brown said.

"Well, sure, but why would I want to do that?"

"Where were you on February the fourteenth at two in the morning?" Kling asked.

"I told you. Right here."

"Anybody with you?"

"If this is an Article—"

"Anybody with you, Andrew?"

"We were shooting a little dope, okay?" Fleet said. "Is that what you want to know? Fine, you got it, man. We were shooting dope, I'm still a junkie, okay? Big deal. Go through the place if you want to, you won't find anything but a little pot. Not enough for a bust, that's for sure. Go ahead, take a look."

"Who's *we?*" Brown asked.

"What?"

"The person who was with you on Saturday night."

"It was Johnny, okay? What are we gonna *do* here, get the whole *world* in trouble?"

"Johnny who?" Kling asked.

A knock sounded on the door. Fleet looked at the two cops.

"Answer it," Brown said.

"Listen—"

"Answer it."

Fleet sighed and went to the door. He turned the knob on the lock and opened the door.

"Hi," he said.

The black girl standing in the hallway couldn't have been more than sixteen years old. She was wearing a red ski parka over blue jeans and high-heeled boots. She was not unattractive, but the lipstick on her mouth was a shade too garish, and her cheeks were heavily rouged and her eyes were made up with shadow and liner that seemed far too nocturnal for twenty minutes past noon.

"Come in, miss," Brown said.

"What's the beef?" she asked, recognizing them immediately as cops.

"No beef," Kling said. "Want to tell us who you are?"

"Andy?" she said, turning her eyes to where Fleet was standing.

"I don't know what they want," Fleet said, and shrugged.

"You got a warrant?" the girl asked.

"We don't need a warrant. This is a field investigation and your friend here invited us in," Brown said. "Why? What've you got to hide?"

"Is this an Article Two-Twenty?" she asked.

"You both seem pretty familiar with Article Two-Twenty," Brown said.

"Yeah, well, live and learn," the girl said, shrugging.

"What's your name?" Kling said.

She looked at Fleet again. Fleet nodded.

"Corrine," she said.

"Corrine what?"

"Johnson."

The dawn broke slowly. It illuminated first Brown's face, and then Kling's.

"Johnny, is it?" Brown asked.

"Yeah, Johnny," the girl said.

"Is that what you call yourself?"

"If *your* name was Corrine, would *you* call yourself Corrine?"

"How old are you, Johnny?"

"Twenty-one," she said.

"Try again," Kling said.

"Eighteen, okay?"

"Is it sixteen?" Brown said. "Or even younger?"

"Old enough," Johnny said.

"For what?" Brown asked.

"For anything I've got to do."

"How long have you been on the street?" Kling asked.

"I don't know what you're talking about."

"You're a hooker, aren't you, Johnny?" Brown asked.

"Who says?"

Her eyes had turned to ice as opaque as that on the window. Her hands were in the pockets of the ski parka now. Both Kling and Brown were willing to bet her unseen fists were clenched.

"Where were you last Saturday night?" Kling asked.

"Johnny, they—"

"Shut up, Andrew!" Brown said. "Where were you, miss?"

"*When* did you say?"

"Johnny—"

"I told you to shut *up!*" Brown said.

"Last Saturday night. Two A.M.," Kling said.

"Here," the girl said.

"Doing what?"

"Shooting up."

"How come? Was it slow on the street?"

"The *snow,*" Johnny said angrily. "Keeping all the johns in they own beds."

"What time did you get here?" Brown asked.

"I *live* here, man," she said.

"Thought you lived here alone, Andrew," Kling said.

"Yeah, well, I didn't want to get anybody else in trouble, you know, man?"

"So you were here all night, huh?" Brown said.

"I didn't say that," the girl answered. "I went out around . . . what was it, Andy?"

"Never mind Andy. *You* tell us."

"Ten o'clock, musta been, usually that's when the action starts. Damn streets was empty as a hooker's heart."

"When did you get back?"

"Around midnight. We started partying around midnight, wasn't it, Andy?"

Fleet was about to answer, but Brown's stare silenced him.

"And you were here from midnight till two?" Kling asked.

"I was here from midnight till the next *morning*. I told you, man, I *live* here."

"Did Andrew leave the apartment at any time that night?"

"No, *sir,*" Johnny said.

"No, *sir,*" Fleet repeated, nodding emphatically.

"Where'd you go the next morning?"

"Out. See if I could score."

"What time?"

"Early. Around eleven o'clock, I guess it was."

"*Did* you score?"

"Snow's hinderin' the traffic," she said. She was not talking about automobile traffic. "You get your junk comin' up from Florida, minute they hit North Carolina, they're ass-deep in snow. I tell you two things it don't pay to be in this weather, man. One's a hooker, the other's a junkie.''

Brown could think of a lot of other things it didn't pay to be in this weather. "Bert?'' he said.

Kling looked at the two kids.

Then he said, "Yeah, let's go.''

They walked down to the street in silence. The two old men were still standing around the gasoline drum, trying to warm themselves. When Kling started the car, the heater began rattling and clanging.

"They look clean, don't you think?'' Brown asked.

"Yeah,'' Kling said.

"Didn't even know the man's *name,*'' Brown said.

They drove downtown in silence. As they were approaching the station house, Brown said, "It's a goddamn crying shame,'' and Kling knew he wasn't talking about the fact that they'd come up blank on the Edelman killing.

10

The superintendent of Sally Anderson's building had been pestered by cops ever since her murder, and now there was a monk to contend with. The super was not a religious man, he did not give a damn about Heaven *or* Hell, and he did not feel like cooperating with a monk while he was sprinkling rock salt on the pavement outside the building, trying to melt the sheet of ice there.

"What's she got to do with you?'' he asked Brother Anthony.

"She ordered a Bible,'' Brother Anthony said.

"A what?''

"A Bible. From the Order of Fraternal Pietists,'' he said, figuring that sounded very holy.

"So?''

"I am of that order,'' Brother Anthony said solemnly.

"So?''

"I would like to deliver her Bible. I've been upstairs to the apartment listed in her mailbox, and there's no answer. I was wondering if you could tell me—''

"You bet there's no answer,'' the super said.

"That's right,'' Brother Anthony said.

"Ain't *never* gonna be no answer up there,'' the super said. "Not from *her,* anyway.''

"Oh?'' Brother Anthony said. "Has Miss Anderson moved?''

"You mean you're not in touch?''

"In touch?''

"With God?''

"With God?"

"You mean God doesn't send down daily bulletins?"

"I'm not following you, sir," Brother Anthony said.

"Doesn't God have a list he sends down to you guys? Telling you who expired and where she was sent?" the super said, flinging rock salt onto the sidewalk with atheistic zeal. "Whether it was Heaven or Hell or in between?"

Brother Anthony looked at him.

"Sally Anderson is dead," the super said.

"I'm sorry to hear that," Brother Anthony said. "Dominus vobiscum."

"Et cum spiritu tuo," the super said; he had been raised as a Catholic.

"May God have mercy on her eternal soul," Brother Anthony said. "When did she die?"

"Last Friday night."

"What was the cause of her death?"

"Three bullet holes was what was the cause of her death."

Brother Anthony's eyes opened wide.

"Right here on the sidewalk," the super said.

"Do the police know who did it?" Brother Anthony asked.

"The police don't know how to blow their noses," the super said. "Don't you read the papers? It's been all over the papers."

"I wasn't aware," Brother Anthony said.

"Too busy with your Latin, I suppose," the super said, hurling rock salt. "Your kyrie eleisons."

"Yes," Brother Anthony said. He had never heard those words before. They sounded good. He decided to use them in the future. Toss in a few kyrie eleisons with his Dominus vobiscums. Et cum spiritu tuo. *That* was a good one, too. And then it occurred to him that this was a remarkable coincidence here, Paco Lopez buying a couple of slugs on *Tuesday* night, and his supplier taking three of them on *Friday* night.

Suddenly, this did not seem like such small potatoes anymore. All at once, the two murders seemed like the kind of action the big-time spic drug dealers in this city were into. He wondered if he wanted to get involved in such goings-on. He certainly did not want to wake up dead in the trunk of an automobile in the parking lot at Spindrift Airport. Still, he sensed he had stumbled onto something that might just possibly net him and Emma some *really* big bucks. Provided they played it right. Provided they did their sniffing around without getting their feet wet. At first, anyway. Plenty of time to move in once they knew what was going on.

"What did she do for a living?" he asked the super, figuring if this Anderson girl had been into something big with Lopez, then maybe one or more of her business associates were into the same thing. It was someplace to start. Such remarkable coincidences didn't fall into his lap every day of the week.

"She was a dancer," the super said.

A dancer, Brother Anthony thought, visualizing somebody teaching the tango up at Arthur Murray's. Once, a long time ago, when he was married to a lady who ran a luncheonette upstate she had convinced him to go with her to a dance studio. Not

Arthur Murray's. Not Fred Astaire's, either. Something called—he couldn't remember. To learn the cha-cha, she'd been crazy about the cha-cha. Brother Anthony got an erection the first time he was alone in the room with his instructor, a pretty little brunette wearing a slinky gown, looked more like a hooker than a person supposed to teach him the cha-cha. The girl told him he was very light on his feet, which he already knew. He had his hands spread on her satiny little ass when his wife walked in and decided maybe they should stop taking cha-cha lessons. Step Lively, that had been the name of the place. That was a long time ago, before his wife met with the untimely accident that had cost him a year in Castleview on a bum manslaughter rap. All water under the bridge, Brother Anthony thought, kyrie eleison.

"In that big musical downtown," the super said.

"What do you mean?" Brother Anthony asked.

"Fatback," the super said.

Brother Anthony still didn't know what he meant.

"The show," the super said. "Downtown."

"Where downtown?" Brother Anthony asked.

"I don't know the name of the theater. Buy yourself a newspaper. Maybe they got one printed in Latin."

"God bless you," Brother Anthony said.

The phone on Kling's desk began ringing just as he and Brown were leaving the squadroom. He leaned over the slatted rail divider and picked up the receiver.

"Kling," he said.

"Bert, it's Eileen."

"Oh, hi," he said. "I was going to call you later today."

"Did you find it?"

"Just where you said it was. Back seat of the car."

"You know how many earrings I've lost in the back seats of cars?" Eileen said.

Kling said nothing.

"Years ago, of course," she said.

Kling still said nothing.

"When I was a teenager," she said.

The silence lengthened.

"Well," she said, "I'm glad you found it."

"What do you want me to do with it?" Kling asked.

"I don't suppose you'll be coming down this way for anything, will you?"

"Well . . ."

"Court? Or the lab? D.A.'s office? Anything like that?"

"No, but . . ."

She waited.

"Actually, I live down near the bridge," Kling said.

"The Calm's Point Bridge?"

"Yes."

"Oh, well, good! Do you know A View From the Bridge?"

"What?"

"It's *under* the bridge, actually, right on the Dix. A little wine bar."
"Oh."
"It's just . . . I don't want to take you out of your way."
"Well . . ."
"Does five sound okay?" Eileen asked.
"I was just leaving the office, I don't know what time—"
"It's just at the end of Lamb Street, under the bridge, right on the river, you can't miss it. Five o'clock, okay? My treat, it'll be a reward, sort of."
"Well—"
"Or have you made other plans?" Eileen asked.
"No. No other plans."
"Five o'clock then?"
"Okay," he said.
"Good," she said, and hung up.
Kling had a bewildered look on his face.
"What was that?" Brown asked.
"Eileen's earring," Kling said.
"What?" Brown said.
"Forget it," Kling said.

By three o'clock that afternoon, they had been through Edelman's small second-floor office a total of three times—four times, if you count the extra half hour they'd spent going through his desk again. Brown wanted to call it quits. Kling pointed out that they hadn't yet looked inside the safe. Brown mentioned that the safe was locked. Kling put in a call to the Safe, Loft & Truck Squad. A detective there told him they'd try to get somebody up there within the half hour. Brown lighted a cigarette, and they began going over the office yet another time.

The office was the first in the hallway at the top of the stairs, which probably accounted for the fact that Andrew Fleet had chosen it for his stickup last July, a junkie robber being interested only in expediency and opportunity. A frosted-glass panel on the front door was lettered in gold leaf with the words EDELMAN BROS. and beneath that PRECIOUS GEMS. Mrs. Edelman had told them her husband worked alone, so both Brown and Kling figured the firm had been named when there *was* a brother-partner, and that either the brother was now dead, or else no longer active in the business. They each made a note, in their separate pads, to call Mrs. Edelman and check on this.

Just inside the entrance doorway, there was a space some four feet wide, leading to a chest-high counter behind which was a grille fashioned of the same steel mesh as that on the squadroom's detention cage. A glass-paneled door covered with the same protective mesh was to the left of the counter. A button on the *other* side of the counter, when pressed, released the lock on the door to the inner office. But the mesh, somewhat like what you might find in a cyclone fence around a school playground, could not have prevented an intruder from sticking a gun through any one of its diamond-shaped openings and demanding that the release button for the door be pressed. Presumably, this was what had happened on that night last July.

Andrew Fleet had barged into the office, pointed his gun at Edelman, and ordered him to unlock the door. The steel mesh grille had been as helpful as a bathing suit in a blizzard.

The office side of the dividing counter resembled an apothecary chest, with dozens of little drawers set into it, each of them labeled with the names of the gems they presumably contained. No one had been in this office since the night of Edelman's murder, but the drawers were surprisingly empty, which led both Kling and Brown to assume that Edelman had locked his stuff in the safe before heading home that night. The men were both wearing cotton gloves as they went through the office. It was unlikely that the murderer had been here before heading uptown to ambush Edelman in the garage under his building, but the Crime Unit boys had not yet been through the place, and they weren't taking any chances. If they found a residue of anything that even remotely resembled cocaine, they would place a call downtown at once. They were working this by the book. You didn't summon the harried Crime Unit to a place that *wasn't* the scene of the crime, unless you had damn good reason to suspect this other place was somehow *linked* to the crime. They had no reason to suspect that as yet.

The detective from Safe, Loft & Truck arrived forty minutes later, which wasn't bad considering the condition of the roads. He was wearing a sheepskin car coat, a cap with earflaps, fleece-lined gloves, heavy woolen trousers, a turtleneck shirt, and black rubbers. He was also carrying a black satchel. He put the satchel down on the floor, took off his gloves, rubbed his hands briskly together, said, ''Some weather, huh?'' and extended his right hand. ''Turbo,'' he said, and shook hands first with Brown and then with Kling, who introduced themselves in turn.

Turbo reminded Brown of the pictures of Santa Claus in the illustrated version of ''The Night before Christmas,'' which he ritually read to his kid every Christmas Eve. Turbo didn't have a beard, but he was a roly-poly little man with bright red cheeks, no taller than Hal Willis, but at least a yard wider. He had retrieved his right hand, and was again rubbing both hands briskly together. Brown figured he was going to try the combination, the way Jimmy Valentine might have.

''So where is it?'' Turbo said.

''Right there in the corner,'' Kling said.

Turbo looked.

''I was hoping it'd be an old one,'' he said. ''That box looks brand new.''

He walked over to the safe.

''I coulda punched an old box in three seconds flat. This one's gonna take time.''

He studied the safe.

''You know what I'm gonna find here, most likely?'' he said. ''A lead spindle shaft with the locknuts *away* from the shaft so I won't be able to pound it through the gut box and break the nuts that way.''

Brown and Kling looked at each other. Turbo sounded as if he were speaking a foreign language.

''Well, let's see,'' Turbo said. ''You think he may have left it on day combination, no such luck, huh?'' He was reaching for the dial when his hand stopped. ''The Crime Unit been in here?'' he asked.

"No," Kling said.

"Is that why you're wearing the Mickey Mouse gloves?"

Both men looked at their hands. Neither of them had removed the cotton gloves when shaking hands with Turbo, a lack of etiquette he seemed not to have minded.

"What *is* this case, anyway?" he asked.

"Homicide," Kling said.

"And no Crime Unit?"

"He was killed uptown."

"So what's this, his place of business?"

"Right," Brown said.

"Whose authority do I have to open this thing?"

"It's our case," Kling said.

"So what does *that* mean?" Turbo asked.

"That's your authority," Brown said.

"Yeah? You go tell that to my lieutenant, that I busted open a safe on the authority of two flatfoots from the boonies," Turbo said, and went to the phone. Mindful of the fact that the Crime Unit hadn't yet been here, he opened his satchel, took out his *own* pair of white cotton gloves, and pulled them on. The three detectives now looked like waiters in a fancy restaurant. Brown expected one of them to start passing around the finger bowls. Turbo lifted the phone receiver, dialed a number, and waited.

"Yeah," he said. "Turbo here. Let me talk to the Loot." He waited again. "Mike," he said, "it's Dom. I'm here on North Greenfield, there's two guys from uptown want me to open a safe for them." He looked at Kling and Brown. "What's your names again?" he asked.

"Kling," Kling said.

"Brown," Brown said.

"Kling and Brown," Turbo said into the phone, and listened again. "What precinct?" he asked them.

"The Eight-Seven," Kling said.

"The Eight-Seven," Turbo said into the phone. "A homicide. No, this is the guy's place of business, the victim's. So what should I do? Uh-huh. Uh-huh. I just want my ass covered, you understand, Mike? 'Cause next thing you know, I'll be doing time on a Burglary Three rap." He listened. "*What* release form, who's got a release form? Well, no. I *don't*. So what should it say? Uh-huh. Uh-huh. You want both of them to sign it, or what? Uh-huh. Uh-huh. And that'll do it, huh? Okay, Mike, you're the boss. I'll see you later," he said, and hung up. "I need a release from you guys," he said. "Authorizing me to open that thing. One signature'll do it, whoever caught the squeal. I'll give you the language."

He dictated the words to Kling, who wrote them down in his pad, and then signed the page.

"Date it, please," Turbo said.

Kling dated it.

"And you'd better let me have your rank and shield number, too."

Kling scribbled his rank and shield number under his signature.

"I'm sorry to get so technical," Turbo said, pocketing the sheet of paper Kling tore from his pad, "but if there's anything of value in that safe, and it happens to disappear . . ."

"Right, you're just covering your ass," Brown said.

"Right," Turbo said, and shot him a glare. "So let's see if this guy left it on day comb." He went to the safe again. "Lots of guys who are in and out of a box all day long, they'll just give the dial a tiny little twist when they close it, you know? Then all they have to do is turn it back to the last number, saves a lot of time." He turned the dial slowly, and yanked on the handle. "No such luck," he said. "Let's try the old five-ten."

The detectives looked at him.

"Lots of guys, they have trouble remembering numbers, so when they order a safe, they'll ask for the combination to be three numbers in a multiplication table. Like five, ten, fifteen. Or four, eight, twelve. Or six, twelve, eighteen, or whatever. Hardly ever the *nine* table, that's a bitch, the nine table. What's nine times three?" he asked Kling.

"Twenty-seven," Kling said.

"Yeah, well, that's the exception that proves the rule. So let's give it a shot."

As he began trying the multiplication-table combinations, he said, "Would you know this guy's birthday?"

"No," Brown said.

" 'Cause sometimes they use their birthdays, you know, anything to make it easy to remember. Like if he was born on October 15, 1926, the combination would be ten left, fifteen right, and then twenty-six left again. But you don't know his birthday, huh?"

"No," Brown said.

"Take a look at the phone there, what's the number on it?"

"What?" Brown said.

"The *phone.* The phone I just *used* there. On the guy's *desk.* What's the first six digits? Sometimes they'll use the first six digits of their phone number."

"You want me to write this down, or what?" Brown asked.

"Yeah, write it down. I'm still only up to the six table. I usually only take it to eleven, because after that the tables get too tricky. Who the hell even *knows* what fourteen times three is?" he said.

"Forty-two," Kling said, and Turbo gave him a sour look.

"Okay, give me that phone number," he said.

Brown handed him the slip of paper on which he'd written down the first six digits of the number. Turbo tried them.

"No such luck," he said. "Okay, let's bring up the heavy artillery." He opened his satchel, and took from it a small sledgehammer and a punch. "Best burglars in this city are on the Safe, Loft & Truck Squad," he said, proudly, and with one swift blow knocked off the combination dial. "Looks like a lead spindle," he said, "we'll find out in a minute." He began pounding on the exposed spindle. The spindle started mushrooming under the hammer blows. "Lead, sure as hell," he said. "This here is what you call a money box here. That means it's made of heavy steel layers, with a punch-resistant spindle, and sometimes a boltwork relock device, or even a copper sheet in the door so an acetylene torch on it don't mean nothing. If I'da known what this was gonna be, I'da brought nitro.'' He smiled suddenly. ''I'm kidding. Your best burglars these days hardly *ever* use explosives. What I got to do here is I got to peel back the steel until I can get a big enough hole to force a jimmy in. Once I get to that lock, I can pry it loose and open the door. Make yourself comfortable, this may take a while.''

Kling looked up at the clock. It was ten minutes past four, and he had promised Eileen he'd meet her at five. He debated calling her, decided not to.

''Can we get a little light in here?'' Turbo asked. ''Or were you partners with this dead guy?''

Brown flicked on the wall switch.

Turbo got to work.

He opened the box in twenty minutes. He was obviously very pleased with himself, and so both Brown and Kling congratulated him effusively before getting down on their hands and knees to see what was inside there.

There were not very many gems in the safe. Several pouches of rubies, emeralds, and sapphires, and one small pouch of diamonds. But on a shelf at the rear of the safe, stacked neatly there, the detectives found $300,000 in hundred-dollar bills.

''We're in the wrong business,'' Turbo told them.

Detective Richard Genero had been very leery about answering the telephone ever since he'd inadvertently yelled at a captain from downtown two days ago. You never knew who was going to be on the other end. That was the mystery of the telephone. There were other mysteries in life as well, which was why his mother constantly advised him to ''mind his own business,'' a warning that seemed absurd when directed to a policeman, whose business *was* minding other people's business. When the telephone on Carella's desk rang at four-thirty that Tuesday afternoon, Genero debated answering it. Carella was at the other end of the squadroom, putting on his coat, preparatory to leaving. Suppose this was that captain again? Carella and the captain seemed to be good friends. Carella had laughed a lot when he was talking to the captain on the telephone. Suppose the captain yelled at Genero again? The phone kept ringing.

''Will somebody please pick that *up?*'' Carella shouted from across the room, where he was buttoning his coat.

Since Genero was the only other person in the room, he picked up the receiver, very gingerly, and held it a little distance from his ear, in case the captain started yelling again. ''Hello?'' he said, not wanting to give his name in case this was the captain again.

''Detective Carella, please,'' the voice on the other end said.

''Who's this, please?'' Genero asked, very carefully.

''Tell him it's Danny,'' the voice said.

''Yes, sir,'' Genero said, not knowing whether or not Danny was the same captain who'd called on Sunday, or perhaps even *another* captain. ''Steve!'' he yelled, ''it's Danny.''

Carella came across the room to his desk. ''Why does it always ring when I'm on my way out?'' he said.

''That's the mystery of the telephone,'' Genero said, and smiled like an angel.

Carella took the receiver from him. Genero went back to his own desk, where he was working on a crossword puzzle, and having trouble with a three-letter word that meant feline.

"Hello, Danny," Carella said.

"Steve? I hope this ain't an inconvenient time."

"No, no. What've you got?"

Meyer came up the corridor from the men's room, zipping up his fly. He pushed his way through the gate in the slatted rail divider and went to the coatrack. The woolen hat his wife had knitted for him was in the right-hand pocket of his coat. He debated putting it on. Instead, he took his blue fedora from the rack, seated it on his bald head, shrugged into his coat, and walked to where Carella was on the phone.

"What do you mean, 'interesting'?" Carella said.

"Well, I thought I might be able to talk to this chick who wouldn't give you the right time, you know the one I mean?" Danny said.

"The Quadrado girl, yes."

"Right. The one who used to live with Lopez. Give her a song and dance, tell her I was looking to buy some dope, whatever. Just to get her talking, you know what I mean?"

"So what was so interesting, Danny?"

"Well . . . you probably know this already, Steve, but maybe you don't."

"What is it, Danny?" Carella said, and looked at Meyer and shrugged. Meyer shrugged back.

"She was cut to ribbons Sunday night."

"What?"

"Yeah. She died at Saint Juke's yesterday morning, around eleven o'clock."

"Who told you this?"

"The lady who lives next door to her."

"Danny . . . are you *sure?*"

"I always check at the source, Steve. I called Saint Juke's the minute I left the building. She's dead, all right. They're still waiting for somebody to come claim the body. Has she got any relatives?"

"A cousin," Carella said blankly.

"Yeah," Danny said, and paused. "Steve . . . you still want me to look for a thirty-eight? I mean . . . the lady was *cut,* Steve."

"Yes, please keep looking, Danny," Carella said. "Thanks. Thanks a lot."

"See you," Danny said, and hung up. Carella held the receiver a moment before replacing it on the cradle.

"What?" Meyer said.

Carella took a deep breath. He shook his head. Still wearing his overcoat, he walked to the lieutenant's door and knocked on it.

"Come!" Byrnes shouted.

Carella took another deep breath.

The ceiling of A View From The Bridge was adorned with wineglasses, the foot of each glass captured between narrow wooden slats, the stem and bowl hanging downward to create an overall impression of a vast, wall-to-wall chandelier glistening with reflected light from the fireplace on one wall of the room. The fireplace wall was made of brick, and the surrounding walls were wood-paneled except for the one facing the river, a wide expanse of glass through which Kling could see the water beyond and the tugboats moving slowly through the rapidly gathering dusk. It was 5:30 P.M. by the clock over the bar facing the entrance doorway. He had made it downtown as quickly as possible, leaving Brown to contact the lieutenant with the startling news Edelman's safe had contained three hundred thousand smackeroos.

The wine bar, at this hour, was crowded with men and women who, presumably, worked in the myriad courthouses, municipal buildings, law offices, and brokerage firms that housed the judicial, economic, legal, and government power structure in this oldest part of the city. There was a pleasant conversational hum in the place, punctuated by relaxed laughter, a coziness encouraged by the blazing fire and the flickering glow of candles in ruby red holders on each of the round tables. Kling had never been to England, but he suspected that a pub in London might have looked and sounded exactly like this at the end of a long working day. He recognized an assistant D.A. he knew, said hello to him, and then looked for Eileen.

She was sitting at a table by the window, staring out over the river. The candle in its ruby holder cast flickering highlights into her hair, red reflecting red. Her chin was resting on the cupped palm of her hand. She looked pensive and contained, and for a moment he debated intruding on whatever mood she was sharing with the dark waters of the river beyond. He took off his coat, hung it on a wall rack just inside the door, and then moved across the room to where she was sitting. She turned away from the river as he moved toward her, as though sensing his approach.

"Hi," he said, "I'm sorry I'm late, we ran into something."

"I just got here myself," she said.

He pulled out the chair opposite her.

"So," she said. "You found it."

"Right where you said it'd be." He reached into his jacket pocket. "Let me give it to you before it gets lost again," he said, and placed the shining circle of gold on the table between them. He noticed all at once that she was wearing the mate to it on her right ear. He watched as she lifted the earring from the table, reached up with her left hand to pull down the lobe of her left ear, and crossed her right hand over her body to fasten the earring. The gesture reminded him suddenly and painfully of the numberless times he had watched Augusta putting on or taking off earrings, the peculiarly female tilt of her head, her hair falling in an auburn cascade. Augusta had piece ears; Eileen's earrings were clip-ons.

"So," she said, and smiled, and then suddenly looked at him with something like embarrassment on her face, as though she'd been caught in an intimate act when she thought she'd been unobserved. The smile faltered for an instant. She looked quickly across the room to where the waiter was taking an order at another table. "What do you prefer?" she asked. "White or red?"

"White'll be fine," he said. "But list, *I* want to pay for this. There's no need—"

"Absolutely out of the question," she said. "After all the trouble I put you to?"

"It was no trouble at—"

"No way," she said, and signaled to the waiter.

Kling fell silent. She looked across at him, studying his face, a policewoman suddenly alerted to something odd.

"This really *does* bother you, doesn't it?" she said.

"No, no."

"My paying, I mean."

"Well . . . no," he said, but he meant yes. One of the things that had been *most* troubling about his marriage was the fact that Augusta's exorbitant salary had paid for most of the luxuries they'd enjoyed.

The waiter was standing by the table now, the wine list in his hand. Clued by the fact that she was the one who'd signaled him, and no longer surprised by women who did the ordering and picked up the tab, he extended the leather-covered folder to her. "Yes, miss?" he said.

"I believe the gentleman would like to do the ordering," Eileen said. Kling looked at her. "He'll want the check, too," she added.

"Whatever turns you on," the waiter said, and handed the list to Kling.

"I'm not so good at this," he said.

"Neither am I," she said.

"Were you thinking of a white or a red?" the waiter asked.

"A white," Kling said.

"A *dry* white?"

"Well . . . sure."

"May I suggest the Pouilly Fumé, sir? It's a nice dry white with a somewhat smoky taste."

"Eileen?"

"Yes, that sounds fine," she said.

"Yes, the . . . uh . . . Pooey Foo May, please," Kling said, and handed the wine list back as if it had caught fire in his hands. "Sounds like a Chinese dish," he said to Eileen as the waiter walked off.

"Did you see the French movie, it's a classic," she said. "I forget the title. With Gerard Philippe and . . . Michelle Morgan, I think. She's an older woman and he's a very young man, and he takes her to a fancy French restaurant—"

"No, I don't think so," Kling said.

"Anyway, he's trying to impress her, you know, and when the wine steward brings the wine he ordered, and pours a little into his glass to taste it, he takes a little sip—she's watching him all the while, and the steward is watching him, too—and he rolls it around on his tongue, and says, 'This wine tastes of cork.' The wine steward looks at him—they'll all supposed to be such bastards, you know, French waiters—and he pours a little of the wine into his little silver tasting cup, whatever they call it, and *he* takes a sip, and rolls it around in his mouth, and everybody in the place is watching them because they know they're lovers, and there's nothing in the world a Frenchman likes better than a lover. And finally, the steward nods very solemnly, and says, 'Monsieur is correct, this wine *does* taste of cork,' and he goes away to get a fresh bottle, and Gerard Philippe smiles, and Michelle Morgan smiles, and everybody in the entire place smiles."

Eileen was smiling now.

"It was a very lovely scene," she said.

"I don't much care for foreign movies," Kling said. "I mean, the ones with subtitles."

"This one had subtitles," Eileen said. "But it was beautiful."

"That scene *did* sound very good," Kling said.

"*Le Diable au Corps,* that was it."

Kling looked at her, puzzled.

"The title," she said. "It means 'Devil in the Flesh.' "

"That's a good title," Kling said.

"Yes," Eileen said.

"The Pouilly Fumé," the waiter said, and pulled the cork. He wiped the lip of the bottle with his towel, and then poured a little wine into Kling's glass. Kling looked at Eileen, lifted the glass, brought it to his lips, sipped at the wine, rolled the wine around in his mouth, raised his eyebrows and said, "This wine tastes of cork."

Eileen burst out laughing.

"Cork?" the waiter said.

"I'm joking," Kling said, "it's really fine."

"Because, *really,* if it's—"

"No, no, it's fine, really."

Eileen was still laughing. The waiter frowned at her as he poured the wine into her glass, and then filled Kling's. He was still frowning when he walked away from the table. They raised their glasses.

"Here's to golden days and purple nights," Eileen said, and clinked her glass against his.

"Cheers," he said.

"My Uncle Matt always used to say that," Eileen said. "He drank like a fish." She brought the glass to her lips. "Be funny if it *really* tasted of cork, wouldn't it?" she said, and then sipped at the wine.

"*Does* it?" Kling asked.

"No, no, it's very good. Try it," she said. "For *real* this time."

He drank.

"Good?" she said.

"Yes," he said.

"Actually, it was Micheline Presle, I think," she said. "The heroine."

They sat silently for several moments. Out on the river, a tugboat hooted into the night.

"So," she said, "what are you working on?"

"That homicide we caught when you were up there Saturday night."

"How does it look?"

"Puzzling," Kling said.

"That's what makes them interesting," Eileen said.

"I suppose."

"*My* stuff is hardly ever puzzling. I'm always the bait for some lunatic out there, hoping he'll take the hook."

"I wouldn't want to be in your shoes," Kling said.

"It does get scary every now and then."

"I'll bet."

"So listen, who asked me to become a cop, right?"

"How'd you happen to get into it?"

"Uncle Matt. He of the golden days and purple nights, the big drinker. He was a cop. I loved him to death, so I figured *I'd* become a cop, too. He worked out of the old Hundred and Tenth in Riverhead. That is, till he caught it one night in a bar brawl. He wasn't even on duty. Just sitting there drinking his sour mash bourbon when some guy came in with a sawed-off shotgun and a red plaid kerchief over his face. Uncle Matt went for his service revolver and the guy shot him dead." Eileen paused. "The guy got fifty-two dollars and thirty-six cents from the cash register. He also got away clean. I keep hoping I'll run into him one day. Sawed-off shotgun and red plaid kerchief. I'll blow him away without batting an eyelash."

She batted both eyelashes now.

"Tough talk on the lady, huh?" she said, and smiled. "So how about *you?*" she said. "How'd *you* get into it?"

"Seemed like the right thing to do at the time," he said, and shrugged.

"How about now? Does it *still* seem like the right thing?"

"I guess so." He shrugged again. "You get sort of . . . it wears you down, you know."

"Mm," she said.

"Everything out there," he said, and fell silent.

They sipped some more wine.

"What are *you* working on?" he asked.

"Thursday," she said. "I won't start till Thursday night."

"And what's that?"

"Some guy's been raping nurses outside Worth Memorial. On their way to the subway, when they're crossing the park outside the hospital, do you know the park? In Chinatown?"

"Yes," Kling said, and nodded.

"Pretty big park for that part of the city. He hits the ones coming off the four-to-midnight, three of them in the past three months, always when there's no moon."

"I gather there'll be no moon this Thursday night."

"No moon at all," she said. "Don't you just *love* that song?"

"What song?"

" 'No Moon at All.' "

"I don't know it," Kling said. "I'm sorry."

"Well, this certainly isn't the 'We-Both-Like-the-Same-Things' scene, is it?"

"I don't know what scene that is," Kling said.

"In the movies. What's your favorite color? Yellow. Mine, too! What's your favorite flower? Geraniums. Mine, too! Gee, we both like the same things!" She laughed again.

"Well, at least we both like the *wine,*" Kling said, and smiled, and poured her glass full again. "Will you be dressed like a nurse?" he asked.

"Oh, sure. Do you think that's sexy?"

"What?"

"Nurses. Their uniforms, I mean."

"I've never thought about it."

"Lots of men have things for nurses, you know. I guess it's because they figure they've seen it all, nurses. Guys lying around naked on operating tables and so forth. They figure nurses are experienced."

"Mm," Kling said.

"Somebody once told me—this man I used to date, he was an editor at a paper-back house—he told me if you put the word *nurse* in a title, you're guaranteed a million-copy sale."

"Is that true?"

"It's what he told me."

"I guess he would know."

"But nurses don't turn you on, huh?"

"I didn't say that."

"I'll have to show you what I look like," Eileen said. Her eyes met his. "In my nurse's outfit."

Kling said nothing.

"It must have something to do with white, too," Eileen said. "The fact that a nurse's uniform is white. Like a bride's gown, don't you think?"

"Maybe," Kling said.

"The conflicting image, do you know? The *experienced* virgin. Not that too many brides today are virgins," she said, and shrugged. "Nobody would even *expect* that today, would they? A man, I mean. That his bridge's going to be a virgin?"

"I guess not," Kling said.

"You've never been married, have you?" she said.

"I've been married," he said.

"I didn't know that."

"Yes," he said.

"And?"

Kling hesitated.

"I was recently divorced," he said.

"I'm sorry," she said.

"Well," he said, and lifted his wineglass, avoiding her steady gaze. "How about you?" he said. He was looking out over the river now.

"Still hoping for Mr. Right," she said. "I keep having this fantasy . . . well, I really shouldn't tell you this."

"No, go ahead," he said, turning back to her.

"Well . . . really, it's *silly*," she said, and he could swear that she was blushing, but perhaps it was only the red glow of the candle in its holder. "I keep fantasizing that one of those rapists out there will *succeed* one night, do you know? I won't be able to get my gun on him in time, he'll do whatever he *wants* and—*surprise*—he'll turn out to be Prince *Charming!* I'll fall madly in love with him, and we'll live happily ever after. Whatever you do, don't tell that to Betty Friedan or Gloria Steinem. I'll get drummed out of the women's movement."

"The old rape fantasy," Kling said.

"Except that I happen to deal with *real* rape," Eileen said. "And I know it isn't fun and games."

"Mm," Kling said.

"So why should I fantasize about it? I mean, I've come within a *hairs*breadth so *many* times . . ."

"Maybe that's what accounts for the fantasy," Kling said. "The fantasy makes it seem less frightening. Your work. What you have to do. Maybe," he said, and shrugged.

"We've just had our 'I-Don't-Know-Why-I'm-Telling-You-All-This' scene, haven't we?"

"I suppose so," he said, and smiled.

"Somebody ought to write a book about all the different kinds of clichéd scenes," she said. "The one I like best, I think, is when the killer has a gun on the guy who's been chasing him, and he says something like, 'It's safe to tell you this now because in three seconds flat you'll be dead,' and then proceeds to brag about all the people he killed and how and why he killed them."

"I wish it was that easy," Kling said, still smiling.

"Or what I call the '*Uh*-Oh!' scene. Where we see a wife in bed with her lover, and then we cut away to the husband putting his key in the door latch, and we're all supposed to go, '*Uh*-oh, here it comes!' Don't you just *love* that scene?"

The smile dropped from his face.

She looked into his eyes, trying to read them, knowing she'd somehow made a dreadful mistake, and trying to understand what she'd said that had been so terribly wrong. Until that moment, they'd seemed—

"I'd better get the check," he said.

She knew better than to press it. If there was one thing she'd learned as a decoy, it was patience.

"Sure," she said, "I've got to run, too. Hey, thanks for bringing the earring back, really. I appreciate it."

"No problem," Kling said, but he wasn't looking at her, he was signaling to the waiter instead.

They sat in silence while they waited for the check. When they left the place, they shook hands politely on the sidewalk outside and walked off in opposite directions.

"I hate scenes that are played offstage," Meyer said.

"So why didn't you come in there *with* me?" Carella said.

"It was bad enough listening to him yell from outside," Meyer said. "You want to tell me what it was all about?"

They were sitting side by side in the front seat of one of the precinct's newest sedans. Each time they checked out the car, Sergeant Murchison came out back to list any scratches or dents on it. That way he would know who was responsible for any *new* scratches or dents. The car was cozy and warm. The rear tires were snow tires with studs. Hawes and Willis, who had last used the car, said that it actually ran on *ice*. Carella and Meyer—heading downtown for Timothy Moore's apartment— were having no difficulties on the city's frozen tundra.

"So let me hear it," Meyer said.

"Very simple," Carella said. "Paco Lopez's girlfriend was stabbed Sunday night."

"What!"

"Died yesterday morning at Saint Jude's."

"Where'd this happen?" Meyer asked.

"That's just it. Charlie Car found her outside her building on Ainsley Avenue. It's all on the Activity Report spindle, Meyer. A Ten-Twenty-four described as a cutting, victim taken to Saint Jude's."

"Who was catching Sunday night?"

"That's not the point. The blues didn't find her till Monday *morning*. The graveyard shift had already been relieved, this was the eight-to-four."

"That's when *we* were catching!" Meyer said.

"You're beginning to get the message."

"So why the hell didn't the blues call it in?"

"They did."

"Then why didn't *we* get it?"

"Officer's discretion," Carella said. "Charlie Car called for a meat wagon, and then accompanied it to the hospital. The girl was still alive when they delivered her. That's the way it appears on the activity report they wrote up at the end of their tour."

"At four *o'clock,* you mean? What time did the girl *die?*"

"Around eleven."

"Is *that* on an activity report, too?"

"How could it be? I found out from Danny Gimp."

"Great! A snitch pulling together the pieces!"

"Exactly Pete's words."

"So what now?"

"Now we ask Timothy Moore about the 'extra' cash his girlfriend was making."

"I mean, what about the Quadrado girl?"

"She was *cut,* Meyer. Does that sound like the same M.O. to you?"

"Maybe the guy's running out of bullets."

"Maybe. Or maybe this was just another one of the hundred cuttings we get every day of the week. I want to talk to her cousin later, the kid who first put us onto her when we caught the Lopez murder. Maybe *he'll* know something."

"If this is related to cocaine . . ."

"It might be."

"Then it's starting to look like gang shit," Meyer said. "And gang shit, I can do without."

"Let's talk to Moore," Carella said.

Well, they knew it was a big city. And in a big city, mistakes were bound to occur. Chances were that even if they'd known of Judite Quadrado's condition *before* she'd died, the girl might not have been able to tell them anything of value in cracking their case—or *cases* as the case happened to be. Knowing about her in time to have questioned her, and perhaps to have elicited a deathbed statement, might have proved a pointless exercise, anyway. Even in a big city, though, it was nice to know things.

Carella was very happy, for example, to have learned from Lieutenant Byrnes (between his readings of the Riot Act) that Brown and Kling had found $300,000 in hundred-dollar bills in the safe of Marvin Edelman, the last—or at least the most *recent;* they *hoped* he'd prove to be the last—of the murder victims killed with the same .38 Smith & Wesson revolver. The presence of such a large bundle might have been attributed, of course, to the very nature of the man's business: a precious-gems merchant did not normally accept subway tokens in exchange for his commodity. But why such an *awesome* amount of money had been kept in his office safe, instead of in a bank account, or even a bank's safety deposit box, was something that troubled the detectives. It might not have troubled them so much if Edelman's fellow victims hadn't been involved, in one way or another, with cocaine. When cocaine was on the scene, big bucks were mandatory. And the bucks in Edelman's safe were very big indeed.

In street parlance over the years, cocaine had been known under various names: C, coke, snow, happy dust, sleigh ride, gold dust, Bernie, Corrine, girl, flake, star dust, blow, white lady, and—of course—nose candy. When combined with heroin, it was called a speedball, although the street jargon for this combination had recently changed to "Belushi Cocktail." Whatever you chose to call it, cocaine was a headache. Up in the Eight-Seven, the heroin dealers had taken to giving their wares "brand" names. You bought your little glassine bag, and it came with a label pasted on it, and the label read Coolie High or Murder One or rush or Jusey Whales or Quick Silver or Rope of Dope or Cousin Eddie or Bunny or Stay High or Crazy Eddie Shit or Good Pussy, hardly names that would ever be considered by General Foods. But since the people selling dope were criminals, and since there truly *was* no honor among thieves, within hours after a reputable dealer's terrific stuff hit the street with a brand name like "Devil," for example, or "Prophecy" or "New Admissions," some slimy little pusher at the bottom of the ladder would be selling you a bag with the same brand name on it, but with the heroin cut almost to nothing—a "beat bag," as it was known to addicts and dealers alike. But that was heroin.

Cocaine was something else.

The most recent federal report handed around the squadroom estimated that an approximate sixty metric tons of cocaine had been smuggled into the United States in the past year, at a wholesale value of fifty billion dollars.

Cocaine was fashionable.

That was the biggest problem with cocaine. You didn't *have* to be a raggedy-pantsed slum kid to snort a line. You could be running a big Hollywood studio, making multimillion-dollar decisions about the next movie you'd be foisting on an unsuspecting public, and that night you could sit around your Malibu beach house listening to the pounding of the surf and the pounding of your own head as you inhaled coke from the little gold spoon you wore on a slender gold chain under your custom-tailored silk shirt. In fact, if you wanted to start doing cocaine, it *helped* to be among the nation's biggest wage earners. Every working cop knew the mathematics of cocaine. Every working cop was also an expert on the metric system of weights and measures. To understand the economy, you had to know that an ounce of cocaine was the same thing as 28.3 grams, and a kilo was the equivalent of 35.2 ounces, or 2.2 pounds by avoirdupois measure. Your average Colombian coca farmer sold his leaves to a trafficker for about a dollar a pound—two bucks a kilo, give or take a penny. By the time this raw material was transformed into cocaine hydrochloride, and then diluted again and again—"stepped on" or "whacked" or "hit"—and then sold in little packets about the size of the one you might find in a sugar bowl, a *gram* could cost you anywhere between a hundred and a hundred and twenty-five bucks, depending on the quality. The astronomical bucks to be realized in the cocaine trade were attributable to the extraordinary number of middlemen between the source and the consumer, and the ruthless dilution—all the way down the line—from a high of 90-to-98 percent pure in South America to a low of 12 percent pure on the city's streets.

Both Meyer and Carella had mixed feelings about a possible cocaine connection to the murders. On the one hand, they were eager to close out the Lopez/Anderson/ Edelman (and possibly Quadrado) file. On the other hand, if the murders had anything to do with the South American gangsters who operated out of Majesta across the river, in a neighborhood dubbed Baby Bogotá by the police—well, they just weren't sure that was a can of peas they particularly cared to open. Organized crime wasn't their bag, and the Colombian underworld was perhaps something more than a pair of flatfoots from an undernourished precinct could cope with effectively. As they knocked on the door to Timothy Moore's second-floor apartment on Chelsea Place, they were hoping he *would* be able to tell them Sally Anderson was into some big-time drug dealing that was netting her the "extra" cash the black dancer Lonnie had hinted at—but they were *also* hoping the lead was a false one; better a bona fide crazy than a Colombian hit man.

There was music playing behind the door. Classical music. Lots of strings. Both of the detectives were musical ignoramuses; neither of them could identify it. The music was very loud. It flooded out past the wooden door and into the corridor. They knocked again.

"Hello!" a voice yelled.

"Police!" Carella yelled back.

"Okay, hold on!"

They held on. The music was all-pervasive, strings giving way to brasses and then to what Carella guessed was an oboe. Beneath the melodious din, he heard a lock being turned. The door opened. The music swelled more loudly into the hallway.

"Hey, hi," Timothy Moore said.

He was wearing a gray sweat shirt imprinted in purple with the name and seal of Ramsey University. He was also wearing brown corduroy trousers and frayed house slippers.

"Come on in," he said, "I just got home a few minutes ago."

Home appeared to be a three-room apartment, living room, bedroom and kitchen;

in this section of town, so close to the school, it was probably costing him something like six hundred dollars a month. The entrance door opened onto the small living room, furnished with a thrift-shop sofa, chairs, and lamp, and unpainted bookcases brimming with thick tomes Carella assumed were medical texts. A human skeleton hung on a rack in one corner of the room. On an end table near the battered sofa, a telephone rested alongside the portable radio that was blaring the symphony or concerto or sonata or whatever it was. The radio was one of those little Japanese jobs like Genero's, similar in every respect except one: Genero's was usually tuned to a rock station. Beyond the sofa, a door opened into a bedroom with an unmade bed. On the opposite wall, another door opened into the kitchen.

"Let me turn this down," Moore said, and went immediately to the radio. As he lowered the volume, Carella wondered why he simply didn't turn it *off*. He said nothing.

"There," Moore said.

The volume was still loud enough to make it annoying. Carella wondered if Moore was a little hard of hearing, and then wondered if he wasn't overreacting. All Teddy had to learn was that he'd been annoyed by the listening habits of someone who might be a bit *deaf*.

"We didn't want to bother you at the school," he said over the sound coming from the radio. Clarinets now, he guessed. Or maybe flutes.

"I wonder if you could lower that a bit more," Meyer said, apparently unburdened by any guilt over hurting the feelings of the possibly handicapped.

"Oh, sorry," Moore said, and went immediately to the radio again. "I have it on all the time, I sometimes forget how loud it is."

"There've been studies," Meyer said.

"Studies?"

"About the rock-and-roll generation growing up deaf."

"Really?"

"Really," Meyer said. "From all the decibels."

"Well, I'm not deaf *yet,*" Moore said, and smiled. "Can I get you anything? Coffee? A drink?"

"Nothing, thanks," Carella said.

"Well, sit down, won't you? You said you tried me at the school—"

"No, we didn't want to *bother* you at the school."

"Well, thanks, I appreciate that. The way I'm falling behind these days, all I'd have needed was to be yanked out of class." He looked first at Carella and then at Meyer. "What is it? Is there some good news?"

"Well, no," Carella said. "That's not why we're here."

"Oh. I thought for a moment . . ."

"No, I'm sorry."

"Do you think . . . is there still a chance you may get him?"

"We're working on it," Carella said.

"Mr. Moore," Meyer said, "we had a long talk with a girl named Lonnie Cooper yesterday, she's one of the dancers in *Fatback.*"

"Yes, I know her," Moore said.

"She told us all about the party that took place in her apartment a week ago Sunday—the party you missed."

"Yes?" Moore said, looking puzzled.

"She confirmed that there was cocaine at the party."

"Confirmed?"

"We had previously heard it from three separate sources."

"Yes?" Moore said. He still looked puzzled.

"Mr. Moore," Carella said, "the last time we spoke to you, we asked if Sally Anderson was involved with drugs. You told us—"

"Well, I really don't remember exactly what—"

"We asked you, specifically, 'Was she involved with drugs?' and you answered, specifically, no. We also asked if she was involved in any other illegal activity, and you answered no to that one, too."

"As far as I know, Sally was not involved in drugs or any other illegal activity, that's correct."

"You still maintain that?"

"I do."

"Mr. Moore, four different people so far have told us that Sally Anderson was sniffing coke at that party."

"Sally?" He was already shaking his head. "No, I'm sorry, I can't believe that."

"You knew nothing about her habit, huh?"

"Well, you know, of course, that cocaine isn't habit-forming. I'm speaking from a strictly physiological standpoint. There's absolutely no evidence of any dependence potential for Methylester of benzoylecgonine. None whatever."

"How about a *psychological* dependence?"

"Well, yes, but when you ask me whether or not Sally had a *habit*—"

"We asked whether you *knew* about her habit, Mr. Moore."

"I take exception to the word *habit,* that's all. But in any event, to answer your question, I do not believe Sally Anderson was using cocaine. Or any *other* drug, for that matter."

"How about marijuana?"

"Well, I don't consider that a drug."

"We found marijuana fibers and seeds in her handbag, Mr. Moore."

"That's entirely likely. But, as I just said, I do not consider marijuana a *drug,* per se."

"We also found a residue of cocaine."

"That surprises me."

"Even after what we told you about that party?"

"I don't know who told you Sally was sniffing cocaine—"

"Do you want their names?"

"Yes, please."

"Tina Wong, Tony Asensio, Mike Roldan, and Lonnie Cooper."

Moore sighed heavily, and then shook his head. "I don't understand that," he said. "I have no reason to doubt you, but—"

"She never used cocaine in your presence, is that it?"

"Never."

"And this all comes as a total surprise to you."

"Yes, it does. In fact, I'm flabbergasted."

"Mr. Moore, in your relationship with Miss Anderson, did you ever see her on Sundays?"

"Sundays?" he said, and the telephone rang. "Excuse me," he said and lifted the receiver. "Hello?" he said. "Oh, hi, mom, how are you?" He said. He listened and then said, "No, nothing new. In fact, I have the two detectives with me right this minute. The ones working on the case. No, not yet." He listened again. "Still very cold," he said, "how is it down there? Well, mom, sixty-eight isn't what I'd consider *cold.*" He listened, rolled his eyes toward the ceiling, and then said, "I'm really not sure. Right now, I'm in the middle of exams. Maybe during the spring break, I'll see. I know I haven't been down there in a while, mom, but . . . well, August wasn't all that long ago, really. No, it *hasn't* been eight months, mom, it's only been *six* months. *Less* than six months, in fact. Are you feeling okay? How's your arm? Oh? I'm sorry to hear that. You did, huh? Well, what did *he* say it was? Well, he's probably right. Mom, he's an orthopedist, he'd certainly know better than I what . . . Well, not yet, mom. Well, thank you, but I'm not a doctor *yet.* Not for a *while* yet. An opinion from me wouldn't be worth much, mom. Well . . . uh-huh . . . uh-huh . . . well, if you want to think I saved that boy's life, fine. But that doesn't make me a doctor yet. And besides, anyone could have done what I did. The Heimlich Maneuver. Heimlich. What difference does it make *how* you spell it, mom?" He rolled his eyes again. "Mom, I *really* have to go now, I have these detectives . . . what? Yes, I'll tell them. I'm sure they're doing their best, anyway, but I'll tell them. Yes, mom. I'll talk to you soon. Good-bye, mom."

He put the phone back on the cradle, sighed in relief, turned to the detectives, and said, unnecessarily, "My mother."

"Is she Jewish?" Meyer asked.

"Mother? No, no."

"She sounded Jewish," Meyer said, and shrugged. "Maybe *all* mothers are Jewish, who knows?"

"She gets lonely down there," Moore said. "Ever since my father died . . ."

"I'm sorry," Carella said.

"Well, it was a while ago. Last June, in fact. But they say it takes at least a year to get over either a death or a divorce, and she's still taking it pretty hard. Sally was a tonic for her, but now . . ." He shook his head. "It's just that she misses him so terribly much, you see. He was a wonderful man, my father. A doctor, you know. A surgeon, which is what I plan to be. Took care of us as if we were royalty. Even *after* he died. Made sure my mother wouldn't have to worry for the rest of her life, even left *me* enough money to see me through medical school and set up a practice afterward. A wonderful man." He shook his head again. "I'm sorry for the interruption," he said. "You were asking me . . ."

"What was that about the Heimlich Manuever?" Carella asked.

Moore smiled. "When I was down there last August, a kid began turning purple in a restaurant. Twelve-year-old Cuban kid, all dressed up for the big Sunday dinner with his family. I realized he was choking, and I jumped up and did the Heimlich

on him. My mother thought I'd lost my mind, grabbing the kid from behind and—
well, I'm sure you know the maneuver.''

"Yes," Meyer said.

"Anyway, it helped him," Moore said modestly. "His parents were very grateful. You'd have thought I liberated Cuba single-handedly. And, of course, I've been
a hero to my mother ever since.''

"Her son the doctor," Meyer said.

"Yeah," Moore said. He was still smiling.

"So," Carella said.

"So, yeah, what were we talking about?''

"Sundays and Sally.''

"Uh-huh.''

"Did you ever see her on Sundays?''

"Occasionally. She was usually pretty busy on Sundays. Her day off, you know,
no show that night.''

"Busy doing what?''

"Oh, getting her errands done, mostly. Running here and there. We *saw* each
other, of course, but only rarely. Did a little window-shopping together, went to the
zoo every now and then, or the museum, like that. For the most part, Sally liked her
privacy on Sundays. During the *day*time, anyway.''

"Mr. Moore, did you ever go uptown with her? On the times you saw her, those
Sundays you saw her, did you ever go uptown?''

"Well, sure. Uptown?''

"*All* the way uptown," Carella said. "Culver and Eighteenth.''

"No," Moore said. "Never.''

"Do you know where that is?''

"Sure.''

"But you never went up there with Sally?''

"Why would I? That's one of the worst neighborhoods in the city.''

"Did Sally ever go up there alone? On a Sunday?''

"She may have. Why? I don't under—''

"Because Lonnie Cooper told us that Sally went uptown every Sunday to pick up
cocaine for herself and several other people in the show.''

"Well, now we're back to cocaine again, aren't we? I've already told you that as
far as I know, Sally wasn't involved with cocaine or any other drug.''

"Except marijuana.''

"Which I don't consider a drug," Moore said.

"But *definitely* not cocaine. Which you don't consider habit-forming.''

"That's not *my* opinion, Mr. Carella, it happens to be . . . look, what *is* this, can
you please tell me?''

"Did you know that Sally was supplying the cast with cocaine?''

"I did not.''

"She kept this from you, did she?''

"I didn't think there were any secrets between us, but if she was engaged in . . .
in this . . . illicit traffic or whatever you want to call it . . .''

"That's what we call it," Carella said.

"Then, yes, she kept it from me. I had no idea."

"How big a spender was she, Mr. Moore?"

"Pardon?"

"Did she ever seem to spend beyond her means?"

"Her means?"

"What she was earning as a dancer."

"Not that I noticed. She always dressed well, and I don't think she denied herself much ... Mr. Carella, if you can tell me what you're *looking* for, perhaps—"

"Someone we talked to hinted at Sally earning extra cash. We're certain she was supplying cocaine in at least a limited way. We'd like to know if her activities in the drug market extended *beyond* that."

"I'm sorry. I wish I could help you with that, but I really didn't know until just now that she was in *any* way involved with drugs."

"Except marijuana," Carella said again.

"Well, yes."

"Can you think of any *other* way she might have been earning extra cash?"

"I'm sorry, no."

"She wasn't hooking, was she?" Meyer asked.

"Of course not!"

"You're sure about that?"

"Positive. We were very close, we spent virtually every *day* together. I'd certainly know ..."

"But you *didn't* know about the coke."

"No, I didn't."

"Did she ever mention *any* kind of outside activity to you? Anything that might have been bringing in this extra cash?"

"I'm trying to remember," Moore said.

"Please," Carella said.

Moore was silent for what seemed like a very long time, thinking, his head bent. Then, suddenly, as if the idea had just occurred to him, he nodded and looked up at the detectives.

"Of course," he said. "I didn't realize what she was saying at the time, but of course, that has to be it."

"Has to be what?"

"How she was getting the extra cash you're talking about."

"How was she getting it?" Meyer said.

"What was she into?" Carella said.

"Ice," Moore said.

11

They had not been able to reach Allan Carter the night before, and when they called his apartment early this morning, they learned that he had already left for his office. They considered the delay a stroke of good luck; it gave them time to do a little homework on the subject they planned to broach with the producer. The sky was clear and the temperature was surprisingly mild on that Wednesday, February 17. This was bad news. If they knew this city, and they did, the springtime bonanza would be followed immediately by a howling blizzard; God gave with one hand and took away with the other. In the meantime, the snow and the ice were melting.

Carter's office was in a building a block north of the Stem, in Midtown East territory. The building was flanked by a Spanish restaurant on one side and a Jewish delicatessen on the other. A sign in the restaurant window read: We Speak English Here. A sign in the deli window read Aqui Habla Español. Meyer wondered if the Spanish restaurant served blintzes. Carella wondered if the Jewish deli served tortillas. The building was an old one, with massive brass doors on the single elevator in the lobby. A directory opposite the elevator told them that Carter Productins, Ltd., was in room 407. The elevator was self-service. They took it up to the fourth floor, searched for room 407, and found it in the middle of the corridor to the left of the elevator.

A girl with frizzied blond hair was sitting behind a desk immediately inside the entrance door. She was wearing a brown jump suit and she was chewing gum as she typed. She looked up from the machine, said, ''Can I help you?'' and picked up an eraser.

''We'd like to see Mr. Carter, please,'' Carella said.

''We're not auditioning till two o'clock,'' the girl said.

''We're not actors,'' Meyer said.

''Even so,'' the girl said, and erased a word on the sheet she'd typed, and then blew at the paper.

''You should use that liquid stuff,'' Meyer said. ''You use an eraser, it clogs the machine.''

''The liquid stuff takes too long to dry,'' the girl said.

''We're from the police,'' Carella said, showing his shield. ''Would you tell Mr. Carter that Detectives Meyer and Carella are here?''

''Why didn't you say so?'' the girl said, and immediately picked up the phone. As she waited, she leaned over the desk to study the shield more carefully. ''Mr. Carter,'' she said, ''there's a Detective Meyer and Canella here to see you.'' She listened. ''Yes, sir,'' she said. She put up the phone. ''You can go right in,'' she said.

''It's Carella,'' Carella said.

''What did I say?'' the girl asked.

"Canella."

The girl shrugged.

They opened the door to Carter's office. He was sitting behind a huge desk littered with what Carella assumed were scripts. Three walls of the office were covered with posters advertising his shows before *Fatback,* none of which Carella recognized. The fourth wall was a window wall streaming early-morning sunlight. Carter rose when they came into the room, indicated a sofa facing the desk, and said, "Sit down, won't you?" The detectives sat. Carella got straight to the point.

"Mr. Carter," he said, "what is ice?"

"Ice?"

"Yes, sir."

Carter smiled. "What water becomes when it freezes," he said. "Is this a riddle?"

"No riddle," Carella said. "You don't know what ice is, huh?"

"Oh," Carter said. "You mean *ice.*"

"That's what I said."

"*Theater* ice, do you mean?"

"Theater ice," Carella said.

"Well, certainly, I know what ice is."

"So do we," Carella said. "Check us and see if we're right."

"I'm sorry, but what—"

"Bear with us, Mr. Carter," Carella said.

"I have an appointment at ten."

"That's fifteen minutes away," Meyer said, glancing up at the wall clock.

"We'll make it fast," Carella said. "First *we'll* talk, then *you'll* talk, okay?"

"Well, I really don't know what—"

"The way we understand this," Carella said, "ice is a common practice in the theater—"

"Not in *my* theater," Carter said.

"Be that as it may," Carella said, and went on as if he hadn't been interrupted. "A common practice that accounts for something like twenty million dollars a year in cash receipts unaccountable to either the tax man *or* a show's investors."

"That figure sounds high," Carter said.

"I'm talking citywide," Carella said.

"It still sounds high. Ice isn't practical unless a show is a tremendous hit."

"Like *Fatback,*" Carella said.

"I hope you're not suggesting that anyone involved with *Fatback*—"

"Please listen, and tell me if I've got it right," Carella said.

"I'm sure you've got it right," Carter said. "You don't seem like the sort of man who'd come in unprepared."

"I simply want to make sure I understand it."

"Uh-huh," Carter said, and nodded skeptically.

"From what I can gather," Carella said, "a great many show business people have become rich on the proceeds of ice."

"There are stories to that effect, yes."

"And the way it works—please correct me if I'm wrong—is that someone in the box office puts aside a ticket, usually a *house* seat, Mr. Carter, and later sells it to a broker for a much higher price. Am I right so far?''

"That's my understanding of how ice works, yes," Carter said.

"The going price for a choice seat to *Fatback* is forty dollars," Carella said. "That was for sixth row center, the house seats you generously made available to me."

"Yeah," Carter said, and nodded sourly.

"How many house seats would you say are set aside for any performance of any given musical?" Carella said.

"Are we talking about *Fatback* now?"

"Or *any* musical. Take *Fatback* as an example, if you want to."

"We've got about a hundred house seats set aside for each performance," Carter said.

"Who gets those house seats?"

"I get some of them as producer. The theater owner gets some. The creative people, the stars, some of the unusually big investors, and so on. I think we already discussed this once, didn't we?"

"I just want to get it straight," Carella said. "What happens to those seats if the people they're set aside for don't claim them?"

"They're put on sale in the box office."

"When?"

"In this city," it's forty-eight hours before any given performance."

"For sale to whom?"

"Anyone.

"Some guy who walks in off the street?"

"Well, not usually. These are choice seats, you realize."

"So who *does* get them?"

"They're usually sold to brokers."

"At the price printed on the ticket?"

"Yes, of course."

"No, *not* of course," Carella said. "That's where the ice comes in, isn't it?"

"If someone connected with a show is involved in ice, yes, that's where it would come in."

"In short, the man in charge of the box office—"

"That would be our company manager."

"Your company manager, or someone on his staff, would take these unclaimed house seats and sell them to a broker—or any number of brokers—at a price higher than the established price for the ticket."

"Yes, that would be the ice. The difference between the legitimate ticket price and whatever the iceman can get for it."

"Sometimes *twice* the ticket price, isn't it?"

"Well, I really wouldn't know. As I told you—"

"Eighty dollars for a forty-dollar ticket, wouldn't that be possible?"

"It would be possible, I suppose. For a tremendous hit."

"Like *Fatback.*"

"Yes, but no one—"

"And the broker would then take this ticket for which he's paid eighty dollars, and he'll sell it to a favored customer for something like a hundred and fifty dollars, isn't that so?"

"You're talking about scalping now. Scalping is against the law. A ticket broker can legally charge only two dollars more than the price on the ticket. That's his markup. Two dollars. By *law*."

"But there are brokers who break the law."

"That's *their* business, not mine."

"Incidentally," Carella said, "ice is *also* against the law."

"It may be against the law," Carter said, "but in my opinion, it doesn't really hurt anyone."

"It's just a victimless crime, huh?" Meyer said.

"In my opinion."

"Like prostitution," Meyer said.

"Well, prostitution is another matter," Carter said. "The girls themselves *are,* of course, victimized. But with ice . . ." He shrugged. "Let's assume someone in a show's box office *is* doing ice. He doesn't *steal* those house seats, you know. If the ticket costs forty dollars, he'll put forty dollars in the cash drawer before he sells that ticket to a broker."

"For twice the price," Carella said.

"That doesn't matter. The point is the show *got* the forty dollars it was *supposed* to get for the ticket. The *show* doesn't lose any money on that ticket. The *investors* don't lose any money."

"But the people running the ice operation *make* a lot of money."

"There's not that much involved," Carter said, and shrugged again. "I'll tell you the truth, on some shows I was involved with, I've had general managers come to me proposing ice, but I always turned them down cold—no pun intended," Carter said, and smiled. "Why risk a brush with the law when peanuts are involved?"

"Peanuts? You said there were a hundred house seats—"

"That's right."

"At a forty-dollar markup per seat, that comes to four thousand dollars a performance. How many performances are there a week, Mr. Carter?"

"Eight."

"Times four thousand is thirty-two thousand a week. That comes to something like . . . what does it come to, Meyer?"

"What?" Meyer said.

"In a year."

"Oh. Close to two million dollars a year. Something like a million six, a million seven."

"Is that peanuts, Mr. Carter?"

"Well, you know, the ice on a show is usually split up. Sometimes four or five ways."

"Let's say it's split five ways," Carella said. "That would still come to something like two, three hundred thousand dollars a person. That's a lot of money, Mr. Carter."

"It's not worth going to jail for," Carter said.

"Then why are you doing it?" Meyer asked.

"I beg your pardon?" Carter said.

"Why are you taking ice on *Fatback?*"

"Is that a flat-out accusation?" Carter said.

"That's what it is," Carella said.

"Then maybe I ought to call my lawyer."

"Maybe you ought to hear us out first," Carella said, "You always seem to be in a hurry to call your lawyer."

"If you're accusing me of—"

"Mr. Carter, isn't it true that Sally Anderson was a courier in your ice operation?"

"*What* ice operation?"

"We've been told Sally Anderson delivered house seats to various brokers, and collected cash for those seats, and then brought the cash back to your company manager. Isn't that true, Mr. Carter? Wasn't Sally Anderson, in effect, a bag lady for your ice operation?"

"If someone in my theater is making money on ice—"

"Someone *is,* Mr. Carter."

"Not me."

"Let's take this a step further, shall we?" Carella said.

"No, let's call my lawyer," Carter said, and picked up the phone receiver.

"We have proof," Carella said.

He was lying; they had no proof at all. Lonnie Cooper had hinted that Sally had been earning extra cash someplace. Timothy Moore had told them she'd been running ice money for Carter. None of that was proof. But Carella's words stopped Carter dead in his tracks. He put the receiver back onto the cradle. He shook a cigarette free from the package on his desk and lighted it. He blew out a cloud of smoke.

"What proof?" he said.

"Let's go back a bit," Carella said.

"What proof?" Carter said again.

"Why'd you tell us you hardly knew Sally?" Carella asked.

"Here we go again," Carter said.

"Once more 'round the mulberry bush," Meyer said, and smiled.

"*We* think it's because she was involved in this ice operation with you," Carella said.

"I don't know anything about any ice operation."

"And maybe wanted a bigger piece of the pie—"

"Ridiculous!"

"Or maybe even threatened to blow the whistle . . ."

"I don't know what you're talking about," Carter said.

"We're talking about murder."

"Murder? For *what?* Because you think Sally was somehow involved with *ice?*"

"We *know* she was involved," Meyer said. "And not *somehow*. She was involved with *you,* Mr. Carter. She was your goddamn courier. She delivered tickets and she picked up—''

"*Once!*" Carter shouted

The room went silent.

The detectives looked at him.

"I had nothing to do with her murder," Carter said.

"We're listening," Meyer said.

"It was only once."

"When?"

"Last November."

"Why only once?"

"Tina was sick."

"Tina Wong?"

"Yes."

"What happened?"

"She couldn't make the rounds that day. She asked Sally to substitute for her."

"Without your knowledge?"

"She checked with me first. She was sick in bed with the flu, she had a fever. I told her it would be okay. Sally was her closest friend, I figured we could trust her."

"Is that why you denied knowing her?"

"Yes. I figured . . . well, if any of this came to light, you might think—''

"We might think exactly what we *are* thinking, Mr. Carter."

"No. You're mistaken. It was just that once. Sally *never* wanted anything more, Sally *never* threatened me with—''

"How much did she get for her services?" Meyer asked.

"Two hundred bucks. But that was the one and only time."

"How much do you give Tina? Is she your regular bag lady?"

"Yes. She gets the same."

"Two hundred for each pickup and delivery?"

"Yes."

"Twelve hundred a week?"

"Yes."

"And your end?"

"We're splitting it four ways."

"Who?"

"Me, my general manager, my company manager, and the box-office treasurer."

"Splitting thirty-two thousand a week?"

"More or less."

"So your end is something like four hundred grand a year," Meyer said.

"Tax free," Carella said.

"Weren't the show's profits enough for you?" Meyer asked.

"Nobody's getting hurt," Carter said.

"Except you and your pals," Carella said. "Get your coat."

"Why?" Carter said. "Are you wired?"

The detectives looked at each other.

"Let's hear the proof," Carter said.

"A man named Timothy Moore knows all about it," Carella said. "So does Lonnie Cooper, one of your dancers. Maybe Sally wasn't as trustworthy as you thought she was. Get your coat."

Carter stubbed out his cigarette and smiled thinly. "Let me put it this way," he said. "*If* there's ice—and I don't remember having this conversation today, do you?—and *if* Sally Anderson, once upon a time very long ago, really and truly delivered some tickets and picked up some cash, it seems to me you'd need more proof than . . . hearsay, do you call it? So let's say you run over to my box office straight from here. Do you know what you'll find? You'll find that all of our brokers, from this minute on, are getting only their legitimate allotments of tickets, and anything we sell them *beyond* their usual quotas will be at box-office prices. Our top ticket sells for forty dollars. If we send a house seat to a broker, that's what he'll pay for it. Forty dollars. Everything open and honest. Now tell me, gentlemen, are you going to try tracking down whatever cash has changed hands since the show opened? Impossible."

The detectives looked at each other.

"You can go to the attorney general with this," Carter said, still smiling, "but without proof you'd only look foolish."

Carella began buttoning his coat.

Meyer put on his hat.

"And, anyway . . ." Carter said.

The detectives were already heading for the door.

". . . a hot show *always* generates ice."

In the corridor outside, Meyer said, "Nothing ever hurts anybody, right? Snow isn't habit-forming, and ice is a time-honored scam. Marvelous."

"Lovely," Carella said, and pressed the button for the elevator.

"He knows we have no proof, he knows we can't do a damn thing. So he walks," Meyer said.

"Maybe he'll clean up his act, though."

"For how long?" Meyer asked.

Both men fell silent, listening to the elevator as it lumbered slowly up the shaft. Through a window at the far end of the corridor, they could see that the sunshine was waning, the day was turning gray again.

"What do you think about the other?" Carella asked.

"The dead girl?"

"Yes."

"I think he's clean, don't you?"

"I think so."

The elevator doors slid open.

"There ain't no justice in this world," Meyer said.

Years ago, when Brother Anthony was spending a little time at Castleview State Penitentiary on that manslaughter conviction, his cellmate was a burglar. Guy named Jack Greenspan. Big Jack Greenspan, they used to call him. Jewish guy. You hardly ever ran into any Jewish burglars. Big Jack taught him a lot of things, but Brother Anthony never figured any of them would help him on the outside.

Until today.

Today, all the things Big Jack had told him all those years ago seemed of immense value to Brother Anthony because what he planned to do was break into the Anderson girl's apartment. This was not a sudden whim. He had discussed it thoroughly with Emma yesterday, after he'd learned that the Anderson girl had been killed. The reason he had gone to see her in the first place was because Judite Quadrado had told them she was the source from which the sweet snow flowed. It was one thing to have a list of customers, but customers weren't worth beans without what to sell them. So he had gone there yesterday hoping to strike up a business relationship with the girl, only to discover she wouldn't be doing business as usual no more, someone had seen to that.

The reason he wanted to get into her apartment—well, there were two reasons, actually. The first reason was that maybe the girl had stashed away a whole pile of dope that cops hadn't found. He didn't think that was likely, but it was worth a shot. Cops were as careless as anybody else in the world, and maybe she'd stashed away a couple of kilos someplace, which would be like found money with a key going for something like sixty grand before it was stepped on. The second reason was that if the girl was an ounce dealer, which Judite Quadrado had said she was, then she was sure as hell getting those ounces from somebody *else,* unless she was in the habit of running down to South America every other weekend, which Brother Anthony doubted. The super of the building had told him she was a dancer in a hit show, right? Well, dancers couldn't go running off whenever they wanted to. No, the way he figured it, she was being supplied by somebody else.

So. . .

If she was getting her stuff from somebody else, then wouldn't there be something in the apartment that might tell him where she was getting it? If he could learn where she was getting it, why then he would just go to the man and tell him he'd bought out Sally, or some such bullshit, and would the man care to do business with him instead? Unless the man turned out to be the one who'd killed her, in which case Brother Anthony would make the sign of the cross, pick up his skirts, and disappear like an Arab in the night. One thing he didn't want was any heavy action from a guy who lived in Baby Bogotá.

He was carrying in the pouch at the front of his cassock two things that were essential to a successful break-in, again according to Big Jack, and assuming that the lock on the dead girl's door was a Mickey Mouse lock. If the lock looked like something Brother Anthony couldn't handle, he'd find some other way of getting in—like maybe climbing up the fire escape and smashing a window, although Big Jack said that was Amateur Night in Dixie, smashing windows, something only junkie burglars did. The two things Brother Anthony had in his pouch were a box of toothpicks and a strip of plastic he had torn from one of those milk bottles with a handle and a screw-top cap.

The toothpicks were his own portable burglar alarm.

The strip of plastic was to open the door.

The way Big Jack explained it, a credit card was the best way to loid a Mickey Mouse lock, but any thin strip of plastic or celluloid would do. That was where the expression *loid* had come from: before credit cards were even invented, the old-time burglars used to use strips of celluloid to work open a lock. Brother Anthony didn't *have* any credit cards, and he wasn't sure the plastic he'd torn from the milk bottle would work; still, Big Jack had said *any* strip of plastic, right?

He had checked out the lobby downstairs before entering the building; no security, and the old fart superintendent was nowhere in sight. He had been up to the girl's apartment yesterday, when he'd knocked and got no answer, so he knew she was in apartment 3A, but he checked the mailboxes in the lobby just to make sure, and then he took the steps up to the third floor, and stepped out into an empty corridor, not a sound anywhere, Big Jack was right about apartment buildings being mostly empty during the daytime. If he played this right, according to Big Jack's rules, he should be inside the apartment in maybe a minute and a half.

It took him half an hour.

He kept sliding the plastic shim into the crack where the door met the jamb, working it, jiggling it, trying to find purchase on the bolt, turning it this way and that, beginning to sweat, removing it from the crack, inserting it again, worrying it, pushing at it, glancing over his shoulder down the hallway, coaxing it, whispering to it (Come on, baby, come on), positive some lady would come out of her apartment down the hall and start screaming at the top of her lungs, jerking the plastic shim, catching the bolt, losing the bolt, sweating more profusely now, the heavy cassock clinging to his body, his hands working feverishly, a full half *hour* before he finally felt the latch beginning to yield (Careful, don't *lose* it now!), felt it beginning to slide back as the plastic insinuated itself between the steel of the bolt and the wood of the jamb, twisting the shim slowly now, feeling the bolt give and then surrender entirely. He seized the knob and turned it, and the door was open.

He was drenched with sweat.

He stepped quickly into the apartment, closed the door immediately behind him, and leaned against it, breathing hard, listening, pouring sweat. When he had caught his breath, he fished in his pouch for the box of wooden toothpicks, opened the box, took a toothpick from it, and then carefully opened the door just a crack and peered out into the hallway, looking, listening again. Nothing.

He opened the door wider.

He wedged the toothpick into the keyway on the lock, and then broke it off flush with the cylinder. He closed the door again, and turned the thumb-bolt, locking it. The way Big Jack had explained it, if anybody came to the apartment with a key, they'd try to put the key in the lock, not knowing a toothpick was wedged there in the keyway, and they'd keep fumbling with the key, trying to get it in there, and the guy inside the apartment would hear all the clicking noise of metal against metal and would go out the window or whatever he'd chosen for his escape route. Your kitchen was a good escape route, Big Jack had told him. Some kitchens had service doors, and most kitchens had fire escapes. He didn't know why so many kitchens had fire escapes, they just did. Brother Anthony went into the kitchen now.

He leaned over the kitchen sink and looked through the window. No fire escape. He began roaming through the apartment, looking out over the windowsills for a fire escape. The only fire escape was outside the bedroom window. He turned the latch on the window, opened the window just a trifle so he could throw it *all* the way open in a second if anybody came in here, and then walked into the living room. This was a nice place. Carpet on the floor, nice furniture, he wished Emma and him could live in a place like this. Posters on all the walls, nice black leather sofa with pillows. There were some framed pictures of a girl wearing tights and one of those little short frilly skirts ballet dancers wore. He figured she was the dead girl. Good-looking broad. Blond hair, nice figure, but a little on the thin side. He wondered where you could buy those little skirts ballet dancers wore. There were probably places in the city you could buy them. He'd like to buy one of them for Emma, have her run around the apartment naked except for the little skirt.

There was a poster for some ballet company hanging on the wall outside the bathroom. He figured he'd start with the bathroom first because Big Jack had told him lots of people stashed their valuables in the toilet tank, in the water inside the tank. He lowered the toilet seat and lifted the top of the toilet tank and put it down on the seat. He looked inside there. A lot of rusty water. He stuck his hand down into the water, felt around. Nothing. He pulled his hand back, wiped it on a towel hanging on a rod across from the toilet bowl, and then put the top of the tank back on again, trying to remember where else Big Jack said a person should look.

Well, let's try the bedroom, he thought. Big Jack had told him that a lot of bedroom dressers, the bottom drawer rested just on the frame of the dresser itself. There wasn't a shelf or anything under the bottom drawer. This meant there was a space of about two, three inches between the drawer and the floor of the room. What a lot of people did, they pulled out the drawer, and then put their valuables right on the floor itself before they put the drawer back in. An inexperienced burglar would go through the drawer, but he wouldn't think of pulling *out* the drawer to look on the floor.

Brother Anthony pulled out the bottom drawer. It was full of the girl's panties and brassieres. Little nylon bikinis in all colors. Tiny little brassieres, she must've had small tits. He tried to visualize her in just her panties. She was really too skinny, but some of those skinny ones, the closer the bone, the sweeter the meat. He picked up a pair of panties, the purple ones, and held them in his hands for several moments before throwing them back into the drawer. He was here to find two things: either a stash of cocaine, or something that would tell him where the girl was getting her stuff.

He got down on his hands and knees and looked into the empty space where the drawer had been. He couldn't see a thing. He stood up, turned on the lamp on the dresser, and got down on his hands and knees again. He still couldn't see anything. He reached into the dresser and began feeling around with both hands. There was nothing on the floor. He picked up the drawer from where he had left it on the floor, carried it to the bed—nice big bed with a patchwork quilt—and dumped the contents on the bed. Nothing but brassieres and panties, damn girl must've changed her underwear three times a day. He guessed maybe dancers did that. Worked up a sweat, changed their underwear a lot.

He took out all the other drawers in the dresser and dumped them on the bed, too. Nothing but clothes. Blouses and sweaters and tights and T-shirts, a whole pile of girl stuff. No cocaine. Not a scrap of paper with anything written on it. The cops had

probably fine-combed the place, taken anything that looked interesting. They probably sold whatever dope they confiscated, the cops. Worse crooks than the *honest*
crooks in this city. He put his hands on his hips, and looked around. *Now* where? he
wondered.

Big Jack had told him you could sometimes find heroin in a person's sugar bowl,
that's if you got lucky enough to bust into some dealer's apartment. You found a
stash of dope, it was better than finding cash or credit cards or even coin collections.
He went back into the kitchen again, looked for the sugar bowl, found it on the
bottom shelf of one of the cabinets, took off the lid, and discovered that the bowl
was full of pink Sweet 'N' Low packets. So much for that, may God have mercy on
your soul. He went through all the cereal boxes in the cabinet, figuring she might
have hidden a plastic-wrapped kilo inside one of the boxes, dumping out cornflakes
and wheat germ and whatever, but he couldn't find a thing. He went through the
refrigerator. Nothing but an open container of yogurt and a lot of wilted vegetables.
He went through every drawer in the living room, and felt under every tabletop,
figuring the stuff might be taped under one of them. Nothing. He went back into the
bedroom, and opened the door to the closet.

Girl had more clothes than a Hall Avenue department store. Even a fur coat.
Raccoon, it looked like. Must have been making a bundle selling the snow, so where
the hell *was* it? He began pulling dresses and coats from the hangers, patting down
all the coat pockets, throwing everything on the floor behind him. Nothing. He
opened all her shoe boxes. Sexy whore shoes, some of them, with high heels and
ankle straps. He thought of her panties again. Nothing but shoes in any of the boxes.
So where *was* it? He dug deeper into the closet.

He found a man's clothes hanging on the rod, pushed to the far corner of the
closet. Well, sure, it figured. Little whore with her sexy panties and her high-heeled
shoes, of *course* there had to be some guy putting it to her. Nice cardigan sweater,
brown, Brother Anthony would have taken it with him except that it looked too
small. Pair of checked slacks, wouldn't be caught dead in them even if they *did* fit
him. A black silk robe with the monogram TM over the breast pocket. Little kinky
sex, T. M.? You put on your black silk robe, she puts on her silk panties, and her
high-heeled hooker shoes, you sniff a little blow, and it's off to the races! Very nice,
T. M. Nice clothes you got here, T. M. But not too *many* of them, so you couldn't
have been *living* here with her, could you? Maybe you just dropped in every now
and then, maybe you're some married stockbroker who was knocking off an uptown
piece every Wednesday afternoon when the market closed. No more nookie, T. M.
The lady's dead and gone.

Nice cashmere jacket, soft, tan. Another pair of pants. Green! Who would wear
green pants except an Irishman on St. Patrick's Day? A down ski parka. Blue. A
small one, though. Must've been the girl's, with one of those zipper collars that had
a hood folded up inside it, in case you got cold on the ski lift at St. Moritz, my dear.
He wouldn't strap a pair of skis to his feet if you paid him a million dollars! Yeah,
here was the guy's parka, a black one, like the robe. Are you a skier, T. M.? Did you
take your little sweetheart skiing every now and then? He patted down all the
pockets in the cashmere jacket, and then threw it on the floor behind him. He patted

down the girls' ski parka, the blue one. Nothing. He was about to toss it on the floor with all the other clothes when he felt something strange about the collar.

He took it in both hands and twisted it.

Something felt a little stiff in there.

He twisted the collar again. There was a faint crackling sound. Something was zipped up inside the collar, something in addition to the hood. He carried the parka to the bed. He sat on the edge of the bed, the panties and brassieres scattered everywhere around him. He felt the collar again. Yes, there was definitely something in there. Quickly, he unzipped it.

At first, he was only disappointed.

What he was holding in his hands was an envelope folded lengthwise, once and then again, so that it formed a narrow oblong that had easily fitted inside the zipped-up collar of the parka. He unfolded the envelope once. He unfolded it again. The letter was addressed to Sally Anderson. He looked at the return address in the upper left-hand corner. The name there meant nothing to him, but the *place* triggered an instant reaction, and he suspected at once that whereas he hadn't found the coke itself, he *might* have found the primary *source* of the coke. He reached into the envelope and took out the handwritten letter. He began reading it. He could hear the ticking of his own watch. He realized he was holding his breath. Suddenly, he began giggling.

Now we *move*, he thought. Straight up into the big time, man, Cadillacs and Cuban cigars, champagne and caviar, man! Still giggling, he tucked the letter into his pouch, considered whether it was safe to go out the way he had come in, decided it was, and headed uptown to share the wealth with Emma.

Alonso Quadrado was naked when they walked in on him at four o'clock that afternoon. They considered this an advantage. A naked man feels uncomfortable talking to a person who is fully dressed. This was why burglars had an edge whenever they surprised some guy asleep in his bedroom, and he jumped out of bed naked and stood there with everything hanging out, facing an intruder who was wearing an overcoat and holding a gun in his hand. Alonso Quadrado was taking a shower in the locker room at the Y.M.C.A. on Landis Avenue when the two detectives walked in. The two detectives were both wearing overcoats. One of them was wearing a hat. Quadrado was wearing nothing but a thin layer of soapsuds.

"Hello, Alonso," Meyer said.

Quadrado got soap in his eyes. He said, "Damn it!" and began splashing water onto his face. He was an exceptionally thin man, with narrow bones and a pale olive complexion. The Pancho Villa mustache over his upper lip was almost bigger than he was.

"Few more questions we'd like to ask you," Carella said.

"You picked some time," Quadrado said. He rinsed himself off, turning this way and that under the needle spray. He turned off the shower, picked up a towel, and began drying himself. The detectives waited. Quadrado wrapped the towel around his waist and walked into the locker room. The detectives followed him.

"I just got done playing handball," he said. "You play handball?"

"I used to," Meyer said.

"Best game there is," Quadrado said, and sat on the bench, and opened the door to one of the lockers. "So what now?" he said.

"Do you know your cousin's dead?" Meyer asked.

"Yeah, I know it. The funeral's tomorrow. I ain't going. I hate funerals. You ever been to a Spanish funeral? All those old ladies throwing themselves on the coffin? Not for me, man."

"She was cut, do you know that?"

"Yeah."

"Any idea who did it?"

"No. If Lopez was still alive, I'da said it was him. But *he's* dead, too."

"Anybody else you can think of?"

"Look, you know what she was into, it coulda been anybody."

He was drying his feet. He reached into the locker, took out a pair of socks, and began putting them on. It was interesting the way people dressed themselves, Meyer thought. It was like the different ways people ate an ear of corn. No two people ate corn the same way, and no two people got dressed the same way. Why was Quadrado starting with his socks? *Black* socks, at that. Was he about to audition for a porn flick? Meyer wondered if he would put on his shoes next, before he put on his Jockey shorts or his pants. Another of life's little mysteries.

"What *was* she into?" Carella said.

"Well, not *exactly* into it, not yet. But *working* on it, let's say."

"And what was that?"

"The only thing she inherited from Lopez."

"Spell it out," Carella said.

Quadrado reached into the locker again. He took a pair of boxer shorts from where they were hanging on a hook, and pulled them on. "Lopez's trade," he said, and reached into the locker for his pants.

"His dope trade?"

"Yeah, she had the list."

"What list?"

"Of his customers."

"How'd she get that?"

"She was living with him, wasn't she?"

"Is this a *real* list you're talking about? Names and addresses? Written down on a piece of paper?"

"No, no, what piece of paper? But she was living with him, she knew who his customers were. She told me she was gonna move on it, get the coke the same place *he* was getting it, make herself a little extra change, you know?"

"When did she tell you this?" Meyer asked.

"Right after he got shot," Quadrado said, and put on his shirt.

"Why didn't you mention this the last time we talked?"

"You didn't ask me."

"Did this sound like a *new* thing for her?" Carella asked.

"What do you mean?"

"Dealing."

"Oh. Yeah."

"She wasn't working with him *before* he got killed, was she? They weren't partners or anything?"

"No, no. Lopez? You think *he'd* share a good thing with a chick? No way."

"But he told her who his customers were."

"Well, he didn't say, 'This guy takes four grams, and this guy takes six grams,' nothing like that. I mean, he didn't hand her the list on a platter. But when a guy's livin' with somebody, they *talk,* you know what I mean? He'll say, 'I got to deliver a coupla three grams to Luis today,' something like that. They'll talk, you know?"

"Pillow talk," Meyer said.

"Yeah, pillow talk, right," Quadrado said. "That's a good way of putting it. Judite was a smart girl. When Lopez talked, she listened. Look, I'll tell you the truth, Judite didn't think this thing was gonna *last* very long, you know what I mean? After the guy hurt her . . . I mean, how much can a chick put up with? He was a crazy bastard to begin with, and he still had other women, never mind just Judite. So I guess she listened a lot. She had no way of knowing he was gonna get killed, of course, but I guess she figured it wouldn't hurt to—"

"How do you know that?"

"How do I know what?"

"That she didn't know he was going to get killed?"

"I'm just assuming. You guys mind if I smoke?"

"Go right ahead," Meyer said.

" 'Cause I like a little smoke after I finish playing," Quadrado said, and reached into the bag on the floor of the locker, and pulled out a Sucrets tin. They knew what was in the tin even before he opened it. They were surprised, but not *too* surprised. Nowadays, people smoked grass even on the park bench across the street from the station house. They watched as Quadrado fired the joint. He sucked on it. He let out a stream of smoke.

"Care for a toke?" he asked, blithely extending the joint to Meyer.

"Thanks," Meyer said drily. "I'm on duty."

Carella smiled.

"Who were these other women?" he asked.

"Jesus, who could *count* them?" Quadrado said. "There's this one-legged hooker he was putting it to, you know Anita Diaz? She's gorgeous, but she's got only one leg, they call her *La Mujer Coja* in the neighborhood, she's the best lay in the world, you ever happen to run into her. Lopez was making it with her. And there was . . . you know the guy who owns the candy store on Mason and Tenth? His wife. Lopez was making it with her, too. This was all while he was living with Judite, who knows why she put up with it for so long?" He sucked on the joint. "I figure she was scared of him, you know? Like, he was all the time threatening her, and finally he burned her with the cigarette, so that must've *really* scared her. So I guess she figured she'd just keep her mouth shut, let him run around with whoever he wanted to."

"How'd she plan to supply these people?"

"What do you mean?"

"Lopez's customers. Where'd she plan to get the stuff?"

"Same place Lopez got it."

"And where was that?"

"From the Anglo ounce dealer."

"What Anglo ounce dealer?"

"The one Lopez used to live with. The way Judite figured it, bygones are by-gones, and business is business. If the chick was supplying Lopez, why couldn't she *also* supply Judite?"

"This was a woman, huh?"

"The blond he used to live with, yeah."

Carella looked at Meyer.

"*What* blond?" he said.

"I told you. The Anglo chick he used to live with."

"A *blond?*" Meyer said.

"Yeah, a blond," Lopez said. "What is it with you guys? You're hard of hearing?"

"When was this?" Meyer said.

"A year ago? Who remembers? Lopez had them coming and going like subway trains."

"What's her name, would you know?"

"No," Quadrado said, and took a last draw on the roach before dropping it on the floor. He was about to step on it when he realized he was still in his stocking feet. Meyer stepped on it for him. Quadrado sat, pulled on a pair of high-topped black sneakers, and began lacing them.

"Where'd they live?" Carella asked.

"On Ainsley. We still got a handful of Anglos living up here . . . the rent's cheap, they're mostly people trying to make it, you know? Like starving painters, or musicians, or these guys who make statues, you know?"

"Sculptors," Meyer said.

"Right, sculptors," Quadrado said. "That's a good way of putting it."

"Let me get this straight," Carella said. "You're saying that a year ago—"

"Around then."

"Lopez was living with a blond cocaine dealer—"

"No, not then."

"He *wasn't* living with her?"

"He *was* living with her, but she wasn't dealing coke. Not then."

"What *was* she doing?"

"Trying to make it. Same as anybody else."

"Trying to make it *how?*"

"I think she was a dancer or something."

Carella looked at Meyer again.

"I think she finally moved away because she got a part in a show," Quadrado said. "Last summer sometime. Moved back downtown, you know?"

"And surfaced again dealing coke," Carella said.

"Yeah."

"When?"

"The coke? Musta been last fall sometime. October, sometime."

"Began supplying Lopez with coke."

"Yeah."

"Who told you this?"

"Judite."

"Are you sure the girl wasn't coming up here to *buy* coke?"

"No, no. She was an ounce dealer, she was selling it. That's how come Judite figured she could pick up the trade now that Lopez was dead and gone. Same customers, same ounce dealer."

"How often did she come up here?"

"The blond? Every week."

"You know that for a fact?"

"I know it because that's what Judite told me."

"And this started in October sometime?"

"Yeah, that's when Lopez went into business. Again, this is all according to Judite. I got no personal knowledge of it myself."

"When did she come up?"

"On Sundays, usually."

"To deliver the coke."

"And maybe a little something else besides."

"What do you mean?"

"Renew old times, you know? In the sack."

"With Lopez?"

"According to Judite. Who knows if it's true or not? You get a chick taking all kinds of shit from a guy, she begins to imagine things, you know? She starts finding panties that ain't hers under every pillow, you know what I mean? She starts smelling other women on her sheets. It gets to her. Listen, my cousin was a little nuts, I'll tell you the truth. You *have* to be a little nuts to take up with a guy like Lopez."

"But you don't know the girl's name, huh?"

"No."

"Do you know the name of the show she was in?"

"No."

"But you're *sure* she used to live with Lopez."

"Positive. Not at first. She had an apartment in this building where there's a couple other Anglos. But then she moved in with him. Yeah, I'm sure of that. I mean, *that* I seen with my own eyes."

"What did you see?"

"Him and her coming and going out of the building together, all hours of the day and night. Look, it was common knowledge Lopez had himself a blond chick from downtown."

"What building was this?" Meyer asked.

"The building he was living in."

"When he got shot?"

"No, no. That's where he was living with *Judite*. That was on *Culver*. This was on *Ainsley*."

"Do you know the address?"

"No. It's near the drugstore there. On the corner of Ainsley and Sixth, I think it is. The Tru-Way drugstore."

"Would you recognize the girl if you saw her again?"

"The blond? Oh, sure. Nice-looking chick. What *she* saw in Lopez is *another* mystery, right?"

"Alonso, would you do us a favor?" Meyer said. "Would you come over to the station house with us? For just a minute?"

"Why? What'd *I* do?" Quadrado said.

"Nothing," Meyer said. "We want to show you some pictures."

12

Arthur Brown did not want to be doing what he was doing. Arthur Brown wanted to be watching television with his wife.

He did not want to be wading through all this stuff he and Kling had got, first, from Marvin Edelman's widow, and next, from Marvin Edelman's safety deposit box. If Arthur Brown had wanted to become an accountant, he would not have taken the patrolmen's test all those years ago. Accounting bored Brown. Even his *own* accounting bored him. He normally asked Caroline to balance the family check-books, something she did marvelously well.

It was twenty minutes past eleven.

The news would be over in ten minutes, and Johnny Carson would be coming on. Brown sometimes felt that the only two things uniting the people of the United States were Johnny Carson and the weather. Nothing short of a nuclear war could make everyone in the good old U.S. of A. feel more united than Johnny Carson and the weather. This winter, the weather was rotten all over the country. If you flew from here to Minneapolis, the weather would be the same. It gave you a feeling that here and Minneapolis were one and the same place. It united the people in adversity. If you flew from here to Cincinnati, the weather would be rotten there, too, and you'd step off the plane and immediately feel this enormous sense of brotherhood. Then, when you got to the hotel room and ordered your drink from room service, and unpacked your bag, and turned on your television set, why there would be old Johnny Carson at 11:30 P.M. sharp all over the country, and you knew that in Los Angeles they were watching Johnny Carson at the very same time, and in New York they were watching him, and in Kalamazoo, and Atlanta, and Washington, D.C., they were all watching Johnny Carson, and it made you feel like an essential part of the greatest people on earth, all of them sitting there with their fingers up their asses, watching Johnny Carson.

Brown figured that if Johnny Carson ran for the presidency, he would win hands down. What he wanted to do right now—well, ten minutes from now—was watch Johnny Carson. He did not want to be cross-checking the contents of Marvin Edelman's safety deposit box against Marvin Edelman's bank statements and canceled checks for the past year or so. That was something for an accountant to be doing. What a *cop* should be doing was sitting on the sofa with his arm around Caroline while they watched Lola Falana, who was scheduled to be Johnny's guest tonight, and whom Brown considered the most beautiful black woman in the world—next to Caroline, of course. He had never mentioned to Caroline how beautiful he thought Lola Falana was. After all these years on the force, he had learned that you never opened a door until you knew for certain what was behind it, and he wasn't quite sure what might be lurking behind Caroline's door these days. Brown had once mentioned that Diana Ross wasn't bad looking, and Caroline had thrown an ashtray at him. He had threatened to arrest her for attempted assault, and she had told him he could damn well glue the ashtray together *himself.* That had been a long time ago, and he hadn't tried opening that particular door since. He had the feeling he might find the same familiar tigress behind it.

He was very happy that Mrs. Edelman had found the duplicate key to her husband's safety deposit box, because the discovery had saved him and Kling the trouble of going all the way downtown to apply for a court order to open the box, which application might or might not have been granted depending on which magistrate they'd have come up against that afternoon. Some of the judges downtown, you got the feeling they were on the side of the *bad* guys. You got a judge like Walking Wilbur Harris, you could go into his courtroom with a guy holding a machete in one bloody hand and a severed head in the other, and old Wilbur would cluck his tongue and say, ''My, my, we've been a naughty boy today, haven't we? Prisoner released on his own recognizance.'' Or he'd set a ridiculous bail like ten thousand bucks for somebody who'd killed his mother, his father, his Labrador retriever, and all his pet goldfish. You got a judge like Walking Wilbur, it sometimes made you feel you were on the job for no reason at all in the world. You worked your tail off out there, you made your collar, and Wilbur let the man walk, sometimes clear to China, never to be heard from since. So what was the use? He was happy he hadn't had to go downtown today to beg for a court order to open that box.

He had not been happy when he'd seen the *size* of the safety deposit box, and he had been even less happy when he and Kling discovered just how many papers were *inside* the damn thing. Those papers were scattered before him on the desk in the spare room now, together with Edelman's bank statements and canceled checks and a can of beer. From the other room—his daughter Connie's playroom during the day, his and Caroline's television room at night—he could hear the identifying theme song of the ''Johnny Carson Show.'' He kept listening. He heard Ed McMahon announcing the list of guests (Lola Falana *was* one of them, sure as hell) and then he heard the familiar ''Heeeeeere's Johnnnnnnnnnny!'' and he sighed and took a long swallow of his beer, and then started separating the various documents they'd taken from the safety deposit box.

It was going to be a long night.

*   *   *

When the telephone ran, it startled Kling.

The phone was on an end table beside the bed, and the first ring slammed into the silence of the room like a pistol shot, causing him to sit bolt upright, his heart pounding. He grabbed for the receiver.

"Hello?" he said.

"Hi, this is Eileen," she said.

"Oh, hi," he said.

"You sound out of breath."

"No, I . . . it was very quiet in here. When the phone rang, it surprised me." His heart was still pounding.

"You weren't asleep, were you? I didn't—"

"No, no, I was just lying here."

"In bed?"

"Yes."

"I'm in bed, too," she said.

He said nothing.

"I wanted to apologize," she said.

"What for?"

"I didn't know about the divorce," she said.

"Well, that's okay."

"I wouldn't have said what I said if I'd known."

What she meant, he realized, was that she hadn't known about the *circumstances* of the divorce. She had found out since yesterday, it was common currency in the department, and now she was apologizing for having described what she'd called an "uh-oh!" scene, the wife in bed with her lover, the husband coming up the steps, the very damn thing that had happened to Kling.

"That's okay," he said.

It was not okay.

"I've just made it worse, haven't I?" she said.

He was about to say, "No, don't be silly, thanks for calling," when he thought, unexpectedly, Yes, you *have* made it worse, and he said, "As a matter of fact, you have."

"I'm sorry. I only wanted—"

"What'd they tell you?" he asked.

"Who?"

"Come on," he said. "Whoever told you about it."

"Only that there'd been some kind of problem."

"Uh-huh. What kind of problem?"

"Just a problem."

"My wife was playing around, right?"

"Well, yes, that's what I was told."

"Fine," he said.

There was a long silence on the line.

"Well," she said, and sighed. "I just wanted to tell you I'm sorry if I upset you yesterday."

"You didn't upset me," he said.

"You sound upset."

"I *am* upset," he said.

"Bert ..." she said, and hesitated. "Please don't be mad at *me,* okay? Please *don't!*" and he could swear that suddenly she was crying. The next thing he heard was a click on the line.

He looked at the phone receiver.

"What?" he said to the empty room.

The trouble with Edelman's records was that they didn't seem to add up. Or maybe Brown was just adding them up wrong. Either way, the arithmetic didn't come out right. There seemed to be large sums of money unaccounted for. The constant factor in Brown's calculations was the $300,000 they'd found in Edelman's safe. To Brown, this indicated at least *one* cash transaction. Possibly a *series* of cash transactions, fifty thou a throw, say, allowed to accumulate in his safe before—

Before *what?*

According to his bank statements and canceled checks, Edelman had not made any truly large deposits or withdrawals during the past year. His various outlays for business expenses were for trips to Amsterdam, Zurich, and other European cities— the air fares, the hotel rooms, the checks written to gem merchants in the Dutch city. But the purchases he'd made (and he was, after all, in the *business* of buying and selling precious gems) were relatively small ones: five thousand dollars here, ten thousand here, a comparatively big check for twenty-thousand dollars written to one Dutch firm. The subsequent bank deposits here in America seemed to indicate that Edelman turned a good, if not spectacular, profit on each of his purchases abroad.

From what Brown could figure, Edelman did a business somewhere in the vicinity of $200,000 to $300,000 a year. His current tax return had not yet been prepared— this was still only February, and it was not due till April 15—but on the last return he'd filed, he'd indicated a gross income of $265,523.12 for the year, with a taxable income of $226,523.12 after allowable deductions and business expenses. A little calculation told Brown that Edelman had deducted about 15 percent from his gross. With Uncle Sam, he was playing it entirely safe: the tax due had been $100,710.56; a check written on April 14 last year indicated that Edelman had completely satisfied his obligation to the government—at least on the income he'd *reported.*

It was the $300,000 in cash that kept bothering Brown.

Doggedly, he turned to the documents they had taken from Edelman's safety deposit box.

Kling looked at the telephone for a long time.

Had she been crying?

He hadn't wanted to make her *cry,* he hardly *knew* the girl. He went to the window and stared out at the cars moving steadily across the bridge, their headlights piercing the night. It was snowing again. Would it ever stop snowing? He had not wanted to make her cry. What the hell was *wrong* with him? *Augusta* is wrong with me, he thought, and went back to bed.

It might have been easier to forget her if only he didn't have to see her face everywhere he turned. Your average divorced couple, especially if there were no kids involved, you hardly ever ran into each other after the final decree. You started to forget. Sometimes you forgot even the *good* things you'd shared, which was bad but which was the nature of the beast called divorce. With Augusta, it was different. August was a model. You couldn't pass a magazine rack without seeing her face on the cover of at least one magazine each and every month, sometimes two. You couldn't turn on television without seeing her in a hair commercial (she had such beautiful hair) or a toothpaste commercial, or just last week in a nail polish commercial, Augusta's hands fanned out in front of her gorgeous face, the nails long and bright red, as if they'd been dipped in fresh blood, the smile on her face—ahh, Jesus, that wonderful smile. It got so he didn't want to turn on the TV set anymore, for fear Augusta would leap out of the tube at him, and he'd start remembering again, and begin crying again.

He lay fully dressed on the bed in the small apartment he was renting near the bridge, his hands behind his head, his head turned so that he could see through the window, see the cars moving on the bridge to Calm's Point—the theater crowd, he guessed; the shows had all broken by now, and people were heading home. People going home together. He took a deep breath.

His gun was in a holster on the dresser across the room.

He thought about the gun a lot.

Whenever he wasn't thinking about Augusta, he was thinking about the gun.

He didn't know why he'd let Brown take all that stuff home with him, he'd have welcomed the opportunity to go through it himself, give him something to do tonight instead of thinking about either Augusta or the gun. He knew Brown hated paperwork, he'd have been happy to take the load off his hands. But Brown had tiptoed around him, they all tiptoed around him these days, No, Bert, that's fine, you just go out and have a good time, hear? I'll be through with this stuff by morning, we'll talk it over then, okay? It was as if somebody very close to him had died. They all knew somebody had died, and they were uncomfortable with him, the way people are always uncomfortable with mourners, never knowing where to hide their hands, never knowing what to say in condolence. He'd be doing them all a favor, not only himself. Take the gun and . . .

Come on, he thought.

He turned his head on the pillow, and looked up at the ceiling.

He knew the ceiling by heart. He knew every peak and valley in the rough plaster, knew every smear of dirt, every cobweb. He didn't know some *people* the way he knew that ceiling. Sometimes, when he thought of Augusta, the ceiling blurred, he could not see his old friend the ceiling through his own tears. If he used the gun, he'd have to be careful of the angle. Wouldn't want to have the bullet take off the top of his skull and then put a hole in the ceiling besides, not his old friend the ceiling. He smiled. He figured somebody smiling wasn't somebody about to eat his own gun. Not yet, anyway.

Damn it, he really *hadn't* wanted to make her cry.

He sat up abruptly, reached for the Isola directory on the end table, and thumbed through it, not expecting to find a listing for her, and not surprised when he didn't.

Nowadays, with thieves getting out of prison ten minutes after you locked them up, not too many cops were eager to list their home numbers in the city's telephone books. He dialed Communications downtown, a number he knew by heart, and told the clerk who answered the phone that he wanted extension 12.

"Departmental Directory," a woman's voice said.

"Home number for a police officer," Kling said.

"Is *this* a police officer calling?"

"It is," Kling said.

"Your name, please?"

"Bertram A. Kling."

"Your rank and shield number, please?"

"Detective/Third, seven-four-five-seven-nine."

"And the party?"

"Eileen Burke."

There was a silence on the line.

"Is this a joke?" the woman said.

"A joke? What do you mean?"

"*She* called here ten minutes ago, wanting *your* number."

"We're working a case together," Kling said, and wondered why he'd lied.

"So did she *call* you?"

"She called me."

"So why didn't you ask *her* what her number was?"

"I forgot," Kling said.

"This isn't a *dating* service," the woman said.

"I told you, we're working a case together," Kling said.

"Sure," the woman said. "Hold on, let me run this through."

He waited. He knew she was making a computer check on him, verifying that he was a bona fide cop. He looked through the window. It was snowing more heavily now. Come *on,* he thought.

"Hello?" the woman said.

"I'm still here," Kling said.

"Our computers are down, I had to do it manually."

"Am I a real cop?" Kling said.

"Who knows nowadays?" the woman answered. "Here's the number, have you got a pencil?"

He wrote down the number, thanked her for her time, and then pressed one of the receiver rest buttons on top of the phone. He released the button, got a dial tone, was about to dial, and then hesitated. What am I starting here? he wondered. I don't want to start anything here. I'm not *ready* to start anything. He put the phone back on the cradle.

The contents of the safety deposit box were very interesting indeed. The way Brown was finally coming to understand it, Edelman's precious-gems business was a mere avocation when compared to what appeared to be his *true* business—the accumulation of real estate in various foreign countries. The deeds to land, houses, and office buildings in such diverse countries as Italy, France, Spain, Portugal, and England were dated from as far back as five years ago to as recently as six months ago. In July of last year alone, Edelman had purchased forty thousand square meters of land in a place called Porto Santo Stefano, for 200 *million* Italian lire. Brown did not know where Porto Santo Stefano was. Neither did he know how much the Italian lira had been worth six months ago. But a look at the financial pages of the city's morning paper told him that the current exchange rate was one hundred lire for twelve cents U.S. Brown had no idea how much the exchange rate had fluctuated during the past six months. But basing the purchase price on *today's* money market, Edelman would have spent something like $240,000 for the land he'd bought.

All well and good, Brown thought. A man wants to buy himself a big olive grove in Italy, fine, there was no law against that. But where was the canceled check, in either U.S. dollars *or* Italian lire, for the deal Edelman had closed in Rome on the eighth day of July last year? $240,000—more than that, when you figured in the legal fees and closing costs and taxes listed on the Italian closing statement—had exchanged hands last July.

Where had the $240,000 come from?

Kling kept pacing the room. He owed her an apology, didn't he? Or did he? What the hell, he thought, and went back to the phone, and dialed her number.

"Hello?" she said. Her voice sounded very small and a trifle sniffly.

"This is Bert," he said.

"Hello," she said. The same small sniffly voice.

"Bert Kling," he said.

"I know," she said.

"I'm sorry," he said. "I didn't mean to yell at you."

"That's okay," she said.

"Really, I'm sorry."

"That's okay," she said again.

There was a long silence on the line.

"So . . . how are you?" he said.

"Fine, I guess," she said.

There was another long silence.

"Is your apartment cold?" she asked.

"No, it's fine. Nice and warm."

"I'm freezing to death here," she said. "I'm going to call the Ombudsman's Office first thing tomorrow morning. They're not supposed to turn off the heat so early, are they?"

"Eleven o'clock, I thought."

"Is it eleven already?"

"It's almost midnight."

"Another day, another dollar," Eileen said, and sighed. "Anyway, they're not supposed to turn it off *entirely,* are they?"

"Sixty-two, I think."

"The radiators here are ice cold," she said. "I have *four* blankets on the bed."

"You ought to get an electric blanket," Kling said.

"I'm afraid of them. I'm afraid I'll catch on fire or something."

"No, no, they're very safe."

"Do *you* have an electric blanket?"

"No. But I'm told they're very safe."

"Or electrocuted," she said.

"Well," he said, "I just wanted to make sure you're okay. And really, I *am* sorry for—"

"Me, too." She paused. "This is the 'I'm-Sorry-You're-Sorry' scene, isn't it?" she said.

"I guess so."

"Yeah, that's what it is," she said.

Silence again.

"Well," he said, "it's late, I don't want to—"

"No, don't go," she said.

Silence again.

"Well," he said, "it's late, I don't want to . . ."

"No, don't go," she said. "Talk to me."

It seemed evident to Brown, as he studied the purchase prices on Edelman's various real estate documents—and translated the French francs, Spanish pesetas, Portuguese escudos, and British pounds to U.S. dollars—that Edelman had been involved in cash transactions that totaled some $4 million over the past five years. His *recorded* transactions, the purchases and sales covered by his various checks and subsequent deposits, amounted to some $1,275,000 over that same period of time. That left almost three million bucks unaccounted for—*and* unaccountable to the Internal Revenue Service.

The trips to Zurich, five in the past year alone, suddenly seemed to make sense, especially in view of the fact that the only expenses he'd incurred there had been for food and lodging. Apparently, Edelman conducted no business in the city of Zurich, no *gem* business, anyway. Then why did he go there? And why had his visits there been followed invariably but side excursions to *other* cities on the continent? His itineraries, based on the flow of checks in each city, seemed to follow a consistent pattern: Amsterdam, Zurich, Paris, London, with an occasional side trip to Lisbon. Brown guessed that Edelman's trips to Zurich were prompted not so much by a desire to visit the Alps as they were by need to visit his money.

There was no way of finding out whether or not he had a Swiss bank account; Swiss bankers were as tight with information as hookers were with free trade. Perhaps *Mrs.* Edelman knew something more about her husband's various trips abroad and his ownership (in *his* name only, Brown noticed) of real estate in five foreign countries. Perhaps *she* knew why Zurich had been an essential stop on all of his little journeys. Or perhaps, faced with what now looked like a simple case of tax evasion, she would claim she was an "innocent spouse" who knew nothing about her husband's business activities. Perhaps she didn't.

In any case, it now looked as if they had a mildly prosperous gem merchant who kept honest books on the little baubles he bought and sold here and there, deducted his operating expenses from his small profits, and then paid the tax man whatever was due on his net income. In the meantime, this same guy was spending large sums of cash for the unreported purchase of gems abroad, selling those gems for cash here in the United States—again without reporting the transactions—and then using his huge profits to buy not only *more* gems for resale later, but real estate as well. It did not take a financial genius to recognize that a cash buyer in today's real estate market, when mortgage interest rates both here and abroad were astronomical, would be welcomed with open arms in any country on the face of the earth. Edelman had been buying like a drunken Arab; his *real* business was netting him millions of dollars, none of it reported to Uncle Sam.

Brown reached for the phone on his desk, and dialed Kling's home number.

The line was busy.

She had asked him not to go, she had asked him to talk to her, and suddenly he could think of nothing else to say. The silence on the line lengthened. On the street outside, he heard the distinctive wail of a 911-Emergency truck, and wondered which poor bastard had jumped off a bridge or got himself pinned under a subway train.

"Do you ever get scared?" she asked.

"Yes," he said.

"I mean, on the job."

"Yes."

"I'm scared," she said.

"What about?"

"Tomorrow night."

"The nurse thing?"

"Yeah."

"Well, just don't—"

"I mean, I'm always a *little* scared, but not like this time." She hesitated. "He blinded one of them," she said. "One of the nurses he raped."

"Boy," Kling said.

"Yeah."

"Well, what you have to do . . . just be careful, that's all."

"Yeah, I'm always careful," she said.

"Who's your backup on this?"

"*Two* of them. I've got two of them."

"Well, that's good."

"Abrahams and McCann, do you know them?"

"No."

"They're out of the Chinatown Precinct."

"I don't know them."

"They seem okay, but . . . well, a backup can't stay *glued* to you, you know, otherwise he'll scare off the guy you're trying to catch."

"Yeah, but they'll be there if you need them."

"I guess."

"Sure, they will."

"How long does it take to put out somebody's eyes?" she asked.

"I wouldn't worry about that, really, that's not going to help, worrying about it. Just make sure you've got your hand on your gun, that's all."

"In my bag, yeah."

"Wherever you carry it."

"That's where I carry it."

"Make sure it's in your hand. And keep your finger inside the trigger guard."

"Yeah, I always do."

"It wouldn't hurt to carry a spare, either."

"Where would I carry a spare?"

"Strap it to your ankle. Wear slacks. Nurses are allowed to wear slacks, aren't they?"

"Oh, sure. But they like a leg show, you see. I'll be wearing the uniform, you know, like a dress. The white uniform."

"Who do you mean? Rank? They told you to wear a dress?"

"I'm sorry, what—"

"You said they like a leg show . . ."

"Oh. I meant the lunatics out there. They like a little leg, a little ass. Shake your boobs, lure them out of the bushes."

"Yeah, well," Kling said.

"I'll be wearing one of those starched things, you know, with a little white cap, and white panty hose, and this big black cape. I already tried it on today, it'll be at the hospital when I check in tomorrow night."

"What time will that be?"

"When I get to the hospital, or when I go out?"

"Both."

"I'm due there at eleven. I'll be hitting the park at a little after midnight."

"Well, be careful."

"I will."

They were silent for a moment.

"Maybe I could tuck it in my bra or something. The spare."

"Yeah, get yourself one of those little guns . . ."

"Yeah, like a derringer or something."

"No, that won't help you, that's Mickey Mouse time. I'm talking about something like a Browning or a Bernardelli, those little pocket automatics, you know?"

"Yeah," she said, "tuck it in my bra."

"As a spare, you know."

"Yeah."

"You can pick one up anywhere in the city," Kling said. "Cost you something like thirty, forty dollars."

"But those are small-caliber guns, aren't they?" she asked "Twenty-twos? Or twenty-fives?"

"That doesn't mean anything, the caliber. A gun like a twenty-two can do more damage than a thirty-eight. When Reagan got shot, everybody was saying he was lucky it was only a twenty-two the guy used, but that was wrong thinking. I was talking to this guy at Ballistics . . . Dorfsman, do you know Dorfsman?"

"No," Eileen said.

"Anyway, he told me you have to think of the human body like a room with furniture in it. You shoot a thirty-eight or a forty-five through one wall of the room, the
slug goes right out through another wall. But you shoot a twenty-two or a twenty-five
into that room, it hasn't got the power to *exit,* you understand? It hits a sofa, it ricochets off and hits the television set, it ricochets off that and hits a lamp—those are
all the organs inside the body, you understand? Like the heart, or the kidneys, or the
lungs, the bullet just goes bouncing around inside there doing a lot of damage. So you
don't have to worry about the caliber, I mean it. Those little guns can really hurt
somebody."

"Yeah," Eileen said, and hesitated. "I'm *still* scared," she said.

"No, don't be. You'll be fine."

"Maybe it's because of what I told you yesterday," she said. "My fantasy, you
know. I never told that to anyone in my life. Now I feel as if I'm tempting God or
something. Because I said it out loud. About . . . you know, *wanting* to get raped."

"Well, you don't *really* want to get raped."

"I know I don't."

"So that's got nothing to do with it."

"Except for fun and games," she said.

"What do you mean?"

"Getting raped."

"Oh."

"You know," she said. "You tear off my panties and my bra, I struggle a little
. . . like that. Pretending."

"Sure," he said.

"To spice it up a little," she said.

"Yeah."

"But not for real."

"No."

She was quiet for a long time. Then she said, "It's too bad tomorrow night is for
real."

"Take the spare along," Kling said.

"Oh, I *will,* don't worry."

"Well," he said, "I guess—"

"No, don't go," she said. "Talk to me."

Suddenly, and again, he could think of nothing else to say.

"Tell me what happened," she said. "The divorce."

"I'm not sure I want to," he said.

"*Will* you tell me one day?"

"Maybe."

"Only if you want to," she said. "Bert . . ." She hesitated. "Thank you. I feel
a lot better now."

"Well, good," he said. "Listen, if you *want* to . . ."

"Yes?"

"Give me a call tomorrow night. When you come in, I mean. When it's all over.
Let me know how it went, okay?"

"Well, that's liable to be pretty late."

"I'm usually up late."

"Well, if you'd like me to."

"Yes, I would."

"It'll be after midnight, you know."

"That's okay."

"Maybe later, if we make the collar. Time we book him—"

"Whenever," Kling said. "Just call me whenever."

"Okay," she said. "Well," she said.

"Well, good night," he said.

"Good night, Bert," she said, and hung up.

He put the receiver back on the cradle. The phone rang again almost instantly. He picked up the receiver at once.

"Hello?" he said.

"Bert, it's Artie," Brown said. "You weren't asleep, were you?"

"No, no."

"I've been trying to get you for the past half hour. I thought maybe you took the phone off the hook. You want to hear what I've got?"

"Shoot," Kling said.

13

It was nine o'clock in the morning, and the four detectives were gathered in the lieutenant's office, trying to make some sense of what they now knew. It had snowed six inches' worth overnight, and more snow was promised for later in the day. Byrnes wondered if it snowed this much in Alaska. He was willing to bet it didn't snow this much in Alaska. The detectives had told him what they knew, and he had taken notes while they spoke—first Meyer and Carella, and then Kling and Brown—and now he guessed he was supposed to provide the sort of leadership that would pull the entire case together for them in a wink. The last time he had pulled an entire case together in a wink was never.

"So Quadrado identified the girl, huh?" he said.

"Yes, Pete," Meyer said.

"Sally Anderson, huh?"

"Yes, Pete."

"You showed him her picture yesterday afternoon."

"*Four* pictures," Meyer said. "Hers and three we pulled from the files. All blonds."

"And he picked out the Anderson girl."

"Yes."

"And told you she used to live with Lopez and was supplying him with coke."

"Yes."

"He got this from his cousin, huh? The girl who was stabbed?"

"Only the coke part. The rest came from him."

"About Lopez and the girl living together?"

"It checks out, Pete. We located the building Lopez used to live in—right next door to the drugstore on Ainsley and Sixth—and the super confirmed that the Anderson girl was living there with him until last August sometime."

"Which is when *Fatback* went into rehearsal."

"Right."

"So there's our connection," Byrnes said.

"If we can trust it," Meyer said.

"What's not to trust?"

"Well, according to one of the dancers in the show, the Anderson girl went uptown every Sunday to *buy* coke."

"So now it looks like she went up there to *sell* it," Carella said.

"Big difference," Meyer said.

"And Quadrado got this from his cousin, huh?" Byrnes said.

"Yes."

"Reliable?"

"Maybe."

"Told him the girl went up there every Sunday to sell coke to Lopez, huh?"

"*Plus* a roll in the hay," Meyer said.

"How does that tie in with what her boyfriend said?" Byrnes asked.

"What do you mean?" Carella said.

"On one of your reports . . . where the hell is it?" Byrnes said, and began riffling through the D.D. forms on his desk. "Didn't he mention something about a deli? About the girl picking up delicatessen on Sundays?"

"That's right, but she could've been killing two birds with—"

"Here it is," Byrnes said, and began reading out loud. " 'Moore identified word "Del" on calendar as—' "

"That's right," Carella said.

" 'Cohen's Deli, Stem and North Rogers, where she went for bagels and lox, et cetera every Sunday.' "

"That's doesn't mean she couldn't have come *farther* uptown afterward, to deliver the coke to Lopez."

"He didn't know anything about this, huh? The boyfriend?"

"The coke, do you mean? Or the fact that she was still playing around with Lopez?"

"Take your choice," Byrnes said.

"He told us there were no other men in her life, and he told us she wasn't doing anything stronger than pot."

"Reliable?" Byrnes asked.

"He was the one who tipped us off to the ice operation," Meyer said.

"Yeah, what about *that?*" Byrnes asked. "Any connection to the murders?"

"We don't think so. The Anderson girl's involvement was a one-shot deal."

"Are you moving on it?"

"No proof," Meyer said. "We've put Carter on warning."

"A lot of good *that's* gonna do," Byrnes said, and sighed. "What about Edelman?" he asked Brown. "Are you sure you read all that stuff right?"

"Checked it three times," Brown said. "He was screwing Uncle, that's for sure. And laundering a lot of cash over the past five years."

"Buying real estate overseas, huh?"

"Yes," Brown said, and nodded.

"You think that's what all the money in his safe was for?"

"For his next trip over there, right."

"Any idea when he was going?"

"His wife told us next month sometime."

"So he was stashing the money till then, is that it?"

"That's the way it looks to us," Brown said.

"Where'd he get three hundred grand all of a sudden?" Byrnes asked.

"Maybe it wasn't all of a sudden," Kling said. "Maybe it was over a period of time. Let's say he comes back from Holland with a plastic bag of diamonds stuffed up his kazoo, and sells them off a little at a time, sixty grand here, fifty grand there, it adds up."

"And then goes to Zurich to put the money in a Swiss account," Brown said.

"Till he's ready to buy either more gems or more real estate," Kling said.

"Okay," Byrnes said, "a nice little racket. But how does it tie in with the other two murders?"

"Three, if you count the Quadrado girl."

"That was a cutting," Byrnes said. "Looks like a wild card to me, let's concentrate on the ones with the same gun. Any ideas?"

"Well, that's the thing," Carella said.

"*What's* the thing?"

"We can't find any connection but the one between Lopez and the girl. And even *that* one . . ." He shook his head. "We're talking peanuts here, Pete. Lopez had a handful of customers, the girl was maybe supplying him with . . . what? An ounce a week, tops? Tack on what she was selling to the kids in the show, and it still adds up to a very small operation. So why kill her? *Or* Lopez? What's the motive?"

"Maybe it *is* a crazy, after all," Byrnes said, and sighed.

The other men said nothing.

"If it's a crazy," Byrnes said, "there's nothing we can do till he makes his next move. If he knocks off a washerwoman in Majesta, or a truck driver in Riverhead, then we'll know the guy's choosing his victims at random."

"Which would make the Lopez and Anderson connection—"

"Coincidental, right," Byrnes said. "*If* the next one is a washerwoman or a truck driver."

"I don't like the idea of waiting around till the next body turns up," Meyer said.

"And *I* don't buy coincidence," Carella said. "Not with Lopez and Anderson both moving cocaine. Anything else, I'd say sure, the guy picked one victim here, another one downtown, a third one up here again, he's checkerboarding all over the city and shooting the first person he happens to run across on any given night. But not with cocaine involved. No, Pete.''

"You just told me the cocaine was a lowball operation," Byrnes said.

"It's *still* cocaine," Carella said.

"Was Lopez the *only* person she was supplying?" Byrnes asked.

The men looked at him.

"Or was this a bigger operation than we know?"

The men said nothing.

"Where was the *girl* getting it?" Byrnes said. He nodded briefly. "There's something missing," he said. "Find it."

Emma and Brother Anthony were celebrating in advance.

He had bought a bottle of expensive four-dollar wine, and they now sat drinking to their good fortune. Emma had read the letter, and had come to the same conclusion he had: the man who'd written that letter to Sally Anderson was the man who was supplying her with cocaine. The letter made that entirely clear.

"He buys eight keys of cocaine," Brother Anthony said, "gives it a full hit, gets twice what he paid for it."

"Time it gets on the street," Emma said, "who knows *what* it'd be worth?"

"You got to figure they step on it all the way down the line. Time your user gets it, it'll only be ten, fifteen percent pure. The eight keys this guy bought . . . he sounds like an amateur, don't he? I mean, going in *alone?* With four hundred grand in *cash?*"

"Strictly," Emma said.

"Well, so are we, in a way," Brother Anthony said.

"You're very generous," Emma said, and smiled.

"Anyway, those eight keys, time they hit the street up here, they've already been whacked so hard you're talking maybe thirty-*two* keys for sale. Your average user buying coke doesn't know *what* he's getting. Half the rush he feels is from thinking he paid so *much* for his gram."

Emma looked at the letter again. " 'The first thing I want to do is celebrate,' " she read. " 'There's a new restaurant on top of the Freemont Building, and I'd like to go there Saturday night. Very elegant, very continental. No panties, Sally. I want you to look very elegant and demure, but no panties, okay? Like the time we ate at Mario's down in the Quarter, do you remember? Then, when we get home . . .' " Emma shrugged. "Lovey-dovey stuff," she said.

"Girl had more panties than a lingerie shop," Brother Anthony said. "Whole *drawer*ful of panties."

"So he asks her not to *wear* any!" Emma said, and shook her head.

"I'm gonna buy you one of those little things ballet dancers wear," Brother Anthony said.

"Thank you, sir," Emma said, and made a little curtsy.

"Why you think she saved that letter?" Brother Anthony asked.

" 'Cause it's a love letter," Emma said.

"Then why'd she hide it in the collar of her jacket?"

"Maybe she was married."

"No, no."

"Or had another boyfriend."

"I think it was in case she wanted to turn the screws on him," Brother Anthony said. "I think the letter was her insurance. Proof that he bought eight keys of coke. Dumb amateur," he said, and shook his head.

"Try him again," Emma said.

"Yeah, I better," Brother Anthony said. He rose ponderously, walked to the telephone, picked up the scrap of paper on which he'd scribbled the number he'd found in the directory, and then dialed.

Emma watched him.

"It's ringing," he said.

She kept watching him.

"Hello?" a voice on the other end said, and Brother Anthony immediately hung up.

"He's home," he said.

"Good," she said. "Go see the man, dear."

The odd thing about the lunchtime skull session the boys of the Eight-Seven held in the squadroom at ten minutes past one that Thursday afternoon was that someone who wasn't even a policeman already knew the missing "something" that would have proved extremely valuable to their investigation if only *they'd* known it, which they didn't. They were *still* trying to find it, whereas Brother Anthony already knew it. Brother Anthony, as it were, happened to be a few steps ahead of them as they chewed, respectively, on their hot pastrami on rye, tuna on white, sausage and peppers on a roll, and ham on toasted whole wheat. They were drinking coffee in cardboard containers, also ordered from the diner up the street, a habit Miscolo tried to discourage because he felt it was an insult to the coffee he brewed and dispensed, gratis, in the Clerical Office. As Brother Anthony pushed his way through the subway turnstile some six blocks away, and ran toward the waiting graffiti-camouflaged train, managing to squeeze himself inside the car before the doors closed, the boys of the Eight-Seven were chewing on the case (*and* their sandwiches) from the top, trying to find the missing something that would take them exactly where Brother Anthony was heading. It did not speak well for the police department.

"I think the Loot is right," Meyer said. "We should scratch the Quadrado girl."

"Except she was looking to inherit Lopez's trade," Kling said.

"That *can't* be why Lopez was killed," Carella said. "For his *trade?* We're not dealing with Colombian hotshots here, we're—"

"How do you know we're not?" Brown asked.

"Because none of that crowd would even *spit* on a two-bit gram dealer like Lopez."

"Please, not while I'm eating," Meyer said.

"Sorry," Carella said, and bit into his sausage-and-peppers sandwich.

(It was funny how things broke down ethnically in this squadroom: Meyer was eating the pastrami on rye, Kling was eating the tuna on white, and Brown was eating the ham on toasted whole wheat.)

"So okay, let's scratch the Quadrado girl for the time being," Kling said.

"And start with the Anderson girl," Meyer said. "We know more about her than any of the other victims—"

"Well, that's isn't true," Brown said.

"*Relatively* more," Meyer said.

"Relatively, okay," Brown conceded. "But don't forget that three hundred G's in Edelman's safe."

"You done good work, okay, Sonny?" Meyer said. "What do you want, a medal?"

"I want Detective/First," Brown said, and grinned.

"Give him Detective/First," Meyer said to Carella.

"You got it," Carella said.

"So here's the girl—" Meyer started.

"Who are we talking about?" Kling asked. "The Quadrado girl, or the Anderson girl?"

"The Anderson girl. She comes up here every Sunday after she buys her deli at Cohen's, and she hops in the sack with Lopez—"

"Well, we don't know that for sure," Carella said.

"That's not important, whether she was still sleeping with him or not," Kling said. "What's important—"

"What's important is that she came up here to sell him *coke*," Meyer said. "You think I don't know that's the important thing?"

"Which her boyfriend knew nothing about," Carella said.

"Her boyfriend doesn't know his ass from his elbow," Brown said. "He's the one who thought she was into ice full time, isn't he?"

"Yeah," Carella said.

"Sent you on a wild goose chase," Brown said.

"It doesn't *matter* what he knew or what he didn't know," Kling said. "*We* know she was coming up here to sell dope."

"A little *shtup* in the hay," Meyer said, "move an ounce of cocaine at the same time, nice way to spend a Sunday afternoon."

"It's funny he didn't know anything about it," Carella said.

"Who're we talking about now?" Kling asked.

"Moore. Her boyfriend."

"That she was *shtupping* Lopez?"

"Or coming up here with coke. That's something she'd have told him, don't you think?"

"Yeah, but she didn't."

"Unless he was lying to us."

"For that matter, why'd he lie about the *ice?*" Kling asked.

"Who says he lied?" Brown asked. "Maybe he thought she really *was* running those tickets on a regular basis."

"Yeah, but it was a one-shot deal," Carella said. "Wouldn't he have *known* that? He was practically *living* with the girl."

"That makes *two* things he didn't know," Meyer said.

"That she was coming uptown with coke," Kling said, "and that she only ran the ice tickets once."

"Three things, if you count the hanky-panky with Lopez."

"Plus he didn't even know she herself was tooting."

"Said she only smoked a little grass."

"Practically living with the girl, but didn't know she was snorting coke."

"Or moving it."

"I keep remembering that a guy with three hundred thousand bucks in his safe was one of the victims," Brown said.

"Here he goes with the safe again," Meyer said.

"You're thinking cocaine numbers, am I right?" Kling asked.

"I'm thinking somebody had that kind of money to hand over to Edelman. And I'm thinking, yes, there's cocaine in this damn case, and those *are* the kind of numbers cocaine brings."

"Not in the small-time trade the Anderson girl had," Meyer said.

"Which is what we *know* about," Carella said.

"We have no reason to believe there was anything more," Meyer said. "Unless—"

"Yeah?"

"No, skip it. I just remembered—"

"Yeah, what?"

"He said they rarely spent Sundays together, didn't he? During the day, I mean. He said he was always busy on Sundays."

"Who's this?" Brown asked.

"Moore. The boyfriend."

"So what does that mean?"

"Busy doing *what?"* Meyer asked.

"Running to the deli," Kling said.

"And making it with Lopez."

"And selling him a little pile of nose candy."

"And that's what kept her busy all day long, huh?" Meyer said.

"It could keep a girl busy," Brown said. "Lopez *alone* could've kept a girl busy."

"The thing is," Meyer said, "If she was so damn *busy* all day Sunday . . ."

"Yeah, that," Carella said.

"What?"

"What the hell was she *doing* all that time? She writes *Del* on her calendar each and every Sunday, is that something important to write on your calendar? That she's coming uptown to get delicatessen? Cohen's is terrfic, I admit it, but does she have to list that on her *calendar?"*

"Steve, she listed *everything* on her calendar. Visits to her shrink, calls to Moore's mother in Miami, dance classes, meetings with her agent—so why not deli?"

"Then why didn't she just write *deli?* Do you know anybody who would write *del* for *deli?* We're talking about a single letter here, the letter *i,* the difference between *del* and *deli.* Why'd she write *del* instead of *deli?"*

"Why?" Brown asked.

"I don't *know* why, I'm just asking."

"Moore said it stood for 'deli.' "

"But Moore hasn't turned out to be so reliable, has he?" Kling said.

"First he tells us she only smoked grass, then he tells us she was involved in Carter's ice scam, then he tells us she went uptown for deli every Sunday ..."

"Too busy to check up on her."

"Too busy with his schoolwork."

"Too busy weighing hearts and livers."

"Busy, busy."

"Everybody busy."

"Doing *what?*" Brown said.

"On Sundays, you mean?"

"The girl, yeah. On Sundays."

"Deli and coke," Kling said, and shrugged.

"And Lopez in the sack."

"Moore had no reason to be lying to us," Meyer said. "He was probably just mistaken."

"Still," Carella said, "they were close."

"Very close."

"The girl even called his mother every week."

"Nice rich widow lady in Miami."

"So if they were *that* close, how come he was *mistaken* about all these things?"

"You'd think he'd have known."

"Miami, did you say?" Brown asked.

"What?"

"Is that where his mother lives?"

"Yeah."

"Miami," Brown said again.

"What about it?"

"I keep thinking of that three hundred grand in Edelman's—"

"Forget the safe for a minute, will you?"

"But just *suppose,*" Brown said.

"Suppose what?"

"That the three hundred was coke money."

"That's a long suppose."

"Not when we're dealing with two victims who were *moving* coke."

"Okay, so suppose the money *was* coke money?"

"Well, what do you think of when you think of Miami?"

The other detectives looked at him.

"Well, sure," Meyer said.

"But that's a long stretch," Kling said.

"No, wait a minute," Carella said.

"Just because a guy's *mother* lives in Miami—"

"That doesn't mean—"

"He isn't even Hispanic," Meyer said. "If he went down there looking to buy cocaine—"

"Anyway, what *with?*" Kling asked. "We're talking three hundred in the safe. To realize that kind of money *here,* he'd have needed at least *half* that to make his buy in Miami."

"His father just died," Carella said.

"When?" Brown asked.

"Last June. He told us he inherited some money, enough to set him up in practice when he gets out of school."

"How much did he inherit?" Kling asked. "Remember the number we're dealing with. There was three hundred grand in cash in that safe."

"What we're saying," Meyer said, and shook his head. "Just because Moore's mother lives in Miami, we're saying he went down there and spent whatever his father left him—"

"What's wrong with that?" Brown said. "That sounds pretty damn good to me, you want to know."

"Bought however much coke," Carella said, nodding.

"A *lot* of coke," Brown said. "Enough to turn over for three hundred G's."

"Which ended up in Edelman's safe."

"Bought diamonds from Edelman, or whatever."

"No record of the transaction."

"They both come out clean. Moore launders his dope money by trading it for diamonds, and Edelman launders his cash by buying real estate in Europe."

"Very nice," Meyer said. "If you believe in Peter Rabbit."

"What's wrong with it?" Carella said.

"First, we don't even *know* how much the guy inherited. It could've been ten, twenty thousand dollars. *If* that much. Next, we're saying a medical student could find his way around those Colombian heavies down there in Miami, and make a big guy without having his head handed to him on a platter."

"It's possible," Carella said.

"Anything's possible," Meyer said. "The sun could shine at midnight, why not? We're *also* saying he made contact with a guy dealing diamonds under the table—"

"Come on," Brown said, "that's the *easiest* part. There must be hundreds of guys like Edelman in this city."

"Maybe so. But even assuming *all* of it's possible—Moore inherited a lot of money, made contact somehow in Miami, doubled his money buying pure there and selling it cut here, laundered the money buying diamonds or rubies or whatever— let's accept *all* of that for the moment, okay?"

"It doesn't sound bad," Carella said.

"No, and it would explain why he was *mistaken* about so many things," Kling said.

"Fine," Meyer said. "Then maybe you can tell me how a man can be in two places at the same time."

"What do you mean?" Carella said.

"How could he have been outside the Anderson girl's apartment, shooting her dead, and be in his own apartment at the same time, studying and listening to the radio? You talked to this Loeb guy yourself, Steve, he confirmed that there were calls going back and forth all night long, he told you Moore's radio was on, he told you—''

And just then, Detective Richard Genero walked into the squadroom with his little Japanese radio in his hand. The detectives looked at him. Genero walked to his desk, set the radio down, glanced toward the lieutenant's open door—a certain sign that Byrnes was still out to lunch—and turned on the radio full blast.

"Okay," Meyer said. "Let's go."

There was very loud music coming from inside the apartment. Brother Anthony knocked on the door again, not certain his first several knocks had been heard.

"Who is it?" a voice inside called.

"Mr. Moore?" Brother Anthony said.

"Just a second," the voice called.

The music became softer, the guy inside had lowered the volume. Brother Anthony heard footsteps approaching the door.

"Who is it?" the voice said again, just inside the door this time.

He knew that in this city people did not open the door for strangers. Brother Anthony hesitated. He did not want to have to break down the door. "Police," he said.

"Oh."

He waited.

"Hold a second, will you?" the voice said.

He heard the footsteps retreating. He put his ear to the wooden door. A lot of moving around in there. He debated breaking down the door, after all. He decided to wait it out. The footsteps were approaching the door again. He heard the lock being turned, the tumblers falling. The door opened.

"Mr. Moore?" he said.

Moore took one look and started closing the door. Brother Anthony heaved his full weight against it, knocking it open, the imploding door forcing Moore away from it and back into the room. Brother Anthony followed the door into the room, slammed it shut behind him, and locked it. Moore was standing several feet back from the door now, nursing his shoulder where the door had hit him, staring at Brother Anthony. Behind him, the radio was sitting on an end table, still playing softly. Brother Anthony decided he would steal it when he left.

"Anybody here with you?" he asked.

"Who the hell are *you*?" Moore said.

"I have a letter you wrote," Brother Anthony said.

"What letter? What are you talking about?"

"From Miami. To a girl named Sally Anderson. Who is now dead," Brother Anthony said, "may God rest her soul."

Moore said nothing.

"Sally was getting cocaine from you," Brother Anthony said.

"I don't know what you mean."

"She was getting cocaine from you and selling it uptown," Brother Anthony said. "To Paco Lopez."

"I don't know anybody named Paco Lopez."

"But you *do* know Sally Anderson, don't you? You wrote to her in August saying you'd made a big cocaine buy in Miami. Where's that cocaine now, Mr. Moore? The cocaine Sally was dealing uptown."

"I don't know anything about any cocaine Sally was—"

"Mr. Moore," Brother Anthony said quietly, "I don't want to hurt you. We got Sally's name from a lady named Judite Quadrado, who got hurt because she wasn't quick enough to tell us what we wanted to know."

"Who's *we?*" Moore asked.

"That's none of your business," Brother Anthony said. "Your business is telling me where the coke is. That's the only business you have to worry about right now."

Moore looked at him.

"Yes, Mr. Moore," Brother Anthony said, and nodded.

"It's all gone," Moore said.

"You bought eight keys . . ."

"Where'd you find that letter?" Moore said. "She told me she'd burned it!"

"Then she was lying. And so are you, Mr. Moore. If all eight keys are gone, where was she getting the stuff she sold uptown?"

"Not *all* of them," Moore said. "I sold off six."

"And the other two?"

"I gave them to Sally. She took them out of here, I don't know where they are."

"You gave away *two* kilos of cocaine? For which you paid a hundred thousand *bucks?* Mr. Moore, you are full of shit."

"I'm telling you the truth. She was my girlfriend, I gave her—"

"No," Brother Anthony said.

"Whatever *she* did with it—"

"No, you didn't give away no two keys of coke, Mr. Moore. Nobody loves *nobody* that much. So where are they?"

"Sally took them out of here, they're probably still in her apartment. Unless the police confiscated them."

"That's a possibility," Brother Anthony said. "I can tell you for sure they're not in her apartment, so maybe the police *did* take them, who knows with those thieves?" Brother Anthony smiled. "But I don't think so. I don't think you'd have let a hundred thousand bucks worth of coke out of your sight, Mr. Moore. Not when it would've already been worth *twice* what you paid for it in Miami, nossir. So where is it?"

"I told you—"

Brother Anthony reached out suddenly. He grabbed Moore's hand in his own right hand, pulled Moore toward him, and then joined his left hand over Moore's so that the three hands together made a sort of hand sandwich, with Moore's hand caught between both Brother Anthony's. Brother Anthony began squeezing. Moore began yelling. "Shhh," Brother Anthony cautioned, and began squeezing harder. "I don't want no yelling, I don't want no people coming up here," he said, still squeezing. "All I'm going to do is break your hand if you don't tell me where the coke is. That's for starters. After that, I'll figure out what to break next."

"Please," Moore whispered. "P . . . please . . . let go."

"The coke," Brother Anthony said.

"The bed . . . the bedroom," Moore said, and Brother Anthony released his hand.

"Show me," he said. "How's your hand?" he asked pleasantly, and shoved Moore toward the open door to the bedroom. A suitcase was on the bed.

"Were you going someplace?" Brother Anthony asked.

Moore said nothing.

"Where is it?"

"In the bag," Moore said.

Brother Anthony tried the clasps. "It's locked," he said.

"I'll get the key," Moore said, and went to the dresser across the room.

"Taking a little trip, were you?" Brother Anthony asked, smiling, and then the smile froze on his face when Moore turned from the open dresser drawer with a gun in his hand. "Hey, wh—" Brother Anthony said, but that was all he ever said because Moore squeezed the trigger once, and then again, and both bullets from the .38 caught Brother Anthony in the face, one entering just below his left eye, the other shattering his teeth and upper gum. Brother Anthony reflexively clawed the air for support, and then fell in a mountainous brown heap at Moore's feet.

Moore looked down at him.

"You stupid son of a bitch," he whispered, and then he tucked the gun into his belt and went out of the bedroom, through the living room, and into the kitchen. There was no time to pack anything else now, the shots would bring suspicious neighbors. He had to get out of here fast now, take the diamonds, take what was left of the coke, just get out of here as fast as he could.

He opened the door on the refrigerator's freezer compartment.

There were two ice cube trays on a small shelf toward the rear of the freezer. He pried the tray on the left loose, and turned on the sink's hot water tap. He let the water run for several minutes before putting the tray under the faucet. The ice cubes began to melt. They took forever to melt. He kept listening for sounds in the hallway outside, someone coming, anyone coming, waiting for the ice cubes to melt. At last, he turned off the tap, carefully spilled the water from the tray into the sink, and removed the plastic dividing grid from the tray. The diamonds glistened wetly on the bottom of the tray. He spread them on a dish towel on the counter top, and was patting them dry when he heard the sound of wood splintering. He turned toward the living room. A voice shouted, "Moore?"

He came out of the kitchen with the gun in his hand, recognized Meyer and Carella, saw that both men were armed, saw two other armed men behind them, one white and one black, and might have put up a fight even then if Carella hadn't said, very softly, "I wouldn't."

He didn't.

14

They realized, by eleven o'clock that Thursday night, that he was going to tell them only what he wanted to tell them, and nothing more. That was why he waived his right to have an attorney present during the questioning. That was why he was flying in the face of the Miranda-Escobedo warnings, telling them whatever they wanted to know about the dope they'd found in his apartment, and the letter he'd written to Sally Anderson back in August, knowing they had him cold on the dope charge, but figuring he'd bluff his way out of the murders. *They* were looking for four counts—maybe five, if he'd also killed the Quadrado girl—of Murder One. He was looking for a Class A-1 Felony charge for possession of four or more ounces of a controlled substance, punishable by a minimum of fifteen to twenty-five years and a maximum of life. With a good lawyer, he could plea it down to a Class A-2 Felony, hoping for a minimum of three, and expecting to get out in two. As for having shot and killed Brother Anthony, he was claiming self-defense and hoping to get off scot-free. *They* were looking for him to do consecutive time on at least four homicide raps. *He* was hoping to be out on the street again within the imminently foreseeable future. They were somewhat at odds as concerned their differing aspirations and their separate versions of what had happened over the past nine days.

"Let's hear it one more time," Carella said.

"How often do I have to tell you?" Moore said. "Maybe I *should've* asked for a lawyer."

"You still can," Carella said, making sure for the record that Moore was volunteering all this information of his own free will. They were sitting in the Interrogation Room, a tape recorder whirring on the table between Moore and the four detectives with him. From where Carella sat, he could see past Moore to the two-way mirror on the wall behind him. Moore's back was to the mirror. No one was in the viewing room beyond the wall.

"Why would I need a lawyer?" Moore said. "I'm admitting the cocaine. You found the cocaine, you've got me on the cocaine."

"Two keys of it," Meyer said.

"Less than that," Moore said.

"But you bought *eight* keys in Miami. The letter you wrote—"

"I never should have written that letter," Moore said.

"But you did."

"Dumb," Moore said.

"So's murder," Kling said.

"I killed a man who came into my apartment with a gun," Moore said, almost by rote now. "We struggled, I grabbed the gun from him, and shot him. It was self-defense."

"The same gun that was used in three *other* murders," Brown said.

"I don't know anything about any other murders. Anyway, this wasn't *murder*, it was self-defense."

"I thought you were a medical student," Kling said.

"What?"

"Are you also studying law?"

"I know the difference between cold-blooded murder and self-defense."

"Was it cold-blooded murder when you killed Sally Anderson?" Carella asked.

"I didn't kill Sally."

"Or Paco Lopez?"

"I don't know anybody named Paco Lopez."

"How about Marvin Edelman?"

"I never heard of him."

"Then how do you account for those diamonds we found in your kitchen?"

"I bought them with the money I realized on the sale of the six keys."

"Who'd you buy them from?"

"How is that relevant? Is it against the law to buy diamonds?"

"Only if you later kill the man you bought them from."

"I bought them from somebody whose name I never knew."

"An anonymous diamond dealer, huh?" Meyer said.

"Passing through from Amsterdam," Moore said, and nodded.

"How'd you get onto him?"

"*He* contacted *me*. He heard I had some ready cash."

"How much cash?" Carella asked.

"I bought the eight keys for four hundred thousand."

"A bargain," Brown said.

"I told you, the man was doing me a favor."

"The man in Miami."

"Yes."

"What's *his* name?"

"I don't have to tell you that. He was doing me a favor, why should I get him in trouble?"

"Because you saved his son's life, right?" Meyer said.

"Right. The kid was choking to death. I did the Heimlich on him. The father said he wanted to do something for me in return."

"So that's how you got in the drug business, right?" Brown said.

"That's how."

"Where'd you get the four hundred thousand?"

"From my mother. The money my father left her."

"She had four hundred thousand bucks under her mattress, huh?"

"No. Some of it was in money market funds, the rest in securities. She was getting something like thirteen percent, I promised her fifteen percent in a month's time."

"Did you pay back the money?"

"Every cent."

"Plus the interest?"

"Fifteen percent."

"You gave back . . . what does that come to, Artie?"

"Fifteen percent on four hundred thousand?"

"For a month."

"It's five thousand dollars," Moore said.

"You returned the four hundred plus five, is that right?" Carella asked.

"I did."

"When?"

"At the end of September. I gave my mother the money shortly after *Fatback* opened."

"Is that how long it took you to cut and resell those eight keys?"

"Only six of them."

"What'd you get for selling off the six?"

"*Twelve,* by the time I cut them. I got sixty thousand a key."

"What does that come to, Artie?" Carella asked.

"It comes to seven hundred and twenty thousand dollars," Moore said.

"And you returned four hundred and five of that to your mother."

"Yes."

"Which left you with—"

"Three hundred and fifteen."

"Three hundred of which you spent to buy diamonds from Edelman."

"I don't know anybody named Edelman," Moore said.

"But that's how much you spent for the diamonds you bought, isn't it?"

"Close to it."

"From this Dutchman who was passing through, right?"

"Right."

"What'd you get for that kind of money?"

"About twenty-five carats. I got a break because it was a cash transaction."

"So how many stones did you buy?"

"About three dozen. Most of them quarter and half-carat stones. A few one-carat stones. Different sizes and cuts, American, European—well, you saw them."

"Just enough to fit in an ice cube tray, huh?"

"I thought of that later."

"First place a burglar would look," Meyer said.

"I don't know anything about burglars."

"Why'd you pick diamonds?"

"A good investment. Over the past thirty years—before the bottom fell out—diamonds have gone up in value more than a thousand percent. I figured they had to start going up again."

"You're just an enterprising young businessman, right?" Brown said.

Moore said nothing.

"Where'd you sell those six keys?"

"I don't have to tell you that."

"Why'd you hang on to the other two?"

"That was Sally's idea. She figured we could get more for it by selling them off to gram dealers."

"Like Paco Lopez."

"I don't know anyone named Paco Lopez. Sally figured it might take a while longer, but over the long run we'd make maybe an extra fifty thousand on those two keys. By ouncing it out to gram dealers."

"*Another* enterprising young businessman," Brown said.

"*Woman,*" Meyer said.

"*Person,*" Kling said.

"So why'd you decide to kill all these people?" Carella asked casually.

"I didn't kill anyone but the man who broke into my apartment," Moore said. "And that was self-defense. The man came in with a gun, we struggled, I took the gun away from him, and shot him. He was trying to hold me up. It was self-defense."

"Knew you had two keys of dope in there, huh?"

"I don't know *what* he knew. Anyway, it was less than two keys. We'd been dipping into it ever since I got back from Miami."

"Selling it here and there around town."

"Sally took care of that."

"Made her deliveries on Sundays, did she?"

"Yes."

"That's what the *del* stood for, right? Not 'delicatessen.' 'Deliveries.' "

"Deliveries, yes."

"Did Paco Lopez put her onto the *other* gram dealers she—"

"I don't know anyone named Paco Lopez."

"Why'd you kill *him* first?"

"I don't know who you're talking about."

"Why'd you kill Sally?"

"I didn't."

"And Edelman."

"I don't know who Edelman is. You've got me on the dope, so charge me with the dope. I killed an armed intruder in self-defense. I don't know what you can charge me with on *that*—"

"Try homicide," Carella said.

"If self-defense is homicide, fine. But no jury in its right mind—"

"You're an expert on the jury system, too, huh?" Meyer said.

"I'm not an expert on anything," Moore said. "I happened across a good investment, and I took advantage of it."

"And then decided to protect it by killing—"

"The only person I killed is the man who broke into my apartment."

"Did he know there'd be diamonds in there?"

"I don't know what he knew."

"Just happened to break in on you, is that it?"

"Happens all the time in this city."

"Didn't know there'd be dope, didn't know there'd be diamonds."

"I never saw him before in my life, how would I know what his motive was? He forced his way in with a gun. We struggled—"

"Yes, and you took the gun away from him and shot him."

"Yes."

"Guy built like a grizzly bear, you took the gun away from him?"

"I can handle myself," Moore said.

"Only too well," Carella said, and sighed. He looked up at the wall clock. It was ten minutes to twelve. "Okay," he said, "let's go through it one more time."

She felt stupid with a gun in her bra.

The gun was a .22 caliber Llama with a six-shot capacity, deadly enough, she supposed, if push came to shove. Its overall length was four and three-quarter inches, just small enough to fit cozily if uncomfortably between her breasts. It weighed only thirteen and a half ounces, but it felt like thirteen and a half *pounds* tucked there inside her bra, and besides, the metal was cold. That was because she had left the top three buttons of the uniform unfastened, in case she needed to get in there in a hurry. The wind was blowing up under the flapping black cape she was wearing, straight from the North Pole and directly into the open V-necked wedge of the uniform. Her breasts were cold, and her nipples were cold and erect besides— but maybe that was because she was scared to death.

She did not like the setup, she had told them that from the start. Even after the dry run this afternoon, she had voiced her complaints. It had taken her eight minutes to cross the park on the winding path that ran more or less diagonally through it, walking at a slightly faster than normal clip, the way a woman alone at midnight would be expected to walk through a deserted park. She had argued for a classic bookend surveillance, one of her backup men ahead of her, the other behind, at reasonably safe distances. Both of her backups were old-timers from the Chinatown Precinct, both of them Detectives/First. Abrahams ("Call me Morrie," he said back at the precinct, when they were laying out their strategy) argued that anybody walking point would scare off their rapist if he made a head-on approach. McCann ("I'm Mickey," he told her) argued that if the guy made his approach from *behind,* he'd spot the follow-up man and call it all off. Eileen could see the sense of what they were saying, but she still didn't like the way *they* were proposing to do it. What *they* wanted to do was plant one of them at either end of the path, at opposite ends of the park. That meant that if their man hit when she was midway through the park, the way he'd done on his last three outings, she'd be four minutes away from either one of them—okay, say three minutes, if they came at a gallop.

"If I'm in trouble," she said, "you won't be able to reach me in time. Why can't we put you under the trees someplace, hiding under those trees in the middle of the park? That's where he hit the last three times. If you're under the trees there, we won't have four minutes separating us."

"Three minutes," Abrahams said.

"That's where he hit the last three times," she said again.

"Suppose he scouts the area this time?" McCann said.

"And spots two guys hiding under the trees there?" Abrahams said.

"He'll call it off," McCann said.

"You'll have the transmitter in your bag," Abrahams said.

"A lot of good *that'll* do if he decides to stick an ice pick in my eye," Eileen said.

"Voice-activated," McCann said.

"Terrific," Eileen said. "Will that get you there any faster? I could yell bloody murder, and it'll still take you three minutes—*minimum*—to get from either end of that park. In three minutes, I can be a statistic.''

Abrahams laughed.

"Very funny," Eileen said. "Only it's *my* ass we're talking about here."

"I dig this broad," Abrahams said, laughing.

"That radio can pick up a whisper from twenty-five feet away," McCann said.

"So what?" Eileen said. "It'll *still* take you three minutes to reach me from where you guys want to plant yourself. Look, Morrie, why don't *you* go in? How about you, Mickey? Either one of you in drag, how does that sound? *I'll* sit outside the park, listening to the radio, okay?"

"I really dig this broad," Abrahams said, laughing.

"So what do you want to do?" McCann asked her.

"I told you. The trees. We hide you under the trees."

"Be pointless. The guy combs the park first, he spots us, he knows we've got it staked out. That's what you want to do, we might as well forget the whole thing."

"Let him go on raping those nurses there," Abrahams said.

Both men looked at her.

So that was what it got down to at last, that was what it always got down to in the long run. You had to show them you were just as good as *they* were, willing to take the same chances *they'd* have taken in similar circumstances, prove to them you had *balls*.

"Okay," she said, and sighed.

"Better take off those earrings," McCann said.

"I'm wearing the earrings," she said.

"Nurses don't wear earrings. I never seen a nurse wearing earrings. He'll spot the earrings."

"I'm wearing the earrings," she said flatly.

So here I am, she thought, ball-less to be sure, but wearing my good-luck earrings, and carrying one gun tucked in my bra, and another gun in the shoulder bag alongside the battery-powered, voice-activated FM transmitter that can pick up a whisper from twenty-five feet away—according to McCann, who, by her current estimate, was now two and a half minutes away at the southeast corner of the park, with Abrahams *three* and a half minutes away at the northwest corner.

If he's going to make his move, she thought, this is where he'll make it, right here, halfway through the park, far from the streetlights. Trees on either side of the path, spruces, hemlocks, pines, snow-covered terrain beyond them. Jump out of the trees, drag me off the path the way he did with the others, this is where he hit the last three times, this is where he'll do it now. The descriptions of the man had been conflicting, they always seemed to be when the offense was rape. One of the victims had described him as being black, another as white. The girl he'd blinded had sobbingly told the investigating officer that her assailant had been short and squat, built like a gorilla. The other two nurses insisted that he'd been very tall, with the slender, muscular body of a weight lifter. He'd been variously described as wearing a business suit, a black leather jacket and blue jeans, and a jogging suit. One of the nurses said he was in his mid-forties, another said he was no older than twenty-five, the third had no opinion whatever about his age. The first nurse he'd raped said he'd been blond. The second one said he'd been wearing a peaked hat, like a baseball cap. The one he'd blinded—her hand began sweating on the butt of the .38 in her shoulder bag.

It was funny the way her hands always started sweating whenever she found herself in a tight situation. She wondered if McCann's hands were sweating. Three minutes behind her now, Abrahams equidistant at the other end of the park. She wondered if the transmitter was picking up the clicking of her boots on the asphalt path. The path was shoveled clear of snow, but there were still some patches of ice on it, and she skirted one of those now, and looked into the darkness ahead, her eyes accustomed to the dark, and thought she saw something under the trees ahead, and almost stopped dead in her tracks—but that was not what a good decoy was supposed to do. A good decoy marched right into it, a good decoy allowed her man to make his move, a good decoy—

She thought at first she was hearing things.

Her hand tightened on the butt of the gun.

Somebody whistling?

What?

She kept walking, peering into the darkness ahead, past the midway point now, McCann a bit more than three and a half minutes behind her, Abrahams two and a half minutes away in the opposite direction, *still* too far away, and saw a boy on a skateboard coming up the path, whistling as he curved the board in graceful arcs back and forth across the path. He couldn't have been older than thirteen or fourteen, a hatless youngster wearing a blue ski parka and jeans, sneakered feet expertly guiding the skateboard, arms akimbo as he balanced himself, a midnight whistler enjoying the dark silence of the empty park, closer, now, still whistling. She smiled, and her hand relaxed on the butt of the gun.

And then, suddenly, he swerved the board into her, bending at the knees, leaning all his weight to one side so that the board slid out from under him, the wheels coming at her, the underside slamming her across the shins. She was pulling the gun from her bag when he punched her in the face. The gun went off while it was still inside the bag, blowing out leather and cigarettes and chewing gum and Kleenex tissues—but not the radio, she hoped, Jesus, not the radio!

In the next thirty seconds, it couldn't have been longer than that, her finger tightening in reflex on the trigger again, the gun's explosion shattering the stillness of the night again, their breaths pluming brokenly from their mouths, merging, blowing away on the wind, she thought, remembered, *Force part of psychological interplay,* he punched her over the breast, *Attendant danger of being severely beaten or killed,* the gun went off a third time, his fist smashed into her mouth, *But he's just a kid.* She tasted blood, felt herself going limp, he was grabbing her right arm, turning her, behind her now, forcing her to her knees, he was going to break her arm, "Let go of it!" yanking on the arm, pulling up on it, "Let *go!*" her hand opened, the gun clattered to the asphalt.

She tried to get to her feet as he came around her, but he shoved her back onto the path, hard, knocking the wind out of her. As he started to straddle her, she kicked out at him with her booted left foot, white skirts flying, the black heel of the boot catching him on the thigh, a trifle too low for the money. She wondered how many seconds had gone by now, wondered where McCann and Abrahams were, she'd *told* them the setup was no good, she'd *told* them—he began slapping her. Straddling her, slapping her, both hands moving, the slaps somehow more painful than the punches had been, dizzying, big calloused hands punishing her cheeks and her jaw, back and forth, her head flailing with each successive slap, his weight on her chest, pressing on her breasts—the gun. She remembered the gun in her bra.

She tried to twist away from him, her arms pinioned by his thighs on either side of her, tried to turn her head to avoid the incessant slaps, and idiotically noticed the nurse's cap lying white and still on the path where it had fallen. She could not free her arms or her hands, she could not get to the gun.

The slapping stopped abruptly.

There was only the darkness now, and the sound of his vaporized breath coming in short, ragged bursts from his mouth. His hands reached for the front of the uniform. He grasped the fabric. He tore open the front, buttons flying, reached for her bra and her breasts—and stopped again. He had seen the gun, he must have seen the gun. His silence now was more frightening than his earlier fury had been. *One* gun might have meant a streetwise lady who knew the city's parks were dangerous. *Another* gun, this one hidden in a bra, could mean only one thing. The lady was a cop. He shifted his weight. She knew he was reaching for something in his pants pocket. She knew the something would be a weapon, and she thought *He's going to blind me.*

In that moment, fear turned to ice. Cold, crystalline, hard. In that moment, she knew she couldn't count on the cavalry or the marines getting here in time, there was nobody here but us chickens, boss, and nobody to look after little Eileen but little Eileen herself. She took advantage of the shift of his body weight to the left, his right hand going into his pocket, the balance an uneasy one for the barest fraction of a second, enough time for her to emulate the movement of his own body, her left shoulder rising in easy symmetry with his own cant, their bodies in motion together for only a fraction of a second, movement responding to movement as though they were true lovers, and suddenly she lurched, every once of strength concentrated in that left shoulder, adding her own weight and momentum to his already off-cehter tilt—and he toppled over.

His right hand was still in his pocket as she scrambled to her feet. He rolled over onto the path, his right hand coming free of his pocket, the switchblade knife snapping open just as she pulled the Llama out of her bra. She knew she would kill him if he moved. He saw the gun in her hand, steady, leveled at his head, and perhaps he saw the look in her eyes as well, though there was no moon. She liked to think later that what happened next had nothing to do with the sound of footsteps pounding on the path from north and south, nothing to do with the approach of either Abrahams or McCann.

He dropped the knife.

First he said, "Don't hurt me."

Then he said, "Don't tell on me."

"You okay?" Abrahams asked.

She nodded. She couldn't seem to catch her breath. The gun in her hand was trembling now.

"I would've killed him," she whispered.

"What?" Abrahams said.

"A kid," she whispered.

"We better call for a meat wagon," McCann said. "It looks to me like she's—"

"I'm all *right!*" she said fiercely, and both men stared at her. "I'm all right," she said more softly, and felt suddenly faint, and hoped against hope that she wouldn't pass out in front of these two hairbags from the Chinatown Precinct, and stood there sucking in great gulps of air until the queasiness and the dizziness passed, and then she smiled weakly and said, "What kept you?"

They had not finished with Moore until almost a quarter past one, and Kling did not get home until two in the morning. They had got from him essentially what they'd expected to get: only what he chose to admit. In approximately eight hours, Carella and Meyer would be accompanying Moore to the Complaint Room at Felony Court, where a clerk would draw up a short-form complaint listing the charges against him. This so-called yellow sheet would follow him later that morning to his arraignment—and indeed become a part of his permanent record. In the meantime, there was not much anyone could do until the wheels of justice began grinding, slowly.

He was exhausted, but the first thing he did when he came into the apartment was dial Eileen's number. There was no answer. He let the phone ring a dozen times, hung up, dialed it again, slowly and carefully this time, and let it ring another dozen times. Still no answer. He thumbed through the *R*'s in his directory, and found the listing for Frank Riley, a man who'd gone through the Academy with him, and who was now a Detective/Second working out of the Chinatown Precinct. He dialed the precinct, told the desk sergeant who he was, and then asked if he had any information on the stakeout outside Worth Memorial earlier that night. The desk sergeant didn't know anything about any stakeout. He put Kling through to the squadroom upstairs, where he talked to a weary detective on the graveyard shift. The detective told him he heard it had gone down as scheduled, but he didn't know all the details. When Kling asked him if Detective Burke was okay, he said there was nobody by that name on the Chinatown Squad.

He was wondering who to try next when the knock sounded on his door. He went to the door.

"Who is it?" he asked.

"Me," she answered. Her voice sounded very weary and very small.

He took off the night chain, unlocked the deadbolt, and opened the door. She was wearing a navy peajacket over blue jeans and black boots. Her long red hair was hanging loose around her face. In the dim illumination of the hallway light bulb, he could see that her face was discolored and bruised, her lip swollen.

"Okay to come in?" she asked.

"Come in," he said, and immediately, "Are you okay?"

"Tired," she said.

He locked the door behind her, and put on the night chain. When he turned from the door, she was sitting on the edge of the bed.

"How'd it go?" he asked.

"We got him," she said. "Fourteen years old," she said. "I almost killed him," she said.

Their eyes met.

"Would you mind very much making love to me?" she said.

15

In some cities, it was called a "first appearance." In this city, it was called an "arraignment." However you sliced it and whatever you called it, it was the first time a person charged with a crime appeared in a courtroom before a judge.

They had talked over their strategy beforehand with the assistant district attorney assigned to the case. They knew Moore's attorney would advise him to plead not guilty to *all* the charges, and whereas they were certain the dope charge would stick, they were on more tenuous ground where it came to the murders. Their fear was that they'd come up against a lenient judge who might accept Moore's contention that Brother Anthony's murder was committed in self-defense, and might set what he thought to be a reasonable bail for the drug offense. Even though the ballistics tests on the Smith & Wesson would not be completed until the case was presented to a grand jury sometime next week, they decided to tack on to their complaint the three additional counts of Murder One, hoping a judge would be intimidated by quantity and weight when it came time to grant or deny bail. If the gun that had killed Brother Anthony turned out to be the same gun that had fired the fatal bullets into Paco Lopez, Sally Anderson, and Marvin Edelman, they felt there was a good chance the grand jury would hand down a true bill on all *four* murder counts. When the case later came to trial, it would then be Moore's word alone that would keep him from spending more time in prison than there were days on an eternal calendar. The important thing now was to make sure he did not walk out of that courthouse. They felt certain that if bail was granted, they would never see him again.

The judge hearing the case was Walking Wilbur Harris.

The court attendant, who was called a bridge in this city, sat before Harris's bench and read off the name of the defendant, and then the charges against him. Harris looked out over his rimless spectacles and said, "Are these charges correct, officer?"

"Yes, Your Honor," Carella said.

The four of them were standing before the judge's bench, Carella with the assistant D.A., Moore with his attorney. Harris turned to Moore.

"You may have a hearing in this court," he said, "or an adjournment for purpose of obtaining a lawyer or witnesses, or waive that hearing and let the case go to a grand jury. Do you have a lawyer?"

"Yes, Your Honor," Moore said.

"Is he here present?"

"I am representing the defendant," Moore's attorney said.

"Ah, yes, Mr. Wilcox," Harris said. "Didn't recognize you."

Wilcox smiled. "Your Honor," he said, in recognition of the recognition.

"How do you plead to these charges?" Harris asked. "First count, Criminal Possession of a controlled substance in the First Degree, contrary to penal law, Section two-twenty point twenty-one."

"Not guilty, Your Honor," Moore said.

"Second, third, fourth, and fifth counts, Murder in the First Degree, contrary to penal law, Section one-twenty-five point twenty-seven."

"Not guilty, Your Honor," Moore said.

"Pending a grand jury hearing," Wilcox said, going straight for the jugular, "may I at this time request bail for the defendant?"

"The man's been charged with *four* counts of First Degree *Murder!*" Harris said, looking surprised.

"He acted in self-defense on the first count, Your Honor, and had nothing whatever to do with the other three murders charged."

"Mr. Delmonico?" Harris said, turning to the A.D.A.

"We have good and reasonable cause to believe the same weapon was used in all four murders, Your Honor."

"What good and reasonable cause?" Harris asked.

"Detective Carella here has ballistics reports indicating the same gun was used in the murders of Paco Lopez, Sally Anderson, and Marvin Edelman."

"What about this other one?" Harris said. "Anthony Scalzo."

"The man was killed—"

"The gun is now with —"

"One at a time," Harris said.

"The man was killed in self-defense, Your Honor," Wilcox said. "He was armed when he broke into the defendant's apartment. There was a struggle during which my client disarmed him and shot him. In self-defense."

"Mr. Delmonico?"

"The gun is now with Ballistics Section, Your Honor. We should have a report sometime before the grand jury hearing next week."

"What makes you think it's the same gun?" Harris asked.

"It's a thirty-eight-caliber Smith and Wesson, Your Honor. That's the make and caliber of the gun used in the previous three murders. The same gun for all three murders."

"But you don't know if it's the same gun that was used in this *fourth* homicide."

"Not yet, Your Honor."

"Your Honor—" Wilcox said.

"Your Honor—" Delmonico said.

"Just a minute here," Harris said. "Mr. Wilcox?"

"Your Honor," Wilcox said, "there *is* no ballistics evidence that would link the gun used in the previous murders with the shooting that took place in my client's apartment yesterday. But even if there *did* exist such evidence, it's our contention that the gun belonged to Anthony Scalzo and *not* my client."

"Mr. Delmonico?"

"Your Honor," Delmonico said, "we feel such evidence will be forthcoming. In any event, given the gravity of the charges before you, I respectfully submit that the granting of bail would be inadvisable in this case."

"Yes, well, that's for *me* to decide, isn't it?" Harris said.

"Yes, Your Honor, of course."

"Bail is granted in the amount of one hundred thousand dollars," Harris said.

"We are prepared to meet that bail, Your Honor," Wilcox said.

"Very well, remand the defendant."

"May I have a few words with my client?" Wilcox asked.

"Take him aside. Next case."

As the bridge read off the name of the next defendant and the charges against him, Carella watched Wilcox in whispered conversation with Moore. Wilcox was a good lawyer; Carella knew he'd have discussed with Moore beforehand the amount of bail he thought he could meet. All they had to come up with now was $10,000 in cash and collateral for the rest, easy enough when you owned twenty-five carats of diamonds worth a cool three hundred thousand bucks. Or would Wilcox simply phone Moore's mother in Miami and ask her to wire him a mere $100,000? Either way, Moore would spend a relaxed day in custody at either the Municipal House of Detention crosstown on Daley Street, or else in the Parsons Island Jail in the middle of the river Dix. By nightfall, he'd be out on the street again. He watched as they led Moore out. He watched as Wilcox exchanged a few words with the bail bondsman. He rarely thought in Italian, but the words *La comedia è finita* crossed his mind. He walked to the back of the courtroom, where Delmonico and Meyer were waiting.

"I told you," Meyer said. "There ain't no justice in this world."

But maybe there was, after all.

There was hardly any packing left to do.

He had done most of his packing yesterday afternoon before he'd been interrupted by the man in the monk's habit, whose name he now knew was Anthony Scalzo. Nothing had changed. He *still* planned to get out of here as soon as possible, out of the city and the state for sure, maybe out of the country as well. The only difference now was that his mother would be out the hundred thousand dollars she'd provided for his bail, a small enough price to pay for his freedom; anyway, he planned to pay her back as soon as he got settled someplace.

As he took his toilet articles from the medicine cabinet in the bathroom, he replayed the little session with the mastermind sleuths of the 87th Precinct, four of them sitting there playing cat and mouse with him, each and every one of them knowing they didn't have a chance in hell of getting him on those three murders unless he decided to fall to his knees in confession. He was tempted—*almost*, but not quite—to forget all about running, take his chances with a jury instead. They'd buy his plea of self-defense, and he'd end up spending a little time—maybe two years—in prison on the drug charge. But he supposed there was no such thing as a *little* time in prison; *any* time in prison was a *lot* of time. Better to do it this way. Jump bail, get out of the country, use the diamonds—but, ah, what a waste. Two years of medical school, what a waste. He wondered what his father would have said if he was still alive. Well, dad, he thought, I saw my opportunity and I grabbed it. It would've all worked out fine, I'd have had the money *and* my medical degree besides, nobody the wiser, nobody hurt, dad, if only . . .

The one person I thought I could trust.

Sally.

Would I have written to her otherwise?

Thought I could trust her. Told me we didn't have to sell off *all* the stuff right away, we could—well, listen, who knew anything at *all* about cocaine? Babe in the woods down there in Miami, Portoles leading me by the hand, I will make you rich, *amigo,* for saving my son. Tested the stuff for me, I didn't even know enough to do that. Paying fifty thousand a key, never thought to ask if it was *real* cocaine. Cobalt thiocyanate. Blue reaction. What'd he say? The brighter the blue, the better the girl. Referring to the coke. Called it girl. Best pure you can find, he told me. Yours now. Mine. Sally's, too, sort of. Told me we could hold back two kilos, ounce them out, she knew somebody uptown who'd be interested, somebody who would put them on to other customers. Knew more about cocaine than I'll *ever* know. Said she'd been shooting it even before it got fashionable, while she was studying dance in London, used to share what she called Cocaine Fucks with an oboe player she was living with. Shared those with her friend uptown, too, but who knew that at the time? Trusted her. One thing you should *never* trust is a woman in bed. Spread any woman's legs, and secrets fly out of her like butterflies. Told him everything. Told him about our little cache, the two keys of cocaine we were milking. Our insurance, she called them. Sure.

He zipped up his toilet kit and carried it to the open suitcase in the bedroom. He stood looking down into the suitcase, as though he'd forgotten something. The gun? Funny how you became accustomed to having a gun around, accustomed to using it. Police property now, evidence tag on it, a lot of good it would do them once they realized he'd packed his tent, twenty-five carats worth of diamonds to turn into cash anywhere in the world. Still, if only . . .

If only she hadn't shared our secret with him, if only he hadn't come to me, slimy little Puerto Rican bastard, wanting a piece of the action, *demanding* a piece of the action, threatening to go to the police if I didn't cut him in on a bigger piece of the pie, those dwindling two keys, greedy little bastard. Give away a piece of what *I'd* taken the risk for? Said he knew I had diamonds hidden someplace in the apartment, said he wanted *those,* too, otherwise he'd go to the cops. Said he had proof, said he knew where he could get proof. The letter, of course, she'd kept the letter. And I'd trusted her. So what was I supposed to do? Spend time in prison because Sally had babbled to the wrong lover, Sally in the heat of passion had—God, she was good in bed! Dancers, Jesus!

Bought the gun two days after he paid me his little visit. Contacted the guy I'd sold the six keys to, told him I needed a gun. Easy, he said. Cost me two hundred dollars. Never used a gun in my life before then. Never even held one in my hand. Wanted to be a surgeon one day, good hands, steady, ah, well. Knew where he lived, hell, she used to *deliver* to him every Sunday, didn't know she was *also* delivering pussy and secrets, waited for him outside his building, followed him, shot him. Easy. Killed him.

But then, you know, you start thinking, you know, you start thinking you've got to *protect* it. Not the coke, not the diamonds, but *all* of it. The *future.* I *did* want to be a doctor, dad, I wasn't just walking through it, you know. I was busting my *ass,* just the way you wanted me to, Doctor Timothy Moore, *that's* who I wanted to be! So it had to be *protected,* you see, and if she'd told Lopez, then she couldn't be trusted anymore, could she? And how long would it have taken her to realize that I was the one who'd killed that greedy little spic? How long before she *herself* went to the police? No, I had to—the radio, he thought. That's what I'm forgetting. The radio.

He went into the living room, where the radio was still sitting alongside the telephone, picked up the radio, held it in the palm of his hand, and looked at it almost fondly. So simple, he thought. No way anyone in a million years could have connected the murder to a small-time coke dealer—well, Sally of course, Sally would have realized sooner or later. Which was why I had to, to, to do the same thing to her, you see. But with her, they'd *find* a connection. With her, they'd begin asking me questions—well, they *did* ask me questions, didn't they? So I needed protection, the radio, needed someone to say I'd been talking to him on the phone and he'd heard my radio going, good old Karl, solid as a rock, make a good doctor one day. Took the phone off the hook before I left the house, called him from a phone booth, radio going, called him twice before I killed her, waiting for her, late as usual, called him again *after* I killed her, when I got home, *kept* calling him, radio going each time, good old reliable Karl.

He carried the radio back into the bedroom, and put it in the open suitcase. Anything else? he wondered. Anything I'm forgetting? So easy to forget things when you're, when you, when you start something like this, all the things you have to do to *protect* it, keep your eye on the main goal, never mind the money, I wanted to be a *doctor!* Almost forgot about Edelman, last link in the chain, remembered him later. Suppose some IRS agent examined his books, wanted to know where he'd sold those diamonds, twenty-five carats, three hundred thousand dollars in cash, who'd you sell them to, *who?* Tie me in with that kind of money, cops would be around asking more questions, where'd you *get* that kind of money, no. Had to protect myself. Had to kill him. Like the others. So I could be a doctor one day. Like my father.

He closed the suitcase.

So, he thought.

He looked around the apartment.

That's it, he thought.

He picked up the suitcase, walked out the bedroom, and out of the apartment, and down the steps to the street.

She was waiting for him in the small dark entrance lobby downstairs.

She said only, "The opera ain't over," and he frowned and started to walk past her, taking her for a crazy bag lady or something, this city was full of lunatics, surprised when he saw the open straight razor in her hand, shocked when he realized she was coming at him with the razor, terrified when he saw his own blood pouring from the open wound in his throat. He clutched for his throat. Blood gushed onto his hands. He said, "I'm sorry," but he was dead before he could say the word "Dad."

*   *   *

The call from Fort Phyllis did not come until Saturday morning. There was only one notorious homosexual cruising street in the entire precinct that surrounded Ramsey University and the neighboring Quarter, but the cops of the 5th Precinct nonetheless called their turf Fort Phyllis. The man phoning was a Detective/Third Grade named Dawson. He asked to speak to Detective Carella.

"This is Dawson," he said, "Fifth Squad."

"What can I do for you?" Carella asked.

"We caught a homicide last night, slashing in a hallway on Chelsea Place. Guy named Timothy Moore."

"What?" Carella said.

"Yeah," Dawson said. "Reason I'm calling, Charlie Nichols here was in court yesterday while you were arraigning this guy, he figured maybe you ought to know about it. Figured maybe this ties in with the homicides you were investigating. The ones you charged this guy Moore with."

"How?" Carella said.

"Well, I don't *know* how," Dawson said. "That's what I'm asking *you.*"

"A slashing, you said?"

"Yeah. Ear to ear. Nice job."

He thought fleetingly of Judite Quadrado.

"Any leads?" he asked.

"None so far," Dawson said. "No witnesses, nothing. Guy had a bag of diamonds in his suitcase. Was he out on bail or something?"

"Yes," Carella said.

"Looks like he was maybe skipping, huh?"

"Looks that way," Carella said.

"So what do you want us to do about this?"

"I don't know what you mean."

"You want us to turn this over to you, or what?"

Here we go again, Carella thought.

"Well, let me see what the lieutenant thinks," he said.

"Maybe you charged the wrong guy, you know what I mean?" Dawson said. "I mean, Charlie told me it was four counts of Murder One."

"That's what it was," Carella said.

"So maybe somebody *else* did it, is all I'm saying," Dawson said. "The four murders. Maybe it wasn't this guy Moore at all."

"It was Moore," Carella said flatly.

"Anyway," Dawson said, and the line went silent.

"I'll talk to the lieutenant," Carella said.

"Sure, let me know," Dawson said, and hung up.

The squadroom was very quiet for a Saturday morning. Carella rose from his desk and walked to the water cooler. Standing near the windows streaming wintry sunlight, he sipped at the water in the paper cup, and then crumpled the cup and tossed it into the wastebasket. He went to the lieutenant's door and knocked on it.

"Come!" Byrnes shouted.

He went into the lieutenant's office, and closed the door behind him. He told the lieutenant that he'd just had a call from Fort Phyllis. He told the lieutenant that someone had slit Timothy Moore's throat in the hallway of his building last night, and that there were no witnesses and no leads, and the cops down there wanted to know what to do about it, whether they should turn this over to the Eight-Seven or what?

Byrnes listened very carefully. He was thoughtfully silent for a long time. Then he said, "No witnesses, huh?"

"None," Carella said.

"The Fifth Squad, huh?"

"Yes."

"We got enough headaches," Byrnes said. "Let *their* mothers worry."

EIGHT
BLACK
HORSES

This is for
VANESSA HOLT

1

The lady was extraordinarily naked.

That is to say, she *looked* extraordinarily naked because she was so very white. There are, after all, no degrees of nakedness. You are either clothed or you are unclothed. The lady was very definitely unclothed, but all the detectives gathered around her agreed that she looked more naked than any naked person they had ever seen in their collective lives.

"It's because she's so white," Monoghan said.

"Looks like an albino," Monroe said.

Monoghan and Monroe were Homicide detectives. They had been called in the moment it was ascertained that the lady lying on the withering leaves off the park path was indeed dead. It did not require much detection to determine that she was dead. The foot patrolman had known she was dead the moment he saw the bullet hole at the base of her skull. When he'd got on the walkie-talkie to the desk sergeant at the Eight-Seven, he had, in fact, said "Sarge, I got a female stiff here in the park." Carella and Brown knew the lady was dead, too. That was why they'd called back to the station house to ask Sergeant Murchison to inform Homicide.

None of the men were wearing overcoats.

After the recent rain the October weather had turned mild enough to permit shorts and sandals, which many of the curious onlookers behind the Crime Scene signs and barricades were, in fact, wearing. In contrast, Monoghan and Monroe were both wearing black suits, white shirts, blue ties, and gray fedoras. They looked like chunky undertakers waiting outside a funeral home to greet mourners.

Arthur Brown was wearing a tan tropical-weight suit. Steve Carella was wearing blue slacks and a darker blue sports shirt rolled up at the cuffs. They could have been two ordinary citizens, a pair of married men—which they were—who had strolled into the park on a lovely Tuesday morning to get away from the wife and kids and discuss football scores.

The gathering crowd knew Brown was a cop, though, because he looked mean. Scowling, he stared down at the body on the leaves. The temperature when he'd awakened this morning was sixty-eight degrees Fahrenheit—or twenty degrees Celsius, as the damn forecasters insisted on translating—and so he'd put on the lightweight tan suit. The suit made him look very brown, which in fact he was. He did not like to think of himself as a black man, which—in today's nomenclature—he also was. He did not know any black men who were really black. Black was an *absence* of color, wasn't it? He had always thought of himself as "colored," in fact, until it became almost mandatory for a black man to start thinking of himself as black. If you didn't think of yourself as black, you were betraying the race. Black power. Bullshit. What Brown had was *brown* power, all six feet four inches and two hundred and twenty pounds of him. The crowd figured he was a cop because anybody so mean-looking, if he was standing with a bunch of cops and he wasn't wearing handcuffs, had to be a cop himself. Also there was a little plastic ID card clipped to the pocket of his suit.

The crowd, what with the World Series still fresh in their minds, thought Carella looked like a baseball player. They deduced this because of his athletic stance and his long slender body. They also thought he looked a little Chinese; that was because his brown eyes slanted slightly downward—or was that Japanese? They doubted there were very many Caucasian Chinese baseball players in America, though, so they figured he had to be a cop, too. A clue to this was the plastic ID card pinned to his shirt pocket, just like the one the mean-looking black guy was wearing. Both men were wearing holstered pistols on their hips, another clue to their identity, though in this city—like in the olden days of the Wild West—you sometimes got cheap street thieves running around with guns right in the open.

Carella and Brown liked being partnered together.

They felt it was effective against the bad guys.

The bad guys took one look at Carella, and they figured *this* one is the pushover, it's the bad-ass nigger you gotta watch out for. Whenever they were partnered together, Carella and Brown played Mutt and Jeff to the hilt. Carella played Mr. Clean—"Golly, Artie, it don't look to me like this nice young man here even knows what marijuana *is!*" Brown played Big Bad Leroy, born in a ghetto garbage can, shooting dope since he was six years old, done time at Castleview upstate, seen the light afterward and became a cop by way of penance for his formerly evil life. Mean, though, still as mean as a hooker's snatch. "You lyin' little punk, I'm gonna kill you right here on the spot, save the state a 'lectric bill. Get your hands off me, Steve, I'm gonna throw this man off the roof!" Mean, oh man, *real* bad-ass. Big Bad Leroy. It worked nicely.

The sky overhead was as blue as a newborn baby's eyes.

The leaves in the trees lining the path were yellow and brown and red and orange.

The leaves under the dead lady were yellow and red. The red was caused by the wound at the base of her skull.

"This city," Monroe said, "you can carry a dead person in a park, she's got a bullet hole in her head and she's starkers, nobody bats an eyelash."

Carella was looking down at the lifeless white body on the blood-stained leaves. They always look all angles, he thought. The thought was short-lived, accompanied by a brief flicker of pain in his eyes. In solitude, on too many occasions, he had sat and wondered why the geometry of death left only angles.

"Let's roll her over," Monoghan said. "See she's wearing some ID pinned to her chest."

He knew they could not roll her over until the medical examiner got there. He just enjoyed hassling the detectives from the Eight-Seven. That was one of life's little joys. The bulls on this squad up here, they took things too serious. In Monoghan's universe a stiff was a stiff, period. Dressed, naked, stabbed, shot, strangled, incinerated, poleaxed, whatever, it was still only a corpse, and a corpse meant paperwork. In this city, though, the appearance of Homicide cops at the scene of a crime was mandatory. The case officially belonged to the detectives who caught the squeal, but the Homicide Division—like a nagging backseat driver—constantly watched over their shoulders, demanding progress reports at every turn in the road.

"What do you say?" Monoghan asked, not sure Carella had heard him. "We roll her over, see what she looks like from the front."

Carella didn't bother answering him. His eyes were scanning the leaves for any sign of a bullet or a spent cartridge case.

"How old you think she is?" Monroe asked. "Judging from her ass."

"That's a twenty-seven-year-old ass," Monoghan said.

"She's got a beauty mark on her right cheek," Monroe said.

"Good firm ass, she's got there," Monoghan said.

"I had a case once," Monroe said, "this guy died from a broken bottle shoved up his ass."

"Yeah, I remember that one," Monoghan said.

"Hemorrhaged to death," Monroe said.

"His boyfriend done it, right?"

"Yeah, his boyfriend."

Both men looked at the woman's buttocks.

"Twenty-seven years old, I'll give you two to one," Monoghan said.

"The legs look twenty-seven, too," Monroe said.

Brown looked up at the sky.

Not a cloud in it.

He took in a deep breath of fresh air.

"Morning gentlemen," a voice said, and they turned to look up the path when a man in his late fifties, wearing dark blue slacks, a seersucker jacket, a pink shirt, and a blue polka dot tie, was approaching. He was carrying a black satchel in his right hand. "Beautiful day, isn't it?" he said. "This the body?"

"No, the body's up in the trees there," Monroe said.

"It's an Indian body," Monoghan said. "They put them up in the trees."

The assistant medical examiner looked up into the treetops. Leaves fell everywhere around them, twisting on the air.

"We've had three naked bodies this week," the M.E. said to no one and then knelt over the dead woman.

"Where'd you hear that?" Monroe asked Monoghan.

"Where'd I hear what?"

"That Indians put dead bodies up in the trees."

"It's a fact," Monoghan said.

"Does Muhammad Ghandi know that?"

"I'm talkin' about *American* Indians," Monoghan said. "Somebody dies, they put the body up in the trees."

"What for?"

"Who the hell knows?"

The M.E. had rolled the body over. He was holding a stethoscope to the dead woman's chest.

"Whattya think, Doc?" Monroe asked. "She dead enough for you?"

"Quiet, please," the M.E. said.

"He thinks he's gonna get a heartbeat," Monoghan said.

The men fell silent. There was only the sound of the flutter of leaves on the sunlit air. The dead woman's eyes were opened wide. They were as blue as the sky above. Her hair was as golden as the leaves beneath her. She appeared to be in her mid-thirties, a not unattractive woman except for the gaping exit wound in the hollow of her throat. Carella wondered if she'd ever been out in the sun, she was so white.

"She's dead, all right," the M.E. said, rising and putting his stethoscope back into his satchel. "You can put it down as a gunshot wound."

"While you're here," Monroe said, "I been having trouble with my throat. You wanna take a look at it?"

The next letter—well, it wasn't really a letter.

The next message—it wasn't *that,* either, not unless it *meant* something.

The next piece of folded paper with, well, *pictures* on it was waiting for them when they got back to the station house. It had arrived, Sergeant Murchison told them, in a plain white envelope with no return address on it. The postmark over the stamp indicated that the letter had been mailed here in the city on the twenty-fourth, yesterday. That spoke well for the Post Office Department; in this city it sometimes took four days for a letter to travel three blocks crosstown.

They did not know if this one was also from the Deaf Man.

That's because there was no ear on it.

They'd been fairly certain that the first letter—message, piece of folded paper, what*ever* the hell—had come from the Deaf Man. That was because they were all expert sleuths, and when their eyes fell upon a deaf ear, they recognized it at once.

The first—communication, they guessed it was—had arrived on Saturday, October 22. It had been addressed to Detective Stephen Louis Carella at the 87th Precinct, and it looked like this:

Well, everybody on the squad knew that those things prancing across the top of the page were horses. They also knew that there were eight of them, and they were black, and if you put all of that together, you got eight black horses. Which meant nothing, of course. Which, of course, if the Deaf Man had sent this thing to them, meant *something*. Because the Deaf Man often sent communications that looked as if they meant nothing until you figured them out and then they meant something. One thing they had learned about the Deaf Man over the years was that he always played the game fair. They didn't know *why* he played the game fair, but then again they rarely understood the workings of the criminal mind, especially the *master* criminal mind. In *their* minds the Deaf Man was a master criminal. That was why he played the game fair and sent communications that looked as if they meant nothing when actually they meant something.

They figured it was the Deaf Man because of the ear with the bar across it.

Most people do not have bars across their ears.

In international sign language, if you saw a cigarette with a bar across it, it meant NO SMOKING. If you saw the capital letter P with a bar across it, it meant NO PARKING. An ear with a bar across it could have meant NO EAR, but they suspected instead that it meant NO HEARING, which further meant DEAF, and since the ear wasn't a delicately shaped shell-like thing but instead a very masculine-looking ear (unless it was the ear of a female wrestler), they concluded that the picture of the ear with the bar across it meant DEAF MAN.

This conclusion was unsettling.

They did not want to believe that the Deaf Man was back in their midst.

They had posted the Deaf Man's message on the bulletin board and hoped it would go away. But this was Tuesday morning, October 25, and it had not gone away. Instead, there was a second envelope addressed personally to Carella. When he opened it, there was another single white sheet of folded paper in it. He unfolded the paper. He looked at it. This time there was no ear with the bar across it. Instead, there was—or were, as the case actually was:

Meyer Meyer was looking over Carella's shoulder.

He was wearing lightweight slacks and a short-sleeved polo shirt with a crocodile over where the pocket would have been if there'd been a pocket on the shirt. Most polo shirts did not have pockets these days. Meyer didn't mind that, now that he'd given up smoking. The shirt was a shade darker than his blue eyes. The trousers were a sort of cream-colored polyester, as pale as his bald pate. His wife, Sarah, had told him this morning that he looked tacky wearing summer clothes to work when it was already the end of October. He'd commented, wittily he thought, that maybe in his head it was October, but in the *rest* of him it was still June. Sarah suspected he was making a sexual remark.

"Is it him again?" he asked.

"I don't know," Carella said.

"So what are those supposed to be, anyway?" Meyer said.

"Radios, I guess," Carella said.

"Walkie-talkies, looks more like," Brown said.

"Five walkie-talkies," Carella said.

"No ear, though."

"No ear."

"Maybe it isn't him," Carella said.

"From your lips to God's ear," Meyer said.

"Five walkie-talkies," Brown said, and shook his head.

"He's giving us arithmetic lessons," Meyer said. "Eight, five . . ."

"He's jerkin' us off," Brown said. "Eight black horses, five walkie-talkies, those things don't have anything at all to do with each other."

The trouble with naked dead bodies is that they are not wearing clothes.

Clothing is an aid to identification.

Clothing is also helpful in determining who the perpetrator or perpetrators may have been. Hair clings to clothing. Stains cling to clothing. Bread crumbs, iron filings, sawdust, face powder, flea powder, gunpowder, all *sorts* of juicy informational tidbits cling to clothing, making a laboratory technician's life a bit easier. Nothing much clings to a dead body. Unless it was raped, in which case there are often wild pubic hairs tangled in the victim's crotch or traces of semen to be found in the vagina.

According to the preliminary report of the medical examiner's office, the lady in the park had not been raped—either before her death or *after* it, a not uncommon occurrence in this civilized city.

She had been shot in the back of the head, gangland style.

A single bullet had done the job, but there were no spent cartridge cases or bullets at the scene. An automatic weapon ejects cartridge cases when it is fired. A revolver retains the spent cartridge cases in its cylinder. But *whatever* type of pistol had been used, if the lady had been shot and killed in Grover Park, there would have been a spent bullet somewhere in the vicinity. The exit wound in her throat told them that. They could find no bullet. Which indicated to them that the lady had been shot elsewhere and only later transported to the park.

It is a myth that the Identification Section of any cosmopolitan police department can immediately identify anyone merely by checking his or her fingerprints against what is known as the base file. The base file in this city was divided into two sections, the largest of which—occupying an entire floor of the Headquarters Building downtown on High Street—was itself subdivided into two sections, one devoted exclusively to maintaining an up-to-date fingerprint record of anyone charged with or convicted of a felony or a misdemeanor, the other composed of latent fingerprints taken at the scene of a crime. The overall section was called the Criminal Section of the Identification Section, or the CSIS, bastardized in police jargon to just plain "Sissies." The Sissies file devoted to known criminals was called the A-file, and the file holding latents was called the B-file.

A check of the A-file revealed no criminal record for the lady found dead in the park.

A check of the B-file came up negative against any latent prints on record.

This meant only that she had never committed a crime for which she'd been caught, and had never left her fingerprints at the scene of a crime.

The second file in the I.S. maintained fingerprint records of anyone involved in the city's vast law enforcement organization, anyone working as a security officer in a municipal jail or prison and anyone who had been granted a carry or premises permit for a pistol.

That was it.

On the municipal level.

But the United States is a big, big country, and it is also a *free* country, which means that *anyone*—even if he is intent on doing criminal mischief—can travel from city to city and state to state without an identity card or a by-your-leave from the local commissar. This is one of the nice things about living in a democracy. It is also a headache for law enforcement officers. The city for which Carella worked was the largest city in the state, but the fingerprint files in its police department's Identification Section were minuscule compared to those in the state depository, some hundred and fifty miles to the north. When Isola's I.S. section came up blank on Jane Doe, a search-and-return request was automatically sent upstate. The prints taken from the corpse were checked against the *state's* base file, and the results were identical: no record.

The buck could have stopped there, but it didn't.

A check with the FBI's *national* files came back with a negative response: no criminal record for Jane Doe. Neither had she ever been fingerprinted for service in the armed forces or for any job considered security-sensitive by the Nuclear Regulatory Commission.

Carella knew that the I.S. routinely ran courtesy checks for any institution whose employees handled large sums of money. Had any *bank* in the city sent Jane Doe's fingerprints to the I.S. for a verification check against Sissies? The I.S. replied that such courtesy checks were made on a search-and-return basis, as opposed to a search-and-*retain* basis. In other words, after either a full or limited search-and-return was made, the I.S. automatically sent the fingerprints back to the financial institution or other commercial entity making the request. They did *not* retain the fingerprints in their files. Even if someone in Jane Doe's immediate or distant past had requested a search against the Sissies file, there would be no record of it.

Period.

End of story.

All of this took the better part of a week.

By that time, though, the police department had circulated to the Missing Persons Section and to every precinct in the city a photograph and description of Jane Doe, together with a copy of the Detective Division report Carella himself had typed up on the morning the body was discovered.

On Wednesday morning, November 2, Carella got a call from a Detective Lipman at Missing Persons.

Lipman told him he had a positive ID on the dead woman.

2

The woman who had identified Jane Doe was staying at a once-elegant midtown hotel that now emanated an air of shabby dignity, like an exiled dowager empress praying for return to the throne. Huge marble columns dominated the lobby, where sagging sofas rested on frayed Persian rugs. The ornately carved and gilded mahogany registration desk was cigarette-scarred. Even the clerk who told them what room Miss Turner was in looked faded, his gray hair a shade lighter than his gray suit, his black tie as funereal as his dark somber eyes. The elaborate brass fretwork on the elevator doors reminded Carella of something he had seen in a spy movie.

Inge Turner was a slender blonde in her late thirties, they guessed, her complexion as fair as her sister's had been, her eyes the same shade of blue. She was wearing a simple blue suit over a white blouse with a stock tie. Medium-heeled blue pumps on good legs. A gold pin in the shape of a bird pinned to the lapel of the suit jacket. Blue eyeliner. Lipstick that was more pink than red.

"Gentlemen," she said. "Please come in."

The room was small, dominated by a king-size bed. Inge sat on the edge of the bed, crossing her legs. The detectives sat in upholstered chairs near musty drapes hanging over a window that was open to the sounds of traffic on the avenue six stories below. Already the second of November, and Indian summer was still with them. It would come with a vengeance, winter. It would come suddenly and unexpectedly, hurling false expectations back into their teeth.

"Miss Turner," Carella said, "Detective Lipman at Missing Persons tells us . . ."

"Yes," she said.

". . . that you've identified a photograph in his files as . . ."

"Yes," she said again.

". . . your sister, Elizabeth Turner."

"That's correct."

"Miss Turner, I wonder if you could look at that picture again . . . I have a print here . . ."

"Must I?" she said.

"I know it's difficult," Carella said, "but we want to make sure . . ."

"Yes, let me see it," she said.

Carella took the photograph from the manila file envelope. As photographs of corpses went, it was not too grisly—except for the exit wound in the hollow of the throat. Inge looked at it briefly, said, "Yes, that's my sister," and then reached for her handbag, took a cigarette from it, said, "Do you mind if I smoke?" and lighted it without waiting for an answer.

"And her full name is Elizabeth Turner?" Carella said.

"Yes. Well, Elizabeth *Anne* Turner."

"Can you tell us how old she was?" Brown asked.

"Twenty-seven," Inge said.

Both detectives thought, at precisely the same moment, that for once in his lifetime Monoghan had been right.

"And her address?"

"Here or in California?" Inge said.

"I'm sorry, what . . . ?"

"She used to live with me in California."

"But she'd been living *here*, hadn't . . . ?"

"Yes. For the past three years now."

"What was her address *here*, Miss Turner?"

"Eight-oh-four South Ambrose."

"Any apartment number?"

"Forty-seven."

"Do you still live in California?"

"Yes."

"You're just visiting here, is that it?"

"Yes. Well, I came specifically to see my sister. We—do I have to go into this?" She looked at the detectives, sighed, and said, "I suppose we do." She uncrossed her legs, leaned over to an ashtray on the night table beside the bed, and stubbed out her cigarette. "We had a falling-out," she said. "Lizzie moved east. I hadn't seen her in three years. I felt it was time to . . . she was my sister. I loved her. I wanted to . . . set things straight again, on the right course again."

"You came here seeking a reconciliation?" Brown asked.

"Yes. Exactly."

"From where in California?" Carella asked.

"Los Angeles."

"And when did you arrive?"

"Last Thursday."

"That would have been . . ."

"The twenty-seventh. I was hoping . . . we hadn't seen each other for such a long time . . . I was hoping I could convince her to come home for Christmas."

"So you came here to . . ."

"To talk to her. To convince her that bygones should be bygones. I think I had in mind . . . I guess I thought if I could get her to come home for Christmas, then maybe she'd stay. In California, I mean. We'd . . . you know . . . pick up where we left off. We were sisters. A silly argument shouldn't . . ."

"What did you argue about?" Brown asked. "If you'd like to tell us," he added quickly.

"Well . . ."

The detectives waited.

"I guess she didn't approve of my life-style."

Still they waited.

"We led very different kinds of lives, you see. Lizzie worked at a bank, I was . . ."

"A bank?" Carella said at once.

"Yes. She was a cashier at Suncoast Federal. Not a *teller,* you understand, but a *cashier.* There's a big difference."

"And what sort of work do you do?" Brown asked.

"I'm a model," she said.

She must have caught the glance that passed between the detectives.

"A *real* model," she said at once. "There are plenty of the *other* kind out there."

"What sort of modeling do you do?" Carella asked.

"Lingerie," she said. "Mostly stockings and panty hose." She reached into her bag, took out another cigarette, lighted it, and said, "I have good legs," and crossed them again.

"And you say your sister disapproved of this?"

"Well, not the modeling as such . . . though I don't suppose she was too happy about my being photographed in my underwear."

"Then what *was* it about your life-style . . . ?"

"I'm a lesbian," Inge said.

Carella nodded.

"Does that shock you?"

"No," he said.

"You're supposed to say something like, 'What a waste,' " Inge said, and smiled.

"Am I?" Carella said, and returned the smile.

"That's what most men say."

"Well," Carella said, "actually we're only interested in finding whoever killed your sister. You don't believe your life-style—quote, unquote—had anything to do with her murder, do you?"

"Hardly."

"But you did argue about it."

"Yes."

"In what way?"

"She disapproved of the friends I invited to the house."

"So she came all the way east . . ."

"Not immediately. She moved into an apartment on La Cienega, a temporary arrangement until she could find work here."

"*Did* she find work here?" Brown asked.

"Yes," Inge said.

"Where?"

"A bank someplace."

"Here in the city?"

"Yes."

"Which bank?"

"I have no idea. This was all hearsay. A friend of mine used to live here in the city, and occasionally she'd run into my sister . . ."

"Does that mean you'd had no word from her . . . directly, I mean . . . in the past three years?" Carella said.

"That's right. Not since she left California."

"But you came here to see her . . ."

"Yes."

"Did you know where she lived?"

"Her address is in the phone book."

"Did you write to her first?"

"No, I was afraid to do that. Afraid she wouldn't want to see me."

"So you just came east."

"Yes."

Carella looked at his notes.

"Would you know your sister's social security number?" he asked.

"I'm sorry, I don't."

"The bank she worked for was Suncoast Federal, did you say? In California, I mean."

"Yes."

"And the bank she worked for here in the . . ."

"I told you. I don't know which . . ."

"Yes, but *when* was this, would you know? When you heard from your friend that she was working for a bank here."

"Oh. Two years ago? Perhaps a year and a half. I couldn't say with any accuracy."

"Would you know if she was *still* working at this bank? Immediately before her death, I mean."

"I have no idea."

"You haven't stayed in touch with your friend?"

"I have. But she's living in Chicago now."

"Then for the past two years—a year and a half, whatever it was—you really didn't know *what* your sister was doing."

"That's right. We lost touch completely. That's why I came here."

"And you arrived on October twenty-seventh, is that right?" Carella said.

"Yes. Last Thursday."

"Checked into this hotel, did you?"

"Yes."

"Planning to stay how long?"

"As long as was necessary. To see my sister, to . . . make amends . . . to ask her to come home."

"For Christmas."

"Forever." Inge sighed heavily and leaned over to the ashtray again, crushing out her cigarette. "I missed her. I loved her."

"When you arrived, Miss Turner, did you try to contact your sister?"

"Yes, of course. I phoned her at once."

"This was on the twenty-seventh of October?"

"Yes. My plane got in at six, a little after six, and it took a half hour to get into the city from the airport. I phoned her the moment I was in the room."

"And?"

"There was no answer."

"Was she living alone, would you know?"

"Yes. Well, I didn't learn that until later. When I went to her apartment."

"When did you do that?"

"Two days later. I'd been calling her repeatedly and . . . well . . . there was no answer, you see."

"So you suspected something was wrong, did you?"

"Well, I didn't know *what* to think. I mean, I'd been calling her day and night. I set my alarm one night . . . this was the night after I arrived . . . for three A.M., and I called her then and still got no answer. I went to her apartment the very next day."

"That would have been . . ."

"Well, the twenty-ninth, I suppose. A Saturday, I guess I was hoping she'd be home on a Saturday."

"But she wasn't, of course."

"No. She . . . was dead by then. But I . . . I didn't know that at the time. I went up to her apartment and rang the doorbell and got no answer. I found the superintendent of the building, told him who I was, and asked if he had any idea where my sister might be. He . . . he said he hadn't seen her in . . . in . . . three or four weeks."

"What did he say exactly, Miss Turner? Three weeks, or four?"

"I think that's exactly what he said. Three or four weeks."

"And he told you that she was living there alone?"

"Yes."

"What did you do then?"

"Well, I . . . I suppose I should have gone directly to the police, but I . . . you see, I was somewhat confused. The possibility existed that she'd met someone, some man, and had moved in with him. That was a possibility." She paused. "My sister wasn't gay," she said, and reached for her package of cigarettes again, and then changed her mind about lighting one.

"When *did* you contact the police?" Brown asked.

"On Monday morning."

Carella looked at his pocket calendar.

"October thirty-first," he said.

"Yes. Halloween," Inge said. "They told me they'd turn it over to Missing Persons and let me know if anything resulted. I gave them an old photo I had . . . I still carried it in my wallet . . . and apparently Detective Lipman was able to match that against the . . . the picture you just showed me. He called me yesterday. I went down there and . . . and made the identification."

The room was silent.

"Miss Turner," Carella said, "we realize you hadn't seen your sister in a long time . . ."

"Yes," she said.

". . . and Los Angeles is a long way from here. But . . . would you have heard anything over the years . . . anything at *all* . . . from your friend or anyone else . . . about any enemies your sister may have made in this city . . ."

"No."

". . . any threatening telephone calls or letters she may have . . ."

"No."

". . . any involvement with criminals or . . ."

"No."

". . . people engaged, even tangentially, in criminal activities?"

"No."

"Would you know if she owed money to anyone?"

"I don't know."

"She wasn't doing drugs, was she?" Brown asked.

The question nowadays was almost mandatory.

"Not that I know of," Inge said. "In fact . . ."

She stopped herself mid-sentence.

"Yes?" Carella said.

"Well, I was only going to say . . . well, in fact, that was one of the things she objected to."

"What was that, Miss Turner?"

"My friends and I did a few lines every now and then." She shrugged. "It's common in Los Angeles."

"But your sister never, to your knowledge . . ."

"Not in L.A., no. I don't know what she might have got into once she came here." She paused, and then said, "L.A. is civilized."

Neither of the detectives said anything.

"You see," Inge said, "this whole thing is so unbelievable. I mean, you'd have to have known Lizzie to realize that . . . that *dying* this way, dying a violent death, someone *shooting* her . . . well, it's unimaginable. She was a very quiet, private sort of person. My friends used to speculate on whether she'd ever even been *kissed,* do you know what I'm saying? So when you . . . when you . . . when the mind tries to associate Lizzie, sweet goddamn innocent *Lizzie* with a . . . with a *gun,* with someone holding a *gun* to the back of her head and shooting her . . . it's . . . I mean, the mind can't possibly make that connection, it can't make that quantum leap."

She looked at her hands. She had very beautiful hands, Carella noticed.

"Detective Lipman said . . . he'd read some sort of report that was sent to him . . . he said she had to have been on her knees when she was shot. The angle, the trajectory, whatever the hell, indicated she'd been on her knees, with . . . with . . . with the . . . person who . . . who shot her standing behind her. Lizzie on her knees."

She shook her head.

"I can't believe this has happened," she said, and reached into her handbag for another cigarette.

She was smoking again when the detectives left the room.

* * *

"His specialty is banks," Carella said.

"Just what I was thinking," Brown said.

They were driving crosstown and downtown to Elizabeth Turner's apartment and they were talking about the Deaf Man.

"That's if you consider two out of three a specialty," Carella said.

He was remembering that once, and only once, had the Deaf Man's attempts at misdirection been designed to conceal and simultaneously reveal an elaborate extortion scheme. On the other two occasions it had been banks. Tell the police beforehand, but not really, what you're planning to do, help them dope it out, in fact, and then do something different but almost the same—it all got terribly confusing when the Deaf Man put in an appearance.

Eight black horses, five walkie-talkies, and one white lady who probably had nothing whatever to do with the Deaf Man, except for the fact that she had worked in a bank.

"Banks have security officers, you know," Brown said.

"Yeah," Carella said.

"And they carry walkie-talkies, don't they?"

"I don't know. Do they?"

"I guess they do," Brown said. "Do you think there might be a bank someplace in this city that's got five security guards carrying walkie-talkies?"

"I don't know," Carella said.

"Five walkie-talkies, you know?" Brown said. "And she worked in a bank."

"The only *real* thing we've got . . ."

"*If* it's a connection."

"Which it probably isn't."

"That's the trouble with the Deaf Man," Carella said.

"He drives you crazy," Brown said.

"What's that address again?"

"Eight-oh-four."

"Where are we now?"

"Eight-twenty."

"Just ahead then, huh?"

"With the green canopy," Brown said.

Carella parked the car at the curb in front of the building and then threw down the visor on the driver's side. A sign was attached to it with rubber bands. Visible through the windshield, it advised any overzealous foot patrolman that the guys who'd parked the car here were on the job. The city's seal and the words ISOLA P.D. printed on the sign were presumably insurance against a parking ticket. The sign didn't always work. Only recently they had busted a cocaine dealer who'd stolen an identical sign from a car driven by two detectives from the Eight-One. In this city it was sometimes difficult to tell the good guys from the bad guys.

It was difficult, too, to tell a good building from a bad building.

Usually a building with an awning out front indicated that there would be a doorman or some other sort of security. There was neither here. They found the superintendent's apartment on the street level floor, identified themselves, and asked him to unlock the door to Elizabeth Anne Turner's apartment. On the way up in the elevator Brown asked him if she'd lived here alone.

"Yep," he said.

"Sure about that?" Carella said.

"Yep," the super said.

"No girlfriend living with her?"

"Nope."

"No boyfriend?"

"Nope."

"No roommate at all, right?"

"Right."

"When'd you see her last?"

"Beginning of October, musta been."

"Going out or coming in?"

"Going out."

"Alone?"

"Alone."

"Carrying anything?"

"Just her handbag."

"What time was this?"

"In the morning sometime. I figured she was on her way to work."

"And you didn't see her again after that?"

"Nope. But I don't keep an eye out twenty-four hours a day, you know."

There is a feel to an apartment that has been lived in.

Even the apartment of a recent homicide victim can tell you at once whether anyone had been living there. There was no such sense of habitation in Elizabeth Turner's apartment.

The windows were closed tight and locked—not unusual for this city, even if someone were just going downstairs for a ten-minute stroll. But the air was still and stale, a certain indication that the windows hadn't been opened for quite some time. Well, after all, Elizabeth Turner had been found dead eight days ago, and perhaps that was a long enough time for an apartment to have gone stale.

But a slab of butter in the refrigerator had turned rancid.

And a package of sliced Swiss cheese had mold growing on it.

And a container of milk was sour to the smell; the SELL-BY date stamped at the top of the carton read "OCT. 1."

There were no dishes on the drainboard, none in the dishwasher.

The ashtrays were spotlessly clean.

The apartment revealed none of the detritus of living—even if the living had been done by a compulsive housekeeper.

There was only one coat hanging in the hall closet.

The double bed in the bedroom was made.

A framed picture of Elizabeth was on the dresser opposite the bed. She looked prettier alive.

The three top drawers of the dresser were empty.

The middle row of drawers contained one blouse.

The bottom row of drawers contained two sweaters and a handful of mothballs.

Only a suit, a pair of slacks, and a ski parka were hanging in the bedroom closet. There were two pairs of high-heeled pumps on the closet floor. They could find no suitcases anywhere in the apartment.

The roll of toilet paper in the bathroom holder was almost all gone.

They could not find a toothbrush in the medicine cabinet.

Nor a diaphragm. Nor a birth control pill dispenser. Nor any of the artifacts, cosmetic or otherwise, they normally would have found in an apartment actively occupied by a woman.

They went back into the bedroom and searched the desk for an appointment calendar.

Nothing.

They looked for a diary.

Nothing.

They looked for an address book.

Nothing.

"What do you think?" Carella asked.

"Flew the coop, looks like," Brown said.

Another envelope was waiting when they got back to the squadroom.

Kling handed it to Carella and said, "It looks like your pen pal again."

Carella's name was typewritten across the face of the envelope.

No return address.

The stamp was postmarked November 1.

"Shouldn't we be checking these for fingerprints or something?" Brown said.

"If it's the Deaf Man," Kling said, "we'd be wasting our time."

He looked very blond standing alongside Brown. He *was* very blond, but Brown made him look blonder. And younger. And more like a shit-kicking farmboy than usual. Born and raised in this city, he nonetheless exuded an air of innocence, a lack of guile or sophistication that automatically made you think he'd migrated from Kansas or someplace like that, wherever Kansas was—the detectives on the 87th Squad all thought Kansas was "out there someplace."

Kling looked as if he'd come from out there in the boondocks of America someplace, where you drove your car two hundred miles every Saturday night to a hamburger stand. Kling looked as if he still necked in the back seat of an automobile. Hazel-eyed and clean-shaven, blond hair falling loose over his forehead, he looked like a bumpkin who had wandered into the police station to ask directions to the nearest subway stop. He was very good at the Mutt and Jeff ploy. In much the same way that any cop teamed with Brown automatically became Jeff, any cop teamed with Kling automatically became Mutt. Together Kling and Brown were perhaps the best Mutt and Jeff act to be found anywhere in the city. It was almost unfair to the criminal population of this city to foist such a Mutt and Jeff team upon it. There was no way you could win, not with Brown playing the heavy and Kling playing the good-natured soul trying to keep his partner from chewing you to bits. No way.

"Even so," Brown said.

"Been handled by ten thousand people already," Kling said. "Postal clerks, letter carriers . . ."

"Yeah," Brown said, and shrugged.

"You going to open it or what?" Kling said.

"You open it," Carella said, and extended the envelope to him.

"It's not my case," Kling said.

"It's everybody's case," Carella said.

"Throw it away," Kling said, backing away from the envelope. "He gives me the creeps, that guy."

"*I'll* open it, for Christ's sake," Brown said, and took the envelope from Carella. He tore open the flap. He unfolded the single white sheet of paper that was inside:

"Huh?" he said.

3

The city for which these men worked was divided into five separate geographical sections.

The center of the city, Isola, was an island; hence its name: *isola* means "island" in Italian. In actual practice the *entire* city was referred to as Isola, even though the other four sections were separately and more imaginatively named.

Riverhead came from the Dutch, though not directly. The land up there had once been owned by a patroon named Ryerhurt, and it had been called Ryerhurt's Farms, which eventually became abbreviated and bastardized to Riverhead.

No one knew why sprawling, boisterous Calm's Point was called that. Maybe at one time, when the British were still there, it had indeed been a peaceful pastoral place. Nowadays it was worth your life to wear a gold chain in some sections of Calm's Point.

Majesta had without question been named by the British; the name rang with all the authority, grandeur, greatness, and dignity of sovereignty, its roots being in the Middle English word *maieste,* from the Old French *majeste,* from the Latin *mājestās,* which was a long way around the mulberry bush.

Bethtown had been named for the virgin queen Elizabeth, but undoubtedly by a British official with a lisp; it was *supposed* to have been called *Bess*town.

Isola was the hub of the city.

Some people who lived there thought it was the hub of the entire *universe,* a belief that did much to contribute to its reputation for rudeness. Even people who lived elsewhere in the city held Isola in awe, invariably referring to it as ''the City,'' as though they lived in the middle of a wheat field on its outer fringes.

There were no wheatfields in any part of this city.

But there *were* a hell of a lot of banks.

In Isola there were 856 banks.

In Majesta there were 296 banks.

In Calm's Point there were 249 banks.

In Riverhead there were 127 banks.

And in Bethtown there were 56 banks.

That came to 1,584 banks, more than a quarter of all the banks in the entire state.

On Thursday morning, November 3, a flyer from the Eight-Seven went out to the main branch of every bank in the city, requesting information on a homicide victim named Elizabeth Anne Turner, who may have been employed as a cashier sometime during the past three years. A photograph and description accompanied the flyer together with the social security number the detectives had got from Suncoast Federal in Los Angeles, where Elizabeth had worked before coming east.

On Friday morning, November 4, a call came from the branch manager of the First Fidelity Trust on Beverly Street downtown.

Carella and Brown were in his office not twenty minutes later.

Arnold Holberry was a man with a summer cold. He thought it was ridiculous to have a summer cold when it was already four days into November.

''I *hate* this weather,'' he told the detectives, and blew his nose. Outside the windows of his office November looked like June. ''This is supposed to be *autumn,*'' he said. ''The first day of autumn was September twenty-first. We are already into the last *quarter* of the year,'' he said. ''The winter *solstice* is almost upon us. We are not supposed to be having this kind of weather. This kind of weather is dangerous for human beings at this time of year.''

He blew his nose again.

He was a trim man in his late fifties, his hair graying at the temples, a gray mustache under his nose—which was very red at the moment. A bottle of cold tablets was on his desk. A box of tissues was on his desk as well. He looked thoroughly miserable, but he told the detectives he was willing to give them all the time they needed. He remembered Elizabeth Turner quite well and had been inordinately fond of her.

"How long did she work here, Mr. Holberry?" Brown asked.

"Almost two years. She used to live in California, excellent credentials out there. Well, a marvelous person all around. I was sorry to have her leave us."

"When was that?" Carella asked.

He was afraid he would catch Holberry's cold. He didn't want to bring a cold home to the kids just when the holidays were about to begin. Thanksgiving was only a few weeks off, and after that Christmas would be right around the corner. He was unaware of it, but his posture in the chair opposite Holberry's desk was entirely defensive. He sat leaning all the way back, his arms folded across his chest. Each time Holberry blew his nose, Carella winced, as if a battery of nuclear missiles were rushing out of their silos, aimed at his vulnerable head.

"In February," Holberry said.

"This past February?"

"Yes."

"When, exactly, in February?" Brown asked.

"On February fourth," Holberry said, and reached for a tissue and blew his nose again. "These pills don't work at all," he said. "Nothing works when you've got a cold like this one."

Carella hoped he would not sneeze.

"We gave her a wonderful reference," Holberry said.

"She left for another job, is that it?" Brown asked.

"Yes."

"Here in the city?"

"No. Washington, D.C."

The detectives looked at each other. They were thinking she had left for Washington in February, and she was back here in October—dead.

"Would you know when she came back here?" Brown asked.

"Gentlemen, I didn't know she *was* back until I got your request for information. You can't know how shocked I was." He shook his head. "Lizzie was such a . . . kind, generous, soft-spoken . . . *elegant* person, that's the word, elegant. To think of her life ending in violence . . ." He shook his head again. "Shot, you said?"

"Shot, yes," Carella said.

"Unimaginable."

Her sister had used the same word.

"Mr. Holberry," Brown said, "we've talked to the super at her building and also to many of her neighbors, and they told us she was living there alone . . ."

"I really wouldn't know about that," Holberry said.

"They described her as a very private sort of person, said they'd rarely seen her with friends of any kind, male or female . . ."

"Well, I wouldn't know about that, either," Holberry said. "She was certainly outgoing and friendly here at the bank. Gregarious, in fact, I would say."

"You didn't know her on a social level, did you, sir?" Carella asked.

"No, no. Well, that wouldn't have been appropriate, you know. But . . . gentlemen, it really is difficult to describe Lizzie to someone who didn't know her. She was simply a . . . *marvelous* person. Always a kind word for everyone, always a smile on her face. Crackerjack at her job, never complained about anything, nothing was too big for her to tackle. When she told me she was leaving for Washington, I was shattered. Truly. She could have gone quite far with this bank. Quite far. Excuse me," he said, and blew his nose again, and again Carella winced.

"You say she asked for a reference," Brown said.

"Yes. Actually she'd told me beforehand she was looking for employment elsewhere. It was not in Lizzie's nature to lie about anything. She was unhappy here, she said, and she . . ."

"Unhappy why?" Carella asked at once.

"She felt she wasn't advancing rapidly enough. I told her these things took time, we all had our eye on her, and we knew what a valuable employee she was . . . but you see, she'd been offered an assistant managership in Washington, and I can understand how that must have appealed to her."

"Which bank was that, sir?"

"The Union Savings and Trust."

"Would you know which branch?"

"I'm sorry, no."

"But it's your understanding that when she left here last February, it was to become an assistant manager at a Union Savings and Trust bank in Washington?"

"Well, yes. Of course. That's what I've been saying, isn't it?"

"What I meant, sir," Carella said, "is whether to your knowledge she actually *took* the job she'd been offered."

"I would have no way of knowing that. I assume . . ."

"Because you see, sir, she was here in this city nine months later . . ."

"Oh, yes, I see what you mean. I'm sorry, but I don't know. I suppose . . . I really don't know. Perhaps she was unhappy in Washington. Perhaps she came back to . . . I don't know." He paused. "This city has a way of luring people back, you know."

A sneeze was coming.

Carella wanted to run for the underground bunker.

Holberry grabbed for a tissue.

Carella hunched up his shoulders.

The sneeze did not come. Holberry blew his nose.

"Sorry," he said.

"Would you know where she was living when she worked here?" Brown asked.

"I'm sure we have the address in our files," Holberry said, and picked up the telephone receiver. "Miss Conway," he said, "can you bring in the file on Elizabeth Turner, please?" He put the phone back on its cradle. "It'll just be a moment," he said.

Carella knew exactly where Brown was headed.

In this city the new phone books came out on the first day of September each year. From past investigations the detectives knew that the closing date for any new listing was June 15. If a phone had not been installed by that date, it would not be listed in the new September 1 directory. Elizabeth's name, address, and number, however, *were* listed in the directory when her sister arrived here on October

27—even though Elizabeth had left the city on February 4. Which meant she'd either kept her old apartment and her old phone when she'd left the city or . . .

The door to Holberry's office opened.

A woman came in and put a file folder on his desk.

He opened it.

He began leafing through papers, stopped to blow his nose, and then began leafing again.

"Yes, here it is," he said, and looked up. "Twelve-twenty-four Dochester Avenue."

Which meant that Elizabeth Turner had taken a new apartment when she'd come back to the city—sometime *before* June 15, the closing date for the telephone directory. The carton of sour milk in her refrigerator had been stamped with an October 1 SELL-BY date. In this city the legal shelf life for milk was eight to ten days; she had to have bought it sometime between September 22 and October 1. On October 29 the super at 804 Ambrose had told Inge Turner that he hadn't seen her sister in three or four weeks. That would make it about right. She had packed her bags and flown the coop, either temporarily or for good, sometime at the beginning of October.

But why?

And where had she gone?

"Thank you very much, sir," Carella said, "you've been very helpful."

Holberry rose and extended his hand.

Carella felt he was gripping the hand of a plague victim.

There were a lot of parks in the city, most of them inadequately lighted after sundown and therefore prime locations for anyone wishing to dispose of a corpse. That this *particular* park—directly across the street from the Eight-Seven's station house—had been chosen was a matter of some concern to the detectives. It indicated either daring or insanity.

Elizabeth Turner had been found naked in the park across the street.

Elizabeth Turner had worked for a bank in Los Angeles, had worked for another bank in this city, and had left employment here to work for yet another bank in Washington, D.C.

The Deaf Man's specialty was banks.

Something was in the wind.

And it smelled mightily of the Deaf Man.

Something was in the mail as well, and it arrived in the squadroom that Friday afternoon, while Carella was on the phone with the manager at the main branch of Union Savings and Trust in Washington.

When Carella saw the white envelope in Sergeant Murchison's hand, he almost lost track of the conversation. Murchison was wearing a long-sleeved blue woolen sweater over his uniform shirt, a sure sign that Indian summer was gone. Outside the squadroom windows the sky was gray and a sharp wind was blowing. The forecasters had promised rain. Shitty November was here at last. And so was another envelope from the Deaf Man, if that's what it was. From the look on Murchison's face, that's what it was.

"... clash of personalities, you might say."

"I'm sorry, sir," Carella said, "What did you ... ?"

"I said you might describe the differences between Miss Turner and Mrs. Hatchett as a clash of personalities."

"And Mrs. Hatchett, as I understand it, is a manager with Union Savings and Trust?"

"Yes, at our Sixteenth Street branch."

"And, as such, was Miss Turner's immediate superior?"

"Exactly."

Murchison was waving the white envelope in Carella's face. Carella covered the mouthpiece, said, "Thanks, Dave," and uncovered the mouthpiece again.

"It's him again," Murchison whispered.

Carella nodded sourly. His name was staring up at him from the envelope. Why *me?* he wondered.

"I recognize the typewriter," Murchison whispered.

Carella nodded again. Murchison kept hanging around, curious about what was in the envelope. Into the phone Carella said, "What sort of personality clash *was* that, Mr. Randolph?"

"Well, Miss Turner was a very gentle person, you know, soft-spoken, easygoing, very . . . well . . . different in every way from Mrs. Hatchett. Mrs. Hatchett is . . . uh . . . aggressive, shall we say? Competitive? Abrasive? Sharp-edged? Appropriately named, shall we say?"

Carella was sure he detected a smile in Randolph's voice.

"In any event," Randolph said, "it became apparent almost immediately that Miss Turner and she would not get along. It was merely a matter of time before the tension between them achieved its full potential, that's all."

"How long did it take?"

"Well, longer than most. Miss Turner gave us notice in April."

"Left the job in April?"

"No. Told us she was quitting. Gave us two weeks' notice in April."

"And left when?"

"At the beginning of May."

"Then she was there in Washington for three months."

"Yes. Well, a little less actually. She began work here on the seventh of February. Actually it was something of a record. We've had nine assistant managers working under Mrs. Hatchett in the past eighteen months."

"She sounds like a dreamboat, your Mrs. Hatchett."

"She's the daughter-in-law of one of our board directors."

"Oh," Carella said.

"Yes," Randolph said drily.

"And that was the only reason Elizabeth Turner left the job? This personality clash with Mrs. Hatchett?"

"Well, Mr. Carella, I'm afraid you'd have to *know* Mrs. Hatchett in order to appreciate the full horror of a personality clash with her."

"I see."

"Yes," Randolph said, again drily.

"Thank you very much, Mr. Randolph," Carella said. "I appreciate your time."

"Not at all," Randolph said, and hung up.

Carella replaced the receiver on its cradle and looked at the white envelope. Murchison was still standing by his desk.

"So open it," Murchison said. "It ain't a bomb."

"How do you know?" Carella said, and nudged the envelope with his pencil. It suddenly occurred to him that the Deaf Man was something of a sideshow for the cops of the Eight-Seven, something that broke the monotony of routine. The Deaf Man arrived, and suddenly the circus was back in town. With a small shock of recognition he realized that he himself was not immune to the sense of excitement the Deaf Man promised. Almost angrily he picked up the envelope and tore off the end on its long side.

Murchison was right. It wasn't a bomb. Instead, it was:

And suddenly it began raining outside.

The rain lashed the windows of the bar on Jefferson Avenue, some three and a half miles southwest of the station house. The tall blond man with the hearing aid in his right ear had just told Naomi he was a cop. A police *detective,* no less. She didn't know the police department was hiring deaf people nowadays. Antidiscrimination laws, she supposed. They allowed you to hire *anybody.* Next you'd have detectives who were midgets. Not that a hearing aid necessarily meant you were deaf. Not stone *cold* deaf anyway. Still she guessed any degree of hearing loss could be considered an infirmity, and she was far too polite to ask him how a man wearing a hearing aid had passed the physical examination she supposed the police department required. Some people were sensitive about such things.

He was good-looking.

For a cop.

"So what's your name?" she asked.

"Steve," he said.

"Steve what?"

"Carella," he said. "Steve Carella."

"Really?" she said. "Italian?"

"Yes," he said.

"Me too," Naomi said. "Half."

"What's the other half?"

"Wildcat," she said, and grinned, and then lifted her glass. She was drinking C.C. and soda, which she thought was sophisticated. She looked up at him seductively over the rim of her glass, which she had learned to do from one of her women's magazines, where she had also learned how to have multiple orgasms, occasionally.

Actually she was half-Italian and half-Jewish, which she guessed accounted for the black hair and blue eyes. The tip-tilted nose was Irish, not that her parents could claim any credit for that. The nose's true father was Dr. Stanley Horowitz, who had done the job for her three years ago, when she was twenty-two years old. She'd asked him at the time if he didn't think she should get a little something done to her boobs as well, but he'd smiled and said she didn't need any help in *that* department, which she supposed was true.

She was wearing a low-cut blue nylon blouse that showed her breasts to good advantage and also echoed the color of her eyes. She noticed that the deaf man's eyes—what'd he say his name was?—kept wandering down to the front of her blouse, though occasionally he checked out her legs, too. She had good legs. That's why she was wearing very high-heeled, ankle-strapped shoes, to emphasize the curve of the leg. Lifted the ass, too, the high heels did, though you couldn't tell that when she was sitting. Dark blue shoes and smoky blue nylons. Sexy. She felt sexy. Her legs were crossed now, her navy blue skirt riding up over one knee.

"I'm sorry, *what* was your name again?" she asked.

"Steve Carella," he said.

"I got so carried away with your being *Italian,*" she said, rolling her eyes, "that I . . ."

"A lot of people forget Italian names," he said.

"Well, *I* certainly shouldn't," Naomi said. "My mother's maiden name was Giamboglio."

"And your name?" he said.

"Naomi Schneider." She paused and said, "That's what the other half is . . . Jewish." She waited for a reaction. Not a flicker on his face. Good. Actually she enjoyed being a Big City Jewish Girl. There was something special about the Jewish girls who lived in this city—a sharpness of attitude, a quickness of tongue, an intelligence, an awareness that came across as sophisticated and witty and hip. If anybody didn't like her being Jewish—well, *half* Jewish—then so long, it was nice knowing you. He seemed to like it, though. At least he kept staring into her blouse. And checking out the sexy legs in the smoky blue nylons.

"So, Steve," she said, "where do you work?"

"Uptown," he said, "at the Eight-Seven. Right across the street from Grover Park."

"Rotten neighborhood up there, isn't it?"

"Not the best," he said, and smiled.

"You must have your hands full."

"Occasionally," he said.

"What do you get up there? A lot of murders and such?"

"Murders, armed robberies, burglaries, rapes, arsons, muggings . . . you name it, we've got it."

"Must be exciting, though," Naomi said. She had learned in one of her women's magazines to show an intense interest in a man's work. This got difficult when you were talking to a dentist, for example. But police work really *was* interesting, so right now she didn't have to fake any deep emotional involvement with a left lateral molar, for example.

"Are you working on anything interesting just now?" she asked.

"We caught a homicide on the twenty-fifth," he said. "Dead woman in the park, about your age."

"Oh my," Naomi said.

"Shot in the back of the head. Totally naked, not a stitch on her."

"Oh my," Naomi said again.

"Not much to go on yet," he said, "but we're working on it."

"I guess you see a lot of that."

"We do."

She lifted her glass, sipped at her C.C. and soda, looking at him over the rim, and then put the glass down on the bartop again, empty. The bar at five-thirty in the afternoon was just beginning to get crowded. She'd come over directly from work, the long weekend ahead, hoping she might meet someone interesting. *This* one was certainly interesting; she'd never met a detective before. Good-looking, too. A naked dead girl in the park, how about that?

"Would you care for another drink?" he asked.

"Oh, thank you," she said. "It's C.C. and soda." She waited for a reaction. Usually you said C.C. and soda to a wimp, he asked, "What's that, C.C.?" *This* one didn't even bat an eyelash. Either he knew what C.C. was, or he was smart enough to pretend he knew. She liked smart men. She liked handsome men, too. Some men, you woke up the next morning, it wasn't even worth the shower.

He signaled to the bartender, indicated another round, and then turned to her again, smiling. He had a nice smile. The jukebox was playing the new McCartney single. The rain beat against the plate glass windows of the bar. It felt cozy and warm and comfortably crowded in here, the hum of conversation, the tinkle of ice cubes in glasses, the music from the juke, the brittle laughter of Big City women like herself.

"What sort of work do *you* do, Naomi?" he asked.

"I work for CBS," she said.

It usually impressed people when she said she worked for CBS. Actually what she did, she was a receptionist there, but still it was impressive, a network. Again nothing registered on his face. He was a very cool one, this one, well-dressed, handsome, a feeling of . . . absolute certainty about him. Well, he'd probably seen it all and done it all, this one. She found that exciting.

Well, maybe she was looking for a little excitement.

This morning, when she was dressing for work, she'd put on the lingerie she'd ordered from *Victoria's Secret*. Blue, like the blouse. A demicup underwire bra designed for low necklines, a lace-front string bikini with a cotton panel at the crotch, a garter belt with V-shaped lace panels. Sat at the desk in the lobby with the sexy underwear under her skirt and blouse, thinking she'd hit one of the bars after work, find some excitement. "CBS, good morning." And under her clothes, secret lace.

"Actually I'm just a receptionist there," she said, and wondered why she'd admitted this. "But I do get to meet a lot of performers and such. Who come up to do shows, you know."

"Uh-huh," he said.

"It's a fairly boring job," she said, and again wondered why she was telling him this.

"Uh-huh," he said.

"I plan to get into publishing eventually."

"I plan to get into *you* eventually," he said.

Normally she would have said, "Hey, get lost, creep, huh?" But he was looking at her so intently, not a smile on his face, and he appeared so . . . *confident* that for a moment she didn't know *what* to say. She had the sudden feeling that if she told him to disappear, he might arrest her or something. For what, she couldn't imagine. She also had the feeling that he knew exactly what she was wearing under her skirt and blouse. It was uncanny. As if he had X-ray vision, like Superman. She was nodding before she even realized it. She kept nodding. She hoped her face was saying, "Oh, yeah, wise guy?" She didn't know what her face was saying. She just kept nodding.

"You're pretty sure of yourself, aren't you?" she asked.

"Yes," he said.

"Walk into a bar, sit down next to a pretty girl . . ."

"You are," he said.

"Think all you have to do . . ."

"Yes," he said.

"Man of few words," she said. Her heart was pounding.

"Yes," he said.

"Mmm," she said, still nodding.

The record on the juke changed. Something by the Stones. There was a hush for a moment, one of those sudden silences, all conversation seeming to stop everywhere around them, as though E. F. Hutton were talking. And then a woman laughed someplace down the bar, and Mick Jagger's voice cut through the renewed din, and

Naomi idly twirled her finger in her drink, turning the ice cubes, turning them. She wondered if he liked sexy underwear. Most men liked sexy underwear. She visualized him tearing off her blouse and bra, getting on his knees before her to kiss her where the cotton panel covered her crotch, his big hands twisted in the garters against her thighs. She could feel the garters against her thighs.

"So . . . uh . . . where do you live, Steve?" she asked. "Near the precinct?"

"It doesn't matter where I live," he said. "We're going to *your* place."

"Oh, *are* we?" she said, and arched one eyebrow. She was jiggling her foot, she realized. She sipped at the drink, this time looking into the glass and not over the rim of it.

"Naomi," he said, "we are . . ."

"Bet you can't even spell it," she said. "Naomi."

Her magazines had said it was a good idea to get a man to spell your name out loud. That way, he would remember it. But it was as if he hadn't even heard her, as if her statement had been too ridiculous to dignify with a reply.

"We *are*," he repeated, giving the word emphasis because she'd interrupted him, "going to your apartment, *wherever* it is, and we are going to spend the weekend there."

"That's what . . . what you think," she said.

She was suddenly aware of the fact that her panties were damp.

"How do you know I'm not married?" she said.

"Are you?"

"No," she said. "How do you know I'm not living with someone?"

"Are you?"

"No, but . . ."

"Finish your drink, Naomi."

"Listen, I don't like men who come on so strong, I mean it."

"Don't you?" he said. He was smiling.

"No, I don't."

"You do," he said.

"Do all detectives come on so strong?" she said.

"I don't know what *all* detectives do," he said.

" 'Cause, you know, you really *are* coming on very strong, Steve. I don't usually like that, you know. A man coming on so strong."

"I'm giving you sixty seconds to finish that drink," he said.

God, I'm soaking *wet,* she thought, and wondered if she'd suddenly got her period.

"Are *you* married?" she asked.

"No," he said, and pushed back the cuff on his jacket. He was wearing a gold Rolex. She wondered briefly how come a detective could afford a gold Rolex.

"Sixty seconds," he said. "Starting *now*."

"What if I *don't* finish it in sixty seconds?"

"You lose," he said simply.

She did not pick up her glass.

"Fifty-five seconds," he said.

She looked into his face and then reached for her glass. "I'm drinking this because I *want* to," she said. "Not because you're looking at your watch."

"Fifty seconds," he said.

Deliberately, she sipped at the drink very slowly, and then suddenly wondered if she could really *finish* the damn thing in whatever time was left. She also wondered if she'd made the bed this morning."

"Forty seconds," he said.

"You're really something, you know that?" she said, and took a longer swallow this time.

"In exactly thirty-eight seconds . . ." he said.

"Do you carry a gun?" she asked.

"Thirty-five seconds now . . ."

" 'Cause I'm a little afraid of guns."

"Thirty seconds . . ."

"What is this, a countdown?" she asked, but she took another hasty swallow of the drink.

"Twenty-six seconds . . ."

"You're making me very nervous, you know that?" she said.

"Twenty seconds . . ."

"Forcing me to . . ."

"Fifteen . . ."

"Slow *down,* will . . . ?"

"In exactly twelve seconds . . ."

"I'm gonna *choke* on this," she said.

"Ten seconds . . ."

"Jesus!"

"You and I . . . eight seconds . . . are going to . . . five seconds . . . walk out of here . . . two seconds . . ."

"All *right,* already!" she said and plunked the empty glass down on the bartop. Their eyes met.

"Good," he said, and smiled.

She had found the ribbons for him in her sewing box. He had asked her for the ribbons. By then she would have given him the moon. Silk ribbons. A red one on her right wrist. A blue one on her left wrist. Pink ribbons on her ankles. She was spread-eagled on her king-size bed, her wrists and ankles tied to the bars of the brass headboard and footboard. She was still wearing the smoky blue nylons, the high-heeled, ankle-strapped shoes, and the garter belt. He had taken off her panties and her bra. She lay there open and exposed, waiting for whatever he chose to do next, *wanting* whatever he chose to do next.

He had put his shoulder holster and gun on the seat of the armchair across the room. That was when he was undressing. Jokingly she had said, "Let me see your badge," which is what anybody in this city said when somebody knocked on your door in the middle of the night and claimed to be a cop. He had looked at her without a smile. "*Here's* my badge, baby," he'd said, and unzipped his fly. She knew she was in trouble right that minute. She just didn't know how *much* trouble. She had looked down at him and said, "Oh, boy, I'm in trouble," and had giggled nervously, like a schoolgirl, and suddenly she was in his arms, and his lips were on hers, and she was lost, she knew she was lost.

That had been four hours ago, before he'd tied her to the bed.

The clock on the dresser now read ten o'clock.

He had insisted that they leave the shades on the windows up, even though she protested that people in the building across the way might see them. There were lights on in the building across the way. Above the building the night was black. She wondered if anyone across the way could see her tied to the bed with silk ribbons. She was oozing below again, dizzy with wanting him again. She visualized someone across the way looking at her. Somehow it made her even more excited.

She watched him as he went to the armchair, picked up the holster, and took the pistol from it. Broad, tanned shoulders, a narrow waist, her fingernail marks still on his ass from where she'd clawed at him. She'd described herself to him, back there in the bar, as half-wildcat, but that was something she'd never believed of herself, even after she'd learned all about multiple orgasms. Tonight . . . Jesus! Afloat on her own ocean. Still wet with his juices and her own, still wanting more.

He approached the bed with the gun in his hand.

"Is there a burglar in the house?" she asked, smiling.

He did not smile back.

"A lesson," he said.

"Is that loaded?" she said. She was looking at his cock, not the gun, though in truth the gun did frighten her. She had never liked guns. But she was still smiling, seductively she thought. She writhed on the bed, twisting against the tight silken ribbons.

"Empty," he said, and snapped open the cylinder to show her. "A Colt Detective Special," he said. "Snub-nosed."

"Like me," she said. "Do you like my nose?"

"Are you ready for the lesson?" he asked.

"Oh my," she said, opening her eyes and her bound hands in mock fright. "*Another* lesson?" The gun was empty, she wasn't afraid of it now. And she was ready to play any game he invented.

"If you're ready for one," he said.

"I'm ready for anything you've got," she said.

"A lesson in combinations and permutations," he said, and suddenly opened his left hand. A bullet was in it. "Voilà," he said. "Six empty chambers in the . . ."

"There's an empty chamber right here," she said.

". . . cylinder of the pistol."

"Come fill it," she said.

"And one bullet in my left hand."

He showed her the bullet.

"I insert this into the cylinder . . ."

"Insert something in *me,* will you, please?"

". . . and we now have one full chamber and five empty ones. Question: what are the odds against the shell being in firing position when I stop twirling the cylinder?" He started twirling the cylinder, slowly, idly. "Any idea?" he said.

"Five to one," she said. "Come fuck me."

"Five to one, correct," he said, and sat on the edge of the bed, resting the barrel of the gun against the inside of her thigh.

"Careful with that," she said.

He smiled. His finger was inside the trigger guard.

"Really," she said. "There's a bullet in it now."

"Yes, I know."

"So . . . you know . . . move it away from there, okay?" She twisted on the bed. The cold barrel of the gun touched her thigh again. "Come on, Steve."

"We're going to play a little Russian roulette," he said, smiling.

"Like hell we are," she said.

But she was tied to the bed.

He rose suddenly. Standing beside the bed, looking down at her, he began twirling the cylinder. He kept twirling it. Twirling it. Smiling.

"Come on, Steve," she said, "you're scaring me."

"Nothing to be scared of," he said. "The odds are five to one."

He stopped twirling the cylinder.

He sat on the edge of the bed again.

He looked at her.

He looked at the gun.

And then, gently, he placed the barrel of the gun into the hollow of her throat. She recoiled, terrified, twisting her head. The metal was cold against her flesh.

"Hey, listen," she said, and he pulled the trigger.

The silence was deafening.

She lay there sweating, breathing harshly, certain he would pull the trigger yet another time. The odds were five to one. How many times could he . . . ?

"It's made of wood," he said. "The bullet in the gun. You weren't in any danger."

He moved the barrel of the gun away from her throat. She heaved a sigh of relief.

And realized how wet she was.

And looked at him.

His erection was enormous.

"You . . . shouldn't have scared me that way," she said. She was throbbing everywhere.

"I can do whatever I *want* with you," he said.

"No, you can't."

"I own you," he said.

"No, you don't," she whispered.

But she struggled against the restraining ribbons to open wider for him as he mounted her again.

They did not budge from that apartment all weekend.

She did not know what was happening to her; nothing like this had ever happened to her in her life.

He left early Monday morning, promising to call her soon.

As soon as he was gone, she dressed as he had ordered her to.

Sitting behind the reception desk at CBS later that morning, she wore no panties under her skirt and no bra under her blouse.

"CBS, good morning," she said into the phone.

And ached for him.

4

If a person is an armed robber and he moves to another state, chances are he'll continue the pursuit of his chosen career. He will not, for example, suddenly become a used-car salesman or a television producer, however similar to felony violators those two professionals might be. He will, instead, buy himself a gun that isn't hot—which is easy to come by in any city in the United States—find himself a mom-and-pop grocery store, and stick it up one fine night. If Mom and Pop are smart and cooperative, they will empty the contents of the cash register into his waiting hands and pray that he departs at once. If Mom and Pop feel that an armed intruder in their store is a *personal* as well as a criminal violation, they might foolishly resist this invasion of their turf, in which case they might lose more than the cash in the register. An armed robber isn't armed because he belongs to the National Rifle Association. He is armed because he knows he is looking at twenty years down the pike if he's caught doing his job, and he is quite ready—and often eager—to use the pistol in his fist. In America the most recent annual figure for deaths caused by handguns was thirty-four thousand nationwide, second only to deaths caused in automobile accidents. That is a whole lot of dead people. Carella sometimes wondered if the members of the NRA, while happily shooting deer in the forest, ever said a silent prayer for all those victims.

Elizabeth Turner had worked for a bank in Los Angeles. She had worked for a bank here in this city, and she had also worked for a bank in Washington, D.C. Honest citizens, like criminals, will most often seek the same line of work when they move from one state to another. Wasn't it likely, in fact almost mandatory, that Elizabeth would have sought a job in yet another bank upon her return here?

The detectives knew that in this state all employers had to fill out a so-called WRS-2 form, which was a quarterly report of wages that had to be filed with the state's Department of Taxation and Finance on April 30, July 31, October 31, and January 31. The WRS-2 form listed the name and social security number of each employee, together with the gross wages earned in that quarter. The detectives were in possession of Elizabeth Turner's social security number. They knew she had left the job in Washington on May 1. They further knew that she had been found dead in Grover Park on October 25. Wasn't it a likelihood that at least one and perhaps two WRS-2 forms had been filed for her since her return to the city? Carella made a call upstate and spoke to a man named Culpepper there. Culpepper said he would check the WRS-2 forms filed on July 31 and October 31 and get back to him.

He did not get back to him until November 11, a dismally gray, wet, and cold Friday, by which time the case was already seventeen days old. He told Carella that none of the forms filed on July 31 reported wages for an Elizabeth Turner in that quarter.

"How about the October thirty-first forms?" Carella asked.

"Those haven't been processed yet."

"Haven't you got a computer up there?"

"Not for these quarterly forms," Culpepper said.

"Well, when do you think they *will* be processed?"

"When we get to them."

"When will that be?"

"When we get to them," Culpepper said again. "Sometime before the next quarter's filing is due."

"You mean in January? Next *year?*"

"The WRS-2's are due on January thirty-first, that's right."

"This is a homicide here," Carella said. "I'm trying to find out where this girl *worked.* Can't you do something to expedite this?"

"I'd be different if the forms were filed under an *employee's* name," Culpepper said. "Or even his or her social security number. But they're not. They're filed under the *employer's* name. You don't know how long it took us to check all those July forms, looking for this Elizabeth Turner. And *those* forms had already been processed."

Carella knew exactly how long it had taken. He had made his request six days ago. "Look," he said, "it's very important for us to find out where . . ."

"I'm sorry," Culpepper said. "I'll have the October thirty-first forms checked once they've been processed, but I can't do better than that."

"Okay, thanks," Carella said, and hung up.

He sat staring at his typewriter for a moment, and then he rolled a D. D. Supplementary Report form into it. He had typed almost a full page when Alf Miscolo came from the clerical office down the hall. There was a plain white envelope in his hand. This one was postmarked November 10. As with the four that had preceded it, the letter was addressed to Detective Stephen Louis Carella, the name neatly typewritten on the face of the envelope.

"I thought maybe he'd forgotten us," Miscolo said.

"No such luck," Carella said and tore open the flap of the envelope.

The same single white sheet of paper inside.

And pasted to it:

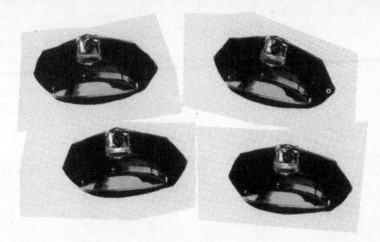

"That looks to me like four police hats," Miscolo said.

"Yes," Carella said.

"You think he's a cop?" Miscolo asked.

"I don't think so."

"Then why's he sending us pictures of all this police shit? Walkie-talkies, shields, handcuffs? Police hats?" He shook his head. "I don't like the idea of somebody sending us pictures of police paraphernalia," he said. "It's spooky."

He was not a handsome man, Miscolo. His nose was massive and his eyebrows were bushy, and there was a thickness about his neck that created the impression of head sitting directly on shoulders. But normally there was an animation to his face and a sparkle to his dark eyes—never more evident than when he was defending the truly abominable coffee he brewed in his office—and this was totally lacking now as he stared disconsolately at the sheet of paper in Carella's hand.

A police station was sacrosanct to men like Miscolo and Carella. Whatever happened out there on the streets, it did not come into the station house except in handcuffs. Although once—as they both remembered well—a woman with a gun and a bottle of nitroglycerin had held this very room hostage for more hours than either of them cared to count. For the most part, though, the precinct was as much a castle to these men as was a shabby row house to a British miner. It was enormously troubling to Miscolo that someone was using *police* equipment to make whatever the hell point he was trying to make. He felt as if he'd wandered into a filthy subway toilet and found his wife's monogrammed towels on one of the sinks.

He knew what the other four messages had—well, *advertised,* if that was the correct word. They were all posted side by side on the squadroom bulletin board in the order in which they'd been received:

Eight black horses.

Five walkie-talkies.

Three pairs of handcuffs.

Six police shields.

And now this.

Four police hats.

Except for the horses, it was as if somebody was putting together a policeman piece by piece.

"They all got to do with cops, you realize that?" he said. "Except the horses."

"Cops still ride horses in this city," Carella said.

"Them shields on the hats got no numbers on them, you realize that? He prolly cut out a picture of a hat someplace and then Xeroxed it."

"There's a number on this picture of the shields, though."

"You suppose that's a real shield?"

"I don't know.

" 'Cause you can Xerox anything nowadays," Miscolo said. "You lay something on the glass there, you close the cover, you press the button, you get a pretty good picture of it."

"Yeah," Carella said.

"If it *is* a real one . . . where'd he get it?" Miscolo asked.

"Maybe I oughta check it out," Carella said. "Trouble is . . ."

"Yeah, I know. You'd feel like a jerk."

"I mean, we're getting these dumb letters . . ."

"I know . . ."

"I make a call to Personnel, ask if a cop lost a potsie with the number seventy-nine on it . . ."

"You'd feel like a jerk."

"Which is how we're supposed to feel," Carella said.

"I don't like this guy, I really don't like him," Miscolo said, and looked at the picture of the four police hats again. "What's he trying to tell us anyway?"

"I don't know," Carella said, and sighed heavily.

"You want some coffee?" Miscolo asked.

"Thanks, not right now," Carella said.

"Yeah, well," Miscolo said, and shrugged and left the squadroom.

The rain lashed the windows.

Carella wondered if he should call Personnel to run a check on shield number seventy-nine.

He looked at the D.D. form in his typewriter. Years ago you had to use carbon paper to make duplicate, triplicate, even quadruplicate copies. Now you just ran down the hall and asked Miscolo to run off Xerox copies for you. The way the Deaf Man—it *had* to be the Deaf Man—had Xeroxed the pictures he'd been sending them. The form—just as he'd typed it, errors, overscoring, and all—read:

DETECTIVE DIVISION SUPPLEMENTARY REPORT	SQUAD	PRECINCT	PRECINCT REPORT NUMBER	DETECTIVE DIVISION REPORT NUMBER	PAGE NUMBER
	87	87	68-8946	DD 72 H-203	1

NAME AND ADDRESS OF PERSON REPORTING

RE HOMICIDE VICTIM ELIZABETH ANNE TURNER (See Jane Doe L-4129)

DATE OF ORIGINAL REPORT

10/25

SURNAME	GIVEN NAME	INITIALS	NUMBER	STREET	VILLAGE

DETAILS

    Subsequent to reports 10/25, 11/2, 11/4.

    1) INGE /TURner, sister of deceased, ELIZABETH ANNE TURNER, returned

       to Los Angeles, California XXXXXXXXXXXXXX on 11/6.

    2) Further canvass of tenants at 804 South Ambrose Street revealed no

       additional significant details regarding deceased's habits or

       relationships with other men or women.

    3) Despite gangland nature of slaying, precinct informers have heard

       nothing significant regarding the murder.

    4) Second pass at banks, brokerage firms, other financial instituutions

       this city incomplete, but majority reporting no employment record

       Elziabeth Anne Turner May 1-October 25.

    5) Check with State Department Taxation and XXXXXXXXXXXXXX Finance

       reveals no record of wages paid Elizabeth Anne Turner as per WRS-2

       forms filed July 31. October 31 search pending.

    6) Considering lack of further evidence, absence of ballistics data,

       witnesses, or motive for murder, it is respectfully submitted

       that xxxxxxx investigation be tempoerarily

DATE OF THIS REPORT

RANK	SURNAME	INITIALS	SHIELD NUMBER	COMMAND	SIGNATURE OF COMMANDING OFFICER

That was as far as he'd got.

He was about to throw the Elizabeth Turner case into the Open File. Open. A euphemism for dead end. A case waiting for a miracle to happen. Open. In that years from now, by some impossible stroke of luck, they might arrest a man dropping another dead woman in yet another park, and he would confess to the first murder and perhaps a dozen murders before that one.

He looked at the form again.

He looked at the Deaf Man's most recent message.

Four police hats.

No faces under them.

Anonymous hats.

The form in Carella's typewriter was about to be thrown into the vast anonymity of the Open File, another piece of paper in a maze of information that confirmed the ineffectiveness of the police in a city where far too many murders were committed. The Open File was a gaping maw that swallowed victims. And in the process swallowed victimizers as well.

The proximity of the Deaf Man's anonymous hats and the imminently anonymous form in the typewriter made him suddenly angry. It was entirely possible that there was no connection whatever between Elizabeth Turner and the Deaf Man. Seeking such a connection would most certainly be time-consuming and, in the long run, perhaps foolish. But she had been found dead in the park across the street. And there had been five letters from the Deaf Man to date, and if he wasn't sticking his finger in their collective eye, then it certainly *seemed* that way. Throw Elizabeth Turner's corpse into the Open File, and he'd be throwing the Deaf Man into it as well.

He ripped the D.D. report from his typewriter.

He carried the Deaf Man's most recent greeting to the bulletin board and was about to tack it up with the others there, when it suddenly occurred to him that perhaps they were meant to be read in *numerical* rather than *chronological* order.

He began shifting them around, retacking them to the board in a single horizontal line.

Three pairs of handcuffs. Four police hats. Five walkie-talkies. Six police shields. Eight black horses.

So what? he thought.

They still meant nothing.

Not realizing how close he'd come to at least a *beginning,* he walked back to his desk, checked his book of police department phone listings, and then dialed Personnel downtown on High Street.

"Personnel, Sergeant Mullaney," a voice answered.

"Detective Carella at the Eight-Seven," he said. "I need a name and address for a possible police officer."

"A *possible* officer?" Mullaney said.

"Yes. All I've got is a shield number."

"What's the number?" Mullaney asked.

"Seventy-nine."

"You gotta be kidding," Mullaney said.

"What do you mean?"

"Seventy-*nine?* You know what number we're up to now? Don't even ask. You know how many cops been through this system since the police department was started? Don't ask."

"Check it anyway, okay?"

"This guy's got to be kidding," Mullaney said to no one. "Where'd you get this number?"

"On a picture of a shield."

"A *picture* of a shield?"

"Yes."

"And it says seventy-nine on it?"

"Yes."

"What's *your* number, Coppola?"

"Seven-one-four, five-six, three-two. And it's Carella."

"That'll give you some idea where we are now with the shield numbers. So you want me to check a shield some guy was a kid when the fuckin' *Dutch* was still here?"

"Just do me the favor, okay? This is a homicide we're working."

"I ain't surprised. A guy with shield number seventy-nine, he's been dead for at least three centuries. Hold on, okay?"

Carella held on.

Mullaney came back onto the line some five minutes later.

"No active shield number seventy-nine," he said. "Just like I figured."

"How about past records?"

"We don't go back to Henry Hudson," Mullaney said.

"Check your past records," Carella said impatiently. "This is a goddamn homicide here."

"Don't get your ass in an uproar, Coppola," Mullaney said, and left the phone again.

Carella waited.

When Mullaney came back, he said, "I got a badge number seventy-nine from 1858. There were eight-hundred thousand people in this city then, and we had a police force of fourteen hundred men. You'll be interested in learning, no doubt, that in those days the police department was also charged with cleaning the streets."

"So what's changed?" Carella said.

"Nothing," Mullaney said. "You want this guy's name?"

"Please," Carella said.

"Angus McPherson," Mullaney said. "He died in 1872. You'll be interested in learning, no doubt, that by then we had a population of a million-four and a police force of eighteen hundred men. Also, by then, there was a street cleaning department. Cops didn't have to shovel horse manure anymore. All they had to worry about was getting shot. Which was what happened to this guy McPherson. Where'd you get a picture of his shield? In an antiques shop?"

"I wouldn't be surprised," Carella said. "Thanks a lot, Maloney."

He had told Charlie Henkins that his name was Dennis Dove, and had asked him to make it "Den" for short. Charlie didn't realize it, but the words *den döve* were Swedish. In Swedish the word *den* meant "the," but *döve* was not a white bird of peace. The word wasn't even pronounced the way it was in English. In Swedish *döve* meant "deaf man." Den Dove, then, was the Deaf Man.

"The thing I still don't understand," Charlie said, "is why you want to do it on Christmas Eve. I mean, the situation is exactly the same on *any* night. The money'll be there in the vault *any* night we pick."

"Yes, but that's when I want to do it," the Deaf Man said.

Charlie scratched his head. He was not a particularly bright human being, but then again most armed robbers weren't. The Deaf Man had chosen him because he knew how to use a gun and was not afraid to use it. Charlie had, in fact, served a great deal of time at Castleview Prison upstate *precisely* because he'd used a gun while holding up a liquor store. The owner of the store was now confined to a wheelchair for life, a minor detail that disturbed Charlie not in the least. The way Charlie figured it, he'd *had* to burn the owner of the store because the man was reaching for his own gun under the counter. Charlie hadn't considered the fact that two cops in a cruising police car up the street would hear the shots and would, within the next three minutes, have Charlie in handcuffs. Those were the breaks. He who hesitates is lost, dog eat dog, and easy come, easy go. Charlie knew all the proverbs and tricks of the trade, and he had learned a few more of them while serving his time upstate. Everybody learned a few tricks in the slammer. The Deaf Man figured Charlie was perfect for the job he'd planned. Charlie had twinkling blue eyes and a little round pot belly.

"What I usually like to do on Christmas Eve," Charlie said, "is I like to watch television. They do a lot of specials on Christmas Eve. Last Christmas Eve I watched Perry Como on television. He used to be a barber, you know that? My cousin Andy used to be a barber, too, before he got into doing burglaries. Not that Perry Como does burglaries."

"You'll be home by seven-thirty," the Deaf Man said. "You can watch television all night long, if you like."

"I go in at a quarter to seven, huh?" Charlie said.

"Into the *vault* at a quarter to seven," the Deaf Man said.

"Yeah, sure, that's what I meant." He scratched his head again. "You sure Lizzie gave you the right numbers?"

"Positive."

"The combinations, I mean."

"Yes, I know what you mean. The numbers are absolutely correct."

"And there's this little push-button pad on the outer door, right?" Charlie said.

"Yes. Set in a panel to the right of the door."

"Steel door, huh?"

"Steel."

"And another door after that one."

"Yes, with another pad and a second set of numbers."

"And inside there's the safe with still *more* numbers."

"Yes."

"Think it was fuckin' Fort Knox they got there," Charlie said.

"Not quite," the Deaf Man said, and smiled.

"Still. Three sets of fuckin' numbers."

"Don't worry about the numbers," the Deaf Man said. "You'll have them memorized long before you actually use them."

"Yeah," Charlie said.

"Before we're through, you'll know those numbers the way you know your own name."

"Well, yeah," Charlie said.

"Does that bother you? Learning the numbers?"

"No, no, I just don't want anything to go wrong, that's all."

"Nothing'll go wrong if we're prepared for the *eventuality* of something going wrong. It's possible, of course, that you'll forget those combinations even after we've gone over them a thousand times. But it's not probable."

"I don't even know what that means, probable," Charlie said.

"A possibility is something that is *capable* of happening or being true without contradicting proven facts, laws, or circumstances. A *probability,* on the other hand, is something that is *likely* to happen or to be true. To put it in simpler terms . . ."

"Yeah, please," Charlie said.

"It is *possible* that our Christmas Eve adventure may go terribly awry, in which case we will both spend a good deal of time behind bars. It is *probable,* however, that all will go as planned, and we'll come out of it richer by half a million dollars."

"Which we split three ways, right?" Charlie said. "You, me, and Lizzie."

"Three ways, yes," the Deaf Man said.

Charlie nodded, but he looked troubled. "Just two broads inside the vault there, huh?" he said.

"Just the cashier and her assistant, yes."

"And you want me to take care of both of them, huh?"

"Immediately. As soon as you're in the vault."

"Well, that's the easy part, taking care of them," Charlie said.

"What's the *hard* part?" the Deaf Man asked.

"Well . . . learning the combinations, I guess. There's eighteen numbers to learn, you know. Six on each of those pads."

"You'll learn them, don't worry. You mustn't think of them as a single set of eighteen numbers. They'll be easier to remember if you think of them as three separate sets of six numbers each."

"Yeah," Charlie said.

"Three separate and distinct combinations."

"Yeah."

"In fact," the Deaf Man said, smiling, "combinations are a good way of differing between possibility and probability."

Charlie looked at him blankly.

"Let's start with something simple," the Deaf Man said. "Take two numbers. How many possible ways are there of arranging those two numbers?"

"Two?" Charlie asked uncertainly.

"Exactly. If the numbers are, for example, one and two, you can either arrange them as one-two or two-one. There are no other possibilities capable of being true without contradicting proven facts, laws, or circumstances. Now let's add another number. The number three. We now have three numbers. One, two, and three. How many possible ways can we arrange those three numbers?"

"Easy," Charlie said. "Three ways."

"Wrong. They can be arranged in six different ways. Here," he said, and picked up a pencil and moved a pad into place on the table. Writing swiftly, he listed the six possible combinations of the numbers one, two, and three:

1-2-3
1-3-2
2-1-3
2-3-1
3-1-2
3-2-1

"Hey, how about that?" Charlie said.

"The way one calculates the possible ways of arranging *any* amount of numbers is to multiply the highest number by the one below it and then multiply the result by the number below that, and so on. For example, we have three numbers: one, two, and three. All right, we multiply three by two and we get six. Then we multiply six by one, and we get six again. The answer is six. And, as we just saw, there *are*, in fact, only six possible ways of arranging those three numbers.''

''I was never good in arithmetic,'' Charlie said.

''It gets more complicated when there are more numbers,'' the Deaf Man said. ''For example, those pads outside each of the doors have nine numbers on them. Do you realize how many possible ways there are of arranging those nine numbers?''

Again Charlie looked at him blankly.

''Well,'' the Deaf Man said, ''do the multiplication. Nine by eight by seven by six by five by four and so on down to one. Nine times eight is seventy-two. Seventy-two times seven is five hundred and four. Five hundred and four times six is three thousand and twenty-four. And so on. If you carry it all the way through, you'll discover that there are three hundred and sixty-two thousand, eight hundred and eighty *possible* ways of arranging nine numbers. What, I ask you, is the *probability*—the likelihood—of anyone accidentally hitting upon the combination of six numbers that will unlock the outer door? And a different combination of six numbers for the inner door? And yet a third combination for the safe itself?''

''There ain't no way to figure that,'' Charlie said, shaking his head.

''Well, there is, but it would take forever. Which is exactly why combination locks were invented.''

''Which is why *Lizzie* was invented, you mean.''

''Yes, of course,'' the Deaf Man said, smiling. ''To *provide* us with the combinations.''

''For which she gets a third of the take,'' Charlie said, looking troubled again. ''You think that's fair?''

''Do I think *what's* fair?''

''Her getting a third.''

''Without her we wouldn't be going in at all.''

''Yeah, well,'' Charlie said, ''it ain't *us* going in, it's *me* going in.''

''I know that.''

''Yeah, but you just said *we'd* be going in.''

''One of us has to be outside,'' the Deaf Man said. ''You know that.'' He hesitated and then asked, ''Would you rather *I* went in?''

''Well, I guess I look more the part,'' Charlie said.

''Exactly.''

''Still.''

''What is it, Charlie?'' the Deaf Man said. ''Tell me everything that's troubling you. I don't want any problems, not now and not later either.''

''Okay, here's what's botherin' me,'' Charlie said. ''I'm the one goes in the vault with a gun. I'm the one has to take care of the two broads in there. You're waitin' outside, and Lizzie ain't nowhere even *near* the scene. So, okay, it was your idea, the whole heist. I ain't begrudgin' you your share, especially since you're the one takes the fall if they catch you with the loot, by which time I'm already home free. But where does Lizzie come off takin' a third when all she done is give the layout?''

"*And* the combinations."

"Yeah, well, the combinations."

"Without which there wouldn't be a job at all."

"It's just a question of what's fair, that's all," Charlie said. "You and me are takin' the biggest risks . . ."

"In a sense, Charlie," the Deaf Man said gently, "*you're* the one who's taking the greatest risk."

"Well, thank you," Charlie said, "I'm glad you said that, I really am. But it's your job, and fair is fair. And also you're taking a risk, too. It's that Lizzie ain't takin' no risk at all."

"Maybe you've got a point."

"I think I do."

"I'll have to talk to her. What would you suggest, Charlie?"

"Well, there's five hundred K in that vault, *supposed* to be five hundred K, anyway . . ."

"Perhaps more."

"So I thought, if we gave Lizzie a hundred thou for setting it up, then you and me split the rest."

"I'll tell you what I'll do," the Deaf Man said. "Fair is fair."

"It is."

"We'll give Lizzie a flat hundred, as you suggest. But I'll take only a hundred and fifty, and you'll get the lion's share, *two* hundred and fifty."

"Hey, no, I wasn't suggesting nothing like that," Charlie said.

"Fair is fair, Charlie."

"Well," Charlie said.

"Does that please you?"

"Well, if it's okay with you."

"It's fine with me."

" 'Cause I didn't want to say nothin' about like I'm the one lookin' at two counts of murder, you know what I mean?"

"I know exactly what you mean. And I appreciate it."

"And I appreciate what you're doin', too, the jester you just made. I really appreciate that, Den."

"Good. Are we agreed then?"

"I couldn't be happier," Charlie said, and then looked troubled again.

"What is it?" the Deaf Man asked.

"You think she'll go along with it? Lizzie?"

"Oh, I'm sure she will."

"I hope so. I wouldn't want her blowin' the whistle 'cause she thinks she ain't gettin' what she *should* be gettin'."

"No, don't worry about that, Charlie."

"Where is she, anyway?" Charlie asked. "Shouldn't she be here when we go over all this shit?"

"She's done her job already," the Deaf Man said. "She's no longer needed."

He looked at Charlie, wondering if he even suspected that once he carried that cash out of the vault he'd have done *his* job and he, too, would no longer be needed.

"Now then," he said, "the combinations."

"Yeah, the fuckin' combinations," Charlie said.

"Think of them as three different sets, Charlie. Forget that there are eighteen numbers in all."

"Okay, yeah." "Can you give me the first set? The six numbers for the outer door?"

"Seven-six-one, three-two . . ."

"Wrong."

"Seven-six-one . . ."

"Yes?"

"Three-two . . ."

"No."

"No?"

"No."

"Three-two . . ."

"No, it's two-three."

"Oh. Yeah. Two-three, yeah. Two-three-eight."

"And the inner door?"

"Nine-two-four, three-eight-five."

"Correct. And the safe?"

"Two-four-seven, four-six-three."

"Good, Charlie. Try it from the top again."

"Seven-six-one, two-three-eight."

"Again."

"Seven-six-one, two-three-eight."

"Again."

"Seven-six-one, two-three-eight."

"And the inner door?"

"Nine-two-four . . ."

5

Eight, four, three, Brown thought.

He was looking at the squadroom bulletin board where the Deaf Man's little billets-doux were tacked in a row under the wanted flyers and a notice advising that the Detective Division's annual Mistletoe Ball would be held on Wednesday night, December 14.

Eight black horses, four police hats, and three pairs of handcuffs.

Six, five, he thought.

In police radio code, 10-5 meant REPEAT MESSAGE.

But this was a *six*-five.

Six police shields and five walkie-talkies.

Goddamn Deaf Man, Brown thought, and went to the coatrack in the corner of the room. He had dressed this morning in a bulky red plaid mackinaw, which made him look even bigger and meaner than he normally did. Blue woolen watch cap on his head. Bright red muffler around his throat. Only the fourteenth day of November, and already it was like Siberia out there. Idly he wondered if the Deaf Man had anything to do with it. Maybe the Deaf Man was a Russian spy. Manipulating the weather the way he manipulated everything else.

The clock on the squadroom wall read ten minutes to eight, but only one man from the graveyard shift was still there. Must've been a quiet night, Brown thought. "Cold as a witch's tit outside," he said to O'Brien, who looked up from his typewriter, grunted, glanced at the wall clock and then said, "You had a coupla calls last night. The messages are on your desk."

Outside the grilled squadroom windows the wind was blowing leaves and hats and newspapers and skirts and all kinds of crap all over the streets. Made a man happy to be inside. Just walking from the subway station to the precinct, Brown thought he'd freeze off all his fingers and toes. Should've worn his long johns this morning. Nice and toasty in the squadroom, though. Even Miscolo's coffee, brewing down the hallway, smelled good. He took off his mackinaw and hung it on the rack, tossing the red muffler over it. He left the blue watch cap on his head. Made him feel like Big Bad Leroy just out of Castleview, where he done time for arson, murder, and rape. Yeah, watch it, man. Cross my path today, you go home with a scar. Smiling, he sat at his desk and looked at the pile of junk the men on the graveyard shift had dumped there.

The squadroom was quiet except for the howling of the wind outside and the clacking of O'Brien's typewriter. Brown leafed through the papers on his desk. A note from Cotton Hawes telling him that a burglary victim had called late last night to ask if Detective Brown had been able to find his stolen television set. Fat Chance Department. That television set had disappeared into the world's biggest bargain basement. The thieves in this city, they gave you a bigger discount than if you were buying wholesale. Some thieves even stole things to *order* for you. Want a brand-new video cassette player? What make? RCA? Sony? See you tomorrow night this time. Coming up with that man's stolen TV would be like finding a pot of gold in the sewer. He wondered if it was true there were alligators down there in the sewers. He once had to chase a thief down a sewer, never wanted to do that again in his life. Dripping water, rats, and a stink he couldn't wash out of his nostrils for the next ten days.

Hawes had been complaining lately that the midnight-to-8:00 A.M. was ruining his sex life. His sex life these days was a lady Rape Squad cop named Annie Rawles. Brown wondered what it was like to go to bed with a Detective/First Grade. Excuse me, ma'am, would you mind unpinning your potsie, it is sticking into my arm. Six police shields. Carella had told him shield number seventy-nine had belonged to a guy named Angus McPherson, long dead and gone. So where had the Deaf Man found it? Goddamn Deaf Man, he thought again. He was looking through the other messages on his desk when the telephone rang.

"Eighty-seventh Squad, Brown," he said.

"Hello, yes," the voice on the other end said. A young woman. Slightly nervous. "May I speak to Detective Carella, please?"

"I'm sorry, he's not here just now," Brown said. "Should be in any minute, though." He looked up at the wall clock. Five minutes to eight. "Can I take a message for him?"

"Yes," the woman said. "Would you tell him Naomi called?"

"Yes, Miss, Naomi who?" Brown said. O'Brien was on his way out of the squadroom. He waved to Brown, and Brown waved back.

"Just tell him Naomi. He'll know who it is."

"Well, Miss, we like to . . ."

"He'll know," she said, and hung up.

Brown looked at the telephone receiver.

He shrugged and put it back on its cradle.

Carella walked into the squadroom not three minutes later.

"Your girlfriend called," Brown said.

"I told her never to call me at the office," Carella said.

He looked like an Eskimo. He was wearing a short woolen car coat with a hood pulled up over his head. The hood was lined with some kind of fur, probably rabbit, Brown thought. He was wearing leather fur-lined gloves. His nose was red; and his eyes were tearing.

"Where'd summer go?" he asked.

"Naomi," Brown said, and winked. "She said you'd know who."

The phone rang again.

Brown picked up the receiver.

"Eighty-seventh Squad, Brown," he said.

"Hello, it's Naomi again," the voice said, still sounding nervous. "I'm sorry to bother you, but I'll be leaving for work in a few minutes, and I'm not sure he has the number there."

"Hold on, he just came in," Brown said, and held the phone out to Carella. "Naomi," he said.

Carella looked at him.

"Naomi." Brown said again, and shrugged.

"You kidding?" Carella asked.

"It's Naomi," Brown said. "Would I kid you about Naomi?"

Carella walked to his own desk.

"What extension is she on?" he asked.

"Six. You want a little privacy? Shall I go down the hall?"

Carella pushed the six button on the base of his phone and lifted the receiver. "Detective Carella," he said.

"Steve?" a woman's voice said. "It's Naomi."

"Uh-huh," he said, and looked at Brown.

Brown rolled his eyes.

"You promised you'd call," she said.

"Uh-huh," Carella said, and looked at Brown again. The way he figured it, there were only two possible explanations for the youngish-sounding lady on the phone. One: she was someone he'd dealt with before in the course of a working day, an honest citizen with one complaint or another, and he'd simply forgotten her name. Or two, and he considered this more likely: the witty gents of the Eight-Seven had concocted an elaborate little gag, and he was the butt of it. He remembered back to last April, when they'd asked a friendly neighborhood hooker to come up here and tell Genero she was pregnant with his child. Now there was Naomi. City-honed voice calling him "Steve" and telling him he'd promised to call. And Brown sitting across the room, watching him expectantly. Okay, he thought, let's play the string out.

"Steve?" she said. "Are you still there?"

"Yep," he said. "Still here. What's this in reference to, Miss?"

"It's in reference to your pistol."

"Oh, I see, my pistol," he said.

"Yes, your big pistol."

"Uh-huh," he said.

"When am I going to see you again, Steve?"

"Well, that all depends," he said, and smiled at Brown. "*Who'd* you say this was?"

"What is it?" she said. "Can't you talk just now?"

"Yes, Miss, certainly," he said. "But police regulations require that we get the name and address of anyone calling the squadroom. Didn't they tell you that?"

"Didn't *who* tell me that?"

"Whoever put you up to calling me."

There was a long silence on the line.

"What is it?" she said. "Don't you *want* to talk to me?"

"Miss," Carella said, "I would *love* to talk to you, truly. I would love to talk to you for hours on end. It's just that these jackasses up here"—he looked meaningfully at Brown—"don't seem to understand that a dedicated and hardworking policeman has better things to do at eight o'clock in the morning than . . ."

"Why are you acting so peculiarly?" she said.

"Would you like to talk to Artie again?" Carella said.

"Who's Artie?"

"Or did Meyer set this up?"

"I don't know what you're talking about," she said.

"Cotton, right? It was Cotton."

"Am I talking to the right person?" she asked.

"You are talking to the person they asked you to talk to," he said, and winked at Brown. Brown did not wink back. Carella felt suddenly uneasy.

"Is this Detective Steve Carella?" she asked.

"Yes," he said cautiously, beginning to think he'd made a terrible mistake. If this *was* an honest citizen calling on legitimate police business . . .

"Who ties girls to beds and plays Russian roulette," she said. "With a wooden bullet."

Uh-oh, he thought, a bedbug. He signaled to Brown to pick up the extension, and then he put his forefinger to his temple and twirled it clockwise in the universal sign language for someone who'd lost his marbles.

"Can you let me have your last name, please?" he said. He was all business now.

This was someone out there who might need help. Brown had picked up the phone on his desk. Both men heard a heavy sigh on the other end of the line.

"Okay," she said, "if you want to play games, we'll play games. This is Naomi Schneider."

"And your address, please?"

"You know my address," she said. "You spent a whole goddamn weekend with me."

"Yes, but can you give it to me again, Miss?"

"No, I won't give it to you again. If you've forgotten where I *live,* for Christ's sake . . ."

"Are you alone there, Miss?" he asked. They sometimes called in desperation. They sometimes asked the department sergeant to put them through to the detectives, and sometimes the sergeant said, "Just a moment, I'll connect you to Detective Kling," or Brown or whoever the hell—Detective *Carella* in this case—but how did she know his first name?

"Yes, I'm alone," she said. "But you can't come over just now, I'm about to leave for work."

"And where's that, Miss? Where do you work?"

"I'm wearing what you told me to wear," she said. "I've been wearing it every day."

"Yes, Miss, where do you work?"

"The garter belt and stockings," she said.

"Can you tell me where you work, Miss?"

"No panties," she said seductively. "No bra."

"If you'll tell me where you work . . ."

"You know where I work," she said.

"I guess I've forgotten."

"Maybe you weren't listening."

"I was listening, but I guess I . . ."

"Maybe you should have turned up your hearing aid," she said.

"My *what?*" Carella asked at once.

"What?" Naomi said.

"What makes you mention a hearing aid?" Carella said.

There was a long silence on the line.

"Miss?" he said.

"Are you *sure* this is Steve Carella?" she said.

"Yes, this is . . ."

"Because you sound strange as hell, I've got to tell you."

"Listen, I'd like to see you," Carella said, "really. If you'll give me your address . . ."

"I told you I'm leaving for work in a few minutes . . ."

"And where's that? I'd like to talk to you, Naomi . . ."

"Is that all you'd like to do?"

"Well, I . . ."

"I thought you might want to fuck me again."

Brown raised his eyebrows. Jesus, Carella thought, he thinks I really *know* this girl! But she had mentioned a hearing aid, and right now he didn't give a damn *what* Brown thought.

"Yes, I'd like to do that too," he said.

"At *last*," she said, and sighed again. "It's like pulling teeth with you, isn't it?"

"Tell me where you work," he said.

"You already know where I work. Anyway, why would you want to come *there?*"

"Well, I thought . . ."

"We couldn't *do* anything there, could we, Steve?" she said, and giggled. "We'd get arrested."

"Well, what time do you get off tonight?" he asked.

"Five."

"Okay, let me have your address, I'll come by as soon as . . ."

"No," she said.

"Naomi . . ."

"You try to *remember* my address, okay?" she said. "I'll be waiting for you. I'll be wide open and waiting for you."

There was a click on the line.

"Miss?" he said.

The line was dead.

"Shit," he said.

Brown was staring at him.

Carella put the receiver back on its cradle. "Listen," he said, "if you're thinking . . ."

"No, I'm not," Brown said. "I'm thinking the Deaf Man."

If this had been a smaller city, the man from the telephone company might have been more conspicuous, arriving as he did at precincts all over town and claiming he was there to clear the trouble on the line. But this was a bigger city than most, one of the biggest cities in the world, in fact, and not many cops paid too much attention to a telephone repairman in their midst. Noticing a telephone repairman would have been like noticing an electrician or a plumber. The man who came and went at will was virtually invisible.

There were rules and regulations, of course, that pertained to anyone entering a police station. Ever since the bomb scares several years back, a uniformed cop stood at the entrance door to every precinct, and he asked any visitor what his business there might be. Or at least he was *supposed* to ask. Not many of them bothered. That was because most cops hated pulling what they called "door duty." They had not joined the force so that they could stand around with their thumbs up their asses waiting for terrorist attacks that never came. Police work meant *action*. There was as much action standing outside a precinct door as there was in an undertaker's shop.

So most cops on door duty, they gauged a citizen coming up the steps, nodded him in, and went back to watching the street, where—if they were lucky—the wind would blow a girl's dress up every now and then. Besides, if a guy was wearing coveralls that had the telephone company's name on the back and if there was a little plastic telephone company ID card pinned to the pocket of those coveralls and if there was a yellow lineman's phone hanging from his belt together with a lot of other wires and crap and if he was carrying a canvas bag with tools in it (some of the door-duty cops actually looked inside the bag to see if there was a bomb or something in it), then they automatically figured the guy was just what he claimed to be, a telephone company repairman there to clear the trouble on the line.

When Henry Caputo entered the Twelfth Precinct downtown, he stopped at the muster desk, just as the sign behind the desk advised him, and he stated his business to the desk sergeant.

"Telephone company," he said. "Here to clear the trouble on the line."

"*What* trouble on the line?" the desk sergeant asked. He had been answering the telephone all morning, and he wasn't aware of any trouble on the line.

Henry reached into a pocket, pulled out a white slip of paper, read it silently, and said, "This the Twelfth Precinct?"

"You got it, pal," the sergeant said.

"Okay, so there's trouble on the line. You want me to fix it or what?"

"Be my guest," the sergeant said, and Henry disappeared into the busy precinct boil.

Henry had hair the color of iodine and eyes the color of coal, and even in his telephone company coveralls he looked like a man who would slit your throat if you didn't hand over your watch the instant he asked for it. He *had,* in fact, once slit a man's throat, which was why he'd served time in a maximum security prison in Oklahoma. He had not slit the man's throat over anything as inconsequential as a watch. He had slit the man's throat because he'd interrupted a conversation Henry was having with a hooker in a bar in downtown Tulsa. The hooker had been a true racehorse, the hundred-dollar variety, not one of your scaly legged dogs who'd do a ten-dollar blowjob in a pickup truck. Henry had not enjoyed having his train of thought interrupted, especially when he had a hard-on. The man was very surprised to find his throat open and blood spilling down the front of his white shirt. All he'd said was, "Excuse me, sister, would you please pass the . . ." and the knife had appeared suddenly in Henry's hand, and the next thing the man knew he was trying to talk through a bubbling red froth in his mouth, and he never did get out the word "peanuts."

Fortunately, for both of them, the man didn't die. Henry was only locked up for the equivalent of what in this city would have been First-Degree Assault, a Class-C felony punishable by a minimum of three and a maximum of fifteen. Henry was now out on the street again, back east again, where he'd been born and raised—the hell with all them cowboys and Indians out west, people with no manners, who interrupted a conversation a person was having with a lady. Henry was ready to take his place in civilized society again, and a good way to start seemed to be the job—or, more accurately, the *series* of jobs—this guy Dennis Dove had asked him to do. Henry did not particularly like cops. Henry thought all cops were crooks with badges. So the idea of *stealing* from cops tickled the shit out of him.

The only thing Henry couldn't dope out was why this Dennis Dove character with the hearing aid in his ear *wanted* all this stuff Henry was stealing from police stations all over town. And paying pretty good for it besides. Two grand up front— plus *another* two grand when Henry delivered all the stuff—wasn't exactly potato chips. Actually Henry would have done the job for much less. A fun job like this one was difficult to come by these days. Besides, being in police stations, he was learning a lot about cops. He was learning they were all pricks, which is just what he'd thought all along. It was terrific to be stealing from these pricks, especially since they kept asking him all the time how the phones were coming along.

He'd go in and unscrew the mouthpiece from a phone, fiddle with the wires, check out some panels in the basement, and then come upstairs again and go into this room and that room and say hello to the prisoners in the holding cells and the squadroom detention cage and pop into the men's room to take a leak and go back to another phone and unscrew another mouthpiece, and meanwhile he was lifting little things here and there and dropping them in his canvas bag, while the cops kept telling rotten jokes about all the crooks out there in the city, never once realizing that a crook was right there in the police station with them, stealing them blind.

So far, Henry had stolen four walkie-talkies from the charging racks they had on the ground floor of the precincts on the far wall past the muster desk, and he had stolen three badges from uniform tunics in locker rooms while some guy was taking a shower or a nap, and he had a nightstick and a whole stack of Detective Division forms from the clerical office in one of the precincts, and he had stolen two police hats and a pair of handcuffs, and when he walked out of here today, he hoped to have another walkie-talkie, which would make five altogether, and maybe another badge or two and also some wanted flyers from one of the bulletin boards, though it was pretty risky to take something from a bulletin board, the fuckin' cops were always reading the bulletin boards like there was something important on them.

He wondered what this Dennis Dove character with the hearing aid in his ear wanted with seven different wanted flyers. That was on the list he'd given Henry: seven wanted flyers. If Henry had known wanted flyers were so valuable, he'd have asked the cops to send him the one of him that had been in a couple of post offices after he'd killed that hooker in New Orleans. They were still looking for him for that one. That one was after he'd got out of prison for slitting that guy's throat in Tulsa. He'd headed back east by way of New Orleans, and he'd got into an argument with this hooker who kept insisting he'd given her a phony C-note, which happened to be true, but it wasn't fuckin' polite to tell a man he was passing Monopoly money, not after you'd just blown him. So he'd slapped her around a little, and when she started screaming she was gonna get her pimp to beat the shit out of him, he juked her, plain and simple. Served her right, the dumb cunt. Accusing him of handing her a phony bill, true or not. A customer was a customer. And anyway it had been a lousy blowjob.

He wondered if there were any wanted flyers of him up here in any of the precincts. Be a real gas if he walked into a station house in his telephone company suit and saw his own face looking down at him from a bulletin board. Well, that's what made his line of work so interesting. You never knew what was gonna happen next.

"Where you got your primary terminal?" he asked a cop who was taking a walkie-talkie from the charging rack in the muster room. Henry didn't know what a primary terminal was. He'd made that up on the spot.

"How the fuck do I know?" the cop said.

"They're usually in the basement," Henry said.

"So go down the basement," the cop said, and hung the walkie-talkie on his belt.

Henry waited until he turned his back. He took a quick look at the muster desk, lifted a walkie-talkie from the rack, and dropped it into his canvas bag.

"Hey, you," somebody said.

His blood froze.

He turned.

A huge guy was standing near the iron-runged steps leading to the second floor. He was in his shirt-sleeves, and a pistol was hanging in a shoulder holster on his chest.

"While you're here," he said, "the buttons on my phone ain't workin'. The extension buttons. Upstairs in the squadroom."

"I'll take a look," Henry said. "You know where the primary terminal is?"

The sixth letter from the Deaf Man arrived in that afternoon's mail.

It was addressed to Carella, but Carella was out of the squadroom, and all the detectives knew it was from their old pal, so they debated opening it for about thirty seconds, and then nominated Meyer as the person to intrude upon their colleague's right to private communication.

There was, to no one's great surprise, a single folded white sheet of paper inside the envelope.

Meyer unfolded the sheet of paper.

The other detectives crowded around him.

What they were looking at was:

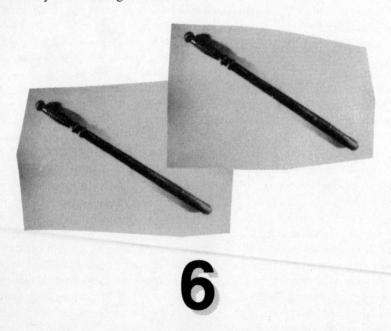

6

Thanksgiving Day always fell on the fourth Thursday in November, and this year it would fall on November 24.

Every detective on the squad wanted Thanksgiving Day off. On Christmas or

Yom Kippur it was possible for detectives of different faiths to swap the duty so that they could celebrate their own holidays. Thanksgiving Day, however, was nondenominational.

The detectives of the Eight-Seven knew of a squad farther uptown that had an Indian detective on it. An *Indian* Indian. Come Thanksgiving, he was in very popular demand because he had come to this country only four years ago—after having served as a captain of police in Bombay—and he did not understand the peculiar ways of the natives here, and he did not celebrate Thanksgiving. Everyone always wanted him to take the Thanksgiving Day duty because he didn't know from turkeys and cranberry sauce.

There were no Indian detectives on the 87th Squad.

There was a Japanese detective, but he'd been born here and knew all about Thanksgiving, and no one would have *dreamed* of asking him to forego his turkey dinner.

Genero asked him to forego his turkey dinner.

"You're a Buddhist, ain't you?" Genero said.

"No, I'm a Catholic," Fujiwara said.

"This is a nondeterminational holiday," Genero sid.

"So what's your point?"

"My point is I got the duty tomorrow," Genero said, "and I'd like to swap with you."

"No," Fujiwara said.

"You people don't celebrate Thanksgiving, do you?" Genero said, "Buddhists?"

"Go fuck yourself," Fujiwara said.

Genero figured he was sensitive about being the only Jap on the squad.

Genero asked Andy Parker if he would like to swap the Thanksgiving Day duty with him.

"You got no family to eat turkey with," Genero said.

"Go fuck yourself," Parker said.

Genero tried Kling.

"You just been through a divorce," Genero said. "Holidays are the worst time of year for people just been through a divorce.

Kling merely looked at him.

Genero figured everybody on this goddamn squad was all of a sudden getting very touchy.

The cops working the day shift on November 24 were Genero, O'Brien, Willis, and Hawes. Genero was annoyed because his mother's big Thanksgiving Day dinner was at two o'clock. The other three detectives didn't mind working on Thanksgiving Day. Like Genero, they were all single, but they'd made plans for later on in the day. Hawes, in particular, was very much looking forward to the plans he'd made for later on in the day; he had not seen Annie Rawles for almost a week.

"Don't any of you guys have mothers?" Genero asked, still sulking.

The detectives on duty were thankful that there'd be no mail deliveries today.

They had not heard from the Deaf Man since the fourteenth, ten days ago. They all hoped they would not hear from him ever again. But they were certain they would not hear from him today. As they ate the turkey sandwiches they had ordered from the local deli, they thanked God for small favors.

The two men sitting at a corner table in a restaurant not ten blocks from the police station were eating turkey with all the trimmings. They were drinking the good white wine ordered by the one with the hearing aid in his right ear. They were talking mayhem.

"How'd you get onto me in the first place?" Gopher Nelson asked.

He'd been nicknamed Gopher during the Vietnam War. His first name was really Gordon. But he'd been a demolitions man back then, and whenever there was any kind of discussion as to whether it was feasible to blow up a bridge or a tunnel or a cache of Cong supplies, Gordon would say, "Let's go for broke," which is how he got the name Gopher. Nothing was too difficult or too risky for Gopher back then. A chopper would drop him and his gear in the boonies someplace, and he'd sneak into a deserted enemy enclave and wire the place from top to bottom and then sit in the jungle waiting for the little bastards in their black pajamas to come trotting back in. Little Gopher Nelson, all by himself in the jungle, waiting to throw the switch that would blow them all to smithereens. Gopher loved blowing up things. He also loved setting things on fire. In fact, Gopher thought back most fondly on the incendiary devices he had wired back then. There's been something very satisfying about *first* seeing the flames and all them fuckin' gooks running for their lives, and *then* hearing the explosions when the fire touched off the ammo in the underground bunkers, all them fuckin' tunnels they'd dug clear across the country. Very satisfying. First you got your roast gook, and then you got the Fourth of July. Gopher wished the Vietnam War had never ended. It was hard for a civilian to find work that was as completely satisfying.

"Well, I make it my business to know what's going on," the Deaf Man said.

"What was it?" Gopher asked. "The Cooper Street job?"

"That, yes. And others."

"Like?"

"I heard you wired the break-in at First National Security."

"Oh, yeah. In Boston."

"Yes."

"Not many people know I was responsible for that one."

"Well, as I say, it's important for me to know such things."

"They're *still* lookin' for us up there."

"What was your end of the take?" the Deaf Man asked.

"Well, that's personal, ain't it?"

"I understand you went in for five percent."

"Ten. And it was just for wiring the place. I wasn't nowhere near it when they went in. There were four guys went in. They were expecting maybe eight hundred thou in the vault, but there was some kind of fuck-up, most of it was in non-negotiable securities. So they came away with two-fifty, which wasn't bad for an hour's work, huh? And I figured my end—at twenty-five—was fair. The other four guys netted a bit more than fifty-six each, and they took all the risk."

"I can't afford twenty-five on this one," the Deaf Man said.

"Then maybe you picked the wrong man."

"Maybe."

He poured more wine into Gopher's empty glass.

" 'Cause, like if you want a Caddy," Gopher said, "you can't expect to pay Chevy prices."

"All I can afford is ten."

"For *both* jobs?"

"A *total* of ten, yes."

"That's only five grand apiece."

"That's right."

"And the first one, that's a compound job, if you know what I mean. There's really nine *separate* jobs in the first one."

"Well, that's a bit of an exaggeration, isn't it?"

"How is it an exaggeration? By my count, nine is nine."

"You wouldn't have to do all nine at the same time."

"But you want them timed to go *off* at the same time, don't you?"

"Yes, of course."

"Or at least *approximately* the same time."

"Within an hour or so, yes. I don't care about the specific hour or minute."

"But all of them on January second, right?"

"Yes."

"Well, who knows what I'll be doin' next year? You're talkin' months ahead here. I was thinkin' I might go down to Miami right after Christmas."

"Well, that's up to you, of course. I thought you might be interested in picking up a quick ten thousand, but if you're not . . ."

"I didn't say I'm not interested. Would I be here if I wasn't interested? I'm saying you're talking low, is all. Especially for the second one. The second one's gonna be risky, all them fuckin' cops up there. Not to mention this'll be three days after the *first* one so they're gonna be on their guard, you know what I mean?"

"I'm not sure you understand," the Deaf Man said. "You won't be anywhere *near* the place when . . ."

"I understand, I understand, you want this all done in advance, I understand that. What I'm saying is after the *first* one they might start snooping around, they'll uncover what I done, they might get onto me somehow."

"How?"

"I don't know how. I'm only saying."

"I hardly think there's any likelihood of that."

"Well, with cops you never know. Also I may have to use a complicated timer. Something like what they used in the Thatcher bombing—something I can set at least a week in advance."

"Will you be using timers on the cars as well?"

"That depends. Does this have to happen during the daytime? Or can it be at night? The cars, I mean."

"That's irrelevant. So long as it's January second."

"And do they have to be totaled?"

"No, that's not important either."

"Well then, maybe I can use a five-pound charge. A charge that size'll open all your doors, your hood, and your trunk and give you a pretty decent wreck. The IRA's been using hundred-pound, even two-hundred-pound charges for their car bombs, but we don't need anything that showy, huh? What they do, they fill their bombs with a mixture of chemical fertilizer and diesel fuel, which I don't like 'cause it's hard to detonate—you need a gun-cotton priming charge or else a few sticks of gelignite to set it off. What I was thinking, I figured a five-pound charge of dynamite would do the job very nice indeed. And if you don't care whether it's day or night, I think I know how I can detonate without a timer. But, for the other, you want a *fire* . . ."

"Exactly."

"Well, that's my point. I'll have to figure on an explosion that'll touch *off* a fire. What's in our favor, this is an old building we're dealing with here, it should go up pretty fast, your old wood and plaster. If I use napalm—which I ain't sure I'll be using yet—I can make it myself, put together the soap chips and the gasoline, make the jelly, you understand? That's if I . . ."

"You can make that yourself?"

"Oh, sure, if I decide to go the napalm route. All you need is your raw materials and a double boiler. Trouble with napalm, it don't like a delay time of more than an hour, 'specially in a hot room. Your gasoline evaporates. Also with napalm they can sometimes smell the gasoline, which is a tip-off. I gotta see. *Whatever* I use, I'm gonna have to figure a small explosion that'll touch off the incendiary, you understand? That's 'cause I'll be working with a timer, you understand? Think of it as a spark first, then an explosion, and *then* your fire. But what I'm saying, the second job ain't as easy as it looks. Even getting *in* there won't be . . ."

"There'll be no problem about getting in."

"That's provided you get me those maps."

"I already *have* the maps," the Deaf Man said. "Believe me, it's all very simple."

"Everything's simple to you," Gopher said, and smiled.

"Yes," the Deaf Man said. "If you choose the right people, everything's simple."

"For the right people," Gopher said, "you've got to pay the right money."

"How much do you want?" the Deaf Man asked.

"Dennis, I'll level with you," Gopher said. "The first job is risky as hell because there's nine of them and because of the proximity. It's not like I'll be working in some empty lot someplace. I'm gonna be right behind the fuckin' *police* station!"

"*Authorized* to work there."

"Sure, if these papers of yours pass muster."

"They will."

"Who's doing these papers for you?"

"You don't need to know that."

"It's my ass, not yours. They smell fish on those papers, the jig's up right that minute."

"All right, I'll grant you that. Someone who once worked for the CIA is preparing the papers for me."

"What *kind* of work for the CIA?"

"He was in their Documents Section."

"Phony passports and such?"

"Phony *everything*."

"So, okay, I'll take your word for the papers."

"Which should calm any fears you have about the risk factor."

"It's *still* risky, papers or not. I can't do nine fuckin' cars in a single day."

"Why not?"

" 'Cause it's not that simple. I'm not talking about the wiring. If I do what I'm figuring on doing, it'll take me two minutes to wire each car. But the charge itself, there'll be nine five-pound charges, and I can't go in with a load like that without somebody noticing. Well, wait a minute, if I do what I'm figuring on doing, I'll *have* to do them all the same day. Yeah. I'll have to plan on making a few trips back to the truck. Yeah. So, okay, it's a day's work is all. But still, there'll be cops comin' and goin' all the time. All it takes is for one of them to ask me what the fuck I'm doin'."

"In which case you show the papers again."

"And pray he don't smell a rat."

The Deaf Man sighed.

"Listen, Den, I'm sorry all to hell, believe me. But like I said, this is my ass we're talkin' about."

"I asked you how much you wanted. I still haven't got an answer."

"For the first job, the nine cars. I want seventy-five hundred."

"And the second job?"

"That's the toughest one, *whatever* you think. I want ten grand for that one."

"So you're asking for seventeen-five total."

"Seventeen-five, right."

"I came here prepared to pay you ten."

"What can I tell you, Den? You were thinkin' too low."

"You've almost doubled the price."

"You can always look somewhere else. No harm done, we drink our wine, we shake hands and say good-bye."

"I'll give you a flat fifteen, take it or leave it."

"Make it sixteen, and we've got a deal."

"No. Fifteen is all I can afford."

"You're getting me cheap."

"Is it a deal?"

"It's a deal. Five up front, five when I'm done on the inside, another five when the cars are wired."

"You're robbing me blind," the Deaf Man said, but he was smiling. He had come here with an offer of ten, but had not expected to get off for less than thirty.

The man reached across the table and shook hands.

"When can you start?" the Deaf Man asked.

"As soon as you get me the maps and the papers and all the other shit. Also I want to look it over first, make sure I ain't steppin' into a lion's den. One question."

"Yes?"

"Why do you want this thing done? I mean . . ."

"Let's say it's personal," the Deaf Man said.

The Carella house in Riverhead was a huge white elephant they'd picked up for a song shortly after Teddy Carella gave birth to the twins. At about the same time, Teddy's father presented them with a registered nurse as a month-long gift while Teddy was getting her act together, and Fanny Knowles had elected to stay on with them at a salary they could afford, telling them she was tired of carrying bedpans for sick old men.

A lot of cops ribbed Carella about Fanny. They told him they didn't know any other cop on the force who was rich enough to have a housekeeper, even one who had blue hair and wore a pince-nez. They said he had to be on the take. Carella admitted that being able to afford live-in help was decidedly difficult these days; the numbers boys in Riverhead were always so late paying off. Actually Fanny was worth her weight—a hundred and fifty pounds—in pure gold. She ran the house with all the tenderness of a Marine Corps drill sergeant, and she was fond of saying, "I take no shit from man nor beast," an expression the ten-year-old twins had picked up when they were learning to talk and which Mark now used with more frequency than April. In fact, the twins' speech patterns—much to Carella's consternation—were more closely modeled after Fanny's than anyone else's; Teddy Carella was a deaf mute, and it was *Fanny's* voice the twins heard around the house whenever Carella wasn't home.

When the phone rang at three o'clock that Thanksgiving Day, Fanny was washing dishes in the kitchen. Her hands were soapy but she answered the phone anyway. Whenever she and Teddy were alone in the house, she *had* to answer the phone, of course. But even when Carella was home, she normally picked up because she wanted to make sure it wasn't some idiot detective calling about something that could easily wait till morning.

"Carella residence," she said.

"Yes, hello?" a woman's voice said.

"Hello?" Fanny said.

"Yes, I'm trying to get in touch with Detective Steve Carella. Have I got the right number?"

"This is the Carella residence, yes," Fanny said.

"Is there a Detective Steve Carella there?"

"Who's this, please?" Fanny said.

"Naomi Schneider."

"Is this police business, Miss Schneider?"

"Well . . . uh . . . yes."

"Are you a police officer, Miss Schneider?"

"No."

"Then what's this in reference to, please?"

It wasn't often that a civilian called here at the house, but sometimes they did, even though the number was listed in the book as "Carella, T. F.," for Theodora Franklin Carella. Not too many cops listed their home numbers in the telephone directories; this was because not too many crooks enjoyed being sent up the river, and some of them came out looking for revenge. The way things were nowadays, most of them got out ten minutes after you locked them up. These days, when you threw away the key, it came back at you like a boomerang.

"I'd rather discuss it with him personally," Naomi said.

"Well, he's finishing his dinner just now," Fanny said. "May I take a message?"

"I wonder if you could interrupt him, please," Naomi said.

"I'd rather not do that," Fanny said. "They're just having their coffee. If you'll give me your number . . ."

"They?" Naomi said.

"Him and Mrs. Carella, yes."

There was a long silence on the line.

"His mother, do you mean?" Naomi asked.

"No, his wife. Miss Schneider, he'll be back in the office tomorrow if you'd like to . . ."

"Are you sure I have the right number?" Naomi said. "The Detective Carella I have in mind isn't married."

"Well, this one is," Fanny said. She was beginning to get a bit irritated.

"Detective *Steve* Carella, right?" Naomi said.

"Yes, Miss, that's who lives here," Fanny said. "If you'd like to give me a number where he can reach you . . ."

"No, never mind," Naomi said. "Thank you."

And hung up.

Fanny frowned. She replaced the receiver on the wall hook, dried her hands on a dish towel, and went out into the dining room. She could hear the television set down the hallway turned up full blast, the twins giggling at yet another animated cartoon; Thanksgiving Day and all you got was animated cats chasing animated mice. Carella and Teddy were sitting at the dining room table, finishing their second cups of coffee.

"Who was that?" Carella asked.

"Somebody wanting a Detective Steve Carella," Fanny said.

"Well, who?"

"A woman named Naomi Schneider."

"What?" Carella said.

"Got the wrong Carella," Fanny said, and looked at him. "The one she wanted ain't married."

Teddy was reading her lips. She looked at Carella questioningly.

"Did you get a number?" he asked. "Did she leave a number?"

"She hung up," Fanny said, and looked at Carella again. "You ought to tell people not to bring police business into your home," she said, and went out into the kitchen again.

Josie was only fourteen years old. That was the problem. She shouldn't have been in the park in the first place, not at one o'clock in the morning, and certainly not doing what she'd been doing. She had told her parents she'd be spending the night at Jessica Cartwright's house, which was true, but she hadn't told them that Jessica's parents didn't care *what* time Jessica came in or that she and Jessica *wouldn't* be studying for a big French exam, as she'd told them, but instead would be out with two seventeen-year-old boys.

Seventeen-year-old boys were exciting.

Actually *all* boys were exciting.

She and Jessica and the two boys had gone to a movie and then Eddie—who was the boy Jessica had fixed her up with—suggested that they take a little stroll in the park, it being such a nice night and all. This was back in October, when the weather was acting so crazy and you could walk around in just a skirt and sweater, which was what Josie was wearing that night. October twenty-fourth, a Monday night. She remembered the date because the French exam wasn't until Wednesday, actually, the twenty-sixth, and she and Jessica *really* planned to study for it on Tuesday, but at *her* house instead of Jessica's. She also remembered the date because of what she had seen in the park.

Josie hadn't wanted to go into the park at all because if you were born and raised in this city, you knew that Grover Park after dark was like a cage of wild animals, which if you walked into it you could get chewed to bits, or even raped, which she supposed was worse, maybe. But Eddie said *this* part of the park was safe at night, which was probably true. In this city the neighborhoods changed abruptly. You could walk up Grover Avenue past buildings with awnings and doormen and security guards—like the building Jessica lived in—and then two blocks farther uptown you were all at once in a neighborhood with graffiti all over the buildings and minority groups hanging around in doorways because they were collecting welfare and didn't want to work. That was what her father told her when he explained why he was voting for Ronald Reagan. "Too many spics and niggers getting welfare," he'd said. Josie didn't know about that, but she thought Ronald Reagan was cute.

So what they did after the movie, they went into the park the way Eddie had suggested. This was around midnight, a little before midnight, and the park entrance they used was a few blocks *downtown* from Jessica's building, which meant this was still a safe neighborhood. Also there was a service road to the right of the entrance, and you could always see parks department trucks parked in there, so it had to be pretty safe if the city parked trucks there overnight. Farther *uptown*, where the police station was, the neighborhood was awful, and if you left your car parked on the street, you'd come back in the morning and find everything gone but the steering wheel. But Eddie promised they wouldn't be going anywhere *near* there; he knew some good spots right here near the service road.

He really knew a lot of things, Eddie. Well, seventeen, you know.

He knew, for example, that what you did, you found a spot that was *dark* but that was also near a *light*. The marauders in this city, they didn't like lights. Darkness was very good for marauders. "That's 'cause all of them are niggers," her father said. "They blend in nice." She didn't know about that, but she thought Eddie was awfully cute, the way he led the four of them past the service road, where she could see a truck parked at the end of it, and then along the path where the lampposts were spaced maybe fifteen, twenty feet apart, and then started climbing up onto a sort of bedrock shelf that had trees around it and was dark, but from which you could still see the path with the lights on it.

It was such a nice night.

Almost like springtime.

She couldn't get over it. She kept telling Eddie she couldn't get over how mild it was for October, almost the end of October.

She didn't even know where Jessica and Aaron—that was the other boy's name—went, they just disappeared in the bushes someplace.

Eddie spread his jacket on the ground for her.

It was very dark there on the rock.

This was now maybe ten after twelve, around then.

Lying on her back, she could look up through the yellowing leaves of the trees and see millions and millions of stars. Eddie told her all those stars were *suns,* he was so smart, Eddie. He had his hand inside her sweater when he told her that all those suns up there maybe had planets rotating around them, that maybe they were solar systems like our own, that maybe there were people like us up there, millions of light-years away, who were in a park just like this one, that maybe there was a green guy with lizard skin, trying to take off a green girl's bra, which was what he was trying to do with Josie's bra. She helped him unclasp it. Boys, even seventeen-year-old boys, could be very smart about a lot of things, but when it came to unhooking a bra they sometimes had trouble.

He started touching her breasts, and kissing them, and wondering out loud if the green girls up there had only *two* breasts—he called them "breasts," which she liked, and not "tits"—like the girls here on earth, or did they have *four* of them or *however* many—the mind boggled when you began thinking about alien life. He wondered, also, if the green guys up there on a planet millions and millions of light years away had a penis—he called it "penis" and not "cock," which she also liked—same as the guys on earth, or did they maybe ask a girl to grab hold of their nose or their armpit or maybe one of their *horns,* if they had horns, maybe they found *that* thrilling, you know?''

"Would you like to grab hold of *my* penis?" he asked.

Well, one thing led to another, you know—he was really very experienced, Eddie—and it must have been around one in the morning when he showed her how to take him in her mouth, which she much preferred to going all the way since she didn't want to get pregnant and have to have an abortion, which her father said Ronald Reagan would do away with damn soon, you could bet on *that,* young lady. She had her head in his lap and was doing it the way he told her to do it when she heard the sound of an engine on the service road. She lifted her head to see if it was a parks department truck, but he whispered, "No, don't stop," and so she kept doing it, not liking very much that he had his hand on the back of her head and was pushing down on it because, as much as she thought this was better than getting pregnant, she sure as hell didn't want to *choke.* He had told her he wouldn't come in her mouth, but of course he did, and she was trying to decide whether she should swallow it or spit it out when she saw the man on the path.

He was very tall and very blond.

He was carrying a naked woman.

The naked woman was draped over his shoulder, like a sack.

The naked woman looked very white in the moonlight.

The man walked right past the rock ledge they were sitting on, five feet below them, no more than that. As he carried the girl under the lamppost, Josie saw blood at the back of the girl's head where her long blond hair was hanging downward.

Then the man moved past the lamppost and into the darkness, and all Josie could hear was the sound of leaves crunching under his feet as he disappeared.

"Did you see that?" she whispered.

In her excitement she had swallowed instead of spitting.

"That was terrific," Eddie said. "Where'd you learn to do that?" He seemed to have forgotten that *he* had taught her how to do that.

"Did you see that *guy?*" Josie said.

"What guy?" Eddie said.

"That guy with the . . . didn't you *see* him?"

"No, my eyes were closed," Eddie said.

"Holy shit, he had a dead girl over his shoulder!"

"Yeah?" Eddie said.

"You mean you didn't *see* him?"

"I saw stars," Eddie said, and grinned.

"Let's get out of here," she said, and got to her feet, and wiped the back of her hand across her mouth, and clasped her bra, and pulled down her sweater, and then whispered into the darkness, "Jessica?"

Before they left the park, she forced the others to walk up the service road with her to where a blue Buick was parked behind the parks department truck. She looked at the license plate and read the number on it again and again, repeating it out loud until she'd memorized it. That was when she still thought she might go to the police and tell them what she had seen. That was before she realized that if she went to the police, she would also have to tell them she'd been in the park at one in the morning, doing something she shouldn't have been doing, which would have been bad enough even *without* swallowing it.

That was a month ago.

She hadn't seen anything on television about the dead lady in the park.

Maybe she'd imagined it.

She did not think she'd imagined it.

Standing outside the police station now, looking at the green globes with the white numerals 87 on each of them, she thought, *My father'll kill me.*

But the girl in the park was *already* dead.

She took a deep breath and climbed the precinct steps.

7

Carella got to the squadroom forty minutes after Hawes called him. Officially the homicide in the park was his and Brown's, and Hawes had called them both at home the moment Josie Sears came into the office with her story. She was only fourteen years old, and the law specified that juveniles could not be interviewed or interrogated anywhere in the proximity of adult offenders. Hawes had talked to her initially in Lieutenant Byrnes's, empty office. That was where Carella found them at ten minutes to four that Thanksgiving Day.

Hawes looked like a sunset against the gunmetal gray of the sky outside. He stood by the meshed window in the lieutenant's corner office, his red hair streaked with white over the left temple, a purple tie hanging on what appeared to be a lavender shirt with a little polo pony over the left pectoral muscle. He was dressed for his date with Annie Rawles, for which he was already late. He had hoped to be out of here by a quarter to four, at which time the shift was relieved. Genero had shot out of the squadroom like a launch from Canaveral. Hawes was stuck with a fourteen-year-old girl who'd maybe witnessed a man carrying a body on the night of October 24.

"So you got this now?" he asked Carella.

"I've got it."

"See you," Hawes said, and disappeared.

Carella looked at the young, dark-eyed, dark-haired girl sitting in the chair opposite the lieutenant's desk. "I'm Detective Carella," he said. "Detective Hawes told me on the phone that you saw something happen in the park last month. I wonder if . . ."

"Well, I didn't see anything *happen,* actually," Josie said.

"As I understand it, you saw a many carrying a dead body."

"Well, I guess she was dead," Josie said. She was biting the cuticles on her right hand. Carella squelched a fatherly urge to tell her to quit doing that.

"Can you tell me what you *did* see?" he asked gently.

"This man parked his car on the service road . . ."

"You saw him parking his car?"

"No, but I heard the car come in, and then the engine went off."

"Go ahead."

"And then he walked past us on the . . ."

She stopped suddenly.

"Yes?"

"We were on this sort of rock. Above the path," Josie said.

"Who?" Carella said. "You and who?"

"Me and this boy."

"I see. What time was this, Josie?"

"Around one o'clock."

"One o'clock in the morning?"

"Well, yeah."

"Go on."

"And this man came by," Josie said, and shrugged.

"What did he look like, this man?"

"He was tall and blond."

"Was he wearing a hearing aid?"

"I don't know. I didn't see any hearing aid."

Of all the detectives on the squad Carella and Willis were the only ones who'd ever seen the Deaf Man face to face. Willis had glimpsed him only fleetingly, in the midst of a shoot-out in the back of a tailor shop. But Carella had remembered him from their *first* meeting . . .

The Deaf Man turning from the hi-fi unit against the living room wall, Carella seeing the hearing aid in his right ear and then the shotgun in his hands. And suddenly it was too late, suddenly the shotgun exploded into sound. Carella whirled away from the blast. He could hear the whistling pellets as they screamed across the confined space of the apartment, and then he felt them lash into his shoulder like a hundred angry wasps, as he fired a shot at the tall blond man who was already sprinting across the apartment toward him. His shoulder felt suddenly numb. He tried to lift the hand with the gun and quickly found he couldn't and just as quickly shifted the gun to his left hand and triggered off another shot, high and wide as the Deaf Man raised the shotgun and swung the stock at Carella's head. A single barrel, Carella thought in the instant before the stock collided with the side of his head, a single barrel, no time to reload, and a sudden flashing explosion of rocketing yellow pain, slam the stock again, suns revolving, a universe slam the stock . . .

"Sorry I'm late," Brown said, coming into the office and closing the door behind him.

"This is my partner, Detective Brown," Carella said. "Artie, this is Josie Sears. She was just telling me what she saw in the park last month." He turned to Josie. "That was on October twenty-fourth, is that right?"

"Well, the twenty-fifth, actually," she said. "It was one o'clock in the morning, you know."

"Right," Carella said. "And this tall blond man you just described . . ."

"Was he wearing a hearing aid?" Brown asked at once.

"I didn't see any," Josie said. She was looking at Brown, remembering all the things her father had said about niggers and wondering if he was a genuine detective. She didn't want to be telling any nigger about what she and Eddie had been doing when she saw the man carrying the body. She hoped they wouldn't ask her what she and Eddie had been doing.

"What was he doing?" Carella asked.

For a panicky moment she thought he was referring to Eddie. Then she realized he meant the man she'd seen.

"He was carrying a girl over his shoulder," Josie said.

"What color was she?" Brown asked.

"White," Josie said, and wondered if that was a trick question.

"What color hair did she have?" Brown asked.

"Blond."

"How old would you say she was?" Carella asked.

"I don't know."

"But you called her a girl."

"Well, yeah. I mean, she didn't look like a *lady,* if that's what you mean. Not like my *mother* or anything."

"How old is your mother?" Carella asked.

"Thirty-eight," Josie said.

He almost sighed. "And this woman was younger than that?" he asked.

"Yeah."

"Can you estimate how old she was?"

"Well, in her twenties, I guess. I only had that glimpse of her when they passed the light."

"How far away from you were they? This man and woman."

"Five feet, something like that."

"You were *where?*" Brown asked.

"On this rock. Above the path."

"Doing what?" Brown asked.

Here we go, Josie thought.

"Sitting with this boy," she said.

"What boy?"

"A boy I know."

"What's his name?"

"Eddie."

"Eddie what?"

"Hogan."

"Did he see this man, too? This man carrying a woman over his shoulder?"

"No, he . . . he didn't see her."

"He was sitting with you, wasn't he?" Brown asked.

"Yes, but . . ."

"Both of you five feet from where the man . . ."

"His eyes were closed," Josie said.

"Eddie's eyes?"

"Yes."

"Was he sleeping?"

"No, but his eyes were closed."

Josie looked away. Brown looked at Carella. Carella nodded almost imperceptibly.

"So you're the only one who saw this man carrying the woman," he said.

"Yes."

"And you say you guess she was dead. What made you think that?"

"There was blood at the back of her head."

"Where?"

"Right here," Josie said, and lifted her hair and touched the nape of her neck.

"You saw blood?"

"Yes."

"At the back of her head?"

"Yes. Her head was hanging down, you know? He was carrying her over his shoulder with her head hanging down. And her hair was hanging, too, and I could see blood at the back of her head."

"Then what?"

"Well, he just kept walking. I mean, I didn't see him after that."

"Where was this?" Brown asked. "What part of the park?"

"You know where the service road is?" Josie said. "Near Macomber?"

"Yes?"

"Right near there. The entrance there. We were a little bit past the service road. That's how come I heard the car when it drove in.

"Did Eddie hear the car?"

"I don't think so."

"Didn't hear the car, didn't see the man."

"No."

"But he wasn't sleeping."

"No, he was awake."

Wide awake, she thought, and remembered the salty taste in her mouth.

"So you were near the Macomber Street service road," Carella said.

"Yes."

"About ten blocks west of here."

"Well, whatever."

"When the man walked off, did he head in *this* direction? Or did he go west?"

"What do you mean?"

"Was he heading *toward* the police station here or *away* from it?"

"Toward it."

"What did you do then?"

"Well, I yelled to Jessica . . ."

"Who's Jessica?" Brown asked.

"My girlfriend. She was with another boy."

"Same place?"

"Well, I don't know where exactly. But nearby."

"Did *she* see this man?"

"No."

"Did her boyfriend?"

"No."

"Okay, you yelled to Jessica . . ."

"Yes, and we went to look at the car. The one that came in the service road."

"You saw the car?" Carella said.

"Yes. A blue car. Eddie said it was a Buick Century."

"Did you happen to look at the license plate?"

"I did."

"Would you happen to remember . . . ?"

"WL-seven," Josie said, "eight-one-six-four."

Brown and Carella looked at each other in surprise.

"Are you sure that's the number?" Carella asked.

"Positive."

"You wrote it down?" Brown asked.

"I memorized it," Josie said.

"Smart girl," Carella said, and smiled.

It was beginning to snow lightly.

Naomi stood under the lamppost across the street from the old house and wondered for perhaps the tenth time whether she should go in or not. Her shrink, whom she used to see three years ago, would have said she was conflicted. That had been one of Dr. Hammerstein's favorite words, "conflicted." If she couldn't decide between the vanilla or the chocolate ice cream, that was because she was conflicted. She once protested about his use of the word "conflicted," and he said, "Good, ve are making progress." That wasn't what he'd really said, he didn't even have a German accent. But Naomi always *thought* of him as having a German accent.

The house across the street looked cozy and warm.

Well, Thanksgiving.

The reason Naomi felt conflicted was because she didn't want to lay this heavy stuff on this bastard Carella's wife, but at the same time nobody should have the right to do to her what he'd done to her, which she wouldn't have let him do if she'd known he was married, which he'd lied about. A cop, no less! A *detective!* Lying to her, taking advantage of her, doing disgusting things to her, and then not even calling her again. She'd called every damn Carella in the Isola phone book and had come down to six Carellas in the Riverhead directory before she'd struck pay dirt earlier today with T. F. Carella. Who the hell was T. F. Carella? Was Steve even his right name? She'd never have gone to bed with somebody who didn't even give a person his right name. A married man. She'd never have gone to bed with a married man who'd picked her up in a bar. Well, maybe she would have. Isadora Wing went to bed with married men, didn't she? That wasn't the point. This wasn't a question of her *own* morality here, this was a question of whether a man sworn to uphold the laws of the city, state, and nation should be allowed to get away with not calling up a person after the person had allowed him to do such things to her. You weren't even supposed to take your gun out of your *holster* without justification, were you? No less what *he* had done with it.

She could imagine telling that to Hammerstein.

Ja? Dot is very inner-estink. Are you avare vot a symbol der gun is?''

She wondered what Hammerstein was doing these days, the crazy old bastard.

Conflicted, she thought, and started across the street toward the house.

The snow was sticking. She shouldn't have come all the way up here. If the snow got really bad, it would raise hell with mass transit. Well, some things simply had to be done. One thing she'd learned about being conflicted was that if you took action, the confliction disappeared. Better you than me, Steve, she thought, and knocked on the door.

A short fat lady with blue hair answered it.

Is *this* his wife? Naomi thought. No wonder he picks up girls in bars.

"Yes?" the woman said.

"I'm looking for Steve Carella," Naomi said.

"I'm sorry, he's not here just now," the woman said.

"He was here an hour and a half ago," Naomi said. "He was here having coffee with his wife."

The woman studied her more closely.

"Are you the person who called here?" she asked.

"I'm the person who called here," Naomi said. "I'm Naomi Schneider. Are you his wife?"

"No, I'm not his . . ."

Another woman appeared suddenly behind her. Dark eyes and hair the color of a raven's wing, good breasts and legs, an inquisitive look on her face. God, she's *gorgeous!* Naomi thought. Why is that son of a bitch fooling around?

"Mrs. Carella?" she asked.

The woman nodded.

"I'm Naomi Schneider," she said. "I'd like to talk to you about your husband. May I come in?"

The other woman was studying her mouth as she spoke. All at once, Naomi realized she was deaf. Oh God, she thought, what am I doing here? But the woman was gesturing her into the house.

She stepped inside.

I'm going to bring this house down around your ears, Steve, she thought, and followed the woman into the living room.

The man from Motor Vehicles got back to them not ten minutes after they'd called.

"Blue Buick Century," he said, "tag number WL-seven, eight-one-six-four. Registered to a Dr. Harold Lasser, One-twenty-seven Hall Avenue."

"One-twenty-seven . . ." Carella repeated, writing.

"This is marked with an 'Auto' flag," the man from Motor Vehicles said. "May have been recovered by now, I don't know. You'd better check with them."

"Thanks," Carella said.

Teddy listened motionless as Naomi told her all about the man she'd met in a bar some three weeks ago, a man she claimed was Steve Carella. Detective Carella had told her he was not married. They had gone to her apartment afterward. Naomi detailed all the things they had done together in her apartment, her eyes unflinching, the words spilling soundlessly from her lips. They had spent the entire weekend together. He had told her he wanted her to go to work on Monday morning without anything under her . . .

Teddy held up her hand. Not *quite* like a traffic cop, but with much the same effect. She rose, crossed the room to a rolltop desk standing near a Tiffany-type floor lamp, and took from it a pencil and pad. She walked back to where Naomi was sitting.

On the pad she wrote: *Are you sure the name was Detective Stephen Louis Carella?*

"He didn't give me his full name," Naomi said. "He just said Steve Carella."

Did he say where he worked? Teddy wrote.

Naomi began talking again.

Teddy watched her lips.

The man—she kept referring to him as "your *husband*"—had told her he worked uptown at the Eight-Seven, right across the street from Grover Park. He'd told her he was working a homicide he'd caught on the twenty-fifth of October. Dead woman in the park, about your age, he'd said.

"I'm twenty-five," Naomi said, a challenging look on her face.

Told her the woman had been shot in the back of the head. Totally naked, not a stitch on her. Not much to go on, he'd told her, but we're working on it.

How can she know all this? Teddy wondered.

On the pad she wrote: *When was this?*

"November fourth," Naomi said. "A Friday night. He left on Monday morning, the seventh. When I went to work that morning—does your husband ask *you* to run around naked under your dress? Does he tie *you* to the bed and stick his goddamn . . ."

Teddy held up the traffic-cop hand again. She rose and went to the desk again. She picked up her appointment calendar. On Friday night, November 4, she and Carella had had dinner with Bert Kling and his girlfriend, Eileen. They had talked about the plastic surgery Eileen was considering. It had been painful for Eileen to discuss the scar a rapist had put on her left cheek. On Saturday, November 5, she and Carella had taken the kids to see a magic show downtown. On Sunday, November 6, they had gone to visit Carella's parents. She went back to where Naomi was sitting. On the pad she wrote, *Please wait,* and then went down the hall to fetch Fanny.

The man at Auto Theft said, "This vehicle is still missing, Carella."

"When was it stolen?" Carella asked.

"We got it down for October twenty-third."

"From what location?"

"Outside the doctor's office. One-twenty-seven Hall."

"What time?"

"Six P.M. Well, that's when he discovered it was missing. He was going home from work, thought at first it might've been towed away by *us*. He had it parked in a no-parking zone. He called Traffic, they told him they hadn't towed his fuckin' car away, and he shouldn't have parked it in a no-parking zone to begin with. He told them he was an M.D. Big deal. They told him to call Auto, which is what he done. Anyway it ain't been recovered yet."

"Thanks," Carella said.

"Mrs. Carella would like me to translate for her," Fanny said. She looked at Naomi sternly, her arms folded across her ample bosom. "Save a lot of time that way."

"Fine," Naomi said, looking just as stern.

Teddy's fingers moved.

Fanny watched them and then said, "This man who picked you up wasn't my husband."

"*Your* husband?" Naomi said, looking suddenly puzzled.

"Mrs. *Carella's* husband," Fanny said. "I'm translating exactly what she signs."

Teddy's fingers were moving again.

"My husband and I were together on the weekend you're talking about," Fanny said.

"You're trying to protect him," Naomi said directly to Teddy.

Teddy's fingers moved.

"What did this man look like?" Fanny asked.

"He was tall and blond . . ."

Watching Teddy's hands, Fanny said, "My husband has brown hair."

"What color eyes does he have?" Naomi asked.

"Brown," Fanny said, ahead of Teddy's fingers.

Naomi blinked. She realized all at once that she couldn't remember what color his

eyes were. Damn it, what color were his *eyes?* "Does he wear a hearing aid?" she
asked in desperation.

This time Teddy blinked.

"No, he doesn't wear no damn hearing aid," Fanny said, though Teddy hadn't
signed a thing. "You've got the wrong man. Now what I suggest you do is get out
of here before I . . ."

Teddy was signing again. Very rapidly. Fanny could hardly keep up.

"This man you met is a criminal," Fanny said, translating. "My husband will
want to talk to you. Will you please wait here for him? We'll call him at once."

Naomi nodded.

She suddenly felt as if she were in a spy novel.

Carella did not get back to the house until six that night.

Naomi Schneider was still waiting there for him. Fanny had brought her a cup of
tea, and she was sitting in the living room, her legs crossed, chatting with Teddy as
Fanny translated, the two of them behaving like old college roommates, Teddy's
hands and eyes flashing, her face animated.

Naomi thought Carella was very good-looking, and wondered immediately if he
fooled around. She was happy when Teddy excused herself to see how the children
were doing. Twins, she explained with her hands as Carella translated. A boy and
a girl. Mark and April. Ten years old. Naomi listened with great interest, thinking
a good-looking man like this, burdened with a handicapped wife and a set of twins,
probably *did* play around a little on the side. She waited for Fanny to leave the room,
grateful when she did. She was going to enjoy telling the *real* Steve Carella all about
what the *fake* Steve Carella had done to her. She wanted to see the expression on his
face when she told him.

The real Steve Carella didn't want to know what the fake Steve Carella had done
to her.

Instead he started questioning her like a detective.

Which he was, of course, but even so.

"Tell me exactly what he looked like," he said.

"He was tall and . . ."

"*How* tall?"

"Six-one, six-two?"

"Weight?"

"A hundred and eighty?"

"Color of his eyes?"

"Well, actually I don't remember. But he did terrible things to . . ."

"Any scars or tattoos?"

"I didn't see any," Naomi said. "Not anywhere on his body." She lowered her
eyes like a maiden, the way she had learned in her magazines.

"Did he say where he lived?"

"No."

"What was he wearing?"

"Nothing."

"Nothing?"

"Oh, I thought you meant when he was doing all those . . ."

"When you met him."

"A gray suit," she said. "Sort of a nubby fabric. An off-white shirt, a dark blue tie. Black shoes. A gold Rolex watch, *all* gold, not the steel and gold one. A gun in a shoulder holster. He used the gun to . . ."

"What kind of gun?"

"A Colt Detective Special."

"You know guns, do you?"

"That's what he told me it was. This was just before he . . ."

"And you met him where?"

"In a bar near where I work. I work for CBS. On Monday morning, when I went to work, he forced me to . . ."

"What's the name of the bar?"

"The Corners."

"Where is it?"

"On Detavoner and Ash. On the corner there."

"Do you go there a lot?"

"Oh, every now and then. I'll probably drop by there tomorrow after work." She raised one eyebrow. "You ought to check it out," she said.

"Had you ever seen him in that bar before?"

"Never."

"Sure about that?"

"Well, I would have noticed. He was very good-looking."

"Did he seem familiar with the neighborhood?"

"Well, we didn't discuss the neighborhood. What we talked about mostly, he gave me sixty seconds to finish my drink, you see, because he was in such a hurry to . . ."

"Did you get the impression he knew the neighborhood well?"

"I got the feeling he knew his way around, yes."

"Around that particular neighborhood?"

"Well, the city. I got the feeling he knew the city. When we were driving toward my apartment later, he knew exactly how to get there."

"You drove there in his car?"

"Yes."

"What kind of car?"

"A Jaguar."

"He was driving a Jaguar?"

"Yes."

"You didn't find that surprising? A detective driving a Jaguar?"

"Well, I don't know any detectives," she said. "You're only my second detective. My *first,* as a matter of fact, since he wasn't a real detective, was he?"

"What year was it?"

"What?"

"The Jag."

"Oh. I don't know."

"What color?"

"Gray. A four-door sedan. Gray with red leather upholstery."

"I don't suppose you noticed the license plate number."

"No, I'm sorry, I didn't. I was sort of excited, you see. He was a very exciting man. Of course, later, when he started doing all those things to me . . ."

"And you say he knew how to get there? From the bar on Detavoner and Ash to where you live?"

"Oh, yes."

"Where *do* you live, Miss Schneider?"

"On Colby and Radner. Near the circle there. If you'd like to come over later, I can show you . . ."

"Did you ask him for any sort of identification? A shield? An ID card?"

"Well, when he was undressing, I said, 'Let me see your badge.' But I was just kidding around, you know. It never occurred to me that he might not be a real detective."

"*Did* he show you a badge?"

"Well, what he said was, "*Here's* my badge, baby." And showed me his . . . you know."

"You simply accepted him as a cop, is that right?"

"Well . . . yeah. I'd never met a cop before. Not socially. Of course, *you* must meet a lot of young, attractive women in your line of work, but I've never had the opportunity to . . ."

"Did he say anything about coming *back* to that bar? The Corners?"

"No, he just said he'd call me."

"But he never did."

"No. Actually I'm glad he didn't. Now that I know he wasn't a real detective. And, also, I might never have got to meet you, you know?"

"Miss Schneider," Carella said, "if he *does* call you, I want you to contact me at once. Here's my card," he said, and reached into his wallet. "I'll jot down my home number, too, so you'll have it . . ."

"Well, I already know your home number," she said, but he had begun writing.

"Just so you'll have it handy," he said, and gave the card to her.

"Well, I doubt if he'll call me," she said. "It's already three weeks, almost."

"Well, in case he does."

He looked suddenly very weary. She had an almost uncontrollable urge to reach out and touch his hair, smooth it back, comfort him. She was certain he would be very different in bed than the *fake* Steve Carella had been. She suddenly wondered what it would be like to be in bed with both of them at the same time.

"How are you getting home?" he asked.

End of interview, she thought.

Or was he making his move?

"By subway," she said, and smiled at him. "Unless someone offers to drive me home."

"I'll call the local precinct," he said. "See if I can't get a car to take you down."

"Oh," she said.

"Thanksgiving Day, they might not be too busy."

He rose and started for the phone.

"Miss Schneider," he said, dialing, "I really appreciate the information you've given me."

Yeah, she thought, so why the fuck don't you come home with me?

The man who arrived at the station house at a quarter past eight that night was wearing a shabby overcoat and a dilapidated felt hat. The desk sergeant on duty looked at the envelope he handed across the muster desk, saw that it was addressed to Detective Stephen Louis Carella, and immediately said, "Where'd you get this?" The Deaf Man was famous around here. There wasn't a cop in the precinct who didn't know about those pictures hanging on the bulletin board upstairs.

"Huh?" the man said.

"Where'd you get this?"

"Guy up the street handed it to me."

"What guy?"

"Guy up the street. Blond guy with a hearing aid."

"What?" the desk sergeant said.

"You deaf, too?" the man said.

"What's your name?" the desk sergeant asked.

"Pete MacArthur. What's yours?"

"Don't get smart with me, mister," the desk sergeant said.

"What *is* this?" MacArthur said. "Guy gives me five bucks, asks me to deliver this for him, that's a crime?"

"Sit down on the bench over there," the desk sergeant said.

"What for?"

"Sit down till I tell you it's okay to go."

He picked up a phone and buzzed the squadroom. A detective named Santoro picked up the phone.

"We've got another one," the desk sergeant said.

"There ain't no mail deliveries today," Santoro said.

"This one came by hand."

"Who delivered it?"

"A guy named Pete MacArthur."

"Hold him there," Santoro said.

Santoro talked to MacArthur until they were both blue in the face. MacArthur kept repeating the same thing over and over again. A tall blond guy wearing a hearing aid had handed him the envelope and offered him five bucks to deliver it here. He'd never seen the guy before in his life. He'd taken the five bucks because he figured an envelope so skinny couldn't have a bomb in it and also because it was a cold, snowy night, and he thought maybe he could find an open liquor store, even though it was Thanksgiving, and buy himself a bottle of wine. Santoro figured MacArthur was telling the truth. Only an exceedingly stupid accomplice would march right into a police station. He took his address—which happened to be a bench in Grover Park—told him to keep his nose clean, and sent him on his way.

These days Carella's mail was everybody's mail.

Santoro took the envelope up to the squadroom and opened it.

He looked at what was inside, shrugged, and then tacked it to the bulletin board:

8

Carella had been shot twice since he'd been a cop, one of those times by the Deaf Man. He did not want to get shot ever again. It hurt, and it was embarrassing. There was something even more embarrassing than getting shot, however, and the Deaf Man had been responsible for *that,* too.

Once upon a time, when the Deaf Man was planning a bank holdup for which he'd fairly and scrupulously prepared the Eight-Seven far in advance, two hoods jumped Carella and Teddy on their way home from the movies. The men got away with Teddy's handbag and wristwatch as well as Carella's own watch, his wallet with all his identification in it, and—most shameful to admit—his service revolver.

The most recent message from the Deaf Man depicted eleven Colt Detective Specials.

The pistol the Deaf Man had shown to Naomi Schneider had been a Colt Detective Special, probably the same one he'd photographed and then Xeroxed for his pasteup. The pistol Carella had been carrying for some little while now was *also* a Colt Detective Special. In fact, this was the pistol of choice for most of the cops on the squad.

Pinned to the bulletin board, slightly to the left of the picture of the eleven revolvers, was the picture of the six police shields.

Carella's shield and his ID card had been used during the bank job the day after they'd been stolen from him. The man who'd gone in claiming to be Detective Carella was also carrying the gun he had taken from Carella the night before.

Was there some connection between that long-ago theft of pistol and shield and the current messages depicting pistols and shields?

There were now seven messages in all, each posted to the bulletin board in ascending numerical order.

Two nightsticks.

Three pairs of handcuffs.

Four police hats.

Five walkie-talkies.

Six police shields.

Eight black horses.

Eleven Colt Detective Specials.

One thing Carella knew for certain about the Deaf Man was that he worked with different pickup gangs on each job, rather like a jazz soloist recruiting sidemen in the various cities on his tour. In the past any apprehended gang members did not know the true identity of their leader; he had presented himself once as L. Sordo, another time as Mort Orecchio, and—on the occasion of his last appearance— simply as Taubman. In Spanish *el sordo* meant "the Deaf Man." Loosely translated, *mort'orecchio* meant "dead ear" in Italian. And in German *der taube Mann* meant "the Deaf Man." If indeed he *was* deaf. The hearing aid itself may have been a phony, even though he always took pains to announce that he was hard of hearing. But whatever he was or whoever he was, the crimes he conceived were always grand in scale and involved large sums of money.

Nor was conceiving crimes and executing them quite enough for the Deaf Man. A key element in his M.O. was telling the police what he was going to do long before he did it. At first Carella had supposed this to be evidence of a monumental ego, but he had come to learn that the Deaf Man used the police as a sort of *second* pickup gang, larger than the nucleus group, but equally essential to the successful commission of the crime. That he had been thwarted on three previous occasions was entirely due to chance. He was *smarter* than the police, and he *used* the police, and he let the police *know* they were being used.

Knowing they were being used but not knowing *how,* knowing he was telling them a great deal about the crime but not *enough,* knowing he would do what he predicted but not *exactly,* the police generally reacted like hicks on a Mickey Mouse force. Their behavior in turn strengthened the Deaf Man's premise that they were singularly inept. Given their now-demonstrated ineffectiveness, he became more and more outrageous, more and more daring. And the bolder he became, the more they tripped over their own flat feet.

And yet, he always played the game fair.

Carella hated to think of what might happen if all at once he decided *not* to play the game fair.

What if those seven messages on the bulletin board had nothing whatever to do with the crime he was planning this time around? What if each of them taken separately had nothing to do with all of them as a whole? In short, what if he was *cheating* this time?

There seemed no question now—if ever there had been—that the man who'd dropped Elizabeth Turner's corpse in the park across the street was the Deaf Man. Josie Sears hadn't seen a hearing aid in the man's ear, but she'd described him as tall and blond. Given the circumstances, that was close enough. No cigar, but damn close.

It was also clear that someone of the same description, and definitely wearing a hearing aid this time, had passed himself off to Naomi Schneider as Detective Steve Carella of the 87th Squad.

The Deaf Man had been driving a stolen blue Buick Century on the night Josie spotted him and a gray Jaguar sedan on the night he'd driven Naomi home. Even before Carella called Auto Theft, he suspected the Jaguar had been stolen, too.

His call to Auto disclosed that a dozen Jaguars, apparently popular cars with thieves, had been stolen in this city since the beginning of November. Four of them had been sedans. One of those had been gray. It had not yet been recovered. Carella now had a license plate number for the car the Deaf Man might still be driving. *If* the same license plate was still on it. And if the car hadn't already been dumped in some empty lot in the next state.

The Deaf Man was a one-man crime wave.

But what was he up to?

What was the goddamn significance of these pictures he kept sending them? Did the numbers themselves mean something? Why all this police paraphernalia with eight black horses thrown in for good measure?

Come on, Carella thought, play it fair. Give us a break, willya?

The next break in the case—if in retrospect it could be considered that—came on the third day of December, a Saturday. It came with a phone call from Naomi Schneider at twenty minutes past three.

"Did you just call me?" she asked Carella.

"No," he said. And then at once, "Have you heard from him again?"

"Well, somebody named Steve Carella just called me," she said.

"Did it sound like him?"

"I guess so. I've never heard his voice on the phone."

"What'd he want?"

"He said he wants to see me again."

"Did he say when?"

"Today."

"Where? Is he coming there?"

"Well, we didn't arrange anything actually. I thought I'd better call you first."

"How'd you leave it?"

"I told him I'd call him back."

"He gave you a number?"

"Yes."

"What is it?"

Naomi gave him the number.

"Stay right there," Carella said. "If he calls again, tell him you're still thinking it over. Tell him you're hurt because you haven't heard from him in such a long time."

"Well, I already told him that," Naomi said.

"You told him . . . ?"

"Well, I really *was* hurt," Naomi said.

"Naomi," Carella said, "this man is a very dangerous criminal. Don't play games with him, do you hear me? If he calls again, tell him you're still considering whether you want to see him again, and then call me here right away. If I'm not here, leave a message with one of the other detectives. Have you got that?''

"Yes, of course, I've got it. I'm not a child," Naomi said.

"I'll get back to you later," he said, and hung up. He checked his personal directory, dialed a number at Headquarters, identified himself to the clerk who answered the phone, and told her he needed an address for a telephone number in his possession. The new hotline at Headquarters had been installed because policemen all over the city had been having trouble getting information from the telephone company, whose policy was not to give out the addresses of subscribers, even if a detective said he was working a homicide. Carella sometimes felt the telephone company was run by either the Mafia or the KGB. The clerk was back on the line three minutes later.

"That number is for a phone booth," she said.

"On the street or where?" Carella asked.

"Got it listed for something called the Corners on Detavoner and Ash."

"Thank you," Carella said, and hung up. "Artie!" he yelled. "Get your hat!"

When the knock sounded on the door to Naomi's apartment, she thought it might be Carella. He had told her he'd get back to her later, hadn't he? She went to the door.

"Who is it?" she asked.

"Me," the voice said. "Steve."

It did not sound like the *real* Carella. It sounded like the *fake* Carella. And the *real* Carella had told her the *fake* Carella was a very dangerous man. As if she didn't know.

"Just a second," she said, and unlocked the door and took off the night chain. There he was.

Tall, blond, handsome, head cocked to one side, smile on his face.

"Hi," he said.

"Long time no see," she said. She felt suddenly weak. Just the sight of him made her weak.

"Okay to come in?"

"Sure," she said, and let him into the apartment.

The Corners at three-thirty that Saturday afternoon was—thanks to the football game on the television set over the bar—actually more crowded than it would have been at the same time on a weekday. Carella and Brown immediately checked out the place for anyone who might remotely resemble the Deaf Man. There was only one blond man sitting at the bar, and he was short and fat. They went at once to the men's room. Empty. They knocked on the door to the ladies room, got no answer, opened the door, and checked that out, too. Empty. They went back outside to the bar. Carella showed the bartender his shield. The bartender nodded.

"Tall blond man," Carella said. "Would have used the phone booth about forty minutes ago."

"What about him?" the bartender said.

"Did you see him?"

"I saw him. Guy with a hearing aid?"

"Yes."

"I saw him."

"He's been in here before, hasn't he?"

"Coupla times."

"Would you know his name?"

"I think it's Dennis, I'm not sure."

"Dennis what?"

"I don't know. He was in here with a guy one night, I heard the guy calling him Dennis."

"There's just this one room, huh?" Brown said.

"Just this one."

"No little side rooms or anything."

"Just this."

"Any other toilets? Besides the rest rooms back there?"

"That's all," the bartender said. "If you're lookin' for him, he already left."

"Any idea where he went?"

"Nope."

"Did he leave right after he made his phone call?"

"Nope. Sat at the bar for ten minutes or so, finishing his drink."

"What was he drinking?" Carella asked.

"Jim Beam and water."

Carella looked at Brown. Brown shrugged. Carella went to the phone booth and dialed Naomi Schneider's number.

"Let it ring," the Deaf Man said.

She was naked. They were on her bed. She would have let it ring even if it was the fire department calling to say the building was on fire. The phone kept ringing. Spread wide beneath him, her eyes closed, she heard the ringing only distantly, a faraway sound over the pounding of her own heart, the raging of her blood. At last the phone stopped.

All at once *he* stopped too.

"Hey," she said, "don't . . ."

"I want to talk," he said.

"Put it back in," she said.

"Later."

"Come on," she said.

"No."

"Please, baby, I'm almost there," she said. "Put it back in. Please."

He got off the bed. She watched him as he walked to the dresser, watched him as he shook a cigarette free from the package on the dresser top. He thumbed a gold lighter into flame, blew out a wreath of smoke. Everything was golden about him. Gold watch, gold lighter, golden hair, big magnificent golden . . .

"There's something we have to discuss," he said. "Something I'd like you to do for me."

"Bring it here, I'll show you what I can do for you."

"Later," he said, and smiled.

*   *   *

They were in the unmarked sedan, heading back toward the precinct. The heater, as usual, wasn't working. The windows were frost-rimed. Brown kept rubbing at the windshield with his gloved hand, trying to free it of ice.

"I told her to stay home," Carella said. "I specifically told her to . . ."

"We don't own her," Brown said.

"Who owns you?" the Deaf Man said.

"You do."

"Say it."

"You own me."

"Again."

"You own me."

"And you'll do anything I want you to do, won't you?"

"Anything."

"You think we ought to stop by there?" Brown asked. "It's on the way back."

"What for?" Carella said.

"Maybe she just went down for a newspaper or something."

"Pull over to that phone booth," Carella said. "I'll try her again."

The phone was ringing again.

"You're a busy little lady," the Deaf Man said.

"Shall I answer it?"

"No."

The phone kept ringing.

Carella came out of the booth and walked back to the car. Brown was banging on the heater with the heel of his hand.

"Any luck?" he asked.

"No."

"So what do you want to do?"

"Let's take a spin by there," Carella said.

"I need you on Christmas Eve," the Deaf Man said.

"I need you right now," Naomi said.

"I want you to be a very good little girl on Christmas Eve."

"I promise I'll be a very good little girl," she said, and folded her hands in her lap like an eight-year-old. "But you really owe me an apology, you know."

"I owe you nothing," he said flatly.

"I mean for not calling me all this . . ."

"For *nothing*," he said. "Don't ever forget that."

She looked at him. She nodded. She would do whatever he asked her to do, she would wait forever for his phone calls, she would never ask him for explanations or apologies. She had never met anyone like him in her life. She almost said out loud, "I'll bet you've got girls all over this city who'll do anything you want them to do," but she caught herself in time. She did not want him walking out on her. She did not want him disappearing from her life again.

"I want you to dress up for me," he said. "On Christmas Eve."

"Like a good little girl?" she said. "In a short skirt? And knee socks? And Buster Brown shoes? And white cotton panties?"

"No."

"Well, whatever," she said. "Sure."

"A Salvation Army uniform," he said.

"Okay, sure."

That might be kicks, she thought, a Salvation Army uniform. Nothing at all under the skirt. Sort of kinky. Little Goodie-Two-Shoes tambourine-beating virgin with her skirt up around her naked ass.

"Where am I supposed to get a Salvation Army uniform?" she asked.

"I'll get it for you. You don't have to worry about that."

"Sure," she said. "You know my size?"

"You can give me that before I leave."

"Leave?" she said, alarmed. "I'll *kill* you if you walk out of here without . . ."

"I'm not walking out of here. Not until we discuss this fully."

"And not until you . . ."

"Be quiet," he said.

She nodded. She had to be very careful with him. She didn't want to lose him, not ever again.

"Where do you want me to wear this uniform?" she said. "Will you be coming here?"

"No."

"Then where? Your place?"

"Uptown," he said. "Near the precinct."

"Uh-huh," she said, and looked at him. "Is that where you live? Near the precinct?"

"No, that's not where I live. That's where you'll be wearing the uniform. On the street up there. A few blocks from where I work."

"We're gonna do it on the street?" she asked, and smiled.

"You have a very evil mind," he said, and kissed her. She felt the kiss clear down to her toes. "This is a stakeout," he said. "Police work. Both of us in Salvation Army uniforms."

"Oh, *you're* gonna be wearing one, too."

"Yes."

"Sounds like fun," she said. "But what do you *really* have in mind?"

"That's what I have in mind," he said.

"A stakeout, huh?"

"Yes, a stakeout."

"Even though you're not a cop, huh?"

"What do you mean?"

"I mean, I know you're not a cop."

"I'm not, huh?"

"I know you're not Steve Carella."

He looked at her.

"And how do you know that?" he said.

" 'Cause I know the *real* Steve Carella," she said.

He kept looking at her.

"I do," she said, and nodded. "I called the station house," she said. "I called the Eighty-seventh Precinct."

"Why'd you do that?"

" 'Cause you told me you worked there."

"You spoke to someone named Carella?"

"Steve Carella, yes. In fact, I met him. Later."

"You met him," he said.

"Yes."

"And?"

"He told me you're not him. As if I didn't know. I mean, the minute I saw him I knew he wasn't . . ."

"What else did he tell you?"

"He said you're very dangerous," Naomi said, and giggled.

"I am," he said.

"Oh, I *know,*" she said, and giggled again.

"And what'd you tell him?"

"Oh . . . how we met . . . and what we did . . . and like that."

"Did you tell him *where* we met?"

"Oh, sure, the Corners," she said.

He was very silent.

"What else did you tell him?" he asked at last.

A good way for a statistician to discover how many policemen are on duty in any sector of the city is to put a 10-13 call on the radio. Every cop in the vicinity will immediately respond. Sometimes even cops from other precincts will respond. That is because the 10-13 radio code means ASSIST POLICE OFFICER, and there is no higher priority.

Carella and Brown were a block from Naomi's apartment when the 10-13 erupted from the walkie-talkie on the seat between them. Neither of the men discussed or debated it. The cop in trouble was ten blocks from where they were, in the opposite direction from the one they were traveling. But Brown immediately swung the car around in a sharp U-turn, and Carella hit the siren switch.

The Deaf Man sat up straight the moment he heard the siren. Like an animal sensing danger, Naomi thought. God, he is *so* beautiful. But the siren was moving away from her street, and as it faded into the distance, he seemed to relax.

"What else did you tell him?" he asked again.

"Well . . . nothing," she said.

"Are you sure?"

"Well . . . I told him what you looked like and what you were wearing . . . he was asking me questions, you see."

"Yes, I'm sure he was. How did he react to all this information?"

"He seemed interested."

"Oh, yes, I'm sure."

"He told me to keep in touch."

"And have you kept in touch?"

"Well . . ."

"Have you?"

"Look, don't you think you should tell me who you *really* are?" she said.

"I want to know whether you and Steve Carella have kept in touch."

"He said you're a dangerous *criminal* is what he actually said. *Are* you a criminal?"

"Yes," he said. "Tell me whether you've stayed in touch."

"What kind of criminal are you?"

"A very good one."

"I mean . . . like a burglar . . . or a robber . . . or . . ." She arched her eyebrows, the way her magazines had taught her. "A rapist?"

"When did he tell you I was a criminal?" he asked.

"Well, when I saw him, I guess. At his house."

"Oh, you went to his house, did you?"

"Well, yeah."

"When was that?"

"On Thanksgiving Day."

"And that was when he told you I was a criminal?"

"Yes. And again today. A *dangerous* criminal is what he . . ."

"Today?" the Deaf Man said. "You spoke to him today?"

"Well, yes, I did."

"When?"

"Right after you called."

Four patrol cars were already angled into the curb when Carella and Brown got to the scene. At least a dozen patrolmen with drawn guns were crouched behind the cover of the cars, and more patrolmen were approaching on foot, at a run, their guns magically appearing in their hands the moment they saw what the situation was. Again neither Carella nor Brown discussed anything. They immediately drew their guns and stepped out of the car.

A sergeant told them a cop was inside there. "Inside there" was a doctor's office. The cop and his partner had responded to a simple radioed 10-10— INVESTIGATE SUSPICIOUS PERSON—and had walked into the waiting room to find a man holding a .357 Magnum in his hand. The man opened fire immediately, missing both cops, but knocking a big chunk of plaster out of the waiting room wall and scaring the patients half to death. The point-cop had thrown himself flat on the floor. The backup-cop had managed to get out the door and radio the 10-13. The sergeant figured the man inside there was a junkie looking for dope.

Doctors' offices were prime targets for junkies. Carella asked the sergeant if he thought he needed them there. The sergeant said, "No, what I think I need here is the hostage team."

Carella and Brown holstered their guns and went back to the car.

The Deaf Man was putting on his clothes. Naomi watched him from the bed.

"I didn't tell him you were coming here, if that's what's bothering you," she said.

"Nothing's bothering me," he said.

But he was tucking the flaps of his shirt into his trousers. He sat again, put on his socks and shoes, and then went to the dresser for his cuff links. He put on the cuff links and then picked up the gun in its holster. He slipped into the harness and then came back to the chair for his jacket.

She kept watching him, afraid to say anything more. A man like this one, you could lose him if you said too much. Instead, she opened her legs a little wider, gave him a better look at her, he was only human, wasn't he? He went to the closet, took his coat from a hanger, and shrugged into it.

He walked back to the bed.

He smiled and reached under his coat, and under his jacket, and pulled the gun from its holster.

Naomi returned his smile and spread her legs a little wider.

"Another game with the gun?" she asked.

It took Carella and Brown five minutes to clear the immediate area around the doctor's office. The police had cordoned off the scene, so they had to stop at the barricade to identify themselves. It took them another ten minutes to get uptown to Naomi's apartment.

They were twelve minutes too late.

The door to Naomi's apartment was wide open.

Naomi was lying on the bed with a bullet hole between her eyes.

The pillow under her head was very red.

Well, now they had a bullet.

The bullet had entered Naomi Schneider's skull just above the bridge of her manicured nose, and angled up slightly and exited at the back of her head, and had gone through the down pillow under her head to lodge in the mattress, where the lab technician dug it out.

The bullet told them that the murder weapon was a Colt Detective Special— similar to any one of the eleven on the picture the Deaf Man had sent them.

But that was all they had.

And until they were in possession of an actual weapon they could test-fire for comparison purposes, the bullet was virtually useless to them.

On Monday morning, December 12, another message from the Deaf Man arrived in the mail:

They were looking at seven wanted flyers.

"Beautiful people, each and every one of them," Meyer said.

"Maybe he's telling us who the gang is," Brown said.

"He wouldn't be *that* crazy, would he?" Carella said. "To *name* them for us?"

"Why not?" Brown said. "If these guys are still loose, their pictures are in every precinct in town."

Which was just the problem.

Even before they tacked the latest message to the bulletin board, the pictures were already there. All seven of them. Plus a dozen more like them. The detectives looked at *all* the Deaf Man's messages now, marching across the bulletin board in a single, inscrutable horizontal line:

Two nightsticks. Three pairs of handcuffs. Four police hats. Five walkie-talkies. Six police shields. Seven wanted flyers. Eight black horses. Eleven Colt Detective Specials.

"What's missing?" Carella asked.

"*Everything's* missing," Brown said.

"I mean . . . there's no *one,* right?" Nothing for the number one. And nothing for nine or ten either."

"Assuming he plans to stop at eleven," Meyer said. "Suppose he plans to go to twenty? Or a *hundred* and twenty? Suppose he plans to keep sending these damn things *forever?*"

"Fun is fun," Lieutenant Byrnes said, "but we happen to have two dead bodies."

He was sitting behind a desk in his corner office, the blinds open to the parking lot behind the police station. Inside the cyclone fence with its barbed wire frosting, pale December sunlight glanced off the white roofs of the patrol cars parked below. Carella thought the lieutenant looked tired. His hair seemed a bit grayer, his blue eyes a bit more faded. Am *I* going to look that way in a few years? he wondered. Is that what the job does to you? Burns you out, grinds you down to graying cinders?

"Technically," Carella said, "the Schneider murder . . ."

"It's linked, it's ours," Byrnes said flatly. "Wherever the hell it actually . . ."

"The Four-One," Carella said.

"So? Are *they* working it?"

"No, Pete. They were happy to turn it over."

"Sure. Christmas coming up . . ."

He let the sentence trail. He was thinking, Carella knew, that there'd be enough headaches ahead in the next two weeks. All the bad guys doing their Christmas shopping. The bad guys didn't need cash or credit cards or charge accounts. The bad guys only needed nimble fingers. He wondered if the bad guys ever got to look as gray and as pale as Byrnes did. Send them to jail, they complained that the swimming pool wasn't properly filtered. If you can't do the time, don't do the crime. They laughed at the old police adage and did their time standing on their heads, laughing. Came out looking healthier than when they went in, all that weight lifting in the prison gym. Came out ready to victimize again. Laughing all the way. Oh what fun it is to ride . . .

"So what've you got?" Byrnes asked.

"Nothing," Carella said.

"Don't tell me *nothing*," Byrnes said, "I'm starting to get heat on this. The cops in New York, they got a dead Harvard graduate, they wrap it in forty-eight hours. We got *two* dead girls, and you tell me *nothing*."

"Well, we know it's the Deaf Man, but . . ."

"Then find him."

"That's the trouble, Pete. We . . ."

"What's all this crap he keeps sending us? What's any of it got to do with the victims?"

"We don't know yet."

"According to this . . ." He picked up the D.D. report on his desk. "According to this, the second girl knew him, is that right?"

"Yes, sir. But only as Steve Carella. That's the name he gave her."

"Used your name."

"Yes, sir."

"Why'd she let him in that apartment? You told her he was dangerous, didn't you?"

"Yes, sir."

"So why'd she let him in? Was she crazy or something? Man like that, she lets him in her apartment?" He shook his head. "What about the first victim? Did this . . . what's her name?" He began leafing through the other D.D. reports.

"Elizabeth Turner, sir."

"Did *she* know him, too?"

"We don't know, Pete. We're assuming she did."

"Still don't know where she worked, huh?"

"No, sir."

"But you're assuming it was a bank."

"That's the line we're taking, yes."

"Which would tie in. His M.O., I mean."

"Yes."

"Maybe planning an inside job, is that what you figure?"

"Something like that."

"Use the girl."

"Yes."

"But you don't know which bank."

"We've checked them all, Pete."

"If he planned to use her, why'd he kill her?"

"We don't know."

"Same gun?"

"We don't know."

"This picture of the guns . . . the one he sent. All Colt Detective Specials, huh?"

"Yes, sir."

"And the Schneider girl was killed with a Colt Detective Special, huh?"

"Yes, sir."

"Eleven of them, huh? In the picture."

"Eleven, yes, sir."

"You think he plans to kill *eleven* girls?"

"We don't know, sir."

"What the hell *do* you know?" Byrnes said, and then immediately said, "I'm sorry, Steve," and washed his open hand over his face and sighed heavily. "I got a call from Inspector Cassidy this morning," he said. "The girl's father—the Schneider girl—her father's a big wheel at some temple in Calm's Point, he's yelling like it's the Holocaust all over again. You think there's an anti-Semitic angle here?"

"I doubt it."

"The other girl wasn't Jewish, was she?"

"No, sir."

"Yeah, well . . . also the Schneider girl worked for CBS, which the newspapers figure to be a glamour job . . ."

"She was a receptionist there, Pete."

"You think he's planning a heist at CBS?"

"Well . . . I'll tell you the truth, that never occurred to us."

"I don't know, do they have cash laying around there?"

"I doubt it."

"Anyway, you get a girl working for a television network, the media automatically makes a big deal of it. Well, you've seen the papers, you've seen television."

"Yes, sir."

"What I'm saying is we're getting a lot of heat on this, Steve. From departmental rank *and* the media. I'd like to be able to tell somebody *something*. And *soon*."

"We're doing our best, Pete."

"Yeah, I know. It's just . . . with Christmas coming . . ."

He let the sentence trail again.

9

Christmas was indeed coming.

And as far as Detective Lloyd Andrew Parker was concerned, it was coming too damn soon. In fact, it *started* coming sooner and sooner each year. This year the stores were already decorated for Christmas a few days before Thanksgiving. You woke up one morning, it wasn't even turkey time yet, and there was Santa Claus in the store windows.

Parker hated Christmas.

He also hated his first name. He doubted that anyone on the squad knew his first name was Lloyd. Maybe no one in the entire world new his first name was Lloyd. He himself had almost forgotten that his first name was Lloyd. Well, maybe Miscolo in the clerical office knew because he was the one who made out the pay chits every two weeks. Lloyd was a piss-ant name. Andrew was better because Andrew was one of the twelve apostles, and anybody with a twelve-apostle name was a good guy. If you were reading a book—which Parker rarely did—and you ran across a guy named Luke, Matthew, Thomas, Peter, Paul, James, like that, you knew right off he was supposed to be a good guy. That was in books. In real life you sometimes got the scum of the earth named for apostles, criminals who'd slit your throat for a nickel.

Parker hated criminals.

He also hated being called Andy. Made him sound like fuckin' Andy Hardy or something. Little piss-ant twerp having heart-to-heart chats with his Judge Hardy father. Parker hated judges. It was judges who let criminals go free. He would have preferred being called Andrew, which was his true and honorable middle name. Andrew had some respect attached to it. Andy sounded like a good old boy you patted on the back: Hey, Andy, how's it goin', Andy? Parker hated his mother for having named him, first of all, Lloyd, and then having reduced his middle name, which he'd got when he was confirmed, to Andy. Parker hated his father for not having stood up to his mother when she decided to name him first Lloyd and then Andrew. Parker was glad both his mother and his father were dead.

Parker wished Santa Claus was dead, too.

Parker wished Rudolph the Red-Nosed Reindeer would get shot some starry Christmas Eve and be served as venison steak on Christmas Day. Or, better yet, venison stew. If he heard that dumb song on the radio one more time, he would take out his pistol and *shoot* the fuckin' radio. The person Parker liked most at Christmastime was Ebenezer Scrooge. Scrooge would've made a good cop. Parker thought of himself as a good cop, but he knew most of the guys on the squad thought he was a lousy cop. He also knew they didn't like him much. Fuck 'em, he wasn't running in any fuckin' popularity contest.

The Christmas songs had started on the radio a couple of days ago, as if all the disc jockeys just couldn't *wait* to start playing them. Same old songs every year. This was only the fifteenth of December, and already he'd heard all the Christmas songs a hundred times over. "Silent Night" and "God Rest Ye Merry Gentlemen" and "Little Drummer Boy"—he wished the little drummer boy would get shot together with Rudolph the Red-Nosed Reindeer—and "The First Noel" and "Joy to the World" and "White Christmas" and "I'll Be Home for Christmas" and "Deck the Halls" and "Jingle Bells" and the worst fuckin' Christmas song ever written in the history of the world: "All I Want for Christmas Is My Two Front Teeth." If Parker ever met the guy who wrote that song, he'd give him his two front teeth all right, on a platter after he knocked them out of his mouth.

Parker hated Christmas songs.

He hated everything about this city at Christmastime.

He hated the city *all* the time, but he hated it most at Christmastime.

All those phony Santa Clauses standing on street corners ringing bells and asking for donations. All the Salvation Army piss-ants blowing trumpets and shaking tambourines. All the fake fuckin' beggars who crowded the sidewalks, guys with signs saying they were blind or deaf and dumb like Carella's wife, or guys on little trolleys with signs saying they lost their legs, all of them phonies like the phony Santa Clauses. Fuckin' phony blind man went home at night, all of a sudden he could see when he was counting the money in his tin cup. Parker hated the street musicians and the break dancers. He hated the guys selling merchandise on the sidewalks outside department stores. If he had his way, he'd lock up even the ones who had vendor's licenses, cluttering up the sidewalks that way, most of them selling stolen merchandise. Parker hated the out-of-towners who flocked to this city before Christmas. Gee, looka the big buildings, Mama. Fuckin' green-horns, each and every one of them, cameras clicking, oohing and ahhing, prime targets for pickpockets, caused more trouble than they were worth. Suckers for all the guys driving horse-drawn carriages around Grover Park. He hated the way those guys decorated their carriages for the holidays, garlands of pine hanging all over them, wreaths, banners saying SEASONS GREETINGS, all the phony trappings of Christmas, when all they were after was the buck, the long green. Hated horses, too. All they did was shit all over the streets, make the job harder for the sanitmen. Hated the idea that there were still some horse-mounted cops in this city, more horses to shit on the city streets, had their stable right up here in the Eight-Seven, the old armory on the corner of First and Saint Sab's, saw them heading downtown each and every morning, a fuckin' parade of horses in different colors, cops sitting on them like they were a fuckin' Roman legion. Hated horses and hated mounted cops and hated tourists who should have stayed home in Elephant Shit, Iowa.

Most of all, Parker hated Alice Patricia Parker.

None of the guys on the squad knew that Parker had once been married. Fuck 'em, it was none of their business.

Around Christmastime he always wondered where Alice Patricia was. He hated her, but he wondered where she was, what she was doing.

Probably still hooking someplace.

Probably L.A. She'd always talked about going out to California. Maybe San Francisco. Hooking someplace out there in California.

On Thanksgiving Day he'd sat alone in his garden apartment in Majesta and watched the Gruber's Thanksgiving Day parade. Watched it on one of the local channels. Not as big or as famous as the Macy's parade in New York, but what the fuck, it was at least the city's *own* parade. Ate a frozen turkey dinner he'd heated up in his microwave oven. And wondered where Alice Patricia was.

And wondered what she was doing.

Blond hair and blue eyes.

A figure you could cry.

Whenever a blond, blue-eyed homicide victim turned up—like the one Carella and Brown had caught in October—Parker wondered where Alice Patricia was, wondered if she was lying dead in an alley someplace, her throat slit by some California pimp.

I'm only doing it as a sideline, she'd told him.

Well, listen, they'd warned him. This was when he was still working out of the Three-One downtown, not a bad precinct, still in uniform down there, learning what it was like to be a fuckin' cop in this fuckin' city. Filth and garbage, that was what you dealt with. Went home with the stink of it on your hands and in your nostrils. He'd met her in a bar, she was dancing topless there, the guys all warned him. These topless dancers, they said, you know what they are. They're either turning tricks already, or else they drift into doing massage parlors part-time, and before you knew it, they were full-fledged hookers. He told them to go fuck themselves. Alice Patricia was maybe dancing topless, but she had ambition and ideals, wanted to dance someday in a legitimate show, make it here and then move on to Broadway and the big time. Took ballet lessons and voice lessons and acting lessons, wanted to make it big. She wasn't what they thought. Parker knew she wasn't. When he married her, he didn't invite any of the guys from the Three-One to the wedding.

It was going good, he thought it was going real good.

Then one night—he had the four to midnight—he went over to the club she was working at, a place called Champagne Bubbles or some such shit, and one of the girls told him Alice Patricia had gone out for an hour or so, and he said, "What do you mean she went out for an hour or so?" This was now twelve-thirty, one o'clock in the morning, the place was almost empty except for some sailors sitting at the bar watching a girl Alice Patricia called the Titless Wonder. "This time of night she went out for an hour or so?" Parker said. He knew what this city turned into after midnight. A fuckin' moonscape full of predators crawling the streets looking for victims. Filth and garbage, the stink of it. "Where'd she go?" he asked.

The girl looked at him.

She was topless. She kept toying with a string of pearls around her neck.

"Where'd she go?" he asked again.

"Leave it be, Andy," the girl said.

He grabbed the string of pearls, ripped them from her neck. The pearls clattered to the floor, rolled on the floor. The sound of the pearls was louder than the sound of the taped music the girl onstage was dancing to.

"Where?" he said.

So, you know, he found her in a hot-bed hotel three blocks from the club. He was in civvies, he had changed in the locker room when his tour ended, the room clerk thought he was a detective when he showed his shield. This was a year before he'd made Detective/Third. He'd made Detective/Third after the divorce, when he had nothing to concentrate on but police work. The room clerk told him a blond, blue-eyed girl had come in with a black man about fifteen minutes ago. The room clerk told him they were in room 1301. Parker would remember the number of the room always. And the stink of Lysol in the hallway.

He beat the black man to within an inch of his life. Kicked him down the stairs. Told him to get his black ass out of this city. He went back to the room. Alice Patricia was still on the bed, naked, smoking a cigarette.

He said, "Why?"

She said, "I'm only doing it as a sideline."

He said, "Why?"

"For kicks," she said, and shrugged.

"I loved you," he said.

It was already past tense.

Alice Patricia shrugged again.

He should have killed her.

He said, "This is it, you know."

"Sure," she said, and stubbed out the cigarette.

He walked out of the room and out of the hotel and into the city. He beat up two drunks who were singing at the tops of their lungs on Hastings Street. He threw an ash can through a plate glass window on Jefferson Avenue. He roamed the city. He was drunk himself when he got back to the apartment at four in the morning. He thought maybe he'd find Alice Patricia there. He thought if she was there, he would kill her. But she was already gone, took all of her clothes with her. Not even a note. Took his lawyer three months to find her. The divorce became final six months after that. And three months after that he made Detective/Third.

He still wondered about her whenever the holidays came around.

Hated her, but wondered about her.

Hated the fuckin' holidays.

Hated the thought of snow maybe coming for Christmas.

He hated snow. It started out white and pure and ended up filthy.

He hated Christmas trees, too. All they did was make a garbage collection problem, even *more* work for the sanitmen, like the horseshit all over the streets. Right after Christmas you had a dead forest of fuckin' Christmas trees, trailing tinsel, stacked up outside the buildings with the garbage. The garbage was bad enough in this city, he sometimes thought it was a city of uncollected black plastic bags. The leftover Christmas trees only made it worse. Saw them all over the city. Dead. Trailing tinsel. She used to dance with this little G-string that looked as if it was made of Christmas tree tinsel, all sparkly and bright, her hips rotating, dollar bills tucked into the waistband. I'm only doing it as a sideline. Could've been a big fuckin' star. He'd have gone backstage, talked to the other people in the cast. Alice Patricia is my wife, he would've said. No kidding? Yeah, I'm a cop. No kidding?

He hated being a cop.

Hated the notes from this guy who had the squadroom in a fuckin' tizzy. The Deaf Man. Who gave a shit about the Deaf Man? In Parker's world they were *all* thieves, some of them smart thieves and some of them dumb ones. Maybe the Deaf Man was a smart one, but he was still a thief. So what was all this fuss about the notes he was sending? Smart-ass thief was all.

Parker wondered what it was like to be young.

Wondered what it would be like to be called Andrew again.

Alice Patricia used to call him Andrew.

He hated her.

Oh, Christ, how he loved her!

On Monday morning, December 19, another note from the Deaf Man arrived.

They were beginning to get tired of him. In six days it would be Christmas. They had other things to do besides worrying about his foolishness. They did not know why he had killed Elizabeth Turner—*if* he'd killed her—and they did not know what his goddamn messages meant. They figured he had killed Naomi Schneider because he may have told her something she had not yet repeated to them, and this something would have been dangerous if revealed. The Deaf Man let them know only what he *wanted* them to know. Anything else was a risk, and he took no unpredictable risks. So good-bye, Naomi.

But both cases were as dead as this year's calendar would soon be, and the latest message from him was only an irritation. They merely glanced at it and then tacked it to the bulletin board with the others:

Cotton Hawes was in trouble.

He felt like calling in a 10-13.

Instead, he said, "I *do* have a Gruber's charge account."

He was embarrassed to begin with. He had just bought Annie Rawles two hundred dollars' worth of sexy lingerie as a Christmas gift. Two hundred and *thirteen* dollars *and* twenty-five cents with tax. He hoped he would not have to explain to this lady on the sixth floor of Gruber's new uptown store that he had bought the underwear for a Detective/First Grade. The store, not six blocks from the station house, was part of the mayor's new Urban Renewal Program. The *real* Gruber's was all the way downtown, on Messenger Square. Hawes should have gone downtown. He should have known better than to shop anywhere in the precinct, even though the new store was very nice and—according to the mayor's office, at least—was doing a very good business and was serving as a model for redevelopment of shitty neighborhoods all over the city.

"Not according to our records," the woman behind the counter said.

Hawes wondered if she would be caught dead in the sort of sexy lingerie he had bought for Annie.

"I've had a Gruber's charge account for three years now," he said.

"Let me see your card again, please," the woman said.

He handed her the card.

He was in the sixth-floor credit office. The woman downstairs on the first floor—where Lingerie was—had told him to go up to the sixth floor to the credit office because when she'd tried to run his card through the computer, she had come up with an INVALID. He had taken the escalator up to the sixth floor and had seen a bristling array of signs pointing in different directions: MANAGER'S OFFICE. CASHIER'S OFFICE. CREDIT OFFICE. RETURNS. PERSONNEL OFFICE, TOY DEPARTMENT. SANTA CLAUS. TELEPHONE OFFICE. REST ROOMS. He had almost gotten lost, fine detective that he was. But here he was in the credit office, handing his card across the counter to a woman who had a nose like a broomstick. And eyes like dirt. Her eyes were dirty. Not brown, not black—just dirty. She looked at his card with her dirty eyes. She almost sniffed it with her broomstick nose.

"I have the new card," he said.

"Where is the new card, sir?" she asked.

"Home," he said. "I haven't put it in my wallet yet."

He realized, as he said this, that claiming to have the card at home was akin to a pistol-carrying thief claiming he had left his permit in a desk drawer someplace.

"If you planned to shop here," the woman said, "you should have put your card in your wallet."

Hawes opened his wallet. "This is where the new card should be," he said. "But I left it home."

He had really opened his wallet so she could see the gold- and blue-enameled detective shield pinned to it. She looked at the shield with her dirty eyes.

"You should have the new card with you at all times," she said.

"I didn't know I'd be shopping today," he said. "I have a lot of things to carry in my wallet," he said. "My police shield," he said. "My police ID card. I'm a detective,'' he said. "I don't like to carry more things in my wallet than I absolutely have to.''

"But you're carrying the *old* card in your wallet,'' she said.

"Yes, I am. By mistake. The new one should be there.''

"The old card went through our computer as invalid.''

"Yes, I know. That's why I'm up here on the sixth floor. But if you run a check through your computer files up here, you'll see that I received a new card in May. And forgot to put it in my wallet.''

"No wonder people get away with murder in this city,'' she said, and left the counter.

He waited.

She came back ten minutes later.

"Yes, you did indeed receive a new card,'' she said.

"Yes, I know,'' he said. "Thank you,'' he added.

"You understand, sir,'' she said, "that the charging of two hundred dollars' worth of lingerie could not go unquestioned when a card came up invalid.''

"Yes, I understand that,'' he said.

She knew it was for lingerie. She had called downstairs. He wondered if she knew what *sort* of lingerie.

"There are a lot of crooks in this city, you know,'' she said.

"Yes, I'm aware of that,'' he said.

"If you'll go downstairs again to Lingerie,'' she said, "the card will go through this time. I hope you are aware, sir, that panties are not returnable.''

"I didn't know that,'' he said.

"Yes. *Especially* our Open City line, which many women wear for special occasions only. I hope you have the right size.''

"I have the right size, yes,'' he said.

"Yes, well,'' she said, and sniffed the air as if smelling something rank, and gave him a last look with her dirty eyes, and left him standing at the counter.

All the way home he thought about his encounter in Gruber's. He wished Gruber's would burn to the ground. He wished the mayor would take his Urban Renewal Program to Dallas, Texas. Or Vladivostok. All Gruber's did was encourage more crime in an area already crime-ridden. More damn pickpocket and shoplifting arrests in that store since it opened last February than in all the other stores along the Stem. Okay, it was making a lot of money. And maybe attracting other businesses to the area. But did the mayor ever stop to think how much time the cops up here were putting into Gruber's? On shitty little arrests? For which they had to travel all the way down to Headquarters to do the booking?

He was still fuming when he reached his building downtown. He stepped into the small entry foyer, took his keys from his pocket, and unlocked his mailbox. There was a sheaf of letters, *including* a bill from Gruber's. He did not look at the mail more closely until he was in his apartment. He was tempted to call Annie, tell her about the hassle uptown, but that would blow the surprise. Instead, he mixed himself a drink and then sat down and leafed through the envelopes. One of them seemed to be a Christmas card. He tore open the flap on the red envelope. It was not a Christmas card. It was an invitation. It read:

YOU ARE INVITED TO A PARTY

FOR:
Detective-Lieutenant Peter Byrnes

DATE: January 5

TIME: 8:00 P.M.

PLACE: 87th Precinct Squadroom

Scrawled on the flap of the card in the same handwriting was the message:

Cotton— I haven't been able to invite everyone, so please keep this a secret, won't you? Harriet.

Harriet was Harriet Byrnes, the lieutenant's wife. Why in hell was she throwing a party for him in the squadroom? Was it Pete's birthday? An anniversary? Twenty years on the force? Thirty? A hundred?

Hawes shrugged and wrote down the date and time in his appointment calendar.

On Tuesday morning, December 20, the Deaf Man's tenth message arrived.

They knew by now that the number of items pasted to each blank sheet of paper had nothing whatever to do with the order in which the messages were received. The eight black horses, for example, were on the very first message. The six police shields were on the fourth message. The eleven Colt Detective Specials were on the seventh message. And so on. And now on the tenth message:

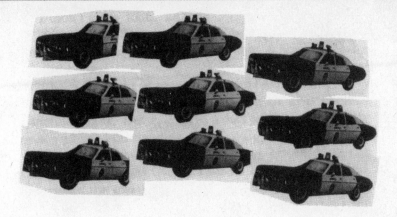

The detectives tacked the sheet of paper to the bulletin board. There were now:
Two nightsticks. Three pairs of handcuffs. Four police hats. Five walkie-talkies.
Six police shields. Seven wanted flyers. Eight black horses. Nine patrol cars. Ten
D.D. forms. And eleven Detective Specials.

They still didn't know what any of it meant.

Did he plan to stop at eleven?

Or would he go beyond that?

If he stopped at eleven, then the number one was still missing in the sequence.

The hell with it, they thought.

Christmas was only five days away.

Bert Kling was looking through his mail when Eileen Burke let herself in with the
key he had given her.

It was close to four-thirty in the afternoon, and the lights on the Calm's Point
Bridge—festooned for the holiday season and visible through his windows—were
blinking red and green against the purple dusk. He sat under a floor lamp near the
windows in an easy chair he'd bought in a thrift shop after his divorce. He had never
discussed his divorce with Andy Parker. He had never discussed anything but police
work with Parker, and even that rarely. He did not know Parker was himself divorced.
He did not know that the two men might have shared common thoughts on the subject,
did not know that Parker, like himself, thought of divorce as a kind of killing.

The holidays, even now and even with Eileen, were the most difficult time for
Kling. Augusta would pop into his mind whenever he shopped the stores, even when
he was shopping for Eileen. Well, the physical similarities, he supposed. In trying to
settle on a color, he'd tell a store clerk that his girlfriend was a green-eyed redhead—
describing Eileen, of course—and immediately Augusta would come to mind. Or in
trying to remember what size Eileen wore, he'd say she was five feet nine inches tall,
and immediately the image of Augusta would come again, unbidden, ghostlike, Augusta as he'd first seen her when he was investigating a burglary in her apartment . . .

*Long red hair and green eyes and a deep suntan. Dark green sweater, short
brown skirt, brown boots. High cheekbones, eyes slanting up from them, fiercely
green against the tan, tilted nose gently drawing the upper lip away from partially*

exposed, even white teeth. Sweater swelling over breasts firm without a bra, the
wool cinched tightly at her waist with a brown brass-studded belt, hip softly carving
an arc against the nubby sofa back, skirt revealing a secret thigh as she turned more
fully toward him . . .

Augusta.

"Hi," Eileen said, and came to where he was sitting.

She kissed him on top of the head. Red and green lights from the bridge blinked into the red and green of her hair and her eyes.

"You look like Christmas," he said.

"I do, huh?" she said. "I feel like Halloween. When did you get in? I called a little while ago."

"A little after four," he said. "I was doing some shopping. What'd the doctor say?"

"He said time heals all wounds."

She took off her coat, tossed it familiarly onto the bed, sat on the edge of the bed, eased off her high-heeled shoes, and reached down to massage one foot. Long legs, sleek and clean, full-calved and tapering to slender ankles. Eileen. Augusta. The knifing would have destroyed Augusta. She was a model, her face was her fortune. Eileen was only a cop. But she was a woman. And a beautiful woman. And she'd been cut on her face. The knifing had occurred on October 21, two months ago. At the hospital they'd taken twelve stitches. The scar was still livid on her left cheek.

"He said I might not need plastic surgery at all," Eileen said. "Told me the hospital emergency room did a very good job. He said the scar may look awful now . . ."

"It doesn't really look bad at all," Kling said.

"Yeah, bullshit," Eileen said. "But it'll heal as a thin white line, he said, if I can live with that. He said it all depends on my 'acceptance level.' How do you like *that* for a euphemism?"

"When do you have to see him again?" Kling asked.

"Next month. He says I shouldn't even be *thinking* about plastic surgery just yet. He said the cut should be entirely healed within six months to a year, and I should wait till then to see how I feel. That's what he means by acceptance level, I guess. How much vanity I have. How ugly I'd care to look for the rest of my life."

"You don't look ugly," Kling said. "You couldn't *possibly* look . . ."

"I'm not winning any beauty contests these days, that's for sure," Eileen said. "You think there are any rapists out there who dig scars? Think they'd go for a decoy with a slashed left cheek?"

"I kind of like the look it gives you," he said, trying to joke her out of her dark mood. "Makes you look sort of dangerous."

"Yeah, dangerous," she said.

"Devil-may-care. Like a lady pirate."

"Like a three-hundred-pound armed robber," Eileen said. "All I need is a tattoo on my arm, Mom in a heart."

"You feel like Chinese tonight?" he asked.

"I feel like curling up in bed and sleeping for a month. Going to see him is exhausting. He's always so fucking *consoling,* do you know what I mean? It isn't *his* fucking face, so he thinks . . ."

"Hey," Kling said softly.

She looked at him.

"Come on," he said, and went to her. He kissed the top of her head. He cupped his hand under her chin and kissed her forehead and the tip of her nose. He kissed the scar. Gently, tenderly.

"Kissing it won't make it go away, Bert," she said, and paused. "I hope you didn't buy me anything too feminine for Christmas."

"What?"

"I don't feel pretty," she said. "I wouldn't want any gifts that . . ."

"You're beautiful," he said. "*And* feminine. *And* sexy. *And* . . ."

"Sweet talker," she said.

"So where do you want to eat?" he said. "McDonald's?"

"Big spender, too," she said, pausing again. "And what?" she said.

"Huh?"

"Beautiful and feminine and sexy and what?"

"And I love you," he said.

"Truly?"

"Truly."

"With all the umpteen million other women in this city . . . ?"

"You're the only woman in this city," he said.

She looked at him. She nodded.

"Thank you," she said softly and rose from the bed. "Let me shower and change," she said. "Thank you," she said again and kissed him on the mouth and then went into the bathroom.

He heard the shower when she turned it on.

He picked up the stack of mail again. He opened several Christmas cards and then picked up a red envelope and tore open the flap. The card inside read:

YOU ARE INVITED TO A PARTY

FOR: Detective-Lieutenant Peter Byrnes

DATE: January 5

TIME: 8:00 P.M.

PLACE: 87th Precinct Squadroom

Scrawled on the flap on the card in the same handwriting was the message:

Bert - I haven't been able to invite everyone,
so please keep this a secret, wont you? Harriet.

The door to the bathroom opened.
Eileen poked her head around the jamb.
"Wanna come shower with me?" she asked.

Christmas Day would fall on a Sunday this year.

This was good for the department stores. Normally sales fell off a bit on Christmas Eve. You had your last-minute shoppers, sure, and the stores all stayed open till six o'clock to accommodate even the tardiest, but the volume was nowhere as great as it was at any other time during that last hectic week before the big event. Unless Christmas Eve fell on a Saturday. Then, miraculously, sales perked up. This may have had something to do with the fact that working people were *used* to shopping on Saturdays. Maybe they felt this was just *another* Saturday, same as all the rest in the year, time to get out there and spend Friday's paycheck. Or maybe the Christmas bonuses had something to do with it, get that big fat extra wad of money on Friday, good time to spend it was Saturday, right? It was funny the way a Saturday Christmas Eve brought out the customers in droves. Statistics showed that it didn't work that way if Christmas Eve fell on a Sunday. Not as many shoppers. Even God rested on Sunday. This year, with prosperity lingering for yet a little while and with Christmas Eve coming on a Saturday, storekeepers all over the city were anticipating a banner day.

On Thursday, December 22, the detectives of the 87th Squad received what they surmised was almost the last of the Deaf Man's communications. It was Arthur Brown, in fact, who guessed this one was the penultimate one. The single white sheet of paper in the now-familiar typewritten envelope showed:

"Number twelve," Brown said.
"Twelve roast pigs," Carella said.
"Only one more to go," Brown said.
"How do you figure that?"
"It's the twelve days of Christmas, don't you get it?" Brown said. "Two night-

sticks, three pairs of handcuffs, four police hats . . . the twelve days of Christmas.''

"He's just wishing us a Merry Christmas, huh?'' Carella said.

"Fat chance,'' Brown said. "But all that's missing now is the first day. It's the twelve days of Christmas, Steve. I'll bet next month's salary on it.''

"So what'll the *first* day be?''

"Take a guess,'' Brown said, grinning.

Brown did not like putting up Christmas trees.

He also did not like what Christmas trees *cost* nowadays. When he was a kid, you could get a huge tree for five bucks. The seven-foot tree he'd bought this year had cost him thirty-five dollars. Highway robbery. He would not have bought a tree at all if it weren't for Connie, his eight-year-old daughter. Connie still believed in Santa Claus. There was no fireplace and hence no chimney in the Brown apartment, but Connie always left a glass of milk and a platter of chocolate-chip cookies under the tree for Santa. Every Christmas Brown had to drink the goddamn glass of milk before he went to bed. He also had to eat some of the chocolate-chip cookies.

The first thing he did not like about putting up a Christmas tree was the lights. It seemed to Brown that if the United States could put a man on the moon, then some brilliant scientist someplace could also figure out a way to make Christmas tree lights that didn't have wires. Brown was no brilliant scientist, but he himself had figured out a very simple way to do this, and if some starving inventor out there wanted to cash in on a bonanza, he was willing to divulge it for a hefty piece of the action. He knew just how it would work in principle, but he didn't have the electrical engineering know-how to put it on paper. He had never discussed his idea out loud with anyone because he didn't want it stolen from him. There were a lot of crooks in this world, as he well knew, and it seemed likely to him that his multimillion-dollar idea would be stolen the moment he talked to anyone about it. He already had a name for the producer: No Strings. If he and somebody went partners on it, they could sell billions and billions of Christmas tree lights every year. No strings. No wires to loop around branches. Each Christmas tree light an individual entity that could be hung anyplace on the tree. All anybody had to do was contact him, write to him care of the 87th Precinct, make him an offer. He was willing to listen.

Meanwhile, he struggled with the damn lights.

Nobody helped him.

That was the *second* thing he disliked about putting up the tree.

His wife, Caroline, was in the kitchen baking the chocolate-chip cookies Connie would put under the tree on Christmas Eve, some of which Brown would later have to eat while he drank the goddamn glass of milk. Connie herself was in the den watching television. All alone in the living room Brown struggled first with the lights and then with the Christmas balls, which was the third thing he disliked about putting up a tree. Not the Christmas balls themselves—except when one fell off the tree and crashed to the floor, leaving all those silvery splinters that were impossible to pick up—but the little *hooks* that held the balls to the tree. Why was it that no matter how carefully you packed all the ornaments away after Christmas, there were always more balls than there were hooks? Brown suspected there was an international ring of ornament-hook thieves.

The smell of baking cookies filled the apartment.

The sound of animated cartoon characters filled the apartment.

Brown worked on the tree.

Only two more days to go, he thought.

His daughter, Connie, suddenly appeared in the doorway.

"How come there's no black Santa Clauses?" she asked. Brown sighed.

The twelve days of Christmas.

Twelfth Night.

The eve of Epiphany.

The first day of Christmas was Christmas Day itself. On Christmas Day the detectives of the 87th Squad would no doubt be celebrating, opening their own meager gifts, and not for a moment expecting the first of *his* gifts. But receive it they would and perhaps recognize at last what all his advance publicity had been about. They would *not,* however—if his notes had been inaccessible enough—realize what lay in store for them on January 5, Twelfth Night, Epiphany Eve.

In lower case the word "epiphany" meant the sudden revelation of an underlying truth about a person or a situation. The English word was from the Greek *epiphaneia,* of course, the gods revealing themselves to mortal eyes, but the Irish novelist James Joyce—one of the Deaf Man's favorites—first popularized the word in modern literature by calling his early experimental prose passages "epiphanies." A sudden flash of recognition. Would the men of the 87th recognize at last? Before the sudden flash? During it? There would be no time for recognition afterward.

He smiled again.

Epiphany Day. January 6. In honor of the first time Jesus Christ manifested himself to the Gentiles. On Epiphany Eve, Twelfth *Night,* as it was called—oh what fun Shakespeare'd had with *that* one—the Deaf Man would reveal himself in spirit to the detectives, making it clear to them for the first, last, and only time that he would brook no further interference with his chosen profession. On three previous occasions he had given them every opportunity to thwart his plans, virtually laying them all out in advance—but never once realizing his plans actually *would* meet with disaster. Oh, not through any brilliant deduction on their part, no, that would be giving them far too much credit for intelligence. But rather through clumsy accidents. Accidents. The bane of the Deaf Man's existence.

Accidents.

The first time it had been a cop wanting to buy ice cream from the Deaf Man's stolen getaway truck. Wanted an ice cream pop. One of the specials with the chopped walnuts. Never once suspected the refrigerator compartment was stuffed with money stolen from the Mercantile Trust. But blew the job anyway—by accident.

The next time it had been two small-time hoods committing a holdup in a tailor shop on the very same night the Deaf Man had planned a little fillip-surprise to his big extortion scheme. There were two detectives in the back of the store, waiting for the hoods. The Deaf Man and his accomplices came in the front door at the very same moment. Fuzz! A stakeout for the two punks, and the Deaf Man had accidentally walked into it. Carella had shot him on that occasion; he would never forget Carella's shooting him, would never forgive him for it.

The last time—well, he supposed he could credit Carella with having doped that one out in advance, though he'd certainly given him enough help with it. That had been his mistake. Laid it all out too clearly, too fairly. Virtually *told* Carella he was planning to rob the same bank twice in the same morning, setting up an A-team for a fall and then going in with his B-team—to find Carella there and waiting.

Carella was smarter than the Deaf Man thought he was. He was maybe even smarter than he *himself* thought he was.

Accidents, not mistakes.

But now—no more Mr. Nice Guy.

There was nothing in the book that said he had to play the game fairly.

They were lucky he was playing it at *all.*

On the night before Christmas the Deaf Man would steal half a million dollars, perhaps more.

And get away with it this time, because this time he had not warned the police in advance. Well, yes, he had not been able to resist dropping Elizabeth's body in the park opposite the station house. Naked, though, and therefore unidentifiable. And that had been the only clue, if it could be considered one, to the job planned for Christmas Eve.

On *Epiphany* Eve, Twelfth Night, he would destroy the detectives—most of them anyway—who worked out of the old building facing Grover Park.

And get away with *that,* too.

Because, although he'd warned them, he had not warned them fairly.

They would die.

Horribly.

He smiled at the thought.

Tonight was December 23.

Tonight there was still some work to be done.

In this neighborhood you had to be careful, even with it being so close to Christmas. In fact, maybe even *more* careful this time of year; people did funny things around Christmastime. Lots of the street people around here, they could remember a time— well, this hadn't been Christmastime, it was in March sometime, years ago—they could remember some young kids setting fire to bums sleeping in doorways. Winos. Doused them with gasoline and set fire to them. Doug Hennesy hadn't lived in this city then, but he'd heard plenty about them long-ago roasts, and he knew you had to be more careful in this city than maybe in any city on earth. Not that Doug considered himself a bum. Or even a wino. Doug was a street person, is what he was.

He didn't particularly enjoy the holiday season because the streets were always too crowded, everybody rushing around, everybody selfish and concerned only with his ownself, never mind dropping a coin in the hand of someone needy like Doug. He'd managed to get four dollars and twenty-two cents today—two days before Christmas, could you imagine it? where was the spirit of giving?—but that had taken him from eight this morning till almost seven tonight. He kept wondering who had given him the two cents. Had it been that well-dressed guy in the raccoon coat and the beaver hat? Two cents. But the money Doug collected had been enough for three bottles of excellent wine at a dollar forty a bottle, including tax, with the two cents still left over. He'd already drunk one of the bottles and planned to savor the remaining two all through the night, huddled in the doorway here on Mason Avenue.

The hookers on Mason Avenue didn't like the idea of street people sleeping in doorways. They felt it made the neighborhood look shoddy, as if anything could make it look shoddier than it actually was. Felt it was bad for business. Downtown johns came up here looking for a little black or Puerto Rican ass, they didn't want to see wino bums sprawled in the doorways. The hookers on Mason Avenue were thinking of getting a petition signed against the street people who made their turf look shoddy. Well, Doug guessed he couldn't blame them much. They worked hard, those girls did. He tried to remember the last time he'd been to bed with a woman, hooker or otherwise. Couldn't remember for the life of him. Back in Chicago, wasn't it? Back when he used to be an accountant in Chicago? Another lifetime ago.

Some of your street people, the men, they took advantage of women living on the streets same as themselves. Found a bag lady curled up in a doorway, threw her skirts up, had their way with her. Doug would never in a million years do anything like that, take advantage of someone unfortunate. He'd seen—this was yesterday morning, it almost broke his heart. He'd seen this young street person, she couldn't have been older than twenty-eight or nine, wearing a pink sweater over a thin cotton dress, woolen gloves cut off at the fingers, Christ, she almost broke his heart. Standing in a doorway. Looking at herself in the plate glass window on the door. Hands clasped over her belly. Exploring her belly. Fingers widespread in the sawed-off woolen gloves. Touching her belly. Her belly as big as a watermelon. And on her face a look of total bewilderment. For an instant Doug visualized her standing in a bedroom someplace, the closet door open, a full-length mirror on the closet door, imagined her standing in a silken nightgown, her hands widespread over her pregnant belly, just the way they were widespread over her belly in that doorway, only with a different look on her face. A look of pride, of pleasure. A young pregnant woman awed by the wonder of it, her face glowing. Instead, a doorway on a cold winter day near Christmas—and a look of utter confusion.

Ah, God, the poor unfortunates of this world.

He unscrewed the top of the second bottle of wine.

It was going to be another cold night.

Maybe on Christmas Day he'd wander over to the Salvation Army soup kitchen.

Well, he'd see. No sense making plans in advance.

He had the bottle tilted to his mouth when the man appeared suddenly out of the darkness. The street light was behind the man; Doug couldn't see his face too clearly. Only the blond hair whipping in the wind. And what looked like a hearing aid in his right ear.

"Good evening," the man said pleasantly.

Doug figured he was a downtown john up here looking for a little poontang.

"Good evening," he answered, and then—in the season's spirit of generosity—he extended the bottle of wine and said, "Would you like some wine, sir?"

"No, thank you," the man said. "I'd like your ear."

At first Doug thought the man wanted to talk. Friends, Romans, countrymen, lend me your ears. But then, suddenly and chillingly, he saw a switchblade knife snap open in the man's hand, the blade catching the reflection of the traffic light on the corner, the steel flashing red and then green as the light changed, little twinkly Christmas pinpoints of light, and all at once the man's left hand was at Doug's throat, forcing him onto his back in the doorway. The wine bottle crashed to the sidewalk—a dollar and forty cents!—splintered into a thousand shards of green glass as the man rolled him over onto his left side, the knife flashing yellow and then red as the traffic light changed again.

Doug felt a searing line of fire just above his right ear.

And then the fire trailed downward, spreading, the pain so sharp that Doug screamed aloud and instantly cupped his hand to his right ear.

His right ear was gone.

His hand came away covered with blood.

He screamed again.

The blond man with the hearing aid disappeared as suddenly as he had materialized.

Doug kept screaming.

A hooker swishing by in red Christmas satin and fake fur, heading for the bar up the street, her stiletto heels clattering on the sidewalk, looked into the doorway and shook her head and clucked her tongue.

10

Christmas Eve dawned bright and clear and sparklingly cold. The Deaf Man was pleased. Snow would not have upset his plans at all, but he preferred this kind of weather. It made the blood hum.

He loved Christmastime. Loved all the Santa Clauses jingling their bells on virtually every corner. Loved the horse-drawn carriages in the streets. Loved the big Christmas tree in Andover Square. Loved all the little runny-nosed toddlers ooohing and ahhhing at the sights and sounds. Loved the thought of all that money waiting to be stolen.

The streets were thronged with holiday shoppers.

That was good.

More cash in the till.

The Deaf Man smiled.

He had put Charlie Henkins up in a hotel some ten blocks from the 87th Precinct station house. Nothing to write home about, and probably a place frequented by a great many prostitutes, but the best to be found in the area. He himself had rented a brownstone miles from the precinct. Charlie had never been there. It was important that he not know where the Deaf Man lived. After the job, when Charlie realized nobody was going to come to the hotel with all that hard-earned cash, the Deaf Man didn't want him paying an unexpected visit. But even if Charlie went snooping, he would never find the brownstone. The Deaf Man had rented it as Dr. Pierre Sourd.

In lower case *pierre* meant stone in French. *Sourd* meant deaf. Together and with a little license—the actual idiom would have been *complètement sourd* or, more familiarly, *sourd comme un pot*—the words meant "stone deaf."

Elizabeth had moved into the brownstone with him at the beginning of October. He'd met her in September at the Isola Modern Art Museum, which the natives of this city affectionately called IMAM. In Moslem countries an imam was an Islamic prayer leader, but in this city it was a museum and a good place to meet impressionable young women. Chat them up over the Matisses and the Chagalls—would you care for some tea in the garden? Shy, she was, Elizabeth. A virgin, he'd thought at first—but there were surprises. There are always surprises.

Learned she'd been working as a cashier since sometime in August. Well, now. Learned she handled large sums of money. Really, Elizabeth? Called her Elizabeth, which she loved. Hated people calling her Lizzie or Liz. Three, four hundred thousand dollars a day, she said. Oh my, he said. Fucked her that very night. A screamer. The quiet ones were always screamers.

The hotel Charlie was staying at was called the Excelsior, a prime example of hyperbole, perhaps, in that the word derived from the Latin *excelsus,* from the past participle of *excellere,* which meant "to excel." Perhaps the Excelsior had once, in a past too long ago to remember, indeed excelled—but the Deaf Man doubted it. On the other hand, "excelsior" was the word used to describe the slender, curved wooden shavings used for packing and also—in the hands of an arsonist—for starting fires. So perhaps the building had been appropriately named, after all, in that it was most certainly an excellent fire trap. The word "excellent" also derived from the Latin— *excellens,* which was the *present* participle of the same word *excellere,* "to excel."

The Deaf Man loved words.

The Deaf Man also loved to excel.

He sometimes felt he would have excelled as a novelist, though why anyone would wish to pursue such a trivial occupation was far beyond his ken.

Charlie Henkins was studying the combinations when the Deaf Man came into the room.

"I was going over the combinations again," he said.

"Let me hear them," the Deaf Man said. "Outer door."

"Seven-six-one, two-three-eight."

"And the inner door?"

"Nine-two-four, three-eight-five."

"Good. And the safe itself?"

"Two-four-seven, four-six-three."

"Good. Again."

"Outer door, pad to the right, seven-six-one, two-three-eight. Inner door, pad to the right again, nine-two-four, three-eight-five. Opens into the vault itself, the cashier and her assistant at two desks, the money in the safe. Pad to the right, two-four-seven, four-six-three."

"You shoot them at once," the Deaf Man said.

" 'Cause there's alarm buttons on both desks."

"*Under* both desks, yes. Foot-activated. You say, 'Merry Christmas, ladies,' and shoot them."

"This silencer's gonna work, huh?"

"It's going to work, yes."

" 'Cause I never used a piece with a silencer on it."

"It'll work, you have nothing to worry about."

"After I pack the money in the bag ..."

"Not only the money. Everything in the safe."

"Checks, everything, 'cause there's no time to do any sorting. I just throw everything in the bag."

"Correct."

"And then I leave by the employees' entrance."

"Correct."

"And you'll be waiting outside on the sidewalk."

"With 'Silent Night' going."

"Yeah, 'Silent Night,' " Charlie said, and smiled.

Detective Richard Genero opened the top drawer of his desk and sneaked another peek at the invitation:

YOU ARE INVITED TO A PARTY

FOR: *Detective-Lieutenant Peter Byrnes*

DATE: *January 5*

TIME: *8:00 P.M.*

PLACE: *87th Precinct Squadroom*

Scrawled on the flap of the card in the same handwriting was the message:

Richard— I haven't been able to invite everyone, so please keep this a secret, won't you? Harriet.

He had received the invitation two days ago. It had taken him a long while to figure out that Harriet was Harriet Byrnes, the lieutenant's wife. He had asked Hal

Willis a discreet question—"Hey, who's Harriet?"—and Hal Willis had winked and said, "Pete's wife." Genero suspected that Hal Willis had been invited to the party, too, but he was sworn to secrecy and so he hadn't said another word. He wondered now what the party was for. It seemed funny to him that Mrs. Byrnes hadn't mentioned what the party was for. Also what should he call Mrs. Byrnes on the night of the party? She had signed the invitation "Harriet," hadn't she? Should he call her Harriet? Should he call the lieutenant Pete? He had never in his life called him Pete.

Genero hated it when things got complicated.

For example, why had Mrs. Byrnes called him Richard? The only person in the entire world who called him Richard was his mother. Nobody on the squad called him Richard. Nobody on the squad called him Dick, either. Nobody in the world called him Dick. On the squad they called him Genero. Always his last name. Genero. They called Carella "Steve," and they called Hawes "Cotton," and Kling "Bert," but they always called *him* "Genero." His last name. Of course, they called Meyer "Meyer," but that was because his first name and his last name were exactly the same. His mother told him that was a sign of respect, people calling him by his last name. He told his mother they didn't call him *Mr.* Genero, they just called him Genero. She insisted it was a sign of respect.

She also insisted that he should find out more about this party because maybe he was expected to bring a present. If he was expected to bring a present and he *didn't* bring a present, this would make him look bad in the lieutenant's eyes.

"Il mondo è fatto a scale," his mother said. *"Chi le scende e chi le sale."*

This meant: "The world is made of stairs, and there are those who go up and those who go down."

This further meant: If Genero ever wanted to get anyplace in the police department, he'd better bring a present to the lieutenant's party if a present was expected.

"Ognuno cerca di portare l'acqua al suo molino," his mother said.

Which meant: "Every man tries to bring water to his own mill."

Which further meant: It was in Genero's own interest to bring a present to the lieutenant's party if he wanted to get anywhere in the police department.

But Harriet Byrnes had asked him to keep the party a secret.

So how was he supposed to *ask* anyone if a present was expected?

It was all very complicated.

Genero sighed and looked out the window to the parking lot behind the precinct. Early afternoon sunlight glinted off the white roofs of the patrol cars parked there.

The forecasters were promising snow for Christmas, but you wouldn't suspect it from today. There were days in this city when you wondered why anyone bothered moving to the Sun Belt. Cold, yes, the day was cold, you couldn't deny that. But the cold merely quickened your step and made you feel more alive. And the sky was so blue you felt like hugging it. And the brilliant sunshine made everything seem like summertime, despite the cold.

The big stores had all taken out full-page ads in the newspapers, announcing that they would be open till six tonight, business as usual. It was a glorious day for shopping. The benevolent sun, the crisp cold air reminding you that this was indeed the day before Christmas, the streets alive with a sense of anticipation and expectation, the welcoming warmth of the stores with their glittering displays, even the shoppers more polite and courteous than they would have been if not sharing the knowledge that this was Christmas Eve.

On the sixth floor of Gruber's uptown store, not far from the 87th Precinct station house, Santa Claus—or rather the man *pretending* to be Santa Claus—was amazed to see a line of kids still waiting to talk to him at five in the afternoon. He told all the little boys who climbed up onto his lap that they had to give him their toy orders real fast because he had to hurry on up to the North Pole to feed the reindeer and get ready for his long chilly ride tonight. The little boys were all in awe of Santa, and they reeled off their requests with the speed of tobacco auctioneers. The little girls took their good sweet time, perhaps because this would be the last shot they had at Santa till he came down that chimney tomorrow morning or perhaps because the man pretending to be Santa encouraged them to take all the time they needed.

Actually the man pretending to be Santa was named Arthur Drits, and the closest he'd ever come to the North Pole was Castleview Prison upstate, where he'd spent a good many years for First-Degree Rape, a Class-B felony defined as:

Being a male, engaging in sexual intercourse with a female:
1. By forcible compulsion; OR
2. Who is incapable of consent by reason of being physically helpless; OR
3. Who is less than eleven years old.

The personnel manager who'd hired Drits to portray Santa for Gruber's uptown store did not know that he had a prison record or that he loved children quite so much as he claimed to love them—especially little girls under the age of eleven. The personnel manager saw only a jolly-looking fellow with a little potbelly and twinkly blue eyes, and he figured he would make a good Santa. Even after Drits started working for the store, the personnel manager never noticed that Santa gave most little boys pretty short shrift while he kept even ugly little girls on his lap for an inordinately long time.

Today, at a little past five now and with the store officially closing its doors at six, Drits kept a little eight-year-old curly headed blond girl on his lap for almost five minutes, his eyes glazed as he listened rapturously to her various requests. He reminded her to leave a cup of hot chocolate for him before she went to bed tonight, and then he helped her off his lap, his big meaty right hand clenched into her plump right buttock as he lifted her to the floor, and then he turned to the next little girl in line—a darling little Hispanic girl with bright button eyes and a mouth like an angel's—and he said, "Come, sweetheart, sit up here on Santa's lap and tell him what you want for Christmas."

Drits wanted *her* for Christmas.

He looked at the clock hanging on the wall across the store and wished this job would never end.

This was what burglars called a lay-in job.

One guy went in the store, he hid himself someplace inside the store, stayed there till they locked up and went home. Then the lay-in man knocked out the alarm, let his partner in, and together they ripped off the joint. Only this wasn't going to be a burglary, this was going to be an armed robbery. And Charlie wasn't going to wait till the place was locked up because then he'd *never* get the fuck out of here. In every other respect, though, it was a lay-in job. Charlie here in the men's room on the sixth floor of Gruber's, waiting for the store to chase all the customers out. Then down the hall to the cashier's office, and Merry Christmas, ladies.

Not many people realized that a lot of department stores had their own vaults, same as banks. The vaults were necessary because department stores did a big cash business, and most of them stayed open later than the banks did. So what did you do with all that cash once the banks were closed? What you did, you had a vault of your own, with security just like a bank's, and you kept the cash locked up overnight till you could go deposit it. *Some* department stores had armored cars picking up the cash to take to a security vault overnight, but Lizzie Turner had told them that Gruber's didn't have any armored cars coming around for any pickups. Gruber's had its own vault with its own safe inside it.

Tomorrow was Sunday.

Under ordinary circumstances Saturday's cash receipts would be tallied in the cashier's office early Monday morning, and then a pair of Gruber's armed square-shields would take it to the bank for deposit.

But tomorrow was not only Sunday, it was also Christmas Day.

Which meant that Monday, December 26, was the *legal* holiday, and the banks would be closed then, too. If all went well, Dennis figured that nobody would even realize the store had been robbed till Tuesday morning, when the cashier's office was opened again.

Charlie was sitting on a toilet bowl with his trousers down around his ankles. He had been sitting on the toilet bowl for close to half an hour now, listening to the traffic in and out of the men's room on Gruber's sixth floor. He was not expected to make his move until six forty-five.

Lizzie had told them that the security in the cashier's office was very good, better than some banks had. Two different combinations on the two steel doors that led into the vault, another on the safe itself. No windows in the vault. Just the two desks, the various adding machines and computers and such, and the big walk-in safe on the far wall. After the store closed at six, it normally took a half hour at most for each department head on the separate floors to tally his or her cash register receipts, put them into zippered plastic bags, and carry them up to the cashier's office on the sixth floor.

Lizzie said that she and her assistant then put the plastic bags of cash in the safe, triggered the safe alarm, and triggered the alarms for both vault doors before they left the office at a little before seven each night. It was rare that any employee, including all the managers, were still in the store after seven. The employees all left by the employees' entrance on the ground floor. The security officer there watched them while they punched out at the time clock. When all employees had punched out, the security officer set the store's external alarm.

She had told them all this while they were laying out the job.

Nice girl, Lizzie. Smart, too. Quit Gruber's early in October, was laying low now till it was time to split the money. That would be tomorrow morning. Christmas Day for the three of them. Christmas in Charlie's room at the Excelsior the minute Dennis arrived with the . . .

A loudspeaker on the wall suddenly erupted with the sound of a woman's voice, startling here in the men's room.

"Ladies and gentlemen, Gruber's will be closing in twenty minutes," the woman's voice said. "We ask you to kindly complete your shopping before six o'clock. Thank you and Merry Christmas."

Charlie looked at his watch.

He rose then, pulled up his undershorts and his trousers, belted the trousers, and reached for the suitcase he'd tucked against one side of the stall.

He checked the lock on the door again and then opened the suitcase.

A huge red banner trimmed in gold hung from a flagstaff and flapped in the wind outside Gruber's side street entrances. Greetings were stitched in gold to the banner, one beneath the other:

MERRY CHRISTMAS
FELIZ NATAL
JOYEUX NOËL
BUON NATALE

Under the banner, and closer to the curb, a man in a Salvation Army uniform stood alongside an iron kettle hanging from a tripod. A sign affixed to the tripod read:

A cassette player blared "Silent Night."

The man in the Salvation Army uniform was wearing a hearing aid in his right ear, but no one could see it because he was also wearing ear muffs.

"God bless you," he said to a man who dropped a quarter into the kettle.

"Ladies and gentlemen, Gruber's will be closing in fifteen minutes," the woman's voice said. "We ask you to kindly complete your shopping before six o'clock. Thank you and Merry Christmas."

In the sixth-floor men's room Charlie looked at his watch again. He had already fastened the pillow to his own not-insignificant potbelly and had put on the red trousers and the black boots, and now he was slipping into the red tunic. He buttoned the tunic. He tightened the wide black belt around his waist and then put on the beard and the red hat with the white fur trim. He would give the beard a final adjustment at the mirrors over the sink before he left the men's room. He reached into the suitcase again, took out the big canvas sack with MERRY CHRISTMAS lettered on it in green and red, and then picked up the gun with the silencer on it. He tucked the gun under the tunic, over the pillow and his own potbelly.

Outside the stall someone was pissing in one of the urinals.

"Ladies and gentlemen, Gruber's will be closing in five minutes," the woman's voice said. "We ask you to kindly complete your shopping before six o'clock. Gruber's will be open again on Tuesday, December twenty-seventh, at which time all items in the store will be on sale at thirty- to fifty-percent savings. Thank you and Merry Christmas."

The sidewalks outside Gruber's looked like an oriental bazaar.

Aware of the fact that the store would close at six o'clock and further aware that this was Christmas Eve and late late shoppers might be willing to plunk down a few bucks for that last last-minute gift, the street vendors were out in droves, the overflow spilling from the choicer locations at the avenue entrances to here on the side street. Standing to the right of the Salvation Army kettle was a Puerto Rican man with a wide variety of wrist watches for sale, all of them displayed on a folding case set up on a folding stand. If the Law showed and the man did not have a vendor's license, he would fold the case and the stand, like an Arab folding a tent, and disappear into the night just as swiftly. The Deaf Man assumed all the watches were stolen. Otherwise, why was the man selling them for five dollars apiece?"

"Fi' dollar!" the man shouted. "Bran' new wriss washes, fi' dollar!"

On the Deaf Man's left, shouting over the strains of "Silent Night" coming from the Deaf Man's cassette player, another sidewalk entrepreneur was displaying on a moth-eaten army blanket two dozen or more scarves in various brilliant colors.

"All silk!" he shouted to the passersby. "Take your choice, three dollars apiece, four for ten dollars, all silk!"

On the corner, where side street and avenue intersected, a man sold hot dogs from a cart. Another man sold pretzels. A third man sold 100% Fresh-Squeezed Orange Juice and Italian ices.

Up the avenue the bell in the tower of the Church of the Ascension of Christ began tolling the hour two minutes too soon.

The personnel manager came into the sixth-floor Toy Department at two minutes to six. Santa was sitting alone on his throne. The personnel manager—whose name was Samuel Aronowitz—went over to him and said, "We won't be getting any more little girls and boys tonight, Santa. Come on, let's have a drink."

Santa sighed forlornly.

They walked down the hall past the bewildering array of signs pointing in every direction of the compass: MANAGER'S OFFICE. CASHIER'S OFFICE. CREDIT OFFICE. RETURNS. PERSONNEL OFFICE. TOY DEPARTMENT. SANTA CLAUS. TELEPHONE OFFICE. REST ROOMS.

As they entered the personnel office, Aronowitz heard the woman's voice over the loudspeakers again.

"Ladies and gentlemen, it is now six o'clock. If you are still in the store, we advise you to use the Fourth Street exit. We take this opportunity now to wish you all a Merry Christmas from Gruber's uptown, downtown, all around the town. Merry Christmas to all and to all a good night."

"That was in our radio ads," Aronowitz said.

"Sir?" Drits said.

"The 'uptown, downtown, all around the town' line. Very effective. Come in, come in, what would you like to drink? I have scotch and gin."

"A little scotch, please," Drits said.

In the cashier's office Molly Driscoll and Helen Ruggiero both looked at the clock at the very same moment. Molly was the cashier. She had been the cashier since the middle of October. Helen was the assistant cashier and was angry that she had not been promoted to cashier when Liz Turner left the job.

It was now a quarter past six, and all but Better Dresses, Housewares, Major Appliances, Juniors, and Luggage had already delivered their zippered bags containing receipts from cash registers all over the store, dropping them into the little steel drawer set into the wall at right angles to the vault's outer steel door. Both steel doors to the vault were closed and locked. The safe door was open. They would lock that and set the alarm on it after the last of the receipts were in.

Helen and Molly were very eager to get the hell out of here.

Molly wanted to hurry home to her husband and three kids.

Helen wanted to hurry over to her boyfriend's apartment. He had told her he'd bought some very good coke that afternoon.

"What's keeping the rest of them?" she asked.

"Mr. Drits, I want to thank you personally for the splendid job you did for Gruber's," Aronowitz said. "Your warmth, your patience, your obvious understanding of children—all added up to the best Santa we've ever had. Would you care for another drink?"

"Yes, sir, thank you," Drits said.

"It was my hope, Mr. Drits, that you would come back to work for us again next year. Frankly we have a difficult time hiring convincing Santas."

"I'd be happy to come back next year," Drits said, accepting the drink.

Provided I'm not in Castleview, he thought.

In the locked stall in the men's room Charlie looked at his watch again.

Six-thirty.

Fifteen minutes before he made his move.

He was beginning to sweat behind the fake beard.

On the sidewalk outside the store the Deaf Man looked at his watch.

Twenty-five minutes to seven.

"Four dollar!" the Puerto Rican yelled. "Bran' new washes!"

"Silk scarves, all of them silk, two dollars apiece, four for six dollars!" the other man yelled.

"Si-uh-lent night," the cassette player blared, "ho-uh-lee night . . ."

The man at the rest room sinks was singing "Silent Night" at the top of his lungs.

In the locked stall Charlie looked at his watch again.

Six forty-two.

"Allllll is calm," the man sang, "alllllll is bright . . ."

In the cashier's office Helen looked at her watch and said, "So where's Better Dresses?"

It was six forty-five.

Charlie had to make his move.

The man at the sinks was still singing.

"Round yon vir-ih-gin, mother and child . . ."

Charlie waited. The man stopped singing. Charlie heard the sound of the water tap being turned on. He looked at his watch again. He couldn't wait a moment longer.

He came out of the stall.

He was looking at Santa Claus.

Santa Claus was washing his face.

His beard rested on the sink top.

Santa turned from the sink.

Charlie was looking at Arthur Drits, who'd served time at Castleview when Charlie was also a resident up there. A short-eyes offender.

"Hey, man," Drits said, looking surprised.

Drits was surprised because he was looking at a Santa Claus just like himself. He hadn't known there were *two* Santas in the store. Charlie, forgetting he was wearing a beard, thought Drits looked surprised because he'd recognized him. Charlie ran out of the men's room before Drits could take a better look.

Molly closed the safe door and pressed the buttons that set the alarm.

"Two-four-seven, four-six-three.

"Well, that's it," she said.
"*Finalmente,*" Helen said.

When Drits came out of the employees' entrance of Gruber's, he was wearing his beard again. Made him feel good, wearing the beard, all dressed up like Santa, best damn Santa the store had ever had—who was that fuckin' imposter in the men's room? What made him feel even better was the quantity of scotch he'd drunk in Aronowitz's office. Very nice scotch. Nice and warm in his little round potbelly.

There was a man selling two-dollar watches on the sidewalk.

There was a man selling scarves at a dollar apiece.

There was a Salvation Army guy standing near a big black kettle.

"Here!" the Salvation Army guy said.

Drits looked at him.

"Ho, ho, ho," Drits said.

"Where's the bag?" the Salvation Army guy whispered. Drits figured he was nuts.

He threw him a finger and walked up the street.

Molly and Helen were about to leave the cashier's office when the inner steel door opened.

They were looking at Santa Claus.

"Merry Christmas, ladies," he said, and shot them both between the eyes.

The silencer worked fine.

The Deaf Man was confused only momentarily.

Of course, he thought, the *real* Santa. Or at least the *store's* Santa.

He looked at his watch.

Five minutes to seven.

Charlie should be coming out that door any minute now.

He glanced toward the corner where the side street intersected the avenue. A uniformed cop was just turning the corner.

"You!" the cop yelled at the Puerto Rican selling the hot watches.

The security officer at the door to the employee's entrance thought he'd seen Santa leave already.

"Two of you, huh?" he said to Charlie.

Charlie was at the time clock. The canvas sack with the red and green MERRY CHRISTMAS lettered onto its side was bulging with the money he'd taken from the safe. He lifted Helen Ruggiero's card from the rack and punched her out.

It was almost seven o'clock.

"Two of us, right," he said.

"Well, have a Merry Christmas, Santa," the security officer said, chuckling at his own little joke.

"You, too, Mac," Charlie said, and stepped out onto the sidewalk, where suddenly all hell broke loose.

*   *   *

The cop wanted to see a vendor's license.

The Puerto Rican didn't have a vendor's license.

The cop said he was giving him a summons.

Somebody in the sidewalk crowd yelled, "Come on, you shit, it's Christmas Eve!"

The cop yelled back, "*You* want a summons, too?"

Everybody in the crowd started razzing the cop.

That was when the Puerto Rican decided this would be a good time to make a break for it.

That was when Charlie came out of the store, carrying the sack of money.

The plan was to put the sack of money down near the kettle, where it would look like a Salvation Army prop.

The plan was for Charlie to disappear into the night, lootless.

The plan was for the Deaf Man to wait five minutes before picking up the sack and walking off with it.

That was the plan.

But the Puerto Rican collided with Charlie as he was coming out of the store.

And the sack fell to the sidewalk.

And zippered plastic bags of money spilled out onto the sidewalk.

And the crowd thought Santa was distributing money for Christmas.

And the cop thought Santa was a fuckin' thief.

The crowd surged forward toward the money on the sidewalk.

The cop's pistol was already unholstered.

"Stop or I'll shoot!" he yelled at Santa.

The crowd thought he was telling them to stop picking up the money.

The crowd yelled, "Fuck you, pig!"

The Puerto Rican was halfway up the block by then.

A gun suddenly appeared in Santa's hand.

The Deaf Man winced when the cop fired at Charlie.

Charlie went ass over teacups onto the sidewalk, a bullet hole in his right shoulder.

A lady dropped a dime into the Salvation Army kettle.

"God bless you," the Deaf Man said.

"Sleep in heav-enn-lee pee-eeese," the cassette player blared, "slee-eeep in heav-enn-lee peace . . ."

Shit, the Deaf Man thought.

And then he melted away into the crowd.

11

Neither Carella nor Brown wanted to be working on Christmas Day.

They had both deliberately chosen to work the four-to-midnight on Christmas Eve so that they could spend the big day itself with their families. But at approximately seven last night a man named Charlie Henkins had inconsiderately held up Gruber's department store, managing to kill two women in the process. Carella and Brown were catching when a frantic patrolman called in to say he'd just shot Santa Claus. The case was officially theirs, and that was why—at ten on Christmas morning—they were questioning Henkins in his room at Saint Jude's Hospital.

"I'm an innocent dupe," Henkins said.

He did look very innocent, Brown thought. In his white hospital tunic, his left shoulder bandaged, his blue eyes twinkling, his little potbelly round and soft under the sheet, he looked like an old Saint Nick without a beard and settling down for a long winter's nap.

"It was the other Santa Claus done it," Henkins said.

"What other Santa Claus?" Carella asked.

"Arthur Drits," Henkins said.

Carella looked at Brown.

"Let me get this straight," Carella said.

"I'm an innocent dupe," Henkins said again.

"What were you doing in that Santa Claus outfit?" Carella said.

"I was going to an orphanage to surprise the kiddies there."

"What orphanage?" Brown said. "We don't *have* any orphanages up here."

"I thought there was an orphanage up here."

"Were you taking a gun to the orphanage?"

"That gun is not mine, officers," Henkins said.

"Whose gun is it?"

"Santa's," Henkins said. "The *other* Santa."

"Let me get this straight," Carella said again. He was having a difficult time getting it straight. He knew only that Henkins had come out of Gruber's with a sackful of zippered plastic bags containing—according to the count made before the cash was delivered to the property clerk's office—eight hundred thousand, two hundred fifty-two dollars in cash plus a sizable number of personal checks. Henkins had drawn a gun—identified and tagged as a .32-caliber Smith & Wesson Regulation Police—and a silencer fitting that gun had been found in the cashier's office at Gruber's, alongside the body of one of the victims, a woman named Helen Ruggiero, who incidentally had four marijuana joints in her handbag. The police officer on duty had shouted the customary warning and then shot him. He was currently at Headquarters downtown, filling out all the papers that explained why he had drawn his service revolver in the first place and why he had fired it in the second place.

"Let me explain it," Henkins said.

Brown knew he was about to tell a whopper.

"I went in Gruber's to use the facilities," Henkins said.

"What facilities?"

"I went up to the sixth floor to take a leak."

"Then what?"

"I ran into Drits in the men's room."

"Arthur Drits."

"Arthur Drits, who I knew from long ago."

"Yeah, go ahead," Brown said.

"Drits was dressed as Santa Claus. Also he had the gun you're now saying was my gun."

"How'd *you* get the gun?"

"Drits gave it to me."

"Why?"

"He said, 'Merry Christmas,' and gave it to me."

"So you took it."

"It was a present."

"So when you came out of Gruber's you had the gun."

"Exactly."

"And you pulled the gun."

"Only to give it to the police officer, because by then I was having second thoughts about it."

"What kind of second thoughts?"

"Who knew but what that gun may have been used in a crime of some sort?"

"Who indeed?" Brown said.

"Where'd you get the sackful of money?" Carella asked.

"That was the Puerto Rican's."

"What Puerto Rican?"

"The one with all the wrist watches. He had the watches in the sack. When he bumped into me, the watches and the money fell out of the sack."

"So the gun belonged to Drits, and the sack belonged to the Puerto Rican."

"You've got it," Henkins said. "I'm an innocent dupe."

Carella looked at Brown again.

"There are barbarians in this city," Henkins said. "You should have seen all those people scrambling to pick up that money." He shook his head. "On Christmas *Eve!*"

"Let's talk about this Arthur Drits character," Brown said.

"Yes, sir," Henkins said.

"You say he was a friend of yours?"

"An acquaintance, sir," Henkins said.

Brown knew from all the "sirs" that he was onto something.

"You said you knew him from long ago."

"Yes, sir."

"*How* long ago?"

"Oh, four or five years ago."

"And you ran into him accidentally in the men's room at Gruber's."

"That is exactly what happened, sir," Henkins said. "I swear on my mother's eyes."

"Leave your mother out of this," Brown said.

"My mother happens to be dead," Henkins said.

"So are two people in Gruber's cashier's office," Brown said. "Who were killed with the gun *you* were carrying."

"Drits's gun," Henkins said.

"Who you met long ago."

"Four, five years ago."

"Where?" Brown said.

"Where what, sir?"

"Where'd you meet him?"

"Well, sir, that's difficult to remember."

"Try," Brown said.

"I really couldn't say."

Brown looked at Carella.

"You understand," Carella said, "that we're talking two counts of homicide here, don't you? *Plus* . . ."

"Drits must have killed those two people," Henkins said.

"Where'd you meet this Drits?" Carella said. "If he exists."

Henkins hesitated.

"Forget it," Brown said to Carella and then turned to Henkins. "You're under arrest, Mr. Henkins. We're charging you with two counts of homicide and one count of armed robbery. In accordance with the Supreme Court ruling in Miranda-Escobedo . . ."

"Hey, hold it just a minute," Henkins said. "I'm a fuckin' innocent *dupe* here."

"It was Drits and the Puerto Rican, right?" Carella said.

"It was Drits gave me the gun. I don't know where the Puerto Rican got all that money those animals were scrambling for."

"Where'd you meet him?" Brown said.

"On the sidewalk outside. He crashed into me on . . ."

"Not the Puerto Rican," Brown shouted. "*Drits!* Where the fuck did you meet him? Was he in on this with you? Did the two Santa Claus outfits have something to do with . . . ?"

"I told you once, I'll tell you again. I was taking a leak in the men's room when Drits . . ."

"The *first* time!" Brown shouted. "Where'd you meet him the *first* time?"

"Well . . ."

"Make it fast," Brown said. "My Christmas is waiting."

"Castleview, okay?" Henkins said.

"You did time at Castleview?"

"A little."

"How much?"

"I grossed twenty."

"For what?"

"Well . . . I got thirsty one night."

"What does that mean?"

"I went in this liquor store."

"Where?"

"Calm's Point."

"And?"

"I asked the guy for a fifth of Gordon's."

"And?"

"He didn't want to give it to me."

"So?"

"I had to persuade him."

"How'd you persuade him? With a gun?"

"Well, I suppose you could call it a gun."

"What would *you* call it?"

"I suppose I would call it a gun."

"What did the *judge* call it?"

"Well, a gun."

"So this was an armed robbery."

"That's what they said it was."

"And you drew twenty for it."

"I only done eight."

"So now you're back at the same old stand again, huh?"

"I keep tellin' you it was *Drits's* gun. It must've been Drits who shot those two ladies. If I'da known the gun was hot, I'd never have taken it."

"Who said they were ladies?" Brown asked.

"What?"

"Who said the two dead people in the cashier's office were ladies?"

Henkins blinked.

"You want to tell us about it?" Carella said.

The room went silent. The detective waited.

"Dennis must've shot those two ladies," Henkins said.

"Dennis who?"

"Dennis Dove. He must've been the one who went in the cashier's office and shot those two ladies. I was nowhere near the place when the robbery went down. I was waiting on the ground floor. I didn't even know a robbery was happening. All I was supposed to do was wait for Dennis and take the gun and the sack . . ."

"*Wait* a minute," Carella said, "let me get this straight." He was having difficulty getting it straight again.

"Dennis asked me to do him a favor, that's all," Henkins said. His twinkling blue eyes were darting frantically. "What he asked me to do was wait downstairs and take this sack he wanted me to bring to the orphanage . . ."

"The orphanage again," Brown said.

". . . to give to the little kiddies there on Christmas Eve."

"And the gun?"

"I don't know how Drits got the gun. Maybe he was in on it, too. An ex-con, you know?" Henkins said, and shrugged.

"Is that why he was in Castleview? For armed robbery?"

"No, he digs kids."

"What do you mean?"

"Short eyes, you know?"

"A child molester?"

"Yeah." Henkins shrugged again.

"But you think he was in on this robbery with Dove, huh?"

"Musta been, don't you think?" Henkins said. "Otherwise, how'd he get the gun?"

"But you were on the ground floor."

"That's right."

"Nowhere near the cashier's office."

"That's right."

"The cashier's office is on the sixth floor," Brown said.

"So's the men's room," Carella said.

"Coincidence, pure and simple," Henkins said.

"Bullshit, pure and simple," Brown said.

"Who's Dennis Dove?" Carella asked.

"Guy I met a while back. Asked me to do him this favor on Christmas Eve."

"Is that his full name? Dennis Dove?"

"Far as I know."

"Where does he live?"

"I don't know."

"What does he look like?"

"He's a big tall blond guy," Henkins said. "Wears a hearing aid."

Both detectives looked at each other at exactly the same moment.

"A while back when?" Brown asked.

"Huh?" Henkins said.

"When you met him."

"October sometime. When Lizzie was filling us in."

"Lizzie who?" Carella asked. He had the sinking feeling that Henkins was not talking about Lizzie Borden.

"Some broad he was banging. Crazy about him. She used to work at Gruber's. Not that I knew what they were planning. I was only there because they wanted me to do them a favor, you see. Whatever else . . ."

"Lizzie who?" Carella asked again.

"Turner," Henkins said.

So there they were.

And where they were . . .

They didn't know where they were.

It seemed as though the Deaf Man had been behind the armed robbery at Gruber's. It further seemed that Elizabeth Turner had worked at Gruber's—they would check to see if she had worked in the cashier's office, a likelihood considering her past employment—and that she had been intimate with the Deaf Man. They did not know how she had met the Deaf Man. They knew for certain that Henkins was lying through his teeth about the robbery itself—the murder weapon had been in his possession, and only *his* fingerprints were on the gun—but they didn't know if he was also lying about this person named Dennis Dove, whose description fit the Deaf Man's. He could not have pulled the name Lizzie Turner out of a hat, though. And on the night of her murder a man fitting the Deaf Man's description had been seen carrying a woman fitting Elizabeth Turner's description. It seemed to make sense. Sort of.

But what did the Gruber's job have to do with the notes the Deaf Man had been sending them?

Nothing that they could see.

Two nightsticks.

Three pairs of handcuffs.

Four police hats.

Five walkie-talkies.

Six police shields.

Seven wanted flyers.

Eight black horses.

Nine patrol cars.

Ten D.D. forms.

Eleven Detective Specials.

Twelve roast pigs.

And then, at eleven on Christmas morning, while Carella was typing up the report on their interview with Henkins, and Brown was on the phone with a parole officer seeking a last-known address for Arthur Drits, a delivery boy arrived at the slatted wooden railing that separated the squadroom from the corridor outside. He was carrying a package wrapped in green paper. It was a rather bulky package, and he was having difficulty holding it in both arms.

"Is there a Detective Stephen Louis Carella here?" he asked.

"I'm Carella," Carella said.

"Di Fiore Florist," the delivery boy said.

"Come in," Carella said.

"Well . . . somebody wanna help me with the latch here?" the delivery boy said.

Carella helped him with the latch. The delivery boy struggled the package into the squadroom, looked around for a place to put it, and set it down on Genero's vacant desk. Carella wondered if he was expected to tip the delivery boy. He dug in his pocket and handed him a quarter.

"Can you spare it?" the delivery boy said. "Merry Christmas," he added sourly and walked out.

Carella tore the green wrapping from the package.

He was looking at what he expected was supposed to be a pear tree. He didn't know if it was a *real* pear tree, but at any rate there were pears hanging on it. They weren't *real* pears, but they were clearly pears. Little wooden pears hanging all over the tree.

There was also an envelope hanging on the tree.

The envelope was addressed to Detective Stephen Louis Carella.

He tore open the envelope.

The card inside read:

On the first day of
Christmas my true love
gave to me a partridge
in a pear tree...

Carella searched the tree for a partridge.

A little package wrapped in red foil was hanging on the tree. Carella unwrapped the package. Something decorated with feathers was inside it. It was not a partridge, but looked like a bird of some sort, feathers glued all over it. Chicken feathers, they looked like. But it was not a chicken either, too small for a chicken. He took a closer look.

The thing was a severed human ear.

Carella dropped it at once.

On December 26, the second day of Christmas, two nightsticks arrived at the squadroom. They were wrapped in Christmas paper, and they were addressed to Carella.

The detectives looked at the nightsticks.

They did not appear to be new ones. Both of them were scarred and battered.

"Still he could've bought them," Kling said.

In this city a police officer was responsible for the purchase of every piece of equipment he wore or carried, with the exception of his shield, which came free with the job—the pin used to hold the shield to the uniform cost him fifty cents. Each officer was given a yearly allowance of three hundred and seventy dollars for his uniform. He bought his own gun—usually a Colt .38 or a Smith & Wesson of the same caliber—and his own bullets—six in the gun and twelve on his belt—and his own whistle, which these days was selling for two dollars. He also bought his own shoes. A foot patrolman wore out at least two pairs of shoes a year. A two-foot-long wooden nightstick cost the police officer two dollars and fifty cents, plus another forty cents for the leather thong. His short rubber billy cost three dollars and fifty cents with—again—another forty cents for the thong. Handcuffs were currently selling for twenty-five dollars.

Most policemen bought their gear from the Police Equipment Bureau downtown near the Police Academy, but there were police supply stores all over the city. Kling himself was wearing a Detective Special he had bought in one of those stores. He'd had to identify himself when purchasing the pistol, but he'd bought uniform shirts and even handcuffs when he was a patrolman, and no one had even asked him his name. He was also wearing, at the moment, one of the ties Eileen Burke had bought him for Christmas. It was a very garish tie, but no one was looking at it. They were still looking at the nightsticks.

"Better run them through for latents," Meyer said.

"Won't be any on them," Brown said.

"I don't get it," Carella said. "He sends us a note with two pictures of a nightstick on it, and then he sends us two nightsticks. Do *you* get it?"

He was addressing all of them, but only Hawes answered.

"He's crazy," he said. "He doesn't *have* to make sense."

"So tomorrow we get three pairs of handcuffs, right? And the day after that . . ."

"Let's see what happens tomorrow," Meyer said.

On December 27 they caught up with Arthur Drits.

Carella and Brown talked to him in the Interrogation Office.

Drits had been inside interrogation offices before. He knew that the mirror he faced was a one-way mirror, and he suspected that someone was sitting in the adjoining office, watching his every move. Actually the adjoining office was empty.

Brown laid it flat out.

"What were you doing in Gruber's department store the night it was held up?"

"This is the first I'm hearing of any holdup," Drits said.

"You don't read the papers?" Carella said.

"Not too often," Drits said.

What he read were the advertisements for children's clothing, the ones showing little girls in short dresses.

"You watch television?" Brown asked.

"I don't have a television," Drits said.

"So you don't know Gruber's was held up on Christmas Eve, is that right?"

"I just heard it from you a minute ago."

"You know anybody named Elizabeth Turner?"

"No."

"She used to work in the cashier's office at Gruber's."

They had already confirmed this with the personnel manager. Elizabeth Turner had begun working there on August 8 and had left the job on October 7—seventeen days before her murder.

"Never heard of her," Drits said.

"How about Dennis Dove?"

"Him neither."

"Charlie Henkins?"

Drits blinked.

"Ring a bell?" Brown said.

"Yeah," Drits said.

"Met him at Castleview, didn't you?"

"Yeah."

"Where you were doing time for First-Degree Rape."

"So they said."

"See him again since you got out?"

"No."

"How about Christmas Eve? Did you see Henkins on Christmas Eve?"

"No."

"Were you in the sixth-floor men's room at Gruber's on Christmas Eve?"

"Yeah?" Drits said, looking puzzled.

"Did you see a Santa Claus in the men's room?"

"Yeah?"

"Did he look like Henkins?"

"No, he looked like Santa Claus."

"That was Henkins."

"Coulda fooled me," Drits said.

"What were you doing in the men's room at Gruber's?" Brown asked.

"Washing my face. This guy come out of the booth, the stall there, he was wearing a Santa Claus suit same as me. I nearly shit."

"*You* were wearing a Santa Claus suit, too?" Carella said.

"Well, sure."

The detectives looked at each other. They thought Charlie Henkins had been lying about Drits and the Santa Clause suit, but now . . .

"As part of the job?" Brown asked.

"Sure."

"The holdup called for *two* guys in Santa Claus suits?"

"What?" Drits said.

"What the fuck were you doing in a *Santa* Claus suit?" Brown asked.

"I worked for the *store,*" Drits said. "I was the store's *Santa* Claus."

Both detectives looked at him.

"I was a very good Santa," Drits said with dignity.

"And you never heard of anyone named Elizabeth Turner? Never met her?"

"Never."

"Or Dennis Dove?"

"Never."

"Did you hand Charlie Henkins a gun in the men's room at Gruber's?"

"I didn't hand him anything. I didn't even know he *was* Henkins till you told me. I was surprised to see another guy in a Santa Claus suit, is all. *He* looked surprised, too. He just ran out."

"What'd *you* do?"

"I dried my face, I put on my beard again, and I left the store."

"To go where?"

"Home."

"Which is where?"

"I live in a hotel on Waverly."

"Were you outside the store when Henkins got shot?"

"I didn't know Henkins *got* shot."

"Didn't see the shooting, huh?"

"No."

"What *did* you see? When you came out of the store?"

"Who remembers what I saw? People. I saw people."

"Who? What people?"

"People. Some guy selling watches, another guy selling scarves, some nutty Salvation Army guy . . ."

"What do you mean by 'nutty'?"

"Nuts, you know? He told me, 'Here.' "

"He told you what?"

"Here."

"H-e-a-r?"

"No, h-e-r-e. I *think*. Who knows with nuts?"

"Here? What'd he mean?"

"I don't know *what* he meant."

"What'd you *think* he meant?"

"I think he was nuts. He asked me where the bag was."

"What'd he look like?" Carella asked at once.

"Tall guy in a Salvation Army uniform. Nuts."

"What color was his hair?"

"I don't know. He was wearing a hat."

"Was he wearing a hearing aid?"

"He had ear muffs on."

Carella sighed. Brown sighed, too.

"All right, keep your nose clean," Brown said.

"I can go?" Drits said.

"Why?" Brown said. "Did you *do* something?"

"No, no, hey," Drits said.

"See that you *don't*," Carella said.

That afternoon three pairs of handcuffs arrived.

They had already questioned George Di Fiore, the proprietor of Di Fiore Florists, about the man who'd ordered the pear tree, and he'd told them first of all that it wasn't a real pear tree, it was in fact a *Ficus Benjamina*, but they were all out of pear trees when the man came in asking for one. Di Fiore had also told them that the man had personally picked out the little wooden pears to fasten to the tree, and then had personally affixed the card and the little wrapped package to the tree. Di Fiore hadn't known what was in the little wrapped package, and did not consider it his business to ask. Carella wanted to ask if Di Fiore—which meant "of the flowers" in Italian—had chosen his profession because of his name. He knew an anesthiologist named Dr. Sleepe—although he pronounced it

Slehpuh—and a chiropractor named Hands. Instead he asked what Di Fiore's pear-tree customer had looked like.

"Tall blond man wearing a hearing aid," Di Fiore told him.

So now the three pairs of handcuffs.

They all looked brand-new.

They could have been purchased, as Kling again suggested, at any police-supply store in town.

December 27, the third day of Christmas, and three pairs of handcuffs.

Tomorrow, Carella knew for certain, four police hats would arrive.

And they did.

Arrived by United Parcel delivery, all boxed and wrapped in festive Christmas paper.

The hats were definitely not new.

Their sweat bands were greasy, and their leather peaks were cracked with age. Moreover, they had police shields pinned to them. And unlike the *pictures* they'd received earlier, *these* shields had numbers on them.

There were four different numbers on the shields.

Carella called Mullaney at Personnel and asked him to identify the shields for him.

"This Coppola again?" Mullaney said.

When he came back onto the line, he told Carella that those shields, and presumably the hats to which they were pinned, belonged to four different police officers at four different precincts. He asked Carella if he wanted the patrolmen's names—one of them, actually, was a female cop, but in Mullaney's world all police officers were patrol*men*. Carella took down the names and then called each precinct. The desk sergeant on duty at each precinct told Carella that yes, indeed, such and such an officer worked out of this precinct, but he—or, in the case of the woman, she—had not reported having lost his, or her, hat. One of the sergeants asked Carella if this was a joke. Carella told him he guessed it wasn't a joke.

But if it wasn't a joke, then what the hell *was* it?

Carella grunted and picked up one of the police hats.

The man or woman who'd worn it had dandruff.

"Those are *police* walkie-talkies," Miscolo said. "Standard issue."

Miscolo was a clerk and not a detective, but it didn't take a detective to see that each of the walkie-talkies that arrived by United Parcel delivery on the fifth day of Christmas, December 29, were marked with plastic labeling tape of the sort you printed up yourself with a lettering gun. Each of the walkie-talkies had two strips of tape on it. The first strip was identical in each case. It read:

RETURN TO CHARGING RACK

The second strips differed. One read:

PROPERTY OF 21ST PRECINCT

Another read:

PROPERTY OF 12TH PRECINCT

And so on:

PROPERTY OF 61ST PRECINCT
PROPERTY OF MIDTOWN EAST
PROPERTY OF 83RD PRECINCT

Five different walkie-talkies from five different precincts.

"Those were stolen from five different precincts," Miscolo said. "This man is entering police precincts all over town."

The six police shields that arrived on December 30, a Friday and the sixth day of Christmas, similarly belonged to police officers from six different precincts. None of the officers had reported his shield missing or stolen; a cop does not like to admit that somebody ripped off his goddamn potsie. Moreover, the six precincts from which the shields had been stolen—Carella was sure by now that they'd been stolen—were not any of the precincts from which the walkie-talkies or the police hats were stolen. In short, fifteen precincts had been entered—four police hats, five walkie-talkies, and six shields for a total of fifteen—and police equipment had been removed from them under the very eyes of the police themselves. There were twenty precincts in Isola alone. Some of the police equipment had been stolen from precincts in Calm's Point and Majesta. None had been stolen from either Bethtown or Riverhead. But someone had been very busy indeed, even assuming that neither the nightsticks nor the handcuffs were similarly stolen, which would have brought to twenty-four the number of precincts whose security had been breached.

For what purpose? Carella wondered.

Toward what end?

The seventh day of Christmas was New Year's Eve, a Saturday.

Naturally seven wanted flyers arrived in that morning's mail.

And naturally there was a power failure at three-thirty that afternoon, fifteen minutes before the eight-to-four was scheduled to be relieved. It would not have been New Year's Eve unless something happened to prevent the outgoing shift from leaving when it was supposed to. The day shift detectives, eager to get the hell out of the squadroom to start the festivities, knew only that somehow the Greater Isola Power & Light Company (formerly the Metropolitan Light & Power Company) had screwed up yet another time, and they would not be able to complete their paperwork before four o'clock. What they did not know was that Greater Isola Power & Light—known to its millions of dissatisfied customers as the Big (for Greater) Ipple (for I.P.L.)—was totally innocent of any malfeasance this time around.

Gopher Nelson had caused the power failure.

The power failure lasted exactly one minute.

Gopher caused it by throwing a switch pinpointed on the "Composite Feeder

Plate Map'' the Deaf Man had provided. The map was one of four the Deaf Man had given Gopher, explaining that he'd acquired them—along with several others—years ago, when he was planning to place a bomb under the mayor's bed. Gopher wondered why the Deaf Man planned such peculiar things, but he didn't ask; the money was good.

The first map was stamped ''Property of Metropolitan Light & Power Company'' and was titled ''60-Cycle Network Area Designations and Boundaries Upper Isola.'' It showed the locations of all the area substations in that section of the city. The area in which the 87th Precinct station house was located was designated as ''Grover North.'' Into this substation ran high-voltage supply cables, also called feeders, from switching stations elsewhere on the transmission system.

The second map, similarly stamped, was titled ''System Ties,'' and it was a detailed enlargement of the feeder system supplying any given substation. The substation on the first map had been labeled ''No. 4 Fuller.'' By locating this on the more detailed map, Gopher and the Deaf Man were able to identify the number designation for the feeder: 85RL9.

Which brought them to the third map, titled simply ''85RL9'' and subtitled ''Location Grover North Substation.'' This was a rather long, narrow diagram of the route the feeders, or supply cables, traveled below the city's streets, with numbers indicating the manholes that provided access to the cables themselves. The cable-carrying manhole closest to the 87th Precinct station house was three blocks away on Grover Avenue and Fuller Street. On the ''Composite Feeder Plate Map'' it was numbered ''R2147-120'ESC-CENT.''

The manhole was a hundred and twenty feet east of the southern curb of Fuller in the center of the street—hence the designation ''120'ESC-CENT''—just opposite the bronze statue of John G. Fuller, the noted balloonist. The cables were five feet below the surface of the street, protected by a three-hundred-pound manhole cover. Gopher set up a Big Ipple manhole stand, raised the manhole cover with a crowbar, went down into the manhole, found the cable switch, opened it, and then closed it a minute later. The lights in the 87th Precinct station house—and indeed in all the surrounding residential houses—were out for only that amount of time. But that was all the time Gopher needed for his purposes.

It was four-fifteen when he arrived at the muster desk, wearing a G. I. P. & L. tag pinned to his coveralls. He presented his phony credentials to the desk sergeant and told him he was here to see about the power failure. The sergeant looked across the desk at this little guy with the floppy brown mustache and the blue watch cap and told him there hadn't been any *real* power failure, lights just went out for a minute or so, that was all. Gopher said, ''A minute or so is a power failure to us.''

''So what do you want to do?'' the sergeant asked. He was thinking that a sergeant from the Eight-Four was having a big bash at his house tonight, and he was hoping it'd still be going strong when he got there. He'd be relieved at a quarter to twelve. Figure fifteen minutes to change in the locker room, another half hour to get crosstown . . .

''I gotta put a voltage recorder on the line,'' Gopher said.

''What's the big fuss?'' the sergeant said. ''We got lights, don't we?''

"For *now*," Gopher said. "You want them to go out again when you got some big ax murderer in here?"

The desk sergeant didn't even want them to go out when they had some little numbers runner in here. The desk sergeant was thinking about putting on a funny hat and blowing a horn.

"That your voltage recorder there?" he asked, peering over the top of the desk to the wooden box at Gopher's feet. Gopher hoisted the box onto the desk. It was about the size of a small suitcase. It looked like a larger version of the sort of box one might use to carry roller skates, with metal edges and a handle and clasps to open the lid. But on the face of the box there was a rectangular dial with a yellow band, a red band, and a green band. The yellow band was marked at the end farthest left with a stamped metal tag reading "60 volts." The green band was marked at its center point with a similar tag reading "120 volts." The red band was marked at the end farthest right with a tag reading "200 volts." A needle was behind the glass covering the dial. Three knobs were under the dial.

"So what's that for?" the sergeant asked.

"It's got a tape disc and graph paper inside it," Gopher said. "It monitors the incoming voltage, lets us know we're getting any surges or fluctuations in the . . ."

"I'm sorry I asked," the sergeant said. "Go do your thing."

Gopher started up the iron-runged steps to the squadroom.

There was no graph paper or tape disc inside the wooden box.

The dial was real enough—Gopher had taken it from a genuine voltage recorder—but it was connected to nothing, and the knobs beneath it, used on a genuine recorder to calibrate the meter, had absolutely no function.

Inside the box there was a timer with a seven-day dial. The timer was normally used for programming heating, air-conditioning, and ventilating equipment, as well as lights, pumps, motors, and other single-phase to three-phase loads. Seven sets of trippers, supplied with the timer, enabled its user to set a different ON/OFF program for each day of the week. The timer looked like this:

When the swing-away cover was moved to the left, the terminals looked like this:

This was December 31, a Saturday.

The timer was already programmed for next Thursday, which would be January 5.

It was set for 8:15 P.M., at which time it would turn on whatever electrical appliance its wires were connected to.

Its wires were not connected to any electrical appliance.

There was a five-pound charge of dynamite inside the box. There was a plastic bag of black powder inside the box. One of the wires from the terminal led to a ground. The other wire was loosely twisted around the first wire. At 8:15 P.M. next Thursday, when the timer triggered the ON switch, a surge of electricity would arc through the loosely twisted wires and cause a spark, which would ignite the black powder and subsequently the fuse leading to the dynamite charge. All Gopher had to do now was plug his phony voltage recorder into an ordinary 110-volt outlet and set up the present time on the timer.

The rest would take care of itself.

In the squadroom upstairs the detectives were discussing the wanted flyers that had arrived in that day's mail.

"These have got to be the real article," O'Brien said.

"Could've got 'em from a post office," Fujiwara said.

"Beautiful crowd, ain't they?" Willis said. "Rape, arson, armed robbery, kidnapping . . ."

"You don't think he's pinpointing them, do you?"

"Pinpointing who?"

"The ones who did the Gruber's job with him."

"What he's doing," O'Brien said, "he's telling us he can go into any goddamn squadroom in this city and do whatever the fuck he wants inside them."

"*If* he got them from a squadroom," Fujiwara said.

"That's where he got them, all right," Willis said.

Gopher stopped at the slatted rail divider separating the squadroom from the corridor outside.

"Electric company," he said. "Got to put a voltage recorder on your line."

"Come on in," O'Brien said.

"Where's your fuse box?" Gopher asked.

"Who knows?" Willis said.

Gopher had no reason to locate the fuse box. He simply wanted an excuse to look the place over. He set the box down near one of the desks and began poking around. Plenty of outlets all over the room, but he needed someplace to plant his incendiaries.

"What's in here?" he asked, his hand on a doorknob.

"Supply closet," Fujiwara said.

A naked light bulb with a pull chain was hanging inside the closet. Gopher pulled the chain. A 40-watt bulb, amazing these guys could *see* anything in here.

"Mind if I smoke?" he asked.

"Long as you don't set fire to the joint," O'Brien said.

Gopher laughed.

He checked the closet baseboard for outlets. Usually you didn't find an outlet in a closet, but some of these old buildings, they divided a big room by throwing up walls wherever they felt like. He found a double outlet on the rear wall of the closet. Good. He could plug in his box right here, where there was plenty of flammable shit. Give it a roaring start with his incendiaries, should have a nice little blaze in minutes flat. Nice old wood all around the room. Oh, this would be a very pretty fire.

"I'll be through in a minute here," Gopher said. "You got an ashtray?"

"Just grind it out on the floor," O'Brien said.

It took Gopher a minute and a half to carry his box into the closet, set it on the floor under a shelf at the rear, and plug it in.

It took him three minutes to set the timer with the present time, which he read off the squadroom clock.

"I have to bring some other stuff up here," he said. "Some chemicals to keep the closet dry. Otherwise, the recorder won't give us a true reading. I'll stack them on the shelves, out of your way."

He went downstairs for his incendiaries.

He stacked three innocent-looking cardboard cartons in the supply closet, one on each of three shelves above the box. As he worked, he listened to the detectives.

"So why's he trying to tell us he can get into squadrooms?" Fujiwara said. "*If* that's what he's trying to tell us."

" 'Cause he's crazy," Willis said.

Over the past several years it had become a ritual.

On New Year's Eve, before they left the house for whatever party they were going to, Carella and Teddy made love. And when they returned to the house again, in the New Year this time, they made love again.

Once a long time ago Carella had been told by a detective of Scottish ancestry that in the northern parts of Great Britain the custom of first-footing is still honored on the first day of the New Year. A dark-eyed, dark-haired person—presumably because Britain's enemies in days of yore were fair-haired and light-eyed—carries a symbolic gift, usually a piece of coal and a pinch of salt, over the doorsill of a friend's house. The gift bearer is the first person to set foot in the house in the New Year: hence, first-footing. His or her gift is a wish for health and prosperity throughout the coming year.

Carella didn't know whether he was recalling the story faithfully or even if the Scotsman had been telling the truth. He suspected, however, that one doesn't kid around when it comes to custom. He liked the story, and he wanted to believe that such a custom, in fact, existed. In a world where too many people came bearing death, it was comforting to know that in some remote little village far to the north, someone—on the very first day of the bright New Year—came bearing the gift of life: a piece of coal for the grate, a pinch of salt for the pot. In a sense, the Scotsman had said, the custom was a reaffirmation of life.

For Carella love making was a similar reaffirmation of life.

He loved this woman completely.

This woman was his life.

And holding her in his arms on New Year's Day—dark-eyed, dark-haired people both, no enemies here in this bed—he silently wished her the best that life could afford.

But New Year's Day was also the eighth day of Christmas.

And someone would come bearing tidings of death.

12

Before the Gruber's holdup the Deaf Man had planned to hire someone else to do the horses—just as he had hired Gopher to do the cars and the squadroom. He did not enjoy messiness. Even cutting off the wino's ear, a necessity if he was to make a point to the clods of the Eight-Seven, had been distasteful to him. The Deaf Man liked things clean and neat. Precise. The festivities he'd planned for the enjoyment of the detectives who worked out of the old station house on Grover Avenue were initially conceived as a fillip to the department store job. First let them know that he could do whatever the hell he wanted to in this precinct, pull off the job, get away clean, and then teach them once and for all that he would no longer tolerate their meddling in his affairs. End the relationship. Good-bye, boys.

He changed his mind after the Gruber's job ended in disaster.

Again by accident.

All that work for nothing.

And now he was angry.

He did not normally enjoy excesses of emotion. A woman in bed was not an object of love to him, but merely something to control. In his lexicon "to love" meant "to risk." Elizabeth Turner had made the fatal mistake of falling in love with him and thereby risking all. She had pleaded with him not to execute the Gruber's job, to change his way of living, move with her to another city, forget the past.

The whiff of danger had been all-pervasive.

Her love for him could have led her into dangerously unexpected paths: perhaps a visit to the police to warn them of the impending job, with a tearful scene later in which she would confess her indiscretion and beg him once again, now that she had made the job impossible, to give it up.

She had never threatened him with such a course of action—she knew better than to threaten him—but he sensed in her shifting moods that she now regretted the information she had given him and, because she "loved" him, might do something foolish to "protect" him. What the Deaf Man dreaded most were the good intentions of well-meaning people, the fools of the world.

But he had not killed her in anger.

Anger was wasteful, a silly energy-consuming extravagance.

He had, in fact, killed her immediately after making love to her, whatever *that* meant. Two people "making" love. Two heavy-breathing individuals—although he hadn't been breathing quite so heavily as she—together constructing a dripping edifice known as—ta-*rah*—LOVE! The architect and the contractor in passionate collaboration, "making" love.

To make.

The verb itself as many-faceted as a diamond, the way most words in the English language were.

To make.

To create, construct, form, or shape: *I made a chair*—or a bomb.

To give a new form or use to: *I made a silk purse from a sow's ear*—or a symbolic partridge from a wino's ear.

To earn: *to make money*—which I failed to do on Christmas Eve.

To prepare and start: *to make a fire*—which I will do on Twelfth Night.

To force or compel: *I made her do my bidding*—which I thought Elizabeth Turner *was* doing until she began to have those fatal second thoughts.

To cause to become: *I made her dead.*

But without anger.

The kiss of death.

When one pimply-faced teenager asks another similarly blossoming pal, "Did you *make* her last night?" is he actually asking, "Did you force her to succumb?"

The Deaf Man had not forced Elizabeth Turner to succumb.

She had offered herself to him of her own volition, and he had casually shot her afterward—she on her knees before him, head bent, expecting God knew whatever further pleasure from behind.

No anger.

But now there was anger.

The old brick armory on First Street and Saint Sebastian Avenue had been used to stable horses for longer than any of the neighborhood residents could remember. At one time in the city's history as many as a hundred horses were kept there, all part of the then-elite Mounted Patrol. The Golden Nugget Squad, as the mounties were familiarly, derisively, and enviously called by their fellow police officers, had been slowly reduced in numbers over the years—two successive mayors believing that men on horseback were too reminiscent of cossacks—and was now virtually defunct. Cops on horseback were used only for ceremonial occasions or events expected to draw huge numbers of crowds. There had, for example, been twelve mounties on duty last night on the Stem downtown, where hundreds of thousands of people watched the red ball's descent into the New Year. The horses those twelve cops were riding were all stabled in the armory up here in the 87th Precinct, together with another twelve, the two dozen being the remnants of a once-proud legion. Most of those horses were brown. Only ten of them were black.

On New Year's Day there was only one police officer on duty at the armory. Even on days that were *not* legal holidays there were three officers there at most. The stable hands—four of them—were civil service employees, but not policemen. On New Year's Day only one stable hand was at the armory. Both he and the patrolman were nursing terrific hangovers.

It was a cold rainy day—a bad harbinger for the year ahead.

The man who arrived at the armory was carrying a pizza in a white cardboard carton. He was also carrying a white paper bag. He approached the big wooden door with its iron hinges, lifted the knocker, and waited.

The patrolman on duty opened the door and looked out into the rain.

"Yeah?" he said.

"Got a pizza and some sodas for you," the man outside the door said.

He was wearing a black trench coat. He was blond and hatless. There was a hearing aid in his right ear.

"Nobody ordered no pizza," the patrolman said, and started to close the door.

"It's from the Eight-Seven," the man said.

"What?" the patrolman said.

"Okay to come in?" the man said. "It's kinda wet out here."

"Sure," the patrolman said.

The delivery man went into the armory. The patrolman closed the door behind him. It thundered shut—or so it seemed to him because of his hangover—with a ponderous roar, which caused him to wince. The armory smelled of horses and horse manure. From somewhere in its cavernous reaches one of the horses whinnied.

"They don't like rain," the patrolman said.

"Where do you want this?"

"Bring it in the office here," the patrolman said.

The office was a small cubicle that still had regimental flags on its walls. The stable hand was sitting in the office, his feet up on the desk.

"That smells good," he said.

"Little present from the boys of the Eight-Seven," the delivery man said, putting the carton down on the desk. "Thought you might be getting hungry all alone here on New Year's Day." He took two Pepsis from the white paper bag and put them down on the desk beside the pizza carton. He reached into his pocket for a bottle opener and uncapped both bottles. The caps came off easily and soundlessly, with no fizzy pop of released carbonation.

"That's very nice of them," the patrolman said.

He did not know anybody at the Eight-Seven. He himself was a Bow-and-Arrow cop, who'd once been a mountie. He was still officially assigned to the Mounted Patrol, but he never rode a horse anymore, nor was he permitted to carry a weapon— hence the sobriquet "Bow and Arrow." The police department had taken away both his horse and his gun three years ago, after he rode a big black stallion into a gathering of some thousand people, firing the gun into the crowd. He was drunk at the time. Nobody got hurt but the horse, who bolted at the sound of the pistol and slammed into a lamppost, breaking his leg. The horse had to be shot. Horse lovers all over the city protested.

"What's on it?" the stable hand asked.

He had already opened the lid of the box. The delivery man was hanging around as if he expected a tip.

"Sausage and cheese," the delivery man said.

The patrolman and the stable hand were looking at each other, wondering how much they should tip for something like this, guy delivering a pizza on a cold rainy day.

"Better eat it before it gets cold," he said.

The stable man took a slice of pizza from the carton. He bit into it.

"Good," he said, chewing.

He reached for one of the Pepsi bottles, tilted it to his mouth, and drank.

"This is a little flat," he said.

The patrolman took a slice of pizza.

"Still nice and hot," he said. "You want a piece?" he asked the delivery man.
"No, thanks."

"You got any change?" he asked the stable hand and reached for the other Pepsi
bottle.

"Yeah, just a second," the stable hand said. He took another bite of pizza,
washed it down with the flat Pepsi, and then reached into his pocket.

"No, that's okay," the delivery man said. "Happy New Year."

"Sure you don't want a piece?" the stable hand said.

"Just want to warm up a little before I go out there again," the delivery man
said.

"Sit down, sit down," the patrolman said, and tilted the Pepsi bottle to his mouth
again.

The patrolman and the stable hand sat eating pizza and drinking Pepsi. Somewhere in the armory another horse whinnied. The delivery man kept rubbing his
hands together, trying to get warm.

Ten minutes later the patrolman and the stable hand were both unconscious on the
floor of the office.

The Deaf Man smiled.

The chloral hydrate had worked swiftly and efficiently.

He reached into the pocket of his trench coat for the pistol. He walked back to the
stalls, where the horses were kept, he affixed the long silencer to its barrel.

The eighth day of Christmas was a legal holiday, and nobody expected anything
from the Deaf Man. No mail delivery on legal holidays. No United Parcel deliveries.
No Federal, Emory, Purolator, or whatever *other* kind of express deliveries. Just
peace and quiet. As befitted New Year's Day.

Car Adam One was dispatched to the armory at one-thirty that afternoon because
someone in the neighborhood had called 911 to report horses screaming.

Sixteen horses were still alive when the two patrolmen got there. They were not
actually screaming. Just white-eyed with terror and—one of the patrolmen described
it as "keening," but he was Irish.

Eight horses were dead.

Each of them had been shot.

They were black horses.

So now it was serious.

Well, maybe the severed ear had been serious, too. Maybe the severed ear hadn't
been merely the Deaf Man's way of announcing himself for certain, but was, in
addition, a promise that this was going to get bloody.

Carella and Brown looked at the dead horses.

There was a great deal of blood.

"It doesn't make sense," Carella said.

He was thinking the horses hadn't done anything.

He was thinking they were beautiful, innocent animals.

Eight of them dead.

All of them black.

Brown was thinking this had been planned all the way back in October. The thought was chilling.

Both men stood looking at the dead horses for a long time.

Outside it was still raining.

The rain stopped on the second day of the New Year, the ninth day of Christmas. It was replaced by clear blue skies and arctic temperatures. Gopher did not mind the cold. Rain would have been troublesome. Explosives had to be kept dry.

Getting in was easier than Gopher had expected.

There was a uniformed cop at the entrance gate in the cyclone fence, but Gopher was wearing a plastic-encased tag on his coveralls, and the tag showed his picture in full color and over that the words ISOLA P.D. DEPARTMENT OF VEHICLES. He was also carrying an order form, printed on an *Isola P.D. Department of Vehicles* letterhead, which authorized him to check the electrical wiring of all fifteen cars issued to the 87th Precinct.

The cop at the gate glanced at his tag and said, "What's up?"

Gopher showed him the order form.

The cop at the gate said, "Did you talk to the sergeant?"

"Told me to come on back," Gopher said.

Actually he hadn't talked to *anybody*. Never ask, never regret, that was his motto. March in as if you belonged wherever you were, explain only if you're questioned. He hadn't wanted to show himself *inside* the precinct again because, even though he'd shaved the mustache he'd been wearing ever since Nam and though he was now wearing windowpane eyeglasses, he didn't want to chance anybody's recognizing him. He figured he could bluff his way through if a sergeant popped out here and asked him what the hell he was doing. Show him the papers again, say he didn't know he was supposed to check inside to service a few fuckin' cars, you'd think they'd be happy to see him here instead of giving him static. If it got tight in any way, he was ready to back out of the job in a minute. No job was worth doing time. Work out here with the puffy lip and the phony glasses, hope nobody made a connection with the guy who'd been upstairs in the squadroom on New Year's Eve. He was counting on the fact that most people—even cops—only noticed the trimmings.

"Most of the junk's on the road," the cop said. "The shift don't change till a quarter to eight."

It was now ten minutes past seven. Full daylight would not come till seven twenty-two. It would get dark this afternoon at four forty-six. The light behind the station house was what Gopher had heard called morngloam in some parts of the country.

"I'll do whichever ones I can get to now," Gopher said. "Catch the others when they come in."

"Since when did you guys start making house calls?" the cop asked. "We used to have to bring them to the garage downtown, anything went wrong."

"The holidays," Gopher said. "We're backed up downtown."

"Well, go ahead," the cop said. "Christ knows, they can use it.

It had been that easy.

The 87th Precinct territory was divided into eight sectors, and a radio motor patrol car was assigned to each sector. The patrol sergeant had a car and driver of his own, which brought the total to nine cars in use at any given time. In addition, there were six so-called standby cars. These six were often pressed into service because police cars—like police stations—took a hell of a beating in any given twenty-four-hour period, and there were a great many breakdowns on the road. A team of officers would often be driving one car at nine in the morning and a different car at eleven.

No differentiation was made between the standby cars and the ones they often replaced. In the jargon of the precinct they were *all* called "the junk." Cops would pile into the junk when their tour of duty started and would drop off the junk when the tour ended. The junk was both singular and plural. One patrol car was the junk. Six patrol cars were the junk. A hundred patrol cars would have been the junk. Whenever a car broke down, it was called "the fuckin' junk." To listen to the motorized cops of the Eight-Seven, you'd have thought they were narcotics dealers. Only one of the cars had ever had a name. This had been the favorite car in the precinct, an old workhorse that rarely broke down. The cops called her Sadie. Eventually Sadie's motor gave out, and the city decided it was cheaper to replace her than to repair her. The cops of the Eighty-seventh held a small ceremony for Sadie when she died. She still remained their favorite.

As a matter of practice all the junk in the precinct—the regularly assigned cars and the standby cars—was used on a more or less rotating basis. There were also several unmarked sedans, which the detectives drove, but these were not considered part of the junk. The junk had white door panels with the city's seal and the number of the precinct painted on them, black fenders, a black hood, and a white roof with a row of lights on it. The unmarked detectives' cars were always parked in the lot behind the station house. The junk was parked either there or in front of the station, angled into the curb.

There were seven cars parked in the lot behind the station house when Gopher got to work—the six standby cars and the sergeant's car. It took him literally three minutes to wire each of the cars. By seven twenty-two, when dawn came, he had already wired four of them. By seven-forty, when the cars on the midnight-to-eight tour began drifting in, he had finished wiring the remaining three and was waiting to do only two more. As soon as a pair of patrolmen left a car to go into the station house, Gopher threw up the hood. Between the grille and the radiator he planted a box containing a plastic bag of black powder and a five-pound charge of dynamite. He attached a ground wire to the chassis. He unplugged the connector wire he knew would be there, and loosely twisted the cleaned ends of both wires. The wires ran into the plastic bag of black powder. The dynamite fuse ran into that same plastic bag.

By seven forty-five, when the cars began pulling out for the eight-to-four tour, Gopher was packing his tools in the truck.

He wished the relief cop at the gate a Happy New Year, got into the truck and drove off.

The first explosion did not come until the four-to-midnight tour was almost a half hour old.

The patrolmen assigned to Charlie Two had checked out the car at ten minutes to four. The patrol sergeant, who was a pain in the ass when it came to the junk, came out to look over the vehicle for dents or scratches, jotting down even the slightest mark for comparison when the car was checked in again at eleven forty-five that night. The sergeant's name was Preuss, but the patrolmen called him "Priss" behind his back. Charlie Two left the precinct at five minutes to four. At four-fifteen, after a single run at the sector, they decided to stop for some coffee. The shotgun cop got back into the car at four twenty-two, a container of coffee in each hand.

"Starting to get dark," he said.

The driver reached for the container of coffee with his right hand and the light switch with his left hand. He pulled the light switch. The plug-in connector wire Gopher had removed from the right front headlight and twisted into his ground wire was suddenly alive with current from the 12-volt battery. The loosely twisted wires lying in the plastic bag of black powder shorted and sparked, the powder flashed, the fuse flared, and the dynamite went up an instant later.

That was at 4:23 P.M.

At 4:27 P.M., nineteen minutes before sunset, the patrolmen riding Boy One saw a man running up Culver Avenue in Sector Two. Patrolmen were normally assigned to the same sector on each of their tours, on the theory that familiarity bred better crime prevention. If a patrolman spotted something that looked unusual to him—a grocery store closed when it was supposed to be open, a snatch of hookers standing on the wrong corner—he immediately checked it out. A running man was always suspicious. If you were a runner in this city, you were supposed to be wearing a track suit and running shoes. Everyone else *walked* fast, but they rarely ran. A running man in ordinary clothing was usually running *away* from something.

The patrolman riding shotgun in Boy One said, "Up ahead, Frank."

"I see him," the driver said.

The time was 4:28 P.M.

The driver eased the car over into the curbside lane. The man was still running.

"In one hell of a hurry," the shotgun cop said.

They kept watching him.

"He's just trying to catch that bus on the corner," the driver said.

"Yeah," the shotgun cop said.

The man got on the bus. The bus pulled away from the curb.

"Getting dark," the shotgun cop said. "Better put on the . . ."

The driver was already reaching for the light switch.

An instant later, Boy One exploded.

Preuss, the patrol sergeant, looked at his digital watch as he came out of the station house and started for his car, his driver immediately behind him. The time was 4:31 P.M. The watch also told him that this was Monday, January 2. Watches could tell you almost anything these days. Preuss knew somebody who had an alarm clock, when it went off, you said "Stop" to it, and it let you sleep for another four minutes.

As Preuss got into the car, he was thinking one explosion could be an accident, two explosions were a conspiracy. He had dreaded a conspiracy ever since he'd made sergeant. He knew that the cops in this city wouldn't stand a fuckin' chance if all the bad guys got together and decided to wipe them out.

The driver put the key into the ignition switch and turned it.

The engine roared into life.

And because it was rapidly becoming dark, he reached for the light switch.

By 4:38 P.M. six of the eight cars on patrol were out of service. The remaining two cars all received an urgently radioed 10-02—REPORT TO YOUR COMMAND. The Bomb-Squad was already on its way to the 87th Precinct.

Neither of them made it back safely to the station house.

Sunset was at 4:46 P.M.

By then nine cars—the eight on patrol and the sergeant's car—had gone up.

Three police officers were killed—one of them a woman—and five were hospitalized, two of them in critical condition for third-degree burns.

"He's telling us to go piss in the wind," Brown said.

It was bitterly cold outside, and frost rimed the grilled windows of the squadroom.

This was the tenth day of Christmas.

January 3 by the calendar on the wall. Five minutes after ten by the clock. Four detectives were on duty that morning, Brown, Kling, Meyer, and Carella. They were all looking at the ten blank D.D. forms that had been delivered by Federal Express earlier that morning. The forms looked innocent enough. Standard police department issue. Printed for the department by municipal contract.

"He's telling us to go write up our reports," Brown said. " 'Cause it won't help one damn bit."

"These forms are legit," Kling said. "You can't buy them anyplace, he had to have got them from a squadroom."

"Or *ten* squadrooms," Carella said.

"Write up your dumb reports, he's saying," Brown said. "File your shit on the eight black horses and the nine cars . . ."

"And he planned that way back in October?" Meyer asked. "To send us ten D.D. forms so we could write up *reports?*"

"Ten D.D. forms, right," Brown insisted. "For the ten separate . . ."

"Are we supposed to write up a D.D. report on *this* shit, too?"

"On *what* shit?" Brown asked.

"On *this* shit. The D.D. forms we got today."

"That's what you write the shit *on*, isn't it?" Brown said, looking at the other men as though Meyer had momentarily lost his wits. "You write the shit on D.D. forms."

"I mean *about* the forms."

"What?"

"Does he expect us to file a report *about* these forms?"

"Who knows what he expects?" Brown said. "The man has a twisted mind."

"So he's telling us to write a report on the pear tree, right? And the two nightsticks . . ."

"Don't go over them again, okay?" Kling said. "I'm tired of hearing all that stuff over and over again."

"*He's* tired," Brown said, rolling his eyes.

"No, *let's* go over it again," Carella said. "This is all we've got, so let's go over it."

Kling sighed.

"First the pear tree," Carella said.

"On the first day of Christmas," Brown said. "I told you all along it'd be the twelve days of Christmas."

"Give him a medal," Meyer said.

"With the ear attached to it," Carella said.

"To let us know it was him," Brown said.

"Then the two nightsticks . . ."

"Easy to come by," Kling said.

"Ditto the three pairs of handcuffs," Brown said.

"Easy stuff."

"Then all that stuff from precincts all over the city . . ."

"Four police hats, five walkie-talkies, six police shields . . ."

"The wanted flyers . . ."

"Seven of them."

"From *squadrooms,* had to be," Brown said.

"Not necessarily. Any muster room bulletin board . . ."

"Yeah, okay, so he coulda got them in a muster room someplace."

"And then it gets serious," Carella said.

"Eight black horses," Kling said. "Six blocks from here."

"And the nine cars. Our *own* cars."

The men were silent.

"Ten D.D. forms," Meyer said.

"You don't find *those* hanging on no muster room bulletin board," Brown said.

"*Those* came from a squadroom," Kling said.

"Or *ten* squadrooms," Carella repeated.

"So tomorrow we get eleven Detective Specials," Brown said.

"And on Thursday we get the big feast. Twelve roast pigs."

"And a hundred dancing girls," Meyer said.

"I *wish,*" Brown said, and then looked quickly over his shoulder, as if his wife, Caroline, had suddenly materialized in the squadroom.

"Maybe he's finished," Kling said. "Maybe the nine cars were the end of it, and now he's telling us it's finished, we can go write up our reports. Like Artie says."

"What about the guns tomorrow?" Meyer asked. "*If* he sends them."

"He'll be telling us to shove our guns up our asses," Brown said.

"He's roasting the pigs, don't you get it?" Kling said.

"Huh?"

"Pigs," Kling said. "Cops."

"So?"

"So didn't you ever watch 'Celebrity Roast' on television?"

"What's that?" Meyer said.

"A roast," Kling said. "It's this testimonial dinner, all these guys get up and rake another guy over the coals. They tell jokes about him, they make him look foolish—a roast. Didn't you ever hear of a roast?"

"Those cops yesterday got roasted, all right," Meyer said.

Carella had been silent for some time now.

"I was just thinking . . ." he said.

The men turned to him.

"My grandmother once told me that in Naples . . . in other Italian cities, too, I guess . . . whenever someone important dies, his coffin is put in a big black carriage, and the carriage goes up the middle of the street . . . and it's drawn by eight black horses."

The men thought this over.

"Was he telling us there'd be some funerals the next day?" Kling asked.

"First the eight black horses and then the dead cops? On the following day?"

"I don't know," Carella said.

The squadroom windows rattled with a fierce gust of wind.

"Well," Kling said, "maybe those cars yesterday *were* the end of it."

"Maybe," Carella said.

The invitation read:

YOU ARE INVITED TO A PARTY

FOR: Detective-Lieutenant Peter Byrnes

DATE: January 5

TIME: 8:00 P.M.

PLACE: 87th Precinct Squadroom

Scrawled on the flap of the card in the same handwriting was the message:

Andy — I haven't been able to invite everyone, so please keep this a secret, won't you? Harriet.

Andy Parker was touched.

He hadn't even realized the lieutenant's wife knew his name.

He wondered if he was expected to bring a present.

* * *

On January 4, the eleventh day of Christmas, eleven .38-caliber Colt Detective Specials were delivered to the squadroom. They were not new guns. Even a preliminary examination revealed that all of them had previously been fired, if only on a firing range. Each of the guns had a serial number stamped on it. A check with Pistol Permits revealed that the eleven guns were registered to eleven different detectives from precincts in various parts of the city. None of the detectives had reported a pistol missing or stolen. It is shameful for a cop to lose his gun.

"Like I told you," Brown said, "he's telling us to stick our guns up our asses."

"No," Carella said. "He's telling us he's been inside eleven different squadrooms."

"Not necessarily," Parker said. "I know blues who pack the Special."

"That ain't regulation," Brown said.

"As a backup," Parker said. "Anyway, what are *you*, a fuckin' Boy Scout?"

The fact remained that the Detective Special was the weapon of choice for most detectives in this city. All three detectives sitting there at Carella's desk were carrying a gun similar to the ones spread on its top like a small arsenal.

"Only an asshole gets his gun ripped off," Parker said, and wondered if Carella and Brown had been invited to the lieutenant's party tomorrow night. "What we oughta do, we oughta wrap them like presents, send them back to those assholes," he said.

And wondered again if he was expected to bring a present.

I don't even *like* the lieutenant, he thought.

13

The Deaf Man would have been the first to agree that most catastrophes were caused by the fools of the world. He would not have dreamed, however, that sometimes a fool can *prevent* a catastrophe, thereby rising above his lowly estate to achieve the stature of a hero.

Genero's first opportunity to become a hero came at two forty-five on the afternoon of January 5, the twelfth day of Christmas. The city had by then taken down all its Christmas trimmings. It looked somehow naked, but there were probably eight million stories in it anyway. The temperature, hovering at twelve degrees Fahrenheit—which was twelve *above* zero here, but approximately eleven *below* zero in Celsius-speaking countries—did much to discourage the fanciful notion (twelve days of Christmas indeed!) that the holiday season had lingered beyond New Year's Day. The citizens knew only that winter was here in earnest, and Easter was a long way away. In between there'd be the short holiday crumbs thrown to a chilled populace: Lincoln's Birthday, Valentine's Day, Washington's Birthday, Saint

Patrick's Day—with only Washington's Birthday officially observed. For now, the city and the months ahead looked extraordinarily bleak.

The cops were nervous.

Only three days ago nine police cars had been blown up. This did not indicate an attitude of civic-mindedness on the part of the populace.

In some quarters of the city, in fact, some citizens were heard to remark that it served the cops right. Now they knew what it felt like to be victimized. Maybe now they'd do something about the goddamn *crime* in this city. Maybe they'd make it safe to ride the subways again. What patrol cars had to do with subways, no one bothered clarifying. The talk was all about the shoe being on the other foot, and turnabout being fair play, and what's sauce for the goose is sauce for the gander. The people of this city, even when police cars weren't being blown up, felt ambivalent about cops. If they came home one night to find their apartment burglarized, the first thing they did was call the cops. And then complain later about how long it took for them to get there and about how they'd never recover the stolen goods anyway. In this city a vigilante could become a hero, even if he was a fool.

To the cops of the Eight-Seven, Genero was not a fool. The word was too elite for their vocabulary. Genero was a complainer and a whiner and an inefficient cop and a dope, but he was not a fool. Just a jackass. Not many of the detectives enjoyed being partnered with Genero. They felt, perhaps rightfully, that if push came to shove, Genero wasn't the candidate they'd elect to help them out of a tight spot. A cop's very life often depended upon the reaction time of his partner. How could you entrust your life to a man who couldn't spell "surveillance?" Or perhaps even "vehicle." Even the worst male chauvinist pig on the squad would have preferred being partnered with a woman rather than with Genero. Tell them that Genero was about to become a hero, and they'd have laughed in your face.

By two forty-five on the twelfth day of Christmas, Genero—because he'd done some splendid detective work at the office—was in possession of the lieutenant's home number. He did not know what he would do if the lieutenant himself answered the phone, but he would cross that bridge when he came to it. He also did not know what he would call Harriet Byrnes if she answered the phone, but he guessed he would think of something.

A woman answered the phone.

"Mrs. Byrnes?" Genero said.

"Yes?" Harriet said.

"This is Richard," he said.

He felt funny announcing himself as Richard, but that's what she'd called him in the invitation, wasn't it?"

"Who?" she said.

"Richard," he said.

"Richard who?" she said.

"Genero. Detective Richard Genero," he said. "Detective/Third Grade Richard Genero."

"Yes?" she said.

"You know," he said.

"Yes?" she said.

"I work with your husband," he said. "Peter Byrnes. Detective-Lieutenant Peter Byrnes. Pete."

"Oh, yes," she said. "I'm sorry, but he isn't here just now. Can I . . . ?"

"Good," Genero said. "I mean, actually I wanted to talk to *you*, Mrs. Byrnes."

"Yes?" Harriet said.

"Am I expected to bring a present?" he said.

"What?"

"Tonight."

"What?"

"To the party."

There was a long silence on the line.

"I'm sorry," Harriet said. "What party do you . . . ?"

"You know," he said, and almost winked.

There was another long silence.

"I'm sorry," Harriet said, "but I don't know what you're talking about."

"I haven't told anybody, you don't have to worry," Genero said.

"Told anybody what?" Harriet said.

"About the party."

Harriet thought one of her husband's detectives had flipped. That sometimes happened during the holidays. Cops had a habit of eating their own guns during the holidays. Some cops even ate their own guns on Halloween. But the holidays had come and gone, hadn't they?

"What did you say your name was?" she asked.

"Genero," he said. "You know. Richard."

"Is there some problem, Detective Genero?" she said.

"Only about whether to bring a present."

"Well, I'll have to ask Pete . . ."

"No, don't do that!" he said at once.

"What?"

"It's supposed to be a surprise, isn't it?"

"What?"

"I thought . . . the invitation makes it sound like a surprise party."

"Well, does it mention a present?" Harriet asked, and wondered why she was entering into this man's delusional system.

"What?" Genero said.

"I said . . ."

"Well, no, that's why I'm calling." He suddenly thought he might have the wrong number. "Is this Harriet Byrnes?" he asked.

"Yes, this is Harriet Byrnes."

"Lieutenant Byrnes's wife?"

"Yes, I'm Lieutenant Byrnes's wife."

"So should I bring a present?"

"Detective Genero," Harriet said, "I'm sorry, but I can't advise you on that."

"You can't?" Genero said.

"Maybe this is something you ought to discuss with someone who can really help you," she said. "If you're deeply troubled about some sort of present . . ."

"Who?" Genero said.

"You," Harriet said. "Aren't you the one who's troubled about . . . ?"

"I mean, who should I *discuss* it with?"

"I think you should call the Psychological Service," she said.

"How do you spell that?" Genero asked.

"Just call the Psychological Service at Headquarters," she said. "Tell them you're extremely worried about this present, and tell them you'd like to make an appointment to see someone. Once you've talked to them, you'll be able to judge for yourself whether . . ."

"Oh, I get it," Genero said. "Okay, don't worry. Mum's the word."

"Meanwhile, I'll tell Pete you . . ."

"No, no, don't blow the surprise, Mrs. Byrnes, that's okay. Thanks a lot, I'll probably see you later, huh? Thanks again," he said, and hung up.

Harriet looked at the telephone receiver.

She found it difficult to believe she had just had this conversation.

She wondered if she should call Pete and tell him that one of his detectives had gone bananas. And then she wondered if perhaps someone really *was* throwing a surprise party for her husband. She sighed heavily. Sometimes police work got very, very trying.

Genero could have become a hero when he spoke to Harriet Byrnes. He could have realized then that she hadn't sent him an invitation at all and that there wasn't going to be any surprise party for the lieutenant. But Genero was a dope, and he didn't realize anything at all, and he *still* didn't know whether he should bring a present or not.

What he figured was that Mrs. Byrnes had told him to use his own judgment.

The thing of it was he didn't have any judgment on the matter. Suppose he *didn't* bring a present, but a present was expected, he'd look like a jackass. Or suppose he *did* bring a present, but he was the only one there with a present, he'd still look like a jackass. The one thing Genero didn't want was to look like a jackass. He sat there in his room in his mother's apartment—he still lived with his mother, which was nice—and wondered what he should do.

If only he knew which of the detectives had been invited.

But he didn't.

If only he knew which of the detectives he could trust.

He figured he could trust Carella, maybe. But he admired Carella, and he didn't want Carella to think he was a jackass, asking whether he should bring a present or not, assuming Carella had even been invited to the party, which maybe he hadn't.

Another detective he admired, perhaps even more than he admired Carella, was Andy Parker.

He called the squadroom and asked to talk to Parker.

Santoro, who was catching, said Parker had the four-to-midnight tonight.

Genero wondered if he should ask Santoro about the party. Instead, he asked for Parker's home number. Parker answered the phone on the third ring.

"Yeah?" he said.

That was one of the things Genero admired about Parker. His gruff style.

"Andy?" he said.

"Who's this?" Parker said.

"Genero."

"What do you want?" Parker said. "I ain't due in till four."

"You're gonna be there tonight, huh?" Genero said.

"What?" Parker said.

"In the squadroom."

"I got the duty, I'll be there," Parker said.

"With or without?" Genero asked slyly.

"What?" Parker said.

"You know," Genero said, and suddenly wondered if he *did* know. "Never mind, forget it," he said, and hung up.

Fuckin' jackass, Parker thought.

In the squadroom supply closet the timer inside the wooden box read 3:15 P.M.

At midnight the timer had moved into the pie-shaped segment marked "Thursday." There were seven such segments on the timer, one for each day of the week. These segments were subdivided into fifteen-minute sectors.

Now, soundlessly, the timer moved into the 3:15-to-3:30 sector.

A giant step on the way to Genero's becoming a hero was his decision to buy the lieutenant a present. He figured he would make it something impersonal. He bought him a pair of pajamas. He also figured he would hide the present under his coat until he saw whether the other guys had bought presents or not. That way, he would be covered either way. If the other guys hadn't bought presents, he would take the pajamas home and wear them himself; he had bought them in his own size, even though Byrnes was taller and heftier than he was.

He wondered whether the other guys would be bringing presents to the party. He wondered how many other guys had been invited.

There were sixteen detectives assigned to the 87th Squad. Of those sixteen, two were on vacation. Of the remaining fourteen, four had pulled the four-to-midnight shift on the fifth day of January and would have been at the squadroom even if they hadn't received an invitation to the party. Unlike the blues, who worked five fixed eight-hour shifts and then swung for the next fifty-six hour, the detectives made out their own duty schedules. Usually—because vacation schedules and court appearances depleted the roster—only four of them were on duty in any given shift. The four detectives who arrived at the squadroom at fifteen minutes before the hour that afternoon were Parker, Willis, O'Brien, and Fujiwara. Each of them had received an invitation to the lieutenant's party. None of them had discussed it with anyone else. Cops were very good at keeping secrets; in a sense secrets were a major part of the line of work they were in.

In the supply closet the timer moved into Thursday's 3:45–4:00 P.M. sector.

It began snowing at six-thirty.

The forecasters were still promising only light flurries. The people of this city knew that when the forecasters promised light flurries, they could expect a blizzard.

All of the other detectives who'd been invited to the party figured they'd better leave for the squadroom earlier than they'd planned.

The other invited detectives were:

Steve Carella.

Bert Kling.

Alexiandre Delgado.

Cotton Hawes.

Richard Genero.

Arthur Brown.

Meyer Meyer

And the guest of honor himself, Peter Byrnes.

Byrnes thought Carella was the guest of honor. That was because his invitation had said it was a party for Steve Carella. The handwritten scrawl on the flap of his invitation had been signed ''Teddy.'' He had been tempted to call Teddy and ask if a present was expected. But he hated talking to that bitchy housekeeper of theirs. Instead, he had bought Carella a pair of cuff links and had hidden them in the top drawer of his desk.

As he dressed that night, he wondered why Teddy hadn't cleared this with him first. A party in the *squadroom?* A squadroom was a place of business. Or had she gone downtown over his head, talked with a deputy inspector or something, asked if it would be okay to give a small party in the squadroom for her husband's . . .

Her husband's *what?*

Was it Steve's birthday?

Byrnes didn't think so.

He was vaguely troubled about the party in the squadroom. He hoped to hell no department rank walked in, and he hoped Teddy hadn't planned to serve anything alcoholic. Only once could he remember a party in the squadroom, and that was when Captain Overman retired, more years ago than Byrnes could count. No booze. Just sandwiches and punch, though Byrnes later suspected one of the patrol sergeants had laced the punch with vodka. Still it wasn't like Teddy not to have checked with him first. He was again tempted to call her, ask if she'd got some sort of clearance. Teddy knew how the goddamn department worked, she'd been a cop's wife for a long time now.

Harriet watched him as he knotted his tie.

''Who's this party for?'' she asked cautiously. She figured the surprise was premised on his thinking the party was for someone else.

''Steve,'' he said.

''You didn't tell me about it,'' she said.

''I wasn't supposed to tell anyone,'' Byrnes said.

''I'm not anyone, I'm your wife,'' Harriet said.

''Still it's supposed to be a surprise.''

She wondered suddenly if the party really *was* for Carella. On the phone the detective who'd called—whatever his name was—had only said, ''It's supposed to be a surprise, isn't it?'' He hadn't said it was a surprise for *Pete.*

''Did you buy a present?'' she asked.

"Yeah, a pair of cuff links."

"Gennario wanted to know if he should bring a present."

"Who?"

"Gennario. One of your detectives."

"Genero?"

"Yes, Genero, right. He called here, wanted to know if he should bring a present."

"What'd you tell him?"

"I said I didn't know."

"He's a jackass," Byrnes said.

The clock on the dresser read six forty-five.

"What time will you be back?" Annie Rawles asked.

"I don't know actually," Hawes said.

Annie was wearing one of his Christmas gifts. He had given her seven pairs of silk panties, one for each day of the week. The panties were in different colors. Blue for Monday. Green for Tuesday. Lavender for Wednesday. Purple for Thursday. Red for Friday. Black for Saturday. White for Sunday. She had asked him why he'd chosen those particular colors for those particular days. He said they had to be blue for Monday because of Blue Monday, and then he'd simply worked his way through the color spectrum until he got to the weekend. Friday was the beginning of the weekend, and the appropriate kickoff color seemed to be red. Saturday was all slinky and sexy, hence black. Sunday was pure as the driven snow—white. Elementary, my dear Watson.

This was Thursday, and she was wearing the purple panties.

She was also wearing a lavender garter belt, a lavender bra, one purple nylon stocking and one black, and a gold chain and pendant, which she never took off. Thirty-four years old with brown eyes and black wedge-cut hair, long slender legs, and small perfectly formed breasts, she stood in high-heeled purple satin slippers, her hands on her narrow hips, and looked more like a Bob Fosse dancer than a Detective/First Grade earning $37,935 a year. She also looked like a woman scorned. Hawes was looking at the clock on the dresser. It read six forty-eight.

"Well, what kind of a party is it?" she asked.

"For the lieutenant," he said.

And it's in the *squadroom?*"

"Yeah."

"Do you always have parties up there at the old Eight-Seven?"

"First one I can think of," he said.

Annie looked at him.

"Are you telling me the truth?" she said.

"What do you mean?"

"Is there *really* a party tonight . . ."

"Of course there . . ."

". . . in the *squadroom,* of all places . . ."

"That's where . . ."

". . . or is there something you'd like to tell me?"

"Like what?"

"Like why you're rushing out of here . . ."

"Who's rushing?"

". . . when I'm all decked out like a whore?"

"A whore? You look gorgeous!"

"Why didn't you tell me about this party earlier?"

"The truth is I forgot about it. I got the invitation a few days before Christmas."

"I'll bet."

"Would you like to *see* it?"

"Yes, I would like to see it," Annie said. "Please," she added. She felt dumb in the sexy underwear. All dressed up for a party of her own, and nobody coming.

Hawes took the invitation from his jacket pocket.

Annie looked at it.

"Why all the secrecy?" she asked.

"I have no idea."

"A small party, huh?" she said.

"It looks that way, doesn't it?"

"How many people?"

"I don't know. I didn't discuss it with anyone. Harriet specifically . . ."

"Well, if it's in the *squadroom* and she's telling you to keep it a secret, then I guess it *has* to be a small party."

"Yeah."

"The reason I'm asking all these questions . . ."

"Mm?"

". . . is not because I'm a mastermind detective trying to figure out why anyone in her right mind would throw a party in a grubby squadroom, but only because I'm standing here half-naked wondering how long the damn party will *last.*"

"Why? Do you have other plans?"

"I'm thinking of making some," Annie said. "So the hooker outfit won't be a total waste."

He went to her. He took her in his arms.

"I don't have to leave here till seven-thirty," he said.

"Great. That gives us what? Half an hour?"

"Hookers can do it in ten minutes," he said.

"Oh, but I'm not a *real* hooker, sir," she said, and clasped her hands together and rolled her eyes.

"I'll break away as soon as I can," Hawes said.

"That may be too late," Annie said. "There's a captain at the Seven-Two who's been making eyes at me."

"What's his name? I'll go shoot him."

"Big talker," Annie said. "Gonna shoot a captain, can't even take off a lady's purple silk panties."

Genero got to the squadroom earlier than any of the others.

This was not because he was normally a punctual person but because he didn't want to keep his coat on and look like a jackass. The pajamas he'd bought the lieutenant were hidden under his coat. If he took off the coat, everybody would see that he'd brought a present, and if none of the other guys had presents, he would look like a jackass. On the other hand, if he kept his coat on in the heated squad-room, everybody would still think he was a jackass. So what he did, he got to the squadroom at a little before seven-thirty, and he went directly to the supply closet without taking off his coat, and he put the present on top of a wooden box that had some kind of meter on its face.

That was the second time he came close to becoming a hero.

The timer inside the box silently moved into the 7:30-to-7:45 P.M. sector.

"Hey, guys," Genero said, taking off his coat and hanging it on the rack. "How's it going?"

None of the four-to-midnight detectives answered him.

Parker was wondering if the lieutenant's wife had been dumb enough to invite this jackass to her party.

Eileen Burke was crying.

Kling looked at the bedside clock, thinking he had to get out of here soon because of the snow. It was snowing like the arctic tundra out there, and the clock read seven thirty-two. Knowing this city, traffic would be stalled for miles—and the squadroom was all the way uptown.

But Eileen was crying.

"Come on, honey," he said.

She was wearing what she'd worn to work that morning. Gray suit, black shoes with French heels, a white blouse. She had stopped wearing earrings ever since the rape. She had always considered earrings her lucky charm. Her luck had run out on the night of the cutting and the rape, and she had stopped wearing them.

They were in her apartment. He had rushed there the moment she called.

"You don't understand," she said.

"I do," he said.

"I was *scared,*" she said. "I turned it down because I was *scared.*"

"You had every right to be scared," he said.

"I'm a *cop!*" she said.

"They shouldn't have asked you in the first place. A gang of . . ."

"That only makes it worse," she said. "A gang, Bert. A goddamn *gang* that's running around raping women!"

"They can't expect you to handle a gang," he said. "Setting up a decoy for a gang is like . . ."

"There'll be backups," she said. "Four of them."

"A lot of good they'll do if you're jumped by a dozen guys. Who the hell requested this anyway?"

"Captain Jordan."

"Where?"

"The Seventh."

"I'll go see him, I'll talk to him person . . ."

"No, you *won't!*" Eileen said. "It's bad enough as it is! Chickening out in front of four hairbags who . . ."

"What four? Are you talking about the backups?"

"From the Seventh Squad. I don't remember their names. All I remember is their eyes. What was in their eyes."

"Let one of *them* go out in drag," Kling said angrily. "Let *him* face a gang of . . ."

"Their eyes said, 'She's scared.' "

"You *should* have been scared."

"No," she said.

"Yes."

"No. I'm a cop. Any other decoy cop wouldn't have batted an eyelash. You got a gang out there? Piece of cake. When?"

"That's not true, and you know it."

"It's true."

"Any woman who'd agree to go out there alone against a dozen men . . ."

"Eight."

"What?"

"It's only eight."

"Terrific. Eight guys dragging a woman into the bushes . . ."

"They're working the subways."

"Better yet. You'll end up on the fucking tracks with another scar on your . . ."

He stopped all at once.

"I'm sorry," he said.

She was silent for a long time.

Then she said, "That's the point, isn't it? I'm afraid I'll get hurt again."

"You don't have to prove anything," he said.

"I'll call Jordan," she said, sighing. "I'll tell him I've thought it over, and . . ."

"No."

"Bert . . ."

"*No*, damn it!" he said, and took her in his arms. "Eileen," he said, "I love you. If anything ever happened to you . . ."

"Who told you to start up with a cop?" she said.

"You did the right thing. I'd have turned it down, too."

"You wouldn't have."

"I would've."

They were both silent.

"I love you, too," she said.

He held her close.

"I don't want anything to happen to either of us," she said. "Ever."

"Nothing will happen to us," he said. "Ever."

"But I'm going to call Jordan . . ."

"Eileen, please . . ."

". . . tell him I want a bigger backup team. All over the platform. Men *and* women. Wall to wall cover."

"You don't have to."

"I want to."

"You *don't* want to."

"I don't want to, right. But I *have* to," she said. "Or I never will again."

She looked at the clock.

"You're going to be late," she said.

"Will you be all right?"

"Yes," she said. "Go. Come back soon."

He kissed her gently and went to the door.

"Be careful," she said.

The clock on the dresser read a quarter to eight.

In the park across the street from the station house the Deaf Man watched them trickling in. Big men, most of them. You could almost always tell a detective by his size. All of them bundled up against the cold. A very cold night. Well, they'd be warm enough soon enough.

He looked at his watch.

Ten minutes to eight.

In exactly twenty-five minutes . . . Armageddon.

He began pacing again.

The snow blew furiously around him.

He hoped none of them would be late.

By five minutes to eight on the squadroom clock, all but three of the invited detectives had arrived. Since none of the detectives knew who had been invited, none of them knew who was missing. But since they knew that anyone there *had* been invited, they felt free to talk about the party.

"What's it for?" Brown asked. "You got any idea?"

"Did you bring a present?" Genero asked.

"No," Hawes said. "Were we supposed to bring presents?"

"Anybody know what it's *for?*" Brown said.

"It said eight o'clock, didn't it?" Delgado asked. "The invitation?"

A man in the detective cage said, "What the hell *is* this?" He had been arrested by Parker not ten minutes earlier. "I'm locked up in a fuckin' cage here, like a fuckin' animal here, and you guys are havin' a *party?*"

"Shut up," Parker said.

"Where's my lawyer?" the man said.

"On the way," Parker said. "Shut up."

Even the four detectives who had the duty were all dressed up. Suits and ties, polished shoes. Parker was upset that he'd got blood on his shirt while arresting the man in the detention cage. The man in the detention cage had slit his wife's throat with a straight razor.

"My wife's dead, and you guys are havin' a *party,*" he said.

"You're the one killed her," Parker said.

"Never mind who killed her, is it right to have a party when a woman is dead? Anyway, I *didn't* kill her."

"No, that razor just jumped off the sink all by itself," Parker said.

"That wasn't even my razor."

"Save it for when your lawyer gets here," Parker said. "You got blood all over my fuckin' shirt."

He walked to the sink near the supply closet, tore a paper towel loose, opened the cold water faucet, and began dabbing at the blood stains.

Inside the box in the supply closet the timer moved into the 8:00-to-8:15 sector.

Carella was just walking into the squadroom.

Genero noticed at once that he was carrying a present.

"Where's Harriet?" Carella asked.

In the park across the way the Deaf Man looked at his watch again. He had just seen Carella going into the station house. Carella, he *knew*. Carella, he *recognized*. In exactly fourteen minutes, though, Carella—and all the others—would be unrecognizable. The moment . . .

There!

Another one.

Blond and hatless, his head ducked against the flying snow.

The Deaf Man smiled.

Alfred Hitchcock, a director whose work the Deaf Man admired greatly—except for *The Birds,* that silly exercise in science fiction—had once described for an interviewer the difference between shock and suspense. The Master had used a parable to explain.

There is a boardroom meeting. Twenty men are sitting around a table, discussing high finance. The audience doesn't know that a bomb has been planted in the room. The chairman of the board is in mid-sentence when the bomb goes off.

That is shock.

The same boardroom meeting. The same twenty men sitting around a table, discussing high finance. But this time the audience *knows* there is a bomb in that room, and they know that it is set to go off—as an example—at 8:15 P.M. The men keep discussing high finance. The camera keeps cutting away to the clock as it throws minutes into the room.

8:08.

8:12.

8:14.

That is suspense.

The detectives in the squadroom across the street did not know that a timer was programmed to set off an explosion and a subsequent fire at 8:15 sharp. They were in for one hell of a shock.

The Deaf Man, however—in this instance, the audience—*did* know, and the suspense for him was almost unbearable.

He looked at his watch again.

8:03.

It was taking forever.

The confusion started the moment Lieutenant Byrnes walked in.

"Where's Teddy?" he said.

"Where's the sandwiches?" Delgado said.

"Where's Harriet?" Carella said.

The detectives all looked at each other.

"You jerks got the wrong night," the man in the detention cage said.

Brown looked at the clock.

8:05.

The invitation had specified eight o'clock.

"Where's my lawyer?" the man in the detention cage said.

All Genero knew was that Carella had brought a present.

He began moving at once toward the supply closet.

Nine minutes, the Deaf Man thought.

He had specifically asked them to arrive at eight because he wanted to be sure they were all assembled by eight-fifteen.

Another man was entering the police station across the street.

The Deaf Man had lost count.

Were all twelve pigs already present and accounted for?

Waiting for the big barbecue?

Which by his watch should happen in eight minutes now.

"I'm Harry Lefkowitz," the man at the slatted rail divider said. "Is that my client I see in the cage there?"

"If your client is Roger Jackson, then that's your client," Parker said.

Lefkowitz came into the squadroom. Genero was opening the door to the supply closet. The clock on the wall read 8:08.

"I hope you read him his rights," Lefkowitz said, and went to the cage."

"They're havin' a fuckin' party up here," Jackson said. "My wife's dead, and they're havin' ...''

"Shut up," Lefkowitz said.

In the supply closet Genero pulled the chain hanging from the naked light bulb. For a moment he forgot where he'd put the lieutenant's present. Oh, yeah, the box there against the back wall, under the lowest shelf.

"Okay, Steve," Byrnes said, "what's this all about?"

"Me?" Carella said.

"Teddy's invitation said ...''

"Teddy's?"

"Harriet's," Brown said.

"What?" Byrnes said.

Genero knelt down and reached for the present. The wrapped pajamas fell off the top of the wooden box and behind it. "Shit," Genero said under his breath and then quickly looked over his shoulder to check if the lieutenant had heard him using profanity in the squadroom.

"'What's the story, Loot?" Willis said.

"Where's the sandwiches?" Delgado said.

"What's going on here?" Byrnes said.

Genero lifted the wooden box by its handle, planning to move it aside so he could get at the lieutenant's present. Something was snagging. The box wouldn't move more than six inches from the wall. He gave a tug. He gave another tug, stronger this time, almost falling over backward when the short cord attached to the box pulled out of the wall socket behind it. Flailing for balance, he banged his elbow against one of the shelves on his right. "Shit!" he yelled, and lost his grip on the box's handle. The box fell on his foot—the same foot he'd shot himself in a long time ago.

"Ow!" he yelled.

The detectives all turned at the sound of his voice.

"*Damn* it!" Genero yelled, and kicked at the box, hurting his foot again. "Ow!" he yelled again.

Carella came to the supply closet.

He looked at the box.

"What've you got there?" he asked.

Genero had just become a hero.

Nothing happened at eight-fifteen.

The Deaf Man looked at his watch again.

Nothing happened at eight-sixteen.

And nothing happened at eight-twenty.

By eight thirty-five the Deaf Man began to suspect that nothing *would* happen.

By eight-forty, when the Bomb Squad truck pulled in across the street, he was *certain* nothing would happen.

The Bomb Squad team rushed into the building.

The Deaf Man kept watching.

The found the cartons of incendiaries in forty seconds flat.

That was after the detectives showed them the open wooden box with the timer and the dynamite inside it. It was Carella who'd unlatched the box. But it was Genero, the hero, who'd found it and yanked it out of the wall socket.

"Lucky thing you pulled this loose when you did," one of the Bomb Squad detectives said to Genero.

"I try to keep my eyes open," Genero said.

"You guys woulda been cinders," the second Bomb Squad detective said. "I never seen so many different kinds of incendiaries in one place in my entire life. Look at all this shit, willya? A dozen fire bottles, six cakes of paraffin sawdust, a whole box full of flake aluminum thermite, eight bottles of mineral oil, five bottles of kerosene—you ever see anything like this, Lou?"

"This timer here was set for eight-fifteen," the second detective said to Genero. "You unplugged it just in time. Very nice little timer here."

"I recognized it right off," Genero said. "Who gets to keep it?"

"What?" Byrnes said.

"I found it, do I get to keep it?"

"What?" Willis said.

"It might work like a VCR," Genero said. "To tape television shows."

"This city has endangered the safety and well-being of my client," Lefkowitz said.

Kling was thinking maybe something *could* happen to him or Eileen. Maybe it *wouldn't* be forever.

Hawes was thinking Annie had come within an ace of wearing the *black* silk panties. To his funeral.

Carella was thinking that maybe the Deaf Man had played it fair after all. On the first day of Christmas he'd announced his intention clearly and unequivocally; they'd be hearing from him on the eleven days to follow. On the second to the sixth days he'd sent them all that police paraphernalia to let them know he was planning something for *cops*. On the seventh day the wanted flyers arrived, a segue from the uniformed force to the plainclothes cops in that the posters could be found in a muster room as well as in a squadroom. On the eighth day he'd let them know he was dead serious, but he'd also told them he was moving into the Eight-Seven itself; the armory was right there on First and Saint Sebastian. On the ninth day he'd started zeroing in. Those nine cars were 87th Precinct cars, no question about it. And on the tenth and eleventh days he'd let them know he was coming into the squad-room itself—ten D.D. forms, which only detectives used, and eleven Colt Detective Specials, a detective's pistol of choice. The twelve roast pigs—by Carella's count, there were twelve detectives in the squadroom right this minute, and they'd just come pretty damn close to being incinerated. He never wanted to come this close again.

"There's a bottle of scotch in the bottom drawer of my desk," Byrnes said. "Go get it, Genero." He turned to Carella. "Also, I bought you a pair of cuff links."

"I bought you a shirt," Carella said.

"I bought you a pair of pajamas, Pete," Genero said, and hurried into the lieutenant's office.

"What'd he call me?" Byrnes asked.

"Do you men plan to drink *alcohol* in this squadroom?" Lefkowitz asked.

The Bomb Squad detectives came out of the station house at a few minutes before nine.

The Deaf Man watched them as they drove off.

Oddly he was neither angry nor sad.

As he walked way into the falling snow, his only thought was *Next time.*